Inspirational Romance Reader

A Collection of Four Complete, Unabridged
Inspirational Romances
in One Volume

• Contemporary Collection No. 3 •

Dance in the Distance
Kjersti Hoff Baez

There's Always Tomorrow
Brenda Bancroft

Free to Love
Doris English

Love's Silken Melody
Norma Jean Lutz

BARBOUR
PUBLISHING, INC.
Uhrichsville, Ohio

© MCMXCIX by Barbour Publishing, Inc.

ISBN 1-55748-952-1

Dance in the Distance
ISBN 1-55748-441-4
© MCMXCIII by Kjersti Hoff Baez

There's Always Tomorrow
ISBN 1-55748-706-5
© MCMXCIII by Brenda Bancroft

Free to Love
ISBN 1-55748-462-7
© MCMXCV by Doris English

Love's Silken Melody
ISBN 1-55748-447-3
© MCMXCIII by Norma Jean Lutz

Published by Barbour Publishing, Inc., P.O. Box 719, Uhrichsville, Ohio 44683
http://www.barbourbooks.com

€CPa Member of the
Evangelical Christian
Publishers Association

Printed in the United States of America.

Dance in the Distance

Kjersti Hoff Baez

Chapter One

"I'm not your birth mother." Anna Silvero's voice trembled and she clutched the flowered handkerchief in her hands.

"Why. . .why didn't you tell me this before?" Clair's words came out with a jerk. She felt the blood rush from her head, and a cold numbness settled over her body.

Anna stretched out her arms to her daughter. "We were so happy with you, your dad and I. When we first saw you, it was love at first sight. We have always loved you as if you were our very own. And you are ours, Clair. We have always felt that way about you. We have never thought of you as adopted, that's how strongly we love you, how close we feel to you." She sighed and looked down at her hands. "We just never had the heart to say anything to you when you were a child. We didn't want to spoil what we had, didn't want to upset you. And the next thing we knew, you became a grown woman."

"What about Danny?" Clair asked woodenly.

Anna hid her face in her hands for a moment and let the tears come. Finally, she lifted her face to her daughter. "Not long after we adopted you, I became pregnant. It was like a miracle. But we never once compared you two or thought of you as different. You were *both* ours."

Pain battered through Clair's defenses. She doubled over with sobs. Anna reached for her, but Clair pulled away.

"No!" she cried. "Don't touch me! You lied to me! All these years you lied to me!" She ran out of the room and up the stairs to her old bedroom.

Clair let the tears flow freely, hiding her face in the bedspread. Her sobs finally quieted, and she sat up on the bed, fingering the purple flowers sprinkled across the white bedspread.

"You're twenty-five years old," the young woman said to herself. "Let's calm down and think this thing through."

Clair quietly surveyed the small room that had been hers from childhood. Even though it had been seven years since Clair had moved to her own apartment, her mother hadn't changed anything.

"Someday I'll make it into a sewing room," Anna would say. Then she would laugh, her eyes twinkling. "But maybe I shouldn't, in case one day we have a granddaughter."

A lavender velvet jewelry box still graced center stage of the white vanity. Clair reached over and gently flipped the clasp, opening the box. A perfect little ballerina righted herself and circled the tiny round mirror that was her stage.

"Perfect little ballerina," Clair whispered. She smiled through her tears, remembering the words her father had often used of her.

"I was a disaster in tights," Clair recalled, "but Daddy always called me his perfect little ballerina, his little dancer." She stopped short at the thought. *Daddy*. For a moment, the familiar word sounded strange to her ears. But then memories began to flood her mind. Trips to the beach. Kickball games that carried on until you could barely see the bases anymore. Birthday parties and chicken pox. Sister and brother fights, sister and brother hugs. First pimples and first proms. Intertwined with every memory was the loving presence of her mother and father, caring for her, cheering her on.

A hesitant knock at the door interrupted the young woman's thoughts.

"Come in."

Anna stood anxiously in the doorway, searching Clair's face for a reaction. Clair dutifully held out her arms, and Anna enveloped her daughter in a long, tearful hug.

"I'm so sorry we didn't tell you when you were little. It would have been better for you to grow up with the truth. I'm sure there are much better ways of handling this than the way we did." Anna looked into Clair's green eyes. "I'm sorry, Clair. We didn't want to hurt you this way."

Clair avoided her mother's eyes. "I know you and Dad did what you thought was best," she said quietly. "I know you love me, and it's true what you said. I never once felt like I was different from Danny. It's just that this is so shocking to me. I'm not sure what to say or do."

Anna looked sadly at Clair's averted face. "I guess it will take awhile for you to deal with this. I regret keeping it from you all these years. Please forgive us, Clair. We love you so."

The sound of the front door opening and closing with a bang made both women jump.

"Where's my two favorite women in the world?" a voice boomed in the hall downstairs.

Tony Silvero stomped up the stairs and burst into Clair's room. "How're my girls?" he asked with a grin. He froze at the sight of the tear-stained women sitting on the bed.

"Anna?" he whispered. "I wanted to be here when you told her. We agreed we should both tell her."

"Tony, I'm sorry, but the words just came out. I couldn't hold it in any longer." Anna's eyes filled with tears again. "I just couldn't wait. . . ."

"It's okay, Dad," Clair intervened. "You're here now, and that's what matters."

Tony rubbed his face with his hand. His voice trembled slightly.

"Clair, honey, you know you are our daughter, no matter what. You know—" His voice broke. Clair stood up and lost herself in her father's arms.

"We did our best, Clair," continued Tony in a voice gruff with suppressed emotion. "We didn't want to hurt you." He stepped back and looked at his daughter's face. "I can see how it hurts you now."

"Please, Dad, it's okay. I understand. I need time, that's all. I know you and Mom love me. There's no doubt in my mind."

Tony hugged Clair again. "That's my girl. It's okay," he said, trying to reassure himself. "We'll be all right. We're Silveros, right?"

The two women struggled to put smiles on their faces.

"Now let's eat," Tony said with false enthusiasm, pretending that everything was back to normal. "What's for dinner, Miss Anna?"

Anna shook her head. "How can you think of food at a time like this?"

"A man's gotta eat," replied Tony. "You should never do anything important on an empty stomach. Except get married," he added. "You know why, Clair?"

"Why's that, Dad?" Clair smiled, waiting for the answer she'd heard a million times before.

"Because I threw up just before our wedding, you know. In the minister's office. On the man's shoes."

Anna groaned. "Now I really feel like eating. Thank you, Anthony Silvero." She nudged him out the door.

"But it's true," the man protested as the women herded him down the stairs.

Clair and Anna deposited Tony in his favorite chair in the living room. They retreated to the kitchen where together they prepared dinner. Anna glanced often at her daughter, trying to read her silence. Clair caught one of her looks and smiled reassuringly. She handed Anna a serving spoon for the vegetables.

"It's going to be okay, Mom," she said.

But Anna's heart ached at the sight of her daughter's trembling hand.

Chapter Two

"Who died?" a young man asked loudly as he entered the dining room of the Silvero home. "You're all so quiet! What's the matter, Clair, did you find a gray hair?" he grinned.

Clair managed a weak smile for her brother.

"Sit down, Danny," his father said firmly.

Danny looked at his father's plate. It was untouched.

"Must be serious," he said.

"Can you please stop joking around for a minute?" Anna's voice was strained. "We have something to tell you."

"All right, I'm listening," Danny said tensely. "But just spill it, okay? I can't stand beating around the bush when it comes to bad news."

Tony Silvero took a deep breath and plunged in. "We want to tell you that your sister—"

"Clair!" Danny gasped. "What's the matter with Clair? Is she sick? What is it?" His voice cracked with emotion.

"Danny! Calm down! It's not that. Will you let me finish?" Tony shook his head with exasperation. "We want to tell you that your sister is adopted. We adopted her when she was a baby."

Danny's mouth dropped open and he slowly studied the looks on his family's faces. He let out a breath of relief. "Is that all? You scared me half to death, I think Clair's on her deathbed, and this is it? The Big Story?" The young man ran a hand through his dark curly hair. "Give a guy a break. I think I just aged ten years."

His reaction to the news comforted Clair in a way. She could see that the news wasn't a big deal to him.

Danny reached over and took Clair by the hand. "Don't get me wrong, Clair," he said softly. "This is news to me, and I know it must be a shock to you. Maybe you even feel angry about it. You may be filled with a mix of emotions that are hard to handle."

Danny's words brought fresh tears to Clair's eyes. He came around to where she sat and put his arms around her. "It's okay to cry," he said softly.

Danny held his sister close while she wept into his shoulder. For several minutes, Clair clung to him, needing the closeness of the brother she had grown up with.

Danny handed her a napkin for her face. "In time, you'll come to grips with this," he reassured her. "And nothing's really changed. You'll always be older than me!"

Clair started to laugh and she took a swipe at her brother. Anna started to cry. Tony took a bite of his food.

"They don't call you the best down at the counseling center for nothing, do they, son!" Tony said through his food.

"Anthony, don't talk with your mouth full!" Anna scolded.

"All right, all right," Tony replied. "Let's all eat. We're together and that's what matters, eh?"

Clair ate her dinner for her father's sake. The Silvero family shared talk about the weather, the Yankees, and the next-door neighbor's poodle to cover the tension and uncertainty that hung in the air like a taut rope straining from a heavy load.

છે

That evening on her way home, Clair stopped by the home of Florence East-man, principal of Anderson Elementary. Clair taught first grade at the school located in Langston, a suburban community sixty minutes north of New York City. Langston was a bustling town along the banks of the Hudson River.

"Don't worry about it," said Florence, when Clair explained her situation and expressed a desire for some time off. Florence valued Clair not only as an excellent teacher but also as a good friend.

"Take Thursday and Friday. That'll give you a long weekend." She studied Clair's profile as she stared out the bay window in Florence's living room. "It must be a strange feeling," she said softly. "I wish I could do something for you. Are you going to try and find her?"

"Find who?" Clair turned to look at her boss with a puzzled look. Then she stopped and her heart leapt up to her throat. Her birth mother. Florence was talking about finding her birth mother.

The look on Clair's face startled Florence. She stuttered out an apology. "I'm sorry, Clair, I guess it's none of my business."

"No, no, it's okay," responded Clair, her voice trailing off into silence. She gathered up her purse and started for the door. "I'll see you Monday," she said over her shoulder as she left.

Florence looked after her with concern in her eyes.

છે

Clair woke up with a start and frantically groped for her alarm clock. Eight o'clock—she'd overslept! Then memories of the previous day flooded her mind, and she sunk back under the covers. What was she going to do with four days off?

Of one thing Clair was certain: She wanted to be alone. And the only way to guarantee solitude was to get away from the phone. After showering, throwing on jeans and a shirt, and drinking some orange juice, Clair grabbed her purse and hurried outside. She got behind the wheel of her red sports car and headed out of town.

Clair spent the morning driving over the back roads of Westchester County. She remembered small incidents from her childhood and discovered they had taken on new meaning. How often had adult conversations been interrupted in midsentence when she'd wandered into a room?

When her growling stomach reminded Clair that she hadn't eaten lunch, she found a diner and grabbed a quick bite. She spent most of the afternoon in a park by the river. As she watched toddlers playing with their young mothers, she wondered why she hadn't taken more seriously the fact that she was the only green-eyed cousin in the Silvero clan. Toward evening, she got in her car and headed back to Langston.

Clair unlocked the front door of the two-family house where she lived and mounted the carpeted stairs to her second-floor apartment. She stood in the middle of her living room for what seemed an eternity. The sun was beginning to fade behind the Hudson Valley. The river glittered in the orange glow of the aging day. Fingers of yellow light poked through the lace curtains, setting the room aglow with golden color.

Are you going to try and find her? Florence's words from the evening before flashed across Clair's mind. "I guess I've been so busy being shocked that I haven't had time to think about my. . .birth mother," she mused. Her mind swarmed with questions.

"I've got to find her," she whispered.

The phone rang, a loud intrusion on her thoughts.

She sat down on the sofa and picked up the white receiver.

"Hello?"

"Clair?" queried a deep voice at the other end of the line. "Where are you? We were supposed to meet at the gym today, remember? You promised."

"Paul, uh, hello." The young woman struggled to collect her thoughts. "I'm sorry. I completely forgot."

"A likely story," the man retorted. "You just chickened out, that's all. I can't believe it! This is the first night of the mixed aerobics class, and you're supposed to be my partner."

Clair let her head rest on the back of the couch. "Paul, really, I forgot." She scrambled for something to say, not wanting to discuss the news of her adoption. "I'm sorry, but I just can't come tonight. Next week."

She heard a groan in her ear. "I'll be the only one there without a partner. I'll look like an idiot. At least if you were here with me, we could both look like idiots."

Clair laughed. "Thanks a lot. How do you know I won't be the most graceful participant there?"

"I've seen you dance," he said flatly.

Clair smiled. "Be brave, Paul. You can do it alone. Remember what your grandfather always said: 'A Carson never retreats.' "

"Leave my grandfather out of this," Paul sighed. "I'll talk to you tomorrow. I can hear the music starting."

"Have fun," said Clair. She dropped the receiver back in place and looked over at a picture of Paul Carson that sat on top of a bookcase. His smile was nice, his hair was nice. He was nice. But that was it. They had been sort of dating for a year, but Clair's heart wasn't in it.

"Right now that's the last thing I want to think about," she said aloud. Her thoughts returned to the strange feelings that surged in her heart and mind. "I'm going to find my mother." The words hung in the air like an unanswered question.

Suddenly Clair felt very much alone.

Chapter Three

The next afternoon, Clair decided to visit her mother and find out if she had any information about Clair's birth parents. Anna handed Clair a faded manila envelope. She smiled and put her hand lovingly on her daughter's shoulder.

"I want you to know I don't feel threatened in any way," she said. "I knew you would want to find your birth mother, and at first it scared me. But I know that my love for you and our relationship as mother and daughter are real. No matter what, I will always be your mother, and you will always be my daughter."

Clair smiled and gave her mother a hug. "You are something else," she said. "I was feeling guilty about my desire to find out about my birth mother. I was afraid it might upset you."

"Don't you worry about me," replied Anna. "The important thing is for you to do what you feel you need to do." Anna looked thoughtfully at her daughter. "Maybe something good will come of all this. You've seemed sort of restless for some time now, even unhappy—like you're looking for something. Maybe this search will help you find that missing something."

Clair looked with surprise at her mother. She certainly was perceptive. It was true. Something was missing in her life. The young woman had been wrestling with vague feelings of boredom and loneliness for over a year.

She turned her attention to the envelope in her hand. A flurry of conflicting thoughts cluttered her mind. Everything was still the same, and yet everything was different. *Even I feel different*, she thought, *a little lost, maybe*. She cleared her throat. "What can you tell me about the adoption?" she asked Anna.

Anna sat down at the kitchen table and signalled Clair to join her. "Your father and I had been married for five years. We had tried right from the start to have children. Nothing happened. We went to several doctors in New York, but no one could help us.

"Uncle Benny, you know, is a lawyer. He found out there was a woman in a small town upstate who was having a baby. She wanted to give the baby up for adoption. So Benny made the arrangements with the woman and a lawyer up there. And the next thing you know, we had a baby girl!"

Anna's eyes misted over. "It was the happiest moment of my life. My own baby girl!" She squeezed Clair's hand. "You were beautiful."

"Upstate New York? Where?"

"Caderville," Anna replied quietly. "It's a small town. Not much to it, really. Kind of quaint, as I remember it."

Clair clutched the envelope in her hand. "I think I'd like to take this back to my apartment and look it over by myself," she said.

Anna smiled at her daughter. "I understand. You need to be alone. Just remember, your dad and I love you with all our hearts."

The young woman nodded and gave her mother a kiss. "I'll talk to you later."

Clair drove home as quickly as she could without getting a ticket. She flew up the stairs and plopped down on her couch. Taking a deep breath, she carefully opened the worn envelope. She pulled out several papers.

One paper looked like a form from a hospital. Her hands trembled as she scanned it for information. She felt like she was unlocking the mystery of a past she had never known. Her birth date was in order. Typed next to the line labeled "name of mother" were the words *Jennifer Wingate*.

"Jennifer," whispered Clair. "What a lovely name."

Next to the line labeled "father" was the word *unknown*. Clair felt a twinge in her stomach.

"Unknown?" she said aloud. "What does that mean, unknown?"

She searched the form for more information, but found none. There was a record of her weight and length, but nothing else.

The loud tone of the doorbell startled the young woman. She quickly put the papers back into the envelope and slipped it into the desk drawer. She hurried down the stairs. Through the lace curtain of the door window she could see Paul Carson standing on the porch.

"Hey!" he called to Clair, peering through the window. "Are you going to let me in?"

Clair turned the lock and let the young man in.

"Hi!" he spoke cheerfully, giving her a light kiss on the cheek.

"Hi," responded Clair, her voice tinged with distraction.

"Well that's a fine how-do-you-do!" Paul huffed. "I know I haven't been away on a dangerous expedition or anything, but it has been over a week since we've seen each other."

Clair mustered up some enthusiasm and gave Paul a hug. "It's always good to see you, Paul."

"You sound like my aunt Sophie. Are you going to pinch my cheek while you're at it?" Paul scoffed. He peered into Clair's face. "Are you all right? And are we going to stand here in the hall and talk or go up to your apartment?"

"Stand in the hall. I can hear you better," a voice cackled from the end of the hall.

Clair and Paul spoke in unison. "Mrs. Hinkle!"

"Oh my, did I startle you? Surely you heard me open my door!" She smiled sweetly at the couple. "Don't mind me, I was just going to sweep the floor." She held out her broom as evidence.

"Nice to see you, Mrs. Hinkle," said Clair. "We were just heading upstairs."

She hurried up the stairs. Paul bowed graciously to the woman with the broom and followed Clair up to her apartment. He headed for the kitchen, where he put the blue teakettle on to boil. Clair brought out a box of cookies and sat down at the table across from Paul.

"Your landlady is something else!" Paul exclaimed. "I wonder how long she stood there listening."

Clair shook her head. "Keep your voice down, Paul, she's liable to hear you."

"I've got a theory about our dear Mrs. Hinkle," Paul whispered. "I think she's got powers beyond the natural realm. I bet she has x-ray vision that enables her to read your mail without opening it. Better yet, she can fly. She probably hovers near your second-story windows and hears every word you say." Paul whistled the *Twilight Zone* theme.

Clair laughed out loud. The picture of her landlady floating outside her windows was funny. "Paul, you are crazy!"

"Now that's better. You're laughing. I was afraid you weren't feeling well. Flo told me you didn't go to work yesterday or today. What's up?"

Clair hesitated. The whistle of the kettle interrupted the conversation. Paul poured the steaming water into the blue and gray stoneware mugs.

"Well?" he continued. "What's going on?"

Clair looked across the table at Paul. His blue eyes studied her face with concern. It wasn't fair to keep it from him, but she wished she could be left alone to pursue her past by herself.

"I just found out I'm adopted," she said squarely to the young man.

Paul leaned back in his chair. "Whoa. That's heavy stuff." He took Clair's hand. "Are you okay?"

"I'm fine," Clair said firmly. "It was a shock at first. I was really upset, but my parents have been super."

"Well, for all we know, you could be some long lost princess. Why, just think—I could be holding hands with royalty right now!" He squeezed her hand and grinned.

Clair pulled her hand away. "Hardly," she said softly. The word *unknown* flashed across her mind, as if to mock her.

"I'm sorry," Paul spoke softly. "That was a stupid thing to say. Is there anything I can do for you?"

"No," said Clair quickly. "I want to handle this by myself. I hope you understand."

Paul shrugged and finished his tea. He looked at his watch. "I better get going. I promised Jerry I'd help him with his new boat. Speaking of boats, my parents want to know if you want to spend a couple of weeks with them at the Cape this summer. You know Mother. I think she's trying to help us get serious."

Clair blushed.

Paul laughed and pushed a wisp of auburn hair away from Clair's eyes. "Don't worry, Clair. I'll hold Mother back! Besides," he said in a more serious tone, "I've been thinking. Maybe we should use this summer as a time to cement our relationship. What do you think?"

"Cement." Clair repeated the word. "It sounds so permanent."

"Very funny. Come on, what do you say?"

Clair stood up and put her mug in the sink. "About this summer," she said, her back to Paul. "I may not be around very much."

"What do you mean?" demanded Paul, irritation in his voice.

The young woman turned around and faced him. "The school year ends in a couple weeks, and I'm going to begin my vacation by trying to find my birth mother. It may take all summer to sort this out."

"Are you sure you want to do this, Clair? What's the point? Anthony and Anna Silvero are the best! Why should you care about who your birth mother is?" Paul's voice stiffened with anger. "And what about us? Are you trying to tell me to take a hike?"

"Paul, please calm down. I'm not trying to hurt you. I'm just so confused and I need to find out—"

"Find out what?" Paul interrupted her. "What if what you're looking for ends up being something painful? Why dig up the past?"

Tears slid down Clair's cheeks. She was losing control. She hid her face in her hands.

"Oh, Clair," Paul said softly. He drew her into his arms. "I'm sorry. I was only thinking of myself. I don't want to lose you. I know our relationship has been pretty casual, but I think that's changing. For me anyway." Pulling a monogrammed handkerchief from his pocket, the young man gently wiped away Clair's tears. "I can see that finding your mother is very important to you. Take all the time you need. Just don't drop off the end of the world."

Clair sighed and gave Paul a hug. "You are so nice!"

"Oh no," Paul groaned. "That's what the girls in high school used to say to me just before they dumped me." He clutched his heart. *"Et tu, Brute!"*

"We'll take it one step at a time, okay?" Clair smiled.

"Okay," Paul conceded. He headed for the door at the top of the stairs. "Hey, wait a minute. What about our aerobic dance class?"

Clair shook her head and shooed him down the stairs. "Forget about it."

"Easy for you to say. You won't be the only one there without a partner." He grabbed the bannister of the carpeted stairwell and gracefully descended. "I'll let myself out. Good night, Mrs. Hinkle," he said loudly.

"Save a dance for me!" Clair called after him.

She closed the door and ran to the window in the living room. She could see Paul bounding down the steps. He turned at the lamppost and looked up at the second-story window. "Good night, Clair!"

Clair waved to him. He blew her a kiss and then disappeared in the dusk. The young woman stood for a long time looking out her window. The sound of Paul's good night seemed to linger in the air. There was comfort in the familiarity of his voice. She almost ran down the stairs after him. The journey she had chosen to take was already making her feel strange and alone.

What if you discover something painful? Paul's words echoed in her mind. "I don't care," Clair said to herself. "I've got to know. I've just got to know."

Chapter Four

Clair's red sports car (the one luxury she allowed herself) carried her smoothly down scenic Route 17. With the passing miles, the hills seemed to gather and come closer, until the highway became a ribbon threaded through the foothills of the Catskills.

Clair was not used to seeing such lovely flowing heights. She drank in their beauty with a thirst kindled by the silent green hills. The June sun washed the air with brightness. A river appeared seemingly out of nowhere, joining the highway in its gently curving journey. Through the open window, fresh country air rushed in and sent Clair's auburn hair flying.

"Danny would love this," she said out loud. "It is absolutely gorgeous and unspoiled!" Her thoughts turned back a few miles to the Hudson Valley and the tearful scene at her mother's house.

"Make sure you call us when you get there," Anna Silvero had said through her tears. "And be careful."

"Drive that dumb little car of yours carefully, young lady," Tony had commanded hoarsely. "If you get a flat, wait for a trooper to come. Don't get out of the car."

Clair had smiled and shaken her head. "Dad, I'm a big girl now, remember? I'll be fine."

Danny had given his sister a quick hug. "You better get out of here, Sis, before they decide to go with you." He looked into his sister's green eyes. "I hope you find what you're looking for."

Her brother's words stirred the sleeping butterflies in Clair's stomach. She glanced quickly at the map. "Exit 84. Dad said to get off at exit 84."

Two-and-a-half hours later, a large green sign heralded the town of Hillside. Another sign loomed in the distance.

"Caderville, 11 miles," Clair read, squinting her eyes. "Lamberton, 93." Her heart skipped a beat. "Almost there," she said lightly, trying to calm herself. As she drove past Hillside, a tall, towerlike building grabbed her attention. It rose above the trees on top of one of the hills surrounding the small village. The sunlight caused the faded yellow bricks of the building to cast a hazy glow. There was something strange, even eerie about it.

"Wonder what it is?" Clair questioned as she left Hillside behind her.

Midway between Hillside and Caderville, another strange sight caught Clair's eye. Across the river, on an open slope, stood a small abandoned oil well. It looked out of place and sad, symbolic of someone's dreams that had come up dry. The rusty spire rose self-consciously from its base. A wooden tunnel, its planks slapped hastily together, trailed crookedly from the rig like a hurried afterthought.

"Who in the world would build such a thing up here?" Clair wondered. She sighed. "Clair, this lovely place is brimming with mystery. I have a feeling this trip is going to be a bit complicated. So much for simple answers to simple questions."

The sign for exit 84 suddenly appeared. Clair pulled off the highway and drove down the ramp. Making a right at the stop sign, the young woman drove slowly down a street marked Rose Avenue. She soon found what she was looking for. A small motel was located on the right side of the street, not far from a green bridge that spanned the river.

"Riverside Motel," Clair read the sign. "Won't Mom be surprised to know it's still here."

Clair parked her car in front of what looked like the main office of the establishment. She brushed her hair and quickly freshened her lipstick. *First impressions only happen once, you know.* Grandmother Silvero's words surfaced in the young woman's mind. She smiled. Grandmother was always so proper and so sweet.

But she's not your real grandmother. The nasty thought intruded. Clair shook the thought from her mind. "Don't be ridiculous," she said aloud, getting out of the car and slamming the door with a bang.

"I wouldn't slam that door that way, lady, if I was you," a voice stated loudly. Clair turned and saw a gangly teenager walking toward her. "You'll ruin it." He looked admiringly at the red sports car. "She's a beaut."

Clair smiled. "Thanks." She extended her hand. "Clair Silvero."

The boy looked taken aback, as if it were rare that someone would address him with such formality. He pushed long greasy bangs away from his blue eyes. "Preston Finch, ma'am. My friends call me Pres." He shyly shook the young woman's hand. "You're not from around here."

"No, I live down in Westchester County. Near the city."

"Oh."

"I was thinking of staying at this motel," she said, pointing to the Riverside Motel sign. "What do you think?"

"It's pretty nice," the teenager replied, feeling a bit shocked that someone would ask his advice. "Mamie Slade runs it. Keeps it clean."

Clair nodded. "Well, thanks for your help, Preston."

"You're welcome, ma'am."

"One more thing, Preston." The young woman smiled.

"Ma'am?"

"Please don't call me ma'am! It makes me feel old. Call me Clair."

Preston laughed. "Okay, Clair." He blushed.

Clair said good-bye and turned toward the office. Preston stood staring at the sporty car, images of speed races and trophies running through his head.

The door jingled as Clair entered the office. The walls were mint green trimmed with white wainscoting. On the wall behind the counter hung a huge painting of a pasture. Lazy cows, brown and white against the grassy field, nuzzled the ground for food. In the distance a tree graced the top of a hill. Clair could see something hanging on the tree. What was it? In an effort to get a better look, she leaned over the counter and squinted.

"It's a swing." A loud, hoarse voice fairly bounced off the walls and knocked Clair over.

"What?" was all Clair could think to say.

"It's a swing in that tree. That's what you were looking at, weren't you?" A short, stout woman faced Clair with her hands on her hips. She wore a white apron over a flowery cotton shift. "There's a little girl on the swing if you look close enough. Most folks think it's a noose or something."

Clair didn't say that that was exactly what she had thought it was.

"I'm looking for a place to stay," Clair said, collecting her wits.

"Rooms are twenty-five dollars a night. It's not the Marriott, but then we don't need a Marriott around here. Most people stay with their families." She scrutinized the young woman who stood before her. "Just passing through?"

"No," said Clair faintly. She wasn't about to explain her presence in Caderville to this stranger. "I'll need a room for at least two weeks, maybe longer."

The proprietor pushed the guest book in front of Clair. "Sign in, and you'll have to pay a week at a time. No pets, no smoking, no drinking."

Clair signed the book and paid for her room. Mamie handed her a key with a big red seven written on it.

"Last one on the left," she said abruptly. "Welcome to Caderville. I'm Mamie Slade." The woman's lips quivered almost imperceptibly. Clair realized it was the closest thing to a smile she was going to get.

"Thank you," responded Clair. She grasped her key tightly in her hand and headed for her car. She almost hoped the boy she'd met would still be out there. At least he was easy to talk to. She would ask him about a good place to eat.

Her car stood alone in the parking lot. *Oh well,* thought Clair. She opened her trunk and pulled out her suitcase. Grabbing a smaller satchel from the front seat, she hurried down the white concrete pathway to her room. The key slipped in easily enough, but when Clair tried to turn it, it wouldn't budge. She pulled and jiggled it to no avail.

"You have to sort of push down and to the right at the same time," a voice barked behind her. Clair almost jumped out of her skin. It was Mamie. The older woman grasped the doorknob and with a flick of the wrist, opened the lock. Clair walked in, put down her luggage, and turned to thank Mamie. She was gone.

"Whew." Clair plopped down on the bed and kicked off her shoes. "Welcome to Caderville."

Chapter Five

The morning light filtered through the venetian blinds and fell across the papers Clair held in her hand. She gently touched the name printed on her birth certificate. Rose. There was no last name. Pulling out the hospital form, she scanned it again for information.

"At least I have my mother's name," she said. The fact that her father was listed as unknown was really beginning to bother her. She had a feeling that the circumstances surrounding her birth were not very pleasant. It all seemed so cold and impersonal.

"Maybe Paul was right," sighed the young woman. "Maybe I should leave it alone. Maybe it will just be a painful dead end."

Clair opened the manila envelope to put back the papers. To her surprise, there was a small envelope stuck at the bottom of the larger one. She dislodged it and opened it with trembling hands. A trace of fragrance faintly slipped from the tiny pocket.

"Why, that smells like a rose!" Clair said aloud. She carefully removed a piece of pale pink tissue paper. Unfolding it, she discovered a cluster of dried rose petals. Nestled inside the dry flower was a gold, heart-shaped locket.

"But it's only half a locket," Clair mused. She fingered the broken hinge. "This must be the cover." The name *Rose* was engraved in flowing letters across the front of the locket cover.

Tears filled the young woman's eyes. Perhaps there was more to her story than cold, hard facts. Maybe her mother loved her, even longed for her, but for some reason could not keep her baby. Clair's heart filled with resolve and she jumped to her feet. She grabbed her purse and the key to her room and pulled the door shut.

"Day one. The search begins," she announced softly to the morning sun. A rustling of leaves drew Clair's attention to a group of trees situated along the edge of the parking lot. The bevy of young beech trees reached for the sky, their leaves shimmering in the morning sun. To Clair it looked as though they were whispering to one another as the wind teased their leaves into motion.

"Ballerinas preparing for the dance," she reflected. The wind surged and the trees bent slightly as if to gracefully bow to the young woman. Clair smiled and turned toward the office.

Having acquired directions from the ever-pleasant Mamie Slade, Clair drove her car across the small bridge and made a left on a little side street. It eventually converged with Main Street, and Clair parked her car in an empty spot near the sheriff's office.

Clair spotted the sheriff standing in front of his office. She gave herself a silent pep talk and then approached the man with as much calm and confidence as she could muster.

"Excuse me, sir," said Clair, "I'm not from around here, but I'm looking for someone. I don't really know where to begin. Perhaps you could help me?"

"James T. Watson, at your service." The sheriff grinned from behind his sunglasses. "Where you from?"

"I live down near New York," Clair responded.

"Figured as much. You've got an accent." The man looked down at the newcomer. "Who you looking for?"

Clair smiled. "It's kind of personal. And it goes back about twenty-five years."

"Oh. No problem. I'm not the snoopy kind. Except, of course, when it comes to crime," he laughed. "Why I'm like a starving hound dog on the trail of a fat rabbit when it comes to illegal activity."

"Oh, I assure you this has nothing to do with the law," said Clair hastily.

"Well, little lady, I know just where to send you for information. You'd want to talk to Ben Wheelock. He's the busiest busybody that ever lived. He's got the snootiest snoot for news this side of the Great Divide. If it's information you want, Ben's got it. His brain's like a filing cabinet that reaches back as far as the Civil War!" He pointed in the direction of the drugstore. "His place is right down there, between the flower shop and the dry cleaner's. Just tell him James T. Watson sent you."

Clair smiled and thanked the officer for his help.

"Don't mention it," he called after her.

The young woman crossed the street and headed for the pharmacy. Just as she reached the building, someone burst through the door and ran past her in a blur of speed. A gray-haired man followed, yelling and waving his arms.

"And don't you ever let me see you around here again!" His voice cracked with the effort. The child disappeared around the corner. "Little termite!" he sputtered under his breath. He was unaware that a young woman was standing behind him.

Clair cleared her throat. "Excuse me," she said politely. "Are you Mr. Benjamin Wheelock?"

Ben turned around and his face reddened at the thought of being seen in such a ruffled state. "Yes, I'm Ben Wheelock." He peered over his glasses at the young lady who stood before him. "Who are you?"

Clair ignored his question momentarily. "I was told you are quite. . . knowledgeable about the people of Caderville."

Ben's eyes narrowed. "James T. Watson. You've been talking to James T. Watson. Let me guess. He said I was the busiest busybody that ever lived and that I had the snootiest snoot for news this side of the Great Divide. Am I right?"

Clair tried her best not to laugh.

"Never mind," the pharmacist smiled and shook his head. He pulled down the pencil that perched behind his ear and tapped it against his hand. "Who are you?" he repeated.

The young woman held out her hand. "Clair Silvero," she said clearly. "I'm visiting from Westchester County."

As he took her hand, Ben shot her a knowing look. "I'd guess you're not really here to visit. You look like a woman with a mission."

Clair's eyebrows shot up. *Am I really that transparent?* she wondered. She couldn't think of anything to say.

"It's okay, you don't have to explain. Come on in to the soda fountain and have a drink of something. It's on me." Ben grinned and opened the door to his pharmacy with a flourish.

Clair settled on a stool at the gleaming white counter.

"You're a very perceptive man, Mr. Wheelock," said Clair.

"Ben. Please call me Ben. I tell all lovely young ladies like yourself to call me Ben," he grinned.

"Ben! Shame on you! I do declare!" Clair swiveled her stool around and caught sight of a short, stout woman wearing an outspokenly purple dress. Her jet black hair was decidedly too black to be natural.

"That's Mr. Wheelock to you," Ben grunted at the purple lady.

"Well, I never!" she huffed. The woman stopped beside Clair and offered her hand. "Violet Cranberry. Pleased to meet you."

"Clair Silvero."

"Why, that sounds like an Italian name!" gushed Violet. "I was engaged to an Italian man once. His name was Salvatore. Oh, he was dashing."

"He was dashing all right," smirked Ben. "He dashed right off to Italy and never came back."

"Benjamin Wheelock! You are a mean-spirited old fox not fit to call yourself a human being! How can you joke about my broken heart!" Violet turned her attention to Clair. "Salvatore's mother was ill. He had to go back and take care of her. I suppose our love was never meant to be," she sighed dramatically. "He never did write me, though."

"Wrote you off, he did," Ben said under his breath.

Clair desperately tried not to smile. Obviously Violet and Benjamin were used to sparring with one another.

"If you'll excuse us, Violet," said Ben. "We were having a conversation before you interrupted."

Violet smiled at Clair. "You are new around here, aren't you, dear. Visiting family?"

Clair was about to answer when Ben jumped in and saved the day.

"That is none of your business," he growled.

"But I'm sure you'll make it yours, won't you, Benjamin?" the woman replied breezily. "Hope to see you again, Miss Silvero." She flicked her wrist to signal good-bye and waddled to the door.

"I'm sorry, Miss Silvero. Now where were we?"

"I'm looking for someone. Her name is Jennifer Wingate. The only information I have is that she lived here in Caderville twenty-five years ago."

"Wingate, Wingate," Ben repeated the name and scratched his head. "Definitely sounds familiar. Now let me see if I—" He stopped short and hesitated. "I remember now." Ben looked as if he had bad news. Clair urged him to speak.

"Well?" she said. "Do you know who she is? Do you know where she is now?"

The pharmacist pursed his lips and looked compassionately into the face of the young woman who sat next to him. Her green eyes pleaded for an answer, but it was an answer that wasn't going to be easy to give. He hoped her link to Jennifer Wingate was not a close one.

Chapter Six

"Jennifer Wingate lives at the Clarkson House on Pine Street."

"So you know her!" Clair said excitedly. "How do you know her?"

"Oh, her family goes way back in Caderville. And I've written prescriptions for her over the years."

"What's wrong? I can tell something's wrong."

Ben sighed. "I never did have a poker face. I'm a terrible poker player. Whenever I play with the sheriff and his deputies, I always lose. It's a shame. The last time I played, I lost nearly five—"

"Mr. Wheelock!" Clair demanded. "Don't change the subject."

"Clarkson House is a home for the mentally ill," the pharmacist spoke gently.

Clair sucked in her breath. She felt as if someone had punched her in the stomach.

"Why do you want to find Miss Wingate?" Ben asked.

Clair stood up in a daze and headed for the door. "I need to be alone," she thought. "Got to get back to the motel."

"Are you okay?" Ben called after her. "I'm sorry if I upset you! Come back if you need to talk!"

Clair left without turning back.

Changing her mind about returning to the hotel, Clair decided a drive down a country road might help clear her mind. She drove down Main Street and made a left. The road swung beneath a small train bridge and climbed up a hill. Not knowing where she was headed—and not caring—the young woman made another turn at the top of the hill.

She discovered a road that followed along the river. Tree branches lush with greenery bent gently over the road creating a fairy-tale tunnel. The tunnel broke open into wide spaces of pastures and open fields that swooped downward from the verdant hillsides. The river snaked lazily along the bottom of the valley, glistening in the morning sun.

Clair let the beauty of the countryside soothe her frayed emotions. Mentally ill. Her mother was mentally ill. Ben Wheelock's words spun around in the young woman's mind like knives, cutting her at every turn. What had happened to her mother? What kind of terrible suffering took her to such a dark corner of the world? Then Paul's words rebounded to Clair. *What if what you're looking for ends up being something painful?*

"Oh, Paul," she whispered. "You were right. Why did I ever come here?"

Her eyes began to blur with tears. She pulled off to the side of the road and let the tears flow freely. Let the dam break, Anna Silvero would always say. It releases the pressure and clears your heart. Then you can untangle your thoughts.

Through her tears, Clair smiled at the thought of her mother. Remembering Anna's lovely face calmed the young woman down.

Maybe I'm just tired and I'm overreacting, she thought. *It certainly wasn't what I was expecting, but still, maybe there's more. . . .* Clair's curiosity nudged her. She looked up through her side window. Across the road was a cemetery. An iron fence skirted the edges of the place, with a small iron archway standing staunchly over the entrance. Bronze letters on top of the arch spelled out Green Meadow Cemetery.

"Ben said the Wingate family goes way back in Caderville. I wonder if any of the family is buried here?" Clair wiped the tears off her face and got out of her car. She crossed the road and pushed open the gate.

The front part of the cemetery was situated on an open field. In back, the land rose in small ripples toward the side of a steep hill. In the older sections, tall evergreens towered above the graves like quiet sentinels. Headstones and statues stood silently in crooked rows, marking the spaces of lives that once were. The air was hot from the July sun, the dry grass crunching beneath Clair's feet. The whirring buzz of a bee sounded loud nearby and then faded. A small white moth zigzagged amidst the stones, finally lighting for a moment on a purple clover.

A whirl of melancholy, peace, and a sense of history hummed in the air. Despite the warm day, Clair felt a shiver run up her spine. It seemed such a sad place. The lives represented here were lives that were over. No more laughter, loving, or seeing the sun bring out the flowers of spring. Clair lamented the fact that she didn't really believe in God or an afterlife. It was a shame that the movement, awareness, and experiences that compose the sentence called life should end so harshly, with a granite period at the end. The young woman ran her finger along the top of one of the headstones. The rough contours made her finger tingle.

Lifting her eyes to the older section of the cemetery, Clair headed for the tall evergreens. She took her time examining each stone, reading each name. Some of the older markers were so faded or covered with moss that she couldn't discern the names carved in them. Others were just as old, but somehow had survived the time and the weather.

" 'Tompkins,' " Clair read aloud from a tall, proud marker. " 'Terrence Adam,

Beloved Husband. Virginia Estelle, Beloved Wife.'" She moved on and crouched down to read a stone set closer to the ground. " 'Lillian Spencer; 1904–1922; Our Fair Flower—Barely Bloomed and Gone from Us.' How sad!" On another slope, the tiny form of a lamb graced the top of a small marker. Its original white color was tainted with soot and lichen. " 'Emily Ann; 1898; Our little lamb—Still in our Hearts.' " Clair caressed the lamb's head. "A little baby. What a shame!"

Clair looked up at the towering evergreens. A summer wind stole between the upper branches of the century-old trees and set them swaying. The soft swooshing sound combed the air with its gentle music. The wind reached down and caught up the gurgle of a nearby stream, drawing it to Clair's attention.

She climbed over the small rise to get a better look. There she discovered the stream that ran along the back of the cemetery, forming a curvy, moving boundary to the resting place. There were several graves situated as near the stream as was prudent. One of them caught the young woman's eye. Wingate. The name was carved in large letters on rose-colored granite.

Along either side of the stone lay several flat stones with names carved in them. Grass had sent its clinging roots across the face of the markers. Clair pulled off as much of it as she could, brushing away the dirt with her hands. The names she discovered there piqued her curiosity. Zacharias Wingate. Rebecca Ann. Jonas Trevor. What were they like? Where did they stand in the family tree, and did their blood run through Clair Silvero's veins? If only there was someone who could answer all these questions, unravel the past.

"Pretty gloomy stuff, wouldn't you say?" A voice spoke from behind the young woman.

Clair nearly jumped out of her skin. She whirled around to see a man dressed in casual brown pants and a white shirt, his brown hair a mass of unruly curls.

"Sorry if I scared you. The name's Jack Thomas." The young man extended his hand to Clair. She cautiously returned the gesture and felt the strength of the stranger's grasp.

"Clair Silvero," she responded. She looked around, realizing she was in the middle of nowhere, alone with a man who for all she knew could be a serial killer.

"Hey, don't look so frightened!" the young man responded to her anxious look. "You must be from the city. Nobody around here gets scared at being alone in the countryside."

Clair blushed and laughed out loud with relief. "I'm afraid you're right. I live in Langston, down in Westchester County. My brother says I worry too much and that I'm as paranoid as a fly in a room full of spiders."

"I promise you I am not a spider. I'm just a lowly journalist, struggling to earn the honor of the prize of all prizes, the Pulitzer."

"You write for a paper? In Caderville?" Clair asked.

"Yes, that's right. But that's not all." Jack stuck his thumbs through imaginary suspenders and puffed out his chest. "I'm the editor, too. You are looking at the brains behind the *Caderville Courier*."

Clair laughed. "Very impressive, Mr. Editor. But do you mind if I ask you a question?"

"Ask away."

"What are you doing in the cemetery? I don't think there's really anything much going on around here, if you know what I mean." She pointed to the silent tombstones.

"Quite to the contrary," Mr. Thomas replied. "There is history to be gleaned here, perhaps clues to several interesting mysteries just aching to be solved, to be told, and told well."

Clair's eyebrows shot up. This man was speaking her language. Suddenly she realized that maybe this Jack Thomas, editor and journalist, could help her solve her own riddle, the mystery of her family background. Maybe he would know where to look for the information, where to find the answers.

"I could ask you the same thing, you know," his words interrupted her mounting thoughts.

"What?" Clair asked, her thoughts in an excited jumble.

"You. What's a lovely young woman like you doing in the Green Meadow Cemetery? It's a long way from Langston, USA."

Clair self-consciously ran her fingers through her auburn hair. Her green eyes sparkled in the sunlight that filtered through the boughs of the evergreens. "I guess you could say I'm searching for my roots."

Jack nodded and bit his lip. "Interesting. Perhaps you're trying to find yourself? Sixties-style?"

"Absolutely not," Clair retorted vehemently. "I know perfectly well who I am, I just don't know who—" She stopped herself and studied the face of the man who stood before her. His brown eyes were warm and lively in a face that looked strong and good. His nose appeared as though it had been broken once. It leant character to his face. At first she wasn't sure about letting this man in on her personal quest for knowledge of her family, but somehow the kindness in his eyes beckoned her to continue her story.

"I don't really know who my family is." She finished her sentence.

A quizzical look from the journalist spurred her on to explain.

"I was adopted years ago from a woman who lived in Caderville. I mean lives. She still lives here," she said quietly, the thought of the Clarkson home muting her enthusiasm to continue.

"I see," Jack replied. "And do you have a name for this woman?"

Clair pointed to the large headstone. "Wingate. Her name is Jennifer Wingate."

"Well, you're way ahead of the game, girl. You've got the name and the place. So what's stopping you?"

Clair turned away and stared into the stream that hurried quickly by the place where there was no hurry to go anywhere. It seemed a paradoxical symbol of life. Life kept going, despite the fact that every day people dropped quietly out of the race. A shawl of sadness enveloped her again, the feeling that none of this made any sense anyway.

"She lives in Clarkson House."

"Oh." Jack was quiet for a moment. "I'm sorry." He paused for a moment, then plunged in. "That shouldn't stop you, you know. You can still find out about your family and its history." He gently put a hand on the young woman's shoulder. "Every life is precious, you know. Even the ones that seem lost in a maze of darkness."

His words shot through Clair's heart like a well-aimed arrow, piercing her, making a space where some light could come through. She turned to face her newfound friend. "Thanks," she said with a smile. "You are absolutely right."

Jack Thomas grinned and folded his arms across his chest. "How about we go back to town and you fill me in on what you know. Then I can see what I can do about sources that might be helpful to you. I know someone who makes the best chocolate shakes in the county. We'll do lunch. Is that how you city folks say it?"

Clair laughed and shook her head. Together they walked back through the metal archway. Clair looked questioningly at Jack. The young man intercepted her thoughts before she could speak.

"I hitched a ride with Sam Jansen. He owns a farm down the road a ways. My car's in the shop." He looked at Clair. "Did you know that your forehead wrinkles up and you sort of frown when you're trying to figure something out?"

"I know," Clair sighed. "My dad calls it my 'thinking face'. 'Watch out world,' he would say, 'my little dancer's got her thinking face on!' He says I've been doing that since I was a baby."

"Sounds to me as if you've got a terrific father."

"I sure do," responded Clair as she got into her car. "I sure do."

Chapter Seven

The chocolate shake was cold and deliciously smooth. Mr. Wheelock hovered over Jack and Clair as they finished their lunch at his soda fountain counter.

"I do apologize for upsetting you, Miss Silvero," said the pharmacist, concern in his voice. "You left in such a hurry, I was afraid I had really knocked you for a loop."

"That's all right, Mr. Wheelock. I was just shocked by the whole thing, that's all. And now you know the whole story. Do you think you can help me?"

Jack pushed his sandwich plate away and crossed his arms. "If Ben can't help you, then no one can. He's got the snootiest—"

"Hold it right there, young man. I'll thank you not to be quoting such nonsense!" He sniffed and stuck his pencil behind his ear. "I consider myself a lay historian."

Jack threw back his head and laughed out loud. "A historian. Yes, I guess you're right about that. Now, dazzle us with your knowledge of the Wingate family."

Clair leaned forward eagerly. "What can you tell me?"

Ben cleared his throat. "Actually, I can't really tell you too much. Jennifer Wingate was the only child of Wendell and Joanna Wingate. They used to live over on Crescent Street, not far from the railroad tracks."

"My grandmother and grandfather," said Clair.

"That's right," smiled Mr. Wheelock. "Wendell and Joanna would be your grandparents. They were quiet people. I guess because Jennifer was their only daughter, they were very strict with her. She couldn't go out much unless her mother was with her." Ben leaned back against the sink.

"I can still see my mother shaking her head and clucking, 'They're way too hard on that girl. Keeping her boxed in can only bring on bad times, you rest assured! Something bad is going to happen!' Of course, I was older than Jennifer and didn't pay much attention to what was going on. Caderville was a small town. It was only natural knowing everybody's business."

"Still is!" muttered Jack.

Clair wanted to know more. "What about boyfriends or a social life? Surely she must have had some friends."

Ben scratched his head and looked pensive. "I do believe there was one young man who used to come around and try to visit Jennifer. Guess he had a crush on her. Can't remember his name, though. At any rate, eventually Jennifer's mother became ill and most of her daughter's time was spent caring for her. In fact it wasn't until Jennifer was in her thirties that—" He stopped and looked at Clair.

"Go on," said Clair.

"It wasn't until Jennifer was in her thirties that she became pregnant," he said quietly.

"And how old are you?" asked Jack, his mind clicking with calculations.

"Twenty-five," responded Clair, her eyes locked on the pharmacist. "But who?" Clair choked on the words.

"Who was the father? No one really knew. They suspected it was the man who used to come and visit Jennifer. But that's about all I know." Ben looked at Clair. "Sorry I can't tell you more."

Clair was wearing her thinking face. "But how can I find out who my father was?"

"Maybe I can help with that," Jack Thomas piped up. "Maybe there's something in the old papers that could shed some light. Maybe a birth announcement or something."

Ben shook his head. "I doubt you'll find anything in the papers. People back then didn't announce the birth of. . ."

"Illegitimate babies?" Clair supplied the rest of the sentence.

"That is such a negative word," Jack jumped in. "I think it's awful. As if there was something wrong with such a child. Ridiculous. All life is precious."

"You'll have to watch out for Mr. Thomas here," Ben said cautiously to Clair. "He's not only a journalist, but at any given moment, when you least expect it (and when you do!) he flashes forth as the Reverend Jack Thomas. He's a preacher, of sorts."

Clair looked over at the young journalist. He was blushing. There was something different about him. And here he was again talking about the preciousness of life. It felt like cool water to her thirsty soul. She enjoyed being alive, teaching, loving her family and friends. But it all just seemed to flow along without any greater purpose and ultimately to an end. Green Meadow Cemetery reminded her of that.

"Anyway, I do know someone who could give you more information. There's a woman named Sadie Atkins who knows more town history than anyone I know."

"Even you!" laughed Jack. "And that's no small feat."

"As I was saying," Ben glared at Jack, "Sadie lives up on Jasmine Hill Road, about five miles from here. She's in her nineties and has a mind like a steel trap. She might be able to tell you more. In fact, she might be able to tell you more about your grandparents and so on."

"It's worth a try," exclaimed Jack. "Let's go!" He jumped off his stool and headed for the door.

"Wait just a minute!" Clair called after him, stopping him in his tracks. "Who said anything about you coming with me? This is something I want to do by myself, thank your very much!"

Jack looked confused. Ben laughed. "Has as much sense as a donkey at a horse show. You can't go busting in on Sadie Atkins. I'm going to have to get in touch with her granddaughter Margret and make arrangements. You're always going off half-cocked, young man."

Jack looked sheepish. "You're right. When there's a news trail to follow, I'm up and running. Sorry, Clair."

"That's okay, Jack," replied Clair warmly. "It's just that this is my story, okay? It's not for the *Caderville Courier*."

"I know, I know. But I would still like to help you, if you'll let me."

"I'll let you know. You've helped a lot already. Thanks." She turned to the druggist. "And many thanks to you, as well, Mr. Wheelock."

"Please, call me Ben!" he smiled. "I'll let you know when you can go see Mrs. Atkins. Why don't you leave me your number at the motel?"

"I don't remember it, but I'll call you here and give it to you then."

They exchanged good-byes and left the pharmacy. Jack offered to give Clair a tour of the *Courier*, but Clair asked for a rain check.

"I'm going to go back to the motel for a while, maybe take a walking tour around Caderville. Get the feel of the place."

Jack handed her a slip of paper. "Here's my number if you need anything. Call any time, day or night." His smile was genuine.

"Thanks. And by the way," the thought occurred to Clair, "you never did tell me why you were at the cemetery."

"Oh yeah," Jack laughed. "Guess you have a nose for news, too, eh?"

"Just curious," said Clair.

"First step to being a good journalist."

"And you are avoiding the question," Clair grinned.

"First step toward being a politician!"

"Jack!" cried Clair with exasperation.

"All right, all right!" He lowered his voice. "I'm investigating the scuttle-butt that's been kicked around here for years that Caderville was a stop on the Underground Railroad. A man named Chester Clayborne was the master mind behind it."

"Clayborne?" quizzed Clair. "Sounds like a Southerner's name."

"Precisely!" hissed Jack with glee. "They say he used to be a slave owner himself, but something happened to change him around. And he ended up here, in Caderville."

"But why so secretive?"

"Because," spoke Jack carefully, "this could be Pulitzer Prize stuff we're talking about. And I want to be the one to write it."

Clair laughed and looked up and down the streets of the small town. "I don't see any outsider journalist creeping around spying on you."

"You never know," whispered Jack with a smile. "I'd like to see Sadie myself, but she's mad at me."

"Why?" Clair asked.

"I did an article on Abby Smith's one-hundred-year birthday party. Forgot to put Sadie's name on the guest list."

"Oh." Clair tried not to laugh. "I'll try and put in a good word for you when I see her."

"Thanks. By the way," remarked the journalist nonchalantly, "you never did tell me when your birthday is."

"June 18," Clair answered without thinking. "Hey, wait a minute, that was sneaky—"

"See you later!" Jack was already strolling down the street, his lanky form moving at a comfortable pace. *Comfortable. There's something comfortable about that man,* Clair thought as she watched him. *He seems to know who he is and where he belongs. It's maddening! Makes me feel even more upside down than I already do.*

Back at the hotel, Clair lay across her bed and let the afternoon breeze stir gently over her. Through the open window she could hear the rustling of the beech trees. The bitter sweet coo of a mourning dove called from the hill behind the motel. Clair tried to sort the information she had gleaned that day. It sounded like a pretty simple chronology of a sad life. Girl meets boy, they fall in love, parents disapprove, and a child is born out of wedlock. Not really much more than that.

A knock at the door startled Clair and pulled her off the bed.

"Who is it?" she called through the door.

"It's me, Preston."

Clair opened the door to find the teenager shyly carrying a bucket and some rags. "Hi. I was wondering if you'd let me wash your car. It looks like it needs it. You've come a long way and, after all, you can't leave that travel dust and grime on a beauty like that." He sort of gulped as if that was the longest speech he'd ever made in the presence of an adult.

"I couldn't agree more, Preston. It's nice of you to offer. Be my guest!" Clair smiled and walked out to the car with her young friend. "She's all yours," she said, pointing to her red pride and joy. "But what about Mrs. Slade? Will she let you use her hose?"

"Yeah. She and my mom are friends. I don't live far from here."

"Great. Have fun." Clair turned to walk away, but then hesitated. "Preston?"

"Yes, ma'am. I mean, Clair."

"Can you tell me where the Clarkson House is located?" She looked intently into the boy's bright blue eyes.

"Sure. But why in the world would you want to go there?"

Clair didn't answer.

Chapter Eight

Clair hesitated for a moment at the gate of the Clarkson home. A wrought-iron black fence surrounded the property in a protective embrace. She wasn't sure if it served to keep the tenants inside the grounds as much as it was to keep visitors out. The well-manicured green of the lawn shimmered in the afternoon sun. Shrubbery, trees, and flower beds decorated the premises with charming dignity. It was obvious that loving and talented hands had successfully corralled the beauty of nature on this spot of land.

As the young woman feasted her eyes on the rainbow of colors, she caught sight of a man digging along the side fence.

"Excuse me!" she called to him.

The man straightened up slowly and looked in Clair's direction. He frowned slightly. Pulling a red kerchief from his pocket, he slowly wiped his face. Clair watched as he ambled toward her.

"The folks are inside taking their naps. It's nap time at two o'clock. Every day." He nodded slowly and rested his hands on the handle of his shovel. "Who are you?"

Clair was getting used to being questioned about her identity.

"Clair Silvero," she said with a smile. "I'm visiting from Westchester County."

"Who?"

"Clair Sil—"

"No, I mean who are you visiting?" he inquired with a piercing look. A flicker of light crossed his face for a moment, as if the young face before him reminded him of someone.

Taken aback, Clair wasn't sure how to answer. "Actually, I'm looking for someone. Jennifer Wingate. I was told she lived here."

The man's face darkened with suspicion. "What would you be wanting with Miss Wingate? She shouldn't be disturbed, you know," he said coldly.

Clair stiffened with what her father called the Great Silvero Stubbornness.

"With all due respect, sir, I think I will discuss this matter with Miss Clarkson." Clair moved to open the gate. The man placed a gnarled hand on the latch and glared.

Great, thought Clair. *I've got to do battle with Quasimoto before I can get to the castle.* She took a deep breath and plunged into a speech about America being the land of the free, when a firm voice stopped her mid-soapbox.

"Grayson! Get away from that gate and let the lady in."

An imposing woman with silver hair swept up to a dizzying height thumped her cane on the front porch. The gardener stepped quickly away from the gate, but not without pointing his finger menacingly at Clair.

Clair lifted the heavy latch on the gate and let herself in. She hurried past the glaring gardener, following the sidewalk trimmed with pink and white impatiens. The woman on the porch signalled Clair to join her.

"Abigail Clarkson," the woman said grandly. "Daughter of Ernestine Clarkson, the founder of this great home." She took Clair's hand in a firm grasp, all the while studying the visitor's appearance.

"Clair Silvero," responded Clair. She suddenly felt very nervous and her heart began to pound. *What am I doing here?* she asked herself. *What do I expect to find?* Her legs began to wobble.

"Have a seat." Miss Clarkson pointed at a white wicker chair. Clair gratefully sat down. "Now, tell me, what brings you to Clarkson House?"

The young woman looked over nervously at the gardener. He stood near the fence, his eyes staring at the two women on the porch.

"Don't mind Grayson," the elder woman purred. "He's just very protective of our people here."

Clair smiled and swallowed hard. "I'm looking for a woman named Jennifer Wingate."

Abigail's eyebrows shot up, and she pursed her lips. "My people (I always refer to them as my people, you know) are special. They are all able to dress themselves and feed themselves. They are all ambulatory. But," and she cleared her throat and frowned, "they do have special needs. Some of the townspeople call my residents crazy."

Leaning forward in her wicker rocker, Abigail placed a hand over Clair's. "They call my people the Clarkson crazies," she whispered.

Clair felt sick to her stomach. "About Jennifer Wingate—"

"I prefer to say that my residents are simply living out their lives in worlds they have chosen for themselves, worlds in which they feel safe. Everyone wants to feel safe, wouldn't you say so, my dear?"

The elder woman smoothed the skirt of her dress. "At any rate, I watch over them with great diligence." She studied the face of her young visitor. "I am especially careful to protect them from people from the outside, people who might upset or harm them." Miss Clarkson's eyes looked beyond Clair into the past.

"My mother, God rest her soul, was a true visionary. She saw the need for such a place as this when she first laid eyes on a man named Kirby Prank.

Years and years ago when my mother was a young woman—about your age—she came upon Kirby Prank sitting on the curb on Main Street chewing on a fried chicken leg. Kirby was considered the local crazy. Well, Mother saw him sitting there, bare feet, bare head, frayed clothes, no place to live, eating his chicken leg as delicately as if it were filet mignon. He looked up at her and smiled graciously, as if he were seated in a fine restaurant."

Miss Clarkson raised her voice in indignation. "Two bullies happened by, and I don't mean children! Two grown men walked up to poor Kirby and began to taunt him. They pushed at him and he dropped his chicken. They called him names and one of them gave him a swift kick. A look of bewilderment covered the man's face, as if he didn't understand what was happening.

"Well my mother understood! She rushed over to those two lumpheads and gave them a piece of her mind. She was yelling her head off, commanding them to leave the man alone. Pretty soon a crowd gathered. Everyone wanted to know what all the ruckus was about."

Abigail's cheeks became tinged with pink as she continued her story. "My mother stood there with her hands on her hips and told them in no uncertain terms that they ought to be ashamed of themselves and they had better stop mistreating Kirby Prank. Well, those two scalawags just gloated at her and huffed, 'And what are you going to do about it?' My mother said at that moment it as was if the Lord Himself had asked that question. What was she going to do about it? In an instant, an idea flashed in her mind, bright as lightning and twice as powerful! Clarkson House. She would found a home where the mentally disabled could live safely and freely."

A smile played across the old woman's face. "My mother marched home right then, as my father tells it, and laid down the law to him. Told him what she was going to do and would he like to be a part of it? My father was a lawyer, a good man, a great man. He loved my mother more than anyone or anything on this earth. He supported her one hundred percent. Together they made plans. They bought the biggest house in Caderville and fixed it up. Father continued to practice law, of course. Set up his office down on Main Street, where Abraham Bennett has his survey office now. Mother even drove to Lamberton and took some nursing courses at the nursing school over there. She wanted to be able to give the best possible care to her residents.

"When all the legalities were settled, Mother went out and sought her first resident. She found Kirby down by the railroad station. It took some doing to get him to understand, but finally she persuaded the gentle soul to come home with her. Word got around that there was help to be found at Clarkson

House. Of course, there were guidelines. Had to be. Mother could not accept any patients who were capable of violent behavior. Eventually she had residents from all over the county and beyond. Over the years we've even housed people from out of state. These are all people with varying degrees of mental illness, whose treatment at the big hospitals has reached its limit. Here, they are able to live out their lives without fear and, best of all, with love. We love our people. They are precious to us."

There was that word again. Precious! *It certainly seems to be the word for the day,* thought Clair.

"That's quite a story," Clair said respectfully. "Your mother was a remarkable woman. And it looks as if you have followed in her footsteps."

"Yes, she was remarkable," beamed Abigail Clarkson, "and thank you for the compliment. Now, about Jennifer Wingate."

At last, thought Clair.

"Why do you want to see her, and what exactly is your connection with her? I must admit I have an idea who you are," the old woman nodded knowingly.

"Well," began Clair hesitantly, "I—"

"Out with it, my dear. Don't be shy!"

"I am Jennifer Wingate's daughter." The words came out swiftly, and Clair suddenly felt relief at sharing this fact with Miss Clarkson.

"Yes, my dear, I knew it all along." The older woman smiled at her visitor. "And you came to Caderville to find your mother and your journey has brought you here."

Clair closed her eyes and took a deep breath. She looked intently into Miss Clarkson's face. "What can you tell me about my mother?"

Chapter Nine

"Jennifer Wingate came to us about a year after she gave birth." Miss Clarkson's voice was gentle. "Apparently, she had been drawing into herself for some time before her parents realized something was wrong. She reached a point where she would not or could not talk. She would sit in the bay window of her home for hours, not moving. Didn't seem to recognize anyone, not even her parents. A doctor at Lamberton said there was nothing to be done. So Joanna and Wendell brought her over here."

Clair shook her head in disbelief. "You mean she's been here for—"

"Twenty-four years."

Clair fixed her green eyes on Miss Clarkson's faded blue ones. "May I see her?"

The head of Clarkson Home pursed her lips. "I'm not sure. I wouldn't want to upset her, you know." She thought a moment and then thumped her cane on the gray porch floor. "I'll let you see her, but we mustn't let Jennifer see you. Give me some time to think over whether or not you two should actually meet." She stood up and signalled Clair to follow her.

They walked through the front door and down a pale blue carpeted hall. A sweeping archway opened into a large room housing two long tables. The rich wood of the tables gleamed in the light that streamed in through three tall windows. Through another archway, Clair followed Miss Clarkson into the kitchen. Everything was white and yellow: white wainscoting, yellow trim, white countertops with white and yellow cupboards underneath. A crystal vase on the windowsill was brimming with daisies.

Miss Clarkson leaned over the sink and peered out the window into the backyard. She nodded her head up and down. "Uh hum." Beckoning Clair to follow quietly, the woman passed through the back door onto a porch. Slowly opening the screen and putting her finger to her lips to insure silence from the young visitor, she pointed to the southwest corner of the backyard.

A double-seater swing stood several feet from the iron fence. The swing was made of oak. The arch that supported the swing was intertwined with a rainbow of Japanese morning glory. A flower bed encircled the swing with baby-blue forget-me-nots and pink phlox. Clair could see someone on the swing, moving slowly and rhythmically. It was a woman. Her brown hair, faded and interspersed with gray, was pulled back in a graceful French braid. Her neck was bowed, as if she were looking at something in her lap.

"That's her," Abigail whispered.

Clair stared at the woman on the swing. Her heart raced. She could only see Jennifer Wingate's back, but it was enough to realize she was seeing her birth mother for the first time. Clair wanted to run around the swing and see her mother's face, but her feet were rooted to the spot. Miss Clarkson laid her hand on Clair's arm.

"We'd better go now. I don't want her to turn around and see us. Don't want to take a chance. You come back next week," Miss Clarkson said cheerfully. "I'll let you know what I've decided about you and Miss Wingate."

Clair could tell by the woman's tone that the interview was concluded. She thanked her hostess and turned to leave. "Miss Clarkson," Clair spoke hesitantly, "what was she doing?"

"Doing? Whatever do you mean, my dear?"

"She kept looking down, as if she were looking at something. Something held her attention. What—"

"It's a doll," Abigail answered quietly. "She has a rag doll she carries everywhere. She's really quite tender with it. It's an important part of her world."

As the two women passed through the dining room, a short round man with thick round eyeglasses hurried up to them. "You're just in time!" he said breathlessly. He straightened his tight-fitting brown vest and fussed at the white hair encircling his balding head. "Hurry now! Don't want to be late! It's in bad taste to be late, of course!"

A bewildered Clair followed Miss Clarkson into a room off the hallway. It was a parlor, warmly decorated in dusty rose and cream. Miss Clarkson sat down in a love seat, pointing Clair to a wing chair, its tapestry splashed with pale pink roses. The young woman seated herself. Their guide busied himself in the center of the room, his toe tapping on the rich rose carpeting. He cracked his knuckles and bowed reverently to the ladies.

"Classical music is one of the seven wonders of the world," he spoke grandly. "The violin, of course, is perhaps the sweetest vessel of such wonderment. The silken voice of the violin has stirred many a heart and exposed the beauty of the classics to even the most untrained of ears." He rested his gaze on Clair, giving her a knowing, forgiving look. "Now, if you please, I will favor you on the violin with a concerto."

Clair waited for the man to produce the instrument, but she soon discovered he already had it in hand. He carefully lifted his invisible violin to his chin, plucking the strings and listening intently. After a minute or two of intense tuning, he rested his bow lovingly on the strings. He was about to begin when an exasperated look crossed his plump face. Still holding the violin under his chin, he freed his hand and tightened the hair of his bow. "Tends to loosen up on me," he said apologetically.

Finally, all was ready. He played feverishly, his fingers flying, his bow dancing across imaginary strings. Sweat dribbled down his temples, his chin contorted with the effort. Clair watched in amazement. She looked over at Miss Clarkson. The silver-haired woman's eyes were closed, her head moving as if to mark the rhythm of a grand and sweeping piece of music. Flabbergasted, Clair set her eyes back on the busy musician. When he finished the piece with majestic chops of the bow, Miss Clarkson opened her eyes as if on cue and began to applaud. Clair followed suit.

"Wonderful, Casper. Vivaldi?"

"*Concerto in G Minor*, of course," he beamed. He looked to Clair for a response.

"Lovely," Clair spoke, unsure of herself. "Such exciting music!"

The man bowed as low as his roundness would permit. He looked engagingly at the young woman with the auburn hair and green eyes. "And now I have a special gift for you," he said shyly.

Clair began to protest the necessity of a gift, but Miss Clarkson quickly silenced her, shaking her head no. Clair sat back in her chair, wondering what was going to happen.

"Music of another kind," announced Casper. " 'To Autumn.' "

A smile lit Clair's face as she recognized the poem from her college days. A poem. What a lovely gift to give.

> *Who hath not seen thee oft amid thy store?*
> *Sometimes whoever seeks abroad may find*
> *Thee sitting careless on a granary floor,*
> *Thy hair soft-lifted by the winnowing wind. . .*

Clair listened as Casper recited the poem in a lilting voice, articulate and clear. When he finished, Clair warmly applauded him.

"Keats! John Keats!" Clair laughed, happy she actually remembered who wrote it.

"Of course," replied Casper. "And now I must be going," he said abruptly. "I'm having lunch with William. Good-bye."

"William?" Clair asked timidly as Casper disappeared through the parlor door.

"Shakespeare," Mrs. Clarkson replied. "They are very close friends." She rose from the love seat and explained. "Casper's world is full of music and literature.

He can 'play' several instruments and actually can read music quite well. But he doesn't know his last name and cannot remember from one day to the next what day it is. He's a dear, sweet soul, unable to cope with reality, as we call it. But he does quite well in his own world."

Clair left with the image of her mother on the swing, loving and nurturing the lifeless rag doll cradled on her lap. Her heart ached with sadness for her mother. A nagging thought emerged as she walked down the front steps of the house. Had something else happened to her mother to trigger her illness—something other than her restricted life and the trauma of giving up her baby for adoption? She frowned, her forehead puckered in thought. Suddenly she realized she was no longer walking the sidewalk alone. The gardener had quietly pulled up beside her.

"I hope you don't aim to cause any trouble around here, miss," he hissed, fire in his eyes. "If I were you, I'd stay away from Miss Wingate, you hear?"

Clair stopped and stared at the man. His face was dark and grizzled, his black eyebrows hovered like dark clouds over his brooding eyes. Icy fingers of fear skipped fiendishly up Clair's spine. She said nothing to the man. Quickening her steps, she hurried through the gate and into her car. The man's menacing looks had only deepened Clair's suspicions that there was more to the Jennifer Wingate story than met the eye.

❧

Jack hunched over his desk, searching the old paper for information. He was about to give up when a small article in the corner of the second page caught his eye. He jotted down a few notes and the date. Grabbing another paper, he searched the contents. Nothing.

He continued for several hours, examining papers dated before and after Clair's date of birth. An elusive pattern was forming as the young detective pulled together snatches of information from various papers. With a push, Jack nudged his chair away from his desk. The wheels on his chair creaked as he leaned back. He let loose a low whistle.

"Could be wrong," he said aloud. "Could be my overactive imagination. I hope I'm wrong."

Chapter Ten

Except for the occasional buzzing of a tree frog and the raucous shriek of a blackbird, the forest was silent. The young man crept stealthily through the underbrush. The ancient trees swept upward, forming canyonlike walls on either side of the trail. Cautiously fingering the weapon at his side, the young man stopped and listened. Up ahead a small clearing stood in a pool of sunlight. A sudden crash in the bushes to the left warned of a lumbering presence. There it was! A huge brown bear. It reared on its hind legs at the sight of the man. With swift, almost reflex action, the man took aim and fired.

"What in thunder!" yelled Ben Wheelock. He was covered with cranberry juice.

"Gotcha!" yelped the young hunter, waving his water gun.

"You!" the pharmacist seethed. "You come back here, Will Tatum! When I get ahold of you—"

"Gotta catch me first!" the dark-haired boy squealed as he scrambled down the aisle and out the door. He stopped to stick out his tongue and then disappeared.

Clair sat at the counter, smothering a laugh. Mr. Wheelock's white shirt was splattered with the red juice. He sputtered and fumed all the way to the back of the store. He returned to the front wearing a fresh shirt.

"That boy aggravates the daylights out of me! I wish someone would—" He stopped and pointed with his head to a woman entering the pharmacy. "That's his aunt coming in now," he whispered to Clair. "She lets that boy run wild."

A woman dressed in faded jeans and a baggy tee shirt walked in, her flip-flops slapping the floor. "Got a prescription needs to be filled, Ben," she said to the pharmacist. "Got a terrible cough." As if to demonstrate her ailment, she began hacking and wheezing.

Ben took the prescription from her, shaking his head. "It would help, Leanne, if you would quit smoking."

"Dr. Stanton says it's bronchitis," she said defensively. "Quit nagging me about my smoking. Every time I come in here, you're railing at me." She smiled, revealing yellow teeth.

"Now Leanne, before I fill your prescription, there's something I want to talk to you about." Ben cleared his throat.

"Will been here again?" She rolled her eyes.

"Will Tatum runs around here, harassing me, stealing candy, and I don't know what all. I wish you'd keep a tighter rein on the boy."

The woman shrugged her shoulders. "He ain't mine. I feed him and clothe him. That's what the judge said I was supposed to do. I can't do nothing more."

Ben could see there was no use talking about it, so he walked to the back room to fill the prescription. Clair watched the woman follow Ben to the back of the store. She felt sad for the boy.

"It's a bad situation," Jack said quietly as he eased into a stool next to Clair.

"Hi, Jack," said Clair. She was glad to see him.

Jack smiled. The warmth in his brown eyes gave Clair a feeling of security, as if this man could make everything work out. *What am I thinking of?* she scolded herself. *I hardly know him and I feel as if I've known him all my life. Calm down, Clair Silvero. You are a sensible woman, not given to romantic notions.*

"Will Tatum's parents were both alcoholics," Jack continued in a low voice. "They were killed in a car accident a couple years ago. Both were drunk. The judge gave custody of Will to his aunt Leanne because she was the only available living relative. As you can see, the situation is less than ideal."

Jack sighed and reached over the counter to pour himself a cup of coffee. "That boy is bright. And what an imagination! If only—" He fell silent as Leanne walked by with her bottle of medicine.

Ben approached Jack and slapped him on the back. "What's doing, Mr. Thomas? Anything new I don't know about?"

Jack shook his head. "What's up with Sadie? Have you talked to her yet?"

"Patience, son, patience. I was just about to tell Miss Silvero the good news when I was attacked." He scowled.

"Let me guess," Jack grinned. "An eight year old with a water pistol."

"With cranberry juice, mind you. Not water like a normal kid. Stained a brand-new shirt." Ben looked at Jack over his glasses. "How did you know?"

"Saw him running down the street."

"His usual mode of movement. Running from the scene of the crime," Ben huffed.

"About Sadie," Clair asked. "What's the story?"

"You're sounding more and more like a journalist every minute," said Jack with a smile. "Maybe I should make you my partner."

His words put butterflies in the pit of Clair's stomach. She tried to ignore their fluttering.

"You can go see Sadie today, if you like," Ben announced. "She'd be happy to meet you and help you in any way she can." Ben looked at Jack. "I even put in a good word for you, Thomas. She said you could come along with Miss Silvero if—"

"Please, call me Clair," the young woman interrupted.

"You can go along with Clair," Ben corrected himself, "if you want to. Although I must say she didn't sound too thrilled."

"Thanks," responded Jack. "I'll be on my best behavior. Let's go." He grabbed Clair by the hand and pulled her gently to her feet. "Where's your fancy chariot?"

❧

Sadie was sitting on the porch when Clair and Jack pulled up the driveway. Sunlight reflected off the old woman's glasses as she leaned forward to watch the shiny red car. The screen door opened and a middle-aged woman came out and joined Sadie on the porch.

Jack bounded up the steps. Clair followed shyly behind him.

"Good afternoon, Sadie." Jack took the soft gnarled hand in his own. "It was good of you to see us this afternoon."

"Humph," Sadie frowned at the newspaperman. She fixed her eyes on the stranger who accompanied him.

"This is Clair Silvero, Sadie," Jack introduced her. "She's from down in Westchester County. That's near New York."

"I know where Westchester County is," snorted Sadie. "Used to have a cousin who taught school down in Dobbs Ferry."

"It's a pleasure to meet you." Clair extended her hand. "I'm a schoolteacher in Langston."

Sadie's face crinkled with a smile. "A schoolteacher, eh? That's nice. Years ago I used to teach. In a one-room schoolhouse, mind you, not in one of these big shiny buildings they have nowadays. And I'm willin' to wager a king's ransom that the children learned a lot more back then. Why, we used to have to memorize all kinds of literature and history. Now all these kids have to memorize is the combination to their lockers. Cryin' shame."

Clair smiled. She was going to like Sadie Atkins. Here was a woman who wasn't afraid to voice her opinion. *I hope it rubs off on me,* Clair thought. Coming up to Caderville by herself was one step toward that goal. She had always been shielded by her family, and now she was doing something on her own. It felt good.

"This here's my granddaughter Margret." Sadie pointed to the woman who stood beside her. "She claims I need takin' care of, but I can take care of myself, thank you very much."

Margret smiled and shook Clair's hand. "It's nice to meet you. Grandma is always happy to tell her stories to anyone interested. I'll be in the kitchen. If you need me, just give a holler."

"I'm going to show you the farm," Sadie announced. She grasped her cane and took hold of Jack's arm. "Let's go."

Sadie directed the steps of the two visitors. She showed them the herb gardens and the old milk house. A nearby field had been newly mown, filling the air with the rich aroma of freshly cut hay. Sadie pointed out the barn and the pigpen.

"You're not wearin' honeysuckle perfume, by any chance, are you?" Sadie asked Clair.

"No, I'm not," responded Clair, puzzled by the question.

"No, her perfume smells like lily of the valley, if I'm not mistaken," Jack chimed in absently.

Clair looked at him in surprise. Jack realized what he had said and shoved his hands in his pockets. "I guess, I mean I think it's lily of the. . .I just sort of noticed once. . ." His voice trailed off.

Sadie's eyebrows shot up. "I see," she said. "Reason I ask is because of Peggy Sue." She pointed toward the pen attached to the side of the barn. "Smell of honeysuckle drives her wild."

Jack and Clair approached the pen and looked over the wooden rails.

"Enormous," was all Clair could say.

"Had a girl here last summer who wore honeysuckle. Had to run for her life, she did." Sadie shook with laughter. "What a sight! A city-slicker running like the wind!"

Jack laughed and patted the pig on the back. "She's a beaut, all right."

Next Sadie led them to a wooden building at the edge of the barnyard. It was smaller than the barn, windowless, with a slanting, tar-covered roof. The door was ajar. Along one side of the door was a wooden bench. Sadie slowly sat herself down on the bench.

"This was the icehouse," Sadie declared. "Back then, there was no such thing as refrigerators. No siree, we had iceboxes." She smiled and the blue eyes behind her glasses twinkled as the memories paraded by.

"In the winter, my father and his brothers would go down to the pond or Blueberry Lake to cut ice. They'd get it from the river if the winter had been cold enough to freeze it solid. They'd cut the ice up and load it in the wagon. The horses would drag their load over the snow and up the road, back to the farm. Then they'd unload the chunks of ice and store them in this building. Between the layers of ice, they'd put sawdust. Worked as an insulator, you know, to keep the ice cold. Why, they fairly filled the place with ice. The chunks were just the right size for the icebox Mother had in the pantry.

"Whenever Mother decided it was time to make ice cream, my father would haul out a chunk of ice and commence to cut off pieces to fit in the ice cream's freezer. He'd have to cut it with a small crosscut saw." Sadie laughed aloud. "While he'd be a-sawin', big flakes of ice would scatter, looking all the world like snowy leaves from some fairyland. We kids would grab them as they scattered and pop them in our mouths. It was a treat!"

Clair was intrigued by the impromptu glimpse into the past. *I must remember this for my classroom next fall. Perhaps I could develop a lesson plan focusing on life in New York before electricity.* A smile tugged at her lips. *Wouldn't the kids love that! We could try to get through the day without it, maybe build a mini icehouse—*

"Go ahead!" Sadie interrupted Clair's lesson plan. "Walk inside a bit. It's still cool in there, always seems to be."

Clair and Jack took a few steps inside the building. It was dark except for the rectangle of light framed by the doorway. Jack walked farther in.

"It is cool in here," his voice said. Clair couldn't see him. "Take a deep breath."

Clair breathed in. "Smells like sawdust," she responded. "Isn't that something? After all these years!"

"Come all the way in," Jack implored. "This is really neat. You can sense the history."

"No thanks," said Clair, keeping close to the door.

"What's the matter, afraid of the dark? Chicken?"

"I refuse to answer on the grounds that it may incriminate me."

Jack reappeared, his face bright with an impish grin. "Clair, I do declare! You are a grown woman and you're afraid of the dark? Tsk, tsk."

"I'm fallin' asleep out here!" Sadie called from the bench. "Let's get movin'. I feel like a cup of tea."

Chapter Eleven

"Wendell Wingate used to work for the railroad," Sadie began her story. "He followed in his father's footsteps. His father's name was Zecharias, if I recall correctly."

Clair nodded and the tombstone in the cemetery flashed in her mind.

"Now Wendell had a brother by the name of Jonas Trevor. Jonas Trevor Wingate never did like the railroad. Disappointed his father to no end because he didn't want to be a railroad man. But Jonas had ideas of his own. He had a real talent for drawin' and paintin'. Why, he could paint a picture of a cardinal so real you'd think it was goin' to fly right off the paper!" Sadie nodded for emphasis. "Right off the paper!"

Clair smiled and jotted down some notes in her notebook. It was wonderful to at last be able to retrieve some information about her family.

"Whatever happened to him?" asked Jack.

"I'm getting to that," glared Sadie. "Hold your horses." Sadie cleared her throat and continued in her soft, sometimes gravelly voice. "Jonas took off for New York City. Found a job with some publishin' company doing illustrations. Proud as a peacock, he was. Lived out all his days in New York. Can you imagine? But when he passed away, they brought him back here to be buried. He's in Green Meadow Cemetery. He never married, never had a family of his own. It was up to Wendell to carry on the family name.

"Wendell bought a house on Crescent Street. It's the dark green one with black shutters. I don't know why anyone would want to live there. It's right near the railroad tracks. Whenever a train goes by, everything rattles and shakes, so with all that racket, you think your teeth'll go flyin'!" Sadie leaned back in her rocking chair. "But I suppose Wendell, bein' a railroad man, he didn't mind. Maybe he even liked it."

"Is the house still there?" inquired Clair.

"Oh yes, it's still there. In fact, I believe it still belongs to Jennifer. Her uncle Jonas and her father's estate have paid the taxes on it all these years. Of course, taxes around here aren't very high, you know. Yes, the house is still there. But it's all boarded up now."

"What about his wife? What was she like?"

"Joanna was a shy slip of a girl. She used to come to the library when I worked there. Loved to read! She'd take out four or five books at a time. Well, Joanna gave birth to a baby boy. They named him Wendell Junior.

Then Jennifer came along. But when Wendell was about five years old, he fell sick with influenza. It took his life." Sadie shook her head and clicked her tongue.

"Cryin' shame. Broke Joanna's heart, but it hardened Wendell Senior. After that, he wouldn't let Jennifer out of his sight. I guess he figured if he kept a strict eye on her, nothin' bad would ever happen to her. Even when Jennifer was older—a teenager and a young woman—Wendell Wingate wouldn't let her go anywhere alone. It was a sad situation." Sadie reached over and covered Clair's hand gently with her own.

"Eventually, Jennifer became pregnant. Her father was outraged and insisted the baby be given away. It broke Jennifer's heart, I guess. A year later, she had to be put in Clarkson House."

"But who is my biological father? Can't you tell me?" asked Clair. "I was hoping you could tell me who he was. What about the man who used to go and visit my mother? Ben Wheelock said there was someone who used to date her, or try to anyway."

"That would be a fellow by the name of Grayson. Robert Grayson."

Grayson. The named sounded vaguely familiar. Where had she heard that name before? Then it came to her. Miss Clarkson on the porch. *Don't mind Grayson.* The formidable gardener at Clarkson House?

"Is. . .is Robert Grayson my father?" Clair stammered.

Sadie looked at Jack. With an almost imperceptible move of his head, he signalled no to Sadie. "Well," Sadie replied slowly. "Maybe. No one knows who fathered Jennifer's baby. I suppose only Jennifer knows." A faint blush appeared on Sadie's wrinkled cheeks.

Clair stared at her, studying Mrs. Atkins's face. "I think you know something you're not telling me. I think you know more about the circumstances surrounding my birth. Why won't you tell me?"

Sadie's blue eyes filled with compassion toward the young woman. "It's not my place to say. It's purely speculation, anyway. I can tell you're a fine young woman and have a fine, loving family of your own. Why don't you just leave it at that?"

"Maybe Sadie's right," Jack chimed in.

Clair fell silent. She certainly didn't want to press the issue with Mrs. Atkins. But Jack! That was another story. If Jack was hiding something, she was determined to drag it out of him.

"Thank you so much for all you've told me, Sadie. I appreciate it," said Clair warmly. "Perhaps we've worn you out! We'd better be going," she said in Jack's direction.

Jack jumped to his feet. "You're absolutely right. It's getting late, after all."

"Now wait just a minute, young man. I'm not through with you." Sadie pointed a gnarled finger at the newspaperman.

"Uh oh," said Jack under his breath.

"My father always used to say holdin' grudges is like eatin' rocks—it tears up your insides. You're forgiven." She nodded, her lips pursed in a firm line, as if to say "case closed." "Now what kind of information are you lookin' for?"

Jack leaned eagerly toward Sadie. "I'm investigating the rumors that Caderville was a link in the Underground Railroad."

"Not a rumor," grunted Sadie. "True as can be. My grandfather used to help out when he could. But it was all kept very secret. They didn't want anyone bollixin' it up. But you'll be wantin' to talk to Abraham Bennett, the surveyor. He can tell you a lot more than I can."

"Thanks for the lead!" said Jack enthusiastically. "This could be the break I was looking for."

"We'd better be going." Clair rose to her feet. "Thanks again for all your help."

"Come and see me again, Clair," the old woman urged.

"I will," promised Clair.

"By the way," said Sadie, "are you two younguns going to the fair tonight?"

"Yes, as a matter of fact we are," answered Jack.

"What fair?" asked a surprised Clair.

"You'll see," Jack replied.

Margret appeared in the door to the parlor. "You stay right there in your chair, Grandma," she ordered. "I'll see your guests to the door."

For once, Sadie didn't protest. She was worn out from all the excitement. She smiled and leaned her head back, closing her eyes. Margret signalled to Jack and Clair to follow her.

On the front porch they exchanged farewells. Margret hesitated for a moment, then spoke quietly to Clair. "Just remember," she said, "sometimes it doesn't matter how a life begins. What matters is how it is lived."

Her words puzzled Clair.

"Let's go," said Jack, taking Clair by the arm. "Thanks again, Margret," he called over his shoulder.

As Clair drove down the bumpy driveway, she gripped the steering wheel tightly. "I have a bone to pick with you, Jack Thomas."

Jack sighed. "Doesn't everybody? Now what?"

"You know something I don't know. So does Sadie, and apparently so does Margret. I want you to tell me what it is!"

Clair spied a little side road, and she pulled her car onto it. The course was narrow and unpaved, more like a path than a road. Trees and head-high weeds clambered for space alongside the path, their leaves and branches plucking at the sides of the car as it passed slowly by.

"Where are you taking me, Alice?" Jack quipped. "I think I just saw a rabbit in a waistcoat run across the road."

"Very funny." Clair stopped the car and turned the ignition off. "You are going to talk now, Mr. Thomas, and you are going to talk fast!"

"Please, please don't shoot me," Jack cried. "I promise, I'll tell it all!"

Clair laughed and stepped out of the car. Jack followed suit and they sat up against the front of the car. The road stretched on until a curve took it out of sight. The weeds were buzzing with insects. A summer wind scooped up the sounds of rustling leaves, whirring bugs, and bird song and poured it over Clair like a warm torrent of music. Clair was discovering that being outdoors relaxed her. Somehow, it soothed her spirit.

"Now Jack," she began. "Sadie is right about my family. I couldn't ask for more love and support than what they give me. I don't feel insecure in any way about them; they are my family. But I do want to know about my birth mother. I need to know about my beginnings. It's already a sad story, I know, but there is some tenderness there, I just know it." She thought of the half locket in the envelope back in her motel room.

"If there is more to it, and obviously there is, then I want to know. I have a feeling it's not a nice story, but I want to know anyway. It's okay, I can take it. Someone once said it was the truth that sets us free. I need to know the truth about my birth."

Jack bit his lip. "Clair, can I ask you something? I know your family's great and everything, and you feel secure about it. That's good. But what about you?" His brown eyes searched Clair's face. "What are you really looking for? Maybe you're not so sure where you fit in this thing called life. And believe me, we all ask that question, whether we've been adopted or not. We all want to find our niche and be who we were meant to be."

"Oh, so finally I get to meet the Reverend Jack that Ben was talking about."

"At your service." Jack bowed to her. "Seriously, I only know of One Person who can free us to be the people we were created to be. And that's Jesus."

Clair rolled her eyes and shook her head. She looked at her new friend with disappointment in her eyes. "Really, Jack, I'm not into religion. It's okay if it works for you, but I never saw a need for it in my life. I don't mean to hurt your feelings, but why don't you keep it to yourself?"

Jack ran his hand through his tangled brown curls. "Sorry. No can do. I can't keep it to myself. It's the kind of thing you have to give away. Can't help it." He smiled and pulled up a bachelor button growing by the side of the road. He fingered the periwinkle-blue flowers, twirling its stem between his fingers. His voice took on a rich, warm timbre. "His love is like nothing I have ever known before. It comforts me, stretches me, makes me think. Shows me who I was, who I am becoming."

His words poured over Clair like the soft summer wind.

"You make it sound so. . ." She searched for a word.

"Real?"

Clair nodded. Jack laughed. "That's because it is real! He's real! He's not just a figure in one of your history books, Miss Schoolteacher. And by the way, it was Jesus who said, 'You shall know the truth, and the truth will set you free.'"

Clair pushed away from the car. She took a few steps down the road and looked back at Jack. He was smiling that engaging smile of his. Not far from the road, a row of oaks and maples caught her eye. They towered overhead, large old branches lifting their leafy crowns to the blue sky. The verdant summit ebbed and flowed in the breeze like a tide unbound by the earth.

The peaceful rhythm of the trees' dance and the peaceful rhythm of Jack's words poked a larger hole in Clair's heart, letting in more light. Her mother's words to Clair before she left suddenly resurfaced: You've been sort of restless, like you're missing something.

Mom was right, Clair mused. *I am missing something.* She looked up again at the swaying trees. Peace in motion, alive. *How do you get that inside? And if you do, does it stay?*

"Hey! A penny for your thoughts," Jack called.

"It'll cost you more than that," she laughed. "What about that carnival Sadie was talking about?"

"I'll pick you up at eight," Jack grinned.

Chapter Twelve

The large empty lot near the lumber mill had been transformed into a gaudy wonderland of lights and action. People bustled in and out between the booths and rides like ants. Children darted in and out of the crowd, bubbling with excitement. The smell of cotton candy, popcorn, and roasted peanuts wafted its tantalizing way throughout the grounds.

Tired parents listened to unending cries for one more ticket, one more ride. Determined, lovestruck boyfriends spent dollar after dollar trying to win over-stuffed monkeys for their girlfriends, while cheerful chords of "She'll Be Comin' Round the Mountain" blared endlessly from the carousel's speakers.

"You did it again, you know," declared Clair. "You managed to weasel out of answering my question. How do you do that?" Clair tried to keep up with Jack's long strides.

"It's a gift," he replied. "What ride do you want to go on first?" he asked, changing the subject.

"Oh no, you don't," Clair objected. "You're going to tell me tonight all you know about—hey look! A Ferris wheel! I haven't seen one of those in years," she exclaimed.

"Ferris wheel it is!" Jack responded. He strode over to buy a ticket. Standing in line, he caught sight of the sheriff. "Here," he said, handing Clair a ticket. "You go on ahead and take a spin. I'll catch up with you in a minute."

"Jack—" she called to him, but he disappeared into the crowd. "I give up!" she said to herself.

She headed for the Ferris wheel. Dusk shrouded the carnival in pre-evening gray. The colored lights glowed a little brighter. The Ferris wheel was revolving at a good pace, the seats swinging with every turn, the lights creating a soft blur of reds, blues, yellows, and greens. Clair could hear the squeals of young children as their seats approached the highest point of the ride.

Clair joined the short line of people waiting for the next ride. The man ahead of her was holding a squirming three year old in one arm, while trying to keep hold of an older boy with his other hand. The older boy turned around to stare at Clair. His upturned face was smeared with chocolate. Clair smiled at him. In return, he stuck out his tongue and sent a flying spray of raspberries in her direction.

"Danny, you stop that," the exasperated father scolded. "That's not polite." He gave an apologetic look to his son's victim.

"No harm done," Clair laughed. "I have a little brother named Danny. I'm used to it." She laughed again, wishing her Danny had been there to hear her. He'd have had a fit!

The line moved up a little. While she waited, a strange feeling crept over her, as if someone were watching her. She looked around. The man standing next to the controls of the Ferris wheel was staring in her direction. His grubby blue jeans, tee shirt, and grimy neck betrayed a disdain for bathing regularly. A red baseball cap covered his dirty blond hair. He looked away when he caught Clair's eye. Clair shivered involuntarily. Where was Jack?

The Ferris wheel bumped gently to a stop. One by one the seats were emptied and replenished with new riders. It was Clair's turn to board. She handed the man her ticket. He took it from her, staring for a long moment into Clair's green eyes. His eyes were black, fathomless.

"Thank you, lady," intoned the man, his voice laced with sarcasm. "Have a nice ride."

Clair sat down in her seat and pulled the bar shut. The man reached a muscular arm over and rattled the bar. "Just making sure it's shut tight, ma'am. Wouldn't want you to get hurt."

"Thank you," said Clair. Her voice sounded small.

A handful of other people boarded the wheel. The man cranked the lever and started the ride. Clair caught her breath as the wheel reached full speed. She had forgotten how high a Ferris wheel could be. She looked cautiously down at the fair grounds. It was dark. Light from under the red-and-white-striped food tent brimmed over into the darkness. The staccato yells of the game vendors punctuated the air.

Suddenly, the Ferris wheel jerked to a stop. Clair's seat swung wildly. She tried to stop it by shifting her weight. Everyone started screaming with delight. *Figures,* she thought. *It breaks down while I'm at the very top.* She peered down to see if she could see Jack. It was impossible to sift him out of the milling crowd. People gathered around to check out the commotion at the Ferris wheel.

Trying her best not to swing her seat, Clair leaned over to see if anyone was fixing the wheel. Looking right up at her was the man at the controls. Clair could see the faint red glow of the cigarette he gripped in his mouth. He stood there, his head turned up toward Clair, staring.

Clair quickly looked away. A thought passed by, leaving in its wake a pit in her stomach. It was as if the man had stopped the wheel on purpose, just to rattle Clair.

No, thought Clair. *I've seen too many movies.*

"Clair! How's the weather up there?" Jack called to her from below.

She waved to him. "Thanks a lot," she muttered.

The wheel jerked to a start. In a matter of minutes, it was Clair's turn to get off the ride. The man in charge opened the bar for her. "How was your ride?" he grinned.

"Just fine, thank you," Clair said abruptly. She walked quickly away, the man's laughter filling her ears.

Jack rushed up to meet her. "Hey, I thought we'd go again. It's my turn!"

"Be my guest," said Clair. "No more Ferris wheels for me."

Jack hurried to catch up with her. "Where are you going?"

"I don't know," she said over her shoulder.

"Wait a minute," Jack laughed. "What happened, Clair? You weren't really scared, were you? Ferris wheels break down all the time—you know that. When I was a kid, that was a big thrill. Especially if you got stuck on the tippy top!"

"Tippy top?" Clair stopped to catch her breath. "I haven't heard that expression since I was a kid."

"That long, eh?"

"Very funny," responded Clair. She looked back at the Ferris wheel. "That man gave me the creeps."

"Who?" asked Jack.

"The guy running the Ferris wheel. He kept staring at me."

"That's Harlow Fleming. He isn't exactly a likeable guy. Come on, I've got just the cure for your frayed nerves."

He took Clair by the hand. She suddenly felt safe. Her fears dissolved into the background. The next thing she knew, Clair was climbing into the golden saddle of a lavender horse. She patted its white mane and admired the white roses painted on its flank. The music was so loud she couldn't hear herself speak. She looked over at Jack. His mount was blue and dappled with silver rhinestones. The carousel began its rounds. The horses traveled up and down, slow and steady.

Jack pulled an imaginary cowboy hat over his eyes. He urged his horse on with an imaginary crop. He shot at rustlers and even lassoed a vagrant cow. He looked ridiculous. Clair couldn't stop laughing. Jack took a bow and proceeded to fall off his horse. Tears streamed from the young woman's eyes as an embarrassed and blushing cowpoke remounted as quickly as he could. "She'll Be Comin' Round the Mountain" clanged merrily in Clair's ears with deafening repetition. Her sides hurt with the hilarity of it all.

"That was fun!" she said breathlessly as they dismounted. She patted her horse good-bye.

"Ain't a playground, you know," the woman who ran the carousel said wryly to Jack as he passed by her. Clair tried not to laugh.

"I'm starving," said Jack. "Want some sausage and peppers?"

"Sounds good to me," Clair agreed.

They made their way to the food tent. While Jack was ordering, Clair waited outside the tent. The nearby hills were dark and silent silhouettes against the night sky. Stars gleamed overhead, while their earthly counterparts flickered in the night air.

"Fireflies! I love those things." Clair ventured out from the tent's light to see if she could catch one of the illusive lights. Someone brushed up against her, almost knocking her over.

"I'm sorry, lady," a voice apologized. "Didn't see you." Clair looked up to see the face of Harlow Fleming. She froze on the spot. He stood there, silent and grinning.

"Here's your sandwich, Clair," Jack's voice called to her. As he walked up to Clair, Fleming sauntered away.

"Did you see that?" Clair hissed. "That's the guy from the Ferris wheel. He bumped into me, almost knocked me over! I bet he did it on purpose."

"I don't think so," said Jack. But as he watched the man disappear into the night, his jaw tightened with anger. "Never mind." He turned his attention to Clair. "Let's eat."

Chapter Thirteen

"Preston!" Clair called to her young friend from the motel parking lot. "Come here!"

Preston loped across the street. "What's up, Clair?" The young man pushed his hair out of his eyes. "Car need washing?"

Clair smiled and shook her head. "No, not yet. Listen, will you take a walk with me? There's something I need to ask you."

The teenager nodded. He tried to act casual, but his chest was swelling with pride. Miss Silvero made him feel like he was a real person.

They stopped at the steel bridge that spanned the Delaware River. Clair leaned over the railing and watched the waves and ripples slide silver-gray beneath the bridge.

Clair looked at the teenager and smiled. "Preston, I wanted you to know a little more about me, since we've become friends. You've probably wondered why I'm even here in Caderville. It's obviously not a hot spot on the map."

"You got that right," Preston snorted.

"Oh, but it's a lovely place!" said Clair hastily. "I like it. Anyway," she continued, "I wanted you to know I came to Caderville looking for my birth mother. I was told her house is on Crescent Street and I'd like to see it. Would you mind showing me where Crescent Street is?"

"Sure," said Preston. "Piece of cake. Hey, this is kind of like that show on TV—*Unsolved Mysteries!* Cool!"

"Don't say that," moaned Clair. "I hate that show! It gives me the creeps. And by the way, let's keep my story to ourselves, okay? I would rather not have all of Caderville in on it."

"Hey, do I look like a blabbermouth to you?" said Preston. He looked offended.

Clair looked at his young face. His greasy hair had fallen into his dancing blue eyes again. Several pimples dotted his cheeks. His lips were two thin lines.

"Of course not," she said warmly. "I trust you."

Clair had no idea the effect she was having on the young man. He had grown several inches on the inside in the short time he had known her. At last, someone took him seriously, talked to him like an adult.

"I'd like to go to Crescent Street now, if it's okay with you," said Clair. "Let's go over and tell your mom you'll be with me."

"I don't have to tell my mother where I'm going!" scoffed Preston.

"Of course you do. You should always tell your parents where you'll be when you go out."

"You sound just like a schoolteacher," moaned the teenager.

"That's because I am!" laughed Clair.

"Uh oh." Preston did a double take of his new friend. "Does that mean I have to call you Miss Silvero?"

"Not unless you're in my classroom. Now, come on, let's go," Clair urged.

Preston rolled his eyes. "Yes, Miss Silvero."

Permission granted from an appreciative parent, the two detectives were on their way. Preston guided Clair through the streets of Caderville until they reached Crescent. Then Clair drove slowly down the street.

"It's green with black shutters and it's all boarded up," she informed Preston.

"There it is!" cried Preston, pointing wildly.

Clair pulled the car to the side of the street. They both looked across the street at the house. The front yard was overgrown with weeds. The front porch sagged forlornly to one side. Green painted siding was faded and peeling. The house wore its windows like cataracts, clouded and dim with filmy dust. Suddenly, Clair got an idea.

"Listen, Preston. I'd like to look around for a while, but I don't want to park the car here. It's too loud, if you know what I mean." She looked at her companion. "How old are you?"

"Seventeen."

"You've got your license, right?"

"Well, sure. I got it when I was sixteen," he said, as if it had happened years ago.

"Great! Why don't you take the car and drive it around a while? Take it to Mr. Wheelock's and have a soda or something, whatever you want to do. Just be back here in about a half hour, okay?"

She turned the car off and got out of the car. Preston exited his side of the car and slid into the driver's seat. He pulled the door shut.

"This is great!" he exclaimed, gripping the black, leather-bound steering wheel. "Are you sure?" he looked anxiously at his teacher friend.

"Of course I'm sure! Take good care of her," said Clair. "I'll see you later."

She waved good-bye to Preston. Then she hurried across the street and stood on the sidewalk in front of the house. The black iron number forty-seven hung crookedly on the front porch next to the door. Clair checked up and down the street. There didn't seem to be anyone out and about. What harm could there be in looking around? Walking up the path to the front porch, Clair placed her hand on the wooden railing of the steps. It was rough with peeling paint. The precarious slant of the porch convinced the young woman not to climb the front steps.

She walked timidly around the side of the house to the back. There she discovered an enclosed back porch. The small backyard was a tangle of high grass and weeds. Someone had discarded a bike in the yard, its blue fenders succumbing to relentless rust. A maple tree rose tall and undaunted by the surrounding decay. Its branches, teeming with green, reached toward the house, creating shade across the back of it.

The door at the top of the steps was partially open, hanging loosely on its hinges.

I think it's okay if I just go in to take a look, Clair convinced herself.

She climbed up the few steps and onto the back porch. Half of the yellowed curtain covering the window of the inside door had fallen away, giving Clair a glimpse inside the house. She peered in through the dusty glass.

"The kitchen," Clair said aloud. The outdated stove and refrigerator stood silently collecting dust. The hands of a clock above the stove pointed endlessly to two o'clock.

Clair tried the doorknob. To her surprise, it turned with a squeak.

It's unlocked, realized Clair. *Either that, or the lock was broken.*

She pushed open the door. It scraped against the gray-and-red-speckled linoleum. "I don't believe I'm doing this," whispered Clair. She walked into the kitchen and quickly shut the door behind her.

The air inside the house was stale and musty. A cobweb fell across Clair's face as she passed through a door into the next room. A long table stood surrounded by six straight-backed chairs sitting at attention. The china closet was covered with a white sheet. Tired strips of pale green paisley wallpaper had let go of the wall and drooped hopelessly downward.

In the living room, Clair discovered a bookcase, still full of books. She knelt down in front of it. There were several books on the railroad. One shelf was dedicated to Reader's Digest Condensed Books, the bindings creating a faded rainbow of color. An oversized book laying on its side caught Clair's eye. She picked it up and read the title: *The Gardener's Treasury of Domesticated Flowers.* The inside leaf had been autographed.

" 'To my niece, Jennifer, a true rose in my book! With affection, Jonas T. Wingate,' " read Clair. "This must be one of the books he illustrated!" Clair read his name printed below the author's name. She turned the pages, marvelling at the detail and color of each illustration. A pink ribbon marked the page describing the garden rose. Clair remembered the rose petals she found with the locket. "It must be Jennifer's favorite flower," mused Clair.

There were several other books with Jonas's illustrations. There were children's books, books on fishing, a reprint of *Tom Sawyer*. Clair delighted in the lively drawings. She felt she was being introduced to Jonas T. Wingate through his art.

A shadow flickered across the floor. Clair looked up at the windows along the front wall. Light streamed in and fell upon the musty floor. She got up from the floor and peered through the window. There was no sign of the red car. She looked at her watch.

"It's been a half hour already. Wonder where Preston is?"

Along the right wall of the living room rose a set of stairs. Clair placed her hand on the bannister and hesitated.

"This is crazy," she scolded herself. "I shouldn't even be in here, let alone going upstairs!" But her curiosity got the best of her and she quickly ascended the steps.

The upstairs was comprised of a short hallway flanked by four doorways. Clair stuck her head in the first room. It was empty except for a few boxes. Furniture in the next room was covered with sheets. It was in the third room that something grabbed Clair's attention. On the wall hung a still-life painting of a vase filled with roses.

"This must have been her room!" Clair whispered. She entered the room. The cherry, four-poster bed was covered with a sheet. Beneath a window that faced the street stood what looked like a desk and chair. Clair pulled the grimy sheet off to investigate. The desk was oak with a narrow top drawer and a row of side drawers along the left side. She opened the top drawer. It was empty except for a few pieces of stationery and a pen. On impulse, the young woman grasped the brass handle of the bottom drawer and pulled. It was stuck. She tugged and got it partway open. She could see what looked like a soft-bound notebook of some kind.

"Maybe it's a journal!" exclaimed Clair. She pulled harder but to no avail. Suddenly she heard a noise from downstairs. It sounded like the scrape of the back door on the linoleum.

Clair froze. She was about to call out to Preston, but she stopped herself. *What if it's not him?*

Looking around quickly, she hurried to what looked like a door to a closet. "Thank goodness!" she breathed. She shut the door as quietly as possible and hid as far back as she could. Several old coats hung on the rod, providing a shield for the frightened woman.

Jack's probably right. I've seen too many movies. It's probably Preston. I'll never live this down if he knows I've been hiding in the closet. She was about to get up when she heard footsteps in the room. Someone walked over to the desk and began pulling on the drawer.

Clair was breathless with fright. *Who would want to get into that drawer besides me? It couldn't be Preston. Besides, he would have called out for me or something.* Her mind searched frantically for an explanation.

With a loud, painful screech of wood against wood, the drawer was forced open. All at once, the house began to shake. A loud rumbling filled Clair's ears as she sat in the dark closet. She could hear nothing else.

What on earth! Clair almost let out a yell, but then she remembered. *A train. Must be a train. Sadie said the house was near the railroad tracks.* She sighed with relief. The train roared past the house for what seemed like a half an hour. Finally the sounds faded into the distance. Clair strained to hear any movement in the house. She waited a few minutes and then decided the person must have gone while the train was rushing by.

Clair cracked open the closet door and looked out. The room was empty. The bottom drawer of the desk lay on the floor. She hurried over to look. "It's gone!" she cried. "The notebook is gone!" Her blood ran cold. "If that's Jennifer's journal, who in the world would want it? I don't like the looks of this," Clair said to herself. "I'd better get out of here."

The tired carpeting in the hall scrunched dryly beneath Clair's feet. She hurried down the stairs. She stopped short at the bottom. To her horror a red baseball cap was hanging jauntily over the end of the bannister.

Clair bolted into a run. She flew through the dining room, the kitchen, and down the back steps, right into the arms of Sheriff James T. Watson.

"Whoa, young lady. Seen a ghost?" The sheriff held the girl at arm's length. Clair was breathing heavily, her eyes frantic with fear. "Calm down," the lawman said gently. "You're coming with me."

Chapter Fourteen

Clair felt ridiculous as she got out of the squad car and entered the sheriff's office. Preston was slumped dejectedly in a chair. Jack jumped up from the top of the desk where he was sitting.

"What in the world were you thinking of?" an exasperated Jack exclaimed.

Clair sighed wearily. "You don't have to shout."

"I'm not shouting," responded Jack vigorously.

"Hello, Miss Silvero," said Preston. "Sorry I couldn't come and pick you up."

"Preston, what happened? And what are you doing here?" Clair looked at the sheriff. "Oh, no! Don't tell me you picked Preston up for driving my car."

The sheriff nodded. "How was I to know he hadn't stolen it for a joy ride?"

"That's ridiculous!" fumed Clair. "Didn't he tell you I gave him permission?"

"Well, uh, yes, he did," the sheriff cleared his throat.

"But they didn't believe me," snorted Preston.

"They? How did Jack get mixed up in all this?" demanded Clair.

"Jim came to my office to tell me about Preston and your car. He knew I knew you and so here I am. Honestly, Clair, didn't anyone tell you curiosity killed the cat?"

Clair glared at the journalist. She turned her attention to Preston. "I am so sorry! Let me take you home. I'll explain to your parents what happened. I am so embarrassed."

"Embarrassed!" exclaimed Jack. "You're in hot water! It's called trespassing around here. Breaking and entering ring a bell?"

"I did not break in," said Clair defensively. "The door was unlocked."

"I'm sorry, ma'am, but it is still considered trespassing," the sheriff chimed in. "And I'm going to have to do something about it."

"Oh, great!" Clair plopped down into a chair. "Just lock me up and throw away the key. Never mind that something strange is going on around here."

Jack's ears perked up. "What are you talking about?"

"Oh, nothing," said Clair sarcastically. "Just that I think someone followed me into the house. Took something from Jennifer Wingate's desk drawer. Left a calling card at the bottom of the stairs." Clair was beginning to look pale.

"How do you know this someone else was in there?" interrogated the sheriff. "And how do you know they took something?"

"I was in the bedroom," started Clair.

"You went upstairs!" cried an incredulous Jack.

"Yes, I went upstairs," huffed Clair. "I made a dumb choice, okay? Now will you let me finish?"

"Yeah, let her finish," piped Preston.

"I was upstairs in what must have been Jennifer Wingate's bedroom."

"How do you know?" asked the reporter.

"Will you let the woman tell her story?" said the sheriff. "Leave your interview for later, Mr. Hot Stuff."

Jack crossed his arms and sat against the desk. "Go ahead, Miss Silvero."

"Thank you, Mr. Thomas. How kind of you to give me permission."

"Don't mention it, Miss Silvero. As a matter of fact—"

"Will you two save your quarrel for later!" interrupted Sheriff Watson. "I have work to do."

Clair continued. "I was trying to open a drawer in the desk. I could see there was some type of notebook in it, possibly a journal. Anyway, I heard someone open the back door, so I hid in the closet."

"You hid—" Jack started.

Clair gave him a don't-you-dare look.

"I heard the person pull out the drawer and then they must have left. A train came by, so I couldn't hear them leave. I decided to go—"

"Finally, some common sense!" muttered Jack under his breath.

"And at the bottom of the stairs, there it was. A red baseball cap."

Jack leaned forward, his face serious. "A red baseball cap. Are you sure?"

"Yes, I'm sure. It terrified me. That's when I ran out of the house."

"We'll check it out," said the sheriff. "Right now we're going to have to go over to Clarkson House and see if she'll press charges."

"Mr. Watson," spoke Clair, "I hardly think my mother is in the position—"

"Miss Clarkson is Jennifer Wingate's legal guardian. It's up to her. Now please come with me, Miss Silvero."

"Will you let me drop Preston off first?" asked Clair.

"Sure," said the sheriff. "I'll wait here for you."

"I'm going with you," said Jack.

"No, you're not," responded Clair.

Preston smiled broadly at Jack as he left the office.

"I'm sorry about the mix-up," the sheriff apologized to the teenager. "It just looked bad, you know."

"Looks can be deceiving," retorted Clair.

"Apology accepted," Preston called over his shoulder. This had certainly turned out to be an exciting day!

Clair explained everything to Preston's parents. To her relief, they thought it was hilarious.

"Sounds like something out of the movies," Preston's father laughed. He slapped Preston on the back. "You sure picked a gem for a friend this time!"

Mrs. Finch smiled shyly at Clair. "I want to thank you for trusting our son. He's a good boy; he just needs to apply himself in school. Do you think you could talk to him about it?"

"Aw, Mom," groaned Preston.

"I'll do my best," declared Clair. "Preston has real potential for a bright future."

Preston blushed, Mrs. Finch glowed, and Mr. Finch slapped his son on the back again. "Well, sport, you heard the lady. We'll be expecting great things from you!"

Clair left with a smile on her lips. As she walked down the front way, she could here the Finches laughing and talking together.

The young teacher had a gift for bringing out the best in children. Their parents inevitably looked at their offspring in a clearer light after Miss Silvero had had her say.

Clair followed the sheriff's car to Clarkson House. She could see that Jack was riding with him. She was actually relieved that Jack had come along. Suddenly Clair knew she needed Jack's support. She had really made a mess of things.

The sheriff knocked on the front door. Miss Clarkson opened the door with a flourish. To her surprise, Caderville's sheriff, the newspaper editor, and a guilty-looking Clair Silvero stood on her front porch.

"Where's the mayor?" she asked, looking for other dignitaries.

The sheriff smiled. "It's just us, Miss Clarkson. We're sorry for bothering you—"

"You should be sorry! It's dinner time, don't you know? I don't like our schedule being interrupted. But do come in," she added graciously. "Obviously, you have something to tell me."

Clair marveled at the woman's calm. If a sheriff had shown up at her doorstep, Clair would have been a nervous wreck.

The mistress of Clarkson House showed her visitors into the lovely rose parlor. Clair warmed at the memory of Casper and his poetry. She could use some soothing words at this point.

The sheriff explained the situation briefly to Miss Clarkson.

"And what I need to know," concluded the sheriff, "is if you'd like to press charges."

Miss Clarkson sat studying Clair's face. "Of course not," came her reply. "But I would like a word alone with Miss Silvero, if you don't mind."

The sheriff nodded and left the room with Jack following behind. Clair shifted nervously in her seat. She wondered if she had ruined her chance to one day meet her mother face to face.

"Are you a Christian, Miss Silvero?"

Miss Clarkson's question threw Clair off guard.

"What does that have to do with anything?" asked Clair, surprised.

"Just answer the question, my dear," replied Miss Clarkson persistently. "Are you a Christian?"

Clair stiffened. "I find that to be a highly personal question."

"Nothing personal about it," the woman responded effortlessly. " 'A city set on a hill cannot be hid,' " she quoted. "If you're talking about prayer time, now that's personal." She continued on, oblivious to Clair's discomfort. "We are to pray in secret. Not make big announcements about it. There is great strength to be drawn from the Lord through prayer. Great strength."

"If you'll pardon me," said Clair formally, "I really don't understand what this has to do with me or the situation at hand. What exactly did you want to discuss with me? I regret my foolish decision to enter the Wingate house without permission. I should have spoken with you or Sheriff Watson first."

"Apology accepted," smiled Miss Clarkson, patting her amazing silver hair. "At any rate, what I'm talking about has everything to do with you. I knew from the moment I met you that you were a determined young lady, determined to know the truth about your birth mother, your biological father. I am a firm believer in truth."

She stood and walked to the lampstand that graced the front of one of the tall parlor windows. With a gentle click, the rose globe of the lamp glowed pink. The lace curtains blushed with the rosy hue. "I believe, however, that it is not just your quest for information that has brought you to Caderville. I believe the Lord has His hand in it. He brought you to Caderville."

Clair sighed and rose to her feet. "Really, Miss Clarkson, I'm not interested in religion. I—"

"I'm not talking about religion. That's for legalistic Pharisees and Sadducees. I'm talking about a Person." Miss Clarkson smiled. "He loves you, Clair, and He wants you to find your home in His heart. Our earthly homes are so temporary and subject to change. To think He wants to dwell with us! It really is amazing. Amazing love."

"You sound just like Jack Thomas," Clair said.

"Jack has a good head on his shoulders. He'd make a fine preacher."

"You're not kidding," muttered Clair under her breath.

"Clair, I can tell you right now your search will most probably lead to a painful discovery. It certainly hasn't been very joyful so far, has it? I want you to know there is Someone watching over you who wants to have you for His own daughter. He wants to adopt you, Clair."

The older woman's words skillfully plunged like flaming arrows into Clair's heart. Tears stung her eyes. The light was becoming so much brighter, things were becoming clearer.

Clair impulsively threw her arms around Miss Clarkson and gave her a hug. "I appreciate what you're trying to say," said the young woman. "I'm not sure I understand. But I'll think about it. Now, please, Miss Clarkson, if there's anything you can tell me about my father, tell me. I need to know."

Miss Clarkson shook her head. "I can't tell you anything. It would only be conjecture on my part. You must find the truth yourself, Clair. I'm sure you will. But please, remember, the Lord has an everlasting strength for you to lean on."

Clair smiled. "You are sweet. I'd better be going. Thank you for being so understanding about my snooping."

The pair headed for the front door. "I almost forgot," said Clair. "I found a book that belonged to my mother. It's all about flowers. Her uncle did the illustrations. They're so beautiful, I thought maybe Jennifer would like to see it. Do you think that would be all right?"

Miss Clarkson thought a moment. "Yes, we'll do it. That's a lovely idea. But we'll take it one step at a time, okay? Perhaps later, after you two have met. I need to see how she reacts to you first. I haven't decided if it would comfort or upset her."

"I understand. And thanks again for all your help."

Miss Clarkson nodded and bade the young woman good night. A bustling in the hall called their attention to someone heading hurriedly in their direction. It was Casper.

"Excuse me, please," he panted, "I hope I'm not too late."

"Late for what Casper?" inquired Miss Clarkson.

"I should like to ask permission to walk our dear guest to the gate," said Casper. His eyes gleamed hopeful behind his round-rimmed glasses.

"That's up to Miss Silvero, Casper," said Miss Clarkson gently.

"I'd be delighted," responded Clair with a smile.

Casper clapped his hands together gleefully. "This way, mademoiselle." He held open the door. Miss Clarkson nodded and the two walked out together.

The sun had slipped behind the hills. Clair and Casper walked down the steps and sidewalk into the dusk. The faint aroma of mock orange blossoms sweetened the air. Casper twiddled his tie and adjusted his wire-rimmed glasses several times before he and his walking companion reached the wrought-iron gate. Suddenly, he stopped short.

"Oh my!" exclaimed Casper. "My, oh my!"

The patrol car was parked in front of the gate. Sheriff Watson and Jack were leaning on the side of the vehicle when Casper and Clair approached. Clair could see the sight of the police car startled her friend Casper.

She gently placed her hand reassuringly on Casper's arm. "It's okay, Casper."

"To jail, are you going to jail?" Casper asked anxiously.

"Oh no," responded Clair. "No jail for me."

Casper smiled broadly. "No matter." He pulled out his handkerchief and wiped his forehead. Pulling himself up to maximum height, he began to recite:

> Stone walls do not a prison make,
> > Nor iron bars a cage:
> Minds innocent and quiet take
> > That for an hermitage:
> If I have freedom in my love,
> > And in my soul am free,
> Angels alone, that soar above,
> > Enjoy such liberty.

"Why, Casper, that was lovely!" cried Clair.

"Richard Lovelace, 1618 to 1658," beamed the old man.

"Thank you for walking me out," Clair smiled.

"My pleasure," said Casper. He tipped an imaginary hat. "Good evening, now."

"Good evening."

Casper hurried back toward the house. Clair stood for a moment with her hand on the iron gate. The words of the poem had pricked her heart. " 'And in my soul am free.' Somehow I don't think that applies to me," she mused.

"You coming?" Jack called to her. "Or do we sit here all night?"

Clair pushed her thoughts aside. "I'm coming. What's your hurry, anyway?"

"Dinner. It's time to eat, in case you hadn't noticed," replied Jack. "Let's get out of here and head for the diner."

"All right," said Clair. "But I'm afraid I'm not too hungry."

"Too much excitement, eh?" said the sheriff. He held open the red car door for the young woman.

"You said it!" sighed Clair.

"Don't worry. I'll eat for the both of us," said Jack.

"I wouldn't be surprised," laughed Clair.

"By the way," said the sheriff as he shut the door to Clair's car. "Jack and I went over to the Wingate house while you were talking with Miss Clarkson. There was no red cap on the bannister. Must've been your imagination." He frowned. "However, there was evidence that the desk drawer you spoke of was tampered with. It was just like you said, lying on the floor."

"Well?"

"So I'll be keeping an eye on the house. We'll see if there's any other activity around the place."

"Thank you, officer," said Clair. "At least you believe me about the drawer!"

"Yes, but we have no way of knowing if it was a journal that was taken. It could have been something else, just an old notebook."

"Why would anyone—" began Clair.

"We'll discuss this later, okay, Clair?" Jack interrupted. "Let the man get back to his office."

"If anything else comes up, let me know," said Sheriff Watson. "Don't hesitate to call or come to the office."

"Thanks," said Clair.

"Next stop, Star Diner. Fried chicken," announced Jack.

Clair put the car in gear. "Fried chicken it is."

Chapter Fifteen

A woman with shocking orange hair and a purple pants suit sped down Main Street. She reached the pharmacy in a streak of color. A steady stream of shrieks and undiscernible words poured forth from the woman's mouth. Store owners up and down the street sprang onto the sidewalk to see the commotion. Clair jumped out of the way as the woman dashed through the drugstore door.

"Benjamin Horace Wheelock, come here this instant!" the woman demanded. Her voice was shaking with indignation.

The pharmacist hurried down the aisle from the back of the store.

"What in blazes is going on? You sound like a banshee caught in a bear trap!" Ben stopped and stared. His mouth dropped open. "Violet Cranberry. What in the world—"

The effect of the blazing hair and purple suit was more than the man could bear. He fought gallantly to keep the corners of his lips from turning upward.

He swallowed a guffaw and nervously turned the pencil behind his ear. "Wha. . .what happened, Violet?"

"You think it's funny, don't you? Thought you'd play a joke on me, did you? Well, this isn't funny!" Tears began to stream down her face. "This is humiliating. In all my years I have *never* been a blond or redhead! I have always had beautiful jet black hair. And you know it! Now look at me!"

"But I didn't—"

"I used the same box of enhancer I always use. The one I buy from you. And would you look at me now! It's a disgrace!" The tears began again until Violet saw Clair by the door. "Oh hello, Miss Silvero," she said politely. "Nice to see you." Then she resumed her tears. "I don't know what I'm going to do!"

Clair approached the trembling woman cautiously. "Excuse me, Violet, but it will wash out. If you go to the hairdresser's, I'm sure they can help you restore your hair. You wouldn't want to do it yourself, though. You don't want to damage your hair."

Violet dabbed her eyes with a lavender handkerchief. "I suppose you're right, my dear. But I'm still going to the sheriff." She glared at Mr. Wheelock.

"Now wait just a minute, Violet Cranberry. I had nothing to do with this. Why in the world would I switch dyes—"

"Enhancer," corrected Violet.

"Dyes," retorted Ben. "Why in the world would I do such a thing? I don't give two hoots about your hair color!"

"Jealous. You're crazy with jealousy. First there was Salvatore," she gazed knowingly at Clair. "And now there's Sam."

"Sam Glass, the sanitation man? The day he decides he's in love with—"

"He's a wonderful man, Sam. And so neat, too," she glowed.

"I tell you I had nothing to do with—" Ben stopped midsentence. Pressed against the glass of the store's window was a round little face. The boy was pointing at Violet and Ben, laughing raucously.

"Will Tatum!" Ben screeched. "I might have known!" Ben headed for the door, growling. "This is the last straw! I'm hauling you to the sheriff's office if it's the last thing I do!"

Violet and Clair followed Ben out the door and watched in amazement as Ben nimbly chased the boy down the street and caught him. Will Tatum looked with shock at the pharmacist.

"I never seen you move that fast before!" he exclaimed, his voice tinged with admiration.

"I've never been so mad at you in my life!" scowled Ben as he hurried the boy toward the sheriff's office. "It's one thing to ruin one of my shirts with your blasted squirt gun, but when you're tampering with my merchandise and affecting my customers, well then by Jiminy you're going to pay, and you're going to pay big."

"Oh my," said Violet breathlessly to Clair, "I've never seen Ben so angry before, not since the time he had a shouting match with Avery Birch over the size of a fish he'd caught. He just loves to fish, you know," Violet babbled.

Clair's curiosity and concern for the child propelled her behind Ben and his captive.

The brick building that housed the *Caderville Courier* was located next to the sheriff's office. Jack Thomas watched the animated parade from behind his desk. He leapt to his feet.

"What's going on?" he asked just as the group reached the sheriff's door.

"That's what I'd like to know," echoed Sheriff Watson.

Jack and the sheriff found themselves staring at Violet.

"Don't tell me. I already know," said the sheriff. He coughed vigorously.

"I want you to do something about this kid," demanded Ben. "Throw him in jail if you have to. No bail."

"Now Ben," said the sheriff, "the boy is only eight years old. It was just a prank. I can't very well arrest him. What would the charges be anyway? Turning Violets into oranges?" He let it go, laughing with his head back.

"Well, I never!" huffed Violet. "I'd like to see you with flaming orange hair, James. For that matter, I'd like to see you with hair!"

"She's got you there, Jim," laughed Ben. He loosened his grip on Will.

The sheriff turned red. He adjusted his ever-present hat. "I'm sorry, Violet. This is not a laughing matter. I will take care of it immediately. Come with me, Will Tatum."

The boy looked nervously up at the sheriff. "What's it going to be, sheriff? Ten years in prison? The chair?"

"You and your imagination," said the sheriff. "Come with me."

The boy was about to bolt when Jack stepped in. "I'm here to represent this young man," he said formally. "You haven't even read him his rights. That in itself is cause for release."

The boy's eyes grew wide. "Yeah, that's just like on TV. You gotta read me my rights."

"Oh for crying out loud," cried Ben. "Are you going to do something about this kid or do I have to file a complaint?"

"Ben, go have yourself a nice cold soda, will you?" said the sheriff. He walked the boy into his office with Jack following.

"I'll take full responsibility for Will," promised Jack. "I'll give him a job so he can pay Violet whatever it costs to have her hair returned to its previous color. And from now on, I'll keep an eye on him. Try to keep him out of trouble."

"Well, Jack, that's real nice of you, but don't you think you ought to ask Leanne first?" asked the sheriff.

"She don't care what I do," scoffed Will.

"I'll talk to her," Jack replied.

"All right. But let me tell you something, young man." The sheriff pointed a finger at the boy. "You'd better mind your p's and q's."

"What?" asked the puzzled boy.

"That's an outdated phrase meaning you'd better behave," explained Jack.

"Oh," said young Tatum.

"You may go now," said the sheriff as sternly as he could. "And I'd better not hear Ben Wheelock complaining about you again!"

The boy nodded meekly. On his way out, he turned around and stuck his tongue out at the lawman. Jack hurried him out of the office and took him next door.

"This is my office," he said to Will. "You like it?"

The boy looked at the piles of newspapers, the brimming file cabinets, and the overflowing garbage can.

"I like it," grinned Will. "It's a real mess."

"It's a sign of genius, you know," Jack defended the disorder.

A knock on the door interrupted their conversation. Jack's face brightened at the sight of Clair. "Come on in," he said. "Miss Silvero, this is Will Tatum. Will, this is Miss Silvero."

"Hello," said the child shyly. He looked down at his frayed sneakers.

"Nice to meet you," said Clair. "What's this I hear about you getting a job, Will? That's pretty good for someone eight years old."

"I'm almost nine," he protested. "July the twenty-eighth I'll be nine."

Clair smiled. "That's great."

"His job will be to come in here once a week and sweep the floor."

"What floor?" joked Clair. "I don't see any floor!"

Will giggled and Jack blushed. "Very funny," said the reporter. "That's just why I need Will to work for me. I can't have people joking about my very important office."

Just as the thirsty soil soaks in new rain, the words "I need Will" fell quickly into the young boy's heart. He looked eagerly around the room. "Where's the broom?"

Jack held out his hand for a high five and Will reciprocated with a firm slap of the hand.

"It's around here somewhere," said Jack. He searched diligently. "Here it is!" He reached behind the filing cabinets. The green-handled broom was covered with dust.

"It must have fallen behind there in the last century," said Clair. She grabbed a nearby rag and wiped the handle off. She touched the boy's shoulders lightly with it. "I dub thee official sweeper of the *Caderville Courier*."

The boy's face lit up with a smile. "I know what that means. That's what the kings and queens used to do when they made somebody a knight. Then they could do battle and stuff and they were called sir."

"Very good!" said Clair. "Do you like to read about knights and kings?"

"Yeah, but I can't read too good. And I don't have a library card. The librarian won't give me one because of the time I put glue in her shoes."

Clair suppressed a smile. "I'll see what I can do about getting you a card, okay?"

"Okay."

"What do you say?" prodded Jack.

"What do you mean? I said okay. Are you deaf?" asked the boy.

"Say thank you to the lady," whispered Jack.

"Oh. Thank you, lady."

"You're welcome," responded Clair.

Clair left the office and headed back toward Ben's. She needed to buy a few things. She stopped to search her purse for the list of needed items. She could hear her brother's voice. "That saddlebag would throw any horse's back out!" he would say at the sight of Clair's bulging pocketbook. She rummaged through her bag.

Suddenly she became aware that someone was standing in the narrow alley between the flower shop and the pharmacy. It was Robert Grayson. He stepped out from the shadowy alley.

"You steer clear of Clarkson House, understand?" he snarled. "You might get yourself hurt."

Clair looked at the man in wide-eyed amazement. "Who do you think you are to threaten me?" she demanded, surprised at her own nerve. "What do you have against me? I've done nothing to harm you or anyone else for that matter."

The man's dark eyes narrowed into slits. "I heard about you breaking into Miss Wingate's house. Had no business doing that."

By this time Clair's blood was boiling.

"What I do is none of your business."

"Just stay away, you hear? You don't belong here. You don't belong. Go back where you came from. Or else."

"Or else what?" countered Clair.

"Just get out of here while you can."

"This is ridiculous," huffed Clair. "I ought to call for the sheriff. This could be called harassment, you know."

The man was undaunted. "You better be careful, miss," he said with a warning tone.

He left Clair standing alone, her list crumpled in her clenched fist. It took her a moment to realize she was trembling.

Chapter Sixteen

"I got it! I got it!" Clair whispered excitedly, waving the library card in her hand.

"That's great!" Jack whispered back. "How'd you do it?"

"Shh!" admonished Miss Fritz, the librarian.

Jack guided Clair into the back room that housed the children's books. They sat down at one of the window seats.

"I just gave her a speech about the importance of nurturing a child's imagination and how reading and education can change a person for the better," said Clair quietly. "Although I think what Will really needs is a lot of love and positive encouragement."

"You said it," sighed Jack. "Most of the time he's getting yelled at for some 'terrible' misdeed. I just know if someone gave him the attention he needs, he'd be less of a rascal."

Clair handed the card to Jack. "You give it to Will when you see him tomorrow. I'm leaving early for Langston. It's my mom's birthday and my dad always throws her a humongous party."

"Do you have to go?" asked Jack, feigning a frown.

"Jack! It's my mother's birthday! I have to go and I want to go," said Clair. "Besides, things are getting a little too weird around here. I think I need some time away to think things through."

"Tell me exactly what you mean by weird."

"Well, the red baseball cap, for instance," replied Clair. "I know you and Sheriff Watson didn't find it, but I know what I saw. And I think I know who it belongs to."

"Who?" asked Jack, all ears.

"That guy at the carnival. The Ferris wheel guy."

"Harlow Fleming?"

"Yes. Don't you remember? He wore a red baseball cap."

"You sure have an eye for detail," said Jack with admiration. "Even I don't remember what kind of hat the guy was wearing."

"Why would that guy be following me? He must have seen me enter the Wingate house. And why would he want Jennifer's journal?"

"Whoa, Clair. Just a minute. First of all, you don't know for a fact who was in the house with you. Secondly, you don't even know if it was a journal or not. It could have been an old school notebook for all we know."

Clair shook her head. "Who in the world would want an old school notebook? That just doesn't make sense. And I did see that cap, whether or not you and the sheriff believe me. And that guy was real creepy at the fair. I bet he stopped the wheel on purpose to scare me. I caught him staring at me. And what about at the food tent? He nearly knocked me over!"

Jack ran his fingers through his curls. "Well, you present quite a case, but it's all circumstantial. You have no way of proving it. Besides, you said yourself you can't figure why that guy would be following you. Why would Harlow Fleming be harassing you? He doesn't even know you!"

Clair looked out the window. The branches of a weeping willow swept gracefully to the ground. A sparrow darted in and out of the pale green canopy of leaves. "I don't know," sighed Clair. "Maybe I'm just paranoid. But I do want to find out about my biological father. Obviously everyone has a theory but me. And no one will let me in on it."

Jack cleared his throat. "I wasn't sure when to tell you what I think," he said quietly. "I've been doing some snooping of my own."

Clair leaned forward eagerly. "Well?"

"Let's go outside where it's more private," he whispered.

Jack led Clair to the grounds in back of the library. A green wooden bench stood waiting for them in the shade of the willow.

Jack hesitated a moment and then began his story. "I looked through the papers dated around the time of your birth, a few years before and after. At first, I didn't find anything. Figured it was a wild goose chase. But then a small article in the corner of page two of one of the papers stuck out to me. I then went back through all the papers again, this time with something to look for. Unfortunately, I think I discovered a pattern."

"A pattern?" asked Clair, giving the journalist a questioning look. "What do you mean?"

Jack reached out his hand to take Clair's. "At least once a year, sometimes twice, for a period of about six years, there were assaults recorded in the *Courier*. It was before I came here. There have been no more reports like that for the last ten years."

"Assaults?" Clair asked. Her heart was beginning to pound against her chest.

"Assaults against young women in Caderville and the surrounding areas," answered Jack.

"Are you trying to say someone was going around attacking women on a regular basis? And this person was never caught?"

"According to the articles, the women or girls couldn't identify their attacker."

"Or wouldn't," breathed Clair. "I don't like the sound of this."

"Yes, but you see it stopped about ten years ago. I talked to Jim Watson about it, showed him the articles. He agreed there seemed to be a pattern. But all this happened before he came to Caderville. He said he wished he'd been around then. Said he wouldn't have rested until the crimes were solved."

Clair turned her attention to the willow once more. She wished she could take flight like the sparrow and flit away to a distant horizon. Life was getting too rough to handle.

"Are you saying you think maybe Jennifer Wingate was raped and that's how she became pregnant? Pregnant with me?" Her last words were in a whisper.

"Clair, I'm sorry. But that is what I think. And from the looks of things, I think Sadie Atkins and Abigail Clarkson feel the same way. I had a little talk with Sadie's granddaughter Margret. She confirmed my suspicions. But Clair," Jack continued earnestly, "it can't be proven. I'm telling you what I think because you seem bent on knowing the truth."

Clair closed her eyes. Tears flowed down her cheeks. To her own surprise, the tears were not for herself, but for Jennifer Wingate. *What a sad life she had*, Clair thought. *So restricted, and then to be assaulted like that.* A sudden flash of insight illumined her mind. *And then to give birth, to hold her baby, probably the only thing she could call her own, only to be unable to care for it.*

Her heart flooded with gratitude. She thought of Anna and Tony Silvero loving her, providing her with love and security. Laughter. There was always laughter in the Silvero home, even in the tough times. Clair wanted to run to Jennifer and thank her.

"Are you all right?" asked Jack with concern. "I know it's rough. Are you going to be okay?"

Clair smiled through her tears. "I'm going to be fine. I feel a little shaky, but I think I'm finally starting to understand. Life is a gift. A gift to be cherished and thankful for."

"There's only One Person I know who can give the gift of life," said Jack warmly.

"I just may be on my way to agreeing with you, Preacher Thomas," spoke Clair. Hope was beginning its lively work in the young woman's heart.

"Hallelujah!" shouted Jack.

"Jack! Control yourself!" admonished Clair.

The young knight approached the enemy's lair cautiously. The slightest sound would betray him. All was quiet. The castle rose starkly against the gray sky, its black walls steep and menacing. Slipping through a secret opening, the warrior made his way quickly to the garden. He hid himself in the far corner of the courtyard. An eerie curtain of cobwebs hung thickly around the brave knight. He parted the webs with a silver-gloved hand. There was the ogre and the princess. The knight checked his pocket. He had only one magic stone left. It must make its mark. The life of the fair princess depended on it. He pulled his slingshot from his belt and took careful aim.

"Hey!" yelped Jack. Something flew by Jack's head. "What in the world?" He retrieved a colorful missile that had been launched his way. A pink jelly bean. "Will Tatum!" Jack leapt up and chased a figure hidden behind the willow branches. Will was giggling hysterically when Jack swooped him up in a big bear hug.

"I'll not put you down until you apologize!" announced Jack.

The boy grinned and whispered in Jack's ear. "I'm sorry I missed."

Jack laughed but didn't let go. "Apologize to me and the nice lady."

Will looked at Clair and blushed. "I'm sorry," he said.

Jack put him down. "Miss Silvero has something for you."

Will looked down at his sneakers. "She does?" he mumbled.

"Look!" said Clair. "Here is your official ticket to high adventure. Your very own library card."

Will took it from Clair's hand. "Thank you," he said. Clair watched him as little lips mouthed his name written in bold type.

"Now you must promise you will behave at all times in the library or Miss Fritz will have a fit. And you might lose your card!"

"Thanks!" The boy took off like a shot.

"Well, we've done our good deed for the day," said Jack. "Time to reward ourselves. Want a milkshake?"

"No thanks, Jack. I better get back to the motel and pack," replied Clair. "Besides, I have a lot to think about. I'm feeling a little drained."

Jack shoved his hands in his pockets. "I'm sorry. Maybe I shouldn't have told you. Sometimes I don't know when to keep my mouth shut." His brown eyes looked apologetic.

"No, Jack. I'm glad you told me. I think it's important for me to know. So much has happened already. I can't put my finger on it, but I just know the truth will come out. And then I can deal with it."

"You know, Clair, you don't have to deal with it alone. The Lord can help you," said Jack.

Clair smiled. "You and Miss Clarkson must go to the same Sunday school class!"

Jack grinned and escorted Clair to her car in front of the library. As he closed her door, he leaned over with a serious look on his face.

"Clair, I'm a little concerned about this journal and baseball cap business. I think you'd better not go exploring anywhere alone, especially at night. If you need to go somewhere, give me a call, or Preston. Okay?"

"Oh, Jack, don't be ridiculous. Whoever assaulted those girls years ago is probably long gone. And I'm not about to be intimidated by whoever stole that journal. I've come too far to back down now," said Clair firmly. "Don't worry, I'll be careful."

"Call me when you get back from your mom's," said Jack.

"I will," answered Clair warmly.

She headed the car toward the motel. She could see Jack standing on the curb, watching her drive away. Maybe Miss Clarkson was right. Maybe the Lord had brought Clair here for reasons other than finding her birth mother.

Stopping at a red light, Clair watched with amusement as a large white dog crossed the street with a little girl in tow. Her little legs were hurrying to keep up with her charge, her pigtails flying with the effort.

The sound of a blaring horn startled Clair. A green car from across the intersection came toward Clair and stopped abruptly next to her. The young woman looked over at the driver. Her heart skipped a beat. It was Harlow Fleming.

"Hello there, Clair," he said with a greasy smile. His face was dark with stubble. "Or should I call you Rose?"

Clair froze. She stared at the man, terrified. He whooped and tipped his red cap. "See you later!"

A car behind Clair beeped and she hit the accelerator. She drove straight to the motel and locked herself in her room. Pulling open the drawer where she'd put the manila envelope, she fished out the locket. With trembling hands she studied the graceful script. *Rose. My name was Rose. How did that awful man know that? I should call Jack right away,* she thought. She reached for the phone. *No. He might do something rash.* Clair took a deep breath.

"I won't be intimidated," she said aloud. She looked in the mirror. "That didn't sound very convincing," she said to her reflection. "Probably that guy is just a creep who likes to go around scaring people. Yes, that's probably all he is."

She packed her things and got ready for bed. She picked up the phone and dialed long distance. Danny answered the phone.

"Hey, Sis, what time you coming?"

"I'll be there around ten o'clock," said Clair, relieved to hear the voice of someone she loved.

"Great. You'll be just in time to help Dad with his ice sculpture."

"Oh no, not again," groaned Clair. "I thought he was going to give that up after last year's disaster."

"Oh yeah, you mean when he tried to carve a huge swan," laughed Danny. "It looked more like a slug waving a flag."

Clair chuckled. "What's he attempting this year?"

"Bambi. A giant Bambi."

"Oh no," said Clair. "I can't wait to see that!"

"Have a safe trip," ordered Danny. "Drive carefully."

"Yes, little brother. I will."

Chapter Seventeen

"It's all in the wrist," said Tony Silvero.

With a quick tap, Bambi's head went flying across the kitchen. It landed in the sink with a bang. Clair stifled a laugh. Danny burst out laughing.

"What in the world!" Anna hurried in from the dining room.

"What was that awful noise? What did you drop?" Anna looked around the room. A woebegone Tony stood staring at his creation.

"Bambi's dead," choked Danny. "He's joined his poor mother in deer heaven."

"Danny! You stop that right now. You'll upset your father," scolded Anna. She turned her attention to her husband. "It's lovely, dear. I'm sure you can fix it up." She kissed him on the cheek and bustled back to her preparations for the party.

Four crooked legs supported a misshapen body. It tilted slightly to the left. The ice glistened in the morning light.

"You'll think of something, Dad," said Clair. She patted him on the back and followed her mother out of the kitchen.

Anna was arranging two cumbersome candlesticks on the dining room table. They were green and shaped like mushrooms. A bright orange ceramic rooster with red combs stood between the candlesticks.

"Why do you do that, Mom?" asked Clair. "Whenever we have a family get-together, you bring those things out. They are the ugliest things I've ever seen. Absolutely gruesome."

"I don't want to hurt anyone's feelings, dear. You know I can't stand the thought of anyone feeling hurt or left out because of me." She dusted the orange rooster. "You know your aunt Flossie gave me those candlesticks. Cousin Sophie gave me the rooster. She made it herself, you know. In her ceramics class."

Clair gave her mother a hug. "I know, Mom. You are a softie to beat all softies. Where's Uncle Herb's giant clam candy dish?"

"It's underneath the place mats in the cupboard over there." Anna pointed to a corner hutch. Clair sighed and hauled out the hideous pink and white clam.

Anthony walked triumphantly into the room. "Another party, another masterpiece," he said grandly. "Danny's taking it over to the deli. Johnny said he'd keep it in his freezer until the party. He'll bring it over with the sandwiches.

This is going to be a great party, eh, Clair?"

"So you salvaged Bambi," commented the dutiful daughter.

"Piece of cake," said Tony. "It's beautiful, if I say so myself. I think it's even better than the swan I made last year. Remember that?"

"We remember," said Danny from the door to the kitchen. "A swan we could never forget."

Clair helped her mother arrange the silverware on the table. "Is Aunt Carmen coming?" asked Clair with resignation.

"Aunt Carmen always comes," replied Danny. "She never misses a family get-together. Where else can she spout her venom at so many Silveros at one time?"

"Daniel! Don't say such things," Anna admonished her son. "Carmen is rather difficult, but she is family."

"Yeah," said Tony. "Like the poet said, 'Home is where they can't put you out, even if they have a good reason.'"

"I think you mean 'Home is the place where, when you have to go there, they have to take you in,'" recited Danny.

"Same difference," grunted Tony.

"Hey, Dad, I'm impressed. That's Robert Frost's 'Death of a Hired Man,'" said Clair. "Since when have you been reading poetry?"

"Since your mother's got me taking a poetry class down at the community center. She drags me there every Tuesday night."

Poetry. Clair could see Casper standing in the rose parlor, shy and eloquent, reciting Keats. It all seemed like a lifetime ago.

The party was in full swing by three o'clock. Clair helped serve and keep order in the kitchen and dining room. Friends and family buzzed in and outside the house. Tony was in his glory, frequently having to explain just what the ice sculpture represented.

"Hello, Clair. Long time no see," purred a voice at the kitchen door.

"Hello, Aunt Carmen," said Clair. "How are you?"

"Just fine, thank you," said Carmen. "I feel great! I go to the club three times a week, you know. That's how I keep my lovely figure." She leaned toward Clair. "Which is more than I can say for Eva. Did you see her?" she whispered. "She looks like she's gained fifty pounds! Honestly, I can't understand that. Doesn't she care how she looks? And don't tell me it's from having kids! Why, look at me. I had my Lindsay and I don't have any residual fat!"

Clair offered her a plate. "Would you like a piece of chicken?"

"Oh no, Clair," said Carmen. "I'll just have some salad, thank you. Have you seen your uncle Herb? I heard he quit smoking, but I don't believe it. He probably sneaks around and smokes behind Sue's back. It's caught up with him you know. He looks perfectly awful."

"Excuse me, Aunt Carmen, I have to see about the other guests." Clair turned to flee out the back door.

"Wait!" insisted Carmen. "I have a picture of Lindsay to show you. She's in the Bahamas with her boyfriend this week. He's a Yale graduate," she bragged. "Isn't she beautiful? Still wears pink all the time. Remember? That was always her favorite color, even when you girls were little. Remember how you two used to play together? Time flies. My Lindsay was always so pretty. And now look how gorgeous she is!"

I would hardly say we played together, thought Clair. Her cousin was always so stuck up. Clair took the photograph from Carmen. There stood Lindsay, with long black hair and pink sweater dress. Her smile was as Clair remembered it—condescending.

A memory pushed its way to the surface. It took Clair by surprise. She quickly handed her aunt the picture and hurried outside. Slipping through the happy crowd, Clair went through the side gate and into the garage.

The memory played itself back with a clarity that was astonishing to Clair. She could see Lindsay's pink cashmere sweater and her black and pink polka-dotted pants.

"I know something you don't know," said a young Lindsay in a singsong voice.

The two cousins were riding the seesaw at the playground.

"So what," said a curious Clair. "I don't care."

"It's about you," Lindsay whispered from the other end of the seesaw.

"What about me?" demanded Clair.

Lindsay smirked and shifted her weight so she could hold her cousin up in the air. "You're adopted!"

Clair squirmed with anger. "I am not! Who says? Let me down!"

"My mother says, that's who. She said you aren't a real Silvero." The girl in pink jumped off the seesaw. Clair's end hit the ground with a thud.

"Liar!" she yelled after her cousin. Lindsay ran away laughing.

Clair remembered riding her red bike home as fast as her skinny legs could pump the pedals. Her mother had drawn her into her arms and assured her it wasn't true.

"Of course you're a real Silvero," her mother crooned reassuringly in her daughter's ear. "You are our very own little girl."

A satisfied young Clair skipped off with a smile and ran to find her cousin. She gave Lindsay a swift kick in the shins and ran back home. All was right with the world again.

Clair looked up at the red bike hanging from the ceiling next to the wall. Anna Silvero couldn't throw away anything. Clair reached up and touched the tire of her old bicycle.

The young woman felt a twinge as she recalled her mother's reassuring words. *To think she had been lying,* thought Clair. *Makes me feel odd somehow. Strange how I'd forgotten all about that time. And now it's so vivid to me. Come to think of it, Aunt Carmen always did have a way of making me feel strange, like I was an intruder or something. It's amazing no one else ever let it slip. I suppose Dad made sure of that.*

"Hey!" Danny walked into the garage. "What are you doing in here, Clair?"

"Reminiscing," answered Clair. "Remember my red bike?"

"That thing!" laughed Danny. "I can't believe Mom hasn't gotten rid of it yet."

"Seems to me you still have your old bike," accused Clair.

"That's different," said Danny. "Mine's a collector's item."

"Oh, brother," Clair rolled her eyes.

Danny took his sister by the hand. "Come on. Dad's about to give his annual tribute-to-Mom-on-her-birthday speech."

Clair could hear her father's booming voice as brother and sister joined the crowd in the backyard. Anthony Silvero was standing on the porch, waving his arms and calling for attention. Anna sat in the chair of honor.

"I have a special presentation to make," announced Tony. "As you know, it is my Anna's birthday we are celebrating today. And as you know, Anna is a special lady. She has been and is a wonderful wife to me and a wonderful mother to our two children.

"Anna is always willing to learn something new, and she usually includes me in the process. Last year it was origami. The year before that, polka dancing. This year it is poetry. And I have taken it upon myself to write a poem for my wife. Happy Birthday, Anna Silvero." Tony pulled a paper from his pocket, put on his bifocals, and began to read:

My love for you is like a song, its melody is mine alone.
>I'll sing it till the end, my dear, until the end, my dear.
My love is like a river, it flows with greater depth
>With passing days and years, my love, it flows until the end.
Other songs may be silenced, other rivers may run dry,
>Not my song, not this river, until the day I die, my love,
Until the day I die.

The crowd was quiet. Anna was wiping tears from her eyes. "It's beautiful,

Anthony," she whispered to her husband.

The crowd erupted into wild applause. "Bravo! Bravo!"

Anthony took several deep bows and handed the poem to his wife. Clair and Danny stood staring at each other. "Dad?" they said. "Dad wrote that?"

"Now he's done it!" moaned Uncle Herb. "Now all these women are going to want the rest of us to write poems for them. Thanks a lot, Anthony!" Herb yelled to his brother.

"Read it again, Antonio!" called out Clair's great-aunt Angelica. She was crying. "Read it again."

"Yes! Encore! Encore!" several voices joined in.

Anthony took a deep bow. He read the poem again, with gusto.

"Oh, boy," muttered Herb to Clair. "First it was the ice sculpting, now it's poetry. He's going to have a new poem every party."

Clair laughed. "You've got to admit, it's pretty good, Uncle Herb."

"Yes, I admit it. My brother always did have a knack for doing a lot of things well. Except, of course, for ice sculpting." He smiled and put his arm around his niece. "Let's go for a little walk."

They walked together to the front of the house. Herb graciously pointed to the steps. Clair took her customary seat. Herb joined her. This was where he always had her sit when he was going to give her a pep talk. Clair smiled at her uncle. He'd given her pep talks before she'd learned to ride a bike, before she'd entered junior high school, high school, and college. "Clair Silvero," he would always say, "never give up. Always do your best. If anyone tries to stop you, remember, you're a Silvero. And Silveros never give up, no matter what."

"Your dad told me that you know now," he said quietly. "You know what I mean?"

"You mean about my being adopted?" asked Clair.

"Yes." He studied his niece's face. "How are you doing?"

"I'm doing okay," said Clair. "I've been up to Caderville. I'm looking around. Sorting things through."

"Clair, if you ever start to feel funny about things, like your life somehow was fake or something—I don't know if you know what I mean. Just remember this: We have all loved you, genuinely loved you, since you came to us. You are a real Silvero—and don't you forget it!"

Tears slipped from Clair's eyes. Uncle Herb wrapped her in his arms and held her tight. The setting sun threw its gold at the front porch, bathing the two loved ones in warm color.

Chapter Eighteen

"Would you look at these things!" Clair exclaimed. "My old dance shoes!" She pulled the faded pink satin shoes from a cardboard box.

"Your feet were that small once!" teased Paul.

"Paul Carson! Don't you tease my daughter or I'll send you home to your momma," said Anna.

"Sorry, Mrs. Silvero," said Paul in a little boy voice. They all laughed.

"Just like old times," sighed Anna. "I think I'll go down and make you two some lemonade." She disappeared down the narrow attic stairs.

"Your mom is a sweetheart," said Paul. He cleared a space on the floor and sat down. Two small windows shed light into the attic. Boxes, books, and a painting or two littered the floor with memories.

"Clair," Paul spoke softly. "How'd it go in Caderville? Did you find anything out?"

Clair smoothed the satin of her old shoes. "Yes, I've found a few things out. But I have to go back. There are some loose ends I need to tie up."

"Did you find your mother? Did you meet her?" inquired Paul.

"Yes, I found her," Clair hesitated, "but I haven't really met her yet."

"Oh." Paul could see Clair wasn't going to explain anything more. He picked up a book from a nearby pile. "Nancy Drew," he mused. "Must be yours."

"Yes, I loved those books," said Clair. "Nancy Drew, Trixie Belden. I used to devour them whole!"

"That's because of your insatiable curiosity. It's a wonder your curiosity hasn't gotten you into trouble yet."

"Oh, it has," countered Clair. "Remember Mr. Wilkins?"

Paul laughed. "Oh yeah! Mr. Wilkins. You thought he was kidnapping all the cats in Langston. So you hid in his tree at night to monitor the man's movements. And whammo. You fell out of the tree and onto Mr. Wilkins and one of his cats. A real-life case of curiosity almost killing the cat."

"How was I supposed to know the man bred cats for a living? All I knew was he bought an awful lot of cat food on a regular basis. And our cat was missing. I thought that was a pretty good deduction for a ten-year-old kid."

Paul grinned. "You were something else."

Clair blushed. "Dad didn't think it was so great. He grounded me for the rest of my life. Or so it seemed to me."

Clair looked at Paul's familiar face. She was glad to see him again. She'd known him a long time. Clair could tell he had something he wanted to tell her.

"You're scratching your ear," she prompted.

"So?" Paul stopped scratching.

"You always do that when you're nervous. When you have something on your mind."

"You know me too well," sighed Paul. He moved over to sit closer to Clair. "You're right. I have some things I want to say to you."

Clair felt a knot in her stomach.

"While you were out at Caderville trying to find yourself, or whatever it is you were doing, I realized maybe I needed to get away myself." He took Clair by the hand. "Look at us, Clair," he said quietly. "Our relationship is so, so. . ." He searched for the word.

"Nice," supplied Clair.

"Exactly!" said Paul with a big sigh of relief. "So you know what I'm trying to say. I don't think either of us wants to stay in a relationship that's just, well. . ."

"Nice."

"Right. We have to both know what we want and want it with all of our being. Does that sound too romantic to you?" he asked.

"No," smiled Clair. "Not at all. I think two people should feel strongly about their relationship. They should want it with all their hearts, if it's the right one for them."

"Ditto," said Paul. "So I've decided this is as good a year as any to go to England."

"England?" said a puzzled Clair. "That's a little out in left field, isn't it?"

"No, actually it's across the Atlantic Ocean. In Europe."

"Very funny."

"Dad's been after me for some time to go over and see how the English branch of our business does things. 'Get a feel for it,' as he always says. So, I thought since things are kind of up in the air with us, I'd go now. It'll be good for me, I guess." He searched Clair's green eyes for a response.

"Paul, I think it's a wonderful idea." Clair smiled at him. "Looks like you and I are both looking for something." She fingered the soft shoes in her hands. "When I was young, my parents put me in a dance class. All the other girls seemed so graceful. They seemed to know what they were doing. I would just stumble along. No matter how hard I tried, I couldn't fit in, couldn't keep up." She paused and pulled at the laces of her old shoes.

"In the last few years, those old feelings have come back. Other people seem to know something I don't. They know the dance. And the dance for me is always in the distance, far away, unattainable. I guess that's how I've been feeling for a long time. Like somewhere, life is happening, like a dance, far from me. Within my sight perhaps, but never within my reach."

The couple sat quietly, listening to the words as they lingered in the air, heavy with meaning.

"There's another reason I want to go to England," said Paul.

"Oh?"

"Do you remember Sally Blake?" he asked.

"Yes. The blond with all the money. Doesn't her dad own that big shipping company? She's the one who carries around her pet dog like it was a security blanket. What was that dog's name? Fufu?"

"Fifi. Yes, that's the girl. Well, I sort of went on a couple of dates with her," he said nervously.

"You what!" exclaimed Clair. "While I was up in Caderville? You went out with someone behind my back!"

"Clair, calm down. It's not what you think!"

"Oh, really," said Clair angrily, not sure why she was so steamed.

"It was all my mother's idea. She had a party, invited the Blakes, made sure I sat next to Sally, etc. It was harmless. And then we went to the movies a couple times. That's all."

"Well, isn't that sweet," said Clair evenly. "I realize our relationship is hardly serious, but really, Paul, for you to go on a date without telling me about it."

"But I am telling you about it!" said a frustrated Paul.

"Yes, but after the fact!" countered Clair. "What's so great about Sally Blake? Just because she never wears the same clothes more than once and she's got more jewelry than Tiffany's, doesn't mean she'd make a great date. After all, I'm just a schoolteacher, but I think—"

"Clair!" interrupted Paul. "You're getting bent out of shape over nothing."

Clair stopped. "What do you mean, nothing?"

"I don't want to go out with Sally Blake. My mom keeps pushing her in my direction. I guess she's given up on you! That's the other reason I want to go to England. To get away from Sally and my mother. And Fifi. That dog makes me sneeze."

Clair started to laugh. "That must have been some date at the movies!"

"Oh yes, a regular riot. I sneezed through the whole movie. They almost kicked me out."

"Why didn't they kick out Fifi?" inquired Clair.

"You don't kick Adam Blake's daughter out of the theater," said Paul.

"Oh, please," moaned Clair. "Must be nice to be privileged. And to think, Sally's set her sights on sorry you."

"You mean my mother's set Sally's sights on sorry me. Hey, a tongue twister!"

Paul and Clair proceeded to see who could out–tongue twist the other. They doubled over laughing with the effort.

"Lemonade!" Anna shouted up the stairs. "Come and get it you two!"

"Coming!" Paul and Clair responded in unison. They laughed together. At the top of the stairs, Paul stopped Clair.

"Promise me something, Clair," he said quietly. "If you find what you're looking for, promise you'll write and tell me what it is."

"I promise, Paul." Clair reached up and kissed her friend on the cheek. "I promise."

"I hope she's got those cookies of hers I like," whispered Paul as they descended the stairs.

"I've got those cookies Paul always liked so much!" called Anna from the kitchen.

Clair laughed. "That's my mom!"

Later that day, Danny dropped by. After dinner, Clair insisted Danny take a walk. They walked down to the park near the river. The sun hung low in the sky, forming a pathway of gold on the shimmering water. The hills across the water rose steeply along the far edge of the Hudson, standing strong and hazy blue in the late day. Clair had always been drawn to the beauty of those mountains.

"So what's up?" asked Danny. He flopped down onto the grassy knoll that overlooked the river. Waves lapped up against the rocks and boulders of the shoreline with steady rhythm. Danny closed his eyes. "You're losing me, Sis. I can feel it. I'm going to fall asleep any minute now."

Clair reached over and pulled her brother's hair with a firm tug.

"Ouch!" he exclaimed, immediately sitting up. "Watch it! This stuff is precious! I don't want to end up with a hairline like Uncle Herb's. Or should I say lack of hairline."

"Well, pay attention then," said Clair. "I didn't bring you down here to take a nap. I need to talk to you."

"I'm all ears. Fire away."

"I haven't told Mom or Dad much about what I've discovered in Caderville. I don't want to upset them. There's no point in giving them all the details. Anyway, I wanted you to know. And I don't want you to say anything to Mom or Dad."

"Okay," responded Danny. "So what did you find out?"

A sailboat skimmed by in the middle of the river. Its white sail was sliced through the middle with a band of red. Clair watched it fly down the river with graceful ease.

"That looks like fun," she said, pointing to the boat.

"Well, if you weren't afraid of the water, I'd take you out on one of those things," volunteered Danny. "Fear can keep us from experiencing a lot of good things, you know."

"Yes, counselor, thank you very much," said Clair wryly.

"Okay, so what's the story. What did you find out up in Caderville?"

"I found out that my biological mother is mentally disabled. She lives in a place called Clarkson House."

Danny sat up. "I'm sorry, Clair."

"But that's not the worst of it. She most probably was assaulted twenty-five years ago. And that's how I came to be."

Clair's brother let out a low whistle. "That is heavy duty, Sis. Do you have proof that she was raped? Who told you all this?"

"No, I don't have proof. And that's why I want to go back. I need to uncover the truth. Then I'll put it behind me."

"How do you feel about all this now?" asked Danny, his voice filled with concern.

"Well, Danny, the strange thing is I feel more upset for my mother's sake than my own. Yes, I feel shocked, I feel sick about it, but I'm more overwhelmed that I was spared so much. I was given life, and I've had a wonderful life."

"You sound like Jimmy Stewart now," said Danny. "Don't tell me you met an angel named Clarence!"

Clair laughed. "Well, maybe close to it!" She thought of Jack and Miss Clarkson. "I have met some very dear people who've been a big help. They've been telling me about something I thought I'd never take seriously."

"What's that?"

"The love of God. They keep telling me He loves me and wants me to be part of His family. I think I'm starting to believe it."

"Be careful, Clair. Don't go off the deep end because of all the stuff you've dug up," said Dan.

"I'm not going off the deep end. I can't explain it, Danny. And I don't expect you to understand. But somehow, I'm beginning to see perhaps there is a God and maybe He loves me. Even Mom has said how restless I've been. Maybe God's love is what I've been looking for."

Danny was quiet for a moment. "I won't discourage you, Clair. I respect every person's search for the truth. I'm just saying be careful. If you need to talk, I'll always be here for you. You know that."

Clair gave her brother a hug around the neck. "I know. Thanks for listening. Now let's go back to the house. Mom was baking a chocolate cake when we left. Must be done by now!"

"I get to lick the dish!" cried Danny, jumping to his feet.

"You are a first-class nut," said Clair affectionately.

"Only when I'm with you, my dear. Only when I'm with you," said a grinning Danny.

As they climbed the hilly streets back to the Silvero home, the sun began to slip behind the mountains. The glow of oranges, reds, and yellows flushed the town with color.

"You know, Clair," continued Danny, "I think faith is a personal thing."

Nothing personal about it. Miss Clarkson's words came back to her. What had Jack said? *It's the kind of thing you have to give away. Can't help it. His love comforts me, stretches me, makes me think. Shows me who I was, who I am becoming.*

The young woman looked up at the town of Langston. Its streets and buildings clung tenaciously to the rolling terrain. The windows flashed like red-orange beacons with the reflection of the sunset.

Clair laughed out loud. Joy was beginning to stir in her heart.

"What's so funny?" demanded Danny.

" 'A city set on a hill cannot be hid,' " quoted Clair with a smile.

Danny looked at his sister and shrugged. "What?"

Clair could see the corner of their street. "First one home gets the dish *and* the spoon!" She started to run.

"Wait a minute!" her brother called out. "I'm too old for this stuff. Wait up!"

Clair dutifully waited, hands on her hips. As soon as Danny was close to her, he bolted into a run.

"Hey! That's not fair!" cried older sister to younger brother.

"Works every time!" he yelled over his shoulder. "Some things never change!"

The Silveros sat around the dining room table enjoying the chocolate cake. Anna looked over at her two grown children.

"I'm so proud of both of you," she said.

"Oh, Mother," said Danny, "you're always saying that."

"But it's true! You both are such good, responsible people."

"At least I am," teased Clair.

"Very funny," said Danny, his mouth full of cake.

"Still having trouble with Manners 101, I see," said Clair.

"Hey, at least I don't park in no parking zones and get tickets on a regular basis," sparred Danny.

"I only got two tickets. And I still say there wasn't a no parking sign there when I parked. I told the officer the same thing."

"Oh, yeah, like the sign appeared miraculously after you left your car there. Really, Clair, grow up."

"You two stop bickering!" said Tony. "You sound like two little kids! Anna, remember how they used to fight? I thought we'd have to keep them in separate houses!" He laughed. "Separate houses!"

Anna smiled. "Oh! That reminds me, Clair. I have something to show you." Clair's mother left the room and returned with a photograph in her hand. "Remember this?"

"Let's remember in the living room, eh?" said Tony.

The family retreated to the comfortable chairs and sofas in the living room. Clair settled down into her corner of the couch. She looked at the picture her mother had given her. It was a picture of Clair and her father. Clair was sitting on his shoulders, her chubby little arms hugging his neck. Tony was smiling broadly, a look of pure relief written all over his face.

"That was taken the day I got lost in the department store!" said Clair.

"Let's hear it," said Danny.

"Not that story!" groaned Tony. "I still feel guilty!"

"I was four years old," recalled Clair, "and it was a Saturday. Daddy needed to buy some things at Larraby's. Remember Larraby's, Danny? It was a huge store."

"It had the best sports department in the county," remarked Tony. "And hunting and fishing, too. That's where I bought you your first fishing pole, Danny, remember?"

"Anyway, we walked around Larraby's, and Daddy got everything he needed. He decided to stop at the sports department and check out the golf clubs. Well, he soon became totally engrossed in the putters. At the same time, a lady walked by with the cutest puppy I'd ever seen. I was delighted! I followed that lady all over the store."

"In the meantime, I turned around and realized Clair was missing," Tony interjected. "I became frantic when I didn't find her anywhere near the sports department. I ran all over the store, calling her name at the top of my lungs."

"Meanwhile, the lady with the puppy walked out of the store. I decided I'd better get back to my daddy. But Daddy was nowhere to be found. So I went to one of the salespersons. I told her I had lost my daddy."

"It was so adorable!" chimed in Anna. "Clair went up to the lady and said, 'Excuse me, ma'am, but my daddy is lost. He's wearing a red tee shirt that's too small because his stomach is sticking out because my mother says he doesn't exercise enough and he yells when he gets 'cited. Can you find him?' "

"Well, just then," continued Clair, "we heard this bellowing sound. I recognized Dad's voice right away. 'That's him!' I said to the saleslady. So she took me by the hand and we followed the sound. When Daddy saw me, he ran up and grabbed me. Hugged me so hard I could hardly breathe. 'Daddy, your face is wet!' I said to him. He told me it was sweat from running around looking for me. But I knew better."

Anna continued the story. "The saleslady thought it was so cute that she took a picture of Clair and your father and sent me a note, telling me what happened." She looked over at Tony. "And *that's* how I found out about it. Your father never told me and I guess he swore his daughter to secrecy."

"He told me it would only upset Mommy and to make up for it he would get me a puppy," confessed Clair.

"So that's how we got old Pepper," said Danny.

"That's right," said Tony. "Now can we change the subject? It was twenty-one years ago, and it still gives me the sweats!"

Clair laughed and blew her father a kiss. "You are the greatest, Dad!"

"And I do not yell when I get excited!" Tony insisted.

"Sure, Dad," said Danny and Clair simultaneously.

"Oh, Anthony!" smiled Anna, shaking her head. "You are impossible!"

There's Always Tomorrow

Brenda Bancroft

Chapter One

Kristin Allen cocked her head and decided that she *had* heard the telephone shrill. She nudged her vacuum sweeper with the scuffed toe of her Reebok, threw down the shiny metal wand, and rushed to answer.

Cloth diapers, not always so easy to find because of the popularity of disposable brands, were the best cleaning rags as far as Kristin was concerned. And as the guiding force behind her own successful cleaning business, she was in a position to know.

Some months earlier, when Kristin had gone into the local Southern Illinois department store and bought four dozen old-fashioned diapers, the smiling sales clerk had trilled such a congratulatory remark that Kristin hadn't the heart to disappoint the woman by admitting that polishing windows and dusting woodwork were probably the closest she'd ever personally come to finding a practical application for diapers.

"Good afternoon, Ms. Allen!" Her caller broke in on her thoughts. "This is Sam Sherman down at the Tip Top Pet Supply and Feed Store here in Camden Corners."

Kristin sighed and frowned at her reflection in the mirror. The call was starting off with all the earmarks of a sales pitch.

"I have no pets," Kristin said quietly, as she prepared to give the man a polite brush-off and idly wondered since when had such specialty stores phoned around town to solicit business?

Mr. Sherman proceeded with what he had to say and Kristin was too startled at finding him on the line to bother to stop him. Her mind was scrambling with facts to the point where she scarcely heard the man's monologue.

Kristin's dark brow drooped into a suspicious frown. She glanced at herself in the spotless mirror, the telephone receiver crushed to her right ear, and her dust rag clenched in her left hand as a sudden thought nettled her.

That afternoon her black, curly, shoulder-length hair was hidden beneath a faded red bandanna. Her face was devoid of makeup because it was her day off—when she cleaned the large Victorian home she rented with an option to buy—and she didn't have to fix herself up in order to feel presentable enough to go out in the world and face the public.

As the jovial feed store owner rattled on, taking the long way around to get to the point of his call, suddenly Kristin's indigo eyes flashed with annoyance when it occurred to her that he—a stranger—had reached her at her *unlisted* number!

Since moving to Camden Corners the year before, she'd literally kept a log of all who possessed her private, unlisted telephone number. It was an odd arrangement for a cleaning woman to have a number that didn't appear in directory listings, she knew, but idiosyncrasies were tolerated in small towns. Her Roving Maid advertisement had provided only her post office box number, contained a request for interested parties to contact her with their numbers, and she'd promised that she would be in touch.

In New York City, where she'd lived before coming to Camden Corners, half a nation away, she could've protected herself by retaining an answering service, something unavailable in the small rural area she now considered home.

Those she'd agreed to take on as clients, she did eventually provide with her home number, but she'd almost made them swear upon a Bible that they wouldn't give it out to a soul.

Just as Kristin's mind was progressing through the roll call of people privy to her number, and she was trying to figure out who was the guilty party, as she was starting to feel the sting of betrayal, she remembered that an unlisted number didn't prevent calls from those telemarketers who dialed consecutive numbers in order to catch the listed and unlisted alike.

But when she recalled that the owner of the Tip Top Pet Supply and Feed Store had addressed her by name, a chill washed through Kristin. She felt the old, familiar sense of vulnerability flood over her, leaving her feeling weak and frightened in its wake.

"On behalf of the fine folks who produce Happy Trails Horse Feed and our local dealership, Ms. Allen, I'd like to offer you sincere congratulations," Mr. Sherman said in an expansive tone.

"What is this? Some kind of joke?" Kristi interrupted in a voice just this side of hostile, but didn't wait for an answer. "If so, it's not funny. I'm a busy person, now if you'll excuse me. . ."

Kristi's words choked off and she felt tears burn in her eyes. Irrationally, she struggled to maintain composure. She hated that she still suffered moments of panic over the silliest, simplest things despite what time had passed since her entire sense of security had been shattered, leaving her feeling helpless and unprotected in a brutal and violent society.

"Oh, it's no joke, ma'am," said the conciliatory gentleman on the other end of the telephone line. "You, Ms. Kristin Allen, are the Grand Prize Winner in the nationwide Happy Trails Horse Feed Sweepstakes contest! You and a companion will get to spend two glorious weeks at the Circle K Dude Ranch, a dream vacation site not far from Rapid City, South Dakota. In addition, you'll receive a check for five thousand dollars—which, I may point out—ain't hay!"

The feed store owner guffawed over his little joke, enjoying it sufficiently for the both of them, Kristin thought. From his manner she almost dared to believe him, then her logical nature came to the fore.

"Bu—but I didn't enter any contests," Kristi persisted. "I haven't been near a horse in years. I've never heard of Happy Trails Horse Feed. There must be a mistake."

"The sweepstakes staff is very careful, doing everything according to regulations, ma'am. As the owner of the dealership listed on the entry stub, I just got the call with the pertinent information. They felt that I'd like to be the one to convey the good news to a local customer."

Kristin swallowed hard, realizing how ungrateful and obstinate she must sound.

"I've never patronized your business, Mr. uh. . .Sherman. It's not that I don't think the prizes are nice, they sound lovely indeed, but I don't feel that I deserve. . ."

"Maybe you didn't enter," Mr. Sherman broke in. "But obviously someone slipped a stub or two bearing your name into the box on the countertop by the cash register in my store. People do that all the time when there's a drawing. It's a neat way to surprise a friend with something really wonderful."

"But who?" Kristin asked, frowning, looking around her as if somewhere she'd locate a clue.

Mr. Sherman's voice was hearty. "It doesn't really matter who, although I'm sure you'll find out all in good time. Meanwhile, just enjoy the fact that you're our Grand Prize Winner. There will be documents from the corporate headquarters arriving by certified mail, and once they're signed, notarized, and returned to the proper officials, we can begin processing the release of your sweepstakes prizes. Have you anything to say? Something we can quote on the radio station and for the weekly newspaper?"

"I–I'm overwhelmed. Shocked. And. . .and. . ."

"Very happy?" the feed store owner prompted.

"Okay," Kristin agreed, the smile on her face reflecting the irony she experienced that made her feel oddly dismal, "very, very happy."

"Got it! Super!" the man cheerfully said, and she thought she heard the lead tip of his pencil snap off as he underlined the quote on a pad of paper. "There'll probably be someone from the local newspaper who'll want to take a picture of us presenting the check to you, Ms. Allen. This is big news in an area like this. It'll likely make the front page of the *Camden Corners Gazette*. It might even be good for two news items if you have a picture of yourself we could have so they can run one announcing you as the winner in this week's edition and another candid photograph when you accept your check. . . ."

"A front-page picture? Wow. . . ," Kristin said and her pulse galloped with a horrible sense of trepidation that sent her adrenaline levels soaring.

And what a comedown, Kris thought, as the silence spiraled, to go from teenage magazine cover girl to small-town front-page news item in two short years.

At the thought Kristin's mind froze. She was spiraled back in time, and suddenly she felt as if she were drowning in nightmarish memories and about to have her most closely guarded secrets held up for public scrutiny and gossipy speculation in an area she'd come to like and regard as home.

"No!" she said, and her voice was a thin gasp. "*No pictures!*" She clarified, trying to control her tone, hoping that the man from the feed store didn't correctly interpret her reaction for the raw terror it was. "I'm sorry. No," she repeated in what could almost be considered a normal tone.

"No picture we can use? What luck. . . . Oh well."

After covering a few more details the man ended the surprise call and Kristin was left with her thoughts.

Pictures? Did she have pictures? He wanted to know. Yes! Portfolios and albums full of them, interred in a coffinlike trunk she could no longer bear to open.

When Kristin was sixteen, her parents had been killed when their plane to Hawaii crashed on takeoff in Chicago. Her aunt Delilah had taken custody of Kristin and her sister, Janice, and moved them to her New York City, Park Avenue apartment.

It was a life unlike either of the small-town girls had experienced. With an important job at the U.N., Delilah traveled and socialized a great deal, so the girls were left alone a lot.

That arrangement was all right with Janice, a flirtatious, outgoing girl who was content to date almost every night, breaking a different heart each month. Jan and Aunt Dee were so busy with their own circumstances, and so alike, that they didn't seem to notice that Kristin was a lonely and introverted girl.

She studied hard, kept the apartment immaculate, read teen romance novels, mysteries, and adventure stories, bought all of the latest teen and fashion magazines, and for hours on end fussed with her hair and makeup while she dreamed of someday having a true love of her own.

Some of Jan's old cast-off boyfriends eventually noticed Kristin and asked her out, but it became her habit to turn them down because she had a feeling that they felt as if they were settling for second best in her. Or even worse, that they were trying to get even with her fickle big sister. Or even worse than *that*, that the boys were asking her out so they could remain nearby in the slim hope that Janice might relent and focus her attention on them again.

Then one day Kristin saw the Beauty Search details in one of her teen magazines. Even though her face was drenched almost fuchsia with embarrassment, and she steeled herself against Janice making fun of her, she got up her courage and begged her big sister to donate an afternoon of her time to taking close-up, color, instant pictures of her.

Janice's grudging attitude hadn't been good.

But the pictures of Kristin, when developed, were great.

Aunt Dee and Janice had exchanged amused smiles when Kristin had sent them off. She suspected that they'd shared whispered assessments that Jan was the true beauty in the family and that although Kristin looked remarkably like her older sister, she lacked the worldly veneer of sophistication that marked Jan's exceptional good looks. Instead, Kristin possessed an innocent patina on her features.

But they were no longer laughing when Kristi, selected as a finalist, was one of the lucky girls to be photographed by a professional and eventually was the judge's final choice.

Kristin was groomed, instructed, made over, made up, coiffed, and presented on the front cover of her favorite teen magazine three months later. It was as if she'd been swallowed up by a whirlwind, for after that her life never seemed the same.

To her surprise, within a week Andre D'Arcy, head of a small but exclusive modeling agency, had contacted her, offering her a contract. His promises were enough to turn any young girl's head, and Aunt Dee warned her about dreaming of pie in the sky. But obedient, hardworking, and pleasant, Kristin did everything Andre required. As a result of her work and dedication, her one-time fantasies became thrilling reality as almost overnight she was in high demand as a teenage model, commanding incredible hourly fees.

Kristin hadn't paid heed to Aunt Dee—or a snickering Janice—about spending so much time with Andre, an older man who obviously didn't return her feelings. She became unaware she existed outside the professional realm, and her social life became almost nonexistent. As her face began to appear in so many ads and on various magazine covers, the few boys she knew who were near her own age acted like they wouldn't dare ask her out, so many nights she remained home alone and lonely.

Fortunately, Kristin now realized, she *had* listened when Aunt Delilah had pragmatically pointed out that Kristin's era of fame might not last. After all, Aunt Dee said, as she got older she might grow out of the teen model category and be unable to make the transition to the world of adult high fashion modeling. She could find herself out of work and untrained to be anything but a pretty face.

An astute woman, Dee had insisted that Kristin invest a healthy portion of her after-tax income. And as a person who'd seen tragedy strike so many times, Delilah arranged for Kristin to take out an insurance policy that would secure her future in case tragedy caused her to become unemployed because of disfigurement.

Aunt Delilah didn't consider herself a seer, but she was intuitive. She was proven all too right when, after four meteoric years, Kristin's modeling career abruptly ended and the rubble of her life made sensationalistic reading for a week or two in every tabloid in the country.

Reading the weekly pulp publications had been like reliving the assault each time the details were disclosed. They detailed the incredible story of a disheveled young man, a wild-eyed drifter, an obsessed fan, who had stalked Kristin, fantasizing that if she just saw him for a few minutes, he could convince her of his love and she would return his feelings and they would live happily ever after. . . .

Instead, when he approached her on the street when she was alone, frightened, and distracted, she'd casually brushed him off. How was she to know that such rejection would provoke unrestrained rage and his attitude that if he couldn't have her, he'd see to it that no one else would want her, either!

She felt the hot, searing slash of the straight-edge razor almost before she had time to recognize the weapon.

The rest was a blur. She remembered screaming and screaming, cupping her face as her life's blood cascaded between her clutching fingers, causing horrible dark blotches to fall to the dusty gray cement sidewalk. She stood there surrounded by people who suddenly seemed not to want to become involved and rushed on by.

The huge insurance settlement was no consolation for the loss of her career and the pain inflicted each time she looked into a mirror. The money did, however, afford her the services of the best doctors available, as they attempted to put her face back together, knowing they would never be able to repair her career.

While undergoing reconstructive surgery, Kristin holed up in Dee's apartment, subletting her apartment to Janice and her new husband, an older man, a Wall Street stockbroker.

Aunt Dee was dating an executive from a foreign company, who wanted her to marry him and live abroad. One doctor told her that Kristin's outer scars would heal. The doctor spoke cautiously of inner scars causing more serious disfigurement. He suggested that Kristin might want to seek help from a counselor or perhaps a member of the clergy.

When the doctor released Kristin from his care, Aunt Delilah freed her, too, declaring her niece well enough and financially stable, to the point where Dee could marry her impatient suitor and make a life for herself abroad.

Kristin, not about to become a burden to anyone or rely on others any longer, agreed with a smile.

Alone, jobless, with no one to talk to about her fears and recurring nightmares, Kristi was unable to bear the city any longer. She slept poorly, lurching awake each time there was an odd scrape or bump in the night, and she felt like a nervous wreck, losing weight from her already slim figure. Andre and his staff had sent her flowers and visited her several times, telling her to come by the agency and see everyone. But it was clear that she was a has-been at age twenty-one.

Briefly Kristin returned to her old hometown northwest of Chicago, but everything seemed changed. Old girlfriends had moved away. Or they'd married and were involved with their husbands and new babies. Or they were engaged and planning their weddings. It was embarrassing to Kris when hometown people still asked for her autograph, shoving old issues of magazines bearing her likeness in her face for her to sign.

And then there were the dreamy-eyed, insatiable teenage girls asking for details about her old, glamorous life and seeking advice on how they could attain fame and fortune just as the older girl-next-door had done.

But the worst were well-intentioned people, many of them shirttail relatives, who leaned forward and peered into Kristin's face, patting her arm as they pronounced the scars were "hardly visible unless you knew just where to look," adding that given time the lines would fade even more.

Kristin wanted only to forget the assault. She wanted to block out those years of her life. And she realized that the only way she could start over was to start fresh. Camden Corners, at the edge of Shawnee National Forest, where she'd once camped as a young girl, seemed the ideal choice.

But now, just as she was growing comfortable with her new life, old specters from the past arose to haunt her.

She'd been in front of the camera so many times that she'd not even allowed herself to be photographed since after her reconstructive surgery. The cosmetic surgeon's photographer had taken pictures of her when Dr. Steinberg considered his work complete. He wanted a before-and-after pictorial to attest to his expertise and assure subsequent patients that he could work miracles for them, too.

There was no way Kristin was going to go before a clicking shutter again. If it was impossible to receive the five-thousand-dollar check without getting her picture taken, they could just keep their money—and for that matter, the dude ranch trip, too!

She didn't need the money. But, elderly Mrs. Stanwyck was right, and she could use a vacation. . . .

Mrs. Stanwyck!

It had to have been her—Kristin's Thursday afternoon client—she realized, and her regular Sunday morning companion at worship services.

The mysterious individual who'd entered her name in a sweepstakes box surely was Mrs. Stanwyck, who claimed that clipping coupons, snipping off proof-of-purchase seals, filling out refund forms, penning contest entries, and sending off for brochures, information, and free samples filled a lot of otherwise lonely, boring, unproductive hours. The widow of a one-time area pastor, Mrs. Stanwyck claimed the activities did wonders for the arthritis in her hands by keeping her fingers limber while ensuring her mind was active and alert. It gave her something to look forward to in the mail, she said, plus, it provided her a source of incoming stamps to save for mission projects and a dream to call her own.

And Mrs. Stanwyck was a firm believer in nurturing dreams. Kristin sighed. Then she laughed with irony and a touch of affection when she found that she couldn't be angry with the elderly widow who'd come to seem like a grandmother to her. After all, Kristin was a young woman who felt as if she had no family, what with Aunt Dee in Europe and a mercenary Janice now relieved of Husband Number One and making it clear she was actively seeking a candidate for Spouse Number Two, provided the appropriate financial profile was provided upon application!

No one aside from dear Mrs. Stanwyck had considered that Kristin had been working for a year without any vacation and no mention of one, either.

Kristin had known that the old woman was concerned. But she hadn't realized to just what extent until that moment, and she was touched over such tangible evidence of another's caring.

A vacation wasn't all that Kristin's Thursday client had made clear she believed the younger woman could put to good use. An empathetic Mrs. Stanwyck probably thought that Kristin Allen needed money. So she'd frequently recommended her services to trusted friends.

An opinionated, unbending romantic, Mrs. Stanwyck believed that Kristin Allen could also use a boyfriend—and handed down the tart verdict that Kristin's vicarious enjoyment of romantic novels and stories didn't count—and what she needed was a good man. A Christian man, of course, because in Mrs. Stanwyck's mind, none other would do.

A pragmatic Mrs. Stanwyck had obviously concluded that Kristin could use a vacation—ideally in a place abounding with handsome, down-to-earth, hard-working men. So quite clearly Mrs. Stanwyck had given it her best shot and filled out who knew how many entry stubs in the slim hope that Kristin would win. . .and no doubt praying over the matter, trusting in God to come through with a miracle of sorts that would propel Kris into the path of Mr. Right.

The next twenty-four hours found Kristin's telephone line frequently busy. She conferred with representatives of Happy Trails Horse Feed, the staff of the Circle K Dude Ranch, made tentative flight plans with a travel agent, and confirmed that it *had* been Mrs. Stanwyck behind her becoming a Grand Prize Winner.

On impulse Kristin had invited the woman out to dinner and they'd gone out for a pleasant meal, then returned to the senior citizens' apartment complex on Sycamore Street. Her residence was just blocks away from the church and parsonage where her husband had pastored for most of his lifetime and where Kristin attended services regularly.

Mrs. Stanwyck asked Kristin in for a cup of coffee. "I have had a wonderful evening, dear. I really appreciated it."

"It was the least I could do to thank you. I enjoyed it, too," Kristin said.

"We should go out more often."

"Maybe. That sounds nice. We will for sure after I get back from South Dakota. I'll have so much to tell you, I'm sure."

"I'll miss you, Kristin. But knowing that you're on vacation and having fun will be a comfort to me," Mrs. Stanwyck said. "And just think of what you can do with five thousand dollars, honey."

"That's something that I've been meaning to discuss with you," Kristin said, feeling suddenly hesitant and searching for tactful words. "I know that you want me to go to South Dakota. But I have decided that I won't go unless *you* accept the prize money check. If you won't agree to take the money, I won't go to the dude ranch."

Mrs. Stanwyck stared, shocked. "I. . .I'm afraid that I don't understand. Honey, I *want* you to have the money. You work so hard. You're young. Why, with five thousand dollars you could—"

Kristin lifted a hand to halt further speech.

"I know that I can trust you to keep a confidence," she said. "The truth is, I don't need the money. I'm financially secure without working. I have my Roving Maid business so that I can fill my hours. It makes me feel as if my life is still worthwhile when I help people by doing what they're not longer able to perform."

"I'm afraid that I don't understand," Mrs. Stanwyck said, frowning. But by the time Kristi finished explaining about her parents' deaths and the value of their estate that had been kept in trust for Kristin, and her sister, her career, and the insurance settlement, Mrs. Stanwyck understood perfectly.

"You'll agree to accept the check?" Kristin pressed for a commitment when she finished her explanations.

Mrs. Stanwyck, who lived on limited means, nodded. "If that's what it takes to get you to the Circle K Dude Ranch."

"Super," Kristin said, relieved, and gave her friend a hug. "Now we'll both be winners. We've had such fun tonight, wouldn't you like to go to the Circle K Dude Ranch for two weeks? It is a trip for two, you realize."

Mrs. Stanwyck laughed. "If I were twenty years younger, honey, I'd be buying boots and a ten-gallon hat. You'd have to lasso me and tie me down to keep me home. Just looking at the brochure from the Circle K Ranch and seeing the exciting events awaiting you there, almost makes me have to reach for my nitroglycerin pills."

"You've got a brochure?" Kristin said, surprised. "For the Circle K Dude Ranch?"

"Oh, yes, I'm almost positive that I do. It's around here somewhere. Probably in the box of travel brochures I've collected from agencies, and some that I sent off for after reading ads in travel magazines. You know me, always sending off for one thing or another. Would you like me to look for it?"

"If it's not too much trouble. The staff at the Circle K is sending me information, but I'd love a sneak preview."

"We could do it right now. Let me get my box of goodies," Mrs. Stanwyck said. "You can put the coffee on to percolate. We can sort through the pamphlets together."

"I'll be with you in a jiffy," Kristin called from the kitchen.

"Here it is!" Mrs. Stanwyck crowed within five minutes and triumphantly waved a glossy, full-color brochure. She took a quick peek, then handed it across to Kristin. "This is even better than I remembered!"

Kristin opened the pamphlet. A collage of pictures vied for her attention. It showed the ranch headquarters, the dining hall, the indoor recreation area and square dance auditorium, the chapel, gift shop, the rodeo chutes, the riding area, a corral full of pleasure horses, a herd of wild horses thundering across the pasture, a swimming pool, a lounge, spa facilities, children playing, and happy, suntanned, glowing people everywhere.

Kristin read the captions, then studied the pictures.

"Are those ranch hands handsome, or are they handsome?" Mrs. Stanwyck said, sighing.

"V. . .very handsome," Kristin said, and felt a strange tightness come to her chest as a warmth flowed to her cheeks. She hoped the pictures had not been posed by professional models but were actually candid photos of the real staff who worked at the Circle K Dude Ranch.

"South Dakota. . .a place where men are men," Mrs. Stanwyck said, "and by the looks of those handsome cowboys, know how to treat a lady like a woman. Kristin Allen, your life may never be the same again. At least that's what we can pray for."

Kristi gave an embarrassed laugh. "There's absolutely nothing wrong with my life right now."

"You've got a nice life, I'll grant you that, except for your distinct lack of a man to love—and a good, upstanding Christian man who loves you. This vacation, my beautiful young friend," she said in an optimistic tone as her eyes sought the brochure and centered on the chapel, "may offer just the solutions to those problems."

"Now let's not let our expectations get unrealistically high," Kristin warned.

Mrs. Stanwyck was thoughtful for a moment.

"Who are you going to ask to go with you, Kristin?"

Kristin shrugged. "Since you won't accompany me, I really have no one to ask but my sister."

"Janice?"

"Yes. The one and only."

At that moment Kristin wasn't so sure that she wanted to invite Jan, but she was even less sure that she could bear going to a dude ranch all by herself.

"It's been a while since you've seen her?"

"Not since I moved back to Illinois. We talk occasionally. But our lives have moved in different directions. We've little in common nowadays except for the same relatives."

"There are few things as wonderful as close family ties. Traditions of faith. The wonderful memories we share with those we love. The special bonds created when He gives us to each other in families who share the same ancestors."

"I know. And that's something I've missed since. . .Mother and Dad died." Kristin brushed her hair away from her face as she found herself unable to go on. A lump that seemed the size of South Dakota suddenly lodged in her throat. "Asking Jan to go with me might be an ideal chance for us to start acting—and feeling—like family again."

"It's a step in the right direction. If she's any kind of sister, Kristin, she'll meet you halfway and there'll be an end to any estrangement that's occurred."

"I think I'll go home right now and give Jan a call," Kristin said, feeling a sudden surge of enthusiastic optimism.

Ten minutes later Kristin let herself into her home, snapped on a lamp, reached for the telephone, looked up Janice's number, and tapped in the sequence.

She tried to recall just when they'd talked last, a perfunctory, obligatory call to be certain. Christmas? Easter? New Year's? A birthday? Kristin realized that she was not sure.

Jan answered on the fourth ring, and Kristin explained who she was—twice—before Janice comprehended that it was her sister on the line.

Kristin winced when she detected that Janice sounded almost disappointed. At that instant she wished she hadn't even decided to call her big sister, but it was too late.

"The reason I'm phoning," Kristin got right down to business when they seemed to quickly run out of idle pleasantries, "is because I've had the most incredible thing happen to me. I won the Grand Prize in a sweepstakes—"

"Terrific, kiddo," Janice said. "Your best move is to contact the sweepstakes officials, tell them that you don't want the merchandise, and then dicker with them for a cash payoff instead of the cars, furs, diamonds, television sets, or whatever they're awarding you."

"But I—"

"They may make you settle for less than the retail value of the items, because they'll get them at wholesale or for the benefit of advertising value, but with cash you're money ahead and you then have liquid funds to take care of the state and federal tax bills due on the amount without—"

"I didn't call for advice!" Kristin quickly spoke up when her sister paused for breath.

"Oh. Then what did you want?"

"Well, my prize is a vacation trip for two at a dude ranch," Kristin began. "I thought that perhaps you'd like to join me for two weeks. It would give us time together so that we can catch up on each other's lives again, and—"

"Oh, I'm sorry, Kristin, but that's not possible. I did a dude ranch right after Bernard and I split up a year ago, and I'm not in the market for that kind of diversion, not after what I went through when a girlfriend and I dallied with the cowboys. I promised myself: *never again!*"

"Oh." Kristin knew that she sounded as deflated as she felt. Janice seemed not to notice.

"But if you ever win a trip to Hawaii, Rio, Tahiti, the Riviera, Europe, or someplace that's nice—by all means give me a ring, darling. I'll be packed and ready to go before we can end the call!"

Miserably Kristin fingered the brochure. "The Circle K Dude Ranch looks very nice," she murmured to fill the blossoming silence.

"Oh, I'm sure it is. Circle K? That sounds familiar. It could be the spread Cissy and I stayed at. But probably not," Janice dismissed. "You know how all of those ranch names get to sound alike after a while."

"Yes," Kristi agreed, and she tried to think of a quick way to end the call that she wished she'd never made.

"Don't get me wrong," Janice said, with sudden warmth as she seemed to realize that the call was fast falling apart. "You'll have a wonderful time. You always were more of a tomboy and girl-next-door than I was. There are lots of things to do on a dude ranch—if you like that kind of activity and don't mind getting dirty, sweaty, sunburned, saddle sore. Oh, the agony of remembering," she said, groaning.

"I thought it looked like a lot of fun."

"And there are guys beyond compare if you go for the rugged, outdoorsy, taciturn type."

"I've seen the brochure. I hope they aren't professional models," Kristin said.

"Trust me. You're in luck. They aren't."

"That's nice to know," Kristi said and felt her spirits lift.

"But you'd better watch out for those dude ranch dudes," Janice offered a worldly warning. "And for Pete's sake, little sister, don't believe everything they tell you. Those cowboys are probably paid to treat every female guest as if she's Miss America, even if she's old, ugly, fat, and worthy of nothing but a healthy dose of pity."

Or scarred? Kristin helplessly added to the list.

"So don't swallow their romantic banter," Janice blithely reminded. "Why, it's very likely memorized repartee, with them having to pass an oral test before they're even hired on!"

"I'm sure I can recognize a line if I hear one. I'm hardly immature and irresponsible," Kristin said, feeling defensive, unable to prevent the chill that entered her tone.

"Well, in my estimation, my dear, you *are* inexperienced for a woman of your age, with your nose in a book when the rest of us discovered boys. And smiling at a camera when we moved on to learn how to deal with men. I don't want to see you hurt. I've been to a dude ranch, don't forget; I've seen the moves those cowboys put to the female guests."

"Do I hear the voice of experience talking?" Kristin muttered, not bothering to hide her needling sarcasm.

"Absolutely!" Janice assured, not even taking offense.

And then, as Kristin listened, held a captive audience, Janice told her about the rich and handsome cattleman who'd wooed her when she was a guest at the dude ranch his family owned.

"Talk about a whirlwind courtship," Janice said. "He was talking marriage almost before I'd unpacked my bags. I couldn't believe he was serious—for I certainly wasn't out for anything but a good time. He was wealthy enough, interesting, educated, and he could've had his pick of the women, and he made it clear that he wanted me. But believe me, little sister, I didn't want him—or that horrible, prissy churchgoing mother and family of his. Believe me, I'd have taken that out of him soon enough and had him sleeping late on Sunday mornings, too. I didn't want what he had to offer enough to move to the wilderness, put up with his mother, brothers, and sisters, plus live on a ranch in the boondocks where they had cows, horses, rattlesnakes, and I'd have to drive miles and miles to attend a so-called cultural event that would've been laughed out of New York City. And not only that, but he wanted children, too. . . . Several." Jan gave a brittle laugh and shudder. "Can't you just see me as *a mother?!*"

The way Jan's tone dropped in disgust, Kristin knew that she'd just wrinkled her nose in distaste, and Kristin thanked God that a child had been spared being born to her cold-hearted big sister.

"I had no idea you'd had a dude ranch romance," Kristi said as she prepared to end the call.

"We really *have* grown apart, haven't we? We never get a chance to talk any more. But do listen to your big sister, huh? I wouldn't lead you wrong, so mark my words about dude ranches."

"Have you heard anything from Aunt Dee?" Kristi quickly asked, changing the subject from Janice's mercenary love life before she could warm to it again while Kristin's toll charges ticked away.

"She and Uncle are due to arrive in New York within the month. They'll be staying at the Plaza. Give me a call when you're at the dude ranch, so I'll have a number where Aunt Dee can reach you when she's stateside."

"Okay," Kristin agreed. "I'll do that."

"Good to talk to you, dear. We really *must* start staying in touch. . . ."

"I'll call you from South Dakota," Kristin promised.

"Good enough, Kristi. Enjoy yourself. And remember what I said, now: *Be on guard!*"

Chapter Two

To Kristin's relief the flight from Lambert Field in St. Louis left on time, under excellent flying conditions. She realized her flight would be on time to Rapid City, South Dakota, where the staff from the Circle K Dude Ranch were waiting to take arriving guests to the ranch.

It was not a direct flight, but it seemed like they'd scarcely departed St. Louis airspace before the pilot instructed them to prepare for landing in Omaha, Nebraska. Although a flurry of passengers disembarked, Kristin remained in her seat. A number of people boarded the craft to continue on to the Rapid City Regional Airport.

Kristin had been involved in a novel she'd purchased at the gift shop at Lambert Field until the pilot taxied to the gate in Omaha, and the sunlight slanting through the window glared in her eyes. She retrieved wraparound sunglasses from her purse, slipped them on, and was content to watch people from behind the mirrored lenses. She watched as a mother and child took the seat ahead of her, and smiled politely, offering help, as the woman confronted difficulty with her child's safety restraint.

Kristin's attention was drawn forward in the cabin when the flight attendant greeted a man as if he were an old friend and asked him how rodeo competition had gone for him.

Kristin didn't hear his reply, but from the championship belt buckle at his waist and the triumphant grin on his tanned face, Kristin suspected that it had gone very well.

His eyes were incredibly blue, turquoise like the brilliant Nebraskan sky. As he sought his seat, for a moment he faced Kristin and she was struck by how handsome he was.

Hair as black as her own, thick and wavy, the kind that seemed to beg a woman to sift her fingers through it, was topped by an expensive Stetson.

The man was tall, much taller than Kristin, broad-shouldered, lean, but solidly muscled. His jeans were faded and fit him almost like a second skin, and his tailored plaid western shirt with pearl buttons skimmed his trim torso. Top-of-the-line custom-made Tony Lama cowboy boots proved that he didn't mind paying for quality and comfort. And a light thatch of chest hair, peeking from the V of his casually unbuttoned shirt, was so blatantly masculine that Kristin felt oddly overwhelmed by the force of his presence.

For a moment their eyes met, or would have, if his glance hadn't been reflected back at him via her mirrored lenses. Then he looked through her and was gone, leaving Kristin realizing that she'd been holding her breath in awe.

If he was an indication of what the western states, South Dakota in particular, had to offer, Kristin thought with amusement, she probably should've borrowed some heart medicine from Mrs. Stanwyck, for just the sight of him had done strange and wonderful things to her pulse!

Minutes later the flight attendant gave them the prepared departure speech and wished them a pleasant flight. A moment later the jet engines whined, the airplane began to move forward, and then catapulted ahead as momentum pressed them back in their seats. Suddenly they were airborne as down below everything became smaller and smaller.

For a while Kristin read from her novel, but soon she slipped the book into her handbag and glanced out the side window so that she could admire the rugged terrain.

Kristin recalled what she'd learned about the region earlier in high school and linked it with what she saw spread out below. She and the other passengers leaned ahead, craning to look out their windows and catch sight of landmarks the pilot mentioned as he entered the airspace of Rapid City, South Dakota.

Kristin marveled at the Black Hills National Forest, heavily forested mountains called the *Paho Sapa* by the Sioux Indians because of the terrain's pine-dark woods. Also in the general area was Mount Rushmore, which Kristin viewed from the air but couldn't fully appreciate. She knew that the tourists down below at the observation point could as they gazed up at the likenesses of George Washington, Thomas Jefferson, Theodore Roosevelt, and Abraham Lincoln. The sculptures were seventy feet high and positioned six hundred feet above the valley floor, chiseled in granite.

The pilot explained that mining was important to the local industry, and he pointed out sightseeing points: the South Dakota School of Mines and Technology, the Museum of Geology, the Federal Sioux Indian Museum, Dinosaur Park, Black Hills Reptile Garden, Wild Cat Cave, Nameless Cave, and Badlands National Monument.

At the Rapid City Regional Airport, the pilot nosed the jet into the slot and workers rolled the ramp into place. Kristin arose, collected her carry-on belongings, and moved into the aisle, filing out behind other passengers.

She went to the baggage carousel and waited patiently for her possessions. When she collected her second valise, she turned away just in time to see the handsome rodeo rider passing through the plate glass doors into the parking lot.

She felt a sense of loss that she would never see him again.

"Anyone else here happen to be going to the Circle K Dude Ranch?" a harried, slightly plump, ginger-haired, freckle-faced young woman asked.

"Yes, I am," Kristin replied, as did several others.

"Great!" the girl said, moving to Kristin's side, no doubt because they were approximately the same age and both by themselves. "Let's stick together. Okay?"

"Good idea," Kristin agreed. "There's supposed to be a van from the ranch to meet us."

"We'll find it," the girl said in a confident tone. "My name's Amanda Gentry. My friends call me Mandy."

"I'm pleased to meet you. I'm Kristin Allen. Friends call me Kristi or Kris or Kristin."

"Call you anything, but don't call you late for lunch, eh?" the round-faced girl teased. Then she frowned. "As slim as you are, you probably don't have a problem with your weight."

"I've eaten my share of cottage cheese and lettuce," Kristin admitted, as suddenly her thoughts flicked back to the old days in New York when she'd had to deny herself so much for the sake of her career.

"In your case it's been worth it," Mandy murmured. "You've got a figure a lot of women would die for. Your face isn't bad, either. You know, for some reason, you really look familiar to me. Have we met?"

At Mandy's remark about her face, Kristin felt as if she'd been slapped, but then realized the girl had meant nothing unpleasant, that it was simply her colloquial way of speaking.

"I. . .I don't think so," she managed to reply. "I'm sure I'd have remembered you."

"Hmmm. I'd almost swear that I've seen you before." Mandy gave her a closer look.

Suddenly Kristin felt self-conscious. She turned away, not wanting to see Mandy scrutinizing her scars, if that's what she was doing, even though Mrs. Stanwyck had assured her that Dr. Steinberg's handiwork was so good that a stranger wouldn't even know she'd once been severely disfigured.

"There I go again," Mandy sighed as silence stretched to the snapping point. "Ol' open-mouth-insert-foot Mandy. The girls in the typing pool and data processing area are used to me, so I forget that you're not."

Kristin managed a bright, warm smile. "But I soon will be. I'm sure we'll see each other around the Circle K spread. Got your bags, Mandy? Let's go."

"I'm glad we met," Mandy said. "I had reservations, no pun intended, about coming to the dude ranch all alone. But now that we've met, I feel like I've already got a friend."

"I know the feeling. Over there's the van," Kristin said.

"And there's an honest-to-goodness-rootin'-tootin'-cowboy. Help me, Kris." Mandy clutched in the area of her heart near where hung a golden cross on a delicate chain. "I think I'm in love!"

Kristin found herself laughing. "Better watch out, Mandy, or instead of the people at the Circle K Dude Ranch letting you have a vacation, they'll *hire* you."

"What are you talking about?"

"My sister came to a dude ranch last year and she said that the cowboys aren't to be trusted, that they have a line for every woman between eight and eighty. They rope, ride, rodeo, and *romance* with equal skill. According to Janice they're absolutely not to be believed. Unfortunately. . ."

Mandy curled a lip, then gave a flip grin. "Oh, who cares?" she joyously asked. "I came here to have a healthy helping of fantasy. I have enough reality back at the office in Kirkwood, Missouri. Cruise ship romances don't seem to last, either. So what? Enjoy it while it lasts, eh?"

The two girls approached the large white van that had the logo of the Circle K Dude Ranch emblazoned on the side. A pleasant ranch hand with a welcoming attitude was greeting the spread's guests, stowing luggage, and directing them inside to find seats in the air-conditioned vehicle.

"Hi, girls!" he greeted Mandy and Kristin as they approached.

"Hello, there!" Mandy boldly replied, grinning, while Kristin offered a demure smile.

The smile froze on her face when the employee of the Circle K Ranch regarded her, did a double take, and gave her an odd and seemingly displeased stare. He looked at her as if he expected her to say something, then as if he considered making a remark himself, but thought better of it.

Without another glance at either of them, he tossed the girls' luggage into the hold and brusquely gestured them into the van.

"He must have a burr under the saddle," Mandy muttered. "Oh well, he's not the only cowboy in the Wild West, even if he is awfully cute."

The suddenly taciturn ranch employee stood outside a moment, tallied up the guest sheet, concluded that everyone was present and accounted for, and that they could proceed east from Rapid City to the Circle K Ranch. The driver wended through traffic and departed the terminal area, passed the Pennington County Fairgrounds, then took the entrance ramp onto Interstate 90. Initially the traffic was thick, but as they left the immediate Rapid City vicinity, it thinned. Mandy kept up a constant flow of chatter, and

Kristin was grateful that she'd connected with the easy-to-like, outgoing, obviously fun-loving girl.

So far her trip was fantastic. If only she could figure out why the nice-looking cowboy from the Circle K, who'd had a distinctly reserved attitude, cool, actually, when he dealt with Mandy and her, kept looking at her in the rearview mirror, sneaking peeks, then quickly pulling his eyes away when Kristin's gaze happened to catch his in the mirror.

"Va-va-va-voom!" Mandy sighed. "Would ya look at *that!*"

Kristin glanced down to where Mandy's brown-eyed gaze lingered and she saw a cowboy, not just any cowboy, but *the rodeo champion cowboy*, cruising alongside the van in a white Corvette.

"I'm in love!" Mandy moaned for the second time in what seemed a matter of minutes. "I wish the driver of this van would peddle a little bit faster! I don't want to lose sight of that 'Vette!"

As if on cue the driver of the Corvette gave a jaunty tap on his horn, the cowboy in control of the ranch's van beeped back, gave a friendly wave, and then the cowboy in the Corvette accelerated and sped ahead.

"Oh, giddyap, buster!" Mandy complained at the driver under her breath. "Don't spare the horses under the hood up there. Or back here. Or wherever the engine in this ol' van is!"

"Too late, Mandy," Kristin said. "He's gone."

"But not forgotten. I may remember that face when I'm old and gray. Oh well, this is South Dakota," the Missourian sighed.

" 'Where men are men, and know how to treat a lady like a woman,' a friend of mine told me," Kristin added.

The idea lifted Mandy's spirits.

"I'm in heaven!" the vacationing computer operator announced.

Twenty minutes later Mandy repeated the remark when the van's driver slowed to negotiate a long, winding drive that led to the headquarters of the Circle K Dude Ranch.

Both girls swiveled around, as did other passengers, to take in all that the dude ranch had to offer.

There was a large main building that housed the offices, lobby, dining room, square dance auditorium, chapel, beauty shop, gift boutique, indoor swimming pool, game room, and western wear store. Outdoors there were tennis courts, a mini-golf course, corrals, riding arenas, a pool, chaise lounges, patio tables, and an assortment of playground equipment for children.

Pristine sidewalks bordered by bright flower beds led to the various compounds where there were units large enough to house complete families and quarters ideal for a person alone.

"What a place," Mandy sighed. "I hope our rooms won't be too far apart. Oh! That's mine!" she sang out as the van's driver flipped a luggage label and called out her name.

"Kristin Allen?"

"Over here," she said and moved forward to collect her bags.

The cowboy consulted the luggage label, looked into Kristin's eyes as if he'd had trouble reconciling the face with the name, then he handed over her bags.

"Have a nice stay, ma'am," he murmured and gave her such a warm smile that her heart skipped a beat. She felt ever so much better after enduring his coldly hostile glances in the rearview mirror for the last forty miles.

"I'm sure I will," she replied in a friendly tone.

Mandy was waiting for her. "Well, ol' Stoneface finally softened up enough to smile at you, eh?" she whispered, leaning close to Kristin. "I wonder what his problem was?"

"I don't know. But whatever it was, he must've solved it."

"Unless your sister's right, and it is a bought-and-paid-for act and now that he's at the headquarters he knows he's got to mind his p's and q's because Big Brother is watching."

"Oh, I don't think so," Kristin said. "It could've been something as simple as a headache."

"You're right. We're all entitled to a bad day now and then."

"It's such a long line waiting in the lobby to check in, Mandy, what do you say that we wait on that bench over in the shade and enjoy the scenery?"

"Sounds good. It might increase our chances of getting rooms near each other, too."

Fifteen minutes later the girls entered the lobby. Mandy excused herself to go to the rest room while Kristin saw to her reservation.

The desk clerk, who Kristin had watched pleasantly deal with the other guests, looked up, and gave her a friendly, generic smile before he'd seemed to focus on her as an individual. When he did, the man's expression seemed to chill ten degrees.

He gave her a barely perceptible nod of greeting.

"Alone this year?" he murmured.

"Yes, I'm afraid so," Kristi said politely. "The name is—"

"Let me see about your—" The man's words trailed off as he riffled through the file box bearing alphabetized reservation cards without even bothering to hear her out. He frowned, but then looked almost gloating. "I'm sorry, but we don't seem to have you registered. Perhaps there's space at the motel in town—"

Kristin's heart leaped to her throat. "Oh dear, that can't be! I made the arrangements myself. I received the confirmation card, although I didn't bring it with me. C. . .could you check again? Please? The name is Kristin Allen. I. . .I'm the person who won two weeks here as Grand Prize Winner of the Happy Trails—"

"Oh, Ms. *Allen,* is it? I'm sorry; my mistake," the man said. He flipped to a different section of the file box. "I don't know where my mind was. I had you confused with a guest I remembered from last year, also a very. . .uh. . .pretty young woman. Ah, here we are. And everything *is* in order, I'm relieved to discover. Sorry about that, ma'am."

Quickly, efficiently, and with genuine warmth, he executed the paperwork and Kristin was affixing her signature when Mandy reappeared.

"Anything else I can do for you, Ms. Allen?" he asked helpfully, as if to make up for the fact that things had gotten off to a poor start.

"Well, if you can put my new friend in quarters close to mine, I know that we'll both be grateful."

"I can put you in rooms right beside each other."

"Super!" Mandy said and favored him with a grin.

Kristin smiled happily. "You can't get any better than that!"

"One of the hands will come for your luggage and show you to your rooms," the desk clerk said. "And tonight to welcome our guests we're having a Texas-style barbecue done up to South Dakota specifications."

Mandy rubbed her tummy. "I *am* in heaven," she whispered to Kristin. "Let them show me to my room, show me where the cowboys are, and point me toward the barbecue pit."

The girls got settled in their quarters, freshened up, changed clothes, and decided to walk around to see what diversions the dude ranch offered. Then they wandered toward the barbecue pit. Delicious aromas crowded the air.

Eventually other guests began arriving, and the festive event began.

The food was excellent, the companionship enjoyable, and as fireflies flickered in the dusky twilight, an area band tuned up their guitars, fiddles, and banjos. Toe-tapping, foot-stomping square dance rhythms filled the cool night air.

People that Kristin realized were area ranch families had been invited to the big celebration to make the city dudes feel welcome. Handsome cowboys of all ages approached women, asking them to dance, while cute local cowgirls took visiting city boys in hand.

There were giggles and protests, but these were met with the assurance that anyone could at least learn to do the simple two-step, that they were there to have a great vacation, and there was no time like the present to get started on enjoying themselves.

Mandy and Kristin were approached and found themselves led to the pavilion with an outdoor dance floor. Mandy was giggling, but giving it her all, and Kristin followed suit. The handsome young ranchers stayed with the girl from Camden Corners and the typist from Kirkwood, and they spent a memorable evening listening to the rollicking country and western music.

Mandy seemed to really like the young cowboy, Billy Joe, who was teasing her and sticking close as a burr. And while Kristin liked the young man, Kerry Kendrick, who was about her age and a student studying mechanics at a technical institute, she could tell that he was liking her a little too much. The way he was regarding her definitely wasn't bought and paid for by the hour by the big boss of the Circle K Dude Ranch. . . .

Kristi liked Kerry Kendrick. In fact, she liked him enough that she didn't want to risk hurting his feelings by seeming to string the kind, flawlessly mannered, quiet young cowboy along. So she'd eventually end up telling him that she wasn't as attracted to him as he seemed to be to her.

In the back of her mind she wondered if she was finding fault with his youthful exuberance so she could make excuses to cut any ties with him before she could find herself involved and unsure of how to proceed. Or if it was simply a lack of that special chemistry. Or perhaps, even, that she often felt old beyond her years from what she'd had to face as a teenager and because she'd worked and mingled with people so much older than she that she wasn't truly comfortable with people generally considered in her peer group.

When Kristin saw a teenager with a thick head of deep auburn hair and intense brown eyes looking incredibly sad as all around her people were so happy, Kristin suggested that Kerry invite the girl to dance.

"I don't want to monopolize your time," she said in a light tone, "and that little girl looks like she'd love to learn how to do a Texas two-step. You're an excellent tutor."

"Oh. . .okay," Kerry said. "If you're sure that you don't mind."

"Of course not. I have to go to my room for a few minutes."

"Okay. See you around, Kristin."

"Sure thing. And thanks for the lessons!"

Kristi threaded her way through the crowd.

"Leaving already?" Mandy cried, as Billy Joe swung her through a vigorous square dance and her face glowed with happiness.

"For a little while. I have some calls I should make."

"Hurry back!" Mandy cried after her.

As Kristin made her way from the pavilion, her footsteps clacked along the sidewalk. She walked through the darkness from one dim carriage lamp to another and was not sure how far she'd gone before she realized that she was not alone.

Someone was walking behind her, rapidly gaining!

For a moment she felt terror ricochet through her as the full horror of the long-ago attack froze her mind before she forced herself to concentrate on the fact that she was at a secure dude ranch, surrounded by convivial vacationers and that there was no one who wished her any harm.

She started to turn off the sidewalk to the path that led to the cluster of rooms where she and Mandy were housed, when a steel-strong grip contained in a smooth leather riding glove snaked out, encircled her wrist, and yanked her back.

Kristin felt her knees grow weak and buckle, then a tall, lean, very strong, and very angry cowboy jerked her upright, lifting her face to within inches of his.

Kristin gasped, then tried to scream, but she was unable to even speak or make any sound. Her eyes widened with fright and she searched the dark for a clue to her attacker's identity.

She stared, stunned, when she saw that it was him. *Him!* The handsome rodeo rider from the flight to Dallas from Kansas City. The cowboy in the white Corvette!

Kristin was trying to collect herself to the point where she could form words and tell the cowboy to take his hands off her, but then his grip tightened and he pulled her into the shadows. He propped her against the clapboard building, leaning one arm against the wall, then glared down at her as she looked up.

He gave a cold smile that was followed by a bitter, cutting laugh. And his eyes, which had been so turquoise on the airplane, became like blue-white lightning flashing to cleave a thunderous summer sky.

"Had to return again, huh?" he drawled mockingly. "Just couldn't stay away? Couldn't leave well enough alone?" Then he seemed about to call her an unflattering name but managed to check himself.

"Please—" Kristin whispered, swallowing hard, as her throat was dry and tight with tension and she felt a heartbeat away from bursting into tears. "There's some kind of mistake—"

He gave another harsh laugh. "You'd better believe there's been a mistake. A passle of them, and most of 'em *mine!* Your reservation should've been refused! You should've been sent away bag and baggage. Haven't you done enough to this family? I saw you dancing and romancing my kid brother, Kerry. Are you trying to get even with me through him?! Well, I'm warning you lady: Stay away from him. I won't have you doing to him what you did to me. Thanks to how you turned my life upside down, I feel that I've all but lost my faith. That's what I get for being so foolish as to let my heart go counter to my head and think that I could have a decent life and healthy relationship yoked with an unbeliever."

"I don't know who you are or what you're talking about—"

"Sure you don't!" The man said in a grating tone and gave Kristin a shake that convinced her to hold her silence.

"But if you think you're going to break Kerry's heart the way you did mine, I won't let you get away with it. This time, you cold-hearted seductress. . .*I'll make you pay!* I know that vengeance is the Lord's, but cross me, sister, and mess up my little brother's heart and mind, and I'll exact my own revenge, too. And consider it as sweet as our relationship that went so sour!"

"Get away from me or I'll report you to the owner of this ranch!" Kristin flared.

For an answer, the man laughed in her face.

"Go away and leave me alone!" Kristin ordered, feeling suddenly angry and frightened to the point of feeling competent to handle him and give as good as she got.

"Gladly," the cowboy said and gave a derogatory laugh. He jerked his touch away as if he'd been burned by her satiny flesh. "No man in his right mind would get within a country mile of a calculating vixen like you. After my father was killed in a rodeo accident, I promised my mother that I'd protect and help raise my brothers and sisters. Kerry's just a kid—a trusting kid—but he's *my responsibility* and I'm not going to have you wrecking him the way you tried to ruin me. Toy with his affections and beliefs, Janice, pretend that you're something special that you're not. It took me a while to figure it out before I came to my senses. Try to get your hooks into the Kendrick money by latching onto Kerry, and you'll answer to me, Janice!"

A shocked Kristin was unable to frame a response, and she sagged with relief when the furious cowboy turned away, leaving her to collapse against the building for support.

"And don't bother going for any moonlight rides with the intention of showing up on my doorstep for old time's sake, either." He tossed another furious stricture over his shoulder. "I can't believe that I was once foolish enough to believe that I loved you." He fixed her with an impaling stare. "I'd sooner be horsewhipped and dragged for ten miles behind a stampeding mustang than spend another moment with you. . . ." He spat the scornful words into the velvety night.

And then he was gone, leaving Kristin shaking.

What on earth was going on? she wondered.

A moment later she flinched and felt even weaker when she recalled that during his tirade, when she'd been too upset to speak, almost too nervous to think, he had called her *Janice*.

All the little clues that she'd encountered that day began to stack within her mind, building a case, from the cowboy looking through her when her features had been hidden behind sunglasses on the airplane, to the van's driver treating her with hostile indifference, to the room clerk gloating as he told her that she had no reservation, and the curious looks from ranch personnel as she and Mandy strolled the grounds.

Added to the fact that they all warmed, instantly and apologetically, when her true identity was revealed, convinced her that she'd been punished for another's cruel and selfish crimes.

Janice's!

Chapter Three

Kristin felt shaky and tense long after she let herself into her room, dead-bolted the door, and secured the chain lock. She felt almost as if she were dreaming and wished that she could awaken to discover a different, less confusing, frustrating reality.

She'd hungered to see the cowboy in the white Corvette again, but most certainly not under the circumstances of their subsequent confrontation.

Trying to calm her nerves, Kristin methodically set about the ordinary unpacking, coordinating outfits, and putting her personal possessions in drawers for the next two weeks.

Soon she gave in to her impulse to call Janice. Kristin reminded herself that she had promised she'd pass along her telephone number so that Jan, Aunt Delilah, and Uncle Benchley could contact her when they were reunited in New York City.

It was a good excuse to dial Jan's number, although she had far more important business, the Corvette Cowboy, to discuss.

Kristin was disappointed when Janice's answering machine took the call. Resolutely she left her name, number, and a brief message that she'd had a pleasant flight to Rapid City.

Sighing, she replaced the receiver in the cradle just as there came a furtive tap at her door.

Kristin's heart leaped to a staccato beat. She crossed to the door, glanced through the peephole, then undid the various locks to allow Mandy to enter her quarters.

"I thought you were going to come back to the dance," Mandy said.

"I was going to," Kristin replied. "But something came up."

Mandy gave her an assessing stare and quirked an eyebrow. "Don't you mean *somebody*?"

"You saw. . ."

Mandy nodded. "What a secret you were keeping from me. I never dreamed that you knew the Corvette Cowboy, Kris."

"I don't, Mandy. He's a stranger, and a rude one at that. It wasn't at all what it might have looked like to you. He wasn't hugging me, he was hurting me. I—I'm afraid of him. . . ."

"Afraid?" Mandy laughed, as if the idea were preposterous. Kristin's new-found friend searched her face, then plopped down on the neat bed. "You really are frightened," she breathed, dazed. "You're shaking with nerves."

"It wasn't pleasant, believe me," Kristin said in a low voice. "Today has been an ongoing nightmare. He, *they*, have all been mistaking me for someone else."

"Is *that* what's been going on?" Mandy murmured. Her brow drooped in consternation. "I'd noticed, Kris, how there didn't seem to be any happy medium for you. People here either loved you. . .or they seemed to. . .hate you."

"I know." Kristin's tone was bleak. "And believe me, it's been upsetting. And the hot-tempered, short-fused, bullying Corvette Cowboy—"

"Dacian Kendrick's his name, by the way," Mandy inserted.

"—thinks that I'm a woman he used to be romantically involved with. And if *that's* any indication of how he treats a woman—"

Mandy almost swooned. "Oh, don't you wish. No, don't *I* wish. I saw him drag you into the shadows," she said, her voice growing husky.

"But how he behaved would not appeal to you. This Dacian Kendrick told me in no uncertain terms to stay away from his brother, Kerry."

"The other guy you were dancing with for most of the night?"

"One and the same."

"After delivering a scathing ultimatum, Mr. Kendrick left. He didn't actually hurt me, but he was threatening, and I don't trust him and certainly don't like him," Kristin said. "People who lose control and have a capacity for violence really upset me. I. . .I've been stewing over this ever since I came back to my room, trying to figure out what to do, Mandy. Do you think that perhaps I should report this Dacian Kendrick to the owner of the Circle K Ranch?"

Mandy looked stunned, then gave a shocked giggle before she began to explain. "Kris, you can't report him to the boss of the Circle K. Dacian Kendrick *is* the owner of this spread."

"In that case, maybe I'd better leave," Kristin said and arose, looking around her as if she didn't know what to repack first. "The way he feels about me—"

"No, silly girl, if it's been a case of mistaken identity, it's not how he actually feels about *you*. It's how he thinks he feels about you because he doesn't know who you are and that's simply how he feels about the person he thinks you are. *Her!* So it's not how he really feels about *you*." Mandy paused and cleared her throat. "If you can follow that. . ."

"Um. . . Perfectly. . . I think. Do you by any chance have a Ph.D. in illogic?"

Mandy grinned. "I haven't done my doctoral thesis yet. But seriously, Kris, it seems to me that the solution is to go to his office and tell him you're not who he thinks you are."

Kristin gave an adamant shake of her head. "I'm not going within one hundred yards of that man!"

Mandy raised a brow. "Honey, if he *owns* this ranch and if he's sitting in his office, you already *are* within a hundred yards of him."

"Do me a favor; don't remind me."

"I could do you a different favor," Mandy offered. "*I* could tell him you're not who he thinks you are." She didn't wait for Kristin to nix or approve the idea. "Who does he think you are, anyway?"

Kristin was about to tell her, but then she shrugged and shook her head.

Old habits were hard to break, and while she liked Mandy and felt comfortable with her, the needs for privacy and protection were too great. Plus, it would be embarrassing to have to admit to Mandy what kind of woman her big sister had obviously become.

"Who knows?"

"Obviously the way people have been giving you dirty looks and snubbing you all afternoon and evening, this despicable, unpleasant someone must look so much like you," Mandy mused, "that she could pass for your sister."

"It would seem so. Truly, Mandy, it might be simplest if I just packed my bags and in the morning arranged for someone to see me back to the airport and I'll return home."

"You can't do that to me, Kris!" Mandy protested. "Don't leave me all alone. We've been having such fun together. Please don't go. There's always tomorrow, and surely things will be better then. In fact, I know that. I've seen God take terrible situations and bring great good from them. I'll bet you've seen that happen, too, no longer than it's been since you made the commitment to Christ as you were telling me about in the van from the airport."

Kristin was forced to nod in agreement. She would never forget that moment when, after church with Mrs. Stanwyck, Sunday dinner together, and continuing on for an afternoon of talking of things of faith, she'd felt such hunger in her heart and such hope that she'd experienced to the core of her soul the knowledge that Jesus Christ, whom she scarcely had met, was her personal Savior and Lord.

Suddenly she wanted to know everything about Him, to understand His life, ministry, and death upon earth and the redemption found in Him. She'd felt frustrated—there'd been so much she wanted to know and understand, and she'd suffered human impatience in realizing it would take *time* to discover the joys, depth, and maturity of faith.

Mrs. Stanwyck had chuckled and admonished her not to be impatient, but to trust in God to give her wisdom in His own way and to know that He would teach her many lessons about faith in her daily walk with Him. The pastor's widow had warned her that she'd learn as much from human failure as she would from Christian triumph. She had said that sometimes the hard lessons that the Lord let us learn, through our own willfulness as we were in His permissive will instead of His perfect will, were those we'd look upon with the most gratitude as truths hard-won.

Kristin knew that suddenly she felt loved, cared for, fed spiritually, and nourished with Scripture while with her friends who were believers. She knew it in a way that worldly acquaintances couldn't ever hope to fill the void within her with any form of edification, for their ways were not those of people committed to God and to strengthening others who had placed their lives and trust in Him.

Could this be, as Mandy seemed to surmise, some kind of lesson from the Lord. . .for her? For Dace Kendrick, too?

Kristin nodded. "I suppose you're right. But if things aren't better within a day or two, I'm definitely leaving."

"The others figured out that you're not *her*, didn't they?" Mandy pointed out.

"Yes, the driver of the van suddenly got very nice when he saw my name on the luggage identification label. And so did the desk clerk."

"See?" Mandy assured. "Why, Dacian Kendrick might have already found out just how wrong he was about you."

"Maybe," Kristin said. "Although I'm not sure I care what that arrogant, egotistical, self-centered, bullying man believes."

"I still think he's perhaps the most handsome man I've seen in all twenty-two years of my life," Mandy admitted. "And if he's anything at all like Kerry, he's probably actually very, very nice."

"That was my first impression of him. And my second impression, too. But if the third one's the charm—he was anything *but* nice," Kristin sourly enumerated.

Mandy smiled and yawned. "At least you can joke about it. That means you're getting better already. By tomorrow it'll have faded like a bad dream."

"It's been a long day for both of us," Kristin said. "Maybe tomorrow will be better."

"I'm going to hit the hay," Mandy said, yawning.

"Spoken like a true cowgirl."

"I'm trying," Mandy said. "And tomorrow, right after breakfast, this city gal's going to ask for a heavy-duty horse and learn how to ride."

"Meet me for breakfast, and we'll get adventurous together. I haven't been on a horse in years, although I used to love to ride when I was a child. After that I couldn't risk costly black and blue marks or, even worse, a broken arm or leg from a fall. I would like to get in a bit of fun before I may be. . .forced . . .to leave. . . ."

Kristin had felt significantly better after talking with Mandy and taking a long, hot, relaxing shower. Although she would've bet that she'd have been too keyed up to sleep, she drifted off within minutes of snuggling down in the comfortable bed.

She hadn't left a wake-up call and the sun slanting through the windows, brightening the room, eventually awakened her.

She dressed, put on makeup, braided her long, black hair, then pulled it up, tucked the tips under, secured it with an ornate butterfly clip, donned her cowboy hat to protect her skin from the sun, and was ready to go.

She was checking her reflection in the mirror when there was a light tap on her door.

"Just a minute," she called.

She crossed to the door, expecting to see Mandy when she glanced through the peephole. She was not anticipating a spray of roses that all but hid the bearer's features.

"What on earth—?" she gasped as she opened the door.

"Ms. Kristin Allen?" the ranch employee asked, and Kristin nodded. "These are for you. The card's attached."

"Why. . .they're beautiful."

"Where do you want me to put them, ma'am?"

"Over there on the table in front of the window would be wonderful."

The ranch employee did as instructed, smiled at Kristin, wished her a nice day, then turned to depart. Mandy was preparing to enter as the staff worker exited.

"Roses? You don't even have to tell me who they're from, Kris. I'll bet the flowers are from *him*. I told you he'd find out how wrong he was and be mortified. A dozen long-stemmed red roses? Obviously he was *very* embarrassed."

"As well he should be after his obnoxious behavior."

"We all make mistakes and need to forgive our trespasses as we would hope to be forgiven. So give the guy a break, Kris. And read the card. See what he has to say."

Kristin had freed the small card from the florist's envelope.

My Dear Ms. Allen:

Apologetic words and flowers cannot convey to you the regret and embarrassment I suffered upon discovering that you were a perfect stranger, while I behaved like a perfect boor. Please accept this as a token of my apology until I can personally express my regrets.

Sincerely,
Dace Kendrick

P.S. For what I did to you perhaps I should be horsewhipped and dragged for ten miles behind a stampeding mustang. . . .

Kristin gave an ironic laugh and handed the card to Mandy, who was unabashedly crowding close to see what it said.

She read it quickly. "What does the P.S. mean?"

"His parting words to me last night," she said. "He warned me not to show up on his doorstep for 'old time's sake,' because he said that he'd sooner 'be horsewhipped and dragged for ten miles by a stampeding mustang than spend another hour' with me."

"Not you, honey, *her.* Boy, she must've been some wicked number, huh? Wouldn't you give a pretty penny to know who she was?"

"Mandy, my dear," Kristin sighed, "I'd pay a small fortune to keep them all from finding out just who she is."

The remark seemed to take a moment to dawn. Mandy's eyes widened and her mouth dropped open. "You mean you *know*? Don't keep me in suspense like this! She must really be something to have gotten under Mr. Kendrick's skin like this."

"Believe me, she *is* something," Kristin said and took a deep, sighing breath. "I have a horrible feeling that the woman everyone loves to hate is none other than my big sister, Janice. And don't you dare tell a soul!"

"Wild horses couldn't drag it out of me!"

"Amanda Gentry. . .I think I'll pardon that pun if you don't mind," Kristin said in a weary voice. "Let's go get some breakfast, see about those horses, and forget all about the big boss man Dace Kendrick."

"Yeah," Mandy said. Her smile brightened. "He's not the only cowboy in South Dakota. Although he may be the most handsome. . . ."

Mandy was such a novice that the foreman in charge of the corral singled her out for individual beginner's instructions. He sent for a big, gentle mare, Molly. Molly was brought from the neighboring residence for one month each summer because she was so sweet-natured and affectionate that she was a favorite of all the children who came to the Circle K for the two weeks reserved especially for youngsters each season.

Kristin, as a more advanced rider, was given Misty, a beautifully marked, dainty Appaloosa, for her mount.

"I'll wait for you in the lounge area of the indoor riding arena," Mandy called after Kristin as Molly was brought out for the lesson to begin.

Two hours later Mandy limped out to meet Kristin and the other returning riders.

Kristin deftly dismounted and handed Misty's reins to a young man, one of many on the payroll, for him to curry, rub down, water, and walk after its use.

"How did your lesson go, Mandy?"

"I think I've figured out everything there is to know about horses. I watched the cowboys in a nearby corral practicing bronco busting on a mustang from the Kendricks' herd of wild horses. They're raised to sell to rodeo contractors."

"Oh? Do tell."

"One, they buck. Two, they bite. Three, they'll stomp on you. Four, they'll kick you when you're down. . . ."

"I saw Molly. She'd do no such things."

"Molly is an ol' sweetheart," Mandy agreed. "The lesson went very well, in fact, super, Jake says. But, maybe he's *paid* to tell all the greenhorns that. . . ."

"What'd you learn today?"

"How to mount up. Neck rein. And start and stop the horse."

Kristin smiled. "Have trouble finding the blinkers?"

"Locating the horn and emergency brake were my big problems. Actually, I had a nice ride. Now I could use a swim. Or," she eased a manicured hand down her side to settle at the small of her back, "a whirlpool bath."

"I think there is one someplace. This ranch seems to offer just about everything."

"Before we go back to our rooms, there's something you really should see, Kris. The Kendrick Family Rodeo Hall of Fame. Actually it is more like the Dacian F. Kendrick Hall of Fame. There are trophies that his father won. And his brothers. Even his sisters got barrel-racing and trick-roping awards. But it's clear that Dacian is the big rodeo talent in the family."

Kristin sighed so hard it riffled her bangs. "Dacian Kendrick! Is that all I'm going to hear today?"

"What's the matter with you? I was only making conversation and talking about my morning."

"I know, Mandy, and I'm sorry if I seem testy. But you're not the only one talking about Dacian Kendrick. Some of the other women along for the ride kept mentioning him, and then the ranch employees sent along to baby-sit us on our maiden ride did nothing but sing his praises. Talk about hero worship! He seems much adored by everyone but Yours Truly."

"Ummm. Maybe we'll convert you yet. The guys in the arena and corral do seem to think he can do no wrong, too, now that you mention it."

"Maybe they're paid to say that. Believe me, Mandy, I could've opened up a few eyes if I'd opened my mouth about how he treated me last night!"

"He did send you flowers this morning and a note of apology."

"That doesn't change how I feel."

"He really hurt your feelings."

"You'd still be smarting, too, if it had happened to you, Mandy. And yes, he hurt my feelings. But worse, he scared me. I. . .I was attacked once." Kristin found herself opening up, even though she wasn't really sure that she wanted to. She threw caution to the wind and continued, "I was held against my will and wounded to the point where I was hospitalized and underwent corrective cosmetic surgery several times."

"How awful, Kris. . . ." Mandy's sympathetic face conveyed her deep dismay. "I had no idea. No wonder you were so shaken last night. An attack would leave you traumatized."

"Mr. Kendrick's actions last night brought back a lot of very unpleasant memories and feelings that I would rather not deal with. I just want to forget them now as I made myself put them from my mind, suppress them, when it happened. I came here to have fun."

"We can skip the Hall of Fame."

"No. We're almost there. That way I can say that I've seen it," Kristin pointed out. "Coming to the Circle K and not visiting the Hall of Fame would be like going to Paris and ignoring the Eiffel Tower."

The girls wandered around the Hall of Fame, which Mandy was viewing for the second time. Kristin, in spite of herself, was impressed.

When she forgot *whose* career she was admiring, she felt a sense of awe. And there was no missing how Dace Kendrick had gone from a sparkly-eyed, cute Little Britches rodeo contestant to become an adult Professional Rodeo Cowboy Association All-Star year after year, walking away with almost every award there was to be won at the biggest rodeo of them all in Oklahoma City.

Although she'd labeled him egotistical, there was a disconcerting expression of poignant humility in his eyes as photographers captured him accepting trophies, belt buckles, and silver-trimmed saddles.

"Quite a guy, isn't he?"

"He's had an impressive career."

"Although he's a rich man, Kris, he's been good to the working man of America," Mandy said. "Why, it's obvious that he's kept all kinds of smelters and metal workers employed producing trophies!"

Kristin laughed. "And probably someone local gainfully employed to dust them all."

Mandy gave Kristin a playful nudge in the ribs. "I'd be his Roving Maid any time."

Minutes later the girls were walking from the cool Kendrick Hall of Fame when the dinner bell clanged, ringing out through the noonday heat.

"Lunch already?" Mandy said and glanced up to check the sun's position.

"How time flies when you're having fun."

"Let's hurry and get cleaned up, chow down, and then go swimming," Mandy suggested.

"I don't know. As hot as it is I'd like to, but—"

"But what?" Mandy prompted when Kristin's voice trailed off.

"There'll probably be so many people in the pool as sunny and hot as it's going to be this afternoon."

"So? That's what the pool is there for."

"I know. But I don't like being seen in a swimming suit."

"Aw, c'mon. What's a little cellulite among friends?"

"I have scars."

"So? I have one from my appendectomy that's a humdinger. No one's perfect, Kris. People at the pool probably won't even notice—or care. And if they do, that's *their* problem. We have to be able to accept that things happen and realize that God allows them in order for us to grow and develop as mature believers. Knowing we are accepted by the Lord can sometimes help us to be able to accept our own human failings and imperfections. If He can accept us, we should learn how to, too."

Mandy had been rattling on, and Kristin wanted to reply, but found herself with such a tight throat that she couldn't form words when she felt the presence of an odd, aching voice that did seem to beg to be filled with deeper Christian growth. Meat was what Mandy offered, not just scriptural milk. Mandy was a young woman, but she had a Christian faith of true maturity, seasoned so deliciously with humor. Then Mandy glanced across and brought the heel of her hand to her forehead.

"There I go again. Maybe I'd better hobble over to that bench so I can sit down and get the required leverage to remove my foot from my mouth again.

I didn't mean to preach at you."

Kristin managed a weak smile. "I was just mulling over what you said. You're not only a very amusing girl, but a truly wise woman in the wisdom of the Lord."

"I try. . . . Sincerely, Kristin, I didn't mean to hurt your feelings or to trivialize something that is obviously of great concern to you. I've accepted that I'll never be perfect. I've learned to live with the fact. And I've decided that I can like myself the way God made me and hope that others will, too. If they don't like me, that's their problem. With Mandy Gentry, what you see is what you get. A committed Christian woman who tries her best but will sometimes fail."

"And what I've got," Kristin said, "is a real friend. I know that you didn't mean to hurt my feelings, Mandy. I'm probably too sensitive about how I look."

Mandy eyed her. "I think that perhaps you are," she agreed in a frank tone. "The scars carried in your memory are probably more easily detected than those on your skin."

"That's exactly what the surgeon told Aunt Delilah," Kristin admitted. "Maybe they do seem so glaringly visible to me because of my background. Once upon a time I used to be a model. . . . I was groomed to be perfect. . . camouflaged to be flawless before the cameras."

For a moment, for perhaps the first time in her entire life, Mandy Gentry was found speechless.

"I remember you! No wonder you looked so familiar to me when we met at the baggage carousel!" She gasped and gave a delighted little squeal of excitement. "Oh, Kristin, you were my all-time ideal. Your face and figure were everywhere, touting makeup, jeans, sportswear, cosmetics. You were my idol. Why, I even taped a picture of you modeling a bikini on our refrigerator to encourage me to stick with my diet the summer I lost ten pounds. Wow, Mom and Dad are going to be amazed when I go back to Kirkwood and tell them who I've been chumming around with!"

"Please don't tell anyone here," Kristin said. "It's odd, and while I've made a whole new life for myself in Southern Illinois and no one's remembered me as the girl I used to be, suddenly, now, it seems as if I'm forced to face and deal with a lot of old issues I'd rather not acknowledge."

"It's a promise," Mandy agreed.

"Thanks. Now, what do you say that we go get something to eat? As hungry as I am, when I leave this ranch I may end up going back to Camden Corners and taping Christy Brinkley's picture to my fridge to discourage me!" Kristin joked.

Laughing, feeling better, the girls joined the other guests for lunch, then trailed toward their quarters to let their meals digest before preparing to go for a swim.

"Want to come in?" Kristin invited as she fished for her room key.

"I may's well," Mandy decided. "Hey! Your phone light's blinking. You've got a message."

"I wonder what it could be?"

"There's one way to find out."

Kristin picked up the receiver and was connected with the desk. "There's a message for me?" she inquired.

"Hang on a minute," the desk worker requested. "I'll connect you."

"Ms. Allen? This is Dace Kendrick. I've been trying to contact you all morning. Thanks for returning my call."

Dace Kendrick?

The mention of his name sent her pulse thudding like the hoofbeats of a runaway horse.

"Oh. I. . .uh. . .you're welcome." *Now what does he want?*

"I'd like to see you, to apologize over last night."

"There's no need," Kristin said, hating how stiff and formal her voice sounded. "The flowers arrived. I've accepted your apology."

"Flowers can't begin to make up for the damage I've done."

No they can't! Kristin thought. *Nothing can!*

"I behaved in a very unchristian manner last night," Dace went on, "that would not be tolerated from any of my employees. They'd have been dismissed immediately for accosting a guest in such a manner. I feel like a fool. So please, Ms. Allen, let me see you personally to apologize. I'll feel better and can hope to undo the shabby example I set for my help. . . ."

"I. . .isn't talking now good enough?" Kristin inquired. "It's quite acceptable to me."

"Our clash occurred in public; it seems suitable that an amicable apology should be a public statement, too. I was thinking more in terms of taking you out to dinner in Rapid City to try to make up for my insulting indiscretion."

"I. . .I really don't know about that," Kristin said.

Mandy, who was seated beside her on the satin-covered bed, was fairly squirming, as she leaned close, listening.

"Tonight, at seven?" he suggested, but with the tone of one accustomed to issuing orders and having them obeyed. "Please—?"

"I'm touched and appreciative, but I really—"

Kristin was not expecting it. Her grip on the receiver was loose, and in no time at all, Mandy had snatched it from her and thrust out her left hand, clamping her finger over Kristin's surprised lips, so she could make only muffled protests.

"I'd really *love* to go, Mr. Kendrick," Mandy cooed in a breathless voice, a passable imitation of Kristin's tone. "I'll be ready at seven. Sweet of you to ask me. Good-bye, now. See you tonight!"

Quickly she hung up before Kristin could react or wrest the phone back and wreck the evening's plans.

Dazed, sputtering with disbelief, Kristin stared at a blushing Mandy, who couldn't even meet her stormy eyes.

"How on earth could you do this to me?" she hissed.

Mandy looked mortified. "I. . .I don't know. It's like something just came over me. I'll admit I'm impulsive, but not to the degree where I ever believed myself capable of being an imposter. Kristin, I'm sorry, but I'm also not sorry, if you can follow that. Something just came over me, and the way you were acting, I knew that you were going to turn him down. And, well, sometimes I'm impulsive. I don't always mind my own business, either."

"Mandy, you were positively brazen. Shameless! And you sounded almost exactly like me. Heaven knows what that man is going to think of me now."

"I really did sound like you, didn't I?" Mandy mused.

"Don't try to change the subject on me, Amanda Gentry!"

"Well, believe me, Kristin, if I could manage to *look* like you I'd gladly take your place tonight."

Kristin moaned at the thought. "I can't do it. I won't do it. I've got to get out of it. Call him back, Mandy, and give him my, your, *our* regrets. Quick! Right now—"

Mandy stared across the room and locked the fingers of both hands around her knees. She gave Kristin a bland smile in the face of her tall, dark-haired friend's distress.

"Among my many flaws is the fact that I'm a bit mulish, too. The answer is no, Kris. If you *really* want out of your date with Dace Kendrick tonight, you'll have to wriggle out of it on your own."

"Nice of you, since it was *you* who got me into it."

"If you really don't want to go, there's the phone."

Kristin stared at it, but did nothing.

Suddenly Mandy let out a whoop and tossed a pillow at Kristin. "You can't fool me, Kristi Allen, you *do* want to go."

"Yes, I suppose I do," Kristin said. "Bu. . .but only to find out a little bit about a man who once upon a time proposed to my sister."

"You really think that *she* is the infamous *her?*"

"Positive. If I'm wrong, I'll eat my hat." She tossed her Stetson toward the dresser. "And my boots, too. . . ." She jerked them off and clunked them to the floor. "Now let's get ready to go for a swim."

"A swim? Kristin, your date tonight changes everything. Won't you want all afternoon to get ready?"

"Mandy, you're forgetting who you're talking to. Why, I know makeup shortcuts that could have me ready ten minutes from now."

"Then let's go!" Mandy said. "I'll meet you outside in five minutes. But we won't swim very long because I'll have to come back and take a nap."

"A nap?" Kristin echoed, confused.

"Uh-huh, because I'm going to be staying up late so you can tell me about every romantic moment of your night alone with the big boss of the Circle K spread. . . ."

Chapter Four

"What time is it?" Kristin asked.

"Six-forty-five," Mandy replied and groaned with vicarious tension. "I'm going to have to go to my room soon. This is just like anticipating Christmas morning when you're a kid. I can't wait for Dacian to arrive. Aren't you excited?"

Kristin thought it over. "Nervous is more like it."

"Well, don't worry about how you look," Mandy said. "This afternoon was fun and the results were worth our combined efforts. You'll be turning heads tonight."

Kristin glanced at the full-length mirror on the closet door. Her shiny black hair hung loose, full, and free, just caressing her shoulders, which were glowing from the afternoon sun's searing kiss. Her makeup, suitable for an evening out, made her features seem intense, vibrant, even mysterious, Mandy concluded.

Kristin's dress of tangerine crepe looked as if it had been made for her. It had a full, flowing skirt, nipped-in waist, and fitted low-scooped bodice with dainty spaghetti straps. A heart-shaped gold pendant on a delicate chain, with a sizable diamond in the center, perfectly accentuated the neckline and rested just above the hint of cleavage.

A year before, Kristin had bought the dress on impulse when she'd gone shopping at the Honey Creek Mall in Terre Haute, Indiana, but she'd never worn it.

When she tried it on for Mandy's reaction, the round-faced girl had almost swooned.

Kristin had studied her reflection. "I can't wear it. . . ."

"Why not?"

"Because. . .just because. It shows a scar. . . ."

Mandy's lips folded into a firm line and she touched her fingertip to the bottle of liquid makeup on the vanity tabletop. She dabbed it to the tiny, white, dimpled scar on Kristin's shoulder and it disappeared as if it had never existed.

"Wear it!" Mandy ordered in a no-nonsense tone.

Now an hour later, Mandy was monitoring the time. "Six-fifty and counting," she announced.

Kristin shivered and goose bumps rippled across her tawny flesh. Mandy noticed, but misunderstood.

"It may get cool tonight, Kris. I have just the exact little cover-up for you to take along. It's a white, lacy shawl with a dainty fringed border. You can secure it with a loose knot. It'll be perfect."

Mandy darted into her room and then rejoined Kristin a moment later, illustrating how the wrap would work effectively.

"You're a dear," Kristin said.

"I've got to go now," Mandy replied and gave Kristin an impulsive hug and an affectionate kiss on the cheek. "He's going to be here any moment. So forget about what happened last night and let this be a new beginning. Incidentally, if Dacian Kendrick wants to keep you out late, stay. You don't have to come home by eleven o'clock to tell me all about it." Mandy gave a good-natured shrug. "I'm going to be seeing Billy Joe tonight. And there's always tomorrow. . . ."

Dace arrived promptly at seven. When Kristin saw his white Corvette pull up in front of her quarters, she was torn between excitement and dismay and seesawed with sensations of eagerness about the evening and an almost overwhelming desire to ignore his knock and hide out for the night.

But she knew that Mandy Gentry would never let her get away with it. Kristin almost laughed when she pictured Mandy next door, peeking from behind the curtain of her darkened room, moaning to herself, "This is heaven. I'm in love!"

When Kristin opened the door to Dacian's knock, for a moment she wondered if that was the emotion that swept over her.

She felt the pulse at her neck throb, probably visible to Dacian, like a butterfly's fluttering wing, as she felt almost overpowered by his appeal. At that moment, his snapshot would've made the perfect inclusion in Webster's Dictionary to illustrate the definition of "handsome."

He was wearing a crisp beige linen summer suit that perfectly accentuated his lean, muscular build and his burnished tan from being outdoors so much. His hair was casually styled, but she knew such grooming did not come inexpensively. His cologne made her feel almost dizzy when she inhaled deeply. And his blue eyes, that had been sparking forked lightning the night before, a barometer that registered the intensity of his anger, were now as calm and open as the cloudless South Dakota sky.

"Dacian Kendrick," he spoke, when Kristin found herself unable. He extended his hand. "You're Kristin Allen?"

"Yes."

He gave a polite, deferential nod. "I'm pleased to meet you. Welcome to the Kendrick Circle K Ranch."

Krista gave a nervous smile. "Thank you. You sound about to give a testimonial to all that the dude ranch offers," she blurted nervously to fill the stifling silence.

Dacian laughed. "Sorry. I was only trying to start fresh with you, Kristin, in the manner I should've greeted you last night."

"Oh."

He paused, then looked hesitant. "Can we begin again? Please? I don't know what came over me last night. It's bothered me all day. . . ."

Kristin was touched by his uncertainty. "I think that's the nicest suggestion I've heard all day. Dacian Kendrick, I'm very pleased to make your acquaintance, and I'm sure I'll enjoy my stay here."

"Now you're starting to sound like a travel brochure," he teased. "Since you already know what the Circle K has to offer, let's head for Rapid City. There's plenty to see and do, and I've got what I think will be a memorable night planned for us."

Kristin's heart gave a sudden lurch when he helped her into his Corvette; and when he was circling around to the driver's side, she sneaked a wave in Mandy's direction.

She realized that no matter where they went or what they did, it would be a truly momentous occasion.

When Kristin's parents were still alive, she'd been deemed too young to date. After finding herself in Aunt Dee's care, she'd been too shy. Eventually, she knew that boys considered her unapproachable. She'd been kissed a few times while she was in high school. And she had gone to the roller rink on group outings. But then such adventures became off limits for a well-paid girl who couldn't afford black and blue marks from falling. So she'd never really had a *bona fide* date.

Until tonight. . .

Dace Kendrick had invited her out because he wanted to make amends. But Kristin was intent on enjoying her first date as if he'd requested her company because he considered her the most beautiful, fascinating woman in the world.

And that's what she tried to be as he drove them toward Rapid City. She listened to him, marveling at the melodious tone of his voice as he explained how the nearby Badlands, considered some of the most beautiful and rugged country in the world, had been formed. He explained about what his ancestors had faced when they'd crossed South Dakota's plains, intent on going further west, how they had confronted the Badlands, turned back in despair, but then carved out a rich and rewarding life.

At the fancy restaurant, they were shown to the table Dacian had reserved for them. The meal progressed flawlessly, and the evening was as perfect as the previous night's confrontation had been ugly.

Over coffee, Dace regarded Kristin by candlelight as the conversation flowed.

Dacian asked about her, and she told him about her Roving Maid business, the people she worked for, but was carefully evasive about anything that could link her to Janice.

When he asked a direct question about her family, she said only that her immediate family was very small, and then she deftly turned the tables by inquiring about his family. He regaled her with fascinating trivia about the close-knit, very accomplished Kendrick clan for most of the meal.

Kristin felt a ripple of pleasure when she realized that Dace was truly enjoying her company, and knowing that he did made her own experience more fulfilling.

As the evening progressed, she felt her breath quicken when he looked at her across the table and she was trying to fathom the inexplicable expression in his eyes.

Amusement?

Admiration?

Affection?

A touch of perplexity?

Eventually he stared at her until she felt a flush spread upward from her cheeks, and the heat disappeared into her hairline.

"A penny for your thoughts, Dace."

"I was just thinking that I can't believe I made such an utter fool of myself last night. Not only was it a stupid mistake, but I must've been blinded by disgust not to see at a glance that you weren't who I thought you were."

"Oh," Kristin said, and took a sip of her coffee, then toyed with her after-dinner mint as she wished she'd left well enough alone and not accidentally turned their talk toward the very topic she'd wanted to avoid.

"At a glance you seemed almost a dead ringer for her, that woman," he went on to explain, "but on closer inspection, that's where the resemblance ends. She had a hard beauty. And she was somewhat older, too. Your looks are fresh, simple. . .vulnerable. . .pure. If I'd looked at you closely last night, I'd have seen the difference."

"You were upset," Kristin dismissed the incident.

"The understatement of the year, Kristin, but when I thought you had the audacity to return to the Circle K after what you had done last year, I became so infuriated that I couldn't see straight."

"It wasn't *me* who did that. It was *her!*" Kristin defended to Dacian just as Mandy had pointed out the same logic to her that very morning, when it seemed as if the line between sisterhood and self had failed to exist to the others.

"Forgive me," he said. "I know that. It's just so uncanny to be sitting across from you, as if I were facing a younger, prettier version of *her*. I suppose that I still find it disconcerting and difficult to take in, although last night if I hadn't been so unhinged, I'd have known that you were not her, Kristin. But I wasn't listening to what you were saying any more than I was listening to how you said it. She had an affected, high society accent. And you sound like. . .a real person."

"I know," Kristin said in a resigned tone.

Janice's la-di-da accent had been one of the first things she'd undertaken to learn when she'd been tucked under Aunt Dee's wing and moved to New York City.

Suddenly Kristin realized what she'd admitted.

"I. . .I mean, I know what those people are like. So often phonies," she quickly clarified.

Dace regarded her a long moment, seemed about to speak further, then looked as if he'd decided against it.

"Last night I committed one terrible indiscretion, and here I am tonight, blundering into another by talking of the other woman to the lady of the moment. I'm sorry. Just let me add that I had no excuse to light into you and take you to task like I did, and I wouldn't have except out of family loyalty and misguided anger. The resemblance is such that you could be that woman's little sister. . . ."

Silence spun out, intense, upsetting, and Kristin's mind swirled as she tried to think of something to say, other than what was on the tip of her tongue: an admission that the infamous other woman had looked like Kristin's older sister because she *was!*

"Everyone gets told that she or he resembles someone else at one time or another, I'm sure," Kristin replied in an offhand manner. "I'm sorry that you were hurt as you were."

"It's over now," Dace said. "And from the experience I learned a few things about myself. . .and how to deal with women. Especially devious, dishonest, calculating Jezebels."

Then Dace fell silent and she knew that he was thinking about what had been, what might have been, and what was now. It was poignantly clear that he'd opened up his life and let himself become vulnerable and placed his love and deep feelings in the care of a heartless woman who had no compassion nor consideration. The set to his lips seemed to warn the world of women that he wouldn't be caught off guard like that again.

"It's late," Dace said as he assisted Kristin from her chair, left a tip, took care of the tab, and escorted her toward his car.

It was a gorgeous night, with a sky like purple velvet, spangled with stars, the perfect background for the full, golden moon. Impulsively Dace took Kristin's hand, and they strolled along, hands swinging. Suddenly Kristin began to laugh.

"What's so amusing?"

"I haven't walked along like this," she said, squeezing his hand, lifting it to gesture what she meant, "since kindergarten, what seems like a century ago."

"As children we resented having to do what we didn't know we'd enjoy as adults," he grinned.

"I hadn't thought of it like that," Kristin said. "I always seemed to get paired with some grubby-handed little boy."

Dacian stopped. He regarded her as her face was bathed in the moon's silvery glow.

"And did any of those grubby-handed little boys grow up to become handsome men? Who'd like to marry you. . .and father grubby-handed little boys who'd grow up to become handsome men?" he asked as if suddenly he found it terribly important to know.

"I'm afraid not."

"Then there's no one in particular?" he asked, his tone careful. "No one waiting for you back home in Illinois?"

The question that would've been embarrassing to answer truthfully to some people was one that she was glad she could give Dacian Kendrick.

"No. . .there's no one."

He brushed a kiss across her cheek, then began walking, swinging her hand, grinning, as if the assurance had been as pleasant for him to receive as it had been for Kristin to give.

"I'm glad," he said. "Very, very happy. You're so young, you probably don't understand the feelings of a man my age. A man who's had to accept the yoke of responsibility when not much more than a boy and live accordingly. Sometimes denying himself the simple things that others take for—" Abruptly he clipped off further words.

"When your father died," Kristin said, remembering information from his lashing out from the night before.

"Yes. At age sixteen, as the oldest son, I had to accept the fact that I had to keep the family together, work so that we could prosper and be secure. Then later on I had to keep in mind that it wasn't only the Kendrick family's fate that relied on my efforts, but the security of the people in my employ, who turned to me, trusted in me. Those are things someone as young as you probably hasn't had to face, if you're fortunate and life's been kind to you."

"Believe me, I've had my moments of trial," Kristin said. "I'm twenty-three. You're not that much older, Dacian."

"Thirty," he replied. "And that's old enough so that I have the urge to—"

Dacian shook his head in apparent confusion of thought or feeling, sighed, and then fell silent.

"Urge to what?" Kristin prompted as he unlocked the Corvette.

"Nothing," he said. "It's not important."

"The way you sighed, I think whatever you feel, or dream, is very important to you."

"Maybe," he said, and gave her hand another squeeze, then leaned toward her, and as the South Dakota breeze blew a wing of hair away from her smooth cheek, he deposited a tender kiss there. "And perhaps sometime I'll tell you all about it. . . ."

Without being told, she sensed that he wanted to find a woman, settle down, and stop being all things to all people so that he could be himself with the woman he loved and the children they would have to carry on a fine Kendrick family tradition in the land that they loved.

All the things, in a slightly different form, that she, too, had dreamed about during the dark lonely nights, wanting them for her own, but fearing she would never possess them.

Kristin's heart squeezed with a painful pang like a stab.

What a fool her sister had been. . .to turn down a man like this. . .scarring him so cruelly in the process that she shaped how he now dealt with all other women. But how lucky Dace had been to escape Janice, delivered from her deceits in time.

And how Dacian Kendrick would hate her, Kris feared, if he knew who she really was. . . .

"Earlier this evening you mentioned a housekeeper," Kristin remarked. "And I sensed you weren't referring to someone on the Circle K's housekeeping staff. Don't you live at the ranch?"

"Uh-uh. I have quarters there if I want to stay, but just as an executive leaves the corporate office and goes home for the night, so do I need to leave the Circle K and get away, too." He gave her a long look, then laid his hand over hers. "But something tells me that for the duration of your stay, I may be staying at the Circle K almost 'round the clock. I have a residence on private property, acreage that adjoins the family concerns." He paused. "Maybe I'll take you there sometime so you can see my ranch."

"I'd like that," Kristin murmured.

Dace didn't respond, and when she said no more, he seemed not to notice. Perhaps he, like she, was thinking of the other woman, Kristin's look-alike, who had probably gone there with him before, with him believing she wanted to share his dreams. Had there been others, too? Was he a womanizer as Jan had hinted all cowboys on dude ranches tended to be? Was Dacian being attentive because it was a good business tactic to romance a guest for the duration of her stay? For the gain of subsequent back-home word-of-mouth free advertising?

Kristin realized with sudden impact that she didn't want to know. Janice had warned her about dude ranch romances. And Mandy had passed judgment that cruise ship romances certainly didn't last.

Was she a fool to believe that she had a future with this remarkable man, when she knew, as he didn't, that the past was waiting in the wings to cause devastation in the present and prevent even the idea of a future?

She knew that all the women eyed the big boss of the Circle K with interest. Surely he wasn't immune. And certainly he frequently looked back with equal fascination. . . .

Kristin found herself feeling insecure and wondering exactly what were Dace's motives. Had he wined and dined her as a public relations maneuver after destructive business behavior the night before? Or had he used it as an excuse to ask her out so that he could set the scene for a seduction and romance her, substituting a look-alike girlfriend for a woman he despised. . .but perhaps still desired?

She would rather never know what it was to feel such longing and desire for a man. . .than to know that he was *using her as a reflection of love.*

Kristin was more confused than ever when Dace stopped in front of her quarters.

"You're quiet," he observed.

"I was just thinking."

"About what?"

Kristin gave a light laugh. "That's for me to know and you to find out."

"Ah, then, I will," he said. "Because nothing happens on the Circle K Ranch that I don't eventually find out about it."

Although it was spoken as light banter, the warning went straight to

Kristin's heart, filling her with dread, as she considered the secret that she, and Mandy, kept.

"It's late. Time for me to go in," she whispered, suddenly desperate to escape his compelling presence.

"I'll see you to your door," he said.

"We'll be quiet," she murmured, "so we don't disturb my neighbors."

He squeezed her hand in silent acceptance.

"Kristin, thank you," Dace said in a solemn tone. "It's been nice."

"You're welcome," she replied. "I enjoyed it, too."

"There will be other nights."

At the promise, her heart leaped, until she reminded herself that it was probably just words, a patly phrased parting promise that actually meant nothing.

"I. . .I'd like that."

"Then starting tomorrow night, if you're agreeable? For the hayride?"

Her heart suddenly soared. All of her misgivings had been in vain!

"Sounds like fun," Kristin said, unable to believe what was happening. Then insecure specters moved into the shadows of her mind. "But is that a wise business move?" She tested him.

"Business move?" He echoed, frowning down at her. "Whatever are you talking about?"

"I think that half of the women at the Circle K are in love with you," Kristin said. "Wouldn't it make more sense to circulate among them all? Keep your guests happy and hopeful?"

Dacian gave a ragged laugh.

"In matters of money, yes. Matters of the heart, no. I've already given so much of myself to the family business, Kristin. It's time that I set about the business of. . .someday having my own family."

Suddenly, as Dace looked into Kristin's eyes, she felt a weak sensation slide through her, leaving her feeling as if she might collapse beneath the weight of the knowledge that Dacian Kendrick was looking at her as if she might be the woman he had been waiting for.

It couldn't be.

She wouldn't let it be.

She couldn't let it be.

For she would not be able to bear it if he ever again looked at her with the threatening hatred that had been in his eyes only twenty-four hours before.

The realization made her feel boneless. Her respiration was thready and insufficient, leaving her feeling short of breath and oxygen starved.

She wasn't sure if she felt dizzy and swayed, or if Dace pulled her into his arms. But suddenly he was embracing her, dropping kisses to her hair, her temples, her cheeks, then his lips sought her mouth and he kissed her with an intensity that she knew she would never forget.

It was as if he were trying to brand her as his, while driving from his tortured mind memories of a woman he'd once wanted by creating equally as heady moments with a woman who looked just like *her* but was her opposite in every other way.

"It's time for you to go in," he said, his voice husky and thick with emotion. "Before I beg you to stay."

"Good night, Dace," Kristin whispered.

"Stay sweet," he ordered.

And then he was gone.

Kristin let herself into her room. She closed the door and collapsed against it, still feeling weak and breathless, but this time from the thrilling forcefulness of Dacian's kisses, not her nervous tension.

She half-expected Mandy to knock on her door and come dancing into her quarters, gasping, "Dacian kissed you! I saw it! The most handsome man in South Dakota kissed you!"

But when Mandy failed to materialize, Kristin realized that either her new friend was fast asleep or she was out with Billy Joe making a few unforgettable memories of her own.

Kristin thought of the person, the other woman, who had given Dacian Kendrick some unforgettable memories he'd sooner not remember, and she glanced at her watch, wondering if it was too late to call Janice.

Then she thought of the kind of hours Janice kept: first as a rich wife whose sole occupation was "shopping 'til dropping," and then as a wealthy divorcee who could sleep until noon and party until the wee hours as she sifted through likely prospects to find her next husband. Kristin decided it wasn't likely her big sister was tucked in for the night.

Although she didn't want to talk to Janice, on one hand, and have her pleasant evening tarnished by condescension, criticism, or cynicism, she knew that she had to put her worries to rest or else clearly define the problem she faced.

"It would be a dream come true to find out that she has never even heard of Dacian Kendrick," Kristin whispered to herself after she reached the switchboard and put through a long-distance call to her sister.

Jan didn't pick up the receiver until the third ring, and she answered in such a tone of voice that Kristin realized that it *was* a wonder Dace hadn't realized his error as soon as Kristin had opened her mouth.

"Hi, Jan? This is Kristin."

"Darling, I got your message—"

"I thought perhaps I'd have better luck catching you tonight."

"I just got in moments ago. You know how it is in New York City: busy, busy. And how are things in the Wild West?"

"I'm having a good time," Kristin said.

"With the sweaty horses, stinging insects, grubby children, scorching sun—"

"I've hardly noticed for all of the romantic men," Kristin interrupted.

"You've been behaving yourself?" Janice asked and gave a naughty sounding giggle.

"Probably better than you have," Kristin retorted.

"*Touche!*" Jan said in a droll tone. "So you've discovered some handsome, *macho* cowboys, have you?"

"Um-hm, although I just arrived yesterday, I went out this evening with a cowboy who has a brand new Corvette."

Jan gave a little croon of approval. "He's rich?"

"Very."

"Handsome?"

"Exceptionally so."

"Intelligent?"

"Top of his college class."

"Ambitious?"

"He runs the family business."

"Kristin, darling, are you *finally* coming to your senses? Aunt Dee will be so happy to hear that you're not only finally dating but keeping company with a man who has solid prospects."

"He seems very nice. A little bit impulsive. And he has something of a temper when he's driven to it. But I really like him."

"And does this Mr. Perfect have a name?" Janice inquired. "So that we'll have something to call him? I know Dee will want to know."

"An unusual name," Kristin said and gave a little yawn. "Dace." She prayed that Janice would gloss over the fact without a bit of alarm and go on to her next question.

But when Kristin's answer earned a startled gasp, her hopes plummeted and she knew that there wasn't going to be a reprieve.

"*Dacian Kendrick?!*" Janice cried, her refined accent forgotten. "Oh, Kristin, how *could* you? How could you be so foolish as to get involved with *him?*"

Kristin feigned innocence. "Simple. We met. He asked me out. I accepted.

And we just spent a wonderful evening together."

Janice muttered an oath. "Oh Kristin—"

"Jan, what's wrong? You seem so upset. Do you know him?"

"It's *him*," Janice said. "The cowboy who wanted me to marry him. The one I turned down. I should have warned you about him, but I didn't think you were going to the same dude ranch Cissy and I went to. The man was a beast when I broke it off with him. He vividly painted a romantic little hearts and flowers picture of our future together, and I tried to play the part for a while but realized there were easier ways to earn a place in society and a right to a man's bank account, without putting up with all Dace would've dished out. I tried, but deep down I just couldn't buy what he was trying to sell me on—"

Kristin wanted to close her ears as her sister railed on, spilling every ugly detail. She pinched her eyes shut, leaned her forehead against the cool wall, and she began to understand perfectly why Dacian despised her sister the way he did.

He'd offered Janice his love.

But she settled for nothing less than cutting out his heart, slashing his private dreams to ribbons.

"You'd better watch out for him," Janice repeated the warning in a grim tone. "You were right when you said that he's intelligent. He's smart enough to benefit from long-range planning. Why. . .he probably knows just who you are. . .and he's romancing you so that he can get back at me. Believe me, Krissie, when it comes to that forsaken ranch of his, nothing goes on that he doesn't know about it. Why, if a leaf turns over in the corral, he's aware of it. And he's just the hypocritical type who'd find this tawdry, tacky little debacle amusing. But if that's what Dace's doing, then he doesn't know me well enough to realize that such juvenile behavior won't bother me at all." She gave a careless sniff. "Let him play his childish games. Such behavior would never win me back. . . ."

Kristin realized that Janice was talking only about herself and seemed not to notice or care if Kristin was wounded along the way.

"As smitten with me as Dacian was, I knew that he wasn't going to get over me fast. Such a. . .passionate man. But impulsive. And he has such a strange sense of loyalty and such an odd set of what he considered 'Christian ethics,' that I'll bet a block of Blue Chip stock that he's still carrying a torch for me! And if *that's* the case, then you're in even worse trouble than if he's got his heart set on revenge, Krissie, because no girl wants to settle for being a substitute for the real thing. Making do with her big sister's hand-me-down love."

Kristin felt near tears.

"Bu. . .but I like him," she protested softly, even as she hated herself for making the admission to a woman who obviously didn't know what it was to enter a relationship without balancing it out in dollars and cents and realizing that a person couldn't attach a price tag to the human heart.

"Of course you like him, dear, because Dace is very good at what he does. He makes every woman between eight and eighty who comes to his ranch feel like the only girl in the world. Why, he gobbles up pretty girls the way I can go through chocolates when I'm depressed. . . . Trust me, darling, you are no match for him. Continue this mad affair, Krissie, and you'll regret your folly. I really hate to ruin your dreams by giving you this down-to-earth advice. But that's what big sisters are for."

"Have you heard from Aunt Delilah?" Kristin changed the subject.

"As a matter of fact, I did. She and Uncle Benchley will be departing Heathrow a week from tomorrow. I'll have a limo meet them at LaGuardia. She told me to give you her love. And we'll be in touch when they arrive, so you and Dee can have a little chitchat."

"All right."

"And I'm not going to tell Aunt Dee that you're mixed up with Dacian, Kristin, and I would suggest that you don't, either. She'd be so worried. She *knew* what I went through last year at this time."

"Well, it's late, and I've really got to go," Kristin said.

"Great talking to you, Krissie. Call again. And remember what I said: Dacian isn't interested in you because of the kind of girl you are, but because of *who* you are. His motives are definitely suspect. Either revenge or trying to mold my look-alike little sister into the sophisticated woman of his dreams so he can enjoy a make-do love affair with a facsimile of his old flame."

Kristin hung up without even saying good-bye, although Janice was too involved in her cooing, kissy noise good-byes to notice.

Kristin took a deep breath and tried to hold in the tears, but they erupted with the force of a sneeze and a painful sob tore from her throat.

She threw herself down on the bed and cried into her pillow as she realized that her big sister, who liked to think that she was so sophisticated and wise, might just be right about Dacian Kendrick. Perhaps they really were two of a kind.

Kristin had known Dace for only slightly more than twenty-four hours. Janice had been involved with him long enough for him to propose marriage.

Was Dacian toying with her?

Kristin thought back over their night together. The way he had said that Kristin looked so much like the other woman, did he know it for a fact? Was he testing Kristin to see if she would confess to the truth? Did he want to see if she would lie to him the way her sister had? And had he warned her that she would not get away with it? Janice had told her that nothing happened on the Circle K Ranch without Dacian knowing about it. That fact wasn't news to her, for the same information had fallen from Dace's lips that very night.

Was he setting her up for an elaborate scheme, despising her sister to the point that he didn't care who he hurt, so long as he could wreak his sick revenge?

Kristin realized she still did not really know if he liked her or loathed her.

And if Dacian Kendrick was truly as farsighted and long-reaching as Janice had insisted, Kristin realized that she would have no idea exactly where she stood with him until Dacian Kendrick decided to make the issue perfectly clear.

Then it dawned on her that even if he did like her, it was only a temporary stay from heartbreak and humiliation, for she couldn't continue on forever keeping it a secret that her only sister was the woman who had spurned Dacian Kendrick and taught him the bitter tenets of faithless, untrue, unreturned love.

Chapter Five

It had been hours before Kristin fell asleep as her mind swirled with the possibilities surrounding her new and chaotic relationship with Dacian Kendrick.

Not long before dawn she drifted asleep, exhausted from crying, too weary to think.

Hours later there came a pounding upon her door.

Kristin sat up, blinked, looked around her, dazed and disoriented, startled to not be in her own bed in Camden Corners.

Then she remembered where she was.

And why.

Her caller knocked a little louder.

"Just a minute," Kristin called out.

She ran her fingers through her sleep-tangled hair, retrieved her robe from the chair beside the bed, scuffed into slippers, and crossed the room, looking out the peephole before she undid the assortment of security devices.

A smiling Mandy was dressed and raring to go.

"Good morning, sleepyhead!" She said in a bright tone.

"Hi. I guess I overslept." Kristin gestured at herself and the rumpled bed.

"If you hurry we can still make breakfast. Pancakes, sausage, and warm, buttery syrup appeal to me this morning."

"It does sound good," Kristin agreed and offered a wan smile as she collected clothing and toiletries, trying to keep her back and profile to her friend.

"You've been crying!" Mandy murmured in a shocked gasp.

She was across the room and tugged Kristin's shoulder, turning her so that they were face-to-face.

"You *have* been crying."

"I. . .I know," Kristin admitted in a quaking voice and squeezed her eyes shut for a moment, hoping to hold back more tears that prickled at her red, swollen eyes.

"The night was that bad?" Mandy said. "That's too bad. I would've been in for details last night, except I was out with Billy Joe until so late I thought it wasn't appropriate to disturb you. But maybe I should've. It looks like you could've used a shoulder to cry on. He was a regular beast, huh?"

"No, actually, Dacian Kendrick couldn't have been more charming," Kristin said.

"What?" Mandy cried, perplexed, as her eyes were telling her one thing and her ears were hearing quite another.

"I had a wonderful time, Mandy. It was perhaps one of the. . .the. . .the. . . most wonderful nights of my entire life."

"Then why are you crying, pray tell?" Mandy asked.

"Because I don't know why Dacian was so nice to me."

"Because he likes you, silly. And you're more than just a little nice to look at, you know. Last night you looked like any man's daydream come true. Oh, and I also suppose you think that he's just being nice in order to fully apologize for his rotten behavior from the night before. But I saw the look on his face when he came to get you. I think apologizing was secondary, Kris. Definitely secondary."

"Dace Kendrick is an intelligent man, shrewd, long-reaching, farsighted—"

"Who am I talking to this morning?" Mandy asked. "It doesn't sound like the girl I know. I feel as if I'm being lectured by some unpleasant stranger."

"Sorry."

"Just what's gotten into you?"

Kristin sighed. "Maybe it's a case of who's gotten through to me."

"Okay. I give. Who?"

"I talked to Janice after I came in last night."

"You didn't! Oh, Kris, *why?* She sounds like nothing but a bucket of bad news."

"Why? Because the way I felt last night. . .I had to know if Janice really was the other woman. Maybe it was foolish, but I entertained hope against hope that she wasn't. Mandy, I feel about Dacian the way I have never felt about a man before. We got along so well last night, had such fun, that I felt as if he considered me the most wonderful woman in the world."

"Your head was swimming," Mandy empathized.

"Yes."

"And then you started dreaming."

Kristin nodded, then sighed again. "Until I woke up and realized what a nightmare it would be if Janice was Dacian's unrequited love. I wanted to know where I stood, Mandy. If Janice had never heard of Dacian, then I'd know that I could risk getting involved with Dace and not fear there being a secret between us."

"And a secret with the capacity to blow your worlds apart," Mandy said, understanding Kristin's inner fears.

"So I called Janice last night. You should've heard her," Kristin said, and she looked ill as she recalled. "She painted a totally different picture of Dacian than the impression he had given me."

"I'm not sure I should ask, and I'd probably be happier not knowing, but what did she tell you?"

"For starters. . .that Dacian was so smitten by her that she doubts that he ever got over her. She feels that he's still carrying a torch for her."

Mandy made a face. "Oh, give me a break. She sounds like she has an ego as big as the outdoors. She couldn't face herself in the mirror in the morning if she thought that he wasn't beating his breast, wearing sackcloth, and pouring ashes over his head on her behalf."

Kristin gave a weak laugh in spite of herself and her worries.

"I'm a glutton for punishment," Mandy said. "Tell me more."

"Well, she also says that he's vengeful. She believes that there's a good chance he knows exactly who I am and that he's stringing me along, being the attentive, affectionate, considerate suitor so that he can make me fall in love with him and then dump me, so that by hurting me he'll somehow get back at her."

"Stuff and nonsense! Pure egotism. And convoluted reasoning." Mandy gestured impatiently. "Go on, go on, surely it gets worse."

Kristin frowned reflectively. "No, basically that's it. Although she expounded on the topics at great length, telling me what she thinks about Dace." Kristin's voice shook. "Excuse me," she said quickly, "while I run in and take a shower."

And have another good cry.

Kristin exited the bathroom ten minutes later, dressed, and toweling her hair.

A definitely nettled Mandy sat with her arms folded over her ample chest.

"You've told me what your sister thinks of Dace. I have a hunch I know how *you* really feel about him, or you wouldn't have cried the night away. Would you like me to tell you what others think about Dacian Kendrick?"

"If you feel compelled to. I don't know if it will make any difference. I feel so confused. . .I wish we'd never met. To think I came here to have fun."

"And you will have it. *With* Dace."

"He did ask to accompany me on the hayride tonight."

"See? Great!" Mandy's expression brightened. "Billy Joe's my date. And, speaking of Billy Joe, he's the source I'm quoting. Last night I asked him about Dace, and he told me about all there was to tell. Listening to him, seeing the expression on his face, I can't believe that Dace is a petty, vengeful, grudge-bearing man. Not someone who loves kids the way he does."

"He's been very good to his brothers and sisters," Kristin agreed. "He told me about them last night. And I know it wasn't an act, like Jan hinted his family loyalty might be."

"If it were an act, kid, he'd have a hard time maintaining it, year in, year out, for two weeks each summer. Especially when you consider that it's costing him dear."

"What are you talking about?"

"The fact that every year, for two weeks of the summer, Dace Kendrick turns down paying guests because he reserves the entire ranch for kids' enjoyment. Not just any kids, *sick children*."

"Mandy, I had no idea. . . ."

"Most of the guests don't know. But the staff, of course, is aware."

Quickly Mandy sketched in the background.

When they were youngsters, Dace Kendrick's older brother had died of leukemia. At the time the Kendricks were not wealthy, there were bills to pay, other children to care for, and the burden of a serious illness had taken a toll on the family's emotional and financial resources.

"An anonymous person knew that Dace's older brother had always dreamed of going to Disneyland. It was a trip beyond the Kendrick family's ability to finance, and this unknown benefactor donated money sufficient not only to take the dying boy to Disneyland, but to send along his family as well."

Mandy was getting misty-eyed, and Kristin suddenly felt that way, too.

"That dream vacation for a sick little boy and his family gave them lasting memories of good times to offset the effects of living daily with inevitable tragedy."

"He's been through a lot," Kristin murmured.

"And that's what makes him such a tough, strong, enduring man, with a compassionate Christian nature to soften the rough edges from his human nature.

"According to Billy Joe Blaylock, Dace, even as a child, had been deeply affected by his brother's illness. He knew what the stranger's generosity had meant to others, and when he was scarcely more than a child himself, he vowed to someday do for other children and their families what was done for the Kendricks.

"He does have a good side," Kristin acknowledged.

"And his word given is a vow that goes unbroken," Mandy said. "Every summer at least one hundred seriously ill children who are in remission or are well enough to come here spend a two-week vacation on a real ranch. All expenses paid."

"They must look forward to it months before they get to go," Kristin said.

"And talk about it for months afterwards," Mandy added. "When I was a kid I can remember the lure horses, rodeos, and ranches held for me. Well, your Dacian Kendrick, my dear, makes dreams happen for a lot of children and their families, and it's been going on for years and years. The Operation: Recovery Rodeo is a tradition in these parts and draws major rodeo riders from all over the United States, who participate and donate their purses to support various children's hospitals nationwide."

"He's hardly 'my Dacian Kendrick,' " Kristin clarified.

"I think he could be," Mandy said. She paused. "And so does Billy Joe Blaylock."

"You've discussed this with Billy Joe?" Kristin cried, embarrassed.

"Actually, no. He asked me about you. So I told him I'd tell him what there was to know about you if he'd respond to my questions about Dace. It seemed a fair swap. And I didn't tell him about your sister, although he's no fan of the infamous Janice, either."

Kristin, who had felt her almost obsessive desire for the protection of privacy slip in the past days, felt suddenly vulnerable.

"I'm not sure I approve of the deal you two struck."

"Billy Joe wants for Dace the same thing that I want for you, Kris, happiness. And we happen to think that you two could find it in each other."

"If it weren't for Janice."

"Do you really think it will, would, make that much difference to Dace if, or when, he finds out?"

"I don't know," Kristin said. "Maybe Billy Joe could tell you, but don't you dare ask him, because I certainly don't have a clue."

"You will after tonight when you go on a hayride and are snuggled on a wagon load of soft, clean straw, beneath a golden moon, with stars twinkling overhead, and—" Mandy broke off her litany of details and leaped to her feet. "So let's get started with our day, concentrate on happy thoughts and positive thinking, and prepare for us both to have the night of our lives this evening."

"Sounds good," said Kristin, who suddenly felt so much better. She cinched her western belt and smoothed her designer jeans over her trim hips. "Mess hall cooks—here we come!"

❧

After breakfast the girls went for a ride. The cowboy in charge of the corral stock gave Mandy a different mount, also gentle, and placed her and the horse in Kristin's more experienced care.

"But I like Molly," Mandy protested.

"Sorry," the cowboy said and gave an amused grin. "She's an ol' pet, and everyone loves Molly, but we keep her up at the corral unless we run short of stock and then we'll only let an experienced rider take her out. You see, the old girl has this bad habit of getting out, becoming a bit headstrong, and heading for home at the neighboring spread, where she lives for eleven months out of the year."

"Oh, okay," Mandy said, laughing, and settled for Waco, a sorrel quarter-horse gelding.

Following the girls' ride, they watched a tennis match, went for lunch, took a swim, and then sunned themselves beside the pool as they talked about plans for the night.

"It'll be fun," Mandy assured.

"I hope so," Kristin said.

"Don't worry. I know so."

Kristin was not as confident as Mandy was. Each time they neared the headquarters that day, she'd glanced to the slot where Dace parked his Corvette. The private parking area was mockingly empty, causing her heart to sink anew each time her searching glance was not rewarded with the presence of his car.

"We probably ought to go to our rooms and think about getting ready for dinner tonight," Mandy said, yawning from the exertion of an hour in the pool combined with the cloying heat.

"You're right," Kristin said and immediately arose, collecting her beach jacket, her leather sandals, her sunglasses, floppy hat, and sunscreen lotion.

A lethargic Mandy was slower gathering her gear.

Kristin walked a few steps ahead of her, hoping that she didn't seem impatient in her desire to cast a quick glance in the direction of Dace's parking slot. Surely as late as it was and with his plans to take her to the hayride, he would have returned to the ranch while she lazed away the afternoon by the pool.

When she saw his parking slot was still empty, she felt drenched with disappointment, and it was an effort to muster passable enthusiasm to respond to Mandy's excited predictions for the hayride.

"See to it that you and Dace sit near Billy Joe and me," she ordered. "We're all going to have such fun together."

"Okay. I promise," Kristin said. "Want to come into my room for a little while? I'll get a soda from the machine and we can split it."

"Sounds great," Mandy said. "I'm parched."

Kristin unlocked the door to her quarters. The telephone on the stand beside her bed blinked a steady rhythm.

"I'll get the soda," Mandy offered, digging in the pocket of her beach robe where coins jingled. "You collect your messages."

Kristin crossed to the telephone and contacted the desk.

"Ms. Allen? This is Marcie at the front desk. Mr. Kendrick called while you were out. He asked me to give you the message that he won't be returning to the Circle K tonight as planned, so he regrets that he will be unable to keep his appointment with you."

"Oh. . .okay," Kristin said, as she heard in reality the message that had been a hidden worry in her heart all afternoon. "Thank you, Marcie!" she said in a bright, upbeat tone that she hoped didn't convey her disappointment. She didn't want it passed on if a callous, caddish Dacian Kendrick should inquire of the girl at the desk what Ms. Allen's reaction to the message had been.

"Anything important?" Mandy asked.

She popped the top from the aluminum can, then was forced to take a quick sip before it could bubble over and spill to the carpet. She divided it between two glasses on a tray on Kristin's dresser.

"Or is it none of my business?" Mandy suggested in a rueful tone when Kristin didn't immediately reply.

"The girl at the front desk told me that Dacian had tried to contact me while we were out, so he left a message with her that he's not returning to the ranch, so he can't keep our, and I am quoting now, 'appointment.' "

"Kind of a stilted word for a date, isn't it?" Mandy mused. "Oh well," she said. "You don't know that 'appointment' was Dacian's choice. That may have simply been the word the girl at the desk selected to get the jist of the message."

"I suppose. But—"

And suddenly Kristin was helpless to contain the worries and insecurities that had plagued her all afternoon, and she blurted to Mandy that maybe it was just a perverse cat-and-mouse game on Dacian Kendrick's part.

"Whatever are you talking about?" Mandy asked.

"He could be toying with me," Kristin said and felt her lower lip tremble. "He could be building me up only to purposely let me down, laughing all the while."

"Don't say such things, Kristin. Don't even think them. They're not true."

"How do you know they aren't?"

"How do you know that they are?"

"Well, Janice did say—"

"I'd call Janice a wicked, lying, envious, troublemaking witch," Mandy said, "except that she's your sister, so I won't."

"In a backhanded way, Mandy, I think that you just did."

"Are you angry with me?"

"I probably should be, but I'm not. I've never been one to argue with the truth," Kristin said and gave a weary sigh.

"So what are you going to do about tonight?" Mandy asked.

"Stay home, do my nails, and read some more on a novel I began on the way here."

"I think that's a mistake. You should go. I want you to go. You can chum around with Billy Joe and me."

"But I don't want to go, not all by myself."

"Billy Joe's got friends. Cute ones, too. Maybe they're not Dacian Kendrick, but they're nice guys."

"I'd sooner stay home than try to be good company, Mandy, when I feel like I'd be anything but pleasant and charming to be around."

"You've got to go," Mandy insisted.

Kristin noticed a grimness about Mandy and a determined set to her lips.

"But why?"

"Just in case it *is* some kind of ugly trick, Kris, then you'll be out having fun and Dacian Kendrick won't get so much as a moment of satisfaction in thinking of you alone and lonely, eating your heart out over him, while he tears your heart out to get even with your sister."

"You believe me, don't you?" Kristin said. "You think it's possible, too, don't you?"

Mandy nodded. "Possible, yes. Likely, no. Billy's told me Dace is a committed Christian, but we believers can all have our moments of falling flat on our faces, being unacceptably petty, because we are human, after all. . . ."

"Maybe I will go with you," Kristin said. "And I'll just put Dacian Kendrick from my mind and concentrate on having a great time."

"Good girl," Mandy said and gave Kristin an encouraging pat on the shoulder. "Don't go off half-cocked, Kris. Don't think about it any more tonight, okay? Wait until tomorrow. Everything may look different then."

Chapter Six

Kristin had felt a sense of trepidation when she tagged along with Mandy and a welcoming Billy Joe. But as soon as they neared the site where workhorses were hitched to racks billowing with fluffy straw, she was glad she'd gone along. She wasn't the only person who wasn't part of a couple.

A worker from the ranch's kitchen staff was carefully tending a bonfire. In coolers laid out on picnic tables were uncooked hotdogs, hamburger patties, and other snacks that would be awaiting the guests when they arrived back at the headquarters of the Circle K Ranch.

"All aboard!" the lead wagonmaster said and snapped the reins over the broad backs of a matched team of Belgian draft horses.

Harnesses clinking, massive heads bobbing, they stepped out, their gigantic hooves raising soft swirls of dust into the hazy evening sky flickering with fireflies lifting from the grassy knolls as stars gleamed in the night.

"Nice, isn't it?" Mandy whispered and grinned at Kristin from where Mandy was in the loose circle of Billy Joe's arms.

"It is pleasant," Kristin said, feeling a pang of disappointment that Dace wasn't beside her, snuggled on the soft bed of straw, with him leaning close to whisper private jokes and observations in her ear.

When they passed a small grove, Kristin saw a jackrabbit dart for cover. And as they moved into the vast expanse of open rangeland, a coyote howled and yipped at the moon. The harrowing, haunting sound that lingered in the cool night air made her shiver and feel oddly lonesome although she was surrounded by people.

"I think we could use a song," someone said.

"Well, we're in luck," one of the ranch hands called out. "Billy Joe Blaylock's got his git-fiddle here somewhere."

Billy, who'd been centering his attention on Mandy, was brought into the spotlight. He tried to protest, but the wagonload of guests and ranch employees wouldn't take no for an answer, and with Mandy's adoring eyes encouraging him, he gave in and agreed to provide the entertainment.

He retrieved his guitar from its sturdy but battered carrying case, quickly tuned it, and then as his calloused fingertips caressed the wires, sliding along the ornate fretwork of the instrument's neck, people began to join in and sing old favorite familiar songs.

The wagons that had drawn ahead of the one where Kristin, Mandy, and

Billy Joe were riding, slowed their pace to narrow the gap, and soon it sounded like almost everyone from the Circle K Ranch was serenading the harvest moon that rose high and huge overhead.

If the coyotes mourned in the night, the guests of Dace Kendrick's dude ranch, including Kristin, were too boisterously happy to even notice.

"I need something to drink," Mandy said when they returned to the ranch and hopped down from the wagons, brushing straw from their clothes and hair.

"Me, too."

"I haven't done that much singing since, since—"

"Kindergarten?" Kristin supplied, feeling another stab when she remembered holding hands and swinging along with Dace.

"Probably," Mandy acknowledged. "But hasn't it been fun?"

"Perfect," Kristin said.

Mandy frowned. "Well, not quite perfect, Kris, because your guy wasn't able to be here."

"I don't want to think about that tonight. Remember?" Kristin said.

"Sorry," Mandy murmured. "I was just having so much fun that I–I—"

"Don't apologize, Mandy. I know that you want me to have what you do. And from my point of view. . .it looks like you have a man who loves you."

"Oh, do you think so, Kris? I've thought that, too, but then I've remembered what your sister told you about the insincere, smooth-talking men at dude ranches, then I hardly dare hope."

"My dear, there is nothing insincere about the way Billy Joe looks at you. Mandy, his eyes regard you as if he thinks that the sun rises and sets on you and the oceans calculate their tides by your desires."

Mandy gave a delighted giggle.

"He does act pretty sweet on me, doesn't he? And I'm *crazy* about him. I know that my family would be, too."

"Billy's easy to like. So nice. So thoughtful. Intelligent."

"Just about everything a girl could ever want," Mandy murmured, her tone wistful.

The two fell into momentary silence as they stood off by themselves and Billy was occupied helping the other ranch employees put the Belgians in their pasture.

"Kris. . .can I ask you something?"

"Sure."

"Do. . .do you think that what I feel for Billy Joe could be love? Or do you think that it'll go away? Die like a cruise ship romance does as soon as a person steps on dry land?"

"I don't know, Mandy. I'm not exactly experienced when it comes to matters of the heart."

"I feel different this time. Real different." She paused and when she spoke again, there was a catch in her voice. "I've never had a life other than the one with my family and friends in Kirkwood, where I feel like I'm marking time hunched over a keyboard tapping data into the company's terminals. I. . .I . . . well, since meeting Billy Joe and getting to like him as I do, I realize that I don't want to go back to that life. I've always believed that God had plans for me since He laid the very foundations of the universe. That there was a special man for me, desired for me by my Lord and Savior. Given time, God would lead me down a path so I'd meet that man. Perhaps I wouldn't recognize him instantly, but the Lord would open my eyes so I'd see him as the perfect mate for me, and he would see in me the woman cherished and desired above all others. I want to stay right here. But I can't. This week will be up in a wink, then there's next week, and after that I have to pack my bags, climb in the van, head for the airport, and. . .Kris, I'm afraid maybe this isn't meant to be, and I want this to be God's plan for me!"

Mandy, who Kristin realized, was too choked up to speak further, fell silent. Kristin put her arm around the shorter girl's shoulder and gave her a comforting hug.

"Don't think about the tomorrows, hun," she advised. "Just live for the moment. Make it through the here and now and the future will take care of itself. If it's meant to be, it'll happen. If not, perhaps you await a fellow who's even more perfect."

"You know, that sounds like something wise that my mother would say," Mandy said, dabbing at her eyes. "You've just made me feel better. Thanks."

Kristin smiled acceptance of the sentiment, then turned away as Billy Joe rejoined them. She wished that a few small words from someone could make *her* feel as relieved and happy as Mandy did now.

She realized that there were three tiny words that could make her world explode in bright, radiant happiness, like a rocket bursting on the Fourth of July.

If only Dacian Kendrick would hold her close, kiss her tenderly, and whisper the sentiment meant for only her to hear: *I love you. . . .*

But why should that ever happen? she realized as she walked back to her quarters and prepared to go to bed. He actually hadn't given her any indication that she was really any more special to him than any other female on his ranch between eight and eighty who was worthy of a bit of flattery to ensure satisfied customers.

To her surprise, Kristin didn't lay awake stewing about it. After all of the exercise, good food, and fresh air, she toppled into bed and slept as if she'd died.

When Kristin awoke the next morning, she was considering getting up early so that Mandy wouldn't have to wait for her when the telephone beside her bed purred.

She got it before the second ring.

It wasn't Mandy, as she had expected, nor was it Dace, as she'd fleetingly, wildly hoped. It was the girl at the front desk, this time a different one, Sonya.

"Just checking to see if you're awake, Ms. Allen," the girl said in a pleasant tone. "There was a package left for you at the front desk early this morning. I didn't want to send someone to deliver it and disturb you."

"Oh, that was thoughtful," Kristin said, as she wondered what could have been dropped off at the front desk for safekeeping.

"You're up and about so I can send someone over with it, then?" Sonya inquired.

"Yes. I'll be waiting."

"Very well. Someone will be there in a jiffy."

Kristin scarcely had time to slip into her robe, brush through her hair with quick motions, and rub the sleep from her eyes before there was a knock at her door.

The young ranch employee checked the number on Kristin's door, then consulted the note on the ornately wrapped package.

"This is for you!" the cute teenage boy announced.

"Thanks," Kristin said.

"Have a nice day, ma'am," the young cowboy said and tipped his hat.

The realization that the package could only be from Dace immediately made Kristin's day much nicer.

There was another knock at Kristin's door as she seated herself in an occasional chair, the heavy but compact box on her lap. She opened the sealed envelope with her name scrawled on it in what she felt certain was Dace Kendrick's handwriting. It seemed to perfectly represent him: large, well-formed, strong, but distinctively his own.

"Just a moment," Kristin called and set the package aside as she rushed to answer. She opened the door to Mandy.

Feeling suddenly on top of the world, she gave her friend an impulsive hug and pulled her into the room.

"I swear, Mandy, if you were a little robin, you'd definitely have all the worms. You're such an early bird!"

"Well, you're in a good mood this morning," Mandy said. "Something happen?"

"I think so."

"You think so? You don't know?"

"I got a package," Kristin breathlessly explained. "I think it's from Dace. And I'll know in a moment."

"Wow, the roses have really opened up overnight, haven't they?" She gave a giggle. "I feel almost like I'm in Pasadena on January first instead of in South Dakota the tail end of July."

Kristin hardly heard her as she carefully opened the envelope.

Dear Kristin,

I was disappointed not to be able to keep our date last night. Something came up. I had to consult with my lawyer in a meeting that went on endlessly. My body and mind were with him, but my heart was with you.

Dace

"Oh, Kristin, see?!" Mandy gave a gleeful squeal. "I told you so. We shouldn't have doubted him for a moment. You know, a place like this spread doesn't run by itself. Someone has to be in charge and make a lot of decisions. And if there are problems, that same someone has to handle them whether it's convenient or not."

"That's true," Kristin admitted and recalled what Dace had said about how demanding his position had been, what it had cost him over the years, the things he'd been denied that others took for granted.

"What's in the box?" Mandy said.

"We'll see," Kristin said.

She slid a fingernail under the transparent tape, freed the glittery foil paper, and folded it back to reveal the bottom of what was obviously a box of chocolates.

"Roses. Chocolates. What comes next?"

"Who knows?" Kristin said, laughing.

She upended the box of candy on her lap, righted it, saw the label, and gasped, dismayed.

Mandy misunderstood. "Wow, do you have any idea how much those chocolates *cost?*" She asked in an awed tone.

Kristin felt suddenly sick to her stomach at seeing the label, a little known but famous brand among chocolate afficionados.

"Yes, when I used to live in New York City, I knew their price right on down to the ounce."

"You had a real sweet tooth, huh?"

"No," Kristin said in a careful tone. "I had a big sister who couldn't resist them and had me pick them up regularly on my way home from the modeling agency offices."

Mandy made a strangled sound of compassionate shock. "Oh, Kristin. . . ."

"These chocolates just happen to be Janice's all-time favorites."

"Really, Kris, they're an excellent, expensive brand. The kind that you'd give to someone you want to impress. The fact that your sister was addicted to them and Dace decided to give that brand to you doesn't mean a thing."

"Doesn't it?" Kristin murmured.

"Does it?" Mandy countered.

"I don't know," Kristin said. "And I wish I did. It's driving me crazy, not knowing where I stand with Dacian, wondering one moment if he sees in me the woman of his dreams and worrying the next instant that he views me as the perfect instrument for his revenge. . . ."

By that evening Kristin had gone from wondering about Dacian's intentions regarding her to feeling that she was the most important woman not only in South Dakota, but in the entire world as far as he was concerned.

For once she happened to be in her room when a call came for her, and she took it, suspecting that it might be Mandy, who was too comfortable to get up and walk to the room next door. Or perhaps, she worried, it was a call from Janice.

When Kristin found Dace on the line, her heart skipped a beat and then her pulse accelerated. She was unable to keep the joy from her voice, and from the way his tone warmed and grew intimate as a caress, Kristin realized he'd noticed and was pleased by her reaction.

When he began to tell her how much he had missed her and how he'd thought of her for what seemed every waking moment when he wasn't occupied with intricate business concerns, Kristin felt as if she'd never been happier in her life.

"You don't have forever here at the Circle K," Dace pointed out, momentarily breaking her heart as he presented the reality she'd tried to forget. "So we're going to make the most of what time you have here, starting tonight. What would you like to do?"

"Well, I've tentatively promised that I'd go out with Mandy and her boyfriend. . .Billy Joe. Billy Joe Blaylock."

"We could all go out together," Dace suggested. "Do you think they'd be interested? Billy's a lot of fun."

"So is Mandy."

"You set it up then," Dace ordered, "and that's what we'll do. Tell them it's my treat."

"Okay. Do you have anything specific in mind?" Kristin asked. "So they'll know what to plan?"

He paused a moment. "The other night was one of the most memorable of my life. Care for an encore?"

"I'd love it."

And Mandy, when she sampled nightlife in Rapid City, South Dakota, did, too.

"I wish this vacation would never end," she sighed when she and Kristin went to the powder room to check their makeup.

"I know," Kristin said and felt a twinge of sadness. "But life goes on. There's no stopping it."

"I'd like to try," Mandy said. "If I could get a job out here, with the least little encouragement from Billy, I'd move to South Dakota bag and baggage to remain near him."

Kristin couldn't help smiling.

Mandy caught Kristin's expression in the mirror and looked stern. "I'm serious, Kris. I'm not clowning around. In my heart," she said and touched the bodice of her pretty, slimming dress, "I feel as if Billy Joe could be the one. The man for me."

"I know," Kristin said. "And some of the looks I've intercepted tonight have seemed to express that Billy Joe feels the same way about you."

"But he's so shy and so steadfast and so sober and so careful, he won't give me encouragement to find a way to stay out here, even if he wants to. Not until he can promise me all the security that a guy like Billy would feel that he should offer a woman before he'd. . ." Her words trailed off to a sigh.

"I know," Kristin said. "I can tell that he's that kind."

"And bold as I can be sometimes," Mandy lamented, "I just don't have it in me to throw myself at him. I'd die if he told me to go back to Kirkwood, that I was just another summer romance."

"I don't think he would. Give him time."

"That's one thing that I don't have and that I can't afford to buy. I have no more vacation time with the company. And I saved all year long to pay the rates this place charges."

"Don't fret over it, Mandy. Perhaps something will come up. You can't let the fact that you may have to leave destroy enjoyment of what time you do have left."

"That's true," Mandy agreed in a morose tone.

"I'm not exactly feeling so perky myself in that area," Kristin admitted. "Our two weeks are up on the same day."

"I know. We can leave together. Misery loves company, they say. But somehow, I have a feeling that Dace is going to be asking you to stay. Kris—the man can't take his eyes off you. He stares at you like he's in a trance, like someone's dinged him on the head, only instead of seeing stars, he's seeing hearts, flowers, butterflies, and hearing bells. Maybe even wedding bells!"

Kristin's heart lurched.

That was exactly what she'd thought, earlier, but then she'd given herself a mental talking-to and told herself that it was an incorrect assessment, one produced by her hopeful mind and romantic heart.

"We've still got over a week left in South Dakota," Kristin pointed out. "We've got lots of time to have fun. And maybe even enough days, hours, and special moments for a miracle to happen for each of us."

"Do you think so?"

"I hope so," Kristin said. "In fact, maybe I even know so."

"What are you getting at?"

"Ummm. Something for me to know. . .and you to find out," she teased.

And Kristin made a mental note that at the first opportunity possible, when she and Dace were alone and he was in the right kind of mood, she was going to mention Mandy's plight and hope that a kind, generous, caring man like Dacian Kendrick might find a way to employ a competent girl like Mandy so that she could remain at the Circle K, a paid employee instead of a pampered guest. But either way, near the man she loved.

For a swift, secret moment, Kristin lamented that she didn't have someone to plead the same consideration on her behalf.

When her two weeks were up, home she would have to go for she couldn't ever humiliate herself by hinting for a job so that she could stay. Although her bank account could stand it, her pride could never afford for her to pay the Circle K's daily rate to be near the man she felt drawn to, dare she call it love, in a way she'd never felt before.

Chapter Seven

The next few days were like heaven on earth for both Kristin and Mandy.

Mandy spent her daytime hours with Kristin, when Kristin wasn't with Dacian, and wiled away each evening with an attentive Billy Joe as they took part in the square dances and other special social events that the Circle K offered to entertain guests.

Both girls maintained long days, arising early for a delicious breakfast and morning ride. They even tried their hand at tennis, neither of them very good, before they adjourned to the mini-golf course. Then they cooled off with a swim as the day heated up with a vengeance.

Their second week was quickly starting to draw toward a close when one morning Mandy didn't appear on Kristin's doorstep, all ready to go.

Kristin waited a while, then, afraid that something was wrong, she stepped outside and knocked on Mandy's door.

"Just a minute," Mandy called out in a weak, warbling, tear-stained tone.

A moment later she opened the door and wordlessly gestured for Kristin to step into her quarters. She hadn't begun to get ready for the day.

"You've been crying!" Kristin gasped. She'd scarcely ever seen the girl with anything but a lovely smile on her sweet face.

Mandy managed an embarrassed, wet-eyed grin that quickly faltered toward a sob. "It seems as if that's become a morning greeting. I remember remarking that to you one day."

Mandy, an ordinarily cheerful, optimistic girl, tried for levity, but failed, as she turned away and helplessly brushed tears from her cheeks, swallowing at sobs that caused her shoulders to heave.

Kristin impulsively put her arms around her unhappy friend. "Mandy, please don't cry. It breaks my heart to see you like this."

Mandy's face crumpled. "Well it b. . .b. . .breaks my heart every time I think about going home to Missouri. And Billy's not himself, either. He's as miserable as I am. But we're at a point where neither of us knows what to do. Maybe there is nothing to do. I talked to Mom and she says that it's my life and my decision to make, because she wants only the best for me and to know that I'm happy. I wish I knew what to do."

"Hope for a miracle. And enjoy the moments together. Anyway, if you have to go back to Missouri, Mandy, you can still come out for a holiday vacation, or surely next summer. It won't mean being apart forever."

"Yeah," Mandy said, brightening a little bit.

"Let's go get some breakfast," Kristin said. "You'll feel better after we have something to eat. Afterwards we'll go for a ride."

"I'm getting good enough that I never get Molly anymore," Mandy said. "And I miss her. I wonder if she misses me?"

"Let her out of the corral with a novice rider and it'll become clear she misses her real home the most. She must have a wonderful home."

"And master or mistress."

Mandy seemed to perk up as they set about their day's activities.

&

All week long Kristin had been letting the matter coast along, waiting for Dace to be in exactly the right frame of mind when she made her suggestion. But she knew that she could no longer postpone taking action with Dacian because time was running out.

Undefined concerns had kept Kristin silent all week. She hadn't wanted to risk their relationship by giving Dacian the impression that she was a meddling woman or that she was trying to tell him how to run his business. But as overworked as he seemed to be, she convinced herself that she'd actually be doing him a favor and she couldn't believe it would be an imposition to suggest that he might want to at least consider hiring a girl as computer competent as Mandy.

As intuitive as she'd come to realize Dace was, and the way he seemed to like to keep his help happy—and Billy Joe *was* visibly miserable—Kristin was a bit surprised that Dace hadn't seen the straits Billy was in and considered a solution himself.

Of course Kristin realized that Dace was a bit preoccupied. He was busy with last-minute details for the arrival of children for the dreams-come-true two weeks of Operation: Recovery and the rodeo. But even so, she'd recognized that there was something about him that caused a worried tenseness to underly his features even when he seemed to be relaxed and was apparently having fun.

She could tell that he was deeply troubled about something. What, she didn't know. And she dared not ask out of apprehension that it might actually regard her and her worst middle-of-the-night fear that he would uncover the family secret that lay between them.

There were moments when, from things Dace said, she had felt certain he knew and he was toying with her to see if she'd be honest enough to admit the situation herself.

Other times, Kristin was so sure that he had no idea Janice was her sister that her heart soared until it as abruptly plummeted when she realized that the fact could not remain hidden forever.

Whatever it was that was bothering Dace, he tried not to let it disturb their times together, and in her heart, Kristin wished that he would confide in her, lean on her a little bit. She wanted him to trust her enough to let his burdens become hers to share. . .even if she found herself unable to believe that he could reciprocate enough for her to be able to count on him to willingly and forgivingly shoulder her problem—Janice—as his own to resolve.

That afternoon when Mandy and Kristin were heading back to their rooms from the swimming pool, Dace exited his office and sought out Kristin.

"I know we have plans for tonight, Kris," he said, after greeting Mandy, too. "But I have to work late in my office. Come there when you get freshened up, and you can wait while I attend to whatever items on my desk can't be ignored a moment longer."

"Okay."

"You don't mind?"

"Of course not," Kristin assured. "I'll bring along a book. Or I could help you if you had something you needed done that I could do. Typing. Filing. That kind of thing."

"What I have to do requires my attention. I know our computer system. You don't, unfortunately."

From the corner of her eye, Kristin saw that Mandy was torn between offering her keyboard services and safeguarding her time with Billy.

Of course Billy Joe won.

"If you can't spare a night away from your work, I'll understand," she said, although the offer was almost unconvincingly delivered as time between them shortened, bringing a quick sting of disappointed tears to her eyes.

"I wouldn't dream of it. Time's passing too fast as it is."

Kristin nodded, relieved, but was suddenly unable to speak as she was struck by how little time remained.

"See you later," Dace said and rushed back to his work.

It was late afternoon and Mandy was primping for her night with Billy Joe when Kristin walked along the pathways to the building that housed the lobby, front desk, Dacian's office, and the gift shop and other businesses.

Dace was on the phone when Kristin gave a light rap on the open door.

Wordlessly he gestured for her to enter.

She sat down, opened her book, but actually watched him as he frowned, listened to his caller for a long time, made undecipherable responses, and ended up agreeing to table the matter for a while and take no action at present.

"Made yourself comfortable, Kristin?" he asked as he hung up. "Can I get you anything? Coffee? Tea? Soda? Perrier?"

"Nothing, thanks. Don't go to any trouble on my account. Just attend to your business. I can wait here. Or. . .if I disturb you, I could go wait in the lobby."

"Don't be silly. Of course you don't disturb me. Well, actually you do," he said, giving a light laugh. "As pretty as you look it's hard to concentrate on the work I have to do. But I wouldn't have asked you here if I hadn't wanted you with me. I'll try to hurry."

"If there's anything I can do to help—"

"I wish there were, but there's not. Now, if you'll excuse me, I'll rush through these contracts and then we can. . ."

His words trailed off as Kristin turned back to the novel she had brought along, and she opened it to where she'd placed the bookmark, but the words swam before her eyes. She was lost in another world and swirling in conflicting emotions as she considered the near future and knew that the time was coming when she would have to leave no matter how badly her heart ached to stay.

And from remarks Dace had made, hints, could it be true that he might actually want her to remain? Even if he did, how?

Suddenly Kristin was lost in thoughts to the point where she stared unseeingly at the page. She was unaware of the passage of time until Dace rolled his chair away from his desk, shut the center drawer, put his pen in its holder, and snugged his chair up against the shiny mahogany desk as he reached for his Stetson on a hat rack.

"Ready to go?" Dace asked, snapping her from her musings.

"Yes. Right away," she said and arose, slipping the book into her purse as she joined him.

He led the way to the hall, closed his office door behind them, but did not lock it.

Kristin, who was so security conscious, was startled.

"Don't you lock your office?" she asked. "I should think—"

"Sometimes the people at the desk have a need for something in the office. I have a reliable staff. I trust them."

"Yes, I suppose so."

Dace gave her an amused glance that seemed to become a scrutinizing stare as he considered her reaction.

"I have no secrets," he murmured. "My life is an open book."

And although the words were kindly spoken, Kristin felt herself flinch as if the remark had been a heartless reminder to her that honest as she wanted to be with him, she was a prisoner of deception, with a necessary lie between them in order that another woman's treatment wouldn't tear their relationship apart, leaving her guilty by association.

Kristin was silent as he led the way to his car. He unbuttoned another button on his western shirt, eased his Stetson back on his head, glanced at her, and gave a helpless yawn.

"You're tired," she said.

"A little bit."

"You've been working so hard. You need someone to help you."

He gave an amused laugh. "Needing help and finding the right employee are not always one and the same, my dear."

It was her chance, Kristin realized, the moment that she'd been waiting for, and praying for, turning to God with a trust deeper than she'd attained before Mandy's ideas had edified her own walk in faith, causing it to expand and enrich.

But before she could open her mouth and make a simple suggestion that might be the answer to Dace's problems, he spoke on.

"What do you want to do tonight?" he asked, changing the subject.

"I'm easy to please. Whatever you'd like to do is fine with me."

"A quiet night appeals to me," he admitted, pausing. "I told you once that I'd take you to my place, my haven. Not very many people have been allowed there. It's where I go to relax. Want to see it? We could fix ourselves something to eat there. Maybe grill out."

She took his hand and squeezed it. "I'd love to see your house. A quiet evening sounds wonderful. You keep us so busy at the Circle K. This'll give me a chance to catch my breath. I feel like I've been caught in a whirlwind for the past week and a half."

"Then it's settled. I have steaks in the freezer, a gas grill, everything for a super meal."

"That'll be enjoyable. And I am hungry."

"You can do the salad while I prepare the steaks. After we finish our meal, we'll have the whole evening together."

"Maybe we could go for a moonlight ride," Kristin said.

"Ordinarily, yes, but at the moment I don't have a horse on the place," Dace admitted. "Although if you really want to, I could call over to the Circle K and have them load a pair into the horse van and they could be here within minutes."

"There's no sense going to all that bother. There's always tomorrow. I'll be riding with Mandy in the morning."

"Then tonight is ours."

At the remark, said in a tone so soft and sensual, Kristin's heart thumped as she wondered if Dace was setting the scene for a seduction. While she wanted him to kiss her again, as he did each night, holding her hand in a possessively thrilling way, she wasn't sure exactly what he had in mind. With Mandy's talk of Dace being a Christian, Kristin had faith he wouldn't try to press beyond certain boundaries.

From things he'd said, and from remarks others had made, he wasn't as totally inexperienced as she was, and she feared that he might be prepared to ask of her more than she was comfortable with. Or would he?

She felt a little shiver of fearful anticipation, but when Dace gave her arm a tender pat, seeming unspeakably happy just to have her beside him in his flashy car, she drew from the companionable touch the knowledge that he wanted to be with her to share. . .not selfishly take from her. . .and she felt a surge of renewed trust for him. He wasn't that kind. But Janice certainly was! Could he be a hypocritical Christian? A chameleon? Showing different colors depending on whom he was with at the moment?

However their evening progressed, no matter what his desires became, she knew that if she asked him to stop. . .he would.

They passed along the rural roads that she'd been on before in the ranch's van and in Dacian's Corvette. Instead of proceeding toward Interstate 90, they turned onto a side road. It wound around a curve, then another, and as they rounded a bend and crested the hill, Dacian's private residence came into view.

It was a big house, but not so huge that it would be difficult for a person to maintain it without help, Kristin's Roving Maid personality realized. It looked to be a house that a person would maintain with a sense of proud fulfillment.

The grounds were beautifully kept with bright flowers, pleasant shrubs, and majestic shade trees. The landscaping accentuated the graceful line of the gently rolling lawn that disappeared into pastureland beyond pristine white board fencing marking the perimeter of the acreage.

A fenced-in private swimming pool graced the rear of the house. A bright red barn was obviously a stable for a riding horse or two, although they did seem somehow empty, with no horses standing in the shade, no welcoming nicker when they arrived.

"Oh, Dacian. . .it's like heaven on earth. You must love it here."

"I do," he admitted. "I had it specially designed and built to suit my specifications. It's handy. It's close enough to the Circle K to be convenient, but far enough away to be serene. And my staff has orders not to disturb me here except in an emergency. Come," he said, and helped her out. "Let me show you around, then I'll start the steaks and you can start making the salad."

The matter-of-fact, sharing way he laid out the plans so that they each contributed as equals made Kristin's heart wrench. She realized now what so many other young women her age had as they built a life together with a man they loved and shared the joys, the sorrows, the work, the leisure. And children. . .

Dace's explanations drew her thoughts away from her private musings as he showed her around his spread and then took her to the house, which Kristin was relieved to learn that he *did* keep locked.

Fifteen minutes later Dace took two T-bone steaks from the freezer and turned on the gas grill, while Kristin fixed a tossed salad in his beautiful, convenient, but quaint country kitchen, a room that was so charming and warm that she had no doubt she was welcome to work there. She looked around and realized that it was a kitchen just like she'd have had designed for herself if she'd been granted every whim, with her smallest wish the contractor's command.

They were enjoying their meal when Dace's telephone rang, disturbing the atmosphere.

"I hope it's not an emergency from the ranch," Kristin murmured.

"Probably not. They haven't called in ages. And this is an unlisted number. So it won't be someone trying to sell me windows, vinyl siding, or a newspaper subscription that I'm not interested in purchasing." He made no move to answer, then explained. "I'll let the machine take it. It's probably my mother, who's visiting her sister in California. Or maybe one of my sisters-in-law wanting to know why I haven't been showing up at one of my brother's ranches for a home-cooked meal and an evening spent wrestling nephews or dandling nieces on my knee."

Hearing the words and knowing what a wonderful family life he had, then comparing it with the wasteland that was her kinship, Kris felt suddenly bleak.

Dace cocked his head, listening, when on the fourth ring his recorded message invited the caller to leave a name, number, date and time of call, and a brief message, then finished with the promise that Dace would return the call.

"Dace? This is Matt Briner. I'm making good progress with the investigation. I've incurred some travel expenses. One trip took me all the way to Illinois. But now I'm onto—"

Dace shot from his chair so fast that he almost upended the small table where they were dining into Kristin's lap.

Roughly he hit the button to stop the machine. He snatched the receiver from the cradle and greeted Matt Briner with a hearty voice, although it bore a hint of strain, and Kristin could tell that Dacian Kendrick was extremely upset.

He glanced at Kristin, lowered his voice, then turned his back to her, mumbling. Then he said, "Hang on a minute, Matt."

He turned to Kris and his eyes were funny, a flat hue, as if he were trying to keep them expressionless and unfathomable.

"Kris?" He spoke to her, but didn't wait for her to reply. "It's pleasant on the enclosed porch. This is going to take me a while. Business. Perhaps you'd like to wait out there?"

It was offered as a suggestion, but she had no trouble discerning it as a direct order.

"Sure," she agreed, even though she felt stung as if she were a banished child, unwanted. "Of course."

Plucking up her plate, she felt numb, and her steps were wooden as she walked from his presence.

She felt a spike of anger surge through her. She considered abandoning her steak and walking out on him. She wasn't a fool. She knew that whatever it was he was talking about, he didn't want her to hear a word of it. And she'd already heard enough. Investigation! Illinois!

She felt pained, miserable, and she glanced at the horizon, not sure how far the Circle K Ranch was from Dacian's private property. They'd had to go out of their way, twisting and turning. As the crow flies, she thought, it couldn't be too far.

She was tempted to strike out walking. She at least was reasonably dressed for it.

But when she regarded her low, rather unsubstantial shoes and considered trekking through rattlesnake country in the dark, her angry resolve became fear and stopped her.

Then a lone coyote howl sealed her fate.

She would have to wait on Dacian Kendrick to see her home, like it or not.

He was a man with no secrets? She recalled his remark time and again as he remained on the telephone for an exceedingly lengthy conversation.

"Obviously he lied," she muttered.

Instead of making her feel better, it made her feel even worse when she recalled that she was living her own lie, too. Not on purpose, of course, but because she'd had no choice. Maybe Dacian was caught up in something bigger than he was, too.

Left alone, her steak finally finished, a puddle of dressing in the bottom of her salad bowl, she began to consider what she *had* managed to overhear.

Dace had an investigator working for him. Obviously it regarded a sensitive matter, the way Dace had sprung from his chair. And it was serious enough so that the man was free to rack up expenses that weren't small enough to be handled from a petty cash fund. He'd even traveled to *ILLINOIS!*

Kristin's heart stopped beating; then when it picked up, it was rapid and arrhythmic. For a long, horrifying instant, she couldn't catch her breath. She felt faint when the full force of the ramifications swept over her.

Why Illinois, if not over her?

Suddenly Jan's mocking remarks came back to haunt her.

Had Dacian been so curious about who she really was that he'd hired a private investigator to check her out? To see if she was who she claimed?

Illinois was a big state, long, from the Wisconsin line north of Chicago all the way down to Cairo, where the Mississippi and Ohio Rivers met and merged.

There were all kinds of reasons why Dace could have sent an investigator to Illinois, she tried to convince herself, but she was unable to comfort herself with logic because women's intuition was signaling to her that something, and something awful, was about to happen.

It was only a matter of time.

While she was living for the moment.

A fool enjoying a fool's paradise.

While tragedy waited, poised to strike. . .

"I'm back," Dace said. "I reheated my steak in the microwave. Want anything for dessert? I think I have some cheesecake in the freezer. I could get it out—"

"No thanks," Kristin said, wondering if he was suddenly conversational because a problem had been solved, or if it was a clever cover-up. Was he trying to prevent her from suspecting that he had a cruel trap in position, just waiting for her to blindly and trustingly blunder into it so that he could leave her tangled up in a web of humiliating facts, enjoying her hurt and shame as she paid the price for her sister's old sins.

But to her relief Dace seemed in better spirits for the rest of the evening.

"Let's leave the dishes," Dace suggested. "They'll still be here tomorrow when Mrs. Appleton arrives."

"Your housekeeper?"

"Umm-hmmm. She's getting older. She's wanting to retire. I have to jolly her to keep her on the job. And I try to be neat so as not to make too much work for her."

"Which I know she appreciates."

"Spoken like a true Roving Maid," Dace teased.

"Well. . .I do know what it's like. I appreciate clients who treat me like a human being and don't consider that they've just hired an indentured servant, expected to do in one day what would take the employer a week of steady labor."

"If Mrs. Appleton is intent on retiring, I suppose that I could let her go. And you could always apply for her position," Dace said. He seemed to study her. "Mrs. Appleton dresses to suit herself. It's none of my business what she wears or if she does housework in the altogether, because I'm never around when she's here. But I think you'd look darling in a maid's uniform—and I might insist."

"Then I won't bother to apply," Kristin warned. "It's Reeboks and jeans for me. No short black dress and frilly white cap and apron," Kristin joked as her heart skittered. "We professional domestic technicians can be an independent lot. We can decide to refuse an account and replace it with a new client immediately. A good cleaning woman deserves to be wooed and won."

"Then perhaps I should practice up a bit," Dace said, "for when Mrs. Appleton gives me my walking papers as a domestic account."

"Maybe you just should!" Kristin warned in a haughty tone, as a smile curved her lips. She was so relieved that he wasn't cranky and cantankerous upon his return from the call as she'd feared he might be.

"In that case. . .I will. But it's been so long since I've seriously wooed. . .I wonder if I remember how. Oh! I think that I do!"

He took Kristin's hand, turned it over, palm up, and placed a tender, feathery kiss in the cup of her hand, closing her fingers around it, as if she could capture and keep it forever.

Then his lips deftly kissed a nibbling trail up to her wrist. The pressure intensified and Kristin wondered if his sensitive lips were pressed against the artery near the bone and he were monitoring her rapidly escalating pulse.

As if he sensed her trepidation, his lightly bussing lips moved up the satiny smooth length of her tanned arm.

"Stop that!" Kristin giggled. "You're embarrassing me."

Dace stopped instantly. "Foiled again. Here I was, thinking that I was managing to woo you, and instead you inform me that I'm only succeeding in embarrassing you. It may be an uphill task to replace dear old Mrs. Appleton when the time comes."

"You could always start doing your own housework."

"Or I suppose that I could get married," he sighed. "It's probably easier to find a wife than it is to locate the ideal cleaning woman."

Then he began to laugh as if he'd just cracked a joke, and maybe he had, because Kristin knew that there were various people who had relied on agents of different sorts, just as she'd once been aligned to Andre D'Arcy. It was common for them to say that a husband or wife could come and go, but an agent-client relationship could be irreplaceable.

But was he serious, serious about her, when he made mention of marriage? Did he pass the reference off as joking banter so that his heart wouldn't be on the line, out in the open, a target for hurting remarks if he was cruelly rebuffed? Had he said what he had said to gain a clue to how *she* felt about their newly developing relationship? Had he, too, been lying awake at night, entertaining thoughts that were a perfect match for the dreams that had captivated her to produce thrilling flights of fancy?

Oh, dear God, could it be the beginning of a miracle, and he'd teased her about wanting her as a maid. . .when he actually was obliquely referring to a desire that she'd agree to one day come to be his wife?

Goose bumps spread over Kristin's skin. Dace saw, put his arm around her, and drew her close.

"Let me warm you," he said, his voice so loving.

Then his arm slid around her and she felt herself being drawn close, her female softness conforming to his angular male body. He drew her even closer, holding her so close that she could scarcely breathe. Then his lips tenderly covered hers, and his rougher male cheeks sensuously and pleasantly abraided her smooth ones.

When she melted against him, he made a sound of delight that seemed to well from deep within him, and Kristin felt a stab of pleasure that she'd found womanly approval with him.

His fingers splayed at the nape of her neck, smoothing the thick dark hair, as his questing fingertips caressed her face, her throat, sifted through her hair, then stopped at the small ridge caused by a scar.

He paused a moment, then continued, caressing even that, and she suddenly felt so accepted by him, feeling that he loved her, imperfections and all.

"Oh, Kristin. . .Kristin," he murmured.

She found herself softly whispering his name, too, as she was lost in the pleasure and power found in his arms.

When Dacian was the first to pull away, even when she knew that he did not want to, her heart almost burst because she was so content, knowing that he cared for her to the point where he would not act selfishly, not considering what might happen to her.

"It's getting late, love," he said. "I really should get you back to the Circle K. Ready to go, dear?"

"Whenever you are."

"We could take the long way back to the ranch."

"Sounds nice."

Enroute back, she decided that she couldn't wait for an opening to plead Mandy's cause, she would have to make one. And there was no time like the present.

"Dace. . .the other day, you mentioned that you'd like to expand your computer operations at the ranch," Kristin said. "I know that this really isn't any of my business, yet I. . .I. . ."

"Go on," Dace urged. "I know anything you'd suggest would be made in good faith and because you wanted the best for me—"

"It's Mandy," Kristin said. "She's a hard worker, she's a smart girl, she's spent several years working with computers for an insurance firm in the St. Louis area. I know she'd be qualified and everything you could hope for in office help. Could you please consider hiring her?" she finished in a burst of words that left her breathless.

"Hire Mandy? Well, it is an idea, but she already has a job, and—"

"She doesn't want to leave here when her—our—two weeks are up, Dace, and I know that Billy Joe doesn't want her to, either. But she has no choice. She can't remain on as a paying guest. But if you could hire her, she'd be earning money instead of spending it, and. . ."

"I see," he mused. "It really is a good idea. And if she's experienced, it would make it so much easier than trying to train a local girl."

"Plus, Mandy's nice. Pleasant. Thoughtful. Hardworking. And the way she and Billy Joe feel about each other, it's not like you'd get her trained, and she'd up and get married and move off, leaving you to retrain someone else. The way things look for Mandy, if you give her a job, Dace, she's here to stay. She's as loyal as they come."

"Sweetheart, I think you just gave me an answer to one of my problems." He sighed. "Too bad the other concerns can't be dispatched with so easily," he added in a bitter tone.

"Then you'll offer her a job?" Kristin said.

"You can take her an application tomorrow; I have plenty of them in the office. Or you can send her in to see me."

"I'd rather not," Kristin said. "I don't want her to know that I asked a favor of you. I think it would make her much happier if she felt that you'd recognized her potential on your own and you offered a job based on merit alone."

"You're right. And it's really commendable for you to want Mandy to feel that it's her own worth that's been recognized, when so many people would've wanted a friend to be left feeling beholden or forever owing a serious favor."

"Mandy will be so happy not to have to go back to Kirkwood."

"And how are you feeling about returning to Camden Corners?"

"Dace, please. Don't even ask. I don't want to talk about it."

"Why I ask is. . .because I think you should stay." He cleared his throat. "You don't have to go back, you know," he said. "You could remain on so that you'd fulfill the contract requirements."

"What?" Kristin asked, puzzled, when the conversation took a sharp turn from matters of the heart to center on business concerns.

"The Happy Trails Feed folks awarded you the Grand Prize. It was two weeks for you *and* a companion. There's only been you. I don't feel right taking the contracted amount from their corporate comptroller without delivering one hundred percent of our agreed-upon services, which is a total of four weeks. Being a man of high ethics, that would mean that I'd have to refund them a portion of the money tendered. You know how it is in the business world, Kris, you'd sooner provide agreed-upon services than refund monies involved in the deal."

"I see," Kristin said. Her heart leaped at the idea of getting to stay, but sank when she realized how unemotionally Dace was arranging for her to be able to stay. Couldn't he just ask? Did he have to go about it as he did, making her feel that she was but a gambit on a playing board, being moved around by two corporate comptrollers?

Was he just buying time at the Happy Trails Feed Company's expense so that he'd be able to spend more time with her and discern if she really was a woman he could love? Or would she prove to be only a pretty facsimile?

"There's only one drawback. The next two weeks the ranch will be full of children, Kristin. They aren't your average youngsters. They're all kids who have been seriously sick. Some of them are disabled. Not one of them will be perfect. And some of them may be so scarred that unthinkingly cruel people would stare, or worse, turn away in disgust. You might not enjoy it. In fact, you might not even be able to handle it."

"I'll have no problem handling it," Kristin said.

If anything, she was a person who knew what many of them had been through. She empathized with their need for affection and dignity, while a callous world of strangers, sometimes with a glance or an unthinking remark, tore away their ability to find acceptance in the everyday world.

"You like children?" he asked, as if he hardly dared hope it.

"I love them. At least what contacts I've had with children in the neighborhood. And the youngsters in the homes I maintain while their mothers manage life in the fast lane. The fast lane by rural Illinois standards, that is."

"Great. Then you'll stay? I mean, I know you planned for two weeks away. Can you manage to make it a full month? I know there was some prize money involved to help make up for lost wages."

"I'll manage," Kristin said. "A few telephone calls, Dace, and I can stay as long as I like."

"Then there's no reason in the world for you not to. And if you're worried about your finances and being an idle guest at the Circle K, let me know. Mrs. Moriarty, the head housekeeper for the dude ranch, could always use a willing worker that time of year. Kids aren't as neat as adults, you know. So don't be proud, Kris. Let me know."

"I might just do that. I'm not used to being a lady of leisure," she admitted, and wondered in passing how Janice endured living the stultifying lifestyle of the idle rich.

"Everything is working out so right," Dace said and on her doorstep swept her into his arms for a quick goodnight kiss. "There's no reason things shouldn't work out."

Wrong, Kristin's heart taunted as the kiss lengthened as if they'd just sealed a sacred pact.

There was one reason why she should leave as planned, why she shouldn't risk remaining so that her daydreams could evolve to become the worst nightmares of her life.

Janice!

Chapter Eight

The next morning when the two girls left the dining hall after breakfast, Dace intercepted them. Although from outward appearances an onlooker would've thought it was a coincidental meeting, Kristin knew better.

"Mandy," Dace said, after greeting them both, "the other night when we all went out to dinner in Rapid City, I recalled you talking about your job back in Missouri and that you worked with computers."

"That's right," Mandy said. "For three years now. . .the keyboard, terminal, myriad programs, and I are old friends."

"I've been considering computerizing additional aspects of the operation. Of course the reservations and billing departments are already automated. But there are other areas where we're buried in paper, photocopying, and, well, I was wondering if perhaps you could spare a few minutes to discuss it with me so that I'd really have an idea of our needs before I—"

"Sure," Mandy agreed before he could speak further. "I'd be glad to help in any way I can and share any insights based on my experiences. When would you like to go over it?"

"Would right now be too much of an imposition?" he asked.

"Well, Kristin and I were about to go riding," Mandy admitted, and she sounded torn between the two choices.

"There'll be horses for us after a while. I'll be in my room when you're done talking," Kristin said, deciding for her.

Mandy faced Dace Kendrick, cheerfully shrugging.

"Then right now is hunky-dory with me. You can't *believe* how much simpler life can be with all records on computer. Unless, of course, the system crashes. But you institute simple safeguards to try to prevent that from ever happening."

"You sound like you're really computer literate."

"I don't know everything," Mandy quickly clarified in a modest manner. "But you pick up quite a bit of education around the office. The insurance firm makes use of several programs, so I'm familiar with a couple of different systems. I might be able to offer suggestions about the various capabilities—"

"It sounds like Mandy is a walking gold mine of information," Dace said to Kristin. "If this takes longer than we planned, I'll take you both to lunch."

"Okay," Kristin said. "And take your time. Don't concern yourselves over me. I have a book I began on the airplane that I've been meaning to read."

When Kristin returned to her room, Mrs. Moriarty herself was attending to the housekeeping duties in her quarters.

"Hi," Kristin said. "Don't let me disturb you."

"Oh, I can come back later when you're not here," Mrs. Moriarty offered. "I noticed that you tend to vacate your room about this time every day. So that's when we've been attending to things."

"Ordinarily my girlfriend and I go riding. But she's meeting with Mr. Kendrick now."

"A nice man," she said. "Salt of the earth."

Kristin listened as one more in a long list of employees sang his praises as an employer.

"I thought you were the girl I'd been seeing with him," Mrs. Moriarty said. "Haven't you been keeping him company?"

"When he has free time."

"Ah, then I don't have to convince you the kind of man he is, do I?" she asked with a laugh. "Do you think you'll stay in touch with him after you leave, Miss Allen? Although I probably shouldn't be asking, since it's really none of my business. But I've noticed that he's been seeing quite a lot of you. And ordinarily, while Mr. Kendrick is very pleasant to the guests, he keeps his distance."

That was news to Kristin, after her own assumptions based on observations of ranch personnel and what input Janice had told her about how Dacian Kendrick supposedly operated.

"Oh really? Well, I don't know if we'll be in touch or not."

The housekeeper frowned as she dusted ledges.

"I thought perhaps you'd have an idea by now." She consulted a sheet on her clipboard. "You don't have many days left here. We'll miss you."

"I'm afraid you're not so easily rid of me, Mrs. Moriarty."

"Oh?"

"It appears I'll be extending my stay," she explained. "Dace told me about the deal with the Happy Trails Feed Company, and they've paid for four weeks' services here. So I'm going to be remaining on for a while. Two more weeks. . . ."

"Then you'll be here for Operation: Recovery?"

"Yes. And I'm looking forward to it. It'll probably be one of the most rewarding experiences of my life."

"As I get old and have my trifling aches and pains, sometimes I feel ashamed of myself, complaining as I do, when I'm around those brave children. They're an inspiration to all of us."

"That's what Dace says," Kristin replied. "But apparently he hasn't told you that he did offer me a job if I get bored. And I might without adults to hang around with during the daytime hours."

"Told me what?" Mrs. Moriarty said.

The aging widow who lived at the ranch seemed a bit puzzled, and Kristin sensed that when it came to her housekeeping department, she was a lot like Dace Kendrick in that nothing escaped her knowledge, either.

"That I could be part of the housekeeping staff if I wanted a job to keep me occupied now and then."

"Oh, well that's interesting," Mrs. Moriarty said.

The expression on her face seemed to reveal that she didn't believe Kristin would know one end of the vacuum sweeper from the other.

"It would seem almost like home. You see, I have a freelance maid service in the town where I live," Kristin added.

"You do?" Mrs. Moriarty asked with fresh interest and the instant empathy found in people who share the same interests or occupation. "You hardly seem the type. You look so pretty and refined and. . .well, like a model or something."

"Believe me, I know what it is to do hard work," Kristin assured.

"Well if you don't mind, when the children are here, we may put you to work. They're not as tidy as adults, and who'd want them to be? They're here to have fun. Sometimes the housework load escalates. Especially when there are accidents. The children here have their ups and downs. But nothing that Dr. Bill, Dace's younger brother, can't take care of. And Melanie, his sister the nurse. She'll be bringing along Tony, her fiance, this year. But of course you know all that."

"No. . .no I'm afraid I didn't. Dace just. . .hasn't happened to mention it."

Kristin fell silent, realizing that as much as she knew about Dacian, there was as much, or more, that remained hidden from her.

She hardly heard Mrs. Moriarty as she departed and only managed what she hoped didn't seem too perfunctory a reply.

As confident as she'd felt the night before, she no longer felt so sure of herself.

He'd said his life was an open book, but so much had not been shown to her. She hated to pry, what with her own penchant for privacy, but maybe a man like Dacian expected that if his life was like an open book, it was up to someone else to read it rather than have it seem, perhaps egotistically, read aloud.

With that thought Kristin turned back to her novel, but she'd scarcely opened the fluttering pages when there came a brisk tap at her door.

"You in there?" an impatient Mandy called out.

"Coming!" Kristin assured.

"Sorry I was away for so long. I hadn't meant to bend Dace's ear about computers so much. But he was full of questions, and I didn't really have any idea that I was so brimming with technical answers."

"You must've been a big help to him. No doubt he was fascinated."

"We didn't talk the whole time I was gone. He got a call—from some investigator. He put the guy on hold and said that it'd be wonderful if I'd go to the dining hall and bring back coffee, so I did."

"An investigator?" Kristin asked, and her heart clutched in her chest until she almost winced with pain. "I wonder what that was about?"

"I haven't the foggiest," Mandy said. "I don't know if he wanted me to get us coffee because he really wanted some—"

"Or to get you out of his office so that he could talk in private," Kristin observed, "to a private investigator, about something he didn't want you to overhear?"

"Right. Although he'd pulled a file while I was gone. And it was on his desk, plain as could be, if I'd wanted to try to read it upside down, I suppose. He didn't act like the paperwork was any big secret."

"Ummmm."

"And in the future I doubt there'll be any secrets kept from me. I just saw Mrs. Moriarty leave," Mandy said. "And guess what, Kris, she's going to be one of my fellow employees of the Circle K Ranch!"

"What?!" Kristin gasped, although Dace had tipped her an unobtrusive wink when he'd led Mandy toward his private offices so she'd known what was in the offing. "What are you talking about?"

"A job, Kristin. Dace just offered me a job and I accepted. With pleasure!"

"Wait until you tell Billy Joe!"

"I can't wait. Will he be surprised!"

"And happy." Kristin frowned. "Mandy! Are you teasing me? Oh, please don't! This is too good to be true."

"No, I'm not teasing. And you mean you actually had nothing to do with it? That Dacian offered me a job because he really wanted to hire me?"

"It would appear so. Anyway, would I do something like that?"

"Yes you would!" Mandy retorted with a frank assessment. "But I'm glad you didn't have to. Wow, to be asked to work at the Circle K. Dace showed me around, and I'll tell you, I'll be in heaven. I'll have my own little office, not a scrunchy cubicle shared with a zillion other data processors. Dace even said that I might become his office manager, because he has a hunch he'll need one."

"Mandy, I'm so happy for you. I told you to pray for a miracle."

"I did. And I've been hoping and praying for a miracle for you, too. Kris, I don't want you to leave the day after tomorrow."

"Didn't I tell you? No, I guess not, because it slipped my mind. We haven't really had a chance to talk today, but it turns out that I will be staying on for a little while."

Quickly she explained about the Happy Trails Horse Feed deal and the fact that she was welcome to become an employee within the housekeeping department if she wanted to.

"You know, your boyfriend is a really nice guy," Mandy said. "I knew that before, yes, but until my job interview, I didn't know just how nice. He thinks the world of you, Kris. I hope you never do anything to change how he feels about you now."

"Meaning?"

"Don't act innocent, dear. What do you want me to do? Draw you a picture to help you understand?"

"First and foremost, I want you to lower your voice," Kristin said, nervously sinking to her bed as Mandy sat in the chair.

Mandy complied, her tone a hushed whisper, her eyes widening with alarmed concern.

"You can't go on like this, Kristin. I saw a side to Dacian Kendrick that I hadn't really seen before. He's going to be a joy to work with. I can see why his help all speaks so highly of him. He makes clear that he considers us all his equals, that his door is always open to talk if there's a problem."

"Yes. I realized that," Kristin admitted.

She'd noticed that his door was never fully closed and that help didn't hesitate approaching him with business that needed his immediate attention, or to check with him regarding a matter, or simply to dart in and retrieve something stored in his office. They obviously felt as at ease with him as any employee would hope to feel with a boss.

"He said that he plays square with his help and that he expects his help to be honest with him. He told me that he knows the computer programs will take me a little while to learn, and he said that he expects slipups and mistakes to happen, but not to get so worried at the prospect that I'm stressed out to the point I make even more mistakes because I'm nervous."

"That's reassuring."

"And he told me, Kris, that if I make a mistake, especially a bad one that could really cause problems, he wants me to come to him with it right away. He told me that he knows that everyone can make errors. That mistakes can happen to anyone. 'A mistake that simply happens,' he said, 'is the way life goes. We start fresh. But what I don't tolerate is someone making a serious mistake and then *making a second, even bigger mistake,* in trying to hide it from me.' Unquote," Mandy said and paused. "He told me that he'll never get angry if I'm a big enough person to confess an error. But that he does not tolerate deceit."

"You won't have a problem in the world, then," Kristin assured. "Because you're not that kind of girl."

Mandy was wringing her hands, as if she'd explained the best parts of the morning but now faced the most difficult. She stared at her lap, then lifted her eyes to give Kristin a penetrating stare.

"I know I'm not that kind of girl, Kris, and neither are you. And *I* don't have a problem. . .but, my friend, *you* really do. And what makes me feel so angry and so helpless is that it's not even your mistake, it's *hers.* After hearing what Dace said, I realized that you're courting disaster by keeping secret the fact that the woman he can't stand is the only sister of the girl he loves."

Miserable silence stretched, the still seeming almost thunderous in the quiet room.

"What do you think I should do?"

Mandy sighed. "Tell him."

"That's easier said than done."

"I know. I don't envy you the prospect. But Kris, you've got to do it. And do it soon. Before—"

"How?"

"God knows," Mandy said. "But you can't risk letting him find out by accident. You've got to find a way, Kristin, you've just got to. The kind of man he is, with ethics that are black or white, no shades of gray for him, I don't know how he'd handle such a deception. Not even from you. . . ."

"Maybe the simplest solution would be to just pack my bags and go home to Camden Corners as planned and let Dace worry about dealing with the Happy Trails people. . . ."

"That would be the coward's way out. Don't you get tired of running, Kris? And hiding? Trying to avoid unpleasantness by locking the doors, real or imagined, and insulating yourself from the world so that you can't risk something out there in the big, wide world hurting you?"

"Old habits die hard," Kristin said.

"Don't I know it," Mandy sympathized.

Suddenly, Kristin, without any warning, cupped her face in her hands and began to soundlessly cry.

Mandy arose and awkwardly patted her shoulder.

"I'll leave you alone to think it out. To pray about it," Mandy said in a soft, sympathetic voice. "Dace isn't terribly busy this morning. You could go to his office and have a talk with him. In fact, that would be the ideal place for you to confess, now that I stop to consider it."

Mandy crossed the room and retrieved a box of tissues, handing it to Kristin, who wiped her eyes and managed to face her.

"What do you mean?"

"Well, because, it's a sort of public location." Mandy, with a degree of reluctance, began to explain her simple logic. "If he really blows up, he'll have to keep it toned down a bit. He can hardly yell at you in front of everyone on the Circle K Ranch so they overhear him, can he?"

"Oh, Mandy. . . ," Kristin whimpered. "Knowing his temper, yes. Yes, he probably could—and would!"

Mandy thought back to the night they'd arrived.

"I guess he could," she was forced to agree.

Kristin's eyes, which had been dabbed dry a moment before, quickly refilled with tears.

"Me and my big mouth," she said. "Please, would you just go see him? Now? And get it over with? Trust me. It'll be way worse constantly imagining how awful it'll be rather than doing it, getting it over with, and facing your reality. People who keep canceling their dental appointments suffer way more anxiety and pain than the ones who make an appointment, keep it, and put the event behind them."

"You're probably right."

"Well, I'm going to go to my room for a while," Mandy said. "And I'd suggest that you go to Dace Kendrick's office."

"I'll think about it," she promised.

And she did think about it.

But she couldn't make herself act.

As one hour passed, then it became two, and that was all she'd meditated on. She knew that she should walk the distance to his office, ask permission to close the door, and in the quiet hush of his office, tell him the truth and get the terrible burden lifted from her mind and off her heart.

But she just couldn't do it. . . .

She realized that she'd reached a decision, probably a bad one, but what seemed the only choice open to her. She prayed that she could keep her act going for two more weeks, at which time she'd return to Camden Corners and take up where she'd left off with her old life and hope that Dace Kendrick, like herself, would look back on it with fond memories and then eventually dismiss it as just a summer romance. . . .

Chapter Nine

Kristin was grateful when Mandy didn't inquire if she'd gone to Dace's office to admit her accidental deceit. But by the way Mandy frowned, Kristin knew that she hadn't been fooled.

As accustomed to sharing their hopes and dreams and their private fears and problems as they were, she realized that Mandy was perfectly aware that she had not attended to the matter, because if she had taken care of it, she'd have told Mandy what had transpired, that is, if Dace's reaction hadn't been such that everyone on the Circle K would know from the force of his explosion his response to the news that she was Janice's sister. . . .

Two days later Mandy's weeks as a paying guest ended, as did Kristin's initial stay.

The day after that Operation: Recovery began. A school bus donated by the local district was used to go to the airport to collect the children. The ranch's van was used to shuttle children from shorter distances who arrived by bus or train. Although the ranch was bustling and the employees were temporarily overworked, their smiles held a hint of happy exhaustion, for the children's smiles and displays of excitement became rewards beyond description.

At first Kristin had noticed how disfigured some of the children were from surgeries and treatments and how others wore turbans that seemed to signify they'd undergone unpleasant bouts of chemotherapy and they needed protection from the sun and stares as their hair grew back in again.

Whatever their situations at home, they'd left a world of poor health behind them, and they did their best to manage the fun activities that average children took for granted.

Dace didn't see much of Kristin the first day, but he did manage to find enough time to introduce her to his brother, Dr. Bill, his sister, Melly, and Tony, whom she was going to marry in a Christmas season wedding.

To Kristin's relief, she liked them as well as she did Kerry, who'd become a friend, and she felt as if she hit it off famously with all the various Kendrick offspring. To her delight, they seemed to have passed approval on her, too, because when Dace was occupied arranging details for the rodeo and was forced into switching livestock contractors at what seemed almost the last moment, his brothers and sisters kept her company.

The more Kristin realized that she liked them, the worse she started to feel; her guilt increased by the day. She wasn't just deceiving Dace, but his family as well.

"You haven't said anything to him yet?" Mandy asked, when she and Kristin took their cups of coffee to a quiet corner of the dining hall during Mandy's break.

"Not yet," Kristin sighed.

"What are you waiting for? Christmas? New Year's? Or the Fourth of July?"

"You know, it's not easy," Kristin said, helpless not to be a bit snappish from stress. "If you were in my shoes, you wouldn't be so—"

"You don't have to blow up at me," Mandy said. "I know it's not easy. I'd tell him for you, but it's not my place to do it. And I really don't want to throw a monkey wrench into a brand-new boss-employee relationship by sticking my noise into other people's business."

"I'd never ask you to. Or allow it. And although it's another deceit, Mandy, I'm going to let Dace think that you had no idea that Janice is my big sister."

Mandy sighed. "Thanks. That's probably for the best."

The way her gaze lowered, then slid away from Kristin's, it was clear to her that Mandy didn't feel any more at ease with a fib than she did.

"I appreciate it. And I understand why it's got to be that way," Mandy spoke a moment later. "But keeping the secret you are from Dace. . .that's courting disaster and tempting the worst possible scenario to come true."

"I know."

"You've *got* to tell him," Mandy insisted.

"Tomorrow. He's got such worries on his mind already today."

"I know. He's had a lot of calls from that fellow who I gather is an investigator. I think it has something to do with the rodeo. And although I'm not certain, maybe even is why Dace switched contractors for rodeo stock. He seemed to act as if he'd accomplished that in the nick of time."

Or that's what he was letting Mandy think, Kristin realized. He knew that his new office help was also Kristin's best girlfriend, and he didn't want Mandy to feel a sense of divided loyalties and warn Kristin what he'd found out about her, causing her to flee without warning. . .so that after carefully laying the trap, it would come up empty, and he'd be denied his moment of revenge. He'd be unable to make her pay for her sister's behavior by humiliating and hurting her the way he'd probably not been able to get at Janice, who could be so thick-skinned at times. Beauty lotions aside, she had the hide of a rhino where matters of the heart were concerned.

"Well, see that you do," Mandy said, jerking Kristin back from her momentary musings about Dace's motives. "I'm a firm believer in tomorrows, new dawns, and starting all over. But time does run out, my friend. And you don't have forever."

"Tomorrow," Kristin promised.

"Good girl."

Kristin took a sip of coffee and then altered her intent as she sighed, "Maybe tomorrow."

But in the upcoming days, that was what she kept reassuringly telling Mandy, and herself, until soon Mandy ceased badgering her about it and only gave her worried looks interspersed with nettled glances.

Kristin noticed that the more closely Mandy worked with Dace, the harder seemed to be the pull of her divided loyalties, as she couldn't help feeling tugged between two opposing viewpoints.

"I hate what you're doing to him, to yourself, and to me!" Mandy protested. "You're driving me crazy!"

"It hasn't exactly been pleasant for me."

"You're going to have to pay the fiddler sometime, Kris. It may as well be now as later. You know that the day of reckoning is going to come. Perhaps it hasn't dawned on you, but it is in your power to select the moment and see to it that Dace is in the right mood and is sympathetic. That's got to be better than having him stumble onto the information, which, I'm warning you, can certainly happen. When it comes to making decisions, that man is meticulous. And he's trying to decide if you're the right woman for him."

"Are you trying to tell me something?" Kristin said and thought about the private investigator and the file folder Mandy had mentioned.

"What I've been trying to tell you for weeks: Come clean! Get it off your conscience and out in the open."

"Tomorrow, Mandy. I promise," Kristin said wearily.

"I wish I could believe you. But I no longer do."

"That's what I'm afraid Dace is going to say if I tell him about Janice, that I'm not like her, and that it doesn't have to be important, that we don't have to let the past, and her, come between a future and us."

"That's an excellent way to put it, Kris."

She wiped a sudden tear that strayed to her cheek. "Have you any idea how many times I've had the conversation in my mind?"

"Then pretend it's a dress rehearsal, instead of the real thing, pretend you're acting a part in the play, and go into his office and put on the performance of your life."

For a harrowing moment Kristin was tempted to do just that, because Dace had been in a super mood that morning after having come in from watching the children being carried around on Molly's back.

Then when she considered what could happen, she lost her nerve.

"Tomorrow."

"Tonight, Kris," Mandy said, as if they were bidding against one another.

Kristin shook her head. "Tomorrow. I won't be seeing him tonight. He's got a meeting in Rapid City."

"That's right. I forgot. Then tomorrow it's got to be."

"And it will. Come morning, Mandy, I promise, I'm going to clear the air so that I can stop living a lie."

She hoped that with the sun's new dawning, she wouldn't find that all resolve would flee again, just as surely as the morning haze was burned away beneath the sun's relentless glare.

But once more, time was running out. Her stay at the Circle K Ranch compliments of the Happy Trails Horse Feed Company would soon come to an end and she would have to leave. . .unless Dacian Kendrick decided to ask her to stay.

She had only known Dace for three weeks. But in some ways it seemed like at least three months, or three years, or the majority of her whole life. And at other moments it was as if she'd known him forever.

"Forever," Kristin murmured as she watched Mandy deposit her empty cup in a tray and then lost sight of her as she rounded a corner to disappear into Dace's office.

Forever was what Kristin realized she wanted so very, very much. And she sensed that it was hers for the taking, if only she dared to risk it all and go for it.

"Tomorrow," she promised herself as she drifted off to sleep, more tired than usual from a long day helping Mrs. Moriarty with the children's quarters. "I'll tell him tomorrow. . . ."

Late that night after spending the evening with Dr. Bill, Kerry, Tony, and Melanie, it seemed as if Kristin had scarcely returned to her quarters, readied for bed, and fallen asleep when there was a pounding on her door.

It wasn't Mandy's knock, she knew. Now that her friend worked at the ranch, she had been assigned a room in a dormitory building. Plus, Mandy didn't keep late hours now that she had to be at her desk early.

The first knock had been harsh.

The raps that followed after it bowed the door beneath a rough, battering, determined pummeling.

"Open up!"

"Just a minute!" Kristin called in a quaking voice. "Who—"

She wasn't about to open her door to an out-of-control madman. She was about to dial the front desk and request help, when she recognized that it had been Dace's fury-soaked tone.

"Open up before I kick the door in!" he growled.

Kristin staggered from her bed, drew on her robe, and when she went to the door, not sure she'd get there before Dace somehow tore it off its hinges, she was shivering from the cool night air and her nerves.

Dace flipped on the light, gave her a long look, an infuriated glare that was so heated she felt an unpleasant warmth flood to her skin. She knew it was a flush of alarm, and shame, of course, but for a moment it had seemed to arrive with the force of Dace's blistering stare.

"What an actress you are," he said, and the mocking words seemed to whistle from him. "Perhaps I should nominate you for an Academy Award. Playing the part of the sweet, lovable, innocent young thing, who's so pleasant and agreeable, when it's clear that you must have a mind like an adding machine, a heart like a cash register, the ethics of a con man, the plans of a swindler, and the bartering skills of a harlot!"

"What are you talking about?" Kristin asked, stalling for time in which to try to shake the sleep from her, as it seemed as if her mental acuities had fled, leaving her without the capacity to provide a convincing, calming defense.

At that moment she felt certain that Dace *had* retained a private investigator to poke into her background, and now he knew the truth after keeping the appointment that took him from her that very night. But a moment later, from the hand held behind him, he produced an answering machine identical to the one she'd seen at his house.

Without bothering to ask permission, he bullied his way into her room, took over as if she had no right to be there, and plugged the device into a wall socket.

"Listen, you vixen," he hissed the order.

Then he savagely punched the button and fumbled to turn up the volume.

Kristin felt her face drain pale as the messages began, and she swirled in an eddying tide of confusion, because none of it made any sense. The messages were just so much gibberish. The evening's calls to his private number meant nothing to her.

"Why are you subjecting me to this?" she demanded to know, her shock and fear giving way to her own fury.

"Be still and listen!"

Then she heard it.

A voice she'd listened to so many times before. Words couched in an accent as phony as the woman who used it!

"Dace, darling, how good to hear your voice, even if it is only on a machine. I've been trying and trying to reach my little sister at the Circle K Ranch. But every time they connect me with her room, no one answers. I decided not to bother with leaving a message at the desk, so I looked in my Rolodex, found your unlisted number, and decided to call your home. I thought that perhaps Krissie would be with you there. . .the way we used to be. I trust you can give her my message? According to Krissie, it's certain that you'll be seeing her because you've been charming her and keeping her very busy indeed, just as you were so wonderful to me last summer when Cissy and I stayed at your ranch. So please tell Krissie that Aunt Dee and Uncle Benchley are in New York City now, and we'll be in touch and to expect our call. Or if she likes, she could telephone us at her earliest con—"

The rest of Janice's message was soon lost in a sickening flurry of kissypoo good-byes that, by the darkening expression that draped to his story features, apparently infuriated Dace to the degree that it sickened Kristin.

"No wonder you look alike. Two peas in a pod. You sprang from the same bloodlines. *Sisters!*" he spat the word. "You're as deceitful as Janice is. But why should I be surprised? After all, the fruit doesn't fall far from the tree, does it? God knows the kind of woman your mother was."

Kristin felt the urge to slap him. "You leave my mother out of this. She's been dead for some ten years."

Kristin fumbled, tried to find words to defend herself and her parentage, to explain, but Dacian was insatiable. There was no stopping him and, she realized, no way to excuse her actions.

"What are you? On the prowl for a rich husband? And Janice is siccing you onto the trail in search of her castoff beaus while she goes on to hunt for bigger game?" He called Kristin a gold digger and other unflattering names. "You're just like your heartless sister."

"I'm not like Janice!" Kristin cried.

"You're more like her than I'm sure even you can see! Fool me once, shame on you. Fool me twice, shame on me. A year ago Janice and her rich divorcee friend showed up. Your sister threw herself at me. It wasn't until I was stupid enough to impulsively ask her to marry me that she ended up revealing what she was really like. She was like something unpleasant to behold that was wrapped up in pretty packaging to fool the consumer. I couldn't believe it when she started offering herself up, for a price, like merchandise for barter. She was interested in marriage, but only on her terms. Trying to flimflam me with phony words of faith that she didn't really possess, and had I been hoodwinked by them, would've found myself unevenly yoked to an unbelieving, wanton woman. . . ."

"I'm sorry," Kristin whispered.

And she was. She knew what Janice at her best was like. She could only imagine her at her worst.

"I'm not so hard up for a woman to love that I had to even consider settling for a plastic personality, and a woman with dollar signs in her eyes, and probably all of the mothering instinct and ability of a turtle depositing eggs on the beach!"

Dace moved a pace away, as if he didn't trust himself, in his anger, to stay in Kristin's proximity.

"I thought I'd learned a lot from her. But apparently I've been a dunce when it's come to matters of the heart. Of course I suppose that she guided you as I helped my younger brothers and sisters. No doubt she trained you, and believe me, she taught you well. You're such an accomplished actress that I even bought your behavior lock, stock, and barrel. I believed you. But, then, I guess all great actresses make the viewers forget where reality ends and fantasy begins. You're the hardworking little maid from Camden Corners?" He gave a scornful, derisive laugh. "What other lies have you told me?"

"I've told you no lies, no lies other than not being able to admit the truth of my sister's identity for fear that you'd behave exactly as you are reacting right now!"

Dace laughed in her face. "You expect me to believe that? Then you must think me an even bigger, more gullible fool than you and your sister obviously already do."

"I have nothing but respect for you, although that's rapidly changing because of the way you won't even let me explain."

"Don't make me laugh. You couldn't ever accomplish that. Not even given all the time remaining in the world."

"I was going to tell you. Tomorrow. Just ask—" She was about to say that Mandy could vouch for her, but then she recalled her promise and out of loyalty bit the words back.

"Yeah, speaking of her message, why'd she call and leave a message on my machine? She would've known it'd blow things sky high. You two have a regular catfight? Do something to tick your big sister off, so she took revenge as she could do it best, by revealing you for a fraud to the man you thought you were going to bamboozle into marrying you so you'd have a cushy existence for the rest of your life, and all the money you could spend, whether you stayed married or whether you didn't?"

"I don't know, but I don't need your money, *that* I do know!"

"Oh, what an act it's been," Dace mused, not even seeming to hear her. "And to think I was taken in." His voice was heavy with self-disgust. "I watched you helping Mrs. Moriarty and thought that I'd found a real lady who could also *work* like a responsible woman, and it made me love you all the more. Now I know that it was just an act, and a necessary evil, so that you could disarm me completely. I'll bet you planned on having a big diamond ring on your finger and would be intent on putting a ring through my nose before Operation: Recovery could come to a close! Then once we were married, instead of being sweet and understanding and easy to please, you'd revert to true form and not bother to hide your colors. You'd nag, complain, whine, and *demand*: Janice's clone, refusing to lift a finger to do anything, while expecting the staff to behave as if they were your personal servants."

"Get out!" Kristin said. "I've listened to enough of this. To think I was fool enough to think you were nice. Naive enough to fall in love with you. *Get out!*"

"I'll go," Dace said. "But when I'm ready. After all, I do own the place," he pointed out in an unpleasant tone.

"Then *I'll* go!" Kristin raged, the effect diminished somewhat by the fact that she also burst into tears.

"Good. The sooner the better."

"I'll leave right now."

"I'm sorry, truly sorry, that that's not possible," he pointed out. "For it's the middle of the night. But there's always tomorrow."

And with that he left and slammed the door behind him. He banged it shut with such force that the picture on the wall was knocked askew. The Roving Maid in her dictated that she automatically right it, the way she was helpless to correctly align her life, it seemed. And at the thought, Kristin began weeping as she furiously packed her belongings while knowing that she'd end up leaving her broken heart behind.

Finally, exhausted, she fell into bed.

But still she could not go to sleep.

She felt an odd relief. At last her horrible secret was out. But it had destroyed her world as surely as she'd believed it would.

Dace had been puzzled why Janice had bothered to phone him at his personal residence, at an unlisted number, and leave the message on his machine instead of with the desk help. He'd known that Janice had realized it would provoke a fight, that it would end what had become a pleasant relationship.

Kristin momentarily wondered why Janice had done something so selfish and so cruel. Then, she admitted what she'd always tried to overlook, and she knew the truth beyond denial.

She'd done it because once again Janice was jealous of her little sister, and she didn't want to risk letting Kristin Allen find the happiness that Jan herself constantly sought but never found because she asked too much and offered so little.

Because she had been so mentally exhausted when she'd gone back to bed after packing and then hadn't been able to sleep until near dawn, Kristin overslept. She hadn't left a wake-up call with the desk employees, and when the cries of children at play awoke her, for a moment she thought that she was in her old neighborhood at Camden Corners. Then she looked around, remembered, and with a horrible, sinking heart, recalled every hurtful, insulting, enraged remark Dace had made the evening before. Numb, Kristin arose, showered, put on makeup, and tried to make herself presentable.

Her stomach was in such a knot that the thought of food made her feel almost ill.

She wanted nothing more than to get away.

She felt a pang of alarm when she saw the van used to transport people to Rapid City Regional Airport was not there. Determinedly she sought out the driver and made a shaky-voiced inquiry about her chances of going to the airport that day.

"The van's in the shop for an overhaul. We don't do much scuttling back and forth between the airport and the ranch while the young'uns are here," Roger explained. "So we usually schedule it for a complete overhaul. The mechanic in town picked it up this morning."

"Oh."

"You sound like you're caught between a rock and a hard place."

"Well, I'd hoped to get to the airport to catch a flight."

The cowboy consulted his watch, then shook his head. "A flight leaves in an hour. We couldn't make it. You'd have to be checking in at the gate right now. There's an evening flight, Kristin, and if it's some kind of emergency, I could drive you in my car. I could take off a few hours of personal leave to do it."

"I'd be so grateful. And I'd pay you for your time so you wouldn't lose your wages."

"Before you get your heart set on it, I'd suggest that you go in and call the airline. You know how airlines are these days. The evening flight tends to get cancelled about as often as passengers can fly out."

Back in her room, Kristin made the call and found out that Roger, who was in a position to know, was right. Her only chance to fly out and away from the Circle K had a departure time minutes away and was booked full.

"There's always tomorrow," she decided, but not with such certainty that she requested passage with the airline for the next day.

Kristin made it a point to leave her room little that day. She unpacked only what she needed. Instead of going to the dining hall, she ate what meals a concerned Mandy brought to her, and when she got hungry, made selections from the coin-operated snack machines near her quarters.

"I wish you'd told him on your own," Mandy commiserated. "I knew that it couldn't help but be so much worse if you let him find out as he did. Your sister is a witch, the type who must make you wish that you had been an only child."

"You can't pick your family, you know," Kristin said in a bleak tone.

"I know it," she said. "Apparently the person who doesn't remember that is Dacian Kendrick."

"He thinks that I'm like Janice. That it's all been an act. And I," Kristin said, "am at the point of not giving a hoot what such an arrogant, opinionated, obstinate, irritating—"

"Hmm. . .as scathing as your remarks, it sounds like you still love him," Mandy sighed teasingly.

Kristin halted. "I suppose that I still do. But believe me, I won't. I'll get over him. You just watch and see. I'm leaving tomorrow."

"Then I guess I won't be able to watch and see, Kris. Because you'll be gone while I'm still here."

"And I'm sure going to miss you."

"It won't seem the same without you."

"You have other friends, Mandy."

"It won't be the same, Kristin."

"I have no choice but to go, the sooner the better. I have to. And now I *want* to." She brushed her hair away from her face. "I don't care if I never see Dacian Kendrick again. . . ."

"That's a lie and we both know it."

"Okay. So it is. But I think I'd rather die than see him face-to-face."

"Don't worry about it, Kris," Mandy said. "No more time than he's spent at the ranch, it's not likely. He's evading you every bit as earnestly as you are zealously avoiding him."

Chapter Ten

Kristin was taken by surprise when a quavery-voiced, almost tearful Mrs. Moriarty called her room and begged her to come to the housekeeper's quarters as soon as she could.

Not one to turn down a request when someone was upset and in need, Kristin put aside what she'd been doing and glanced outside to make sure that Dace was not arriving or departing in his Corvette. She hurried toward the dormitory-like apartment house where Circle K's female staff lived.

Mrs. Moriarty's quarters were on ground level. Her inner door was open although her screen door was closed.

"Knock! Knock!" Kristin called out in a tone much more cheerful than how she felt.

"Come in, child," she invited. "The door's unlocked."

Kristin let herself in and gasped when she saw Mrs. Moriarty, seated in a recliner rocking chair, her right leg elevated, ice packs surrounding it. An accident had swollen it to twice its normal size and colored it an ugly, mottled purple. The skin was stretched tight until Kristin knew how it must throb.

"Oh, how that must hurt," she murmured.

"It's plenty uncomfortable, although the prescription tablets I've been taking have taken the edge off the pain."

"What happened?"

"I forgot to look where I was going. A child left a baseball bat on the sidewalk. I stepped on it and—"

"It was worse than a banana peel is reputed to be."

"Exactly. Thank goodness I'm no worse than this."

"It could've been a disaster."

"Dr. Bill says I'm lucky that I didn't chip my elbow or dislocate a shoulder."

"Or break a hip."

"And I'm no kid anymore," the aging woman remarked.

"Anything I can do to help, Mrs. Moriarty, you just let me know," Kristin said.

"That's why I called you, dear. Dr. Bill says that it's too swollen right now to bother wrapping it. I'm to keep off my feet except when absolutely necessary. And then—" She gestured toward the crutches.

"What rotten luck," Kristin said.

"And it couldn't have happened at a worse time. You know what the children can do to their rooms."

"Oh my. . .I hadn't even thought of what that would mean."

Kristin, who had begun sticking close to her own quarters to avoid Dace until she could manage to leave the ranch, had ceased helping the housekeeping staff. And she'd not gone outside much, staying in her room to the point where she tended to forget that the children were present until something jarringly reminded her.

"I really hate to ask a favor of you, Kristin, because I've heard mumblings around the ranch. I know for a fact that you asked Roger to take you to the Rapid City airport, and that you'd have left us already if you'd been able to get the flight connections arranged. I won't act like I don't know that things are not good between you and Mr. Kendrick, because I believe in telling the truth."

"Well, we're not getting along," Kristin said. "And come tomorrow I will be gone."

"Oh no. . . ."

Mrs. Moriarty suddenly looked so worried that Kristin noticed what dark circles had appeared under her eyes, making her look old, feeble, and very, very tired.

"Oh *yes*," Kristin said. "I've already told the staff at the front desk that I'm leaving."

"You can't go, Kristin. I. . .I mean. . .do you have to?"

"I should. I'm not welcome here."

"I think you are. Perhaps not by Dacian. But you are welcome here as far as the other Kendricks are concerned. As for me, all night long as I laid awake, worrying, I kept telling myself that I could stop stewing because you'd be able to help me out. We desperately need you to help out with the housekeeping again."

Kristin's resolve wavered.

She deplored turning her back on someone in need, especially someone as strong and stoic as Mrs. Moriarty, who would always offer a helping hand quick as a wink but was hesitant about inconveniencing others by letting her needs be known.

"I'd really like to help you, but I've already given notice that I'll be vacating my room."

"It's not likely that there'll be any guests coming in, although I suppose that the staff might have reserved your quarters already. The cowboys who come in for the big rodeo do have to stay someplace. And some of Dace's friends will probably want to get a room here at the ranch." Mrs. Moriarty paused, her face thoughtful. Then she looked up with an expression of last-ditch hope on her pain-filled features. "I'll be sleeping in this chair with my foot elevated," Mrs. Moriarty said. "You can have my bed and bunk here with me. I wouldn't ask such a huge favor of anyone, Kristin, except that I—we—are desperate. There's more work to do, fewer hands to do it, and by the time we could bring some young girls from town and train them to do the house-work our way. . .why I'd probably be back on my feet. I've worked with you. You can do the job of two people. I'd see that you were well compensated."

Kristin felt embarrassed. She gave Mrs. Moriarty a pat.

"I know you would," she said. "But the money doesn't matter. It's painful for me to remain here. I don't know what rumors you've heard, but probably anything you've been told is based on the truth. It's hard for me to leave my new friends here, but it would be more of an agony to remain."

"Many things that are painful are the very things that we should do. I'm not just begging you as a helpless old woman, Kristin. I'm also asking on behalf of the children, who really know what pain is all about, and their par-ents, who are getting a little vacation, too, as we promise to take care of their youngsters as responsibly as we would our own. It's not just me who needs you." Mrs Moriarty gestured beyond the four walls. "The children do, too."

Kristin forced a smile. "You've just made me an offer that I can't refuse. And I will bunk with you, if you don't mind. It'll be good to have some com-panionship. I've truly missed Mandy now that she's working in Dacian's office."

"That was a wonderful thing you did, Kristin. He's been too overworked, but also too stubborn to admit it. He knows Mandy's a competent girl, or he wouldn't have hired her. He thinks that he did something nice for Mandy and Billy Joe. And he's blind to the fact that he also did something pleasant for himself. He needs to relax more."

"Sometimes he seems so. . .driven."

"I think he is. Dacian Kendrick is a very complex man." She paused. "He was a very complex little boy. So serious. So solemn. And always so respon-sible." Her voice dropped off to become low musings that seemed almost more to herself than to Kristin. "I hate to think where I'd be without Dacian Kendrick as my boss."

Kristin sighed inwardly. More testimonials were not exactly what she wanted to hear, as needled as she felt by the wonderful Mr. Kendrick who'd so cruelly railed at her.

"Dacian was just a lad when my Harley was wounded in a rodeo accident.

He didn't die right away. He lingered for a week, and it was awful. My heart broke by inches and degrees every day that he lingered. And the bills, of course, mounted higher and higher."

"That's so sad. It must've been hard."

"It'd have been a lot harder. I managed to hang onto my ranch, but it wasn't easy. About that time Dacian came into his own and began this dude ranch, employing his brothers and sisters, but making sure that each of them went to college, while he, himself, took night classes in the evenings and kept the enterprise going during the day. When he slept, I'll never know."

"I know he's an accomplished man," Kristin admitted.

"Running the ranch was becoming too much for me. One day Dace Kendrick drove in, a handsome young cowboy who'd turn any woman's head. He offered to buy my ranch, which adjoins this spread. Knowing my need, many a man would've dickered for the lowest dollar amount possible. Not Dace Kendrick. He knew how hard it was when his father died, only a few years after they'd lost his brother. If anything, he offered me more than my ranch was worth."

"That's really admirable."

"I needed to sell. I wanted to sell. But I truly hated to leave the area where I'd lived all my life. People are like trees. They set down roots. Rip 'em up and so often they wither, and he told me that he wanted to expand the ranch. But to do it, he'd have to have people he could count on. He allowed as to how he knew that I could be the best manager of the housekeeping staff that he could ask for. And," she said, as pride came into her voice, "I like to think I've never let that boy down."

"I'm sure you haven't."

"I hope I haven't. Because he's been like a son to me, and I don't think I could love him more if I were his mother." She paused. "And it's because I do love that boy that I want to see him happy. You made him happy, Kristin. Now you've made him sad. Or so he thinks. I not only need you to stick around to help us with all of the housework. I'd like you to remain here until that bullheaded young pup comes to his senses and recognizes that you're the woman meant for him. The God-sent woman who'll give him lifelong joy."

Kristin couldn't help the bitter laugh that erupted.

"I'm afraid I must beg to disagree; he made it perfectly clear that he'd be happy if he never laid eyes on me again."

Mrs. Moriarty made a piffling gesture. "What a man says and what he really thinks are often not one and the same. Just because Dace Kendrick rages, it does not mean that you're required to believe it."

"He was very convincing." Kristin wiped her eyes. "I never want to see him again. I've felt like a prisoner in my room, afraid that we'd accidently meet on the sidewalk somewhere."

"Well, you won't have to worry about seeing him if you stay on. When you're not cleaning rooms, you can hole up here. They can bring your meals along with mine. And Dr. Bill won't say anything about your being here. From what I've seen, and the girls tell me, Dacian is making himself scarce. That convinces me that he still feels something for you, Kristin, or he wouldn't stay away. The reason he's not showing hide nor hair is because he's afraid to. Frightened that what he feels will be so strong and true that he'll end up taking back everything he said and having to swallow that pride of his and say that he's sorry."

"Which certainly wouldn't hurt him. But what about his family? I haven't seen any of them. I figured that people would be taking sides. And they are his immediate family. So I'd assumed—"

"It was Dr. Bill who suggested that you might help out again. And he won't tell Dace, I'm sure, because right now he and Dace aren't on the best of terms. Nor is he with Melly. Or Kerry. I would suppose he feels betrayed that they've taken your side instead of his."

"Th. . .they still like me? And believe in me?"

Mrs. Moriarty nodded. "They think you're super, Kris, and just the woman for a man like Dace Kendrick, the big boss of the Circle K spread. They're really hoping that you two will sort out your differences and that Dace will give you the Kendrick family ring that, by tradition, goes to the wife of the oldest son and claim you for his own."

Kristin's thoughts were swirling.

As she listened to Mrs. Moriarty, she remembered so many good things about Dace that it made it easier to overlook his rare forays into unpleasantness.

Although she'd wanted to leave, she now felt drawn to staying, but she could not admit it, not to Mrs. Moriarty, because she wasn't comfortable acknowledging it herself. . . .

"I'll stay," Kristin quietly agreed. "But only for a few days. And for the children's sake. We do have an obligation to them and their parents."

"A few days is all we ask, Kristin, and pray God that's all that's required for Dace to bury his anger, find his good sense, and settle this matter once and for all by realizing that you can't judge a book by its cover nor decide what one girl's like because you've previously met her sister."

For the next two days, Kristin's daytime hours were spent slipping from building to building, working quietly, scrubbing, dusting, vacuuming, and bringing order to the children's chaos.

She talked with the young ranch guests who had to take naps and rest more than other children did. She found them loving, funny, earnest, and so sweet that her heart wrenched when she feared she'd never know what it was like to have a child of her own.

As the days progressed, she was relieved when Dace's parking slot remained vacant, because it meant that she wouldn't have to worry about walking out of a building, her cleaning cart rolling along in front of her, and coming face-to-face with him.

By the time she'd remained for three days, she really wanted to leave. It was torment being so close to Dacian by geography, yet so far apart emotionally that he could've been around the world. But her rashly given promise in the face of Mrs. Moriarty's almost coercive pleading was a vow she couldn't break. The elderly woman worried enough as it was, and if Kristin left, she knew that it was all too likely Mrs. Moriarty would begin putting weight on her badly sprained ankle before Dr. Bill said that it was all right for her to be up and about. That could result in a broken hip, which so often meant the end of good health to older people.

Because she felt a bit uncomfortable, Kristin tried to be away from Mrs. Moriarty's quarters when Dr. Bill Kendrick was due to arrive to check her ankle.

He confronted her when he arrived unexpectedly and caught her sitting with Mrs. Moriarty.

"Can we talk?" he asked.

"Sure," she said with a casual calm she didn't really feel.

"Let's take a little stroll," he suggested. Wordlessly, Kristin followed him outside. "Dace is still in a snit. The rest of us don't agree with him. But, unfortunately, his view is the one that matters to you," he said and eased his glasses up, rubbing the bridge of his nose in a tired gesture. "None of us can change his mind. We've tried. Believe me, we've tried."

"I don't know if I appreciate it or not."

Dr. Bill gave a small smile. "I'm not here hinting for thanks but to extend it, Kristin. We're very grateful to you. I know that the children think you're tops. I'm sure it's not been easy to always give a child a smiling face when inside you feel like crying."

"You're right. And I'll be glad when Mrs. Moriarty is back on her feet so I can go home with a clear conscience."

"It'll be soon, Kristin. Just a matter of a few days. Think you can hang in there for that long?"

"It won't be easy," she admitted. "But I'll try."

"You've been working so hard," Dr. Bill observed. "And by the looks of you, there's a strong chance that you're not eating as you should. Appetite dwindling?" She nodded. "Not unusual when a person is upset. Just do your best. You should try to relax; do something fun."

"You're a great one to give me such advice, Doctor," she said. "I've seen you working almost 'round the clock."

"The cobbler's children do without shoes, and the doctor often ignores his best bits of advice."

"I do get bored staying inside all the time, but it's difficult to be around people, adults, who know Dace, are employed by him, and who he might think are disloyal if—"

"Surely he's not that unreasonable."

"Isn't he? Anyway, I don't want to make use of what facilities the ranch offers for fear that Dacian will return, and he'll see me, and in anger force another confrontation. Thinking that I'm hanging around to be a thorn in his side instead of as a favor to others."

"But couldn't you go for a ride? The pastures are quite private. And the bluffs and plateaus are nice. Serene. Especially in the evening when the children aren't stampeding all over the hills, whooping and shrieking and playing cowboys and Indians. Why don't you start taking a ride each evening?"

"I'll think about it," Kristin said, realizing that the idea appealed to her more than a little.

"Then consider it doctor's orders," Bill said and gave her a grin so much like Dace's during happier times that she turned away, feeling as if her heart was breaking anew.

That night after taking her meal with Mrs. Moriarty and visiting a bit with Mandy when she came to Mrs. Moriarty's quarters, Kristin felt oddly restless.

She didn't feel like watching television, nor did she want to risk an encounter with Dace by going to the large building where children were square dancing to rollicking tunes that could be heard far away from the dance floor.

Kristin had closed her eyes and was listening to the bouncy tunes, when she realized that she detected a different rhythm at counterpoint with the fiddle's lilting beat.

It took her a moment to realize that it was the steady *clip-clop* of horses.

"Whoa," she heard a soft voice outside her door command.

Kristin sat up, then went to the door and glanced out. Dace's younger sister, who was a third-year nursing student, was astride a roan that she tended to select for her mount, and she was leading Molly alongside. The plump mare was saddled up and ready to go.

"Let's go for a ride, Kristin," Melanie said, swinging down. "And I won't take no for an answer," she warned before Kristin could open her mouth. "It'll do you good."

Molly lifted her head, revealed flat, wide, yellowed horse teeth, laid back her ears, looked as if she were smiling, and issued a low nicker.

Melanie slapped her jean-clad thigh and laughed.

"Hear that? We're going for a ride at the special invitation of Miss Molly herself. Even if you thought about turning me down, you *can't* decline an offer like that."

"I guess not," Kristin said, laughing, and suddenly felt at ease with Dace's younger sister. "Let me slip on a pair of boots and grab a jacket and I'll be right with you."

She rejoined Melly moments later after telling Mrs. Moriarty where she was going.

As Kristin took the reins, Molly gave her an affectionate nuzzle, snuffling at the back of her jacket and blowing out her breath in an impatient snort, with the moist gust of air tickling Kristin's skin.

"Now behave yourself, Molly!" Kristin ordered. "We all know that you have a reputation to live up to."

She stuck her left foot in the stirrup, shoved off with her right foot, and swung her leg over, settling into the saddle. She gave Molly a pat.

"The greeting you gave me, old girl, Mandy will be jealous. So would your owner," she said, "whoever he or she is. I'll bet whoever owns you will be glad to have such a sweet old horse return after the children have gone home."

Melly gave Kristin a rather startled look, seemed about to say something, but then apparently thought better of it and did not. The two women slowly rode along the wide street, then out into the vast expanses beneath the twilight South Dakota sky.

At first Kristin felt self-conscious, being with the sister of the man she still loved, while she, and every adult on the Circle K, had been made aware that Dacian despised her. But gradually talk between them became easier.

"Kristin, can I ask you something?"

"I suppose."

"I won't if you think I have no right to get a bit personal."

"If I think you're too personal, I don't have to answer," Kristin replied.

"That's fair enough. So I may's well cut right to the heart of the matter. Are you going to try to get Dacian back?"

"Why do you ask?" Kristin responded to Melly's question by asking one of her own.

"Because we're hoping that you will. And if there's anything that we can do to help, let us know. We care about Dace, but we've also come to care for you. He's not a totally happy man. Dace isn't fit for man nor beast to be around these days. And now, instead of feeling like he's settled the issue, it's as if he's in a worse fettle because, while he's done what he wanted to do and hurt you the way he couldn't wound your sister, deep down he knows he's like the man who cut off his nose to spite his face."

"Sorry to disappoint you. And I can appreciate your concern and sentiments, but the answer is no. I haven't any plans to try to get him back. And I'd appreciate it if you wouldn't do anything to intervene. It could end up making things worse. And of course Dacian would blame me."

"You're probably right," Melanie said in a bleak tone. "We all hate to see you both so unhappy."

"I'll be all right. Don't worry about me. I'll be fine just as soon as we have Mrs. Moriarty get back on her feet so I can go."

Melly seemed to think it over. "Well, never forget that the rest of us are your friends, Kristin, and if you're ever passing through areas where any of us live, we'll be disappointed if you don't stop in to visit."

"I'd like that," Kristin said. "And it's reassuring to know that not everyone thinks I'm an awful person because my sister seems to be."

"I'm glad you're not prejudiced against me because of how my big brother's treating you."

Kristin started to say something, but then their attention was drawn to a rider who was coming across the pasture with his horse going at full gallop.

"That's Tony!" Melanie said. "I'd better go see what he wants. It was his sister's due date today, maybe he's going to tell me that he's just become an uncle. Want to ride back to headquarters with us? Or continue on your ride?"

"I think I'll go it alone, thanks," she said. "The night's still young. And this is the most peaceful I've felt all week."

"Remember, you're on Molly," Melanie warned. "I guess you've heard about her and what she does if she thinks you're not an expert enough rider to show her who's boss."

"I think we'll get along fine."

"Well, she can be a handful. And we're not too far from where her owner lives. Keep a firm rein, because she can be as headstrong as she is lovable. A lot like her owner, I guess."

"I'll be all right. Don't worry. I can take care of myself."

As dusk began to drape over the ranch in the rapidly fading light, Kristin looked for familiar paths. She seemed to remember some of them, but about the time she believed she was on the way home, she'd confront a landmark she'd never seen before, and soon her confusion was complete.

For the better part of an hour she'd let Molly mosey along wherever she chose, and now she regretted it, for the horse was determined to go where she wanted, not where Kristin desired.

"Well, you stubborn old hayburner," Kristin said, "then I guess we'll just go where you want to, and when I meet your master, I'm going to apologize and tell him what you did and ask him if he'll give me a ride back to the Circle K. With any luck he'll be able to deliver me right to Mrs. Moriarty's doorstep."

As the darkness began to descend in earnest, she felt a prickle of alarm. But when the sky grew dark enough, before the moon rose, she saw lights from a house glowing on the adjoining ranch.

When she and Molly climbed a bluff and Kristin was at a vantage point so that she could look out over the area, she saw what had to be myriad lights from the Circle K glowing off in the distance, and she turned Molly in that direction, determined to show the stubborn creature who was boss.

But the chunky horse had other ideas. Molly snorted, stomped, threw her head back, and even threatened to rear.

"Stop it!" Kristin cried, and there was fright in her voice, which Molly probably heard, so she knew that Kristin's order was a command that she need not heed.

At last Molly started to move. Sighing with relief, Kristin thought that they were heading back in the direction of the Circle K until a moment later, when she understood that Molly had taken a shortcut, and the wily mare had instead progressed toward the ranch, where only a few lights glowed in the night.

When the mare increased her pace, Kristin realized that Molly's excitement indicated that she was just about home!

Mentally Kristin rehearsed her embarrassed explanations.

She'd tell the kindly ranch owner, who of course already knew what Molly was like, that she'd been riding the horse, thought she was competent, but found that she wasn't the match for one lovable but stubborn horse.

Molly seemed to know her way around, and with brisk movements so frisky that Kristin had to hang onto the pommel to keep from being thrown off in the darkness, Molly negotiated the dark terrain.

"Oh, no!" Kristin cried in horror when Molly went through an open gate, entered a large yard, then went to stand expectantly at a stable gate. It was not just any stable gate, but the stable gate on *Dacian Kendrick's private property!*

Molly was home. . . .

With a nicker that shattered the still night, she began to make almost mulelike brays. The evening was pleasant, Dace's windows were open, and within a moment he was outside to investigate.

"Who's out there?" he called.

Molly gave a delighted nicker and trotted over to see him as if she were thrilled to at last lay eyes on him. Shameless as a hussy, she nuzzled him while Kristin cowered in the shadows.

Dace touched the saddle and seemed to know from the leather's warmth that it had been unseated mere moments before.

"Whoever you are, you'd better come out. Don't be alarmed. This is Molly's oldest trick. I'll see you back to the Circle K and remind the staff at the corral not to give Molly to a novice again."

Kristin didn't answer. She was frozen with horror beyond the capacity to produce speech.

"Come on, kiddo," Dacian said, his tone having a hint of exasperation. "I'm not going to call your mom and dad and tell on you. You're not in trouble, so be a pal and come out. Okay?"

Still Kristin didn't answer.

She heard Dace mutter under his breath to Molly, then he went into the house while Molly patiently waited. He returned with a powerful lantern. He easily swung into the saddle, jerked Molly around, and she knew better than to disobey *him*.

She started to canter past where Kristin was standing, but the horse sensed her and shied. In the process the all-around cowboy was almost thrown over her head. He flicked on the lantern as he jerked on the reins, making Molly rear, as her front hooves lashed the air not far from Kristin's face.

"Who's there?" he cried out.

Dace swung the light around, and the beam crisscrossed the nearby lawn. Then it came to focus on Kristin's face, blinding her. The look he gave her was beyond description. In the glow of the lantern that reflected up toward his face, she was certain that even in the dim light she saw his complexion drain.

"*You!*" he said. His tone was stunned, disbelieving, as if he couldn't comprehend that she was standing on his property. "What are you doing here?" Startled, miserable, Kristin couldn't answer except for an awkward, defiant shrug. "Don't bother to explain. I'm sure that I know exactly what you're here for. Been talking to big sister, have you? Has she been offering tutelage?

Advising you how to get a man back? Well, my dear girl, *it won't work.*"

"That isn't what I had in mind," Kristin said. "I wouldn't have you if you were the last man on earth. You're the most unpleasant man on the face of the earth."

"And you, my dear, are tied for first place as one of the most devious women I have ever met."

Dacian was poised to say more.

But Kristin decided that she didn't have to listen and wouldn't. With steps that were heavy because of her tough leather riding boots, she sprinted for the pasture and the bushes and shrubs and trees beyond. She was panting for breath as she raced through the darkness, intent on finding cover before Dacian Kendrick could reach her.

"Kristin!" he yelled as he guided Molly around, flashing the lantern here and there, hunting. "Would you come out? This isn't funny. Don't you realize that I'm responsible for you? You're on ranch property."

Kristin pinched her lips shut and said not a word.

"Kristin, please. You don't know your way around. There are animals. And you shouldn't be stumbling around in the dark among the rattlesnakes. Be a good girl, you little fool, and I'll take you home."

For a moment Kristin was tempted. But then she decided she'd rather take her chances with the snakes. She cowered in the bushes until Dace returned to his house after putting a triumphantly nickering Molly back in her paddock. Then he roared away in his Corvette.

Kristin got up, stretching the kinks out of her spine. She looked at Molly, silhouetted in the moonlight, and she was tempted to saddle her up and strike out for the Circle K.

Two things stopped her.

One, Molly probably wouldn't go.

And two, it would provide Dacian Kendrick the right to add "horse thief" to her lengthening list of supposed transgressions.

Grimly Kristin faced toward the lights glaring into the sky to the north and started out walking, step by careful step.

With any luck, she'd be home by dawn.

Chapter Eleven

Minutes after Dace's Corvette shot down his driveway toward the main road, Kristin started walking, intent on putting distance between them before he could return to hunt her down and shepherd her back to the Circle K Ranch like a wayward, incompetent child.

The first few minutes after she'd stepped from the perimeter of Dace's immaculately tended lawn and into the increasingly tangled wilds of the vast pastureland, she was in misery.

Every time a twig snapped, an insect rasped, an owl hooted, a coyote yipped, or a dust devil riffled through the prairie grass, causing it to crackle and saw around her legs, she almost jumped out of her skin. She gasped with alarm, whimpering, when she considered rattlesnakes and other unseen threats hidden by the night.

At the thought of a thick-bodied, diamond-backed reptile silently slithering toward her, forked tongue flitting, rattles whirring a warning, her heart pounded with fright and spurts of adrenaline shot into her system, causing her fingertips to tingle from the effect.

But then she thought about how God was sovereign over His Creation, how He had dominion over all. That He knew when a sparrow fell and the exact number of hairs on her head. Everything was in the Lord's control and no evil would touch her unless the Lord allowed the event to take place in order that He might work good with it one day. There was nothing for her to fear, and she prayed for God to give her relief from the fright she felt welling inside, threatening to erupt with just the right squirmy, startling nocturnal catalyst.

It was enough to make her plaintively cry out for Dace, to beg him to come rescue her, except that he'd already departed as if she were not worth the effort. She'd chosen her course of action; now she had no alternative but to follow it through until she arrived back at the ranch under her own power.

Kristin sighed, halted to get her bearings, then stood, resolute, as she mentally mapped out her strategy. She had a long hike ahead of her, and it would become an almost unbearable ordeal if she attempted it in a state of near hysteria.

"Stop it," she muttered to herself as she tried to convince herself that she had nothing to fear but her own self-induced terrors. She prayed for God to give her courage and serenity.

Instead it seemed to her that she began to recall what Dace had told her about animals in the wild, how they didn't threaten humans unless they felt threatened themselves or were protecting their young. She realized that they, even snakes, would hurry from her approach and that her chances of a startling confrontation were almost nil.

Plus, she was well-equipped for the walk back to the woods. She had on almost knee-high tough leather riding boots, and her rugged denim jeans were tucked down inside. She had a denim jacket against the evening chill and even a small portable spray can of mosquito repellent in her pocket.

Suddenly she felt competent, prepared to cope with almost anything. Or anyone. Except Dace Kendrick.

She suddenly realized that he hadn't just stormed away from his ranch, roaring over the roads in the Corvette because he was piqued with her, but because he was worried and was no doubt at the Circle K Ranch right at that moment, organizing a search party of men on horseback and perhaps even on all-terrain vehicles.

She shuddered at the thought. Her humiliation wouldn't be a matter between her and Dace, it would become public record and probably the talk of the ranch, as workers would be routed from their beds and ordered to go in search of the woman Dace despised, even as he accepted responsibility for her safety.

She'd begun to consider herself an accomplished enough horsewoman, by city slicker standards, and she felt a flush of embarrassment that she'd been bested by a wily old mare, who was as headstrong and singleminded as her owner.

And how shocked she had been to learn that the anonymous ranch owner, the person who shipped the lovable old mare to the Circle K Ranch each summer for a month's use and who lived on an adjoining spread, was none other than Dace Kendrick.

Gradually the facts began to sift through Kristin's mind, and as if she were sorting out data, mentally stacking it in piles, then assembling it in chronological order, she saw the pattern emerge.

And with a startled gasp she realized that she'd been hoodwinked by Dacian's family, just as surely as she'd been outfoxed by that plump, stubborn horse. When she'd given Molly her head, she thought the mare was going to obey and head back to the Circle K, only to realize too late that Molly had taken an alternative route back to the owner she adored.

Kristin had always heard that an individual could fool another person, but that it was impossible to deceive an animal.

At the moment, Kristin thought that Dace was the most impossible man on earth. But obviously Molly thought he was the most wonderful.

"I've heard of horse sense," Kristin mused to herself. "What if she's right?"

Then she realized that both she and Molly were right.

Kristin had to honestly tote up Dace's many wonderful traits, personality aspects that, of course, would cause the old horse he'd probably had since he was a youth to adore him.

Then she every bit as honestly noted his flaws, as if they were jotted in a column in her mind.

While the good traits were many and the flaws were few, she found no comfort in the fact, for the differences that parted them were so serious as to make her all but forget the wonderful moments that they had shared—funny events, tender interludes, heartfelt talks of Christian faith. Kristin's beliefs had solidified and strengthened after Mrs. Stanwyck had helped her to come to know the Lord. Contact with Mandy, Dace, Billy Joe, and others had all had an edifying effect. It was as if all these things were overcome by hurtful memories that had begun compiling since the first moment that they had officially met.

Kristin made steady progress as she strode through the night and reflected on what had taken place. Gradually as she adjusted to the nocturnal sounds in the same way her eyes grew accustomed to the dark, she began to feel as if she were one with the night. Oddly enough Kristin had never felt closer to God, nor more protected by Him, her destiny in His loving care.

Kristin realized that she had to have been heading in a northerly direction for at least the better part of an hour, maybe even more, although it was hard to accurately judge time, as preoccupied as she'd become. It was still too dark to read the face of her watch. To the east a summer moon was rising, pale and coldly white, to cast a thin silvery sheen over the landscape, shedding enough light to inkily outline objects, now that her eyes had grown accustomed to the total dark surrounding her like soft black velvet.

Far away to the north, like a welcoming beacon in a sea of darkness, the outdoor lights of the Circle K Ranch glowed a steady signal, marking her way through the night.

Trying to put the situation with Dace from her mind, Kristin considered what she knew about South Dakota, the wild land she'd come to love and that was as diverse as the people who had settled it.

Bathed in moonlight, she had an appreciation for the timelessness of the land upon which she walked. She thought of the prehistoric animals whose fossils could be found preserved in rocks, with their presence revealed by the steady, eternal flow of water, the force eventually unearthing ancient history to mankind who mastered the land at the moment, marveling at their Creator's timeless touch.

She felt a sudden empathy with the pioneers, Dace's ancestors he'd spoken of, who'd stood on the land, perhaps venturing across the terrain beneath the moon's guiding light because it had been too hot for the women, children, and animals to trek on in Conestogas during the daytime summer hours. Then to proceed west a few more miles, a journey that had probably taken days, only to confront lands so bad, the Badlands, that in despair they'd turned back to settle on grounds more hospitable.

She considered Dace's ancestors and had an idea of the kind of people they'd been, judging by the legacy they'd passed down through the years.

Doubtless, they were a people who didn't give up. When they wanted something, they went after it. And if at first they didn't succeed, they picked themselves up, dusted off, and tried again, having faith in a good outcome. Knowing that with the Lord, joy would follow sorrow, laughter would come in the wake of tears, fulfillment after a time of disappointment, trials and tribulations that God had allowed that it might make straighter the journey of faith that led to peace everlasting.

That is, except where she was concerned. It was unlikely that Dacian Kendrick would ever give her a second chance.

Her steps drew to an abrupt stop and she almost toppled with surprise. Instead, wearily sinking to a boulder that still retained the afternoon sun's blazing heat, she realized that she'd not only been tricked by Molly, but she'd been bested by Melanie and Dr. Bill as well. They'd used the old horse as their most willing conspirator to force her to a confrontation with Dace in hopes that instead of both of them retreating into hurt and disillusionment, they would actually communicate, allowing their mutual interests and shared faith to draw them together for a united walk through life.

Kristin couldn't help uttering a weak laugh when she looked back and, with good old twenty-twenty hindsight, saw with such clarity what had not been obvious until a moment before.

She remembered Dr. Bill's questions, his concerns, and how he'd tried to plead Dace's case and explain his brother to a woman who'd already come to know him so well and to understand him, on down to his occasional fits of irrational unreasonableness.

" 'Doctor's orders,' indeed!" Kristin muttered, sniffing, and idly wondered if she should jokingly tease Bill about considering a malpractice suit for so idly tinkering with matters of the heart, reminding him that a physician was to do a patient no harm.

But, then, he hadn't, she realized. Dr. Bill Kendrick, as the excellent physician that he was, had simply been trying to promote the healing of a relationship, prescribing the only treatment that he saw as having a chance at working a miracle cure.

And Melanie had been a most cooperative nurse practitioner!

Kristin had promised Dr. Bill that she'd consider starting to take rides in the evening. But in truth she knew that that's as far as she'd have taken the matter, mere consideration. She wouldn't have proceeded as far as direct action.

So Melanie, like a nurse bearing an antidote, had, on doctor's orders, appeared on Kristin's doorstep, prepared to see to it that Kristin took her treatments, administering a 'dose of Molly,' knowing it would take effect quickly.

It hadn't been happenstance that Melanie had selected Molly for Kristin, she realized. And it hadn't been an accident that they'd ridden out in the direction they had. Nor, Kristin realized, had it been a matter of fate that Tony had come riding out looking for Melanie. The pretty woman's fiance was surely but another name to add to the list of conspirators.

No doubt they had hoped to force a confrontation and had believed that if Kristin and Dace would just face one another, talk like adults, and with initial fiery angers cooled, *communicate*, the problems and misunderstandings would be resolved. They had hoped for peace and unity for the people at the Circle K Ranch who had been caught in the unpleasant situation of being expected to take sides by the headstrong man and the sensitive woman pitted against one another.

Momentarily, she felt a twinge of regret that she had turned tail and run away from Dace, instead of boldly facing him, *making* him listen to her as it was now so apparent others wanted her to do.

And, as she arose from the boulder and continued walking, a small part of her wondered if he would've listened to her.

She would never forget the expressions that had washed across his face, evolving like shapes in a kaleidoscope, as one emotion gave way to another, seeming to convey everything on the spectrum in a split second.

She'd seen concern when he'd believed Molly had accomplished what would have been nothing short of an equine kidnapping.

She'd seen relief when he'd located Molly's rider, unhurt.

His look had then become shock when he'd focused and recognized the features of Molly's hostage as *her*.

That brief expression had merged with a look that had momentarily sent

Kristin's heart soaring, because it had been a fleeting glimpse of what looked like tender, relieved love, before it was quickly and determinedly replaced by a look of angry contempt, and he'd begun flinging accusations about her actions based on his experiences with her sister.

But what haunted her was that when she had confronted him face-to-face, he'd almost looked overjoyed at seeing her until he forcibly reminded himself that she was a woman he did not like and could not trust. No doubt he believed her professions of a shared faith in Christ a sham, not a maturing way of life and belief. It was that look that had caused Kristin to turn on her heel and run into the night.

And without glancing back, without having to, she knew that the look cast in her direction had then become one of utter exasperation that she'd fled from him, obviously willing to take her chances with snakes rather than remain another moment with him.

The moon was directly overhead when Kristin topped a bluff. She paused to catch her breath after making the uphill climb and was quite certain that she was halfway back to the Circle K Ranch. Although she'd made good time, it was still a long walk ahead of her.

When she saw lights in the distance, roving, jerking about, panning across the terrain, flitting into the sky, she realized that Dace had routed out employees and they had fanned out on the all-terrain vehicles possessed by the Circle K to be used to haul feed, save steps in doing necessary chores, and search for lost riders as they were now doing for her.

Kristin kept walking. The small but rough and durable little vehicles were noisy enough so that she could hear their approach well in advance as they drew near her and she could take evasive actions. She wanted to walk back under her own power, not be taken back, feeling like a recalcitrant child forced to surrender.

Kristin hadn't traveled more than an additional quarter of a mile before she heard unfamiliar sounds in the dark, coming from behind her. She'd been so intent on monitoring the progress of the search party on the vehicles ahead of her that she hadn't stopped to consider that there was also a search party closing in from behind.

She stood stock still, listening.

Men on horseback! And their positions would be hard to reconnoiter because they were letting their horses pick and choose their way, their eyes as accustomed to the light as Kristin's had become, so that they conserved their flashlight batteries and only flicked their lanterns on when they investigated shapes in the pasture.

Kristin, although she was tired, didn't want to be caught and treated like a disobedient child, especially by Dace, who she sensed was one of the riders who'd mounted up after they'd obviously transported horses by van to his spread to begin a search from that direction.

Quickly, panting from the exertion and tension, her hair whipping back and forth as she scanned the immediate vicinity for a hiding place, she moved toward a large area where brambles, briars, and scruffy brush formed an almost impenetrable thicket. To save face she had no choice but to wedge herself into the underbrush, biting her lip to hold back cries of pain as thorns raked at her exposed skin and tangled in her hair, harshly tugging it every time she moved a bit to burrow deeper and wait for the riders to pass by.

"If she's come this way," Dace said in a tired voice, "she must be part Indian, because she's moved through with the grace and finesse of a warrior."

"My thoughts exactly," another rider, who Kristin recognized as Billy Joe, agreed.

"Let's pause a moment to let the horses rest," Dace suggested.

The saddle leathers creaked as the two dismounted.

Kristin frowned and gave an almost inaudible sigh over the fact that they'd accidentally selected the location where she'd hidden herself to confer before they moved out again.

Or was it simply another one of Dace's tricks? Did they know *exactly* where she was? Was Dace toying with her, as he'd probably done with the information being compiled by the private investigator, before Janice's telephone call had presented incontrovertible evidence to confront her with?

The horses stood so close to her that she could hardly breathe for the musky, sweaty odors as they stomped, steadily swished their coarse tails at flies, and huffed and snorted with impatience.

"Well, we'd better mount up again," Dace said. "Perhaps she hasn't come this far from my spread. But she's a plucky woman, and determined. . ."

"Not to mention probably very angry," Billy Joe softly added. "Mandy's going to be an unhappy woman if we don't find her friend. She wasn't happy that Kristin was given Molly, being as Mandy herself was constantly warned about your old horse."

"It was a trick," Dace said, confirming Kristin's suspicions.

"A trick?"

"Compliments of the Kendrick family. It appears that Melly went to the corral and selected two horses. When she picked out Molly, she was reminded that she wasn't to leave the corrals. And you know how Melanie can be. Sweet as could be, she told the ranch hand in charge to mind his own business, that she knew exactly what she was doing."

Billy Joe began to laugh. "And I reckon she did. It was one way to see to it that you and Kristin started talkin' again."

"But we didn't. Why, I'd hardly opened my mouth before she turned tail and ran."

"Hardly opened your mouth?" Billy Joe echoed, slightly mocking disbelief evident in his tone.

Dace sighed, the sound cutting through the darkness to reach Kristin. "Okay, so I said things I shouldn't have."

"Again?" Billy Joe said softly.

"*Again*," Dace admitted heavily. "And if I don't want to keep doing this to Kristin, I have to get to the bottom of my anger. Tomorrow, when all this is over and I know Kris is safe, I'm making an appointment to talk with Pastor Johnson and get some counseling."

"We'd better start looking for her," Billy Joe said. "Obviously the guys on the ATVs haven't had any luck finding her."

"I don't know how I'll ever forgive myself if something has happened to her," Dacian murmured. Kristin felt her heart melt when she detected the tender concern in his voice that seemed to transcend the emotions he'd feel for just any ranch guest who was lost. "I love her, even though a part of me hasn't wanted to. . . ."

"Aw, I'll bet she's okay. Maybe sittin' on a rock somewhere waiting to be rescued."

"I wish we'd find her. Although I don't know what I'd ever say to her."

Billy Joe made an impatient sound of incredulousness. "Why don't you try starting off with 'I'm sorry'?"

"A good idea," Dace said.

"And then you could get real brave and follow it up with 'I love you. . . .' I know how you feel, God knows, but does she?"

"An even better suggestion," Dace said. "And I really do love her, you know."

"Yeah, I know, boss," Billy Joe said and gave a laugh. "Along with everyone else on the Circle K. The only one who doesn't know how you feel about her now is Kristin. And you, before you came to your senses. You now realize it. So convince Kristin."

"Let's move out," Dace softly ordered. "I've got to find her and attend to some personal business."

For a moment Kristin had been tempted to wriggle from her hiding place, revealing herself to them as she'd probably risk spooking their horses. But then she stayed where she was, realizing that she wasn't quite ready to surrender yet. She wanted, instead, to walk through the silent night, treasuring in her heart the things she'd overheard Dace confide to Billy Joe Blaylock.

By the time she'd walked back to the Circle K, perhaps she would know her own heart and have it finalized in her mind just exactly how to deal with the upcoming confrontation that she knew she was destined to have with Dace Kendrick, the big boss of the Circle K Ranch, who could but with the right words become the sole owner of her trusting woman's heart.

When enough time passed, Kristin decided that the riders must have given up and called off any further search until daylight.

Kristin found that her steps seemed to slow as she neared the headquarters, and she recognized her own reluctance to face Dace. She wouldn't be able to bear it if instead of expressing relief, he thundered at her out of the grateful emotion that she wasn't hurt and had scared him so badly that he momentarily lost control again.

As dawn approached, the sky began to lighten as the moon started to sink into the western sky, although the sun had not begun to appear over the horizon.

Able to see much better in the dim morning light, Kristin looked across the hazy pasture and realized that she wasn't very far from the headquarters. When the sky brightened as morning drew nigh, the dusk-to-dawn utility lights that made the Circle K glow like a diamond against the black sky and had served as a beacon to her disappeared.

She glanced at her watch. It was four-thirty in the morning, and she considered what was probably going on at the ranch. The riders who'd been out during the night were probably in the dining hall eating a hearty breakfast, drinking down cups of strong black coffee to shake away their weariness and fuel them to begin another search for her once daylight arrived.

She hurried her steps, wanting to reach the ranch before she inconvenienced them anymore.

As she topped a rise and looked down upon the Circle K headquarters, she thought she'd never seen such a glorious sight, for at that moment the sun had swiftly risen and had cast a fiery glow over the side of one of the buildings that served as children's quarters.

She paused to enjoy the serene moment when suddenly she realized that the orange glow wasn't the sun's reflection. She glanced to the east and discovered to her horror that the sun hadn't arisen yet, and the horizon was showing only the shelly pink promise of a beautiful day.

"No!" Kristin shrieked.

Adrenaline shot through her system again, giving her the swiftness and strength that she'd never have dreamed she could've mustered as her numb legs picked up speed and her boots pounded over the rough terrain. She screamed warnings with every gasping breath she took.

"Fire!" she cried. *"FIRE!"*

Couldn't they hear her? she wondered, almost sobbing in frustration. She increased her speed, almost tripping over her own feet as forward momentum increased.

And the children! Couldn't they feel the heat? Smell the smoke? At the thought of them burning in their beds or suffocating, dying from smoke inhalation, their parents stunned and shocked beyond coping, with a guilty Dace Kendrick forever buried beneath a mantle of crushing unmet responsibility that would ruin what days remained in his life, Kristin found the reserves to run even faster.

She leaped over low thickets of rough grass, dodged prairie dog holes, and thudded on. Her legs felt as if they were lead, and her ribs stabbed her lungs with every breath. She had a stitch in her side that almost made her cry out with the intensity if she hadn't been screaming warnings to those below. They were either sleeping so soundly that they did not hear or were listening to the morning farm forecasts on the radio as their coffee cups banged, the cooks made noise from the kitchen, and the cutlery of hungry men clanked against the durable stoneware plates to obliterate her desperate cries.

Kristin felt as if she were going to pass out when she neared the dining hall, gasping for breath as she raced down the deserted sidewalks and across the empty parking lot.

"Fire!" she tried to scream, but it came out a rusty croak instead.

She looked toward the building and realized just how fast she had run when she saw the flames just beginning to lick at the structure that housed the children, with tongues of fire intent on consumption.

She lunged for the door of the dining hall just as ranch hands prepared to troop out. The force of impact against the door almost knocked her over.

"Good news, boss! She's back!"

They gasped, and everyone started to talk at once and barrage her with questions as they saw her, disheveled, exhausted, almost unable to make sounds as she wildly pointed, trying to signal to them that *she* was all right, but there were children who were not!

"Fire!" she hoarsely croaked.

They looked at each other with uncomprehending amazement, not understanding what she meant. Then the breeze fanned dark smoke toward them as it rolled along on the wind, low to the ground, thick, menacing.

"Oh dear Lord! Smoke! There's a fire!"

"The children—!" Kristin gasped.

Dace rushed past her as if she wasn't even there, yelling over his shoulder for the cook to call the fire department and get pumpers dispatched to the ranch right away.

The cowboys spread like scurrying ants, running toward the extinguishers that had been strategically placed around the ranch while others bolted toward the cabins, praying under their breaths. They fumbled for master keys to let them into the children's rooms so that they could wake the youngsters and prod them toward the door and safety or carry out those who were too groggy to walk.

Women from the ranch staff came running, and they marshalled the children into a stunned group, watching over them.

"Everything's going to be all right," a motherly worker assured and hugged the children nearest her close to her comforting form.

Kristin joined the women, trying to help calm the children, most of whom were shivering from the tension of the horrifying sight of the building shooting flames high into the sky as thick, oily black smoke plumed into the air.

"Don't worry about your clothes, honey," a worker assured a blubbering child. "Why, Mr. Kendrick has insurance so that your mommy will be able to go to the store and buy you beautiful outfits. Nicer than the ones you've been wearing. Brand, spanking new!"

"Sure," another added. "We'll be measuring you children, taking you to town, and buying you shoes before the day is out. We can replace everything. Anything you've lost, we'll get something like it for you."

"But no one can make me another Pooh Bear like Grannie made me," a little girl whimpered. "No one. 'Cause it wasn't store bought. Grannie told me that it was the only one in the whole world like it. She said that I was the only one in the world exactly like me, and my Pooh Bear was that way, too."

"Well, sweetheart, I'll bet that your grannie knows just how much you loved that Pooh Bear, and she'll get out her knitting needles, scissors, fabric, stuffing, and whatever she used, and she'll make you another Pooh just like the one you had."

"She can't," the little girl said, and then began to sob as she realized the full impact of what was happening. " 'C. . .cause Grannie's dead. And now Po. . . Pooh's going to die if I don't save him—"

It took the jolted adults a moment to understand what the child meant, and before they could react, the small child had slipped from the group and begun running toward the room she had just vacated.

"No!" Kristin cried, sprinting after the little girl. "You can't go in there! You can't!"

The child, surely no more than seven years old and scrawny because she'd been so sick, stood in front of the flaming row of once lovely rooms that now were going up in flames, unit after unit.

"Stop!" Kristin ordered as the little girl hesitated.

Kristin thought that she was obeying, but then she realized that her momentary pause had resulted only because she was confused and she wasn't certain which room was hers, as the doors had been left open and there were no helpful numbers to guide her.

Then apparently recognizing something inside the room that was fast becoming illuminated by flames, she darted through the open doorway as the windows gaped blankly, like the vacant eyes in a skull.

Kristin rushed into the unit, trying to grasp the child as she rummaged through the plunder created by the children since the housekeeping staff had cleaned the room the day before. She desperately searched for Pooh.

"Where's Pooh?!" she cried. *"Pooh! Where are you?"*

The child's face was glowing from the flames, drenched in quick sweat from the heat. Fire had crawled up the wallpaper and was encircling the door. Heat radiated from the ceiling, and Kristin realized that at any instant the roof could come crashing in, burying them beneath a flaming pyre.

The draft created by the inferno was so hot that each breath was agonizing, and Kristin's eyes involuntarily closed against the scorching heat. She felt her hair catch on fire, saw the sparkling effect as the child's hair singed, too, making the child shriek and dance about in hysterical fright.

"Come here!" Kristin cried.

The child, suddenly paralyzed with fear, thinking she was in trouble and about to get a spanking for disobeying an adult, evaded Kristin.

Kristin was crying from pain, shock, and frustration. She dove toward the child, grasped her, and the little girl's nightgown tore, almost freeing her, but Kristin wadded the material around her hands, pulled the little girl toward her, then stumbled toward the only faint opening she could see in what had become a wall of brilliant orange, almost blindingly bright flames.

Kristin's legs felt as if they could no longer move as the heat seared up through the heavy soles of her boots. She heard a rumbling sound, knew that it was the harbinger of tragedy, as the nails and bolts holding the rafters groaned and threatened to pull loose, allowing the roof to crash down as support was destroyed by the fire's devastating force.

"Oh, God," she cried. She thought of the little girl's parents, she thought of Dace's grief, the fact that the child had a life to live, perhaps a man whom she'd grow up and one day love as Kristin knew she cared in that special way for Dace. "Please, Lord, no! Oh. . .give me the strength I need."

From somewhere deep within she found the will to plunge toward the wall of flame in front of her, as she was surrounded by fire on all four sides.

Then there appeared a dark staggering form, silhouetted in the flames, as a man bolted ahead, not allowing himself to be driven back by the fire that had become out of control.

Kristin heard mechanical noises, engines whining, and she realized that the pumpers from town were there. There were hissing noises, steam arose, engulfing them, as the firefighters created a wall of water in hopes that it would allow them to walk through the flames alive.

She took a step toward the man—Dace?—surely Dace.

Arms reached out to her. So close, but still seeming so far, far away.

And just when she felt that she should surely die, she clung to the child, intent on protecting her even in their last moments, as the little girl tenaciously hugged her neck, burying her face against the hollow of Kristin's throat the way she'd someday dreamed her own child would.

Kristin felt her oxygen-starved body start to waver, topple, and she was caught in strong arms and pulled toward safety, where suddenly all became dark, wet, and she felt herself buffeted mercilessly by the force of the water that made the skin that moments before had blistered with heat grow so cool that she began shivering.

"Get blankets! Keep her warm. An ambulance is on the way. Don't let her slide into shock from the trauma."

As they wrapped her tightly in the blanket, Kristin tried to protest as the searing heat returned to her skin.

Someone tenderly dabbed her face.

And the touch was cool. . .so blessedly cool.

A moment later she heard the child's cry, knew that she was safe. And then Kristin heard no more.

❧

Kristin didn't know how much time had passed before she flickered her eyes open when a cool compress was pressed to her cheeks. Then she felt the searing pain.

"Looks like it's time for another hypo," a crisp, efficient voice said.

"Where am I?" she whispered through lips that felt so dry and parched.

"You're in the hospital—"

Kristin strained to get up, but the nurse's hands eased her back down.

"You're all right. Everyone's fine. The little girl is okay. She's in better shape than you are, Miss Allen," she murmured.

"Thank God," Kristin said, and began to cry with relief.

"Go ahead and cry. It'll maybe make you feel better," the nurse said. "You've been through a real ordeal. Dace told me what you did—"

"Dace!" Kristin gasped.

"He's been waiting impatiently to see you. Do you feel up to receiving company?"

Kristin's hands touched her cheek, her hair, and she felt a sinking sensation. She'd detected blisters. And a charred odor clung to her. "I must look a sight."

"I'm sure you've looked better," the nurse said. "But I know that seeing you alive is the most beautiful sight Dace Kendrick has ever seen. He's got a few blisters himself to mar those handsome features. . . ."

"Show him in," Kristin said, knowing that at last the moment had come.

A moment later, his towering presence seemed to fill the doorway. He slid off his hat and came into the room, his attitude almost reverent.

"Hello, Dace," she whispered as he stepped to her side.

"Kristin, oh Kris. How can I ever make it up to you for being such a fool?"

She remembered Billy Joe's advice out on the lonesome prairie, as she'd been hidden a mere pace or two away, as the man she loved admitted his mistakes.

"You can start by saying, 'I'm sorry,' " she suggested.

"I am sorry," he whispered, seating himself on the edge of the bed, taking her left hand in his. "More sorry than you'll ever know. But somehow saying that I'm sorry doesn't seem like enough."

"It's not," Kristin said. "I have an even better idea. You might try saying, 'I love you.' "

"I have a disturbing sense of *déja vu*."

"We were close then, Dace, although we were never so far apart, it would seem. I heard what you said, what Billy did."

He gave a relieved smile. "Then you know I'm serious about getting to the root of my anger. I do love you, you know. You have the capacity to irritate me and inspire me like no other woman I've ever met."

"Not even Janice?" Kristin asked, helpless to contain the question, even as she hated to raise her name at a moment like this.

"Who's Janice?" Dace said. "It seems that nowadays when I look at you, Kristin, I don't see Janice or her look-alike. I see only Kristin Allen. . .the woman I love and want more than any other gal I've ever known."

"Oh Dace. . . ," Kristin sighed as tears of happiness came to her eyes. "I love you, too. I love you so very, very much."

"Enough to marry me?" he murmured.

Wordlessly Kristin nodded. From the pocket of his jeans he produced the Kendrick family ring, an heirloom handed down to the eldest son, to give his beloved bride.

"Yes. Oh my, *yes!*" Kristin breathed the happy agreement as he slipped the ring on the finger of her left hand that was closest to her heart.

"It's a perfect fit," he observed.

She squeezed his hand. "We're going to be a perfect fit. Forever and ever."

"When are we going to get married?" he asked.

"That's up to you, darling," she said.

"If I had my way, we'd elope on this very day. But the doctor says you've got to remain in the hospital overnight."

"And you're such an impatient man," she clucked in sympathy.

"But so willing to wait for the woman I love, because I know that now we have a fresh beginning. We'll arrange to be married soon enough."

"Ummmm. . .there's always tomorrow. . . ," Kristin reminded.

Free to Love

Doris English

Chapter One

Dread lay inside Stephanie Haynes like a weight of cold steel as she sat alone on her small balcony and stared into the mist that shrouded the boulder-strewn New England coast. Needles of morning light penetrated the grayness as the sun struggled to bring in the new day. This greeting of the morning was her daily ritual, but today anxiety clung to her like a rain-soaked blanket.

The aroma of fresh coffee wafted through the air, and she turned toward a soft rustling noise behind her. Stephanie's eyes met the steady gaze of Martha Newton, her aging housekeeper, who stood in the open French doors separating the balcony from Stephanie's bedroom. She held a breakfast tray in her hands.

Martha set her heavy burden down on a green wrought-iron table beside Stephanie. "I heard you up, child, and knew you'd be needing this. With all the decisions you'll be making today, you'll need every ounce of strength you can muster."

"Decisions? Seems they have been made for me." Stephanie smiled wryly.

"The good Lord always gives us an option," Martha responded softly.

Silence held sway for a moment, as the steaming coffee added its vapor to the mist surrounding them and its pleasant odor to the pungent smells of sea and morning. Her voice husky, Stephanie responded, "I do have one, but I have a difficult time believing it's from Him."

"If you mean selling Boulder Bay to that Jay Dalton, then there must be another you haven't considered," Martha replied with a snort.

"There is, lose it to the bank." Stephanie turned toward the older woman and away from the roar of the invisible breakers, discouragement etched in the fatigue binding her young face.

"If you could just hold out a few more months, surely the inn would be on a paying basis," Martha encouraged.

One corner of Stephanie's mouth curved slightly upward in a sad, patient smile. "I can't. I don't have enough operating capital to see us through the month. The money I borrowed for renovations is due, and the bank has turned down an extension."

"Something about that situation sounds peculiar to me. This place should be ample collateral, and your plan to turn it into an inn is a good one. I thought banks were interested in sound investments." Martha's fine brows were drawn almost together in a disapproving frown.

"They seem to think my inexperience hinders the soundness of it."

"Pshaw! What's that got to do with it? You're a hard worker, I can vouch for that. I know the Lord don't want you to lose your home place to the bank. Why, it's been in the family for generations," Martha insisted.

Stephanie smiled sadly. "Ancestors don't count with a bank, profits do."

"Are you sure it's not someone who has his eye on this property trying to force you out?"

"I don't think so. It does take more than just hard work to make a business venture successful," Stephanie explained wistfully.

If only her father had followed through with his dream of turning Boulder Bay into a bed and breakfast! He, however, had refused to face the inevitable: The upkeep on the old inn was too expensive unless it could bring in a substantial income.

Martha, tall and slender as a willow reed, pursed her lips and sat down in a wrought-iron dining chair beside the table. The intricate acorn designs in the back of the chair held the morning moisture like slanted miniature finger bowls. Perched on the edge of the seat, her back ramrod straight, she poured the rich, mahogany beverage into a translucent china cup that had been Stephanie's great-grandmother's.

Martha cupped both her hands over the steaming cup to warm them. A long silence reigned before she remarked thoughtfully, "When you got that loan, Stephanie, I felt uneasy about the short time limit on it."

"That's all the bank would consider, but they did assure me that an extension would be no problem." Stephanie sounded perplexed.

"No one could finish what had to be done around here in six months. And on top of that, they wouldn't loan you nearly what you needed, while demanding the whole place as collateral," Martha insisted.

"The contractor didn't live up to his promised schedule, and then unexpected repairs cost more than anticipated. I guess I should have sold it." Stephanie shrugged her shoulders in defeat.

"Sold the old Haynes home place? Heaven forbid."

"What do you think I'm going to have to do today?" Stephanie asked, her brow creased, her wide blue eyes cloudy.

"Not sell it to Jay Dalton. Your parents, God rest their souls, would turn over in their graves if they knew a man like him was going to own Boulder Bay. Anyway, I heard he isn't buying it to live in," Martha rejoined as she reached over to replenish her cup.

"He told me he wanted it for a summer home. Don't you believe him?" Stephanie questioned, her eyes narrowed.

"No. I'd take anything that man said with a grain of salt until I had more proof than just his word. You just be careful about him."

Stephanie looked at the older woman, warm affection lighting her eyes. "If I sell, then I can salvage something from it, enough to live on until I can get a job. He's promised a place for you and John."

"What if we donated our services to you? We have a little nest egg we could loan you until you could get on your feet. . . ."

"No," Stephanie interrupted.

"Why not?" Martha's quiet voice insisted.

"I won't take advantage of you, that's why not. The decision was mine, and I will not allow you to suffer for my mistakes."

"I won't listen to talk like that, Stephanie Haynes. No one knows better than a bank that it takes time and money to get a business started. Surely they'll give you an extension, but if not, then use our money. Anything to hold out a little bit longer. A little time, maybe more advertising, and I know we'd make it."

"But I haven't any more time. Even if we were ready to open right now, which we aren't, there's nothing to carry us until we're on a paying basis."

"I don't know why you're so stubborn about letting John and me help you." Pain was reflected in her eyes.

"Well, I can't let you take that risk. Boulder Bay has got to go. This is, after all, just a house. Sometimes life requires us to give up things that are important to us." Stephanie's brave words denied the bereavement she felt as a fresh onslaught of pain surged through her. She closed her eyes tightly, willing the truth away before her beloved friend could see it.

But Martha did see, and her gray eyes clouded as tears threatened. "Don't deny your feelings, my dear. This house and us are all that you have of your past. You've been too busy to let the grief of your parents' death catch up with you. Now it's all wrapped up together."

Stephanie's mouth felt dry and faintly tasted of salt from her tearful struggle throughout the night. Now her eyes stung as they held Martha's. "What am I ever going to do without your wisdom?"

Martha answered briskly, "You're not. We're family, and you aren't rid of us yet, little lady."

Stephanie smiled through a mist clouding her eyes. "Is that a fact?"

"Sure is. Tell you what, since you don't seem much in the mood for food, why don't you go down to the cove for a swim? Always did make you feel better. Now, mind you, be careful, it's a lonely place," Martha cautioned.

"Maybe it would help. I'll be careful. Anyway, since Dad died, no one but us even knows about the place. Maybe a swim will get the cobwebs out."

Martha smiled as she went out the door. "You need all the cobwebs out today, girl."

Stephanie was into her suit and out of the house in record time. The sun had won its victory, and now her world shimmered in a soft golden radiance. She ran toward the bluff, which towered over the crashing breakers, and paused at the edge. A brisk breeze ruffled her long, silvery-blond hair, caressing her skin. To shield herself from the salty spray, she wrapped her arms around herself, hugging her form-fitting white swimsuit. Her eyes, now the color of the sky above, searched the horizon as if hoping to find in the clouds the answer to her dilemma.

She sighed and turned toward the house behind her. The brilliant morning light reflected off fresh paint and polished windows. From the widow's walk to the broad front porch with spindled railings and ornate fretwork, she took in every detail. She lingered, reluctant to tear herself away.

Finally she shook her head and took a deep breath, relishing the faint fragrance of an early blooming rose as it mingled with the briny sea. She turned to walk across the cold, smooth rock ledge toward a stone shelf that flared and swept out toward the sea, making a small crescent. Within the inner arc of the crescent, the path led downward through an opening like the eye of a needle, between huge boulders, then dropped steeply in natural cuts resembling shallow steps. The passageway ended at the edge of a secluded inlet of emerald green water.

Stephanie dropped the towel she held loosely in her hand and executed a perfect dive into the deep pool just below her. She surfaced and turned over onto her back, letting the warm sun caress her face. Minutes slipped away before the knot in her stomach eased and peace usurped anxiety.

Here in her own private cove her father had taught her to swim; here at Boulder Bay he had taught her about a God of love who watched over her and wanted to guide her. Stephanie knew then that God had calmed her fears.

She rolled over in the water and put her head down, channeling her newly found energy into slow, powerful strokes. The water barely rippled as she glided through the pool. She relished the gentle resistance, the challenge of her body against its silken embrace. At last ready to face the day, she reached out for the handholds, chiseled out years before.

Instead of touching smooth stone, strong hands grabbed hers and lifted her out of the water. Startled, Stephanie looked up into the bluest eyes she had ever encountered.

"I didn't know we had mermaids in the area." His voice, deep and resonant, bounced off the rock wall while his eyes danced with merriment.

Speechless, Stephanie strained to pull away from the stranger, but he held her firmly in his grip. One small foot landed on the narrow step and then the other as he swung her into the steps below him. When she gained her balance, he loosened his hold.

"Where did you come from, and who are you?" she inquired, her voice weak with apprehension.

"Lancelot, at your service. I rescue pretty maids, er, mermaids, that is," he replied with a crooked grin.

"I didn't need rescuing," she offered weakly. Alarm and curiosity battled in Stephanie's pounding heart. He released her hands.

"Perhaps not, but would you rob me of that pleasure and cheat both of us?"

Stephanie ignored his question, retorting sharply, "I don't know what you're doing here, but you are trespassing. This is private property, very private, in fact."

"Oh, not really, I have business here. I just didn't know it would be so pleasant."

"The only business you could have here would be at my invitation. I'm positive I didn't invite you."

Laughter lines crinkled at the corner of his eyes. "That's only because you didn't know me."

"Since I don't know you, would you be good enough to leave? You're blocking my exit, and I'm in a hurry." Her teeth began to chatter as rivulets of cold water ran down her body and formed puddles on the hard stone.

"You didn't seem in a hurry."

Stephanie held his eyes while her mind groped. She was alone in this hidden cove; no one could hear her if she cried out. Yet something about this stranger with electric blue eyes and sun-streaked hair intrigued more than frightened her.

"I watched you from there." He pointed to a shelf in the cliff. "You passed me and didn't even glance my way. Such deep thoughts!"

His eyes held hers. Her heart thudded strangely.

"I didn't expect an intruder."

"I'm intruding?"

She nodded, adding softly, "And now you're detaining me. Please let me pass."

The one-sided grin again parted his face as mischief burned in his eyes. "Come ahead."

Undaunted, the stranger stood with his feet firmly planted on the steps above her, leaving no room for escape.

Anger stirred in Stephanie, mysteriously mixing with fascination. Her flush deepened as she clinched her hand into a tight fist.

Obviously enjoying his advantage, the intruder crossed his arms and pursed his lips. Then tilting his head to the right, he calmly surveyed her from head to foot. He smiled slightly and nodded in a gesture of approval.

Fury blazed in Stephanie's narrowed eyes as she lifted her chin defiantly. She had two choices. She could continue standing here so close she felt the heat from his sun-warmed body or retreat to the pool below. Not one to retreat, she reached up and grabbed for her towel now draped across the man's bare, bronzed shoulder. The violent movement proved too much for her narrow footing. Losing her balance, she fell backward, and the bright world of sun and sea gave way to silent blackness.

Chapter Two

"Stephanie Haynes, what are you doing out of bed?" Martha's question seemed to echo off the walls of the airy Victorian bedroom. "You just turn right around and get yourself settled back in that bed of yours. Doc Andres said you're to take it easy for the next few days."

"Take it easy? What happened?" Stephanie rubbed her head gingerly, her hand encountering a mass of wet curls.

"You had a nasty fall. Don't you remember?"

"No, at least I don't remember falling, only. . ." Stephanie hesitated, unwilling to reveal more.

"Only what?"

"Oh, nothing. How did I fall?"

"When you went swimming. I shouldn't have suggested you go off by yourself. That always has worried me, but you were in such a state this morning and a swim always does you so much good." She paused with a long sigh, regret etched in her face. "If that Mr. Donovan hadn't been there to rescue you, then you'd not be worrying about anything else."

"Mr. Donovan rescued me? I don't know any Mr. Donovan." A puzzled frown wrinkled her brow as something in her subconscious tried to surface.

"Well, I don't either, but the good Lord surely sent him along at the right time. You know, the Good Book says the Lord looks after widows and orphans. All I know is I'm glad He sent that nice man your way just in time." Martha seemed to breathe a sigh of relief.

Suddenly with blinding clarity the brilliant blue eyes and laughing mouth of the morning took on substance. Weakly, Stephanie sat down on the bright-flowered chintz boudoir chair. "What did this rescuing angel look like?"

"Hmm, he was tall, real tall, berry brown skin with red-blond hair and blue eyes, the kind that send shock waves through a body." Martha felt her cheeks blush as if the handsome stranger were in the room.

"Some rescuing angel! He's the reason I fell. Didn't you wonder how he just *happened* to be there when I needed help?"

"Never thought much about it. Seems to me the Lord provides in strange and wondrous ways. I figured He knew you'd be needing help so He just sent it on ahead."

"Martha, I hate to dampen your faith, but the man caused me to fall," insisted Stephanie, her mind clamoring with the morning's events.

"Well, 'pears to me you're up here in this room and not at the bottom of the ocean," Martha retorted, unconvinced.

Stephanie stared at the older woman, nettled by her simple explanation. "If you could have seen your good-looking angel a few minutes ago, you wouldn't be so certain who sent him."

The slender young woman took a deep breath and continued, her eyes pleading. "He nearly scared me to death. I didn't know he was anywhere around until I started to get out of the water. There he was, like some unwelcome, arrogant apparition, watching me swim. Furthermore, he blocked my path, refusing to leave. When I tried to pass him, my foot slipped, and that's the last thing I remember."

"All the same, he saved your life."

Exasperated, Stephanie responded shortly, "Didn't you hear anything I said? If he hadn't been there, I wouldn't have fallen."

"Now we don't know that for sure, do we? All we do know is if he hadn't been there, you wouldn't be here now."

Recognizing the impossibility of convincing Martha of anything once her mind was made up, Stephanie asked, "Who is this 'angel' and what was he doing here?"

"Child, I didn't have time to ask him all that. I was too busy getting my heart to settle down when I looked at you all limp and dead looking in his arms. Then I called the doctor and Mr. Donovan left, saying he'd see you, us, later. He called about thirty minutes later to see what the doctor said."

"He must not have been too concerned or he would have stayed," Stephanie pointed out wryly.

"No," said Martha hesitantly, her voice less convincing, "he was late for an appointment."

"Don't you think it was a little strange he didn't give you his full name?"

"I was so flustered, perhaps he did and I just can't recall."

"Probably not. He knew he had some responsibility in that accident."

"Well, just leave be. You're safe, and I'm more thankful than you could ever know. Me and John never had any children of our own and living here with you, watching you grow up, has made up for it. I can't tell any difference than if I'd really given birth to you. It's just like you are part ours." Martha reached out her hand to touch Stephanie's arm in an uncharacteristic show of affection.

A lump swelled in Stephanie's throat when she encountered the unvarnished love in Martha's eyes. "I know. I couldn't have made it without you. I realize the sacrifices you've made for me, especially after Dad's death and through Mother's illness."

"Sacrifices, humph!" Martha paused and cleared her throat. "I have been giving some more thought about your predicament while you've been laying here so still and helpless in this bed. What if John and I weren't around? You know, we aren't getting any younger! It's time you started thinking about settling down somewhere and raising a family. Let some good man do the worrying for you. Today just proves my point." Martha punctuated the last with a brisk nod of her head.

Stephanie's smile faded and a guarded look replaced the brief sparkle in her blue eyes. "You're wrong on both counts, Martha. I don't need a man to do the 'worrying' for me. That's what happened to my mother. She couldn't cope when she lost Dad. She lived life from the passenger's side, but that's not for me. I want a career and independence, and that's what I intend to have. If I ever marry, it will be on my own terms, not because I'm looking for someone to take care of me."

"Not even someone like Todd Andrews?"

"Todd?" Warm memories brightened Stephanie's eyes. "Todd was like a big brother to me, but I haven't seen him since I was fifteen and his family moved to Texas. Strange you should mention him, Martha. I received a letter from him yesterday."

"Not so strange. I saw the letter on your desk; made me think of him. Fine youngster as I recall."

"Todd was a dear. Did you know he graduated from law school at the top of his class? He's thinking about going into politics. Yet I wonder if I'd even recognize him. Sometimes the man doesn't fulfill the boyhood promise."

Stephanie stood up slowly and made her way gingerly to the bureau. Opening the top narrow drawer, she released a subtle fragrance of potpourri that Martha had made from crushed rose petals. Beneath the satin container she found a picture of Todd. He had been seventeen when the picture was taken. Tall and slender with broad shoulders, dark hair, a finely shaped nose, and a lopsided grin, he was a handsome teenager. The picture had failed to do justice to him, Stephanie mused silently. She couldn't see that special spark in his laughing eyes.

Martha gave her a quizzical look as she gazed intently at the photograph. "You can't make me believe he hasn't fulfilled all his promise, both in looks and character. His eyes fairly twinkled all the time, especially when he looked at you. Yes, mighty fine boy, that one."

"Martha!"

"Just observing, just observing. Don't get all riled up again. A body's got a right to some observations."

Stephanie's sternness dissolved in laughter. "Anyway, he's probably engaged by now although he didn't mention it in his letter. A while back he was pretty serious with the governor's daughter."

"That wouldn't surprise me any; he would be a real catch for any girl."

"Well, I'm not fishing, now or ever."

Ignoring Stephanie's retort, Martha remarked dryly, "Be that as it may, you'd better quiet down a little if you're going to make your appointment."

"I'd forgotten all about my appointment! Nothing like a brush with death to put things into perspective. What time is it? Oh, I've already missed it!" Stephanie glanced at her watch on the bureau beside her.

The older woman smiled warmly. "I called Mr. Jarrett and told him you couldn't make it this morning and asked him to give you another appointment. He said fine, how about middle of the afternoon? I said only if you felt like it. He sounded kinda eager, if you know what I mean. Said if you couldn't make it down to the bank, perhaps he'd just drop by with the papers, but it's only ten thirty so you have plenty of time to rest. Maybe by this afternoon your headache should be easing off."

"Thank you for taking care of that," Stephanie replied softly, visibly touched by the older woman's care and concern.

"There's a lot more John and I could do for you to ease your burden if you'd let us. Your independence is going to cause you real heartache one of these days, I fear. Why don't you want anyone's help, honey?"

"Mom's love for Dad crippled her. Dad always handled everything, and Mom let him. He was her whole world, and when he died she didn't know how to survive." Involuntarily Stephanie shuddered, remembering her mother and the tragic year after her father's death.

"After she died, I had to make decisions for which they hadn't prepared me. If I'd had any idea about how critical our financial situation was, I'd never have stayed at college the last year. I could have invested that money in Boulder Bay. I guess there's no use in rehashing the 'what might have beens'."

"I told you we would forego our pay until you could afford it," Martha reminded.

"You've already helped out more than you should have." Stephanie closed her eyes, fighting to control her emotions. "I won't, I can't, take advantage of anyone, most of all someone I love." She paused, adding firmly, "This is my problem, not yours. You will not suffer because of my mistakes."

The older woman looked sadly into Stephanie's eyes for a long moment, then walked over to her and patted her hand. Stephanie dropped her head, refusing to look into Martha's eyes. Why was she afraid to accept people's help? Was she, as Martha indicated, afraid to love and be loved?

She shuddered slightly and pulled her light robe closer as the thought sent a chill through her in the room warmed by a late spring sun.

Martha looked pensively at Stephanie, sympathy and affection mingling in her blue-gray eyes. As she walked toward the door, she gave one last gentle command. "You get back in bed. I'll awaken you in plenty of time for lunch and your meeting."

Hours later at Martha's light tap, Stephanie was aroused from a deep sleep. Struggling to dispel the grogginess that plagued her, she opened her eyes wide and stretched her arms high above her head, noting with pleasure that her headache was only a memory.

A pot of steaming tea greeted Stephanie as Martha revealed a lunch tray filled with chicken salad and fresh fruit. Her stomach growled a hearty welcome to the tantalizing aroma of fresh baked bread and apple muffins.

When she had finished, she lingered at the window, putting off her shower, reluctant to get ready for her dreaded appointment. She could see no way out. The quarterly mortgage payment came due on Monday, and not only did she not have the money to pay it, she did not have enough operating capital to carry her through the next month. Once the sale was completed and the mortgage paid off, she would see what was left to finish her education.

She sighed and stood up slowly, pausing to glance in her bureau mirror. *"What will I do when I sell Boulder Bay?"* Shaking her head at her reflection, she wrinkled her nose. *"Mr. Jarrett has been too evasive about how much Mr. Dalton is willing to pay,"* she thought.

After a leisurely shower, Stephanie applied her makeup sparingly. Her even tan emphasized her blue eyes so she only needed a light shadow on her eyelids and a brief touch of mascara. The weight she had lost made her high cheekbones more prominent.

In college she had been dubbed "the beauty," but she never gave it much thought. She was accustomed to the approving appraisal of men, but she chose to ignore such gestures, dismissing them as a fact of life rather than a tribute to her true beauty.

That is, until today. The encounter at the cove disturbed her in more ways than one. True, the invasion of her special sanctuary had annoyed her. But if she admitted the truth, it was the man himself, the way he looked at her and the way she felt when her eyes met his, that was the real problem. Even now the memory brought a blush to her face. She grinned sheepishly. "Martha was right. Those cobalt eyes do send shock waves through you."

His eyes as they met hers were daring, challenging, yet admiring all at the same time. Was that what triggered the angry response so uncharacteristic of her? Or perhaps it was fear, but fear of what? Her safety? The light bronze of Stephanie's face deepened. Or was it her heart? Was she afraid of the woman's heart that thundered a response her actions denied? Did the encounter stir up embers she had buried long ago under heartache and furious activity?

Stephanie paused to consider her reflection before carefully placing the mascara wand into its small cylinder. She tilted her head to one side and leaned closer to the mirror. "Stephanie, my dear, you acted like an outraged spinster," she said out loud with a brittle laugh.

The sound of her voice startled her in the silent room. Yet not even this moment of truth could wipe out the memory of her first encounter with those deep blue eyes. She continued her conversation with the young woman in the mirror. "I'm not some love-starved female who thinks the primary purpose of life is to find a man. So what if he was extraordinary looking, I've never behaved like that before!" She shook her head, denying that the vitality emanating from the man, even his very nearness, had disturbed her.

An overwhelming curiosity forced her to search her image for what had caused him to look at her as he did. After gazing at her reflection for several seconds, she shrugged as she grabbed her shining mass of golden curls and captured them in a tight chignon. *I don't know what he saw because I don't know what he was looking for*, she thought suddenly.

As she surveyed her reflection one last time, a wry smile of acknowledgment looked back. From this day forward, life would never be the same. She turned and reached for a jacket to cover her pale blue linen dress. She squared her shoulders, ready to meet her destiny, oblivious that she was a remarkably beautiful and elegant woman.

Chapter Three

The heavy oak side door leading to the outside groaned as Stephanie pushed it open. She made a mental note to oil the hinges, then winced as she remembered what today would bring. Her dream had ended, or at least it would when she arrived in town and finished her business. After today any repairs or problems would be up to Mr. Jay Dalton.

She looked longingly toward the path that hugged the bluff and made its way into town following the curve of the shore below. A slight smile tugged at one corner of her mouth, dimpling her cheek as she yielded to the temptation to walk to town instead of drive. Impulsively she found herself overlooking the sea on her way.

The bluff was high above the water, and the low tide left a wide strip of sand and rocks far below her. The salty breeze that blew in felt cool against her skin and an occasional gust set her skirts whirling around her legs.

Anyone who enjoyed the rugged beauty of a long, oceanfront property with relative seclusion, yet still conveniently close to town belonged at Boulder Bay. How could she blame Jay Dalton for wanting it? Stephanie sighed. Maybe he would buy it, but the walk to town reinforced her resolve to get all that she could from her place. If she had to lose it, she would fight for what it was worth.

Stephanie arrived at the offices of Brown, Jarrett, and Garrard in good spirits and calm of heart and mind. She had come to terms with herself and accepted the inevitable. Every eye in the plush offices turned toward her as she entered. Some appraised furtively, and some openly, but none ignored her beauty and sun-kissed radiance.

Stephanie approached the desk nearest the door where the only woman in the room sat. A sign on her desk designated her as executive assistant, and the expensive perfume she wore teased the air around her desk, giving Stephanie a moment of envy.

For an instant she wished for the trappings of success, a designer suit and accessories to match, an expensive perfume, something to lift her from the rural, homespun image she felt she presented.

The young woman looked up and smiled with a disarming friendliness, dispelling her cool mystique. "May I help you?"

Stephanie hesitated, glancing around the room, as she looked for Mr. Jarrett among the men seated at the adjacent desks. Her eyes went to each desk and every man, in turn, lowered his head, reluctantly taking his eyes from her.

"Mr. Jarrett? I had an appointment?" she asked, a perplexed look darkening her eyes.

"Oh, you must be Miss Haynes. Mr. Jarrett's expecting you. I'm Abigail Burnes, his assistant. Mr. Dalton is not here yet. Would you like to go on in anyway?"

"Yes, I would, thank you," Stephanie responded.

Abigail pushed her chair away from her desk of finely crafted cherry and stood up. "I'll show you to his office. I need a break. Would you like a cup of coffee?"

"No, thank you. This is the first time I've been to your new offices. Are you enjoying them?"

"Well, yes and no," replied the pretty brunette, her voice lowered intentionally. Her smile invited camaraderie, dispelling the last remnants of Stephanie's uneasiness.

"How's that?"

The young assistant looked over her shoulder and then said in a voice just above a whisper, "In our old office the decor was fluorescent lights and utility working space, you know, metal desk and blinds, but I had my own private cubicle. In here the esthetics are wonderful, but the open work area can be distracting, not to mention my hair has to be in place and my makeup perfect all the time. I feel like one of the company's displays."

Stephanie laughed at the amused indignation mirrored on her face and commented, "I can see your point, but then they have a very impressive display with you. You fit right into these plush surroundings, but I guess it would be difficult working in a room full of men and having so little privacy."

"Yes, it's my privacy that I miss. Working for Mr. Jarrett is a dream, though; I couldn't have a better boss. Are you a secretary?"

"Not at the moment, but I will be needing a job shortly. Do you have an opening?"

The young woman looked at Stephanie and smiled warmly. "Not right now, but I've heard rumors of expansion. If my workload increases, I'll need an assistant. Why don't you check back with me?"

"You say you've heard rumors of expansion?"

"Oh, yes, we are going to handle all the real estate for the area from North Shore to Emerald Shore, about a five-hundred-square-mile area. With all the new plans underway, we're expecting a virtual boom."

"What new plans?"

"Didn't you know this area just legalized gambling?"

"I would hardly call that an asset."

"Well, that's a surprise, I mean, since your business is with Mr. Dalton." Abby nervously twisted her single strand of creamy white pearls.

"What do you mean?" Stephanie asked, her eyes narrowing slightly as Martha's warning echoed in the corridors of her mind.

"Didn't you know he is the biggest casino owner on the East Coast?" Abby's voice was insistent, tinged with a slight impatience.

Stephanie stopped midstep. "No, as a matter of fact, I didn't. I only talked to him once when he came to look my place over."

"Some of the guys in our firm said if he moves in here, the sky's the limit on development property. This coastline is beautiful and undeveloped. With a casino as a drawing card, we could have a thriving tourist trade all year long. Consider what that would do for land values."

"Pardon me, Abigail, but where would you put a casino in Emerald Cove?"

"Well, you know, your. . ." The color drained from Abigail's face as she looked directly into Stephanie's puzzled eyes, understanding replacing impatience. "You really didn't know?"

"Know what?"

Abigail stopped just as they arrived outside Howard Jarrett's door. "Sometimes I talk too much. Miss Haynes, do me a favor. Don't let Mr. Jarrett know I said anything to you. It could cost me my job."

Stephanie took a deep breath as she reached for the door. "Of course not. You've done me a real service, but you're wrong on one count. Gambling, legalized or not, can never be a boon to a community. It brings crime and greed and they're no assets ever, land values notwithstanding."

Abigail paused before turning away and looked steadily at Stephanie. "I never thought of it like that. Maybe we could talk again sometime."

"I'd love to. How long have you lived in Emerald Cove?" Stephanie probed.

"Only six months. I came here from the home office and so far I don't know anyone my own age." Abigail sighed.

"Well, we'll have to remedy that, Abigail. Call me, and we'll get together," Stephanie said over her shoulder as she turned to open the door that led into the large, cherry-paneled office of Howard Jarrett.

His back was to her as he talked on the phone and stared out a window behind his desk. From the floor-to-ceiling window Stephanie could see a lush green lawn sloping gently to meet a rocky bluff that then fell sharply to the sea. Stephanie's heart constricted at the thought of this gentle hamlet being transformed into a "Las Vegas-by-the-sea." That would explain why this large and prosperous firm had chosen this little village to build its fine imposing offices.

Howard Jarrett, a handsome man in his midfifties, whirled around when he heard the door close and rose from his desk as he placed the telephone in its cradle.

Stephanie watched the distinguished-looking man with salt-and-pepper hair walk briskly around his imposing mahogany desk, his hands outstretched. They were as smooth and well manicured as a woman's. A gold watch embossed with diamonds encircled his wrist while a plain gold wedding band gleamed softly on his ring finger. He smelled faintly of pipe tobacco.

"Stephanie, my dear, are you all right?" he asked, concern showing in his hazel eyes.

"I'm fine, Mr. Jarrett," Stephanie said assuredly as she offered her hand to him.

"Please call me Howard. Dalton will be here shortly, but I wanted to talk to you about his offer before he arrives. It really is quite generous, and since you seem anxious to sell, my advice is to accept it. I can assure you that it exceeds the average price of land in the area by several hundred dollars an acre."

"How much is he offering, Mr. Jarrett?"

Howard Jarrett paused, then with a confident smile pointed to the tufted leather wingback chair. "Have a seat, my dear. That one's comfortable. Would you like a cup of coffee?"

"The offer, Mr. Jarrett?" Stephanie insisted as she sat down.

"Oh, yes. Your house is quite large, twenty-five rooms, I believe. However, its age and the renovations and upkeep have to be considered. Even though you have twenty acres of oceanfront property, much of it is quite rugged, you know."

"Mr. Jarrett!"

"Howard, my dear."

"Howard, I'm familiar with my property. What I'm not acquainted with is Mr. Dalton's offer. I can't understand why you wanted to have this meeting before you had even given me an offer to consider. If I'm not interested, then you've wasted all our time," Stephanie responded firmly.

"You'll be interested," he said confidently.

"How much?"

"How about a million dollars?" he responded, his eyes burning with triumphant expectation.

Stephanie wrinkled her brow and narrowed her eyes. The silence grew heavy as she purposely delayed her response.

Howard Jarrett's confident stance weakened slightly. As the seconds passed without comment from Stephanie, he began to squirm and finally blurted out, "Well, what about it?"

The young woman widened her eyes and said softly with a cool smile, "I'm interested." The sum was three times what she needed to clear and over twice as much as she had even dared hope for. Yet, a warning signal sounded deep within her, and she added firmly, "Now tell me this. Why is he willing to pay that much for an old house on twenty acres of rugged property?"

Howard Jarrett's handsome, tanned face flushed slightly and his well-manicured fingers drummed a nervous rhythm on his desk. He had not expected her response. "Well, Stephanie, it's just a matter of his seeing it and falling in love with the quaint old place. It's secluded, and he needs a quiet place away from his many business ventures. You know what I mean, a place to get away."

"But what precisely does he want to do with Boulder Bay?"

"I just told you."

"No, you told me why he likes it, but you didn't actually say what he was going to do with it."

Howard Jarrett's suave facade cracked as he answered thinly, "He will repair it and use it for a summer home. Now let me tell you, Miss Haynes, you will never get a better offer, and if you don't accept this, you'll have to find another agent."

Stephanie's composure remained unruffled. "You're telling me that if I don't accept this offer, you will no longer work for me and our agreement is broken?"

The agent nervously put both hands to his temples and ran them back through his hair. "Yes, that is exactly right. I'm a very busy man, and I have many other clients who know what they want and follow my advice."

Stephanie nodded her head and said pleasantly, "Fine. I just wanted to make certain I understood what you meant."

"Well?" Jarrett asked with one eyebrow slightly arched.

"Well, what?"

"Are you ready to sign this contract?" he asked, irritation elevating his voice.

"Not until Mr. Dalton arrives," she replied.

"I see," he snapped. "Just understand this. Mr. Dalton won't put up with delaying tactics, so you better make up your mind before he walks in that door. If you keep Jay Dalton waiting for an answer, he'll just go buy someplace else."

"There is no place like mine, Mr. Jarrett," Stephanie quietly reminded him. "Except for the town and my property, the government owns all the adjacent shoreline. No, he'll have to go to another state."

Howard Jarrett narrowed his eyes. "Who's been talking to you, Stephanie?"

"What do you mean, Howard? Did you think I was totally uninformed about the value and desirability of my property?" If the truth were told, Stephanie was amazed that these words had come from her mouth. Sometime during her walk to town she had decided to fight for what the place was worth. Her inner alarm, which had sounded earlier, propelled her through this confrontation.

With a knock on the door, Abigail ushered in Jay Dalton. Stephanie had only seen him once, and the encounter had been too brief to form an opinion. Now she studied him carefully, bearing in mind Martha's warning. He was a handsome man in a flamboyant sort of way. The cut of his clothes reflected a designer's touch, but he lacked the natural grace to wear them with ease. His dark, longish hair complemented his rugged features and swarthy complexion. Only his eyes captured Stephanie's attention. They were the lightless color of aged steel.

He breezed in the room with an outstretched hand and blustery greeting to Jarrett. However, when he turned his attention to Stephanie, he paused midsentence and looked at her from head to toe. With a smile of approval, he murmured, "How could I have forgotten such beauty? Howard, this is one deal I should have handled myself."

Stephanie smiled coolly, never taking her eyes from his. "Mr. Jarrett tells me I must not delay. Shall we get on with it, Mr. Dalton?"

"Howard is sorely mistaken. I'll always have time for you, Miss Haynes. Shall we say dinner this evening?"

"Oh, I think we can surely finish before then, Mr. Dalton."

"That would disappoint me. Perhaps we should view the property again?"

"Are you reconsidering your offer?"

"No, no, just a joke. Where are the papers? We sign, yes? Then we go to celebrate our good fortune. I get what I want, and you get a good price for it, eh?"

"I have one question, Mr. Dalton. What are you going to use Boulder Bay for?"

"Like I told your housekeeper, as a summer home."

"There are rumors that you want to turn it into a casino."

"Rumors, rumors, why would I want another? I have more than I can look after now. No, just a home."

"I see. Well then, I guess we have a deal. The price is very generous. Where are the papers, Mr. Jarrett?"

"Howard," corrected the agent, regaining his composure.

"Howard, I'm ready to sell. It's a hard thing for me to sell my home. My family has owned it for generations."

"Yes, yes, I'm sure it must be. Now if you will sign right here, Stephanie, and Jay has his check, then we can finish this business satisfactorily for all of us." Relief washed across his face.

"One more thing, Mr. Dalton." Stephanie paused, pen in hand. "If you are going to use my place for a summer home, then you'll have no objection to signing an affidavit that you do not intend to use it for a casino. Is that right?"

The rhythmic tick of the ornate walnut wall clock pierced the silence like a dagger. Alarm seized Jarrett's face as Jay Dalton responded smoothly, "My dear, I can't possibly see what that has to do with our deal. I refuse to sign an affidavit, because if my word isn't sufficient, then the deal's off."

Stephanie cocked her head, smiled sweetly, and stood up. "Thank you for your time, gentlemen. We don't have a deal."

Jay Dalton turned his intense gaze on Stephanie, his former good humor replaced by an icy stare. "Miss Haynes, if this is a ploy for more money, it won't work."

"Believe me, it isn't. Your offer is fair, and I have no complaints. I only require an affidavit."

He paused for a long moment, then as Stephanie took a step toward the door, he spoke. "How does two million dollars sound to you, along with relocating you anywhere you wish to live?" A low gasp escaped the realtor and he slumped in his seat.

"An affidavit *and* one million dollars is the deal, Mr. Dalton."

Jarrett looked in helpless frustration from one to the other, then jumped to his feet and exclaimed in disbelief, "Stephanie, what are you doing? I have the information on your loan before me. You are going to lose your place to the bank if you don't sell it. Be reasonable!"

"I know it doesn't seem sane to either of you, but there can be no other terms. I must have an affidavit, or I won't sell."

"I don't understand, Miss Haynes. Why can't you sell on my terms? I've doubled the price, and you've got to sell."

"Because I couldn't live with myself if I gained at the expense of a community I love."

"Who set you up as judge and jury to decide what's best for this town?" Jarrett asked.

"No one, Mr. Jarrett, but I do have a responsibility to others for my decisions."

He looked at her, his hazel eyes now cold with malice and anger. "Are you your brother's keeper?"

"Sometimes" was her sad response.

Dalton interrupted with a sneer. "You can't stop me."

"Perhaps not, but I refuse to aid you."

Then he laughed coldly. "Well, Miss Haynes, I tried to do you a favor. Now I'll just wait for the bank to repossess it and sell it on the courthouse steps. I'll buy it then and save myself a bundle. You'll get nothing."

Stephanie walked toward the door. "No, you won't, Mr. Dalton. Somehow I'll keep it." She closed the door without a backward glance toward the two stunned men and walked quickly down the hall past Abigail Burnes's vacant desk. Desire to leave this coastal compound of plush offices consumed her, but her trembling legs refused to cooperate. Seeking a place of escape, she turned toward town and the Hotel Atlantic Tearoom. There she could get a strong cup of tea and a place to sit until somehow her strength renewed.

Now what am I going to do, Lord? That was my only way out. Dalton's right, he can buy my place cheaper if it's repossessed. Yet, how can I sell it knowing what it will be used for? her mind questioned.

Stephanie stepped into the welcoming coolness of the tearoom and walked toward a table next to the window. A few white sails visible on the horizon prompted a fleeting urge to rig up *Carefree*, her sloop, and go for a sail.

Stephanie shook her head. No, she couldn't escape. She was trapped with no apparent way out. What was she to do? *Lord, You promised to meet all our needs, and I really have a need right now*, her heart pled silently.

Stephanie ordered tea and scones from Janie, the hostess, and, as an afterthought, requested the afternoon paper. The tea and scones revived her, and with a deep sigh, she turned to the want ads. Job opportunities appeared few and far between.

"I didn't know mermaids drank tea," said a voice behind her that set her heart to racing.

Stephanie turned and looked up into the mocking eyes of the man at the cove. Before she could respond, he lifted one long leg over the low-backed chair and sat down at her table.

"You!" she said through clenched teeth.

"Yep, it's me!" Undaunted by her narrowed eyes and bristling anger, he gave her a maddening grin.

"Why don't you have a seat, Mr. Mystery," she responded sarcastically.

"Donovan, Lance Donovan is my name and, thank you, I don't mind if I do. How are their scones?" he asked, taking the last one and smearing it liberally with strawberry jam. "Nearly good as my mother's, but of course nobody could hold a candle to hers."

"Won't you have the rest of my tea also?" she invited, her outrage at the man's arrogant boldness growing by the second.

"No, thanks, that won't hurt you. I'm eating this scone because you've had enough calories. Don't want you to gain any weight; you're just right!"

Stephanie's mouth flew open, shock at his impudence widening her eyes. For a moment the memory of a sneering Jay Dalton evaporated as she felt her early morning rage stir once again.

Donovan leaned across the table, placed his finger under her chin, and pushed upward, closing her mouth. "Don't gape. We need to talk. I've got a proposition for you."

Stephanie closed her eyes, her long dark lashes resting on her cheeks, and shook her head as if to clear her mind of this disturbing apparition. When she opened her eyes, he still sat there, munching on the last remnant of her scone and smiling jauntily.

"A proposition?" Then Stephanie slowly nodded her head. "That figures."

"Good, now we can get down to business."

"Mr. Donovan," she responded weakly, "you'd be the last man I'd be interested in."

Lance looked at her, his brow slightly wrinkled. "Oh!" he exclaimed, laughing, understanding brightening his countenance. "Not that kind of proposition. I mean a business proposition."

"Business, what kind of business? You don't look like a businessman to me," she retorted, then added, "or act like one."

"Why? Is Jay Dalton your idea of a businessman?" he queried, his head cocked to one side.

Stephanie sighed with disgust. "Okay, okay. Tell Mr. Dalton I am not interested, and your, er, charm won't convince me, either."

"Well, that's a relief. I'd heard rumors, and then when I saw Dalton go into Brown, Jarrett, and Garrard right after you did, I thought I was too late."

"Have you been following me?"

"Well, yes and no, but not intentionally. You see, I had some business in town, and when I saw you go in their offices, I just decided to wait around."

"I still don't understand. Don't you work for Dalton?"

"Not on your life. I make an honest living. I'm Lancelot Donovan, movie producer."

"Yes, and I'm Joan of Arc."

"No, seriously, here's my card."

Stephanie took the card and read, *Century Production, Lancelot Donovan, President, Hollywood, California.* An amused smile momentarily softened her eyes as she looked up. With one side of her mouth twisted upward, she gave a derisive half chuckle. "Lancelot? You mean your name is really Lancelot?"

Donovan's jaunty confidence weakened, and he gave a crooked smile. "Yeah, my mom liked to read medieval novels." He shrugged before continuing quickly. "I'm Lance to my friends, but being in the movie business I felt that Lancelot had a certain show biz ring to it."

"Around here a name like Lancelot wouldn't be to your advantage. Anyway, anyone can print business cards."

"True, but these are genuine. I am who it says."

"You're a long way from home" was her skeptical retort.

"I am producing a new film and have been searching the northeastern coast for the right location. When I discovered Boulder Bay, I went to the courthouse and found out that it belonged to one Stephanie Haynes, but local gossip said she had sold it to Jay Dalton."

"What if I don't believe you, Mr. Donovan? You know a name like Lancelot makes it a little more difficult." Stephanie pressed her advantage, suddenly enjoying piercing the arrogance of this handsome stranger.

"Well, call Hollywood and check me out, but meanwhile read your local paper. Don't you keep up with the news?" he asked pointedly, attempting to divert the conversation.

"I've been preoccupied lately."

"Look on page one, or do you only read want ads?" Sarcasm dripped from his words like jam from a warm scone.

Stephanie pressed her lips together tightly and glared at him as she turned the paper. True to his prediction, a small blurb announced in bold letters, FILM COMPANY SEARCHES.

"That's old news now. I've found what I want. It's Boulder Bay and you!" he exclaimed with boyish exuberance, extinguishing all traces of his former attitude.

"Really?" Stephanie asked, curiosity softening her retort.

"Yes, really. If you read the article you'll see I was searching for a location and a new face for the ingenue role. I've spent these past weeks walking shorelines, sailing in and out of coves, and auditioning women. I saw your place from a copter last week, and after I rented a sailboat and looked at it from the sea, I was fairly sure I'd found it. Today when I 'trespassed' and walked over it, I knew my search was over. How much do you want for it?"

Pausing, he looked at her with mischief dancing in his eyes and added, "By the way, that cove is perfect for a love scene, don't you think?"

"I'm not believing this conversation!" Stephanie replied, trying not to laugh.

"So? Just name a price. I'll make a believer out of you!"

"It's not for sale to you at any price!" she responded as visions of gambling tables in her parlor came crashing back.

"Why? You'd rather do business with Mr. Dalton?"

"No, but what would be the difference between you and him?"

"I don't want it for the same reason he does."

"How do you know what he wants it for?" Stephanie queried, her brows furrowed.

"I told you, Ms. Haynes, I did a thorough investigation," Donovan assured. "It is for sale, isn't it?"

"I'm—I'm not sure," she stammered.

"Oh, it's me." He laughed as his steady gaze locked on hers. "Lovely lady, you'd better get used to me. I see a great future for us."

Stephanie stared at him in wide-eyed disbelief, then dropped her eyes before he could see her obvious embarrassment. She had read something in his eyes that stirred a strange, disturbing emotion within her. "This is all so sudden, Mr. Donovan. I need time to think."

"How about my coming by later this evening? Give you time to check out my credentials," he suggested pleasantly, all his former arrogant jauntiness missing.

Stephanie slowly nodded. "I guess that would be all right."

"About eight-thirty, then?" he pressed and acknowledged her fleeting nod. "Would you like a lift home?"

"No, thank you. I need the walk and time to think," she replied.

He reached across the table and picked up the check. Standing up, he almost whispered, "See you tonight."

Chapter Four

The shadows lengthened and the breezes cooled as dusk arrived. Stephanie paced restlessly in the large parlor of Boulder Bay, her heart stirred by a faint hope that her head battled to deny.

On one side of the parlor nestled into the alcove formed by the three bay windows was a large storage chest of fine, old walnut. She sat down on it and listened to the distant roar of the tumultuous sea as it broke against the rocks. The intensity of the waves matched her mood. The answers she sought still eluded her; the steadfast faith that usually calmed her was missing.

Lance Donovan's credentials had checked out, and she had no problem with his intended use of the place. Furthermore, his films were notably wholesome and family oriented. So, what was her problem?

The doorbell interrupted her thoughts, and she stood up. She saw Donovan's profile outlined behind the lace-curtained glass of the old front door. Reluctantly, Stephanie walked across the heart pine floors of orange and gold as the lingering fragrance of lemon oil polish of antique furniture gave an inaudible welcome.

Tonight, however, her eyes saw nothing but the waiting profile, while her heart knew nothing but the anguish of indecision.

Lance stared quietly for a moment into Stephanie's eyes. A softer, warmer expression replaced his usual arrogance and somehow it comforted and reassured her. As if he sensed her indecision, he suggested, "Let's go for a walk. I find sitting by the sea sometimes clears my mind."

She nodded, and they walked together silently, each deep in thought. They approached a bench placed strategically at the highest point of the property with a commanding view of the coast. Sitting a few inches apart, they lingered in a companionable silence until Lance turned to her, carefully choosing his words. "Stephanie, I've thought a great deal about our conversation this afternoon. I am withdrawing my offer to buy Boulder Bay."

Stephanie turned her face toward him and bit her bottom lip, waiting for his explanation. She knew then that caution had lost its battle with hope. Lance Donovan's profile had become a beacon in the gathering twilight, but with these words despair threatened to engulf her.

He smiled when he saw her expression, some of his jauntiness returning. "I have a better plan. What would you like to do if you didn't sell your place?"

"If you've done your homework, you know I have to sell it."

"You didn't answer my question," he gently insisted.

Stephanie turned away from him before he could see tears of longing mist her eyes. "I'd live here and have the most unique inn on the North Shore."

He put his hand under her chin and turned her face around to meet his, lifting it so he could look deeply into her eyes. "Then do it."

"I can't."

"Suppose you had a partner?"

"I don't know anyone who would be interested."

"But I do," he smiled.

"You? I thought you wanted to buy it for location."

"I did, but leasing it would be better for me and, I believe, for you in the long run. I thought it would be nice for a personal retreat, but the property is really too valuable to leave idle. Leasing it wouldn't give you enough money for your immediate needs, but what if I bought in as a partner and supplied the funds for renovations? Then I'd have an investment in an income-producing property. We'd both get what we want. I could have it when I wanted it, and you could have it after we leave. The movie company could stay on location and rent the facilities. Do you think your staff could handle accommodations for thirty-five or forty people?" Eagerness raised the timbre of his voice a pitch and washed his face in boyish anticipation.

"We don't have enough room in the main house to lodge them, but if the cottages were renovated we would. But Mr. Donovan, are you sure? What kind of money are you talking about?" She would leave no stone unturned.

"As much as you need," he gently assured.

"Sounds too good to be true," Stephanie responded, doubt darkening her eyes.

"There is one condition. I want to give you a screen test for the supporting actress role in my film. When I saw you this morning, I knew you were the lady of my dreams."

"Me, a movie star? I'm not the type," she objected, shaking her head.

"Depends on what you mean," he said.

"Glamorous, beautiful, sophisticated." Stephanie sighed.

"If you mean a glittering facade, no, you're not. What you have is the very essence of beauty: all the physical attributes put together with an intangible inner radiance that I had given up on finding," he explained, his tone one of sincere persuasion.

Stephanie tilted her head and stared at him. "Are you putting me on?"

"No, why did you think I looked at you the way I did this morning?"

"I don't know, but I felt like a side of meat that had just passed inspection," she retorted, pulling her mouth in a thin line as she relived her morning encounter.

"You had passed my wildest expectations. The world of films is a marketplace for beauty."

"Mr. Donovan, I'm not for sale," Stephanie responded primly.

"Miss Haynes, you've made that abundantly clear more than once today," he agreed with a chuckle. "Now what about my proposition, are you interested?"

"Could you call it something else? That particular term just doesn't appeal to me." She gave him a timorous smile, and for the first time the glow of expectation widened her eyes.

"How about 'business venture?' "

"That's better," she laughed, turning to look up at him with her eyes shining.

"Careful, don't look at me like that; you'll take my breath away," he said, smiling. "Well? I'm still waiting for my answer."

"The first part about leasing the inn for a filming location and housing the crew sounds wonderful, almost too good to be true. But I'm having problems with the other part about your financing it and my being in the movie."

"Why?"

"Lance, I won't take advantage of anyone and that plan sounds like you would be carrying 80 percent of the load. It's either charity or. . .what's in it for you? You see, I would be dependent on you."

He gave her a mock leer but said nothing.

"No, I'm serious. I refuse to be dependent on anyone. I've got to carry my load." Suddenly anxiety and weariness dimmed her eyes.

"Okay, I'm serious, too. In the first place I'm not a very charitable person even for beautiful damsels in distress. I'm a businessman. Here I see an opportunity for a profitable business venture, and you must have thought so, too, or you wouldn't have attempted it." Lance's eyes held hers, willing Stephanie to see she had nothing to fear.

"Well, yes, but I didn't have the capital."

"I do," Lance assured.

The final light of day had exited and a tall security light behind their bench bathed the couple in gold. For a moment silence reigned as Stephanie considered what Lance had said. The ocean's roar and a whippoorwill's loud rhythmic call from the woods interrupted her brief reverie. The brisk sea breeze ruffled her hair and lightly kissed her lips with salt as she breathed in the familiar smell of seaweed. She shivered and Lance moved cautiously toward her.

Taking off his jacket, he moved his arm across the bench behind her and draped his jacket over her shoulders. Then with a disarming smile, he kept his arm around her. Stephanie turned toward him, seemingly unaware of his jacket, his arm behind her, and even oblivious to his nearness. Circumstances had invaded her comfort zone, threatening extinction of life as she knew it. Now Lance offered a promise of rescue that seemed too good to be true. Carefully she weighed the issues, groping for an answer as she searched for the right questions.

"What if there isn't a return on your money?" Stephanie probed.

"That won't happen, Stephanie. I'll be around often enough to go over the books and make suggestions. About the part in the movie, you would do well to read the magazines. Several articles have described in detail what I was looking for. . . ." He paused and took her face in his hands once again. "Go look in the mirror, Stephanie, and don't fail to thank God for what He's done for you."

"What if I can't act?" she insisted, willing him to persuade her.

His somber look gave way to a confident smile. "Then I'll teach you."

Stephanie turned from him and looked toward the navy horizon where stars twinkled like millions of diamonds. She sat transfixed for several moments, drinking in the familiarity, the beauty. Now she fought the urge to give in, to end the probing, but she knew she couldn't. Her decision had to be right.

Stephanie pulled her eyes from the stars and, dropping her head, asked hesitantly, almost inaudibly, "But what if you really want to do something else with Boulder Bay, something that I wouldn't approve of? How could I stop you?"

Lance shifted on the bench beside her and stretched his long legs out in front of him as he put his hands behind his neck. "You have a valid point. You don't know me, and I could have other plans for the place. What if I just lease it from you for the duration of the film and loan you the money for renovation and advertising? Then I will have the mortgage on it instead of the bank, and you can pay me back with interest or with part ownership of the inn, whichever suits you better. That way you retain control."

"Like I just asked, what's in it for you? That looks like a rather lopsided deal to me."

"Don't forget, you have to promise to be in my film if the screen test is okay. But beyond that, I see an opportunity for a business investment. You see, I'm confident when you observe firsthand my business acumen, and, of course, fall victim to my many charms, you will beg me to come into the business with you. We could have a real winner up on this bluff with the gorgeous view. Well, what do you think?"

Without warning, relief coursed through Stephanie, washing away all vestiges of doubt. A sense of direction and confidence replaced the turmoil that had buffeted her off and on since she turned down Jay Dalton's offer. She sighed as if a heavy weight had lifted from her, and her shoulders relaxed against Lance's arm.

He felt the tension ease from her as she turned to look him squarely in the face. "I think I'm very interested." Then a mischievous grin suddenly lighted her face as she added, "I think you are an answer to prayer."

Lance flinched and raised his eyebrows. "Baby, you are full of surprises. I've been called a lot of things in my brief life, but an answer to prayer has never been one of them."

Laughing gently, she remembered her earlier conversation with Martha and observed, "Lance, sometimes the Lord chooses strange avenues to perform His works."

With mock disappointment, he responded, "Oh shucks, I thought I had just gotten a promotion."

"Sorry, Lance, we don't have to be special, just available," she explained, her face earnest, excitement lighting her eyes.

"Available?" he queried.

"Yes, being at the right place at the right time and willing for God to use us."

"Well, I guess I don't mind God using me, if that's what happened. But as far as my being at the right place at the right time, God didn't have anything to do with that. I was the one who decided where I was going." His eyes refused to meet hers directly, but in them she read determination and apprehension.

Stephanie's eyes twinkled, mischief playing in them. "Don't you know the verse, 'The steps of a good man are ordered by the Lord?' "

"A good man, eh? Maybe I'd better end this conversation while I'm ahead. As for this availability business, I still don't understand it, but perhaps someday we can talk about it again. Meanwhile, what kind of partners are we going to be?" Lance responded deftly, piloting the conversation to safer and more familiar waters.

"What about a limited partnership with an open book policy?" Stephanie was delighted for the opportunity to use something she had learned at the university.

"I'll get my attorney to draw up the agreement." Glancing at his watch, Lance slowly rose to his feet as he held out his hand to her.

She took it but lingered another moment on the bench as she looked up into his eyes, searching his face. "This has been the strangest day of my life. I've handed over my future to a man I've just met, yet I'm not even nervous about it."

"Did you have any other choice, Stephanie?"

"No, not an acceptable one," she agreed as she stood.

"Then accept it as if fate smiled on you. This is going to be a good deal for both of us."

"I believe that, but Lance, it isn't fate."

"Oh, yeah, I forgot, I'm an answer to prayer!" He chuckled aloud.

"Don't worry, I won't let you forget!"

"How can I entertain any ulterior motives if you keep reminding me of that?" Lance's teasing nature was never far from the surface.

"That's what I'm counting on to keep you in line."

"It won't be easy, you know. You're very beautiful." He grinned easily, but the look in his eyes was so intimate, it sent tingles down her spine.

Her face flushed in the early moonlight as she responded lightly, "I bet you say that to all the Hollywood starlets. Aren't we supposed to be beautiful?"

Lance paused midstep and took both her hands in his and looked down for a long moment. "Yes, but your beauty is so different. It has a mysterious quality that intrigues and challenges me to solve it. Will you let me, Stephanie?"

As Stephanie saw the tenderness in his gaze, she felt her heart leap in response. For the first time in her life, someone had pierced her independent spirit and touched the woman's heart beneath, setting it aflame.

❧

The staccato ring of the telephone startled Stephanie, who was engrossed in pleasant reflection. Once again she sat in the window sea, but now night's inky curtain concealed her view. The day's excitement had denied her both sleep and the ability to read the magazine resting in her lap.

She glanced down at the gold watch whose precious gems embedded in its face colored the hours, mutely proclaiming the passage of time. Her grandmother had worn it as a bride, then her mother, and now she wore it and cherished the memories.

A frown furrowed her smooth brow briefly as she saw the hour was late for a casual call. Apprehensively, she approached the phone, remembering other times when late-night calls had heralded tragedies.

"Hello, Boulder Bay, Stephanie Haynes speaking."

A deep, slightly slurred voice responded. "Yes, Ms. Haynes. I've called to see if you have reconsidered my offer."

Stephanie paused before answering. The voice, though slightly familiar, eluded identification. "I beg your pardon. Who is this?"

"You know me. I'm the man who is going to make you rich. What a dynamite team we will make! I liked the way you performed this afternoon." A deep chuckle punctuated his voice as he added, "I'll have to say, though, you really fooled old Jarrett."

"Mr. Dalton?" she asked hesitantly, recognition finally dawning.

"Who else? Your benefactor." The slurring of Dalton's speech now seemed ridiculously exaggerated.

"Who else, indeed? It is very late, and we've completed our business."

Dalton delayed his response for a few seconds. "You are mistaken, Ms. Haynes. We've just begun our business. You do business just like me. You took a big gamble this afternoon. At first you kinda riled me, but when I cooled down, I figured out your game. Anyway, it would be better for me and for you if we leave Jarrett out. Say, since you're still up, I'll just drive up, and we'll finish this business."

"Our business is finished, Dalton. Let me make myself clear: I will not sell to you on any terms or at any price."

"That's all right, St–Stephanie, I—"

"You bet it is, and that finishes this conversation."

"Wait! I just told you, sweetheart, I know what your game is and I'm all for it. I'll just come on up and we'll strike a deal and leave Jarrett out of it altogether. . .better for me, better for you."

"Mr. Dalton. . ."

"Jay."

"Mr. Dalton, I don't want to talk to you tonight or any other day or night. I want you to understand. . . ." Stephanie paused slightly before continuing. "I'm not selling to you or anyone."

A low chuckle filled her ear. "Now that's one bill of goods I won't buy. You've got to do business with me. I was willing to bargain, but you've pushed me too far now."

"Fine. If I were you, I wouldn't bargain, either. In fact you should just withdraw your offer." Stephanie's voice dropped softly, and she spoke much as she would to a small child she hoped to convince. Dalton's altered speech pattern alarmed her, but his threat to arrive on her doorstep in the middle of the night galvanized her into action.

Cool, common sense now replaced her former irritation with the man as she continued, her voice honeyed. "Jay, it's late and I'm exhausted, besides I really meant it. I've decided not to sell, so you would be wasting a trip. Now you wouldn't want to waste a drive up here, would you?"

"But I was gonna offer you three million dollars! Wha-what about that, and you won't even have to give old Jarrett part of it." He chuckled. "Guess you could use all that dough, eh? I'll be right on out."

"No!" Stephanie answered, more sharply than she intended, panic teasing her composure. Then with a deep breath she said softly, in what she hoped was a persuasive voice, "Not tonight, Jay. Come tomorrow. I'm just too tired to think tonight. I'll explain all about it, and we can talk when we're both fresh."

"You really don't want me to come tonight? Not even for three million dollars? Why, I've got my check all made out."

"No, I'm really too tired. And besides, we can't go behind Mr. Jarrett's back, that's illegal," she reasoned.

"You just leave Jarrett to me. He'll do anything I say, if he knows what's good for him," Dalton threatened.

"Well, Jay, since I don't feel comfortable about dealing like that, maybe you'd better talk to Howard first and make it right before you come out," Stephanie hedged, praying he would forget the conversation come morning.

"Well, all right, but I'm telling you Jarrett will agree to anything I say. But if you're too tired, I'll see you at ten in the morning at your place."

"Sure, that will be fine," Stephanie reluctantly agreed, then added, "but I'm still not promising you anything, Jay. You understand that, don't you?"

"Little lady, you are going to sell to me. See you in the morning, Ms. Stephanie Haynes." His answer, brisk and confident, now without a trace of his former slur, sent shivers up and down Stephanie's spine.

She slowly replaced the receiver in its cradle and, with arms crossed, leaned against the wall for a moment. Then with a long sigh of relief, she made her way down the hall and up the stairs to her room, wondering all the while if this latest turn of events in her day would allow her to sleep at all.

Kneeling before her bed, she thanked her Heavenly Father for His miraculous answer to her prayer for assistance. A smile teased the corner of her mouth as she observed that God's answer to her dilemma had certainly come wrapped in a handsome package. Then sleep met her full force, fear and worry swallowed up in the victory of resolution.

Chapter Five

Stephanie hummed a quiet tune and hugged herself as she watched the golden streaks of dawn pierce the eastern sky, heralding the dawn of a new day. Sometime during the evening hours with Lance, her worry had eased. Facing the future and deciding to take the risk to fight for her dream had lifted the fog of indecision that had enveloped her.

Eager to get on with her plans, Stephanie had worked during the predawn hours preparing financial statements and renovation lists for Lance. With the whole plan down in black and white, she discovered her financial needs were not as great as she had feared. Martha's assumption had been correct. Her main need was time, and Lance would buy that for her.

If the inn ran with a capacity crowd for six months out of the year, it would carry itself with some profit. With guest houses in use and snaring some of the ski tourism, the prospects for Boulder Bay looked as rosy as the eastern sky.

Moving toward the porch's ornate spindled railing, Stephanie leaned against a column. She turned her head toward the horizon to watch, entranced in the beauty. Breathing deeply of the fragrant sea air, she said aloud, "What a difference a day makes. Yesterday seemed so hopeless and today—yes, today so filled with hope. Oh, God, how could I ever doubt Your goodness and loving care?"

So immersed was Stephanie in the beauty before her that she failed to hear the creaking of the old door or see Martha step quietly onto the porch. She jumped and turned wide, questioning eyes when Martha asked, "What was that you were saying, girl?"

Stephanie smiled sheepishly. "Didn't know I was talking out loud."

"Well, girl, you're sure up bright and early—is it good news or bad that's got you up and out?" Martha asked, her face creasing with concern as she searched the younger girl's face for an answer.

Spontaneously, Stephanie grabbed Martha and danced her around the porch. "That's what I was talking about when you startled me, Martha. I was thanking our good Lord for His miraculous blessings."

"Good news, I. . .I ga. . .gather," she stammered as she struggled to gain her composure. "Now you leave me be, Stephanie. I'm too old for such shenanigans. Besides, are you going to tell me all about it before I explode? John and me went to bed while that nice Mr. Donovan was still here."

"How did you know it was Lance?"

"Er. . .I just. . ." The old woman dropped her gaze in embarrassment. Then gaining her usual aplomb, she lifted her head and looked steadily into Stephanie's eyes.

"I could tell you that I had an errand out at the springhouse about the time you and he took your walk, but that wouldn't exactly be the whole truth. You see, I wanted to size him up and to make sure you'd be all right. I didn't see who it was when he came. I can tell you right now it was quite a surprise when I saw who you were with and all so friendly like. Guess 'twas a little presumptuous of me, just being an employee and all, but seeing's we were so worried about you, I just thought to ease our minds a bit."

"Presumptuous?" Stephanie stepped back and looked at the older woman, her eyes bright with grateful tears. "Only if love is. You and John are the only family I have—your love and care my anchor."

The creases of concern that had bound the older face relaxed, and the beauty etched by a lifetime of loving responses took control. "Stephanie. . ." Martha could go no further. A slender hand, its skin like fine parchment, reached down and picked up the corner of her snow-white apron as a tear escaped. "I told you yesterday, you're the child we couldn't have. Nothing in this world could mean as much to me and John as caring for you."

"I know that now, but I only realized it yesterday. I had felt so guilty taking advantage of you. But now it looks as if we can go on with our plans, and you can get the pay you so deserve."

"You don't say, now." Martha narrowed her eyes and cocked her head to one side. "You must've had some really good news. Come on in the kitchen and eat while you tell me and John all about these miraculous happenings."

"I'll take you up on that. I'm hungry as a bear."

"All that dancing 'round, I'll wager. Anyway, you surely sound different from yesterday."

"Oh, Martha. Everything is different today!" Stephanie said, closing the front door on the bright orange orb peeping over the eastern horizon.

❧

Breakfast proved to be a celebration feast. The three lingered over the meal as Stephanie shared each detail of her new plans. The previous day she had told them only that she had turned Dalton's offer down and was considering an alternative. Her agitation after the meeting with Dalton had been so evident that Martha and John had not pressed her for more information.

"Stephanie, it sounds too good to be true, and if I wasn't a believer in the goodness of our God, I'd plumb be scared." Martha remarked as John nodded his head silently beside her.

Stephanie looked at him and smiled. He, too, was tall and wiry, with blue eyes that could be piercing or warm and lively as the occasion warranted.

"What do you think, John? Martha and I have done all the talking."

"It sounds like just the answer you've been searching for. The only thing is. . ." He hesitated, uncomfortable in the new role of advisor.

"Go on, John. She wants to know what we think," Martha encouraged proudly.

"I don't like that telephone call you got from Dalton last night. He might show up around here and cause trouble."

Stephanie breathed a sigh of relief. "No, I don't think we'll have to worry. I feel sure he was in his cups too much to remember he even called. Anyway, he's too shrewd a businessman to act the way he did last night when he's sober. Is that the only thing that's bothering you?"

"I've got to admit I would feel better about the whole thing if I'd joined Martha at the springhouse and got a look-see at your Mr. Lancelot."

"Lancelot Donovan," Stephanie smilingly corrected. "You did. When he brought me back to the house yesterday morning."

"I wasn't looking at him, young lady. I saw him, but I wasn't 'looking' at him, if you know what I mean."

Stephanie laughed, "You mean, look him over! Martha, were you surprised when you saw that it was Lance?"

Martha's Mona Lisa smile revealed more than her words, "Not too much."

Stephanie cocked an inquisitive eyebrow at her, but before Martha could respond, the doorbell rang.

A few moments later John ushered in Lance, and soon he was devouring the last remnants of breakfast. By the time the final muffin was gone, Lance had completely charmed the couple. He dispelled any lingering doubts in John's mind by inviting him for a tour of the property to assess the repairs and improvements while the women cleaned up the kitchen.

Stephanie wrinkled her brow, her ready retort aborted when he turned to her, smiling with a strange intimacy that stirred her to her bones. "And then, young lady, you're mine for the rest of the day, understand?"

She nodded her head slowly, mesmerized by his clear, blue eyes. Her heart pounded in furious response.

The two women worked efficiently and silently, both lost in their own thoughts. Stephanie tried to think ahead to the plans she needed to discuss with Lance, but a curious joy that she couldn't explain kept drawing her to introspection.

Stephanie had been on tenterhooks since her mother's death. Tension from all the new and difficult decisions had intensified during the last few days. From her adventures in the cove the previous morning to her confrontation in Jarrett's office, Stephanie had felt every emotion from fear to anger.

Truly that must explain her current euphoria—just plain old relief—and yet she hadn't felt this curious feeling before breakfast. No, if she were candid with herself, she'd have to admit that the strange sensation arrived shortly after her front doorbell rang—at the exact moment she had encountered the vivid blue of Lancelot Donovan's eyes.

Stephanie stooped to put the bread tins she had just dried into a lower cabinet, glad for the movement to cover the sudden flush tinting her face.

"Why, Stephanie, those pans belong up here. You must be wool gathering," Martha exclaimed. Modifying her tone when she saw Stephanie's face, the older woman added, "And I'd say you've got a right to—there's a lot to think on, all these goings-on in the last twenty-four hours."

"Oh, Martha, I'm afraid it's more than wool gathering. The excitement of the past two days seems to have given me butterflies. It just disgusts me. I'm always so cool and collected. I guess keeping Boulder Bay meant more to me than I realized."

"Boulder Bay, hmm?" Martha asked.

Stephanie flushed and lifted an inquisitive eyebrow. "What's that about?"

"Just hmm. That's all."

"No, that's not all. It was steeped in meaning. You might as well be out with it. You will anyway," Stephanie laughingly persisted.

Martha cut her eyes toward Stephanie and said over her shoulder, "Maybe it's Boulder Bay and maybe it's not."

"I'm just relieved, that's all," Stephanie insisted.

"Yup!" Martha's noncommittal answer came brisk and short.

"Why shouldn't I feel relief?"

"You should and probably do, but butterflies don't mean relief. They mean something else."

"What?" Stephanie frowned.

"Anticipation. Butterflies mean anticipation."

"I guess that's right. I have relieved anticipation!"

"Humph!" snorted Martha.

"My dear lady," Stephanie urged, this time in a serious vein, "will you speak your mind? I *want* you to."

"You're surely relieved, girl, and I know you're excited about the help you'll be getting, but I'm more a mind to attribute the butterflies to the helper than to the help."

"You mean Lance?"

Martha responded with a firm nod of her head. "That's exactly what I mean."

"Martha, you're an incorrigible matchmaker! I have known Lance Donovan less than twenty-four hours. Don't you think you're a little premature?"

The older woman paused before answering. "Tell me this: When did your butterflies arrive? Before or after the doorbell?"

Stephanie's eyebrows shot up in shocked amazement, but before she could answer, the doorbell rang again, ending their lively exchange.

The two women stared at each other and simultaneously looked at the wall clock. It chimed ten times before Stephanie started toward the door.

"I guess I was wrong. Dalton must've remembered. I'll face the music," she sighed.

Stephanie glanced down at her bare feet and brief denim shorts topped with a Boulder Bay T-shirt. She paused to glance in the mirror and gathered her abundant locks into a barrette.

"You're prompt, Mr. Dalton. Please come in. We can talk in the parlor."

The swarthy, dark-haired man had shed his business suit in favor of a kelly golfing shirt and pale yellow, close-fitting trousers, which accented his deep tan and muscular physique.

Stephanie had to admit that he was an attractive man in an overpowering way. He flashed a vivid smile beneath a dark, neatly trimmed mustache, and his manner proved impeccably charming as he entered the room with a slight swagger. His actions last night had not dampened his confidence; he appeared completely at ease.

Stephanie's courage faltered.

"Please be seated, Mr. Dalton," she directed with an outward poise that belied her thumping heart. She became acutely aware of her shorts and shirt as Jay Dalton's deliberate gaze took her in from head to toe.

An appreciative smile began at one corner of his mouth and spread to a wide, full grin. "Can it be possible? You're lovelier than I remembered."

"Thank you, Mr. Dalton—"

"Jay," he corrected.

"Jay, but I don't believe the way I look has any bearing on our business."

"You're wrong. It makes it much more pleasant, and I have to confess my only weakness is beautiful women. You might say, I'm putty in their hands. You see, I will enjoy doing business more, but you will have the advantage," his eyes slid over her once more as he nodded. "A decided advantage."

The man's boldness stirred a cauldron of anger within Stephanie, setting her countenance in disgust. "Who I am or how I look will not affect our business, Mr. Dalton," she replied coldly.

She fought to control her anger as she softened her tone, realizing the potential danger in her situation. Jay Dalton was a powerful man, perhaps with unsavory connections. "Jay," she amended, "I tried to explain last evening, but you seemed, uh. . .preoccupied."

He smiled knowingly, acknowledging nothing. "Not too preoccupied to remember what you said or to understand the game you're playing. Stephanie, let's get to the bottom line. I intend to have Boulder Bay, one way or the other. I know you need the money, and I'd rather you have it than the bank. Just how much will it take to satisfy you?" The dazzling smile parted the dark face once again, but the eyes remained cold and calculating.

"Not anything you have. Boulder Bay is not for sale."

A humorless laugh interrupted her. "Anything has its price. Tell me what's yours. Let's quit playing games and finish our business."

Her eyes rounded in amazement, and she paused before replying. "I wish I could make you understand, Mr. Dalton. You can't buy Boulder Bay."

"Because you don't approve of what you think my plans are for it?"

A slow smile softened Stephanie's face and warmth touched her eyes. "I don't expect you to understand, and I can't explain it any better than I did yesterday. If I aided you in doing something that violates my convictions, then all the money in the world couldn't compensate for it. What price can even you put on peace of mind, Jay?"

He stared back at her, incredulity written on his face, yet his eyes for an instant were unguarded, warmed by a puzzled admiration. Then his hooded eyes grew cold and hard as if rejecting what he'd recognized. "Ms. Haynes, I've found the only way to assure my peace of mind is to buy it."

"That's unfortunate, Jay Dalton, for if having Boulder Bay is important to your peace of mind, you'll lose out. I won't sell to you, now or ever."

Anger flared briefly in the cold, ebony eyes, and he clenched his jaw, but quickly had himself under control. In a gentle, persuasive voice, he remarked, "This is a strange turn of events. Yesterday you seemed willing until I refused to agree to your ridiculous stipulation. Took me a few hours to realize it was a ploy. I think you're still playing."

Stephanie threw up her hands in exasperation and walked away from her visitor to the window. She looked out over the rolling lawn. The grass, a lush green, extended to a rock ledge that plunged straight to the breakers below.

"It's easy to see why you're so persistent," she remarked without facing him. "This is a place of resplendent beauty and the only gem of privately owned property on this section of the coast. A valuable investment for whatever your plans may be. My reasons for turning you down yesterday haven't changed, but my circumstances have. I don't have to sell now."

"You're mistaken. You have to sell it—to me."

Stephanie whirled around, patience at an end and an angry retort on her lips. "That's—"

The words hung in midair as she collided, face to chest, with the bright green shirt. The pungent herbal fragrance of Jay Dalton's aftershave overpowered her. He had moved silently from his seat and now stood squarely boxing her in. Stephanie retreated. With her back pressed against the window, she held her head high, eyes questioning, but her stomach churned with alarm.

Dalton smiled darkly, enjoying his advantage, and crooned softly, "Are you ready to talk business or play games?"

"I'm. . .I'm. . .," Stephanie stammered hesitantly. Then squaring her shoulders, she threw her head back and looked him squarely in the eye. They stood so for a moment, eyes locked in combat, piercing black ones against icy blue.

From across the room a deep-timbred voice spoke with calm authority. "Mr. Dalton, I believe my partner has spoken for both of us. Boulder Bay is not for sale."

Jay Dalton whirled, astonishment written on his craggy features. Stephanie slipped quickly from her cornered position.

"Who are you, and why are you interfering?"

"I'm Lance Donovan, movie producer and business partner with Stephanie Haynes. I have been informed of your offer, and we are in complete agreement. No sale." Lance spoke amiably as he strolled across the room toward Stephanie. With three long strides, he reached her and put a possessive arm around her shoulders, offering a haven of protection.

He cast a reassuring smile at Stephanie and added, "I wholeheartedly agree with you, Dalton. She is an enchanting creature, but she's more than that. She knows what she wants and can't be swayed. Admirable quality, don't you think?"

Jay Dalton recovered his composure more rapidly than Stephanie and looked Lance steadily in the eyes. A charged message coursed between them as he silently acknowledged the challenge in Lance's soft statement.

With an abrupt change in tactics, he spoke in a conciliatory tone as he turned to Stephanie. "I guess I owe you an apology, Ms. Haynes. In my business, bluff is the name of the game. I sincerely thought you were holding out for more money."

He paused and once again looked Lance squarely in the eye, this time issuing his own challenge to the younger man. "Are you Ms. Haynes's social secretary as well as her partner? I had intended to invite her to dinner this evening. Surely she doesn't have to work night and day."

"No, but she's spending the evening with me. In fact, from now on she'll be spending all her free time with me. Tonight we're going out to dinner. Could you recommend a good restaurant, some place extra special? You know, I'm new to the area."

Stephanie remained silent, her eyes round in disbelief as Dalton raised his eyebrows in surprise, then threw his head back and laughed heartily.

"Donovan, you're all right. Why don't both you and Ms. Haynes be my guests at the yacht club? It's the best place in town, and you can only dine there if you're with a member."

"Thank you, but no. Tell me, Dalton, would you want to share the attention of this lovely lady if you were me?"

"No, but I thought I'd try anyway. I don't give up easily," he responded lightly and, turning his head toward Stephanie, he added with a pleasant smile, "I meant what I said. You are a lovely lady, and I'd enjoy doing business with you. You have my number if you change your mind."

"She won't," Lance interrupted.

Jay Dalton's smile broadened, and he shifted his gaze toward Lance. "Don't be too sure. I intend to have Boulder Bay, and I always get what I want."

Stephanie shivered as she looked from one man to the other. Dalton's smile did not hide the determination his voice conveyed.

Lance tilted his head to one side and stroked his chin before replying softly, "But you have never wanted anything that was mine before." The warm blue of his eyes had turned to steel gray.

Stephanie found her voice. "Lance is quite right, Mr. Dalton. I won't be changing my mind. I appreciate your interest and am sorry we've taken up so much of your time. I know that you, as we, have a busy morning ahead. Therefore, I won't detain you any longer."

"Yes, I need to be going. Never mind showing me out," he responded as Stephanie walked toward the door. "I know the way. Until later, have a pleasant evening."

Stephanie let out a long sigh when she heard the front door close. "Thank you, Lance. It was very kind of you to intercede like that. But I'm afraid you gave Dalton the wrong idea about us."

"How's that?"

"That somehow you are in charge of my life."

"In a way I am."

"We are partners—business partners."

"I know that. So what's the problem?"

"Well, you made him think. . ."

"Think what?"

"You know."

"Know what?"

"That you had control of other parts of my life."

"So?"

"I don't want him to think that."

"Think what?"

"That you have any other interest in me than business." Stephanie's voice edged with impatience.

"But I do."

"Now, Lancelot Donovan!"

"Honorable. Completely honorable," Lance responded with a look of mock horror on his face.

"Lance, please be serious."

"I am."

"Then let me be serious. I appreciate your help this morning—more than I could tell you—but I don't want anyone, including Jay Dalton, to think that there's anything about our relationship that's not aboveboard."

"He doesn't. Unless the man is totally blind and without a smidgen of understanding, he knows you are a woman of principle. Your whole countenance glows with innocence. Why do you think he was giving you such a hard time? He thought you'd be easy to intimidate," Lance explained.

"Well, I'm not easily intimidated, and I hope you're right about his understanding," came Stephanie's doubtful reply.

"Take it from a man of the world. Who you are shows. That's why I'm here, to protect you."

"I thought you were interested in a business deal."

Lance paused and looked at her, all traces of his lighthearted teasing gone. "I was, but suddenly I find that each time I look at you, I forget about our business. I meant it when I told Dalton to forget seeing you. I plan to take up all your time. You see, I'm going to marry you someday, Stephanie Haynes."

Words of protest died on Stephanie's lips as she encountered the tender resoluteness in the vivid blue eyes that held hers. Only her heart thundered an utterance.

Chapter Six

Stephanie barely noticed when spring gave way to summer. After Lance assessed the needs and potential of Boulder Bay, he made swift plans and began immediate execution of them. He had a movie to get under production, and the major improvements had to be completed before he could begin. Stephanie shared his determination, eager to prove the confidence he had in her.

They saw each other often but had no time to talk intimately again, nor did Lance seem inclined to elaborate on his earlier, startling statement. Warm friendship and respect permeated their relationship.

Lance's uncanny business sense discovered potential revenue-producing projects that Stephanie had either overlooked or had lacked the money to pursue. He mapped out the improvements he wanted and gave Stephanie a budget to work from. Her large, blue eyes widened in disbelief when she saw the size of it. She protested vehemently.

He silenced her with his reasonable explanation that it takes money to make money. His eagerness to release the untapped potential of the property knew no bounds. Stephanie, cautious by necessity and by nature, felt anxious at first, but gradually her anxiety eased as she caught Lance's vision. Determined to contribute her part, she threw herself wholeheartedly into getting the best job done the most economically.

Following Lance's master plan to the smallest detail, she supervised the project and developed skills of bargaining and supervision that she hadn't known she possessed. The workmen came early, but they always found Stephanie there before them. However late they left, she was still busy, planning and inspecting their work. The inn reached its last stages of completion just as the date for Lance's production approached.

Stephanie felt relieved that business had left little time for intimate conversation. Disturbing questions hammered at her mind, but she ignored them, glad she could throw her heart into the work at hand and fall exhausted into bed at night. She told herself a thousand times that Lance had been teasing and the sheer jubilance she felt was the result of seeing her dream of Boulder Bay come alive before her eyes.

Like the proverbial phoenix rising from the ashes, the whole place took on a new dimension. Where it had been a large, comfortable, rambling house, it now resided in a gown of splendor. The crew painted the old, white clapboards a pastel blue and repaired and replaced the ornate Victorian trim, painting it a dazzling white.

Craftsmen cleaned the stained glass windows, restoring them to their original beauty. Antiques and authentic reproductions furnished the rooms, adding irresistible charm. Workmen replaced old plumbing and modernized the kitchen with every convenience needed for serving capacity crowds. A garden room was added to enlarge the dining facilities, and a large grand piano sat in regal splendor in one corner.

Because of Martha's culinary artistry, Lance decided to establish the inn as a gourmet paradise, pulling in local diners as well as tourist and inn guests. His aim: an expensive night of epicurean delight in an elegant atmosphere topped off with good entertainment.

He turned the coach house into a coffee shop, equipping it with a fireplace built from boulders found on the property. From the terrace, diners could overlook the new pool and tennis courts.

Professional landscapers added gardens and rock pathways along the deserted bluff above the rugged coast, but Stephanie's private cove was fenced off. As if by unspoken agreement, Lance let it remain as it was, Stephanie's private sanctuary.

Where the coast curved gently inward to form a protected inlet, they built a dock and boathouse. Soon Stephanie's forty-foot sloop, *Carefree*, sat anchored in readiness. Her teak deck sparkled, cleaned and refurbished by a part-time college crew, eagerly awaiting their first customer to charter her for an hour, day, or week.

As the final weeks approached, Stephanie and Lance saw less and less of one another, each absorbed with the work at hand. Even so, their friendship strengthened with each passing day. They were two people who had deep respect for one another and shared a common goal.

Martha had been too busy to engage in her matchmaking pursuits, but she'd noticed Stephanie's growing radiance and caught Lance's lingering glance when Stephanie walked away from him. She smiled knowingly; a business venture alone couldn't light up a woman's eyes like that. Martha told John as much, adding that she could rest easy if Stephanie had a man like Lance to look after her.

Before Stephanie was quite prepared, summer waned and a hint of fall teased the air. She redoubled her efforts and worked even longer hours. When darkness swallowed up the long twilight shadows, she worked on her accounts in the light of an old seaman's lamp on her small rosewood desk.

The size of the invoices and payroll astounded her, but when she checked her budget, it remained well below Lance's estimate. Her excitement grew. Already there was a sizable income from the chartering of *Carefree*. The college crew had been so excited about the adventure that they had taken care of the advertising. Demand had exceeded the number of trips they could run.

It was Lance who had realized the charter potential of Stephanie's sloop, but it was her idea to channel the energy and enthusiasm for sailing of the local young people. The success was just another example of how well Lance and Stephanie worked together.

Once she had caught Lance's vision for Boulder Bay, Stephanie knew that he was right. She determined to bring that vision to reality, but substantially under the budget. Now it looked as if she would have a sizable amount to give back to Lance on completion of the project.

After the first month, he had not looked at the books with her. At first the responsibility he had entrusted her with worried her, but now it gave her a sense of satisfaction.

When refurbishing the cottages got under way, Lance took a personal interest in them. Without explanation, he enlarged one to include an office, extra bedroom, kitchen, and solarium. Since it was the cottage nearest the sea, it seemed reasonable to Stephanie that it should be enhanced for a honeymoon cottage, and Lance's personal involvement in it puzzled her.

Shortly before its completion, Lance arrived late one afternoon in a bright red truck, loaded with his personal belongings. Stephanie, brown as a berry from her busy weeks outdoors, met him and raised an inquisitive brow.

The bright afternoon sun caught the merry lights flashing in Lance's vivid blue eyes. One side of his mouth turned up in a lopsided grin. "I can't stand being so far away from you, so I'm moving in."

Stephanie smiled, not believing him. "Sure you are."

"If you won't marry me, what choice do I have?" he countered, attempting a pitiful countenance.

"You poor little lamb," she laughed as she impulsively reached up and patted his cheek. "Seriously, what are you doing?"

"Just like I told you—moving in. I can't go on living without seeing that beautiful face every day," he responded, putting his hand over his heart in mock seriousness. "Oh, to see those beautiful eyes across the breakfast table from me every morning—it must be thus or I die."

"Lance, you're incorrigible," Stephanie laughed.

"Yeh, but ain't I fun?" he quipped, his face alight with laughter.

"You still haven't answered my question. What are you doing?" she insisted.

"Moving in."

Stephanie's smile faded and she looked at him, the question in her eyes turning them dark and wary.

Lance stepped over to her and, taking her chin in his hand, tilted her face upward to his. He was standing so close to her that she could see the spidery fine laughter lines around his eyes and hear his steady breathing.

Lance bent his head and kissed her lightly on her upturned lips. "The cottage, sweetheart. The cottage. I fixed it up for me. It's perfect. Save me time, rent, and the best thing of all—I *can* have breakfast with you every morning." He smiled gently, reassuringly at her, then with an impish grin added, "Course, to be honest—Martha's cooking had a great deal to do with my decision. She does cook breakfast every morning, doesn't she?"

Stephanie stepped back from his kiss as if an electrical current had coursed through her body. Embarrassment and relief flushed her face. "I'm sure. . . ," she stammered, dropping her eyes.

He lifted her chin again, "You're sure, what?"

"That Martha'll be glad to have you!" she finished, her voice shrill in her ears.

He stepped even closer, never releasing her chin. Her head came to just below his shoulder, and she could see the even rise and fall of his broad, muscular chest. Lance tilted her head farther back, forcing her to meet his eyes. "And what about Miss Stephanie Haynes? How does she feel about it?"

The look in his eyes, his very nearness, returned the disturbing emotions that she had pushed away all summer. How could she deny the joy, desire, and even terror that he stirred within her? Did she want him to stay at Boulder Bay where she could see him every day, hear his voice, see the way the sun caught the copper glint in his hair, feel the warmth of his eyes as intimate as an embrace when they rested on her?

The truth. He wanted the truth, but how could she tell him? It was what she wanted, God help her, with all her heart. Instead she closed her eyes, wrinkled her nose, and remarked with as much nonchalance as she could muster, "I might be able to put up with you, Mr. Donovan—if you'll behave yourself."

His smile broadened as he released her. "I knew you'd see it my way, my dear. I'll do my best to behave, but it won't be easy. You'd better be thankful we have more work to do than hours to finish it, 'cause otherwise you might prove to be a fatal distraction, and I'd be tempted to break my word to you— sweep you off your feet and look for a preacher. . . ."

"Lance. . . ," she began, trying to look stern.

"No, no, I know we're not ready for that yet—neither of us. I just said it would be tempting." The laughter in his eyes muted and he added, his tone softly serious, "You're a delicious woman, Stephanie Haynes, like none other I've ever met. Someday I'll tell you just how much you mean to me; but right now, we've dragons to slay."

"Dragons?" she asked puzzled.

"Jay Dalton. Has he approached you again about Boulder Bay?"

"No, why?"

"Several evenings lately the workmen said they've seen him parked up on the bluff watching the progress down here. I feel sure that he will make another offer. He doesn't give up easily, and I want to know how you feel about it. The place is still yours, and if you decide you want to sell, it's okay."

"I still feel the same way. Why, Lance? Has there been some change in your financial status? Do you need your money back?"

"No, I just wanted to be sure that you still feel the same."

"I do. I couldn't sell it to him for what he wants to do with it, but aside from that, seeing it transformed like this—why it exceeds my wildest dreams. The only worry I have is how soon you will get a profitable return on your investment. You've spent a lot more money than I had anticipated. The improvements have been so much more elaborate than I had envisioned."

"It will take longer to pay for the improvements, but in the long run your revenue-producing potential is much greater. Using the inn as a location for the film will be a windfall for me. It will cost the film less, and we will be making a profit at the same time. By enlarging the facilities, we can open the inn up to other guests while we are filming, and that will be a drawing card."

"How do you plan to get the word out?" Stephanie questioned, marveling at Lance's innovative ideas.

"News releases. Hollywood and the surrounding area are interested in the movie project, so we'll just casually include our plans for using this place as a location."

"You're pretty sharp, Lance Donovan."

"Did you ever have any doubts about that?" he quipped.

She chuckled. "Well, I did have a moment or two at the beginning, if you recall."

Lance threw back his head and laughed. "Especially about my proposition. Boy, did you get your dander up about that. Did I ever tell you how beautiful you are when you're angry? You're like fire and ice—absolutely breathtaking."

"Lance, you're impossible!"

"No, I'm an artist, among all my other wonderful attributes. I'm an expert on beauty—and I can tell you something else, I can read emotion."

Stephanie shot him a quick look and warned, "Be careful that you don't read too much into them. You might get hurt."

His gaze was steady as it met hers. "Don't worry. I won't. Anyway the time's not right yet. By the way, would you happen to have any leftovers for a homeless man?"

"Leftovers?" she responded, her brow wrinkled.

He grinned at her, "Yeh, the kitchen kind. I couldn't eat, thinking about Martha's cooking just waiting for me."

"You're in luck. There's soup and salad in the kitchen and a strawberry pie in the oven. Come on, hungry man, let's feed you before you suffer the vapors."

He bent in a mock bow and lifted her hand to his lips, murmuring, "Lead on, fair maiden, and sit thee before me or I perish."

After an ample meal, Lance unloaded his belongings with Stephanie's help. Martha had sent over cookies and a large pitcher of lemonade, and the two had just sat down on the large porch overlooking the sea when a smart, yellow sports car drove up the drive and stopped outside. Stephanie watched the immaculate brunette walk hurriedly up the rock walk and recognized her just before she reached the door.

"Hello, Abigail," Stephanie called from the porch. "Just follow the walk on around. We're here on the porch. Come have a glass of lemonade." Lance looked at Stephanie questioningly and she replied softly, "Abigail, Mr. Jarrett's secretary."

He rose from his chair when she opened the door and smilingly acknowledged the brief introduction.

Abigail smiled shyly. "I hate to interrupt you. . . ."

"You're not interrupting anything, Abigail. I'm glad to see you," Stephanie responded, realizing she felt genuinely glad to see the young woman. "I told you to come out anytime, you know."

"Yes, thank you, I remembered. That's one of the reasons why I'm here. I'm on my way back home."

"A visit?" Lance questioned.

Tears filled the somber, dark eyes. "No, to stay. I've lost my job."

"What happened, Abigail?" Stephanie asked, concern clouding the bright blue of her eyes.

"Do you remember the conversation we had before you went in to see Mr. Jarrett?"

"About your job?"

"No, about what Mr. Dalton wanted to do with your place."

"Yes."

"That started me to thinking. The fact that your convictions were so strong you'd risk losing your place rather than compromise made an impression on me. I began to question what went on in the office. Some things happened, some business deals that—well, I won't elaborate. I'll just say I couldn't in good conscience participate in them. Mr. Jarrett told me to do it or to leave; so I left."

"I'm sure that you did the right thing, and you'll be better off for it," Stephanie soothed.

A wan smile appeared briefly, lifting Abigail's countenance. "It's rather embarrassing for me. Everyone will ask questions, and there's no telling what Mr. Jarrett will tell them. You're the only two I've talked to, and the only reason I've come to you is to warn you. I've really struggled with this—trying to evaluate if I should betray what I heard while in the employ of Mr. Jarrett."

"Something that affects Stephanie, Abigail?" Lance asked. Stephanie could see him tense beneath his warm, hospitable stance.

"To both of you. You are her business associate, aren't you?"

"Yes. Now tell us," Lance responded, his voice edged with urgency.

"It's Dalton. He and Jarrett were talking. He's determined to get your place. When you paid off the bank, and he realized that hope of a default was gone, he went into a rage. About a week ago he came back, and I heard him tell Jarrett that he'd found a way, and it would be only a matter of time before Boulder Bay was his. He laughed and said that it had worked out better for him anyway; the improvements were superb, and he'd gotten all the benefit of your time and expertise without having to pay for it."

"Abigail, how did he say he was going to accomplish this?" Lance asked.

"He didn't. He just said there were more roads to Rome than one and something about his trip to Las Vegas. Then they noticed the door was ajar and closed it. That's all I could hear."

"Lance, what could he mean?" Stephanie asked, her face creased with worry.

"Don't let it worry you, honey. He's just blowing off steam."

"I don't think he was," Abigail disputed with a shake of her head. "They talked a long time after that, and he was too jubilant not to have a solution."

"I can't think of anything he can do to us, can you, Lance?" Stephanie puzzled.

"Nope, not if you've been paying the bills on time," Lance replied with a reassuring wink, but not before Stephanie could see a vestige of doubt in his usually confident eyes.

"By the way, Abigail. Speaking of paying the bills, how would you like a job here with us?" Lance continued.

Stephanie looked from Lance to Abigail and back again questioningly.

"Production is about to start, and I need a good secretary," he explained. "Stephanie will be involved in the picture soon and could use some administrative help running the lodge and inn. What do you say, Steph?"

"You know what you need better than I do, Lance. I'm sure Abigail would make you an efficient secretary," Stephanie answered stiffly.

"It's not me that I'm thinking of. I know you. You won't get anyone to help you. I don't want my ingenue to look tired and haggard." He looked at her, mild pleading in his eyes.

Relieved, she smiled her assent and asked, "Can we afford it?"

"Sure we can. Taking care of you is my first priority." Once more the message in his vivid blue eyes sent chills of fear and delight straight to Stephanie's heart.

The three quickly worked out the details of Abigail's job. She would live on the premises, taking her room and board as part of her compensation. Her salary was less than it had been at Brown, Jarrett, and Garrard's, but Stephanie suggested profit-sharing options and bonuses that would make up the difference. Soon a happy Abigail unloaded her little sports car, and Boulder Bay had another resident.

Chapter Seven

Abigail settled into her new job with ease and efficiency, and within a month she proved indispensable to both Lance and Stephanie while garnering a reluctant Martha's affection. John observed her in wary silence, but soon her sincerity and good humor had won him over completely.

The dining room opened with a flourish, and the first week the crowds overflowed. They came to experience a culinary treat and lingered to enjoy the romantic dinner music. Stephanie and Martha opened the coach house and used it as a secondary dining room. Music from the solarium wafted across the pool, and diners sat beneath the stars on the terrace. Each left having experienced an evening of outstanding quality. They told their friends and their friends came. Crowds upon crowds—and they were never disappointed.

Lance was too busy with the final preparations of his film to take an active part in the opening of the restaurant, but Stephanie filled in as needed, sometimes as hostess and sometimes in the kitchen. Every evening, she and Abigail totaled up the receipts, and after only a month, she saw the wisdom of Lance's investment in Martha's culinary genius. The dining room proved an unqualified success, and thanks to Abigail's attention to careful shopping, it promised to be a very profitable endeavor.

Each night, Stephanie fell into bed past midnight in happy exhaustion. She had yet to take a meal in the dining hall, preferring to catch a bite in the kitchen with Abigail and Lance.

One afternoon, Stephanie strolled over to Lance's bungalow to see how it looked after he had furnished and decorated it. Her time had been so involved at the main inn that she had left the completion of the cottages to Lance and Abigail.

She heard a deep baritone voice singing gustily as she approached the porch facing the ocean. A warm smile parted her face when she recognized Lance's voice singing one of the old love songs played the night before. She joined her sweet lilting soprano with his, and they finished the chorus together.

He rose from his seat on the porch when he saw her, delight flaring in his eyes. Meeting her at the door, he opened it and motioned her in. "Wow, we ought to be in show biz—the Dynamo Duo. Do you reckon we could get a job at Boulder Inn?"

"I don't know. I think we ought to practice, don't you?"

"I've been for that from the beginning." His eyes held hers. "Give me a kiss—"

"To build a dream on," she chimed in, her eyes soft and shining. Happiness bubbled inside her.

Suddenly the singing died as she looked up into his vivid blue eyes. The mirth in them faded, exchanged for something undefinable that left her breathless.

Lance moved closer and without taking his eyes from hers, he lifted her hand and pressed it to his lips. "Stephanie Haynes, if you look at me like that one more time, I can't vouch for your safety. I was thinking of you while I sang, and then you appeared like a beautiful vision. It's almost more than this lovesick man can stand."

Stephanie's brow wrinkled as she searched his face. Was he teasing her again? His words sounded light, but his eyes betrayed him. She saw apprehension, almost fear in them. But of what? His own emotions? Her response?

She laughed softly, trying to relieve the tension between them. "I bet you say that to all your beautiful female visitors. Never fear, I can take care of myself, but I will watch these expressive eyes. I wouldn't want to tempt you unduly." She lowered her long lashes in a mock apology.

A low chuckle started in Lance's throat and spread to a full laugh, clearing the emotion-charged air.

Stephanie sighed with relief as he remarked, "Well, you little vixen, you wouldn't come in second to Miss Scarlett herself with those fluttering lashes. Yes, ma'am, I've got myself a little actress on my hands."

"Lance, all you talk about is business, business, business, and here I came looking for a break," she teased.

He raised his eyebrows and searched her face, blandly replying, "Where you are concerned, that's the safest subject. By the way, you need to set aside tomorrow afternoon and evening. The camera crew arrives in the morning, and I need to set up your screen test."

"Will it take that long?"

"No, but afterwards I want to take you out to dinner. How about a date?"

"Any place in particular?"

"How about that new place over at Boulder Bay?"

"You mean the dining room or kitchen?"

"The choice dining room table, so put on your best duds. We're dining in style."

"That sounds like fun."

"Time we had some fun, don't you think?"

"Well, yes, I. . ." Stephanie hesitated, a faint blush tinting her cheeks.

Lance raised an eyebrow, waiting. When she failed to continue, he gently urged, "Any problem?"

A timid smile touched her lips and she finished softly, "Working with you *has* been fun. More fun than I've ever had in my life."

"I'm talking about a different kind of fun, Steph. I mean the strictly 'me and you' kind of fun. Where I can stare at you in the candlelight, with love songs in the background, listen to the sweet sound of your voice as it speaks my name, and afterwards hold your hand while we walk in the moonlight. Nothing to do with our joy of accomplishment this time; just the plain joy of being alone with you." His eyes were soft, and his voice held a gentle intensity as he added, "There's more to life than work."

A lump constricted Stephanie's throat. Lance had opened a floodgate of longing. She turned from him toward the door when she could finally speak and, nodding her head, said simply, "I'll be ready."

৯

The next morning the atmosphere at the inn crackled with excitement. By midmorning, the first vans and trucks arrived, bringing camera crew and equipment. Then came the wardrobe van and the makeup artists.

Stephanie worked swiftly and efficiently with Abigail to get them settled. By early afternoon, every crew member had his room assignment and had enjoyed a sumptuous lunch, enabling Stephanie to report promptly to the basement production department for her wardrobe and makeup, then on to the filming room.

The morning's activities had kept her too busy for anxiety to creep in, but now her palms dampened and her heart beat wildly when Lance met her in the narrow hall. His encouraging smile calmed her and, much to her surprise, she thoroughly enjoyed the filming session.

Lance's relaxed instruction brought her through step by step, and when he called an end to the session, she experienced a fleeting moment of disappointment.

Lance's features were animated with controlled excitement. Stephanie raised her eyebrows, tilting her head to one side as she waited for an explanation.

He offered none. With a wave of his hand, he dismissed her, saying nonchalantly, "I think this'll do, kitten. See you at seven!"

Stephanie walked slowly from the room, her small white teeth pulling absentmindedly on her bottom lip. She felt let down. Why? It seemed natural that she should. After all, she'd been working toward this day since early spring. She sighed. What happened to the happy sense of accomplishment?

Perhaps the screen test traumatized her more than she realized.

Apprehension knotted her stomach. What if it didn't turn out well? Did it really matter? She didn't want to disappoint Lance, yet she'd never had any desire to be a movie star. She pulled at her lip again. She had enjoyed the screening, though.

On down the hall she strolled, head down, deep in thought. With a shrug of her shoulders, she reached out to take the railing of the stairs, her foot paused on the first step. It wasn't her work or her test! It was Lance. He had been so. . .so businesslike with her. Encouraging, accommodating, but that special way he looked at her. It hadn't been there! And she'd missed it. Had she ever missed it!

Stephanie smiled and walked up the stairs. Amused at herself, she acknowledged that by necessity her relationship with Lance would have to change. They would have to put aside the casual atmosphere they had enjoyed all summer or risk a morale and discipline problem on the set. This movie was big business, and Lance was the boss.

Her smile broadened at the thought. This Lance she'd not seen before— one with a controlled energy that commanded respect and response. A competent business mind whose attention remained fixed on the project at hand had replaced the slightly impudent young man with the teasing eyes. The metamorphosis intrigued her, yet she couldn't shake the uneasy feeling in the pit of her stomach. How would this affect their relationship?

For the first time, Stephanie acknowledged her dependence on Lance. Her delicate brows knit together in a frown as her emotions sought safer ground. How could she allow that? Dependency meant enslavement. Hadn't she made that decision a long time ago? Yet her heart refused to listen as the image of Lance's laughing blue eyes danced before her. She hurried up the stairs, breathless in anticipation of the evening ahead.

❧

Stephanie smiled at her reflection. Her hair hung loose to her shoulders in a golden cloud with silver lights. Her long, white dress draped her body. A silver belt clasped her narrow waist, and the silky material lay softly across her small rounded hips in a gentle caress before falling gracefully to the floor.

The vivid white set off Stephanie's sun-bronzed skin, and her eyes, wide with excitement, sparkled like sapphires. Tonight, she wanted to be beautiful. The mirror told her that she was.

So did Lance's eyes. He saw her the moment she left her room. She walked across the open balcony and, pausing, she looked down at him over the ornate rail. Her full, pink lips parted in a half-smile. Then with queenly grace, she slowly descended the curved staircase. She felt the warmth of Lance's approving gaze and enjoyed the pleasure it stirred inside her. Then their eyes locked and her heart raced. His eyes smoldered a passionate message, and Stephanie saw yet another Lance.

She walked up to him, and he briefly rested his hands on her small, square shoulders. Running his fingertips in a light caress down her arms to her hands, he lifted them and pressed each one to his lips. "You are the most beautiful woman I've ever seen." His voice was husky with emotion.

"You approve?" she dimpled up at him, reveling in this strange new power she possessed.

"I think you could say that," he said with a half-smile. "Is—the dress—new?"

"Yes. Abigail saw it when she was in town and brought it home on approval. I was going to take it back, but when you said you wanted me to get my best duds on, I couldn't resist the temptation."

Tucking her hand inside the curve of his arm, Lance pulled her closer to him, and they walked out the door. "I'm glad you didn't. I've never seen anything to compare with you in that dress."

"Thank you, Sir Lancelot. I aimed to please."

He smiled at her. No words were needed. His eyes burned his appreciation.

The evening continued with the same promise that it began. From the meal of seafood delicacy to the softly throbbing romantic songs from a bygone year, Stephanie's senses were filled with heady delight.

Later Stephanie couldn't remember what they discussed during dinner. She could only recall Lance's eyes blazing into hers with a message that needed no utterance.

They were enjoying their after-dessert coffee when Lance asked her how she felt about her screen test.

"I really enjoyed it. Although I was nervous at first, before long I forgot about the camera and just enjoyed the experience."

"I thought you did."

A shy smile teased her lips, and she traced the intricate designs on the damask cloth with her finger, then glancing up at him through her lashes, she added, "I couldn't have done it without you. Your instructions were perfect."

He chuckled, "You just keep believing that, sweetheart."

She turned her full, wide eyes on him questioningly.

"That you need me," he explained, his mouth curving with tenderness.

She dropped her head, not wanting him to see the response that flamed in her eyes. But he had, and rising, he took her hand and pulled her to her feet. "It's time for that moonlit walk."

The night sky blazed with stars, and a gentle breeze cooled the air. Soft strains of music drifted after them as they strolled across the lawn toward the bluff and the bench they had shared so many months before. Stephanie shivered, partly from the cool night air and partly from the heady excitement of the moment.

Lance stopped and, taking off his coat, draped it around her and pulled her to him in a gentle, undemanding embrace. Unresisting, she rested her head on his shoulder.

They stood thus for a long moment. Stephanie could hear the beat of his heart, echoing the thundering sea beneath them. The scent of his aftershave teased her nostrils, and the towering strength of his tall, masculine body gave her a quiet sense of security and safety.

She stirred and tried to pull away, suddenly afraid of this haven, her dependence, her need for it.

Lance felt her resistance and tightened his hold. "Don't pull away, Stephanie. I've waited an eternity to hold you like this. Tonight is our night. No other world exists but ours, no others but us; nothing else matters but our love."

Stephanie lifted her head and stared intently into his eyes, longing and fear battling in hers. Her long blond hair, silver in the moonlight, cascaded down her back.

With a low guttural groan, Lance bent his head to hers and kissed the soft, full mouth turned up to him. The kiss lingered. It throbbed with the passion of demand, yet flowing with a tender love that finally ended in a crescendo of victory as two hearts united in spirit while time and space receded. Stephanie forgot her fears. In that moment only Lance existed, the safety of his arms, the power of his kiss, the rivers of delight he sent flowing through her with his love, with his embrace, with his kiss.

Finally, he released her and a knowing smile crinkled his eyes. "Stephanie, I love you, and you love me."

A frown wrinkled her wide, smooth brow, and her eyes looked dark in the bright moonlight. She shook her head and said breathlessly, "Lance, don't push me. The night, the moonlight—it's too romantic to rely on."

He chuckled softly in her ear. "It isn't the moonlight, darling. It's me and you. We were made for each other. I never believed that was possible before I met you. If you'll tell the truth, you'll have to admit it, Steph." Slipping his arm around her waist, he picked up her hand and, placing it on his heart, laughed. "It's like a herd of wild horses every time you come near me whether it's in the moonlight or broad daylight."

"That's not love, Lance."

"I don't need a biology lesson, Stephanie. This is love—heart, mind, body, and spirit. A love that says it wants you and only you, now and always. A lifetime commitment—the 'until death do us part' kind."

She shuddered. The euphoria of the previous moment receded, leaving reality with all its fears and apprehensions. "Lance, don't."

Releasing his hold on her, he demanded, "Why?"

"Because you are complicating things. You know me, you know our agreement," she hedged, closing her heart to him.

"Our agreement is a business arrangement, pure and simple—good for you and me. The way I feel about you is something entirely separate. I want to spend every moment with you—for the rest of my life and down through eternity if that is possible."

Why couldn't they remain friends—partners with a common goal, a comfortable relationship based on mutual respect? So much safer, the warm esteem of friendship than these searing emotions of love.

She pushed against him, fighting to be free—free from an emotion that might enslave her. "You don't know what you mean. It will completely destroy what we have."

"Stephanie, how can the way I feel about you destroy you, destroy us?" His eyes, usually alert and confident, pleaded for an explanation he could understand. "I will never take advantage of you—I want the best for you, to take care of you—"

"I never want anyone to take care of me—don't you see? I never want to be dependent on anyone, not you, not *anyone*," she said, her teeth clenched, trying to bring her conflicting emotions under control.

Lance dropped his arms, his handsome features sharp as he fought his own battle with bewilderment and frustration. This was a Stephanie he'd never seen. "Why are you afraid of me, Steph? Is it because we've only known each other a few months? Have I done anything to cause you to distrust me?"

"This talk of marriage frightens me."

"Why, Stephanie?"

"I'm not sure you'd understand."

"Was it another man? Have you been hurt?" he gently probed, determination set in his face.

"No."

"What, then? What *are* you afraid of?"

"I. . .I don't like what love can do to a person," she answered uneasily as memories of her mother pierced her heart. She dropped her head, unable once again to meet the intensity in his gaze.

His dark brows lifted questioningly, but he remained silent, his eyes demanding an explanation. She turned away from those disturbing eyes. How could she make him understand that years before she'd determined not to love? She tried to calm her racing heart—to put substance to the old resolutions that ruled her—yet it was hard when he stood so near.

She walked away from him, putting more distance between them. His very nearness stirred a response in her that was stronger than her stubborn will. She must have time to sort out her answer, to make him know that they had no future together beyond a warm friendship and a business venture.

Her tortuous thoughts propelled her on. Finally she almost ran down the rocky pathway, stopping only when she reached the end of the path. There a rock wall separated it from a sheer cliff that fell straight to the rocks and pounding surf below. A stiff northeastern breeze blew, and she knew despite the cloudless sky that a late summer storm brewed somewhere out in that vast ocean. It blew her silken hair in wild profusion around her head, whipping her face, then lifting it to trail behind her, catching the light in silver ribbons. She caught her breath in a ragged shudder, half-sob. *Why does he have to complicate things? Why can't he just accept things as they are?* Her eyes mirrored the sea's stormy turbulence. She clenched and unclenched a tiny, competent fist, frustration framed in every movement.

Suddenly a quiet, firm voice spoke in her ear and two strong hands gripped her shoulder. "Steph, you can't run far enough to get away from me."

Lance gently turned her to him. With her back to the ocean, her heart pounded her ears in cadence with the power and force of the water below. "Darling, tell me what you're afraid of. Let me help you," he pleaded as he searched her eyes for an answer.

Stephanie was powerless to answer. Her stubborn will weakened as her demanding heart threatened to betray her.

A half-smile brushed Lance's lips, but only fierce determination lighted the eyes that held hers.

"I'm not afraid," she denied. " It's just that I'm not ready for this. . . ."

"Ready for what—love? I love you, Stephanie. That's the simple truth. I'm not talking about any other relationship but that. I've never been in love before. I've been infatuated by beauty and charm, but never this. Honey, you turn the morning on for me!"

Stephanie, mesmerized by the raw emotion she saw in his eyes, reached up and pressed her fingers against his lips. She moaned softly, "No, don't. Don't, Lance. You mustn't talk that way—feel that way. I can't."

"You can't what? You feel the same way I do. I can tell—the way your eyes look at me when I come in a room, the soft smile that's mine alone. You can deny it with your lips, but that doesn't change your heart."

Stephanie opened her lips to speak, but the denial died in her throat.

Lance rushed on in a torrent of words, releasing his pent-up emotions. His eyes were midnight blue with intensity as he tried to convince her. "I'm not pressing you now—it's too early in our relationship for that. I just want to spend more time with you—time for our love to grow. It's only just beginning. It's fragile, but it's there. Give it time—give us time." His eyes were smiling, filled with a pleading, tender patience that melted Stephanie's heart.

"No pressure?"

"No, just time together—sharing our work, our hopes and dreams, the summer sunsets, the morning mists rolling in from the ocean." He beamed an encouraging smile. "Agreed?"

She narrowed her eyes, once again able to look him in the face, a tenuous smile tugging at her mouth. "Time. I need time to sort things out. To search my heart. If you'll give me time."

"Are you ready to tell me what you meant about not loving anyone?"

"Not just yet, but someday."

"I'll wait until you're ready, and Steph, you're worth waiting for and so is our love."

Stephanie turned wide, troubled eyes to his. "I don't want to hurt you, Lance."

A broad grin parted his face. His eyes danced as with some mysterious knowledge that spelled victory. "You won't, my dear. You love me too much, whether or not you know it." Then putting his hands on each side of her face, he lifted it up, locking her eyes to his. "Stephanie, I'll never take advantage of you. I only want your happiness. Trust me. Follow your heart."

His eyes darkened once again with emotion before he bent his head and claimed Stephanie's lips in a long kiss.

Lance released her with a slight smile. The warmth of her response had answered his question. A soft mist in her shining eyes proclaimed a woman on the brink of love.

Chapter Eight

By midafternoon, the storm, which had announced its coming in the gentle ocean breeze of the night before, hit full blast. It deposited its fury on the manicured lawns, and its gale force winds bowed the tall, stately trees as if they were young saplings. High water flooded the main road leading to the inn, and the small group of people housed there were like an island.

Stephanie paced up and down the parlor. Every few minutes, she glanced out the window and shuddered.

The lights flickered, and she prayed the power would stay on, but she breathed a silent thanks that Lance had insisted on putting in the auxiliary power unit. He was right again. Accommodating guests was a big responsibility.

Abigail walked through the room, pausing to speak to several people. Stephanie noticed her usual bright smile appeared forced. When she arrived at Stephanie's side, she turned to look out the window, worry written on her face.

"Have you seen Lance?" Abby questioned, her voice tense.

"No, I imagine he is stranded in his cottage. Told me he had a lot of paperwork to do."

"I helped him, so he finished about midmorning. *Carefree's* crew had asked him to check on a little problem they were having with the sloop so he left for the boathouse," Abigail explained.

"He what?" Stephanie's voice rose in alarm.

"That's not the worst of it," Abigail exclaimed, her eyes bright with anxiety. "He said he thought he'd take *Carefree* out. You know how much he'd wanted to."

Fear and regret descended on Stephanie, almost suffocating her. She remembered. How many bright and shining days of summer had she put Lance off when he'd asked her to go? She had been too busy working, trying to prove to him her worth, her independence, and now. . .

She rejected the thought. He mustn't be lost. She could call the rescue unit. But how? The telephones were out and only the boathouse housed the ship-to-shore and short-wave radios.

Abigail tugged at her arm. "Stephanie, did you hear me? I said Lance may be on *Carefree*. What can we do?"

Darkness settled around Stephanie's eyes, and she turned back toward the voice of her friend. The only thing she could see was Abigail's face, her worried eyes. "Didn't he know. . .about. . .the storm?" The words stumbled out haltingly.

"No. Just laughed when I warned him. Said I was talking to a sailor who'd been in some real storms before. You know how he is."

Out of Stephanie's anguish, a bitter smile tugged at her mouth and she answered softly, "Oh, yes. I know how he is."

Maybe, maybe he was still in his cottage. She strained to see it. No lights. No Lance. No happiness, only pain. She turned from the window.

"Abigail, I'm going to borrow Randy's Jeep and go to the boathouse."

"You can't—" Abigail started to protest.

"I have to."

❧

Stephanie refused to allow anyone to go with her. Knowing the risks involved did not prepare her for the perilous journey. Trees blocked the lane, and the Jeep slid as she left the road to drive around them. Without four-wheel drive, the trip would have been impossible. At times, the wind almost set the small vehicle off its wheels. Stephanie strained to see through gray sheets of rain.

Finally, the lane began its gentle descent to the inlet and boathouse. Water cascaded down the ramp with such force that Stephanie feared the vehicle would be swept into the inlet. Finally reaching the safety of the buildings, she peered anxiously toward the small sound. Her long white sloop with the bright blue stripes was not in its slip. Hope for Lance disintegrated in one long shuddering sob.

Cold rain mingled with warm tears streamed unnoticed down her face, leaving a salty taste on her lips. As she ran toward the building and her one beacon of hope, she uttered a pathetic prayer of confession, "Oh, God, protect him. I do need him. I've fought it so hard—bring him back to me."

All through the night, Stephanie kept watch by the radio. It crackled and popped and occasionally voices spoke, but no message came for her.

The inlet offered some protection from the wind, and she was thankful for the sturdy comfort of the building. It resembled a clubhouse with its fireplace and kitchen area.

She built a fire and put on a pot of coffee—for her and for Lance. He'd need it when he came back. She surveyed the well-stocked cooler for food. Satisfied, she noted that it had eggs. He'd be hungry as a bear.

A smile softened the lines of worry and fatigue that bound her face. His hearty appetite amazed her, yet his body remained lean and trim. Abigail said he ran every day—she hadn't known that. Her heart constricted and she felt a pang of jealousy toward her friend. How many other things about him did she take for granted? The wan smile faded, and she put her head in her hands.

Had she been so involved with their project, with proving her worth, her independence, that she'd failed in a more important issue? Like the brilliance of a lightning bolt, the answer came. If she'd failed, it had been because of fear—fear to let herself love. That fear had set her priorities and driven her to prove her independence, to deny her need for anyone.

Stephanie's eyes filled with tears that slowly made a warm, wet pathway down her cheeks. She wept bitter tears of regret—the regret of wasted moments. Now, too late, she knew her feeling for Lance superseded the fear that held her in bondage. He had wanted to help her, to show her that love didn't always enslave, but she'd refused and now she might never know the joy of love as God had intended it. Oh, yes. Her fear had been wrong, so wrong. If God would only give her another chance.

With shuddering sobs, she emptied her heart to God, pouring out her fear and confusion. Slowly, Stephanie's sobs subsided, and a quiet assurance calmed her. God would give her another chance.

The hours dragged on, but she refused to doubt. Come morning, Lance would return.

❦

A gray dawn proclaimed morning. Stephanie had dropped off to sleep from sheer weariness, but a strangely familiar sound jerked her awake. The wind and rain had ceased their howling. She ran to the door facing the water and saw a mist rolling in from the sea.

The light of a coast guard cutter sliced through the mist and raked the shore. The boat continued its unswerving course straight toward her dock.

With her heart in her throat, Stephanie opened the door and stepped through just as the boat pulled up and a tall, bedraggled figure dressed in jeans and a plaid shirt stepped onto the slick boards of the landing.

Lance bent his head to look back into the boat and, with a nonchalant salute, bid the crew good-bye. His wet clothes were plastered to him, and his hair was flat and dark with water. A day-old beard darkened his face, and he walked with a slight limp.

A cry of sheer joy wrenched from Stephanie's throat as she ran down the slippery dock. Giving no heed to her safety or his, she hurled herself into his arms, sobbing.

With an impudent grin, he lifted her head and lightly kissed her cheek. "What's the matter, Steph? You lose something?"

The emotions of fear and worry that she had battled all night exploded in angry relief. "Lancelot Donovan, where have you been? Don't you tease me about this. I thought. . .I thought. . ." A heart-wrenching sob escaped and she could go no further.

"You thought what, my darling?"

"I. . .I thought. . .I'd lost you," the independent Stephanie Haynes confessed between sobs.

The impudent light left Lance's eyes. Holding her like a small child, he brushed the damp blond curls from her face and crooned softly, "Never. Nothing can take me away from you."

She looked up, her eyes shining with soft radiance, and whispered, "I know." Then dropping her head on his shoulder, she nestled in the warm security of his embrace.

While Lance changed into some dry clothes he had left in his locker, Stephanie cooked a quick breakfast. As they ate, he told her about his afternoon adventures.

He'd sailed out of the inlet into the sea for about an hour when he'd discovered a problem with the rudder. Nearing Evergreen Island, he'd decided to dock on the leeward side and fix it. Finding a protected inlet, he anchored and lowered the sails.

He failed to notice the approaching storm until he finished the repairs. "Even for a daredevil like me, that storm was too rough, so I hoisted the storm sail to keep her pointed into the wind. Then I dropped both anchors, making sure they were on the bottom securely about fifty yards offshore so she wouldn't blow aground. I had one cold swim back to shore." Involuntarily, he shuddered.

Lance continued, "When I reached the island, I headed for higher ground. My ship-to-shore radio wouldn't work, but I did have emergency flares, so I climbed the one high bluff on Evergreen and found a small cave to ward off the elements. I weathered the storm there until the coast guard came and picked me up. They said they saw my flare because you had radioed them. They were a welcome sight. The cave kept the trees from falling on me, but the water blew in. I thought I'd never be warm again—that is until I stepped on the dock."

Stephanie blushed and dropped her head, suddenly shy with him. "What . . .what about *Carefree*?"

"I think she survived it okay. I didn't have time to examine her before I left. They are going to carry me back over there to pick her up this afternoon. Do you think you could find time to help me bring her back?"

Although thoughts of her responsibilities bombarded Stephanie's mind, she nodded her head without a moment's hesitation. Her priorities had changed. God had given her that chance. The chance to know Lance better, to test their love.

As it does so often after a storm, the sun shone that day with an added radiance, and the sky hung a cloudless blue. Lance arrived at the lodge shortly after three with a picnic hamper. He looked as if he'd not missed a minute of sleep.

His eyes brightened at the sight of Stephanie. With her blond hair pulled back in a ponytail and denim shorts and red shirt, she looked like a teenager. Had anyone cared to ask her, she could have told them she felt like one. Something strange had happened to her during the tortuous hours before dawn. She was able to walk across the storm-wrecked lawn without a backward glance at the work waiting to be done. Somehow it would get done, but for right now, her only thought was the man beside her and the adventure of being together that awaited them.

A radiant smile greeted Lance, and Abigail, noting it, said mischievously, "You sure you don't want me to go so you can stay here and direct the clean-up crew?"

"Absolutely sure, Abby. I put this off for a whole summer. Lance and I are going for a sail." Slipping her hand in Lance's outstretched one, Stephanie added with eyes large and dark, "I almost waited too long."

The cutter met them at the dock, and a half hour later they were pulling into the calm inlet where *Carefree* bobbed up and down in the gentle swells.

Pulling up beside the sloop, the cutter soon had maneuvered in position to enable Lance and Stephanie to climb aboard her. After thoroughly checking the boat for damages, the couple smiled in agreement. The storm had taken no toll on their lovely boat. They would not be spending precious hours making repairs.

Lance looked at Stephanie mischievously. "Too bad you don't have your swimsuit. I'd race you to the shore."

Stephanie laughed up at him, her eyes dancing. "You don't get off that easily, Sir Lancelot. I have my suit on, and I challenge you." She stepped from her shorts and removed her shirt, revealing a brightly colored maillot. Diving overboard, she swam swiftly through the cold water.

Before she reached shallow water, her teeth were chattering, and she shuddered at the thought of Lance's swim in the storm. Just then he swam up beside her. His powerful brown arms propelled him through the water, barely rippling the surface. Stephanie paused to marvel at Lance's strength and expertise. When he pulled half a length ahead of her, he turned on his back and splashed water in her face. "I win. Admit it. What's the prize?"

"I admit it—and the prize is you get to spend the afternoon with me, you lucky man."

"The most delightful prize I could imagine, my dear," he replied as they reached shallow water and ran splashing to shore.

The afternoon passed too quickly. They laughed, explored the island, and raced along the beach. Stephanie learned about Lance's family, his boyhood, and the things he liked to do. She discovered they shared many interests.

She reveled in the warm sense of contentment that she felt in these shared moments with Lance. Other than hold her hand, he didn't touch her, but the warmth of his gaze was as tender as an embrace, setting her heart aglow.

Was this love? This total joy in being in the presence of the beloved. Not touching, yet united in spirit? This feeling of completeness? Was this why it could enslave?

For the first time since she had lost her parents, Stephanie understood her mother's tragic grief. Her eyes clouded.

Lance noticed. "What's the matter, Steph?"

She shook her head in half-denial.

"You can't fool me. You've left me again. That mysterious something that keeps taking you away from me like some gate to your past slams shut, and you close me out. I don't like that. Don't you think it's time you told me?"

"Yes, but it's getting late, and I think we'd better get back to the boat. Besides, aren't you hungry yet?"

"Sure. Love makes you that way. Aren't you hungry?" he countered.

"Come to think of it, I am. I believe I could eat a bear."

"There, that proves my point! See what love did for your appetite?" he insisted.

"You really think I'm in love, Lance?"

"No think to it. I know it. This one thing I know: We were meant for each other."

She remained quiet for a long moment, looking down at the sand. Her heart raced, but her lips refused to respond.

Lance placed his hand under her chin and lifted her head, forcing her eyes to meet his. Emotions struggled in the clear blue depths of hers. Then, hesitantly, she asked, "What do you mean by that?"

"I mean, pardner, we'll need to be finding a preacher man and get married up," he drawled in a perfect cowboy mimic.

Stephanie's brow creased, and she pulled her chin from his hand. "I don't think that's something to tease about."

Lance looked at her long and hard. "I'm not teasing. I plan to marry you. I meant it when I told you that last spring, and I mean it now. The only thing I don't know is when. Two problems to that: your agreement and the success of these business ventures."

Stephanie shot him a puzzled look.

"Most of my worldly goods that I could 'thee endow' are tied up, and my success is riding on this film," Lance explained.

"You mean you couldn't afford to do these improvements on Boulder Bay?"

"Not if I didn't know it would pay off. Leasing it to the film company will get us the majority of our initial investment, and the free advertising the film will give us insures a successful season next year. No, my dear. It isn't the inn that's the problem; it's the film. In order to get the film rights I had to act quickly, and I invested far beyond what I usually do. I didn't have time to get a substantial number of investors, but I believed so strongly in the film's potential that I took the risk. Big investment means big return—or big loss."

"You mean you're the only investor?"

"No, I don't have that much capital or credit. Alana DeLue is the other major investor, and then we have a cartel of small investors."

"I thought she was the star."

"Yeh, that's part of the deal and great for me. Her name means box office clout, and that's the way she wanted it. Every producer in Hollywood wanted this story. It was a bidding situation, and when I got the opportunity, I had to move swiftly."

"You *outbid* everybody else?"

He looked sheepish. "Not exactly."

"Well?" she persisted.

"Strange set of circumstances. Guess you might say it was my unbeatable charm." He grinned disarmingly.

"Charm must be worth a lot in Hollywood."

"It is, but to tell you the truth, I think it must have been being at the right place at the right time."

"You mean divine appointment?"

"I'd say coincidence."

" I don't believe in coincidences, Lance."

"Yeh, I remember. You thought I was an answer to prayer." He smiled, but a hint of uncertainty touched his usual confident gaze.

"You were—and are."

"For whatever the reason, I got the script. I'm glad for the opportunity, but its success is not assured. I believe in the project, but even if production is finished on time and within the budget, it awaits a fickle public's response. No, until the cash registers start jingling substantially, I couldn't think of offering myself to you. Too much risk involved."

"Risk?"

"Yes, that I couldn't look after you the way I want to. Lady, I want to put the world at your feet debt free." His eyes crinkled with a merry grin, but Stephanie could see beyond the mirth. His eyes were serious.

Stephanie bit the corner of her lip, revealing the tips of her even white teeth, and remarked hesitantly, "I sincerely pray that it's going to be a success for your sake, but not for me, Lance. You mustn't do it for me. I don't want you or anyone to lay the world at my feet. In fact, I never intended to fall in love."

Stephanie whirled from Lance and ran into the surf, diving in just beyond the breakers. She swam fiercely, fleeing her unstable emotions. What had destroyed the peace and contentment of the afternoon? Why had fear reared its ugly head once more? And fear about what?

Chapter Nine

Stephanie arrived at the boat before Lance and went below to towel off and change her clothes. She pulled her hair back in damp ringlets and touched her lips lightly with color.

The sun rested low over the horizon, and she pulled her jacket closer to her as she stepped out onto the deck. The evening breeze had a chill in it, and she was thankful she had brought the additional jeans and jacket.

Lance had *Carefree* under way by then. She went to sit beside him at the wheel. He'd exchanged his suit for white denim pants and a bright blue shirt that turned his eyes to cobalt. The power of his masculine good looks played havoc with her studied composure.

She took a deep breath and looked up at him. He ignored her presence, devoting his attention to the job at hand. Stephanie watched, entranced, then shifted uncomfortably. Seconds turned into minutes, and only the wind snapping the sails broke the silence. Stephanie understood. Lance was determined that she would take the initiative. Stubbornly she kept silent. Didn't he care? What had happened to the warm rapport of this afternoon?

She flinched. She had destroyed it by running away. Now it was up to her, not Lance, to restore that intimacy.

They had crossed the open water between the small island and the mainland. The dock and boathouse loomed ahead. Stubbornly, Stephanie remained silent, the words she needed to speak locked in her mind and heart.

Finally Lance maneuvered *Carefree* into her slip. Without speaking, Stephanie threw herself into assisting him by dropping the sails and securing the boat.

When they had finished, Lance nodded toward the picnic basket and asked tersely, "Would you like to eat here or at the boathouse?"

"The boathouse, but. . ." Stephanie walked up to Lance and stood in front of him. She placed one small hand on his chest and toyed with one of his buttons, refusing to look up.

"Yes?" he asked.

"I'm sorry if I ruined our afternoon."

"I am, too, Stephanie. I love you and you love me, but our future relationship depends on you. I don't understand your fear, and until you deal with it or at least trust me enough to let me help you with it, we're at a stalemate."

"I have—did deal with it—last night."

"That doesn't explain what happened today."

She smiled slightly and raised her head to look directly at him. "Old responses are hard to break. I didn't want to talk about it, but I owe you an explanation. It was what you said—about laying the world at my feet, taking care of me. In a way it sounds like enslavement."

"Enslavement?" His eyebrows came together, astonishment sharpening his countenance.

"My idea of marriage is partnership," Stephanie continued.

Lance shook his head, puzzled.

"It was my parents," Stephanie explained. "What you said reminded me of their relationship. You can't imagine what that did to my mother."

"Not unless you tell me," he encouraged gently, his eyes softening.

"My mother was so dependent on my father that when he died, she couldn't go on living. He was her world, her only world—almost her god."

"Darling, that wasn't a normal or healthy love."

"I know. I felt disgust for what I thought was my mother's weakness—until I met you. Lance, the way I feel when I'm with you is overpowering. It frightens me because, how do I know that I won't react like she did? After all, she's my mother."

"Did she have a strong faith?"

"I don't know. She never discussed it with me. She was religious, but somehow it didn't influence her life."

"There you're altogether different. Who taught you about faith?"

"My father. He had a strong faith in Jesus Christ. He had accepted Christ as his Savior, but beyond that, my dad trusted Jesus as the Lord of his life."

"You mean he was a strong man who had confidence in himself and could handle problems?"

"Not exactly. Lance, do you ever have a moment of self-doubt?"

"Nope. I know what it takes to get a job done, and I'm willing to pay the price. I haven't had a problem yet I couldn't solve, and I'm confident now. I just don't quite know what the timing will be."

"Doesn't God-given talent have anything to do with it?"

"Uh, maybe, but I'm inclined to think God leaves it up to us to make a success of it, don't you?"

"Well, yes. I think He wants us to be diligent and work at what He gives us to do, but it's more than that. He has a purpose for us—a special place for us to fill. That's why He gives us talent. Don't you think so?"

"No, not really. I think God is too busy to be concerned about whether or not I produce a certain movie. I think He gives us the talent, and it's up to us to get out and find the opportunities."

"Then why are you filming this particular story?"

"Just like I said. I think it's outstanding enough to be a blockbuster. That means money, prestige, and success—not to mention being in a position to offer myself to you."

Stephanie couldn't suppress a smile at his candor. "The story is uplifting. It will leave the world a better place. Don't you think that God might have a reason for wanting it produced?"

"I dunno. Never thought about it before."

"Why have you produced the films that you have?"

"Because I believe that wholesome entertainment is a better investment. It'll bring in more dollars."

"Lance!"

"Okay. I don't want my name on anything that would violate my moral principles, but I don't think God has time to read scripts. It'd be hard for me to believe that He's interested in the movies I produce. Seems to me He's got more important matters to contend with than my day-to-day affairs."

"I guess you've never learned just how important a person is to God, Lance."

"Nope, I guess I haven't. Where did you get that notion?" he asked lightly, but his eyes probed yearningly.

"When I had nowhere else to turn. That's where most people learn, Lance—out of desperation—and that's a pity. We could save ourselves so much anxiety and pain if we were willing to discover God's love and concern earlier."

"Perhaps you're right, Stephanie. I've just never encountered anything I couldn't handle. I've never questioned it. Now I understand that God had to have a plan for salvation. I accepted Jesus Christ when I was a child. I knew that He had paid the price for my sin on the cross and I needed to ask forgiveness for that and invite Him into my life."

"Well, where's He been since?"

Lance chuckled humorlessly. "I've acknowledged my responsibility to Him for moral decisions, but the rest of my life. . . I sort of thought He just equipped me in the beginning and the rest was up to me—you know, direction, sink or swim, all those issues."

Stephanie smiled at him sadly. "I hope you discover the truth before you get in a desperate situation. God is interested in every area of our lives. His interest gives us purpose, an excitement in everything that we do—an added dimension as it were."

"Is that what's different about you? The secret that gives you that special glow?"

"I didn't know I had one." She wrinkled her nose at him, her blue eyes wide and questioning.

"Most of the time. Sometimes it gets clouded over—like a few moments ago. For someone so strong in her faith, you seem to have short-circuited it where love is concerned. How can fear and faith live together?"

The truth of his question probed Stephanie's soul, and she paused before answering. Tears filled her eyes as she explained haltingly, "I struggled with that question all last night when I thought you might be gone. I asked God for another chance, and He gave it to me."

"What are you going to do with it?"

"Not run away from it again. That was just an emotional reaction earlier this afternoon. I know now that I can learn not to fear love—and you're right. The love Mom had for Dad was not the way God planned love to be. But I think I must blame Dad some, too."

"Why?"

"Because he let my mother depend on him. He never prepared her for eventualities."

"He took good care of her."

"Too good. That's what I'm talking about. Our ideas of love and faith, too, are so different. Even when I put aside my fears, I don't know how we can reconcile our differences."

"Don't you think my faith can grow?"

"Are you willing for it to?"

"I don't know if I can ever see life as simply as you" came his honest answer.

"You mean you want to be in charge of your life and mine?"

"I want to take care of you."

"You want to take care of me, but I want a partnership—a relationship where I can contribute, do my part."

"What if I do want to take care of you? I don't see that your father did anything wrong. That's a man's pride, taking care of his woman."

"To the point she can't survive without him?"

"Sounds romantic."

"I'm not talking about a Hollywood script. I'm talking about a tragedy that I don't want to repeat. If you can't understand what I'm talking about, then perhaps we don't have a foundation for a lasting relationship. Lance, I will have to be able to share my faith with the man I marry, and he'll have to need me as much as I need him. He must be someone who'll let me share his heartaches and defeats as well as his victories. I never want to be on a pedestal to be adored and worshiped. I want a man who's strong enough to let me help him."

"You want a weak man, Stephanie?"

"No, a strong man who needs me."

"I need you."

"How?"

"I need your love."

"That's not enough."

"Stephanie, I don't want you to support me. I want to look after you. I have a need to take care of you."

"What if something happens and you can't? Will you stop loving me? Will I stop loving you?"

"Nothing is going to happen. I'll see to that!"

"That's just my point. Will our relationship be based on your ability to take care of me? If you take care of me well, then I'm to love you lots, and if you take care of me less, I love you less? Do you see what you're reducing love to?"

"Is it so wrong for a man to want to provide for the woman he loves?"

She smiled, shrugging sadly. "No, Lance. That's a God-given instinct within a man—to be the protector and the provider. But with some men, it has evolved into a macho self-image that's destructive. Failures are bound to happen. They come to every life. I don't think you would let me share them with you. Lance, the real mark of a strong man is one who can admit he needs help—from God and from his wife."

Pain sharpened Lance's handsome features, and his thick dark brows knit together. Stephanie saw uncertainty and something akin to anger flare in them briefly before he answered tersely, "Maybe you're right. Perhaps I'm not the man for you because with every fiber of me, body and soul, I want to love, protect, and take care of you. If that weakens me in your eyes, then I'm weak." He turned abruptly and walked away toward the road home, his hunger and the filled hamper forgotten.

Tears of frustration streamed down Stephanie's cheeks as a sob caught in her throat. She wanted to run after him, but instead she watched him walk away. All her resolutions had dissolved. She knew the heart-wrenching truth—weak or strong, success or failure, she loved Lance and always would. Enslaved or free, he was the only man she could ever love. But did she dare?

Stephanie did not know how long she sat huddled on the dock after Lance left, but unnoticed, night had descended.

Car lights bounced off the wide drive and curved downward as a vehicle started its descent to the landing. Stephanie ran her hand through her tousled curls, muttering, "I must look a sight." She did. With eyes red from weeping and rumpled clothing, she squared her small shoulders and stood up, dreading to face anyone, except Lance. Maybe, just maybe, he'd returned.

Abigail's bright little car dispelled that hope.

"Stephanie, you down there? I can't see. Why don't you turn on the dock lights?" Abby called as she alighted from the car. As soon as her eyes became accustomed to the darkness, she spotted Stephanie.

"Oh, thank goodness! Martha needed you so I came for—you look a mess!" she exclaimed as Stephanie stepped into the harsh circle of car light.

Stephanie retorted with a bitter smile, "If you ever need a lift, call for Abigail."

"Oh shucks, Stephanie, don't complain. You're the only woman I know who can still look beautiful when she's a mess. What happened? You and Lance, wasn't it? I knew it. I saw him come storming home without you."

Stephanie smiled ruefully at her friend's nonstop conversation.

Abigail saw the smile. "That's better. I knew it couldn't be the end of the world. Just a lover's quarrel. Happens all the time."

Much to Stephanie's chagrin, the tears she thought she had exhausted began again. "It's more than that—much more."

"Well, Steph, it can't be as bad as that. You two are the greatest people I've ever known. You seem made for each other."

"Don't sa. . .say that, Abby. That's what he said," Stephanie sobbed.

"Seems to me he's right. Want to tell me about it?" Abigail gently probed as she started the car and expertly maneuvered it up the gentle grade.

Stephanie gave Abby an abbreviated account of what had occurred.

Her friend remained silent until Stephanie had finished and then observed, "I can understand where you're coming from, Stephanie, but the problems don't seem insurmountable."

"I think Lance thought so."

"Oh, he was just mad. You had injured his male ego, and he's stubborn, too. One of the reasons he's been so successful is his stubborn will."

"That's what worries me, Abby. He has such a strong will, how can his faith grow when he doesn't even think he needs any?"

"Well, it's harder for men to let go and step out on faith. It's a male characteristic. They like to be in control. But from my experience, God has His own way about putting us in situations that we can't handle any other way. And as for you—you're pretty independent, too, young lady. Do you have any idea how many girls would give their right arms and twenty years of their lives to have a man like Lance Donovan want to take care of them like he wants to take care of you?"

"I know. The way I feel doesn't make sense. But, Abby, I feel so overpowered when Lance is near. I find myself forgetting everything but him. I can't let that happen. Marriage is forever, and I believe there are certain ingredients that are basic for its survival—a shared faith and a shared concept of life. Other differences can be worked out by compromise, but not those."

"I admire your stamina, Stephanie. It's not the first time I've seen you risk everything for your convictions. If there's anything I can do to help, just let me know. I think the world of you both."

"Both?" Stephanie looked squarely at her friend, a question, not voiced, in her eyes.

Abigail flushed and answered firmly, "Yes, both. Stephanie, I'd be deaf, dumb, and blind if I hadn't noticed how handsome Lance is, but believe me, he's not my type. Even if he were, his eyes see only you. You've got nothing to worry about there, anyway. Now you go wash and get all dolled up. Dinner is served in an hour. It's a special bash tonight—all Boulder Bay people—and Martha prepared a treat."

Stephanie took a long leisurely soak in the oversized tub with claw feet. After placing witch hazel pads over her eyes to reduce the swelling, she deftly applied a little makeup to cover the emotional ravages of the afternoon. She piled her hair high on her head in a cascade of curls and put on a long black evening gown that molded her slender body and emphasized her blond beauty. She put on her mother's teardrop diamond earrings and dabbed perfume behind her ears.

Glancing in the mirror, she gave herself a wry smile. "Head held high, Stephanie, and no one will guess the pain searing your insides. Not even Lance."

Tears welled in her eyes, and she whispered his name softly, caressing the sound of it with her lips.

Soft music played as she descended the stairs, and voices raised in animated conversation. People stood in groups drinking hot cider and eating hors d'oeuvres. Abby had been right. Tonight was special. Looking around her, Stephanie frowned. There were some faces she didn't recognize and one face she looked for and didn't find.

Stephanie reached out and took the crystal cup that John handed her. She smiled up at him—he, too, looked handsome and distinguished in his dark suit. There was Martha in her best gray taffeta. A celebration of sorts, but for what?

A bell tinkled, and Abigail, dressed in a short, pale yellow gown, stood on the stairway. "Friends, I would like to propose a toast to Martha and John. It's their fiftieth wedding anniversary."

She turned her head toward them and raised her cup high. "May your second fifty be as lovely as your first. By the way, how old were you when you got married? You're much too young to have been married that long."

"I married her when she was a girl of sixteen and I was a lad of seventeen, but it's been my love what's kept her young," John spoke up with uncharacteristic boldness. Then he planted a kiss firmly on the mouth of his blushing bride, and the crowd roared with good-natured laughter and cheers of "Hear, Hear!!"

A lump knotted in Stephanie's throat at the mist of love softly shining in Martha's eyes. What would it be like to share a love like theirs for half a century and longer? What would it be like to share a love with Lance for. . . She didn't finish the thought, for she heard familiar deep tones behind her as he entered the room and she turned to meet him, a warm greeting on her lips and soft shining eyes.

It died without utterance, for she turned to meet a pair of fiery ebony eyes in a small face with perfectly chiseled features. Abundant dark hair set off the woman's exotic beauty, and her red gown clung sensuously to every curve, dipping low at the bodice. Diamond bracelets graced her arms as did diamond rings her hands. Around her slender ivory neck hung one exquisite diamond, large and brilliant.

The beauty paused, one arm entwined in Lance's, as the dark eyes raked Stephanie from head to toe. A malicious smile played at one corner of her mouth, and she remarked in perfectly modulated tones for all to hear, "So this is the little country girl you're going to turn into a princess, Lance, darling."

Stephanie bit back an angry retort, but before she could answer, Lance winked at her, responding smoothly, "She's already a princess. Stephanie Haynes, may I present Alana DeLue. Her bark is much worse than her bite."

Alana gave Lance a throaty laugh. "Lance, you will completely destroy my image."

He bent his dark golden head to hers attentively and replied, "Not a chance, my dear. Your beauty and grace speak for you."

"Now that's the Donovan charm to which I'm accustomed." She smiled up at him. Turning to Stephanie, Alana held out her hand. "Miss Haynes, glad to have you on board. I'm looking forward to working with you. It seems that our Lance here is fairly moonstruck with you. Now I can see why."

Stephanie stared in disbelieving wonder. As quickly as a stage curtain can be drawn, the facade disappeared from Alana DeLue. The fiery eyes now contained genuine warmth and friendliness, but tinged with something else—pain, longing. Stephanie couldn't decide. Alana's beauty was genuine, and if Stephanie were any judge, it had been forged in pain.

Lance had known Alana for years. Their affection for each other was obvious to the most casual observer. Stephanie's observance was anything but. How had he resisted her, or had he?

Looking into the eyes of the beautiful woman, Stephanie experienced a new kind of fear. Cold, icy fingers gripped her heart as she responded stiffly, "I don't know what Lance has told you, but we're *all* excited about having you and the rest of the crew here. I didn't expect you until next week. I'm afraid you have caught us in the aftermath of a storm."

Alana raised a hand as if to brush such concerns aside. "Lance told me all about it. The place is lovely, and Lance's cottage will be just perfect for me."

Stephanie's face blanched, and she turned questioning eyes toward Lance.

"Guess I fixed it up too well. I hope you don't mind a cluttered office, Alana, because that's a working apartment, and I'm not moving that office even for you, my lovely," he warned, tweaking her chin with his finger.

"No bother. Having you around again will be wonderful. It's been a long time, darling," she answered softly.

"Too long," he agreed.

Stephanie stirred uncomfortably. Unable to respond, she was grateful when Abby's voice broke in. "Miss DeLue, I'm Abigail Burnes, Lance's secretary. If you need anything, just call and I'll get it. I'm sorry your cottage was damaged by the storm."

Alana smiled at Abigail, giving her the same appraising look she had given Stephanie. "Thank you, Abigail, but I'll be fine. I've taken possession of Lance's cottage."

Abigail's lips smiled, but her eyes flew to Stephanie in alarm. "Uh—"

Stephanie found her voice and smoothly replied, "That's quite all right, Abby. If it suits Lance, how can we object? Right, Lance?"

Alana turned her dark eyes on Stephanie, wide and knowing. They sparkled with amusement. Stephanie flushed, realizing the beautiful star had read her heart.

Lance, oblivious to the undercurrent going on, responded, "Right. Now where's dinner? Seems I missed mine somehow, and suddenly I'm hungry."

Lance's remark pierced Stephanie's heart as the painful memories of their afternoon together blinded her. She turned from the striking couple before they could see the pain in her eyes and mumbled, "I think dinner will be served momentarily."

"Alana, I can't wait for you to try the food here. But mind, you'll have to be very careful. I won't have a chubby leading lady," Lance chortled as they moved across the room and away from Stephanie without a backward glance.

Abby looked at Stephanie and raised her eyebrows. In a low voice, she remarked, "Wow! She'll certainly liven things up around here."

"Well, she's the star," Stephanie responded with a sad shrug. Squaring her shoulders, she lifted her head and moved across the room with the art and grace of a seasoned performer.

That night Stephanie gave the first performance of her life, and it dazzled. While inside she mourned with the regrets of what might have been, outside she sparkled with wit and beauty. Periodically, she looked up to catch Lance's questioning eyes on her. This was a Stephanie he'd never seen—a chic and sophisticated beauty whose charm had completely captivated the cosmopolitan group. Had he just witnessed the metamorphosis of a country girl?

Chapter Ten

Lance would never know what Stephanie's performance cost her or the agony of uncertainty that she carried to bed with her that night.

The memory of Lance walking away from her in anger and the image of his head bent to the flashing-eyed beauty in his cottage seared her mind and denied her the oblivion of a dreamless sleep. Even in slumber, she wept.

Despite a fitful rest, her weary body demanded restoration after two nights without sleep, and Stephanie stirred only when Abigail pounded at her door.

"Sorry you missed the hot breakfast, Steph. This was the best I could do. Kitchen is all cranked up for lunch," Abby explained cheerfully, a breakfast tray in her arms.

Stephanie smiled weakly and ran her hand through her tousled hair. "Why didn't you wake me?"

"Because you haven't had any sleep in two nights."

"How do you know that?"

"Because I'm a woman, and I've been in love."

Stephanie raised an inquisitive brow as she took a sip of coffee. "You were in love?"

Abby shrugged nonchalantly while pain shadowed her eyes. "Yeah, loved and lost."

"I'm sorry, Abby. I didn't know."

"It was for the best—totally incompatible. But painful all the same. It still hurts sometimes. I'm sure, despite the pain, that I made the right decision. Anyway, he's married now."

"I guess that's some consolation—that you made the right decision. Do you think I did?"

"Only you can determine that, Stephanie. Certain things are essential for a happy marriage—a shared faith is one of them. But if Lance tries to have a faith like yours just to please you, that won't work, either."

"Oh, I know, Abby! But the issue is too vital to ignore. I guess I've lost him."

"Stephanie Haynes, you have forgotten something. God is in the life-changing business, not you. It's not too late for that, you know."

"Maybe not, but won't it be hard for even God to work in Lance's life with that beautiful Alana DeLue on his arm, not to mention in his apartment—maybe his bed?"

Abby burst into laughter at the woebegone look on her friend's face. "Boy, are you borrowing trouble. You know Lance! Now trust him."

"Well, he's a man, and how could any man resist a temptation like that?"

"He loves *you!*"

"Does he? You weren't there when he walked away."

"No, but I know Lance. He's aggressive and used to getting what he wants. Your conditions angered and frustrated him. He'll be back. He loves you too much."

"But it wouldn't do any good, Abby. I don't want him to change just to please me. He'd end up resenting me. There just isn't any solution."

"The game's not over yet. Now you pull yourself together and get dressed. We've got two days' work to do in three hours. I could strangle Miss Hollywood for showing up with her entourage a week early!"

Stephanie laughed despite herself. "Did she say why she arrived early?"

Abby shrugged her shoulders. "She didn't talk it over with me. Are you going to get dressed, or are you coming down in that robe? I mean it. We've got to hurry!"

"Okay. It won't take me any time to shower and change."

"That's more like it. Work hard—it helps. I found that out," Abby responded as she closed the door behind her.

❦

Abby's assessment proved correct. The early arrival of the rest of the crew pushed the Boulder Bay staff almost beyond endurance. The sets were readied and production started a week ahead of schedule, pleasing Lance. He rushed from set to set and barked commands to the crews. Alana DeLue stuck to him like his shadow.

Stephanie managed to miss Lance at meals. She ate early or late and stayed as busy as did he. She and Abby managed the herculean task of repairs and cleanup after the storm.

One evening while Stephanie pored over the additional invoices, Abby slipped quietly into her office. As Stephanie ran a tape totaling up the final expenses, Abby peered over her shoulder and gave a low whistle. "That storm was expensive."

"Yes, it looks like I'm going to have to ask Lance for more money instead of giving some back to him. I hate that—for more reasons than one. At least I'd hoped to prove acceptable as a business partner."

"Stephanie, you couldn't help the storm."

"All the same. . ."

"All the same, I have good news for you. The insurance company called earlier today and said that we had full coverage after all. I went into town this afternoon and picked up the check. Here you are, boss lady. Now let me see you smile."

"Abby, how did you manage that?" Stephanie gasped.

"I've been negotiating with them for days. Finally, I called the insurance commissioner, and we got our check."

"What would I ever do without you, Abby?"

"My aim is to be indispensable. By the way, you need to be thinking about adding to our staff. Before the summer's out, you and I won't be able to handle this business efficiently."

"Who do you think we need?"

"A comptroller and legal help, but I don't know where to find them since Emerald Cove is short on professional people—at least when it comes to finding someone who isn't already buttonholed by Jay Dalton or Howard Jarrett." Abby shuddered involuntarily.

"You still think they haven't given up on us?"

"I know they haven't."

"Well, we haven't had any problems so far."

"Restorations weren't complete until now. I think Dalton's been biding his time. By the way, I'm almost positive that he passed me on the road to town when I was coming back."

"Could be. Some of the workmen said he'd been observing our progress."

"But that's not all. It looked like Alana DeLue was in the car with him."

"You must be mistaken, Abby. How could she know Jay Dalton?" Stephanie questioned.

"I don't know. You tell me."

Stephanie held the insurance check in her hands for a long time after Abby left, staring at it unseeingly as she considered what her friend had said. Hiring more personnel was something she'd have to discuss with Lance. Her hands grew cold. They had not talked since the day at the dock; she'd deliberately avoided him. But even if she hadn't, it would be difficult to deliberate business concerns with Alana DeLue glued to his side.

Stephanie grimaced in distaste, then laughed aloud. "I'm acting like a high school sophomore who's been jilted. Despite our personal problems, Lance and I are very compatible business partners. I think I'll walk over there tonight and talk to him or at least make an appointment for tomorrow."

She slipped quietly from her office and walked slowly across the lawn toward the bluff and the cottages. Reaching Lance's cottage, her sneakers propelled her silently across the wide brick porch. Just as she raised her hand to knock, she saw a man and woman silhouetted in the dim light filtering through the old beveled sidelights. They were locked in each other's embrace. Stephanie backed away, her heart in her throat, suppressing the sob that threatened to erupt.

❧

Stephanie toyed with her breakfast. She had arrived earlier than usual—determined to avoid Lance at any cost. She knew their business relations would have to continue and soon they would be forced to meet. But not just yet—not until she had had time to make peace with her sorrow.

Stephanie didn't blame Lance. After all, she had set terms that he couldn't accept. But how could he go straight from her arms to those of another woman if he loved her? She shuddered and reached for her coffee cup. Its warmth felt good to her cold hands.

Deep in thought, Stephanie failed to see the door open and a tall man, light catching the burnished copper lights in his thick hair, slip in behind her. She picked up her fork and pushed the food around her plate.

"I thought you looked like you were losing weight. Now I know why!"

Stephanie jumped and turned toward the voice behind her. His eyes were warm and merry, but concern played in them, too.

She flushed and dropped her head, not willing to meet his eyes.

"Have you added not speaking to me to your list, Stephanie? I know you've been avoiding me lately."

She managed an offhanded shrug and remarked, "We've both been busy."

"I know, dear," Lance remarked. "You've performed a miracle getting this place back in shape after the storm."

Stephanie flinched at the endearing term. With studied determination she kept her voice steady. "I didn't do it by myself. Abby's help was invaluable."

"Steph, I came early on purpose, hoping I could catch you. We've got to talk."

Stephanie faced him squarely, a shield of indifference turning her eyes gray. "Yes, we need to discuss several things—business matters."

"Yes, that too."

She smiled coolly. "What can I help you with?"

"Get that cold look off your face for one thing! This is Lance, remember?"

"Oh, yes, I remember," she replied ever so softly, her eyes still hooded.

Lance sighed, then spoke in short, clipped tones, anger evident in the clinch of his jaw. "I don't know how much time you've had to study, but we start shooting your scenes next week. We'll go over your part as soon as you feel comfortable with it. It'll have to be at night or early morning, since I'll be tied up during the day."

"Fine. Do you think it'll be necessary for you to take up your time with me? It's just a small part."

"Don't you understand? I want to."

"No, I don't."

For a moment, Lance's familiar impudent grin broke the grimness of his countenance. "Just say my professional judgment is at stake here. The part is small, but it's vital to the picture."

Her face closed tighter against him. "I see. Whenever and wherever, you just let me know. Now I'd really better get busy."

Stephanie half-rose from her chair. Lance's hand shot out and grabbed her arm, forcing her back into her chair. "Stephanie, I think this has gone far enough."

"What's gone far enough?"

"This ice maiden bit. You've avoided me, and now you act like we're strangers. I don't like it. In fact, I won't have it. What's happened to us?"

"Don't you know, Lance?"

"I know you gave me some silly ultimatum that I can't live up to, but we can work that out."

"With Alana?"

"With Alana—what do you mean by that?"

"Like sharing your quarters with her?"

"My what? You mean you think—"

"What else could I think?"

Lance narrowed his eyes and snapped his mouth shut. A muscle twitched in the side of his tense face. Very slowly and precisely he spoke. "You could think I love you and you could trust me. Obviously you have graver reservations about me than I knew. Maybe someday you'll find someone worthy of you, Miss Haynes—but you'll *never* find a man who loves you more."

Lance stood up abruptly and moved resolutely toward the door. Then as an afterthought, he said over his shoulder, "Abby talked to me last week about the need for additional staff. Do whatever you think best. From now on you make all the decisions concerning Boulder Bay. I'll be too busy with the film. If you need additional money in the account, let me know."

Stephanie sat motionless, staring straight ahead. In an instant, Lance was gone, and the door slammed behind him with a sense of finality that broke her heart. His outrage—could she be mistaken about Alana? Had she misjudged him, failed to give him the trust he deserved?

Stephanie dropped her head in her hands and pushed her blond hair back with her hand as if she could clear her mind. She had seen them in the dimness of Lance's cottage, and he let Alana live in his cottage—what else could it be? Stephanie shook her head. There *was* no other explanation. How could he expect her to believe anything else?

&

For all Lance's good intentions and finely tuned scheduling, weeks passed and still he had not called for the filming of Stephanie's scene. She avoided the set but picked up bits and pieces about mysterious production problems involving both equipment and crew. Even the usually cooperative leading lady seemed destined to delay production. Gossip had it that she spent too many hours in the hotel casino and was too tired to remember her lines.

On rare occasions when Stephanie ran into Lance, his face was lined with fatigue. Dark circles shadowed his eyes. She never saw him laugh, and she heard the crew talk about the boss's short temper.

A brilliant fall had come and gone. The winds had a winter chill in them and the trees had dropped their leaves, but Stephanie had been too busy by day and too troubled by night to note the passing seasons. One thing she did notice—the film was weeks behind schedule. When winter arrived in all its fury, outside filming would have to be suspended. The scenes scheduled for completion by late fall would have to be rescheduled for spring.

Stephanie ached for Lance. When she saw him across the crowded dining room, she wanted to take her hands and smooth away the tired lines, to make him laugh, to see the warm, merry lights shine in his eyes again.

Alana no longer lived in Lance's bungalow. Shortly after the storm repairs were finished, Abby enhanced one of the cottages according to the star's detailed instructions. It had been expensive, but necessary. Abby said Alana had objected fiercely every time the office was used, so Lance had directed Abby to fix Alana a place that suited her—whatever the cost.

Abby laughed when she told Stephanie. "Just think what a drawing card that cottage will be. We can charge three times as much to rent it. It's very plush, and Alana ended up paying for most of the cost. I don't know how Lance managed that, but he did. Too bad he can't manage her on the set as well—but then, who could? I'd never heard she was so difficult to work with. You know, I've been helping her with her lines and she couldn't be sweeter, but does she ever give Lance a hard time. Complains all the time about this dull hamlet—says she's dying of boredom."

Stephanie bit her lip and frowned. "You know, I've had dinner with her several times. She's always been real pleasant to me. Have you ever noticed her eyes, Abby?"

"They're large and beautiful, is that what you mean?"

"No. When she's off guard, there's a sadness in them. Almost wistful, a little childlike. Sometimes I feel like she needs protecting, that she's vulnerable."

"Well, that's a charitable reaction to her, I dare say. I wish I had your forgiving spirit."

"As far as I know, she's done nothing to need my forgiveness."

"She and Lance—"

"I really don't know about that. Sometimes I wonder—"

"If you weren't too hasty?"

"Yeah. It's just, who could resist her? They've known each other a long time, you know."

"That's right, and if Lance had wanted Alana DeLue, he's had ample opportunity to get her before Stephanie Haynes ever appeared in the picture."

"What you say makes a lot of sense, Abby. I'd find it easier if only I hadn't—" Stephanie stopped, not willing to share what she had seen in the darkness on Lance's porch.

"Only what?" Abby probed gently.

"Nothing. What I think is no longer the problem. Lance has decided our differences are irreconcilable. Perhaps he's right. Better to find out now rather than later." Stephanie plopped down on the sofa. "I do wish I could help him some way with all these production problems."

Abby wrinkled her nose. "Short of straightening out Alana, I don't know what would help. All these minor accidents and delays seem so strange. Everything went like clockwork while the restoration work was underway, but as soon as the movie started, everything went haywire. I surely wouldn't want to be in Lance's shoes. It must be costing him a mint!"

Stephanie nodded her head in agreement as cold fear clutched her heart. Lance had risked his future on this film; what if he failed? She shook her head, rejecting the thought. Lance never failed at anything.

A week later Lance met Stephanie in her office.

"Stephanie, you're aware of my problems—we're way behind schedule. Somehow my leading lady just can't get it together. She seems to be unhappy here, so she's going to fly back to Hollywood for a break."

"Why do you put up with that, Lance? Can't you replace her? Surely you could find another actress who would do as well?"

"That isn't an option. You know she's a major investor. I had hoped to run a tight ship and use as little of her money as possible so I would retain full control of the venture, but because of these delays, I'm about to run out of the money that I and the other small investors had put into the deal. If I replace Alana, I'll lose her backing and won't be able to finish the film.

Needless to say, I'll be ruined, and the others will lose their investments. I don't want that to happen!"

Stephanie looked up at him, her eyes full of pain.

Lance, misinterpreting her look, chuckled bitterly. "Don't worry about Boulder Bay. You should be fine. As long as we keep the location here, the income from that will make the inn self-supporting. I don't have any more capital to invest in the improvements, though."

Stephanie bit her lip, hurt that Lance thought her only concern was the future of Boulder Bay. She replied coolly, "I see. Boulder Bay can make it financially, but if you need your investment back—well, that's another story."

Lance's eyes hardened and he spoke curtly. "That isn't a consideration. I didn't even imply that. I'm going to be fine and so is this movie. I'll see to that. I really came over here to tell you that I have restructured the filming schedule to work around Alana's scenes."

"How much of her footage do you have?"

"Usable footage? Zilch!"

"Is this the first time you've worked with her?"

"No. In the past she has been completely cooperative. Oh, she demanded her status symbols as a star, but on the set, she was totally professional."

Stephanie frowned, puzzled. "Do you have any idea what her problem is?"

Lance nodded. "I think so. She lost her husband tragically eighteen months ago. She almost went off the deep end. Maybe she's not ready to handle the stress." He sighed, discouragement bleeding through his determined countenance.

"Well if she's not, maybe she'll voluntarily relinquish her part," Stephanie probed, seeking to find a solution to Lance's problems and restore the jaunty self-confidence that usually sparkled in his eyes.

"No, I had a long talk with her today. No luck. I hope her trip will help."

"I hope so, too, Lance." Genuine concern lighted Stephanie's eyes. "Now what about the new schedule?"

"Oh yes. Almost forgot why I came. Meet me tonight downstairs where you made your screen test, and we'll go over your part until you're comfortable with it. We'll start your filming tomorrow."

The fear Stephanie had expected with this announcement didn't materialize. Her main concern was assisting Lance. "Fine," she said. "I'm ready."

Lance studied her a moment and smiled. His eyes lingered on her briefly with a touch of the old tenderness in them. "You amaze me, Stephanie Haynes. With all your other duties, you're still prepared."

Her lips curved slightly upward, her eyes soft in response. "Anything for you, Lance."

꙳

Stephanie was waiting, script in hand, when Lance arrived, fifteen minutes late. He shot her a look of apology as he rushed in, removing his tie and unbuttoning his collar. "I took Alana to the plane. The drive is farther than I realized. Are you ready?"

Stephanie raised an eyebrow. "Where is Doug? Isn't he going to read his part?"

"No, I'm going to, but we're going to do more than read. I want to make sure you have the movements right."

"How can you watch and act at the same time?"

"I just have a feeling about this. Let's get into position."

For the next two hours, Lance gave Stephanie acting lessons. Masterfully he pulled from her inner being joy or sorrow, agitation or exhilaration. With a natural ability she didn't know she possessed, she conveyed a mood with the blink of an eye or the flick of her hand.

When they approached the final scene, Lance was jubilant. Stephanie had surpassed his expectations. Tomorrow the cameras would roll and discover a new star.

By his direction she turned her back to him and began her lines. This was the parting love scene.

Stephanie began the lines softly, emotion and pain reflected in her voice. Lance walked up behind her and, placing both hands on her shoulders, turned her around slowly and pulled her into the circle of his arms. Tears streamed down Stephanie's face as she spoke the parting words of the script. Lance stared intensely into her face, responding softly, pleading. Finally, with pain and anger blazing in his eyes, he crushed her to him in a defiant kiss.

Stephanie shuddered and tried to push away from him as the script directed, but Lance only tightened his hold. His kiss lingered, and suddenly Stephanie forgot the script. She felt the sanctuary of Lance's arms around her, the warmth of his lips on hers, remembered the joy of their earlier shared moments. Her arms moved up around his neck. All resistance ceased as she returned his kiss.

When Lance finally raised his head, his breathing was ragged, his eyes bright. He searched her face, caressing it with his eyes. "Steph?"

She moved her fingers, pressed them gently against his mouth, and shook her head. "Not now, Lance. I can't think straight."

He gave a low, throaty laugh. "You think too much. I told you—follow your heart."

She shook her head once more, agony in her eyes. "It has to be head and heart, Lance."

He dropped his arms down by his side and stepped away, a bitter smile on his face. "Love involves compromise, Stephanie. Since you're not willing to give a little, perhaps you *are* following your heart."

Stephanie flinched at his caustic tone, but she replied firmly, "That's why I can't compromise on some issues, Lance. I love you too much to see you miserable. Don't you understand? Love is for a lifetime. I'm afraid we don't have enough building blocks to make it last. Anything less, I'm not willing to settle for."

Lance stared at Stephanie and said harshly, "I understand. I don't measure up to your preconceived notions of what a man is supposed to be. Very well, Miss Haynes. May I congratulate you? You play a love scene exceptionally well."

Stephanie's face flushed with anger and pain. "Thank you, Mr. Director. That's what you're paying me to do, isn't it?"

Lance clamped his jaw together, setting his mouth in a hard line and giving her a mock salute. "Touché, my dear. At least my professional judgment has been vindicated."

Stephanie moaned, "Oh Lance. Stop it. Why are we saying these things to each other? I don't want to hurt you. I told you that. Remember?"

"Oh, yes, I remember," he replied softly.

"Then what's happened?"

"I made an error in judgment."

Stephanie stepped back as if he'd slapped her. An icy mask shielded Lance's blue eyes, and the man she knew and loved removed himself from her reach.

She took a deep breath and spoke calmly, her voice flat. "I'm sorry you feel that way, Lance. I so wanted you to understand."

A knock interrupted her, and a tall, handsome young man in his early thirties opened the door and walked in. He glanced uncertainly from Lance to Stephanie as Lance barked, "Yes?"

The young man smiled broadly, showing even white teeth beneath his close-cut, dark mustache. "I was looking for Stephanie Haynes, and I think I've just found her." His large brown eyes crinkled with pleasure as he gave her a warm, appreciative look.

Stephanie stared at him without responding. There was something familiar about this handsome stranger. Something in his mannerisms that drew her, but her mind, so filled with Lance, refused to place him.

By this time he was crossing the room, his eyes glued to hers. "Stephanie Haynes, the ravages of time have been generous with you. The pretty little girl is a beauty who takes my breath away!"

A joyous exclamation broke from Stephanie, and she rushed forward to meet him with outstretched arms. "Todd!" she managed before all sight and sounds were muffled in a rib-crushing embrace that lifted her off her feet.

"I can't believe it. Where, when, how?" she babbled unintelligently as he laughed freely.

"I told you I'd be back."

"Yes, but that was so long ago." She leaned her head back, still encircled by his arms, and added softly, "So very long ago."

Behind her Lance stirred, remarking, "Stephanie, I suppose that'll be all."

She whirled from Todd, her face pink with embarrassment, her eyes alight with excitement.

"Oh, excuse me, Lance. This is an old childhood friend. Todd Andrews, meet Lance Donovan, my. . .my partner and. . .my boss."

"If you can be her boss, you must be a rare individual. Unless this girl has changed, she's a handful."

Lance took the outstretched hand and remarked sardonically, "She hasn't changed a bit."

Stephanie spoke quickly. "Lance is a movie producer and director. He's filming a movie here at Boulder Bay."

Todd nodded his head. "Yes, I know. That's why I'm here. Your assistant wrote me and told me everything that was going on here and some of your needs. I just couldn't resist coming to see for myself."

Lance moved toward the door and spoke amiably. "Good meeting you, Andrews, but I have an early call in the morning. If you two will excuse me, I'll leave you to catch up on old times."

As he passed Stephanie, Lance remarked, "Don't stay up too late. I don't want the makeup lady to have to cover all that natural beauty trying to get out fatigue lines."

Stephanie searched Lance's face. His nonchalant manner conveyed indifference, and the vibrant eyes that had glowed with love and tenderness now looked at her with the coolness of a casual acquaintance. She ached for her loss.

Chapter Eleven

Despite Lance's warning, Stephanie and Todd sat in the old kitchen replete with childhood memories and talked, filling in the long years that had separated them.

Martha sat with them for several hours, and her matchmaking bent couldn't resist asking the handsome young lawyer about the governor's daughter. Todd responded with the sad story of two people from different worlds who held conflicting values. The experience left him leery of politics and skeptical of women.

Todd reached out and took Stephanie's hand, adding, "I needed to come home to lick my wounds. And when I thought of home, I thought of you, Stephanie. You're the nearest thing to a family I have left, so when Abby called, I came running home to you."

A lump swelled in Stephanie's throat as the longing and pain of the past weeks rushed out. "Oh, Todd. I need you so. We all do."

Todd leaned over and, too overcome with emotion to speak, took Stephanie in his arms, and she began to sob on his shoulder. She rested in the haven of his arms as the emotional storm buffeted her, providing an overdue and much-needed release.

Todd patted the blond head on his shoulder and stroked the long silken hair that streamed down her back. They sat thus until the sobbing subsided. The young attorney lifted Stephanie's chin and wiped away the trail of tears and smeared mascara that ran down her cheeks. Placing a light kiss on her forehead, he teased, "You look like a blue-eyed raccoon, Stephanie."

With a sigh, Todd continued his story. "The decision hurt; I won't say that it didn't. But marriage is for a lifetime. Our differences were so basic that a marriage wouldn't have endured. I fully believe God closed the door for me in Texas. And, if He did, then I know He has something better for me.

"I just hope it isn't politics," he added with a wry smile, his arm still cradling Stephanie. "Maybe it's here. Emerald Cove is a long way from state house politics. Just a simple country lawyer in a community with traditional values is what I'm looking to be. I'm excited about the things Abigail has told me."

"Now that Abigail, she's a *real* girl. One that'd make any man proud," Martha interrupted.

Stephanie and Todd burst into relief-giving laughter. Martha, the irrepressible matchmaker, was at work again.

"By the way, Martha, how did Abigail know about Todd?"

"Um, er, we were talking one day, and I sort of mentioned Todd, and then later on she asked me about him again. And you know Abby. The next thing I knew, Todd was standing on the doorstep. Not that I mind a bit, you know," Martha explained, nodding her head for emphasis. She reached over and patted Todd's hand reassuringly.

"I know that, Martha. You've always had a knack for making me feel welcome."

"That's because you are."

"That means more than I could ever tell you, especially since I lost my parents. It's real strange—Stephanie and I both being all alone in the world. Guess you and John are going to have to be our folks." Todd grinned infectiously at Martha, and she blushed while unspoken appreciation glowed in her eyes.

"Nothing John and I would like better. It's like having children of our own, having Abby and Stephanie in the house." Then her face clouded and she added as an afterthought, "But mind you, me and John won't live forever. You need to be making a home of your own. Maybe have a few babies these old arms could rock."

She stopped, embarrassed that she had revealed her innermost longings.

"You've got plenty of time for that, Martha. And don't you worry. Someday I plan to have a houseful, and you'll be so busy rocking, you'll wear the rockers off your chairs," Todd declared.

"Who's going to have a houseful of what?" called Abby as she bounded down the back stairs, her crimson robe setting off her dark beauty, and her eyes sparkling with the excitement of life.

"Me. Don't I look like the fatherly type?" Todd asked with a grin.

"Is this something that's supposed to be immediate?" Abby teased.

"There're a few other items on the agenda first," he confessed.

"I'm relieved to hear that, Mr. Attorney! If you decide to stay here, we're going to have you so busy you'll not have time for outside activities. Look at Stephanie and me—we're strictly working girls."

"That's sure true, and if I might add a word, I think it's a shame," Martha said, her lips in a disapproving line.

"Yeah, I can see all work and no play has made them dull girls." With a laugh at Abigail, who made a face at him, Todd added, "You leave them to Uncle Todd, Martha. I'll have these two straightened out before you know it. They just need a firm hand. You've spoiled them."

Abby nodded her head, "That's a fact."

Her exuberance dispelled the last vestige of sadness, and the three young people continued a merry exchange for several hours after Martha had retired to her quarters. Stephanie and Todd entertained Abigail with childhood tales of their misadventures. She laughed until tears streamed down her cheeks.

As the wall clock chimed three times, Stephanie jumped up from the table, exclaiming, "Lance Donovan will have my hide. I'm afraid I'll be forced to leave this stimulating company."

"If you think you must. I'm just getting started. It's two hours earlier in Texas, you know," Todd reminded.

"Well, don't wear Abby out, Todd. She's not on Texas time, either."

"I'll be on up in a little while, Steph. You'd better get a couple of cold cucumber slices to put on your eyes. Lance won't like a red, puffy-eyed starlet," Abby commanded.

Stephanie placed the back of her hand on her forehead and gave a mock frown. "Oh, what sacrifices we must make to preserve our beauty. But then, that's show biz."

She exited with the gentle laughter of her friends following her up the stairs. For the first time in weeks, Stephanie felt relaxed. For a few moments, her heart had thrown off its pain, and the brooding face of Lancelot Donovan had not haunted her every thought. In the shelter of Todd's arms, she had felt warmth and protection.

The hour was late, but the evening had been therapeutic. Yes, she hoped Todd stayed. She breathed a silent prayer, *Please, God, I need him.*

❧

Stephanie's first session before the camera went smoothly, and her self-confidence grew. Her hardest adjustment had been her audience.

Since she had spent little time observing the film crew at work, she didn't realize so many people were involved in the process. Not only the actors, but stand-ins stood by as the makeup and wardrobe people hurried to and fro with touch-ups and assistance readily available. Along with Abigail and Todd, several crew members stood on the sidelines observing. Stephanie suspected they were curious about their hostess-turned-actress, but their faces revealed they were here to cheer her on.

Her mind wandered for a moment before she realized a hush had come over the set. Lance walked up and curtly asked the bystanders to move back and the actors to take their places. He, too, had noticed the size of the audience, and his face registered disapproval.

Stephanie walked to the center to meet Douglas McNeil, the young man who would play her love interest. She smiled at him, genuine affection crinkling her eyes. If ever a man met the criteria of a romantic hero, Doug did. He stood tall, blond, and handsome, like a hero from a Viking epic. His every movement flowed with masculine grace and magnetism. Lance had, once again, chosen his character with great care.

Stephanie had just inquired about the health of Doug's wife when Lance curtly interrupted, "Miss Haynes, if you and Doug are finished with your conversation, I believe we need to get started."

Stephanie looked up into the cool eyes of the director and replied calmly, "We're quite finished, thank you. What would you have us do?"

"We'll begin with the scene at the front door."

Stephanie nodded and obediently turned to the makeshift door. Her first experience as a professional actress began.

Soon she forgot everything except her part, the hero, and the director barking orders. Lance no longer was her Lance, but rather someone whose command she instantly obeyed as he fine-tuned her performance. He skillfully brought her through the scene several times, and shortly before lunch, the cameras rolled, recording Stephanie's first scene.

When it was over, they became Lance and Stephanie again, and her heart yearned to know he had approved. She watched him covertly to see if she could gauge his feelings about her performance. She couldn't. After his first curt words to her, his attitude had been one of impeccable professional aloofness. While they had been filming, she relished his professionalism; now she longed for that intimate smile that told her she was special, that he'd been pleased. It was not forthcoming.

Lance had patiently explained what he wanted and at times had walked through the scene with her. There was no difference between the way he treated her and Doug. His explanations were explicit, and he expected them to be followed. They were. He had not boasted vainly of his abilities. He was good at his job. Stephanie marveled at his communication skills and wondered why he'd had so much trouble with Alana. Surely an experienced actress would appreciate and respond to his outstanding ability.

The crew broke for lunch, and Stephanie headed toward her friends. Suddenly she felt hungry. Breakfast had been scant. She'd been too excited to eat.

Abby praised her abundantly. Todd reached over and gave her an enthusiastic hug and kiss, congratulating her. Stephanie laughed with relief, thankful for her friends and their encouragement. Putting her arm around Todd's waist, she walked buoyantly toward the inn and the meal that awaited.

Unseen by Stephanie, Lance had started toward her until he witnessed the tender scene. To his eyes, it looked more like a reunion between lovers than the affectionate encouragement between friends. His eyes clouded before pain brought down an icy curtain of studied indifference. Perhaps here was the man who could meet Stephanie's standards.

≥≥

During the next few days, Lance drove Stephanie and Doug unmercifully. He filmed every inch of footage he could, with an eye on the weather. Unseasonable warmth blessed production, so he pressed to complete the outdoor scenes before winter arrived in earnest. He squeezed every moment of progress he could from the daylight hours. After dark, he went inside and perfected each scene for the next day.

Miraculously, the weather held as well as Lance's luck. The earlier problems that had delayed him abated, and he finished all the outdoor scenes the day before the weather broke.

Tension showed in his face, and dark circles deepened under his eyes. He ate his meals on the run and talked little. Stephanie had a hard time relating this Lance to the easy-going man she had fallen in love with. But she didn't love him any less. The more she worked with him, the more her heart ached.

She longed to smooth his brow, to do something to ease his burden. But even more than that, she longed to hear him call her Steph and caress her face with eyes warmed by love.

Instead, Lance remained cool and aloof. As a boss, he couldn't be faulted. As the man she loved, he broke her heart. How could real love change so rapidly to indifference? Her heart wrenched. She didn't want to know the answer.

Todd and Abigail apprehensively watched tension drain the energy from another face and they puzzled. Martha watched, too, and finally broached the subject. "Stephanie's getting too thin."

"She must be working too hard. I noticed she looks kind of tired. Lance won't like that. He almost gave me a lecture about keeping her up the first night I was here," Todd reasoned.

"Yes, she's working hard. But she's worked hard before," Abigail hedged.

"Yep, that's worried tired, not working tired," Martha tersely observed.

Todd raised his eyebrows inquisitively. "Worried? Worried about what? She seems a real winner in front of the camera, and as for the inn, I've been over the books, and you're covering operating costs and even making a little profit."

"It's not the inn or her acting. It's Lance," Abigail inserted.

"What do you mean, Lance? He seems fair enough and satisfied with her performance."

"It isn't business, it's her heart."

"You mean Stephanie's in love with Lance?"

"I mean they are both in love with each other."

"You must be kidding. He doesn't appear interested in anything but his business. He's a genius in his job, though. I considered him a mighty cold chap, myself. Tried to be friendly to him. He appeared congenial enough, but withdrawn. Are you sure?"

"The Lance you see now is not the real Lance. He shut himself away from everyone behind a wall of determination."

"Why?"

"Two reasons. For one thing, the production is in trouble. It's way behind schedule and substantially over budget, not to mention the leading lady has gone AWOL."

"That's too bad, but if it's a success, then he'll have no problem with losses."

"That's a big if. You see, Lance put most of his assets into this picture, and he's about out of money. That's why he pushes the crew so hard. He contacted Alana and told her to come back and release some of her funds—she's the other investor. So far she's refused both requests."

Todd gave a low whistle. "No wonder he's worried. If he's out of money and production stops, he'll not be able to finish the picture—"

"And he'll lose the right to the script. One of the conditions was that the film be released next summer. We don't have any usable footage of Alana."

"Well, why doesn't he get other backers and another star?"

"There isn't time, and I don't know if he can get out of his agreement with her."

"Do you think he'd let me look at his contract?"

"I don't think so. Not in the mood he's in right now. He's fighting the inevitable."

"Poor guy. I know the feeling. A man's career is vital to his self-esteem. If I hadn't recognized God's hand in the problems I had in Texas, I don't know how I would have survived it. Looking back, I can see it was the best thing for me. But what does this have to do with Stephanie?"

"It's all wrapped up together. He asked her to marry him, but only after the movie was a success so he could take care of her in royal style."

"What's wrong with that?"

"Men! There's nothing wrong with wanting to, but sometimes things happen that make it impossible. She feels like love is sharing the good times and the bad. He feels a relationship like that makes a man weak. He's very self-sufficient and, I might add, so is Stephanie. They were bound to collide, and now they are both miserable."

"Well, what can we do to fix it?"

"Mr. Fix-it, don't you know there are some things we just can't fix?" Abigail's bright eyes danced merrily.

"Isn't that the pot calling the kettle black?"

Abigail wrinkled her nose thoughtfully. "You've got a point there, counselor."

Todd touched the tip of her nose with his finger and added, "We're a lot alike, you know."

"Oh, no. Batten down the hatches. There'll be trouble ahead," she laughed.

The smile left his face, and he looked steadily into the liquid brown eyes turned up to his. "I think it's enchanting, Abigail."

His soft drawl gave her name a musical sound, and in his eyes, she could see the memory of a Texas girl fading.

*

The winter winds howled outside while inside the crew prepared to finish the final scenes they could shoot without Alana.

Guests at the inn watched, fascinated, as the crew worked. Lance proved amazingly cooperative in working around them, and even let some participate as extras, much to their delight.

They shot party scenes in the Victorian parlor and moved to the carriage house to film beside a roaring fire. Meanwhile, Lance's face grew more drawn and haggard. Even the crew began to question the whereabouts of their leading lady.

Lance battled his own private agony with that question. Alana had refused to come back, and only one scene was left to shoot without her. He mulled over a million options, but none of them proved viable. He was out of time and money.

His last call to Alana proved futile. She didn't relish the cold weather, so neither the money nor Alana arrived. Threats and pleading accomplished nothing. *If she didn't cooperate soon*—he couldn't finish the thought. He clinched his fist tight, and a tiny muscle twitched in his jaw. He'd find a way, he always had. Somehow, too much was at stake: his career and maybe Stephanie.

A bitter smile played at the corner of Lance's mouth. No, not Stephanie. He had lost her already. He closed his eyes, and images of her intruded. He saw her thin and pale. She had lost weight recently, but it only enhanced her beautiful features. Her confidence had improved, and now she projected on screen that inner radiance that had captivated him from the first moment he'd seen her. If things were different, he'd be jubilant with his discovery, but unless Alana came through, the world would never experience Stephanie's radiance and beauty.

Lance knew with proper management Stephanie could become a star who would far exceed the Alanas in the industry. He cringed inwardly. What would stardom do to her? Would it destroy the very radiance that made her unique? He thought not, but it wasn't worth the chance. She was too special, too innocent.

He growled and tried to thrust her from his mind. He had not allowed himself this indulgence in weeks, not since the night Todd had arrived. He was probably the reason she looked thin and pale, too many late nights catching up on old times. Well, he'd warned her.

Suddenly his mind burned with the memory of that night. In a few minutes he would leave to direct the scene they had rehearsed. He'd watch her in the arms of another man, but he'd be remembering how she'd felt in his arms, the sweet fragrance of her hair, the warmth of her response. He whirled and slammed the wall with his fist, his tightly controlled indifference dissolved.

A knock interrupted and a voice informed him that the set waited. Lance took a deep breath and squared his shoulders. A scowl darkened his face as he walked out his door and toward the cottage where the crew waited. Determination to put memories aside set his face like a flint.

He cleared the set of visitors and sent the makeup and wardrobe women away. There would be no audience today. No curious eyes would observe this scene.

The tension in Lance transmitted itself to the set, and for the first time, Stephanie had trouble with her lines.

After many attempts, Lance abruptly called for an hour's break and remarked scathingly to Stephanie, "Maybe you can learn your lines by then."

Stephanie flushed, but she looked directly in his eyes until he returned her gaze. "I did learn these lines," she said softly. "I knew them earlier, remember?"

Lance turned on his heel and stalked away without answering, but not before Stephanie saw his mask of icy indifference slip, revealing the pain beneath. Somehow it comforted her.

During the break, Stephanie didn't study her lines. She studied her heart and her reluctance to play the scene. Forcibly, she recalled that night weeks ago when Lance had held her. She experienced once again every emotion that had engulfed her. When she finished, she walked back to the set, ready to begin. Out of her reservoir of memories, she would play the scene with the power and pathos it deserved.

Soft firelight reflected on the warm cherry walls of the cottage. A man and woman stood at the door, encased in the aura.

Her face, translucent in the firelight, glowed with a love that revealed her soul, yet in her eyes an agony of pain blazed. Her voice spoke soft words of a final farewell.

The blond giant gathered her tenderly into his arms and wiped away the tears that streamed down her face. Then lowering his head, he claimed her lips in a long, gentle kiss. The camera moved in and captured the face of the woman as it revealed the gamut of her emotions from sheer ecstasy to agonizing despair.

The shoot ended with a fade-out of the woman's wide blue eyes looking up into the face of her beloved. A hushed silence followed, only broken when the director's husky voice pronounced it a take.

Without a word, Lance left the room, the door slamming forlornly behind him. Spontaneously, everyone broke into applause. Stephanie tried to respond, but finding she couldn't speak, she simply nodded in appreciation to her friends as she, too, turned and walked away.

For those few moments it had been Lance who held her. There had been no cameras for her, no other people present, only the memory of his arms, the pain and ecstasy of that night. Now it was captured on film for the world to see. She sighed, glad it was over.

The days grew shorter as winter tightened its hold on the New England countryside. Winds blew in from the sea, biting and stinging all who dared to venture outdoors.

Stephanie watched and waited, but Alana did not return. Lance spent his time in the basement workrooms going over the footage they had completed. Had he been on schedule, he would have been ecstatic with what they had shot. Unfortunately, without the leading lady and her scenes, they only had bits and pieces of a collage.

He smothered his distress by perfecting what he had. Little by little, his aloofness thawed, and he joined the group in a game of Scrabble or lively conversation. He looked morose, but the fatigue lines eased, and Stephanie knew he must be getting more rest.

Their relationship improved. They now discussed business, the inn, its potential. The suggestions Lance gave Stephanie for the coming holidays resulted in a large number of reservations for Thanksgiving.

Stephanie relished the opportunity to talk to Lance. Despite the congenial companionship of her friends, she missed him. Todd and Abigail were efficient and thorough when it came to business, but neither possessed Lance's foresight and creativity.

One afternoon, the distant sound of jingling bells drew Stephanie to the front window. Her eyes rounded in bewilderment as a horse-drawn sled pulled up in front of the porch. She laughed when Todd leaped out and bounded up the porch. "Todd, there's barely a half inch of snow out there. Aren't you pushing the season a bit?"

Todd's face fell, but his eyes held their excitement. "I just couldn't help it, Steph. Lance told me to find one, and I did. An old farmer in Bay Side had what we needed, so I went after it. You get bundled up. We're all going for a ride."

Todd went in search of Lance, and soon four bundled-up adults arrived on the porch anxious for the new adventure. Todd sat in the driver's seat as Stephanie moved to the back seat. Lance climbed in beside her. Puzzled, he looked from Stephanie to Todd but said nothing. He helped Abigail in beside Todd, and the sled glided over the icy layer of snow while the foursome laughed and talked like children.

The wind grew steadily stronger, and Stephanie shivered, pulling her stocking cap down farther over her curls. Lance placed his arm protectively around her, and she nestled in the curve of his shoulder, putting her face down on his chest and away from the stinging wind.

Lance's arm tightened, and Stephanie could hear the thundering of his heart. A longing to recapture the precious moments of last summer flooded her. Memory transported her back to when their lives were filled with the rapture of simply being together, before the conflicts and questions began. She felt so warm in Lance's arms, so safe and protected. So complete.

Darkness came too swiftly for Stephanie. Before she was willing, the sled arrived back at the inn's front door. When Lance handed the girls out of the sled, Stephanie noticed he treated Abigail with the same warm courtesy as he did her. Perhaps she'd been mistaken about the flicker of pain in his eyes, the thundering of his heart.

Stephanie gave Lance a shy smile. If she couldn't have his love, she'd cherish his friendship. He winked in return, and for the first time in weeks, the old Lance peeked out from behind his troubled countenance.

Chapter Twelve

Lance sent the crew home for Thanksgiving and told them they could stay on through Christmas unless they heard from him. Stephanie knew he'd given up on Alana's return, and she waited for the inevitable, wishing he'd talk to her.

After the sleigh ride, Lance had seemed in better spirits, a fact which mystified Stephanie. One night the foursome decided to go into town for a movie. Once again, Lance looked puzzled when Abigail took the seat next to Todd in the car, but he made no comment. The movie turned out to be one of Lance's, and he balked at going in, but his friends dragged him, laughing and protesting, into the theater.

Walking from the auditorium afterward, Stephanie impulsively took Lance's hand and squeezed it, her eyes bright and moist. "Lance, you're so good at your job. I wish all movies left you feeling uplifted like that."

He stopped and turned to her. With a strange light in his eyes, he searched her face. Then he frowned and faced forward. Still holding her hand, he placed it in the crook of his arm before replying, "I'm glad you liked it."

For the rest of the evening, Lance remained subdued. They headed for the coffee shop, the college crowd's usual hangout, which for once was deserted. Todd challenged Stephanie to find some suitable music on the jukebox. She took the challenge, and pulling Todd after her, left Lance and Abby at the table alone.

Abby stood the gloomy silence as long as she could. "Lance Donovan, will you tell me what's the matter with you?"

"I've got a lot on my mind. Some big decisions to make."

"I know. But what happened in the movie tonight?"

"It just reminded me of what I'm facing."

"What, Lance?"

"Losing my career."

"You're not going to lose your career," Abby protested.

"Yes, I am, Abby. Tonight's film reminded me of what I stand to lose in my career, not to mention. . . ," and he nodded his head toward Stephanie.

"Lance, don't be foolish. Stephanie loves you."

"What about him?"

"Todd?" Abby asked, incredulity written on her pert features.

"Yes, Todd. He's a fine man with all the characteristics that Stephanie's looking for in a man."

"That's right, but she isn't in love with Todd. He is like a big brother to her. It's you she loves, you big lug."

"Aside from all that, our other differences are too great."

"Can't you change a little?"

"Maybe, but if I change just to please her, it won't work, and I refuse to be a hypocrite for her or anyone."

Tears brightened Abby's brown eyes, and she reached over to pat her friend's hand. "Stephanie wouldn't want you to. She told me as much."

"What did she tell you?"

"That she'd never want you to change your mind just to please her. Change must come only because you believe it for yourself. Now what about your career, Lance?"

"I can't give it up. I had decided to walk away from it, find something else to do. Without Stephanie, I thought success didn't matter anymore, but I realized tonight it does. I can't walk away. It's my life and I'm good at it. Somehow, I'll find a way to finish this film—I will finish it."

"Can't walk away from what, Lance? Making movies or success?"

"Isn't it the same thing?"

"No. One has to do with purpose, the other ambition."

"You, too, Abby?"

"Me, too, what?"

"Think we have some purpose we were born to or God created us for, as Stephanie put it."

"As a matter of fact, I *know* it."

"How can you know it?"

Abby laughed ruefully. "I guess you could call it trial and error."

Silently, his blue-gray eyes questioned.

"I had my life mapped out," Abby explained. "I didn't consult God about His plans for it, and He allowed me to fall on my face to get my attention."

"That doesn't sound much like the loving God Stephanie talks about."

"On the contrary," Abby disputed. "He wants what is best for us. When we suffer defeats, that's His way of protecting us from a decision that would lead to a miserable or unproductive life."

"I wouldn't say I've had an unproductive life, and I've never consulted Him."

"Maybe up till now you've sort of stumbled on the same path He'd have you take."

"Up until now?"

"Well, you're having some second thoughts, aren't you?"

"You think God's interested in helping me out of this mess?" Lance asked with a mirthless chuckle.

"Maybe." Abby's eyes flared with sympathy. Her voice hesitated as she weighed her words.

Lance rushed on with a compelling need to share his feelings. "I truly wish I could believe that, but I can't think something like this would matter to Him."

"Lance, it's not the 'something like this' that matters to God."

He shot her an inquisitive glance. "Then what does?"

"It's you, Lance. Lancelot Donovan matters to God. Sometimes He lets us suffer defeats before we can learn that. I can't promise He'll pull this deal out of the fire for you—I wish I could." Abby paused, her brown eyes pleading for his understanding. "He won't if it's not the best thing for you."

Lance shook his head obstinately. "There's no way failing in this could benefit me or anyone else. I'm sorry, Abby. I don't buy it. Failure and defeat can never be anything but bad."

"Lance," her voice and her eyes pleaded with him. "He *can* turn our defeats into victory when we give Him our lives and determine to follow His direction, no matter what."

"That's what bothers me about all this, Abby. I believe God's given us enough equipment to run our lives without bothering Him."

"I know, Lance. I thought that, too, until I ended up in some situations I couldn't handle."

"You seem pretty happy now."

She laughed. "That's because I found out that God knows how to run my life better than I do."

Lance smiled in response, warm wistfulness touching his eyes. "You sound like Stephanie. I wish I could believe what you said was true, but the way I see it, I got myself into this situation, and I'll have to get myself out."

"What if you can't, Lance?"

"I will, somehow."

"What if you have to compromise your principles?"

Lance sighed deeply. "I'll have to face that when and if the time comes."

Abby impulsively reached over and patted Lance's hand with an encouraging smile. "When the time comes, and it will, I know you will make the right decision."

Lance's eyes brightened. "Thanks, Abby, for that vote of confidence. It felt good to talk to somebody."

Abby cocked her head toward Stephanie, who was returning to the table and added, "As for her, you aren't going to lose her. You two were made for each other."

Memory of a warm summer night and Stephanie in his arms flooded Lance and he winced. "I remember saying that to her on a lovely evening a thousand light-years ago."

Lance stood up and pulled out a chair for Stephanie as she reached the table. Their eyes collided, his were open and vulnerable while hope dawned in hers.

The ride home was quiet. Just before Todd turned off the main road where the lane began, Lance moved his arm to the back of the seat, his hand resting lightly on Stephanie's shoulder. Suddenly she felt his eyes on her. Lifting her head slowly, she turned toward him. His head was bent down to hers, their lips almost touching. Even in the dimness, she could see his eyes filled with pain and longing.

Without thinking, she put her hand to his cheek, caressing it as she whispered his name. She felt his warm breath on her cheek and then his lips claimed hers. Gently, ever so gently at first, his kiss told her what his words had been reluctant to express. Stephanie's arms crept around Lance's neck, as her lips responded with her own heart's message.

Suddenly his arms swept around her, pulling her to him in a close embrace. The wool of his topcoat scratched her face, and she reveled in the smell of his aftershave mingled with wood smoke from the night's walk in town. Her heart thundered as his kiss turned from gentle to intense. His lips told her that he never wanted to let her go; hers pliant beneath his answered in kind. Their desperate embrace spoke of an uncertain future, but their lips proclaimed a love that had past and present.

When Lance finally released Stephanie, the inn was in view. Both were so overcome with pent-up emotion that neither could speak until Todd drove up in front of Lance's cottage.

"Okay, Donovan, here's your lodging. You're back all in one piece thanks to the superb driving skill of one Todd Andrews, not to mention an evening of delightful entertainment. Now what could you find in Hollywood that would top this?"

Lance took Stephanie's hand and kissed her fingertips out of Todd's view. Looking straight into her eyes, he answered, "Not anywhere this side of heaven could I find anything to top this."

Todd cocked an eye in the rearview mirror and retorted, "Now you don't have to get carried away. I know I'm a lot of fun but. . ." His retort died as his eyes met Lance's.

Lance turned to Stephanie once again. "Stephanie, would you get out and stay a few minutes? We could have a cup of hot chocolate—or something."

Stephanie smiled reluctantly and shook her head. "I don't think it would be wise, tonight. Could I have a rain check?"

Disappointment sharpened Lance's features. "Sure, anytime."

Stephanie touched Lance's cheek again, creating privacy with her soft voice. "Don't, Lance. We need time to think. The hot chocolate would be fine, but I don't think either of us are up to handling the 'or something.' Do you?"

He looked at her, his eyes dark with emotion, then smiled. "You're right."

Hope and longing transformed Stephanie's features as Lance bid goodnight to his three friends and disappeared behind the cottage door.

❧

The Thanksgiving weekend passed in a flurry of activity, leaving Lance and Stephanie no time to talk. Many of the inn staff had taken the day off, so Abigail, Stephanie, and Todd pitched in to make the holiday a memorable one for their guests. By the end of the day, their ears were ringing with guests' promises of return visits the following year.

Stephanie missed Lance at supper. Abigail told her he had some loose ends to tie up and would get a snack later on. On impulse, Stephanie loaded up a tray with enough leftovers for two and braved the cold wind to carry them to Lance's cottage.

He answered her soft knock at the door with a curt, "It's open."

She pushed against the heavy door and stumbled into the room, a vision of loveliness in her bright red coat and mittens, with eyes shining and cheeks rosy from the cold.

Lance leaped to his feet and took the tray from her. "What did I do to deserve this?"

She wrinkled her nose at him and replied, "Not a thing. I'm hiding out from the chores. You won't give me away, will you?"

He chuckled, "What's it worth to you?"

"I brought my bargaining power with me. You see all the goodies on this tray? If you're not good, I'll sit here and eat them all in front of you and not give you a mouthful."

"Now would you treat a poor starving man that way?"

"I might. You can never tell about me."

Their eyes met and held; the lively bantering stopped. "I've missed you, Steph."

She turned quickly from him, her heart in her throat. She shouldn't have come. Those old feelings would engulf her again, and she'd be powerless.

He set the tray down and took her shoulders, turning her to face him. The firelight illumined his features, but his eyes burned from an inner fire. She closed her eyes and shook her head. "I. . .I shouldn't have come. I'd better leave."

"Don't, Stephanie. I need to talk to you. We've wasted so much time. Open your eyes. Look at me," he commanded softly.

She opened her eyes and shook her head. "Nothing has changed. You're still you, I'm still me." Her voice faltered.

Lance pulled Stephanie toward the sofa, and they sat down on its soft pillows. The fire licked at the oak logs and cast long shadows on the wall.

"Why were you sitting in the dark?" Stephanie asked.

"I had a lot to think about, and before I knew it, night had fallen. Now I'm not going to turn on a lamp; you're too beautiful for words, sitting here in the firelight."

"Are you hungry?" she asked as his arm slid down the back of the sofa and cradled her head.

He pressed two fingers against her lips and said, "Shh. Yes, but later. First we'll talk."

"About what?"

"About why you came over here tonight."

"Because I thought you might be hun—"

"The real reason, Stephanie."

Her voice quivered, and her eyes locked in his gaze. "Because I didn't stop to think about it. I just wanted to be with you."

"Thank you," he said.

"For what?"

"Your honesty for one thing. I needed to hear that tonight."

Her eyes, wide and wondering, stared back at him.

"I'm leaving tomorrow."

She nodded her head, pain touching her eyes. "I wondered when you'd be going. Will you be back?"

"Someday."

"Where are you going?"

"To Hollywood. I talked to Alana tonight. She's refused to return, so I'm going to see her and perhaps salvage the film."

"How will you do that?"

"Either by getting her to go through with her agreement or by finding other backers."

"Will you have time before your option is out?"

He shrugged. "At least I have to try. Completing what we did here will give me a little edge if I don't have to use it up looking for financing. Of course, the best thing is for Alana to go on with it."

"If she doesn't, you'll have to find another actress."

"Yes, but I hope Alana will be more cooperative in Hollywood."

"Do you have any idea why she hasn't been?"

"Who knows? Said she couldn't stand it here. Made her depressed. She told me on the phone that she's ready and eager to get back to work if we can get together on the terms. I can't imagine what she's talking about—other than maybe filming her sequences in California. That'll cost more money since we have the lease here to pay, and we'd have to move everything to California."

"Don't worry about the lease here, Lance."

"Hush, Stephanie. We decided from the beginning that the only way you could make it this year would be with the income from the lease and what you'd make from the movie yourself. I haven't forgotten."

"It's just that I don't want you to worry about us here—if I can't make it, I can't. The inn's worth a lot more now than it was. If I have to sell it, at least you could get your investment back."

"And you'd be left with very little."

"Maybe I could borrow the capital to operate on."

"Too big a financial burden for the inn to carry. No, your survival depends on my honoring our lease, which is one reason I want to get this thing settled. I can't pay you the final installment until Alana or someone comes across with the capital." He squeezed her shoulder reassuringly.

"I didn't realize things were that bad for you, Lance. If you hadn't invested in the inn. . ."

Lance smiled ruefully. "Compared to movie expenses, that's just a drop in the bucket. It would only put off my decision by a few weeks."

She searched his face for the truth. Was he trying to protect her at his expense? She couldn't tell.

"Anyway," Lance continued, "if I'm not successful, this may be the only business venture I have left."

She shuddered. "Don't say that, Lance. You mustn't fail. It means too much to you."

"You're probably right, Steph. It means too much, but that's not what I wanted to talk to you about. I think we need to talk about us."

Her face guarded, she asked, "What about us? Has anything changed?"

"Something has. I'm sharing my problems with you."

"You won't let me help you."

"I don't know how you could."

"Would you, if I could?"

He chuckled bitterly. "Probably not."

"Then nothing's changed." Stephanie moved to stand up, but Lance held her back.

"I don't want to quarrel our last night together."

Stephanie dropped her head on his shoulder, shielding her eyes from his probing. "I never want to quarrel with you. It hurts too much. Why do we?"

"Because we're stubborn, and our pride gets in the way. That's one of the things I want to clear up with you before I go."

She raised her head, surprised.

"Do you remember that morning in the kitchen when you suggested I had spent the night with Alana?"

Stephanie bit her lip. Anger briefly flamed in her eyes. "Well, didn't you?"

"No. I have principles, too, Stephanie. That's what angered me, and my pride wouldn't let me explain."

"Then where did you spend your nights?"

"In the unfinished cottage next door. The boys moved a cot over there. That's where I slept. I worked, when Abby was with me, in my office. There was nothing and never has been anything between Alana and me. I wanted you to know that before I went to California to see her."

"But what about that night—"

"What night?"

"I went to your cottage to talk to you about some business, and I saw you and her silhouetted through the door, embracing."

His eyes widened, and then he frowned. "I don't know what you're talking about."

"Lance, it wasn't just a friendly, sympathetic hug. I can recognize passion, even through the door."

His frown disappeared, and he looked at her keenly, then threw back his head and laughed.

Embarrassed, she defended heatedly, "I didn't think it was a laughing matter then, and I don't now."

By the time Lance brought his laughter under control, Stephanie sat primly on the edge of the sofa, her lips pressed together in a tight line.

"Darling, you must be mistaken. I only went in that cottage with Abby, and I never went there after dark."

"I wasn't mistaken, Lance. Now you tell me the whole truth."

His eyes still danced with amusement. "Believe me, I am. There was no more between Alana and me than between you and Todd."

Stephanie's eyes rounded in surprise. "Todd and me? What are you talking about?"

"For months I labored under the notion that you and Todd had sort of taken up where you'd left off all those years ago. It's plain to see you and he are more. . .er. . .compatible."

"You were jealous, Lance?" Her smile dazzled.

"You could say that," he reluctantly agreed.

"Well, in part you were right. We did take up where we had left off. Todd's the brother I never had."

"So Abby told me."

"And Lance?" Stephanie looked up at him through lowered lashes.

"Yes?"

"There's more to a relationship than compatibility."

"Yeah?" He looked down at her, his eyes dangerously alive.

"Yes, like the sheer joy and excitement in simply being alive that I've felt with you."

"Felt, Stephanie?"

"Feel," she confessed, her head dropped.

Lance reached out and lifted her chin, forcing her eyes to meet his. Neither spoke, neither dared move, afraid to destroy the beauty of the moment. The clock ticked the seconds away and finally chimed the hour, breaking the spell.

Stephanie stirred reluctantly and said, "We'd better eat, Lance."

He nodded his head and answered, his voice husky with emotion, "Perhaps, we'd better."

They took their meal in silence. When they finished, Lance gathered the dishes and placed them on the tray while Stephanie put her coat and mittens on. He carried the tray and walked to the door with her. When they reached the door he turned, the tray between them, and looked deeply into her eyes. His darkened with emotion; hers caught the dancing firelight.

"I won't see you in the morning."

"This is good-bye?"

"I don't like good-byes," Lance responded.

"All the same, it is," she gently insisted.

"I guess so."

"For how long?"

"I don't know. Even a day will seem like an eternity."

Stephanie pressed his lips with her fingertips and shook her head. "It's in God's hands."

"And us?"

"Us, too. If we're meant for each other—if He means for us to be together—then He'll work out our differences."

She reached for the tray, and their hands touched. Fire and ice collided.

"What if He doesn't?"

"Then we'll have to trust that we—you and me together—would have been a miserable mistake—for both of us."

Misery blazed in Lance's eyes, and he groaned, "How can you be so trusting, Stephanie? So passive?"

She looked up at him, her eyes shining brightly through a veil of tears, and said, "Because I know He loves us more than we even love each other."

A particle of hope ignited within Lance, and the misery left his face. His eyes caressed hers. Spellbound, he saw in her eyes the struggle between joy and pain. He recognized the emotions the camera had captured weeks before. But now, seeing, he understood and was humbled.

Chapter Thirteen

A dozen long-stemmed roses arrived for Stephanie. Tears stung her eyes as she read the card, "May God grant us a lifetime of memories, my darling."

Tears turned to laughter when she noted the signature, scrawled boldly in his own handwriting, "Your Lance." Did he think she still worried about Alana? How could she after last evening?

She glanced in the mirror. Could this be the same Stephanie Haynes that had been afraid of love? Eyes illumined with a soft tenderness peered back at her. She trusted Lance. He loved her. In fact, she hadn't given Alana DeLue another thought—until now.

Stephanie's fine brows knit together, and she turned from the mirror. She gathered the roses to her and, putting her nose down into their crimson, velvet petals, sniffed the delicate fragrance while her mind wandered. Lance hadn't explained what she had seen through the window. She closed her eyes, and the scene appeared as real as it had that night.

If it hadn't been Lance, and she knew that it wasn't, then who? One of the crew? No, Alana remained aloof, having very little social contact with them, or anyone, for that matter. Her only outlet had been her trips to town, but there was no man in Emerald Cove that could interest a beautiful woman like Alana, or was there? Incredulity washed over Stephanie's face as understanding dawned.

❧

Stephanie's face was not the only one to register disbelief that cold November evening. Thousands of miles away in a sun-warmed solarium on the California coast, Lancelot Donovan sat across the table from Alana DeLue. Anger and shock contorted his features as he exclaimed, "You're mad, Alana. I'll. . .I'll—"

"No, darling. I'm in love."

"With Jay Dalton?" Lance growled, shaking his head in disbelief.

Alana nodded, a half-smile frozen on her face. "Surely you of all people can understand. You feel the same way about that little country girl, Stephanie."

"Don't compare what I feel for Stephanie with what you call love."

"Oh, Lance. Don't be so melodramatic. Love is love, wherever one finds it."

"I didn't come here to discuss the various definitions of love, Alana. I came here to discuss our agreement."

"And we have, darling. I just told you my terms. Take them or leave them."

His eyes narrowed, his breathing ragged, Lance protested, "We had an agreement."

"But I can no longer honor it. My circumstances have changed." Alana smiled, and stretching like a cat, she added, "And so have yours."

"Yes, thanks to you!" Lance's voice rose in frustration as he wrestled with his rising panic. He knew better than to negotiate a business deal in the white heat of anger, but Alana had played her hand well.

"May I ask you why?" His words cut the air, his voice now more controlled, icy.

"Because Jay wants it that way, and he's my husband."

Lance stood abruptly and walked to the window. The blue waters of the Pacific sparkled in the sunlight. From this distance it looked deceptively placid, harmless, but when he turned his eyes toward land, he saw where the destructive power of the surf had eroded the shoreline until, one by one, the houses had fallen into the sea. Some day in the future when the stress became too great and the last vestige of foundation had been worn away, even the house he was standing in would fall, destroyed by that very thing it sought—the beauty and magnificence of the ocean.

Suddenly Lance felt tired. Anger drained from him. His shoulders drooped. Alana called his name, but it fell on deaf ears. He saw in the awesome, tragic splendor before him his own life. If he turned around and agreed to Alana's terms, the beauty of success would be his. But at what price?

Lance clenched his fist and pounded his other hand with it. The price? His own soul. And Stephanie.

He turned back to the dark-haired beauty behind him and said slowly, "Now let me get this straight. You want me to film the rest of the movie here?"

Alana nodded.

"And you want me to cancel my lease with Stephanie? And to place a lien against the property for the amount I have invested in it?" He paused, almost choking on the words.

She nodded. "And Stephanie Haynes is to be replaced in the picture."

"I can't do that, Alana."

"Do what?"

"Submit to any of those demands."

"Very well. Then give up your option and lose your entire investment—which I happen to know amounts to all you have in this world, Lance." She shook her head. "You shouldn't have acted so foolhardily, dear. It isn't like you."

"Nor is this like you, Alana. Why? Why?"

"I told you. Love."

"Love doesn't destroy another person."

"If you mean Stephanie, it won't destroy her. She's young and beautiful, a survivor. But she's standing in the way of something the man I love wants, so she'll have to move over."

"How can you love a reptile like Jay Dalton?"

Fire touched the liquid brown of Alana's eyes. "Careful, Lance, he's my husband."

Lance shrugged his shoulders. "Okay, how did you come to fall in love with your husband?"

"Lance, have you ever lost someone you loved?" The hard glitter left Alana's eyes, and they became softer, more vulnerable.

"Not yet," Lance muttered.

"It's torment—the loneliness, the memories. I thought I'd go out of my mind the months after Brian died. Nothing helped. I couldn't work, I couldn't sleep—pills didn't help. I'd take trips only to remember the times we'd gone there together. I'd see someone who looked like him and the tears, the unending tears, would start again. Finally I couldn't stand it any longer so I walled up my emotions and refused to feel anything. This went on for months. I don't know which was worse, the feeling or the not feeling." She shuddered.

Unwelcome compassion for Alana crept into Lance's heart and for a moment he found himself trying to understand her pain. This was the Alana he knew.

She looked up at him and smiled the dazzling DeLue smile, softness evaporating with it, destroying any vestige of empathy that Lance felt.

"My agent had to talk me into that Las Vegas engagement last summer. It was there that I met Jay, and he made me laugh again. He unlocked all those good emotions that I had thought were over, and it was wonderful. When I went to Boulder Bay, we took up where we left off." She smiled, a faraway look in her eyes, remembering. Then the softness hardened. "He told me we had to be discreet because you and that little self-righteous girl of yours didn't approve of him. The stress of loving him and keeping our relationship secret was too much for me, so I flew home. Jay followed the next week, and we were married."

Lance growled something unintelligible, his eyes burning into hers.

Alana sighed and continued, "Now I'm in a position to help him get what he wants. You're a good friend, Lance, but Jay is the most important thing in the world to me." She paused and looked up at him, her eyes pleading for understanding. "Don't you understand? I'd do anything for him."

Lance groaned, "Alana, you *are* mad. You attempt to destroy another person just to satisfy one man's greed."

"No, Lance. Don't you see? As soon as this picture's a success, you can make it up to Stephanie. It's going to be a smash. What's one little old country inn compared to what you'll have to offer her after this? Besides, this wouldn't have happened to her if she'd been reasonable with Jay, but she wasn't. He really needs that property. She doesn't. She has you," Alana rationalized as she leaned toward him, her eyes imploring him to agree.

"She won't want me if I accept your terms."

"Oh, don't be silly. She might pout, but if she really loves you, it won't matter. If she doesn't, then you don't need her anyway."

A cold knot formed in Lance's stomach, and he turned to leave. Even in his turmoil he could see further argument would accomplish nothing. He needed time to sort things out, to bring sanity back. Suddenly the room felt close, the air heavy. His breathing came hard. White-hot anger returned, boiling in Lance until he feared he'd lose control if Jay Dalton walked through Alana's door. Lance left the room without another word, but echoing through the chamber of his mind was another day and another room and the cold voice of Jay Dalton saying, "I always get what I want."

❧

Lance walked the streets for hours. Later, he didn't even know where he'd been. He'd simply tried to outdistance the torment that drove him.

When darkness fell and the city lights glittered, Lance came to himself and hailed a taxi. It was a mystery to him how he'd arrived back in Los Angeles or what he'd done with his rental car. He hoped he had turned it in somewhere.

He sighed and leaned back in the seat. Tomorrow he'd remember. Tomorrow he'd have an answer to this mess. Tonight he'd rest. Suddenly he felt a longing like physical pain. An image of Stephanie's face swam before his eyes. He couldn't bear it, the wide-eyed innocence of the woman who trusted him. He moaned in the darkness, and the driver heard.

"Hey, buddy, you all right?"

"Uh, yeah," Lance lied. "I just remembered a call I need to make." Suddenly, Lance knew he hadn't lied after all. That's what he needed. To hear her voice, to assure her everything was going to be all right—maybe to assure himself? He could bear anything if he could hear her voice.

Lance rushed through the lobby of the hotel and up to his room. Opening the door, he didn't even take off his coat before he had the telephone receiver in hand. He dialed one digit, then two, before he looked at his watch. It was late, after midnight, but not nearly as late as it was on a lonely New England coast.

In his mind's eye, he could see the inn. The house was dark, and inside, upstairs in her room. . . He'd never seen her room. His heart pounded at the thought. He felt bereaved, robbed of the comfort of her presence. With a groan, he fell across the bed face down.

•

Lance slept the sleep of total exhaustion and awoke to morning light streaming in his window. He sat up with a start, forgetting where he was, startled at the strange room, a strange bed. Then he remembered, and he fell back against the pillows with his hands over his eyes. Shut out the world, close down his thoughts. He had rested—the bright light of day blinded him—but his problem remained.

Somehow, somewhere, he'd find an answer. He always had. First he'd call Stephanie. Then he'd settle his problem.

Lance climbed out of bed and reached for the phone. The need to talk to Stephanie was like an unquenchable thirst. The phone rang three times. He drummed his fingers on the table. It rang two more, and he sat down on the bed. Three more times, and he dropped his head in his hand and tapped his foot nervously.

A man's deep voice answered. He recognized Todd's slow, Texas drawl. Irrelevantly he thought how persuasive Todd must be in a courtroom with that pleasant voice. He said curtly, "Todd, let me speak to Stephanie."

"Sure, Lance, right away." No pleasantries, no time wasted—Todd sensed the urgency.

A brief pause seemed like an eternity. Then her voice called out to him. "Lance. Stephanie, here." As if he didn't know, as if he couldn't pick her voice out of an angel choir.

"Darling," he paused. He couldn't go on. How could he inflict her with his pain?

"It's bad news, isn't it?"

"You're not to worry. I'll take care of it, but, yes, Alana is being very unreasonable, and her demands would affect you, and—it isn't only Alana, you see it's—"

"Jay Dalton." Stephanie interrupted him. The two words like an icy, steel dagger fell from her lips.

"Yes, how did you know?"

"Yesterday, I thought about the scene in the cottage. Then I remembered Abby telling me she had seen them together. When she told me, I had dismissed it as mistaken identity until our talk. Go ahead, tell me about it."

"Promise you won't worry?"

"I know whatever decision you make will be the right one, Lance."

The pain in his chest bore down. The burden of her trust was too great. Then he told her the story, leaving nothing out. She'd have to understand his problem, all the implications of his decision, the loss he faced. He expected a reaction—tears or anger, maybe.

His news was greeted with total silence followed by one long, shuddering sigh. "Poor, poor Alana," Stephanie said. "How awful!"

Poor *Alana?* Had the entire world gone mad?

Then Stephanie explained. "She loves him. Lance, he's set her up. He'll destroy her."

Lance muttered under his breath, "She deserves it."

"Darling, she can't help it. That's what I meant. When a woman gives her heart to a man, she's in his power. That's a woman's nature—to submit to the man she loves. That makes her vulnerable. Don't you know that's what I've struggled with all these months? What I've been afraid of?"

Stephanie's words didn't register in Lance's heart. He needed a solution, some sort of action. Who cared what *caused* his problem. The question remained: What could he do about it?

Lance crossed his arms over his aching chest impatiently. "Stephanie, we need to address our problem, not Alana's."

"I know, darling. What do you think your alternatives are?"

"Pound the pavement in search of other financing."

"What if you can't find any?"

"I will. I *have* to."

"I hope so. You'll keep in touch?"

"Yes. I'll call you as soon as I know something. It might be several days. I have a lot of contacts I can make."

"I understand. I'll be waiting."

The line clicked, and he was alone again. Why hadn't he comforted her? Strangely, she didn't seem to need it. Where were the reassurances that he was going to give her? He didn't have any. Why hadn't he told her he loved her? Because he couldn't. He hadn't earned the right. As long as Alana's offer stood unrenounced, how could he be free to love Stephanie?

Lance pounded the pavement for a week. His efforts were fruitless. The tinsel town that had embraced him as her golden boy now closed her heart and her pocketbook to him.

The word was out. The movie was in trouble, the option running out. No one wanted to take the risk. Rumor ran the gamut—his supporting cast was ineffectual, especially the mysterious beauty he'd discovered. The answer was always the same: Thanks, but no thanks. Sometimes they said it with a friendly reluctance, other times with a cold, harsh no. Either treatment netted the same result.

Lance attempted to borrow the money, but his assets were already tied up in the picture, and the lenders considered the production itself too great a risk to accept as collateral.

Friday night arrived. The next day he had to give Alana an answer. Reluctantly, Lance reached for the phone. He knew the hour would be late, but he had to tell Stephanie—had to explain that there was no other way.

She answered the first ring. Yes, she had been sitting by the phone, and yes, she knew he'd call.

In a flat, emotionless voice, Lance relayed the facts. He only had two options: Alana's ultimatum or financial disaster. If he chose the latter, he'd never be able to work in Hollywood again. His credibility would be gone. Someone had seen to that; they had spread the word.

Lance heard Stephanie take a deep breath. He knew she was fighting tears. Were they for her or for him? She didn't know what his decision was.

He rubbed his forehead with his fingers, undecided as to what to do. What had seemed such a cut-and-dried decision a week ago had changed. But how? The price of his success—had it lessened?

Stephanie began to speak. His heart contracted. He could hear the effort it was taking her. "Lance, what have you decided?"

"What do you mean?" he hedged.

"I want you to listen to me." She took a deep breath, and her voice strengthened. "The decision you make—I want you to make it as if I didn't exist."

"You can't mean that, Stephanie," he disputed.

"Lance, I love you. The most important thing in the world to me is your happiness. If finishing this film is what you need to make you happy, then that's what I want for you—at any price."

"What about Boulder Bay Inn?"

"We'll borrow money until we get on our feet."

"You can't with a lien against it. That's the whole deal. Dalton knows you can't keep Boulder Bay Inn if I accept their offer."

After a long silence, she spoke softly, emphasizing every word. "Then so be it. You are more important to me than Boulder Bay Inn or anything else in this world. All I want is your happiness."

Lance had a difficult time understanding. She had spoken the words he had most wanted to hear. She not only loved him, but she had freed him to make his own choice.

"Stephanie, Alana did have a point. She said when this movie is a success, we could buy a dozen other places like Boulder Bay Inn."

"Perhaps, but that isn't the point, Lance. The point is you make your decision on what is best for you. I have total confidence that you'll make the right choice. Now I've got to go. And Lance, I love you."

Lance paced the floor all night. He knew that one phone call would seal his future. He reached for the phone. If he called Alana, the success for which he'd worked so hard would be his. He knew that this new agreement would open up broader avenues of promotion. That alone could spell success or failure. Slowly, he replaced the receiver.

He shook his head, and the pacing began again. What other choice did he have? If he turned them down, Stephanie would still lose Boulder Bay Inn. She couldn't survive without the money from the movie production, and without Alana's money, there would be no film. Either way they would lose. Wouldn't it ultimately be better if they accepted Alana's offer and at least salvaged his investment? So what if Dalton won? Wasn't compromise the essence of life?

Lance reached for the phone again, but his fingers stiffened. He buried his head in his hands, and the raging war within tore at him through the night.

さ。

Lance was not the only one who faced the pink and gold of a sleepless dawn. While darkness still gripped his world, Stephanie bundled up in warm clothing and went to sit on their bench and face the eastern horizon, fighting a battle of her own.

Memories of that first evening with Lance intruded, bringing a sad smile to her lips. They had been so full of promise for the future. That dream had become a reality, at least the physical aspects of it had. Now she surveyed her world as the light of the new day bathed it in a soft, shimmering radiance.

The beauty of Boulder Bay Inn dazzled. Thanks to Lance's foresight and her hard work, they had met their goal and surpassed it. Now Jay Dalton might win, after all. Through Alana, all this could be his. Stephanie's heart fought to deny what her mind acknowledged.

She had meant every word she'd said to Lance the night before. The decision involved more than just her. It meant Lance's future, his happiness. She couldn't let her wishes stand in the way of his success, his happiness. But in the blackest hours before dawn, doubts and fears bombarded her.

Stephanie sighed. Maybe she should have pled with Lance to turn Alana down, to trust God to work things out. No, she smiled ruefully, she was the one who had to trust God to work things out. What had she said? If Lance made decisions just to please her. . .

Stephanie got up slowly, her feet stiff from the cold. She walked toward the lodge. Her friends needed to know about these events. After breakfast, Stephanie called a meeting around the large, old harvest table. She filled everyone in on the decisions to be made and the apparent hopelessness of their situation.

Abigail fumed while Martha and John sat tight-lipped and silent. Todd stroked his chin thoughtfully and finally said, "Let me do some checking, Stephanie. Maybe I can come up with an alternative."

"I appreciate that, Todd, but I can't think of one. If Lance decides to accept Alana's terms, then of course there are none."

"Did Lance tell you how much he needed to pull this movie off?"

"Several million dollars, especially if he has to hire another star."

"I see, well—"

"Todd, you know Lance isn't going to turn Alana down," Abby interrupted. "Success means too much to him. We had a long talk the night we went to the movie. He loves Stephanie, but his career is everything to him. Stephanie, why didn't you just demand that he turn Alana down? After all, you have some rights."

"I really don't, Abby. All this," and Stephanie waved her hand to indicate their surroundings, "is a result of Lance's money. Without it, the bank would own it, or Jay Dalton. I really don't have any right to make demands on Lance. What it would amount to is my telling him that my career is more important than his. Is that love?"

"Well, is it love for him to sell you down the river?" Abby's eyes danced with an angry fire, then regret clouded them. "I'm sorry, Steph. You're right, of course, and I know Lance loves you."

"Yes, he does, but that's not the question. He must decide what he's going to do with his life. That is more important than this place or. . . ," Stephanie hesitated, her voice faltering, "or our love. I had to release both the inn and Lance to God."

The logs burning in the fireplace sizzled as the fire licked up the sap, breaking the deathly quiet that followed Stephanie's words. Finally, Martha reached in the pocket of her snow-white apron for a handkerchief.

When she had finished wiping her nose, Martha stated, "Stephanie, don't worry about us. The good Lord hasn't let us down yet, and He's not planning to now—I oughta know, I've had a good many years with Him—more than I'd admit to."

Laughter broke the heavy silence as a fragile hope revived in the hearts of the friends. Stephanie stood up. "Okay, troops. Let's get busy. We're not out of a job yet. Todd, I want you to hitch up the sled. We're going to cut a Christmas tree. I feel like trimming one tonight. Martha, you make some special goodies, and we'll just have a celebration."

True to Stephanie's word, they found the perfect tree and, with worries momentarily put aside, gathered in the parlor to decorate it with antique ornaments from the attic. Expectancy filled the air as Todd brought a ladder up from the basement and they began.

Laughter, mingled with carols from the radio, rang through the house. The aroma of spiced cider and gingerbread sharpened appetites. Finally the tree was trimmed except for the star on top. Todd asked Stephanie to do the honors. She slowly climbed the ladder and paused before putting it in place.

With her friends laughing gaily in the background, their glass cups clinking as they drank the warm, refreshing beverage, Stephanie paused to look at the exquisite ornament. Tears dimmed her eyes, and she felt a deep loss that Lance was not able to share this simple joy with her. She groped for the top of the tree and put the star in place, then backed down the ladder, never realizing the cheerful sounds of the room had stopped.

With the bittersweet memory of Lance still blinding her, Stephanie missed a step and fell. Alarmed, she reached out to clutch the ladder but missed. Suddenly, strong arms caught her, and she buried her face into the warm embrace of a memory turned real.

"Lance?" she whispered in unbelief.

He smiled his familiar lopsided grin and nodded. "Yes, darling—your Lance, and God's."

❧

The days before Christmas were the happiest of Stephanie's life as Lance shared his renewed faith whose dimensions were forged in a lonely California hotel suite. In the darkness, he had cried out for direction in a decision he seemed powerless to make. When he had admitted his own inadequacy, the answer had come, gently and clearly. The price of his ambition was too high to pay, and he had walked away from it all, not looking back.

The peace and joy he experienced as a result mystified him. How could he relinquish what had driven him all his life and not be destroyed?

Stephanie smiled. "That's real faith, Lance. You've been obedient, now it's God's turn. He'll show you, us. I know He will."

With all that was happening, Christmas Eve seemed almost anticlimactic. Lance, Stephanie, and their friends turned the lights off except for the tree and sat around the fire. Todd recited the Christmas story, and they all sang a few carols. Then they opened their gifts. With laughter and teasing, they admired and appreciated what they received. Finally, the floor lay bare beneath the tree, the paper and boxes discarded.

Lance turned to Stephanie with a mischievous light in his eye and said, "The best for last." Pulling her to her feet, he dragged her to the archway between the hall and parlor, where a large ball of mistletoe hung tied with bright red ribbon. Todd and Abigail, John and Martha watched wide-eyed and laughing.

Stephanie's face turned scarlet as Lance pushed her in the doorway. Slowly, he enfolded her in his arms, then kissed her lightly on the nose. Her eyes flew open in surprise to gales of laughter from her friends.

Lance had something in his hand, "Stephanie, do you remember one time I told you I wanted to lay the world at your feet?"

She nodded, the amusement leaving her eyes.

"Well, darling, I probably will never have a world to lay at your feet, but would you take my heart instead? Will you agree to being an innkeeper's wife?"

Like a flame filling a lantern, love filled Stephanie with a sparkling radiance. "Oh, yes. That's all I ever wanted, Lance."

Opening the small box, he asked, "Will you wear this ring? It was my mother's."

Against the dark velvet, a large, pear-shaped diamond caught the light from the hallway and sparkled with inner fire.

"Yes. It's beautiful!"

There was a moment of silence, and then Todd spoke. "Congratulations, old man. You've got a real winner there." Holding his cup toward Lance, he continued, "To my good friend and business associate."

Lance's brow furrowed in puzzlement.

Todd smiled. "I was going to wait until Monday, but I can't. I've been in touch with some of my contacts in Texas, and I think we have the backing you need to finish your picture."

Lance's mouth gaped. "You're kidding."

"I wouldn't kid about something this serious, Lance. Can you find another star and get the film finished before your option runs out?"

"Er, yes. I know two or three women who wanted to play that part. One of them would play it for a percentage basis rather than for a fixed fee."

"Great, you contact her tomorrow. We're in business."

"But you don't know how much I need."

"You'll have enough," Todd smiled.

"Who? How?

"I went beyond the sphere of Jay Dalton. These backers are wealthy Texas businessmen. I simply presented your case. They know the type of films you make, and they said to go ahead. There was only one stipulation. I had to invest as well to show my good faith."

Lance couldn't speak. He dropped his head, embarrassed at his deep emotions. Finally, he tightened his arm around Stephanie and said, his voice husky, "Thanks, Todd."

Looking toward Abby, Lance confessed, "You were right. God can do a better job with our lives than we can, if we just trust Him with them."

Love's Silken Melody

Norma Jean Lutz

Chapter One

Spotlights refracted into countless glittering stars against the performer's spangled turquoise dress. Deftly she moved out of the wings onto center stage. Her flaxen hair was in its usual simple elegant style—sleek and straight with bangs and the slightest curl at the ends.

Benny Lee's band exploded into throbbings that touched her feet like a magic wand. The muted lights melted from mauves to lavenders. Nervousness, tension, and worry were swept away by force. Roshelle never knew it to fail. Music drew her from the dregs, picked her up, and propelled her into dimensions high and bright.

Benny Lee, sitting at the piano, grinned at her. His smile, peeking through the full frowzy brown beard, inoculated her with confidence. Her step quickened. Why had she not heard it before? Applause—wild and crazy! Applause on an entry? Different. But something she could definitely get used to. Each club on this tour had been better than the last.

She grasped the mike and cold, solid metal contacted her damp palm. Nothing, no one, could stop her now. This was where she belonged. This was where she fit.

Benny Lee worked over the ivories, his bearlike form swaying slightly as he presented her with the smooth intro. Slowly, she raised the mike to her lips and the silken contralto poured forth a rich love ballad. Her slender body turned and moved with rhythmic understated motions. When the music flowed, all else seemed to follow naturally. The melody spun out, a golden cord weaving listeners into a captive trance.

Hadn't Benny Lee told her? "Stick with me," he said. "We'll hit the tops together." He said it only three months ago at that grungy little club in St. Louis where some klutz was so obnoxious she actually cried over the incident. She didn't want Benny Lee to see how upset she was for fear he'd tear the guy apart. But the appearance of an occasional loudmouth wasn't the only problem. It was the whole scene of second-rate places in which they'd played for years.

When? she asked herself over and over. When would the rooms be cleaner? When would there be an audience who listened? Listened and perhaps even appreciated?

Then it happened. "This is it!" Benny Lee whooped when he got the call from their new agent. At last a tour was booked in something more than smoke-filled dives. "Gen-u-wine uptown," Benny said. "Where folks wipe their feet at the door. And," he added, "they kick out the jerks without my help."

ROSHELLE RAMONE AND THE BENNY LEE CAMP BAND—the words were surrounded by flashing pink lights on the marquee out front of the sprawling Miami Beach Hotel. Roshelle had seen it from her hotel window that afternoon as she was working out her nervousness, dancing to an aerobics tape.

If only she could take photos of the marquee and send them to the folks back home in Sandott, Oklahoma. But who would really care? No one back there had ever understood her drive to make it to the top. Besides, how would it look? Hardly the decorum of a famous entertainer, to stand out on the street and take snapshots of her own marquee.

When the last full notes of the ballad unwound and came to rest, sweet applause came again to tickle her senses. Not a polite ripple, but real applause. "They're listening now," she wanted to cry out to Benny. "They're really hearing me."

Abruptly, the band moved uptempo. Benny began to bounce a little and Roshelle leaped into the rhythm like a racehorse at the starting gate—energetic, yet wisely paced. She moved to the golden stairs and descended to her audience, to sing to them personally—and they loved it.

Off the platform now, she executed a few complicated dance routines that caused another wave of rousing applause. At first she hadn't been sure, but now there was a heightened awareness of her control over them. A heady, intoxicating sensation. Benny Lee stopped playing the piano and raised his trumpet to his lips. The horn was now singing along with her in that teasing style of his. The guys in the band were sensing it as well. They were at peak performance, at the beck and call of their talented leader.

Never did Roshelle want another thing in life but to hold an audience spellbound as she was doing this moment. The exhilaration was unmatched in any other realm.

Effortlessly, she soared through several more numbers before taking a break. If only her body could keep pace with her heart's desire. Backstage, she stood for a moment catching her breath and noticed that Benny Lee was talking with the manager. From her vantage point it looked to be an agreeable conversation. Benny Lee was smiling. Then she stepped into the room where the boys in the band were unwinding.

Keel Stratton bent his thin torso into a deep bow as she stepped in the door. "Madam," he said, rising, then bowing again. "Oh, esteemed madam, to what do we owe this visit? That such an exalted celebrity should walk into the presence of these petty commoners?" Off came his coat that he twirled high over his head, then spread on the floor. "Let not your dainty slippered feet touch the floor, your highness, but step only upon my humble cloak."

"Oh, Keel," she groaned. "Don't tease. I'm still in a million knots." She snatched up his coat and pretended to brush it off, then threw it at him. He sidestepped, and it whizzed past him to the bar where Pedro Pedago was pouring a drink.

Pedro's dark eyes flashed as he mopped up the spill. "Hey, look out, Stratton. Maybe you don't care about stains on your jacket, but I do."

"Don't get your Latin blood in a boil, Pedro. Besides, the lady threw it. Awkwardly, perhaps, but she did throw it."

Pedro tossed the jacket back to Keel, who tossed it on the couch where Thorny Thorndyke and Mike Wilson were already engaged in a poker game spread out on the glass coffee table. Mike had pulled his glasses from his pocket and placed them on his nose. His youthful, studious appearance would have been more at home in a college dorm rather than being one-half of a quick poker game in the back room of a nightclub.

"They're heartless," Pedro said to Roshelle as she looked over at them. "Ignore them. Their brains are pickled. Ginger ale?"

Roshelle nodded and took the icy glass from his hand. Why did reality have to be such a comedown? And yet she loved them all.

Mitzi Wilson, Mike's nineteen-year-old sister, rushed in breathless and wide-eyed. "I've never heard you sing like that, Rosh. You were tremendous!"

"You always say that, Mitzi."

"Yeah, but this time I really mean it. Some big recording producer will hear you and you'll be swept away into stardom before our very eyes."

When Mitzi first joined their traveling entourage a year and a half ago, Roshelle was concerned that it wouldn't work out. Mitzi had run away from home—rather from a boring small community college, as she put it—and found them in New Orleans. But, when Benny Lee learned she was a whiz at bookkeeping, he insisted she earn her keep. To Roshelle, the company of another female proved invaluable.

"You really were terrific," Pedro told her.

Before she could answer him, Benny came bursting through the door. He threw his burly arms around Roshelle and gave her a squeeze that lifted her off her feet. One glittery shoe flew off as he whirled her around. "They loved you, Rosh. They're crazy about you. You really wowed them. Just like I knew you would."

"Benny, put me down," she squealed. "I can't wow anybody if I'm seasick." She stood wobbly before him, but didn't move from his embrace. It was so safe to have Benny Lee holding her. He was like a fortress against all that posed a threat.

"I couldn't have done it without the band, Benny Lee, or without your help." She looked up at his puppy brown eyes. "Thanks," she whispered. "I can't believe we're really here."

Something grabbed at her foot and she looked down. Keel bowed down to replace her shoe. "Hold still, your highness. Ah, at long last, one small favor this poor peasant boy can do for thee."

"Keel, let go of my foot or I'll wrap your drumsticks around your skinny neck," she warned, but she laughed as he placed her size five-and-a-half foot back into the slipper. "I'd better hurry if I'm going to get changed for the next number." Breaking away, she headed for the door. She turned back to look at them—her family. "Thanks again, guys. Mitzi, I'm wearing the emerald one next. Come help me zip up."

Minutes later the band was in place once again, playing her intro. By the time the show was closing down, Roshelle's body passed the exhaustion mark and moved into another gear fueled only by excess adrenalin.

"For my last number," her husky voice came over the mike, "I have a tradition that I've never broken in all my years of performing, and that is to close with a hymn."

Thorny and Mike put their guitars on the stands and Pedro laid aside his sax. Keel touched his brushes to the drums and cymbals as Benny Lee picked out the melody of "How Great Thou Art."

The strains seemed out of place, but Roshelle wasn't one to go back on a promise. When Rosh was only sixteen, Grandma Riley had made her promise that no matter where she sang she would always close with a hymn. Many times she'd wished she'd never promised. But Grandma was gone now, and how could she betray that precious old lady?

The applause that followed was a little weaker than previous ones. She gave her most professional smile and blew them kisses, replaced the mike, and disappeared through the curtains.

Still strung out in high gear, she headed for her private dressing room. Benny was beside her almost immediately. "Let me get you something," he said, closing the door.

"Ginger ale's adequate," she laughed, pressing her fingers to her temples.

"Rosh, I've told you a hundred times, you need something stronger at a time like this."

Her soft laugh sounded again. "Don't be so concerned, Benny Lee. I'm fine." She kicked off her shoes and sunk into the couch.

Concern and unconcealed admiration for her shone in his soft brown eyes. "You're much more than fine, Rosh."

She knew by his expression that he wanted to say more, but she held up her hand and gave him a half-smile. "The ginger ale, please. I'm plum dry."

When he returned with the chilled glass, in his hand was a tray on which was placed a nosegay of violets sprinkled with delicate baby's breath. They were lovely in their simplicity. "Benny! You old sweetie you."

"They're not from me, Rosh. You must've knocked somebody's socks off out there." He lowered the tray to her. "There's a card."

She reached out to touch the deep purple violets.

"Hey, does class scare you, Rosh?" He jiggled the tray. "Go on, take it. It won't burn. Probably some producer looking for a star just like you." He pulled the tray away abruptly. "Hey, what am I saying? I can't let someone bundle you off like that."

"Benny Lee!"

"Oh, all right. But you gotta promise to cut me in on a share of the take."

She laughed and shook her head. "You're impossible." Delicately she took the violets and sniffed their fragrance. There was a business card with them. "Victor Moran," it read. "President, Moran Recording Company." The address was Tulsa. She turned it over. In a bold script was penned, "Psalm 69:30, 'I will praise the name of God with a song. . . .' " Below that was written, "May I see you backstage?"

Roshelle stared at the card for a moment. A Bible verse—the last thing in the world she needed was a Bible verse. She gave a light laugh that sounded hollow even in her own ears. "What do you think?" She handed Benny Lee the card.

His expression sobered. "Sounds like a kook. I'll go get rid of him." He turned toward the door.

Roshelle straightened. "No, Benny Lee." She tucked a strand of blond hair behind her ear. "No. Let him come back. You can get rid of him if I give you the high sign."

Benny Lee looked at her. He had loosened his tie and the top button of his shirt was undone. To Roshelle, he always looked like a lovable teddy bear, and she did love him, but not in the way he wanted. She was wise enough to know the difference. Still, there was an unspoken knowing that Benny Lee had wanted their relationship to be more, but Roshelle was determined that it remain on a friendship level. Now, he searched her face. "You sure?" he asked.

"I'm sure."

"Want to change first?"

"No, this is fine."

A moment after he left, there was a soft knock at her door. She rose to answer. There stood a tall man, slender, but not thin. His chestnut brown hair was softly styled back from his face. His impeccable gold-green suit, high-lighting his gentle hazel eyes, was hardly what Roshelle had expected. The guy was a knockout!

"Miss Ramone? I'm Victor Moran. Thanks for seeing me."

Roshelle looked past him to where Benny Lee stood in the hallway, leaning against a doorway. "No problem," she answered, letting him in and waving him toward the couch. "Have a seat."

"Thanks."

"Sure." She stole a glance at him as he sat down. He looked nothing like a Bible-verse type of guy. The suit was obviously custom-made. He had an almost regal look, like a crown prince—narrow face, straight nose, hair per-fectly groomed. A lot she knew about crown princes, she thought as she curled up in a chair across the small room.

"Tell me, Mr. Moran," she said coolly, "what can I do for you?"

"Please, just Vic. First of all, I wanted to tell you what an outstanding entertainer you are. I enjoyed the show tremendously." He leaned forward as he spoke. "I appreciate good music. Your voice has an almost silken quality. Quite unique."

Roshelle shook her hair back from her face. "You know what they say about an entertainer's ego. You certainly know how to feed it. Where did you derive your technique?" Did she detect a slight blush? How long had it been since she'd seen a guy blush? Eighth grade?

"I know it sounds a little plastic, but I'm as sincere as I can be. Your power and thrust are amazing. I also wanted to thank you for closing with a hymn. It takes courage to do that here, and I admire your fortitude. It's refreshing to see. The Lord will honor you for it."

Roshelle felt herself stiffen, as she remembered the verse on the card. "I appreciate the compliments, Victor—Vic, but let's get one thing straight from the beginning. I sing those hymns for one reason and one reason only. It was a request of a dying granny to whom I couldn't say no. I've wished a thousand times that I'd never promised, but I did. I'm not and never will be Miss Goody Twoshoes."

"Still and yet, it does take courage—"

"Oh, sure. Courage to hear the volume of applause go down five decibels whenever I turn on the religious stuff? More insanity than courage, Mr. Moran! Sometimes, it quiets the drunks and makes the old men teary-eyed. I'm far from being a saint and don't even pretend to be. But then, I'm not a hypocrite, either." Why was her heart pounding? Benny Lee was right outside the door and if she merely called his name, he would be dragging this guy out by his ear.

"Please, Roshelle. May I call you Roshelle?"

"That's my name."

"I had no intention of coming back here to upset you." His voice was quiet, even. His eyes were gentle. "On the contrary, I simply wanted to let you know what a blessing you were to me."

"Blessing? You even talk churchy. What's your bag, mister? What is it you really want? Invite me to a local revival?" Maybe he was one of those television ministers she'd heard about. Next, he'd be asking her to do a benefit concert to help raise money for his new multimillion-dollar television outreach. But still, she didn't call for Benny Lee.

Victor rose to his feet. "Scout's honor, Roshelle. No ulterior motives. I meant what I said. I simply wanted the violets to express to you how I felt about your performance. Beautiful flowers for a beautiful performance and a beautiful person. I'll go now, and I apologize if I upset you."

He pulled another card from the pocket of the silk suit and handed it to her. She didn't take it. He gently laid it on the glass coffee table. "Incidentally, you don't need to feel any certain way about a hymn for it to minister. The lyrics are based on Scripture. They minister life no matter how you feel about them." He gave her a quiet smile. "If you're ever in Tulsa, look me up."

"Oklahoma? Fat chance! It's a great place to be from—far away from."

"You're from Oklahoma?"

"Born and raised. No way you can make any money singing like I sing in Oklahoma. They don't like my style."

"On the contrary, I've heard some mighty spirited music in Tulsa."

"Tulsa, maybe; Sandott, hardly. Around my family—never."

He dismissed the negative comments as though she hadn't spoken them. "Thanks for letting me come backstage, Roshelle. I pray for the Lord to bless all that you do."

"Bless? Yeah. Yeah, sure. Thanks." When she closed the door and leaned upon it, she was trembling from head to stockinged toe. He had not called her a beautiful woman—but a beautiful *person*.

Chapter Two

Roshelle paced the length of her hotel room, her nightgown swishing with each step, the carpeting plush beneath her bare feet. The applause had not ceased to thunder in her ears. The frightful exhilaration had wound her to a fevered pitch and sleep had fled. The heavy draperies were drawn against the brightness of the lighted hotel front. She snapped on the light in the bathroom and rummaged in her makeup case until she found the small prescription bottle. She didn't open it yet, but dropped it into the pocket of her nightgown and moved back out into the room. Sleeping pills were a last resort; she loathed the strung-out feeling that came the next morning. She shunned the booze for the same reason. Her body was her friend and she was determined to take care of it.

Mitzi was asleep in the adjoining room. In the days of playing sleazy little dives on the back streets, she and Mitzi roomed together and talked and laughed all night.

"Now, Rosh," Benny Lee had said proudly, "on this tour, you get a room of your own. Class, angel. Lots of class."

But private rooms were intimidating to Roshelle, the solitude threatening. She didn't have to face it in a noisy bus day after day nor in a crowded motel room with the giggling Mitzi. But now. . .

She studied the door that led to Mitzi's room, then turned away. Cupping her elbows in her hands, she paced once more. A breeze had come up. She could hear it sweeping past her windows. Reaching for the fringed cords, she drew open the draperies. Palm trees swayed lazily, and far out from the hotel grounds lay the ocean gleaming like a treasure in the moonlight.

Suddenly, she wanted to walk along that beach and feel the breeze in her hair. Fresh air. . .that's what she needed. She took off her nightgown and let it slip to the floor, hearing the bottle of sleeping pills make a soft thunk as it dropped. She changed into her royal blue sweats and a pair of sneakers.

Hopefully, Benny Lee, in the opposite adjoining room, would not hear her. She slid open the chain latch, wincing as it clanked. The door was heavy and groaned in protest as she pulled it open. The hall was dim and vacant. Just as she started to pull the door closed, she remembered. The room key! Tripping back in, she grabbed it off the dresser and then closed the noisy door behind her.

Now, she could only hope there would be no drunks in the lobby to stop her and offer slobbery comments about the show. First, through the vast resplendent lobby and then to her left, down the hall to the open courtyard. So far, so good. Her sneakers were silent as she crossed the courtyard that also served as an outdoor snack bar; chairs were stacked on the tables now. Finally, the white beach lay before her. The breeze touched her hair and ruffled her bangs; she lifted her face to it. It was sweeter than she had imagined. She didn't slow her steps until she was at the foamy edge of the curling waves.

She stood with her feet planted apart and her hands on her hips looking out at the endless swelling and ebbing waves. In all her years of traveling with the band, seldom had they ever been on the coast. When they were, they were never on a nice stretch of beach like this.

Several times since she received Victor Moran in her dressing room, his quiet hazel eyes appeared in her mind's eye. Now, as she gazed out across the water, she saw them again.

Benny Lee's eyes were gentle and kind, always looking at her with tenderness and admiration, but they were also troubled eyes.

Victor Moran's eyes were not only gentle, but peaceful. They seemed to emit an essence of quiet. . . .

She shook her head to free herself of the clinging thoughts. Surely the breeze would clear away the sticky cobwebs. She turned to walk quickly along the water's edge.

She walked a ways in the silence, then "Rosh!" The voice coming down across the beach toward her made her gasp. She whirled around. It was only Keel.

"Keel, my word! You scared me silly. What're you doing out here at three in the morning?"

Keel slowed his long legs as he fell in beside her. "I might ask our fair celebrity the same question. What would Benny Lee say if he knew you were out here? It's not all that safe, you know."

She gave him a guilty grin. "I know. He'd kill me, wouldn't he? But I couldn't sleep, and the beach looked so inviting from my room. Fresh air won over the pills tonight, Keel. At least so far."

"Great news. But the fresh air didn't win over Benny Lee. I think he's a trifle soused."

"So that's why he didn't hear me sneaking out."

"That's it." There was a moment of silence before Keel asked, "Who was the flashy dude who gave you the posies tonight?"

Roshelle stopped and looked up at him. "Violets."

"Violets. Posies. Same difference."

"How'd you find out about it?" she asked with a trace of irritation.

"It was all Benny Lee talked about after he'd downed a few."

"Really?"

"You sound surprised."

"I guess I am. The guy was some sort of staid religious kook who wanted to make something saintly of my singing a hymn as a closer. That's all there was to it. No big deal. I've already forgotten about him."

Keel gently took her arm. "Let's sit down." He steered her away from the water's edge and sat beside her on the sand. "Did you explain it to Benny Lee?"

She dug her hand down into the sand and felt the fine grains sift through her fingers, and remembered. Remembered how she'd spoken to Benny Lee through the door after Victor had left. "I'm going to change and then rest awhile," she'd told him. She hadn't admitted it before, but she didn't want to see him just then. More honestly, she hadn't wanted him to see her in her unexplainable trembling state.

"No, Keel, I guess I didn't explain. Should I have?"

Keel's voice was steady. The guy who was eternally kidding was now too solemn. "You act like you don't realize what you mean to Benny Lee, Rosh."

"Keel!" She didn't want to hear this. Why should this skinny drummer try to meddle in her life? She started to get up, but he laid his hand on her arm. He didn't grab her, but his voice pleaded. "Just listen, Rosh. For a minute. Please?"

She nodded mutely and relaxed.

"Benny Lee could have handled it if you'd only explained everything. But when you wouldn't see him after the dude left, wild things began to play in his mind. He was even waiting and hoping he could throw the guy out. Those slick kind are a threat to him, Rosh. He's so scared of losing you. Why don't you just—"

"Marry him? Is that what you think I should do, Keel?"

"Why not? You're together constantly anyway."

"Did he send you to talk to me?"

"No! Like I told you, he's potted."

"So why did you decide to play cupid?"

Keel gave his silly laugh. "Honest, I didn't. You decided for me when you just happened to be out on the beach when I was coming out after the bar closed."

Roshelle mulled over what Keel had said. "Marriage is a trap, Keel. Why ruin a good relationship by getting bogged down in a rat race of marriage. Why spoil everything? If you think Benny Lee gets upset over guys like Moran now, what would he do if I were his wife?"

Keel shrugged his thin shoulders and she continued. "You have to under-stand—I'm headed for the top. Marriage has never fit into my plans. The ball and chain bit isn't compatible with a soaring career. I don't want to turn fifty someday and look back on four or five sour marriages polluting my career. I don't need that kind of misery. I'm chicken. I don't like pain. You may not think so, Keel, but Benny Lee understands."

"Do you talk about it?"

She paused. "No. It's just an understanding we have."

"It's an understanding you have, maybe. I don't think Ben understands at all. Maybe you should talk about it."

But that was just the problem, she protested inwardly. She'd never been able to talk about it to Benny Lee because of the way he looked at her. It broke her heart. What if she weakened? What if she couldn't stand strong?

Abruptly, she stood to her feet, brushing the sand from the seat of her sweats. "I think I'll sleep like a baby now, Keel. I'm going back to my room."

"Okay, I can take a hint. I touched a sensitive spot. But do us one little favor?"

"Name it."

"When you agree to see a flashy dude in your room, and then refuse to see Benny Lee afterward, at least give old Ben an explanation. It's a nightmare to get that lunk into the elevator and then into bed."

She laughed, thinking of the boys struggling to get their leader, built like a linebacker, into bed. "It's a deal." They were through the courtyard now and entering the lobby. "And Keel, thanks. I know it wasn't easy to say what you did."

"Psychoanalysis free! What a bargain." He laughed aloud in the empty lobby. She shushed him as the desk clerk looked their way.

"Mike says we're pulling out at ten in the morning," he said in a quieter tone as he put her on the elevator. "Be ready."

❧

Roshelle was awakened out of a heavy sleep by sharp raps on her door. Who could be wanting her in the middle of the night?

"Go away," she muttered through the covers.

"Rosh, get up. It's me, Mitzi. Let me in so we can get you packed."

Turning over, Roshelle strained to focus on the clock. Nine o'clock? She felt as though she'd just fallen asleep. And Mike wanted to be on the road in an hour!

Shaking off the drowsiness, she roused and pulled on her robe and moved to let Mitzi in. On the dresser lay the violets. How awful! She hadn't even bothered to put them in water. How unfeeling she was. Just because she didn't like the giver was no reason to waste such beauty.

Purple violets and baby's breath. Representing innocence? What a joke. Mr. Moran had gotten the wrong idea about her. Courage for singing a hymn? What a laugh. If there was one thing she wasn't, it was courageous.

Still, Victor Moran was quite a mystery. Talking churchy, but looking nothing like the part. Strange. He talked almost like Grandma Riley, or Uncle Jess. . . .

No, she scolded herself mentally, *you're thinking Rachel Rayford thoughts again. You buried Rachel to become Roshelle, remember?*

"Rosh, good grief! Open this door or Mike will have a fit because we're late." Mitzi rattled the knob. "He'll blame me. You know how big brothers are."

"Coming, Mitzi. Keep your shirt on."

She'd heard of people pressing flowers, but what could she press them in? Quickly she tucked the little bouquet between the pages of a Bible she found in the drawer and slipped it into her suitcase, threw some clothes over it, and hurried to open the door. On her way past the front desk, she paid for the Bible.

When they got out front to the bus, Thorny and Keel were loading instrument cases and the drums into the storage bin of the bus. Keel grinned over at her as she and Mitzi approached.

"Our bags are ready and waiting in the lobby," Roshelle announced proudly.

"Terrific." Keel heaved in another case and shoved to adjust it into place. "Mike, go get the girls' things in the lobby."

Mike was sitting in the driver's seat scanning a map. "Get them yourself. I've gotta get this route figured out before we pull out of here."

"Where's Benny Lee?" Roshelle wanted to know.

Thorny jerked his head toward the hotel. "Coffee shop, downing the java. He'll be okay. . .sooner or later."

Roshelle stifled a groan. It was her fault.

"And Pedro's at his usual station," Mitzi added brightly.

Roshelle followed Mitzi's pointing finger to where Pedro sat with a woman on the edge of a fountain in front of the grand hotel. He seemed to be gallantly telling her how he hated to leave. Then he made a great to-do about saying good-bye. *If she only knew*, Roshelle thought. At nearly every stop, the handsome, dark-skinned sax player had a woman at his side.

Actually, Pedro's name was Ralph. But after Benny Lee hired him on and the boys heard his name, they laughed themselves silly over Ralph and promptly changed his name to Pedro!

Just then Benny Lee joined them, looking a bit tired, but hardy as ever.

She gave him her kindest smile. "Good morning, Papa Bear. Have you had your porridge?"

"Food! Perish the thought." He screwed up his bearded face and Mitzi giggled.

Thorny came pushing a loaded luggage cart. "Where's your trumpet case, Benny Lee?"

The hefty band leader came to life. "It was with the other equipment last night. Rosh, have you seen it?"

She shook her head. "Mike," she called, "where's the golden trumpet?"

Mike stuck his head out the bus door, the map still in hand. "I have enough trouble keeping track of my own stuff!" He retreated and a mad search was made throughout the empty club and then through the now-vacant rooms they had occupied. No trumpet.

"Rosh," Benny Lee said, "you know how I love that stupid old thing. We've just gotta find it." They were walking back to the bus.

"I know, Ben. I know. Don't worry. We'll find it."

"You don't think it could have been stolen, do you?"

"Who'd want a battered old trumpet?"

He laughed. "This is true."

"Time to get loaded and head on down the pike," Mike warned as they approached the bus. Pedro was hurrying toward them from the fountain area and in his hand was the missing trumpet case.

"Pedro," Rosh yelled at him. "What are you doing with Benny Lee's trumpet?"

Pedro looked down at the case as though he'd just discovered it and then grinned at them. "I was guarding it. Anyone who would leave their trumpet in the men's room of a bar ought to hire a keeper."

Benny Lee threw back his head and let his deep laughter roll. "Am I a dunce or what? In the men's room! Boy, I must be getting old."

"If that's everything, then let's get rolling!" Mike ordered in the gruffest tone his young voice could muster.

"Give a man some authority," Thorny muttered as he boarded, "and it all goes to his head."

Mitzi shook her head. "Organized confusion as usual," she said with a giggle.

Within minutes they were loaded, settled, and on their way in the spacious bus.

"Hey, Rosh," Keel called out from the back, where he was already raiding the small propane refrigerator. "Hear any more from your religious freak of last night?"

He was doing it for Benny Lee, Roshelle knew. "Why no, Keel. I guess I sent him packing when he found out what a heathen sinner I was."

"Yeah, well," he called back, his mouth full of a ham sandwich. "Good thing you set him straight."

"Religious freak?" Benny Lee looked at her.

"That guy who sent the violets and the Bible verse."

"Oh yeah, I remember."

"He was just a kook like you said. I should have let you throw him out in the first place."

"Wish you had." He slid down in the seat to take a nap.

The next night the little group landed in Mobile for a week's stand. After that, New Orleans. The tour then took them north to Little Rock, St. Louis, and on to Chicago.

In St. Louis, there was a small greeting card waiting for her from Victor Moran. The card was lavender with a dusky photo of violets on the front. The note read: "You've been in my thoughts and in my prayers." Benny Lee didn't see it. She hid it in her suitcase.

It was March and they had left spring behind in New Orleans, where the flowers were blooming. It was snowing in Chicago.

"That crazy agent doesn't even know how to schedule a tour," Roshelle complained to Benny Lee in her dressing room after the first show. "That white stuff out there is definitely a bummer."

"Newt's the best agent we've ever had, Roshelle. If he's crazy, he's only crazy about the way you sing!" He poured her a ginger ale. "Better not complain. This is the best money we've ever earned. Besides it's the Windy City, remember?"

Another lavender card awaited her in Chicago. She wanted to be angry. The nerve of that guy! And how did he know her itinerary? The note read: "Wish I could see how Chicago receives a hymn. Bless you, Vic." She threw it across the room. Later, she tucked it into her suitcase with the other one.

Two days later, she had just returned to her hotel room from a strenuous workout, jogging the marvelous indoor track. The phone was ringing as she came in the door. Still out of breath, she answered. It was Newt, calling from Los Angeles.

"I've been meaning to talk to you," she teased. "Is it sunny there? Well, it's freezing out here. We slipped and slid all the way up here in that old bus."

"Okay, Rosh! You don't like the chill? How does Reno sound? I don't think it's snowing in Reno today."

"Reno? That's a long way from Chicago, Newt. You got us a spot in Reno?"

In her mind's eye she could see him rolling an unlit cigar between his fingers as he talked.

"Tentatively, you're booked in Reno. From there, with a little loose finagling, looks like I could get you into Vegas. This guy's got a club in Vegas and if he likes you—"

"Vegas?" She had gone from breathless to totally winded. Unceremoniously, she collapsed back onto the bed. "You mean it, Newt? I thought it would be years before Vegas."

"It's not one of them flashy joints on the strip," his nasal voice sounded back at her. "But it's not bad for starters. What do you say?"

"Let me talk to the boys. I'll call you back in an hour."

"Hey, Rosh. Hang on. Tell me. Did you hear me say anything about a band?"

Painfully, Roshelle sat up and stared at the phone in her hand. No words came. Her brain refused to compute. "No, Newt," she answered in a weak whisper.

"Now listen, sweets. Bands aren't too big right now. A dime a dozen. Get it? But you? You got class. . .style. . .a powerful voice. I can sell you, easy. Look, I been working on this thing night and day for a week. What do you say? Are we on?"

"The boys and I have been together forever."

"Hey! Look who's getting sentimental. The last time you were in L.A., you told me you wanted to go to the top. Am I right, or was I dreaming on a sauerkraut sandwich?"

"You're right, Newt. That's where I'm heading."

"So what's a few musicians along the way? They was doing fine before you met them. Dump them and get on with the business at hand."

Dump them? It sounded so harsh. . .cruel. . .heartless. She needed them and they needed her. "I'll have to talk to them before I can say yes. Surely you understand that."

"So talk. But make it quick. This guy in Reno just had a cancellation and he's sort of up a creek. I need you out here, pronto. Oh, and by the way, I've been talking with a recording company to boot. They like your sound."

Roshelle ran her fingers through her soft bangs. They settled, featherlike, back onto her forehead. "I'll call you back right away."

"See to it, sweets. I'm in a hurry to make both of us rich."

"Oh, Newt?"

"Yeah?"

"Thanks."

Chapter Three

Had Roshelle been flying alone, she would have pulled down the shade on the plane window. The takeoff from O'Hare in the driving snow was terrifying, adding anguish to her already frazzled nerves. But perky Mitzi insisted on having the window seat and, like a little kid, kept peering out. After all, it was her first flight!

Above the snowstorm, cloud formations spread out like pink marshmallow fluff. Roshelle turned her red-rimmed eyes from the brilliance. Why did things have to turn out this way? she questioned silently. Wasn't this the break she'd waited for since she left home and played her first club in Tulsa?

So why had she let herself get so attached to the band? Like Newt said, they were just a bunch of musicians. But they'd become so much a part of her.

Benny Lee had held her close to his massive chest after she explained everything to him. "Maybe it'll only last a few weeks," she told him. "Even if I go on to Vegas, I'll be with you again after that."

"Rosh," Benny Lee said in his gentlest tone. "Don't you cry, Rosh. You're gonna make it, angel. You're gonna make it big. Just like you always dreamed. And when you do," he dabbed at her tears with his handkerchief, "you call for us and we'll be there in a flash. We'll be coming up to where you are, not you falling back down to where we are."

But the words didn't make the hurt go away and when she left them at the airport, she felt like Dorothy saying good-bye to her friends in the Land of Oz before going home to Kansas. Keel was definitely the Scarecrow. Mike, the Tinman. She'd edit in two crazy new characters for Thorny and Pedro because Benny Lee, of course, was her lovable Cowardly Lion—only with courage unlimited.

But, unlike Dorothy, she wasn't going home. She didn't have a home, really. But it never mattered. With a mobile family, who needed a home?

It was Mike's idea for Mitzi to go with Roshelle. He wanted better things for his baby sister. But, for whatever reason, Roshelle was thankful and Mitzi warmed up to the idea immediately.

"Put her to work," Mike had said. "She knows the ropes. She can be your personal secretary."

It sounded good, personal secretary. Plain old down-home company sounded better.

"Hey," Benny Lee protested to Mike. "What do you think you're doing, giving away my bookkeeper?"

"I guess I'm brilliant enough to keep your simple books," Mike shot back at him.

But they were just going on, as they always did. How she would miss it. The zaniness of it all, the rushing, the hurrying. Mike ordering people around like he owned them. Keel's wit and wisdom. Pedro and his women. Thorny and his poker. And Benny Lee. . .

Roshelle snuggled the luxurious blue fox jacket around her face, more for comfort than for warmth. It was her very first fur. Benny Lee insisted on getting it for her before she left. "You'll have a jillion furs soon enough, Rosh. All I ask is to give you your first one."

"You look great in the fur, Rosh," Mitzi piped up next to her, as though she had a readout on Roshelle's brain waves. Her wide, brown-black eyes were dancing. She reached over and stroked the sleeve. "Feels so. . .so money!"

"It gives me an almost wicked feeling to wear it."

"Wicked? Why? You look terrific."

"Blue fox," Roshelle mused. "Sounds like something at the top of the endangered species list."

"Female vocalists are on the list, too, Rosh. Just figure it was them or you."

"Thanks."

"Oh, don't worry, honey. Mama Mitzi is here to take care of you."

Roshelle looked at her youthful companion, who reminded her of her younger sister, Janey, who was always giggling and joking, too. Mitzi's black, close-cropped curls framed a pixie face. She looked nearer to fifteen than almost nineteen. Roshelle was six years her senior. "Okay, Mama Mitzi," Roshelle mocked, laughing at the irony of it. "Take over."

"I'll be in the wings tomorrow night, Ms. Ramone," Mitzi singsonged, "and I'll have your endangered species jacket ready for you to wear out on your third curtain call. Won't that be flashy?"

"Third? Hey, I like you. You think big!"

"You're that good, Rosh. They'll love you!"

"Forget the wings, Mama Mitzi. I'm planting you in the audience to lead the applause." That led them both into enough giggles to attract stares.

Later, Mitzi asked, "Rosh, are you going to play your own accompaniment like Benny Lee suggested?"

Roshelle thought a moment, running her fingers over the hem of the fleecy jacket. "I guess I can answer that better when I've rehearsed with the combo there. See how we mesh."

"You play a mean piano. Just take over and do your own thing."

"It isn't that, Mitzi. The problem is lack of audience contact when I'm at the keyboard. It stands as a barrier between me and my audience. I love to move among them. The music is ministering to them and I want them to know that I know it."

Mitzi turned to look square at her. "Ministering? That's a funny word coming from you. I've never heard you say that before."

Roshelle hedged. "I don't mean minister exactly."

What was it that Victor had said? That the hymns minister life. Had he planted the word in her brain?

"I guess I mean help," she corrected herself. "Uplift. You know. I give them something they can reach out and take hold of. And what do you mean, funny word? Don't forget, I was raised in church."

"I remember. Your uncle was a minister, wasn't he?"

"Of sorts."

"That's an odd answer. Was he or wasn't he?"

"He had all the right papers, but all the wrong actions."

"One of those who doesn't practice what he preaches? There are a lot of his kind around."

"My grandma Riley preached a better sermon than Uncle Jess, and she never stepped foot in the pulpit."

"Did you ever play the piano in church?" Mitzi wanted to know.

"Almost from the time I could reach the keys." She remembered how proud Daddy had been the first time his little Rachel played for the congregational singing on a Sunday night. For a time, she was only allowed to play on Sunday and Wednesday nights, when the crowds were smaller. But when the regular pianist suffered so badly from arthritis that she could no longer play, Uncle Jess let Roshelle play on Sunday mornings as well. She could play every song in the songbook, and some that weren't.

"Did you play all those years? Until you ran away from home?"

"Actually, no. When I got a little older, I stopped. Sort of in rebellion, I guess."

When Daddy died, she swore she would never do anything for Uncle Jess ever again. Uncle Jess called it "wicked rebellion" that was "bound up in her heart." But she didn't care what he said. She sat staunchly on the back pew of the church and refused to play for him. It made her mother furious.

It was her fault the conversation had veered in this direction and now she wanted out. The memories were as painful as ever. Fortunately, at that moment, the pilot announced their approach to the Cannon International Airport. Thankfully, Mitzi let the subject drop.

"I suppose there'll be a big black limo to pick you up," Mitzi remarked as she stuffed the flight magazine back into the pocket of the seat in front of her and fastened her seat belt. "What a kick."

But there was no limo. Nobody. . .nothing.

"Now, where did I put my women's lib handbook," Mitzi quipped as she grabbed for their luggage and pulled them off the moving carousel. "How did I ever become so dependent upon men?"

"You should have memorized the handbook so you could teach me. What's a good secretary for anyway?"

By the time all of their luggage had been retrieved, a porter had spotted them and offered his assistance. And, with his kind help, they were led to the car rental office and were soon loading the luggage into the trunk of a nice little compact car.

"This is more my speed than a limo, anyway," Roshelle said after tipping the porter and coming around to the rider's side.

"Hey," Mitzi called out. "Where're you going?"

Roshelle stood on the curb and looked at her. "You do drive, don't you, secretary?"

Mitzi raised innocent eyebrows. "Drive, I do. Have my license, I don't."

"Some personal secretary!" Roshelle fumed. "Well, get in and we'll try to find the Supreme Royale Hotel. Shouldn't be too hard. Help me look." As they craned and watched, Roshelle muttered, "First on our list will be for you to take your driver's test and get your license."

Mitzi shrugged, unaffected. "How was I to know I was up for promotion to a chauffeur? Somehow a license never seemed important. I never liked doing things that were legal."

Roshelle shot her a sidelong glance.

"Until now, that is," she added with a giggle.

❧

The Supreme Royale was a new hotel in Reno. Tall and glittering in the sunshine. Not nearly as spectacular as some of the others, but not bad considering where she'd come from, Roshelle thought.

She was scheduled to appear in the cabaret rather than the bigger theater showroom. Obviously, that was why she had to sing with the existing musicians. Rehearsals with the combo were frightful. During a break, she sat down in the front, away from the stage, and pondered her predicament. It was a good combo. . .up-tempo. . .versatile. Not as versatile as Benny, but good enough. Perhaps it was simply the adjustment time. How naive she'd been, leaning so much into Benny Lee's music and style. She should have been developing her own style. . .in her own way. Well, better late than never. Silently, she determined to work hard to adjust and to be her own person and have the band follow her direction and lead.

The stage was the most elaborate setup Roshelle had ever seen—massive shimmering sets in bright luminous colors. She tried not to appear awestruck as she sat there studying it.

The band leader, a short serious man named Truman, came bouncing down the stairs toward her. "Everything to your liking I trust, Ms. Ramone?" he asked politely.

"Thank you, Truman. A little more Latin emphasis on the second number, please. And tone down the drums when I go into the bluesy number near the break."

He nodded and pulled a small notebook from his pocket and took down neat little notes. She would learn to work with others. She really would.

"By the way, I sing a hymn at the close of all my concerts."

Truman cleared his throat and looked at her. "A what?"

"A hymn. A church song, you know, like. . .like 'Rock of Ages.'"

His expression was as unchanging as that rock, as though to say, "One more screwball, more or less, makes no difference." What he did say was, "You want the band to play a hymn?"

She felt herself weakening. "The band doesn't have to play. Why don't you just have the pianist follow along."

He nodded, his face still a mask. "Anything else, Ms. Ramone?"

There were other things. . .several other things. But this was all she could handle at the moment. She shook her head and said, "No."

He rose to leave.

"Thank you, Truman," she called after him, feeling that her last contact with success had been severed.

That evening, she followed a mediocre juggling act that was no buildup for her at all. The band came through tolerably, though not as superbly as Benny Lee's band would have done. There was rousing applause, which was heartening.

The next afternoon, she was able to boldly talk to Truman about the other things that needed altering. He was still amicable, but somewhat distant. If ever she would have given up on the hymns, this would have been the moment. Obviously, the pianist didn't like the idea of playing a hymn and his delight was either to drag it or rush ahead. She simply had to make do.

On the second evening, following the show, Mitzi was rapping on the dressing room door. Roshelle invited her in.

"You have company, Rosh. A group traveling together." She was flushed and giggling. "You'll never believe this."

"Must be the Local Morticians Association."

"Almost. A group of senior citizens. A whole flock of gray-haired women."

Roshelle gave a dry laugh. "What a following. What a way to crack Reno." She let out a deep sigh. "Invite them back, I suppose. But don't leave me. And when I give you the high sign, shoo the hens out. Got it?"

"Got it, boss."

There were only about a dozen of them, all cackling and fussing over her just like a bunch of mother hens. They seemed terribly excited about her dressing room. One in particular reminded her of Grandma Riley. "Bless you, child, for singing the hymn right in the midst of the heathens."

Roshelle wanted to ask her what she was doing in the midst of the heathens, but she refrained.

After Mitzi had "shooed" them out, Roshelle didn't know whether to laugh or cry. . .to feel privileged or humiliated.

What she did feel was a fresh acute wave of loneliness that she couldn't free herself from or even define. That night she took sleeping pills. There was no beach.

⁂

Toward the end of the second week, Newt called to confirm she was booked at the Supreme Royale in Vegas. "Same song, second verse," he quipped. "It's not Caesar's Palace, but it is Vegas. The guy says you did good there in Reno and he thinks you could make it in Vegas as well. He says the audiences like your 'traditional' style. What a break, sweets. We're going places. I'm still working on the recording deal. I'll keep you informed as it progresses." Newt always did most of the talking. Patiently, she listened as his nasal voice talked around a chewed cigar. All the while she strove to keep her heart still. Vegas! She could almost taste it.

"Oh, and Rosh, this fellow won't squawk if you have your own accompanist. I pressed him about it for you. Rosh? You still there? I said—"

"Yes, I heard you, Newt, my own accompanist. Accompanist, not band?"

"Yep."

"So where's Benny Lee so I can call and tell him?" Her heart was hammering hard now. If she could just have Benny Lee with her in Vegas, then everything would be all right again.

She motioned for Mitzi to get her a pen as Newt rattled off the number of a place in Jersey City. She then waved Mitzi out of the room as she punched phone buttons with unsteady fingers. Let him be there, her heart cried out.

In a hollow well, she heard the hotel clerk paging, "Benny Lee Camp! Phone call for Benny Lee Camp!" Eventually, his deep voice was on the other end of the line.

"Camp here!"

"Hi, Benny Lee."

"Rosh! Hey, angel. What's the good word? Super to hear from you!"

"I'll be playing the Royale in Vegas in a few weeks. They like my style, they say."

"Terrific news, Rosh. I knew it. Didn't I tell you? Go for it. Give it all you got."

"Benny Lee, I just got the word from Newt—at the Royale in Vegas I can have my own accompanist." It was quiet for a moment. Now her heart was thudding in her brain. "My own accompanist, Benny Lee. Can you come out? We can work together again."

"Rosh," he said softly. "I can't, Rosh. You know I can't. The boys. Remember what we said? We'll all come when you need us. But I can't just leave them. They'll scatter like the wind. And we're in the middle of a tour, remember?"

Of course she knew all that. She knew from the beginning that he couldn't come. But he should come to her. Wasn't she more important than the band?

"But I need you, Ben. I need you here." She was being totally self-centered, like a spoiled child. If Benny Lee did not come, she would still have her pick of pianists. But if he came to her, the boys would have no leader. . .no band . . .nothing. It was as though she couldn't help herself. The loneliness. . .

"This tour will be over in six weeks, angel. I won't schedule another thing. I promise. We'll hang loose till we hear from you, okay?"

"Six weeks! The world could come to an end in six weeks. I need you now, to play for me in Vegas, Benny Lee. Are you coming or not?"

"Rosh. Please! Be reasonable. Don't ask me something you know I can't do."

"Oh forget it then!" Her voice was high pitched, ugly. "I don't need you or anybody! Forget I ever called!" She slammed the receiver down with a crash.

Now the sobs were coming hard. How could he care more about them than her? What a stinking rotten mess!

"Rosh." Mitzi was banging on the door between their adjoining rooms. "Rosh! Let me in."

"Hold on, will you? Let a person get herself back together."

She stumbled into the bathroom and splashed cold water on her mascara-smeared eyes, then let Mitzi in.

"You should have known he'd say no."

"I don't pay you to listen in on my conversations," she snapped as she slouched into the plush chaise by the bed.

Mitzi was oblivious of the curt manner. "I didn't need to listen, silly. I knew what he'd say. After all, that's what we all love about Benny Lee—his staunch loyalty." She busied herself at the wet bar fixing Roshelle an icy lemonade.

Of course she was right, but Roshelle didn't want to hear it.

"Well, you were right about one thing," Mitzi said calmly.

"What's that?" She sipped on the lemonade, thankful for it's sharp tartness.

"You don't need Benny Lee. Not really. You can do it, Rosh. You can make it on your own. Now, get those gorgeous eyes repaired. Rehearsal's in ten minutes."

Mitzi was turning out to be one great secretary.

🐚

The next week, they caught an evening flight out of Reno. Now it was Roshelle's turn to stare out the window as they circled McCarran Airport. Las Vegas lay as a sparkling, glittering broach on the breast of the desert. She could almost feel the pulsating beat of its vital energy pumping up into the airwaves. Names like Golden Nugget, Horseshoe, Showboat, and the Sahara smiled and winked at her, beckoning her into a new world.

"Get ready," she whispered to the twinkling lights below. "Here I come."

The pair of them rubbernecked like tourists all the way from McCarran to The Strip. Roshelle had been in Vegas one time previously with Benny and the boys, before Mitzi had joined the troupe, so she tried to point out the sights to Mitzi. But even Roshelle was gawking, so much had changed. Neither the Excalibur nor the Mirage existed when she and the boys played a small club off The Strip those many years ago. The five-storied waterfall at the Mirage would make anyone stare. And whether or not they wanted to stop to watch the volcano erupt, they were forced to because the line of tourists ahead of them was stopping.

The Royale was at the north end of The Strip. It was a tall gleaming building with a flashing neon crown above the words SUPREME ROYALE. The causeway was lined with swaying palm trees and curved around and into little bridges spanning man-made lagoons. As they stepped inside from the golden porte-cochere, they entered a fantasy wonderland. A trilevel atrium was accented with bubbling marble fountains laced with lush tropical plants and trees. Massive crystal chandeliers hung suspended from the highest points of the ceiling.

"Bugsy would never recognize the place," Roshelle whispered, looking around.

"Bugsy? Who's Bugsy?" Mitzi whispered back. "We don't know anyone named Bugsy."

Roshelle looked at her friend and smiled. "Bugsy Siegel, silly. The guy who masterminded this city in the first place."

"Oh. Never heard of him."

As soon as the young man at the desk learned who they were, he called management. They were quickly shown to their suite on the tenth floor. The room they walked into was done in tones of autumn gold and forest greens. Soft brocade couches, teakwood furniture, sunken tub in the bathroom—they were both in awe.

When they were alone, Mitzi ran to the window to look out. Roshelle looked, too, but refrained from running.

"Rosh," she cried, pointing like a little kid, "the clown from Circus Circus is over there laughing at us."

"Laughing *with* us, not *at* us. He's happy we're here. And so am I."

❧

Rehearsals the next afternoon went off without a hitch. The band leader was a swell guy, affable and jocular and easy to work with. But Roshelle wasn't going to get caught in a pinch this time. As they conferred privately, she quietly explained that she would need the piano pushed center stage for her last number. He agreed with a smile and a nod.

"Opening night jitters?" Mitzi quipped as they took a few laps in the hotel's indoor pool that afternoon.

"An overextended, exaggerated, extreme case of jitters, if you please."

"Well, cool it. You'll do great."

"Keep telling me." She dove in to challenge Mitzi to another race down the length of the pool.

She won easily, jumping out at the shallow end and grabbing for her towel. Briskly, she wiped droplets from her eyes. As she took the towel from her face, she caught a glimpse of a man dressed in sweats walking through the weight room adjacent to the pool. Her breath caught. It looked exactly like Victor Moran.

She fluffed her hair with the towel and shook her head vigorously. Impossible. If there's one place a religious guy would never be, it was Vegas. There had been no word from him since Chicago. Hopefully he'd forgotten about her. She thought she'd forgotten about him, too. But perhaps she hadn't. Otherwise, why would she be looking at total strangers and thinking it was him?

She was so keyed up by curtain time, she virtually exploded onto the stage and never wavered in thrust or energy throughout the entire performance.

The warm-up group was excellent, setting a mood of expectancy in the audience. Gracefully she moved from one number into the next, talking gently with her audience between each. Her sultry voice cast its spell over her listeners. She felt as though she could sing forever.

She slowed to a low-keyed ballad, and the wailing of the trumpet cried along with her. They forced the music before them in an unhurried blazing crescendo that brought people to their feet.

Now the piano was center stage. Slowly, she moved toward it. It had been years since she'd played in a performance. But some things, she thought ruefully, you never lose.

In a momentary panic, she realized she hadn't planned which hymn to sing. But, as her fingers rambled up and down the keys, she effortlessly moved into the simple strains of "In the Garden." Her voice could do nothing but obey the promptings from deep within.

> He walks with me, and He talks with me,
>   And He tells me I am His own.
> And the joy we share as we tarry there,
>   None other has ever known.

Suddenly, it was as though the showroom of the Supreme Royale had been swept away and she was again Rachel Rayford sitting at the piano in the dusty little white-frame church in Sandott, Oklahoma.

She closed her eyes and the verses rolled forth. But something strange was happening. For when she played in Uncle Jess's church, God had been very real and very near. She *did* walk with Him and talk with Him. He *did* let her know she was His own. No aching loneliness plagued her then.

For a fleeting moment, there was the faintest recollection of His reality. It had been submerged into the darkest corners of her suppressed memories. The very act of playing, the familiar touch of the keys beneath her fingertips allowed her to travel back. It had been so long ago. . .since before her daddy died. But the memory was only a brief taste, then it was gone.

As the last notes of the chorus faded, she sat paralyzed. When she opened her eyes, she found they were damp, and the applause was ringing once again. She rose on shaky legs and went to take her bows. She could make out a few faces in the front row, past the blazing spotlights, and found that some were crying with her.

This was insane. People in Vegas cry only when they lose at the game tables.

Then she saw him—Victor. There, off to the side. He was smiling at her. So he *was* here. This was all his fault! Somehow his being here had done this horrid thing and had yanked her back into the morass of the past. She maintained her facade, smiling, taking bows, and blowing kisses until she made it to the side stage, where Mitzi helped her to her dressing room.

"What were you saying about a piano being a barrier?" Mitzi said. "You weren't at the piano, Rosh. You were sitting in their laps. They loved it!"

Mitzi opened the door and let Roshelle in ahead of her. There, on the counter, beneath the brightly lit makeup mirrors, was a tray with a nosegay of violets and a card.

Chapter Four

Roshelle stood still a moment, staring.

"What's the matter?" Mitzi asked, closing the door. Then she saw, too. "Oh. It's that religious guy again, huh?" She moved past Roshelle to look down at the unpretentious little bouquet. "This is like the bouquet he sent to your room in Miami, isn't it? Violets?"

Roshelle only nodded. She wanted to run. She wanted to cry. She wanted to throw the silly flowers in the trash. What right did he have?

"They're sort of cute." Mitzi reached down for the card. "Shall we. . .?"

"Don't touch that!"

Mitzi drew back her hand as though she'd touched a hot iron. At the hurt look in her eyes, Roshelle was immediately sorry. "I didn't mean to snap at you, Mitzi. But this guy sort of gives me the creeps. I saw him in the audience out there tonight."

"He's right here in Vegas? The religious guy? Don't that beat all."

"Will you stop calling him 'religious'?"

"Well, isn't he? I thought he gave you a Bible verse and stuff. That's what Keel said."

"How about the word 'Christian'?"

"Same difference. You called him a religious freak."

"Correction. *Keel* called him a religious freak." Roshelle recalled the conversation on the bus as though it were yesterday. "I called him a kook," she added softly.

"The guy spooks you and you split hairs about what the nut should be called." Mitzi shook her head in confusion. "What's the deal here? Do we open the card or not?"

"*We* are not going to do anything. I think I just need to be alone for a few minutes, okay? I need to sit down until my head stops spinning."

"Hey, Rosh. Now it's my turn to apologize. Come and sit down here." She hurried to fluff pillows on the couch situated against the far wall. "Do you want to change now? Later? What can I get you? I'll put the flowers in water and then I'll get you a ginger ale."

"Please, Mitzi. I think I really do want to be alone for a few minutes."

"I didn't mean to make you mad," Mitzi said.

"I could never be mad at you." She reached out to give her little partner a hug and felt tears still near the surface.

Mitzi gave a squeeze in return. "I'm glad. I think you're the greatest."

Surely it must just be the excitement of the first performance in Vegas. That's all it was. And yet Roshelle was sure that once the tears started, they'd never stop. That's how uptight she felt. And now this. She wanted to read that note, but she couldn't bare to do it in Mitzi's presence.

"Okay, boss. I'm going. But not far. Just holler if you need me. Got it?"

"Thanks."

Mitzi moved toward the door. She paused and nodded toward the flowers. "Don't let this little thing bug you. You got too much going for you." And she was gone.

How did this guy find so many lavender cards? She opened the lavender envelope and pulled out the card. A picture of violets covered the front. Inside he had written out his praise for her evening performance. At the bottom he added an invitation to lunch the next day. "Call me," it said. "Room 875." Psalm 69:30 was added again as well. Of course, she couldn't go. How she wished Benny Lee were here. She needed his presence to protect her from all the crazies in this world.

There was a soft tap on the door. "Psst. Roshelle. It's me, Mitzi."

Quickly, Roshelle slipped the card back into the envelope. "What is it?"

Mitzi opened the door and stuck her head in, her dark eyes flashing. "The 'Christian-religious-freak-nut-kook' is headed this way! Want me to guard the door?"

Vic? But the card asked her to call. Why would he come back to her room? She needed time to think.

"Quick, he's. . .well, hello, Mr. Moran. How are you tonight? And what brings you to Las Vegas?"

Roshelle could hear him asking if he could see "Miss Ramone."

"I'm not sure," Mitzi told him, hedging. "She's so exhausted after that long performance. Do you realize how much energy it takes to perform that many songs?"

"I won't be long," she heard Vic answer.

"Mitzi," Roshelle called out. "It's okay. I'll see Mr. Moran."

Mitzi stuck her head back inside the door with a questioning look. Roshelle nodded at her. "Just for a minute," she said.

Mitzi shrugged and withdrew. "She'll see you just for a minute, Mr. Moran. Please don't tire her."

Roshelle had to smile at Mitzi's new stance as her guardian. And before she could take a breath, there he stood in the doorway, seemingly twice as handsome as the first time she saw him. Impeccably dressed in a hunter green suit that reflected warmth to his hazel eyes.

He smiled and closed the door. But not before Mitzi raised her voice to say, "I'll be right out here, Rosh."

"You're well taken care of," he said, nodding toward Mitzi.

"Mitzi's great," she retorted. She felt awkward, unsettled. What could he want?

"Did Mitzi replace the big bearded fellow who was with you in Miami?"

"Benny Lee? Oh, no." Then she paused. "Well, sort of, I guess." Mitzi couldn't take the place of her buddies in the band, but she certainly had filled a void.

"The booking didn't include the band?" It was a question and statement combined.

She shook her head, thinking again of the pain of having to leave them.

"Couldn't you have insisted? Held out?"

She looked at him. "You don't do much insisting in this business when you're first starting out. You should know that." But actually, she had no idea what this man did know about the business. Probably very little. "This night has been a big breakthrough for me." She hated being put on the defensive. "Benny Lee and the guys insisted I take the offer."

Vic nodded. "I see you got the violets."

Was he fishing for a response? She inwardly vowed not to give him the pleasure, so she only offered a slight nod. Moving to the mirrors, she poured herself a cup of coffee from the coffeemaker on the counter. "Want a cup?"

"Thanks, I'll pass. I promised your little friend out there I wouldn't keep you. In the note I invited you to lunch tomorrow, but I was wondering if you'd rather make it a picnic out at the lake."

Roshelle emptied a packet of sugar into the mug of coffee and stirred it with the plastic stir rod. "Lake? What lake?"

"Lake Mead. You know, where Hoover Dam is. The area near the lake is filled with nice picnic spots. Less than an hour's drive away. There's more to this region than blazing marquees and roulette tables."

"I never was very good at geography." She sipped at the scalding coffee. Sitting beside a lake sounded glorious to her right now. Water was always so peaceful. Like the beach. Like the pond at Grandma Riley's that was surrounded by weeping willows.

"We could grab sandwiches at a deli and leave at about ten. I'll have you back in plenty of time to be ready for your afternoon rehearsals."

He knew enough to know she was in rehearsals late in the afternoon. But how would a Christian know. . .? "Are you here on vacation?" she asked, letting her curiosity win out.

"Business, actually. One of my clients has a show in town. I wanted to catch it."

"But your card said you had a *Christian* recording company." She wondered how he was going to explain his way out of this. Probably works with gospel quartet groups in Tulsa and several "swingers" out here in Vegas.

"I do. It is." His voice never wavered.

Her own voice was not so steady. "Then what. . .?"

"I understand your confusion. We—meaning my company—don't happen to think the Christian faith is to be imprisoned within the confines of a church building. Several of the stars who record on our label feel we are to 'go into all the world,' as Scripture says. And that includes Vegas."

That was absolutely the dumbest thing she'd ever heard. A Christian singing in a nightclub. In fact, she wasn't sure she even believed him. And why should she? She didn't even know him.

A tapping at the door let them know that Mitzi was getting restless. "Roshelle, can I get you anything?"

"Thanks, Mitzi. I have coffee. Everything's fine."

"Just checking," came the answer through the door.

Vic gave a low chuckle. "She's marvelous." He moved to go. "The picnic? What do you say? A little sunshine, fresh air, and quiet."

Surely he wouldn't be a threat to her. And the offer sounded tempting. "Okay, Mr. Moran, I'll accept that offer of the fresh air."

His smile was soft and subdued, not as though he'd won a victory, but of quiet acceptance. "Great. I'll meet you in the lobby at ten. And the name's Vic."

"Thanks, Vic. And thank you for the flowers."

"My pleasure. I've never seen or felt a more moving moment in a Vegas club as I did during your last number. There wasn't a dry eye in the place. You deserve all the accolades. Bless you now."

Bless me, bless me, she fumed inwardly. Always blessing me. Immediately she wanted to defend herself. But he opened the door, gave a little salute, and was gone.

Give a guy an inch and he'll take a mile every time. Well, she had his room number. She could always call him and cancel.

Mitzi was by her side in a flash. "Man, oh man, that's the best-looking kook I've ever laid my eyes on. Wonder if he has a brother?"

Roshelle collapsed into a chair laughing. "You're hopeless."

"Come on, Rosh. Don't tell me you don't think he's a knockout." Mitzi rummaged in the small refrigerator for a soda, popped the top, and took a long drink. "If you don't, I'll take you in tomorrow and get your eyes checked."

Roshelle avoided a direct answer. "If you're so hep on him, forget about the brother. Vic is obviously not taken."

"Yeah, but he's not sending me darling little bouquets." She picked up the delicate nosegay from the table and arranged them in a cup with water. "There. That'll do till we get them up to your room." She fingered the lace around the flowers. "Wonder how he thinks of something so original? Most men don't have a clue. So what did he want?"

"If you must know, Miss Snoopy, he's taking me on a picnic tomorrow."

"Whoa. You mean you're actually going out with him?"

Roshelle hadn't thought of it like that. . .not like a date. She'd never dated, not really. Her high school years were so abnormal. Uncle Jess always spying on her. . .her mother's strict rules. Then later, there was Benny Lee. "It's not like I'm 'going out with him.' "

"No? So what do you call it?"

"We're just going to take a little lunch and go out to the lake."

Mitzi nodded, drank the last of her soda, and threw it into the waste basket. "Like I said, a picnic-lunch date."

Roshelle picked up a pillow from the couch and slung it toward Mitzi, but she ducked. Mitzi picked up the card from the table, put it under the cup holding the violets, then reached down to help Roshelle up from the chair. "Ta-ta now. Let's get you up to your room, so you'll be fresh for your picnic-lunch date tomorrow."

Roshelle groaned as she rose from the chair. "I think I'll ship you back to your brother."

By the time they arrived at the room, there was a massive bouquet of roses awaiting them. "Congrats on cracking Vegas. From Benny and the boys," the card read. Roshelle felt the tears burning. She'd never known such an ache of emptiness before. When she left home, she never missed anyone. Not Janey, not her mother, and especially not Uncle Jess.

"Let's call them," Mitzi was saying, excitement bubbling in her voice.

Roshelle glanced at her watch. "Do you realize what time it is on the East Coast? About four. They've crashed. And you know how hard it is to get Benny Lee awake." She couldn't bear the thought of actually talking to the guys. Not the way she felt right now. It would only make things worse.

"Oh, yeah." Mitzi looked deflated. "You're probably right. It'd be almost impossible to get any of them awake enough to talk."

Roshelle hadn't even thought of how much Mitzi must miss her brother. Mentally, she kicked herself. "Tell you what. Tomorrow you call Mike and tell him all about our success here tonight. In fact, feel free to call Mike anytime. Newt will always know where they are."

Mitzi's pixie face brightened. "Oh, Rosh. I'm so silly. I didn't even think that it would be okay to call him anytime. I really do miss the nut."

"He's family, Mitzi. You should keep in close contact."

Mitzi moved toward the door that separated their rooms. "They're all family to me, Rosh."

As soon as the door was closed, Roshelle let the tears loose and they didn't stop until she had cried herself to sleep. The next morning, she still couldn't figure out why she had cried.

Chapter Five

The drive to the lake was peaceful, as Vic had promised. They left the bustling city of Las Vegas and entered the rugged countryside. Farther down the highway was the quiet community of Boulder City. Past that lay the mammoth lake.

Roshelle had wanted to wear shorts but, knowing Vic's background, she opted for a comfortable skirt, blouse, and sandals. After all, hadn't Uncle Jess reminded her on countless occasions of the utter sinfulness of wearing shorts? "No decent girl would be caught dead in them," he declared.

When they met in the lobby, she was quite surprised to see Vic dressed in olive shorts with a white knit shirt open at the throat. She was tempted to run back to her room and change, but she let it go. Nothing about this guy made any sense.

"I have a large tablecloth," he said as they spotted the lake in the distance. "Shall we cover a picnic table with it, or spread it out and sit on the ground?"

"Oh, the ground, most definitely. The tables are for the wimps."

He gave a little laugh. "I see."

She craned to see the appearance of the lake, and in a few moments it was spread out before them. The indigo water was ringed by craggy mountains and bluffs ranging in color from sandy tan to blue-black. Wispy clouds hanging low in the sunlit sky seemed to be snagging on the tops of the bluffs as they sailed by them. Situated in the inlet was a large marina with rows of stanchioned sailboats sitting with their masts pointing skyward. In the distance, little sailboats scooted along like feathers across the water.

"Let's sit as near to the water as possible," she said.

"I'm sure that can be arranged."

And it was. He parked in a picnic area that was nearly deserted and pointed down the incline to a wide, flat ledge that jutted out. "How does that look?"

"Great."

Vic handed Roshelle the tablecloth and he followed behind, carrying the cooler.

"Do you always come to Vegas packing a cooler and such a nice tablecloth?" she queried him.

"I confess. I have friends who live here in the city and I went borrowing early this morning."

As she spread the cloth, she felt the lake breeze softly ruffle her hair. She turned her face to it and closed her eyes and breathed in deeply. "M-m-m. Sometimes I forget how much I miss the openness and the fresh air. Clubs and hotels can be pretty stifling at times."

"You're a country girl, I take it?" He was digging in the cooler and pulling out sandwiches, fruit, and cooled bottles of soft drinks. The food looked wonderful. She'd had no breakfast.

"Not really country but definitely small town. Until I was a teenager, anyway."

He handed her a sandwich. "Do you like ham and cheese?"

"I'm not fussy."

Before she could unwrap the sandwich and dig in, Vic said, "Let's take a minute and thank the Lord for the food and for His handiwork at creating this beautiful spot."

She felt her teeth clench. She'd not said grace since she left home. It was always a big joke to hear Uncle Jess pray—no matter what the occasion.

Vic's prayer, however, was nothing like Uncle Jess's. Vic seemed to be talking to more than just the air. But, regardless, Roshelle was glad when he was finished and she could devour her sandwich.

"So," Vic said as he leaned back on one elbow, "when will you have your band back with you?"

She shrugged. She wasn't sure how much she wanted Vic to know about her or her business. "My agent seemed vague about it."

"Is your agent in L.A.?"

Her mouth was full, so she nodded.

"What's his name?"

"Newt."

"Hardcastle?"

"Yes. You know him?"

Vic offered her a bunch of grapes and she took them. "I've had dealings with him in the past. He's good. All business, that's for sure."

"That describes Newt." Roshelle recalled the night he instructed her to dump the band. She still wondered if she had made the right decision. "He sure put us on the map. He seems to have all the right connections."

"I know. That's why it surprises me that he couldn't book all of you together in Vegas."

"He said bands are a dime a dozen."

Vic nodded soberly. "Well, he does have a point there."

"Maybe when we begin recording sessions."

"Maybe what?"

"Maybe Benny can be with me again."

"Don't count on it."

"Why do you say that?" She wasn't sure if it was his words or the wind off the lake that made her shiver.

"Have you been in a recording studio lately?"

"No, not for a few years." Roshelle thought of the small studio in Tulsa where she had spent hours recording ad jingles for everything from car dealerships to furniture stores. But that was nearly six years ago. Six years! Had she been on her own that long?

"Everything is done by computers now. Those keyboards can make a trumpet sound as good as your friend, Benny Lee. And, of course, the percussion sounds are superior to any drummer's."

Immediately in her mind's eye, Roshelle saw loose-jointed Keel banging his drums, ecstatic every minute of every performance. She shook her head. "Imagine that. Tough for the musicians."

"Of course, later on, if you're on a nationwide tour, you'll need them. Or if you have a few big hits. Then you can record in one of the nicer studios with space enough for an entire orchestra if you want one."

That all sounded so far away. She hadn't thought about her time without Benny being so drawn out.

"How did you meet him?" Vic wanted to know. He was gathering up scraps of their trash and putting it in a bag in the cooler.

"Newt?"

"No, Benny."

She had to smile as she thought of it. How Benny practically rescued her from a bar owner in Little Rock. The creep wasn't going to pay her until she came through with a few favors. But Benny saw to it she was paid. And quickly, too. But how could she tell Vic about all that mess? So she simply said, "At a cheap dive in Little Rock," and let it go at that. When she met Benny, she was doing okay. . .not great, but at least okay. She was getting more and more job offers and was traveling more. But joining with the band was a smart move. She helped them, and they helped her.

"When was that? How long have you worked together?"

She had to stop and figure it out. "Almost five years. Boy, it doesn't seem that long."

He studied her face a moment as though he meant to ask another question. She was relieved that he didn't. Instead, he stood to his feet. "Want to walk down by the water?"

She jumped up. "Sure."

They loaded the cooler back into the car and made their way down to the water's edge. "Let's wade," she said, pulling off her sandals. The shore was full of painful little rocks, but she didn't care. Vic kicked off his loafers.

She couldn't help but laugh as she felt the cold waves lapping up against her legs.

"Your laugh is almost as silken as your singing voice," he said softly.

Roshelle felt herself blush. "Thanks."

"How did you learn to sing? To play the piano? Voice lessons? Piano lessons? Your performance last night was a knockout."

Last night was something she was trying to forget—at least the moment when those strange feelings emerged as she played and sang the hymn. Performing nightly for all these years had sharpened her ability to act. She'd learned how to press the emotions down and put on her stage face. No matter how you feel at showtime, a performer puts on the stage face and the stage smile. She did that now.

"I can't remember not singing," she answered lightly. "My mother says I was mimicking the radio when I was about three. They quickly learned to be very selective of what stations they listened to."

Vic chuckled at that remark.

"I even sang all the zany ads. But when I learned how to turn the dial myself, then I did have fun! I sang all the hits."

"Pure and natural God-given talent," he said with a touch of wonder in his tone. "And the piano?"

"My grandma Riley. Mother's mother. She taught piano in her younger days. The trouble was, she taught me solely out of the hymnbook. With a few classics thrown in for good measure."

"What a blessing to have that kind of a background."

She gave a little snort. "I guess it's all in how you look at it. It was like prison to me. At school, I ransacked my music teacher's sheet music stash and played everything I could get my hands on."

He laughed. "That figures. But at least you had God's Word around you as you grew up."

"All I remember is being surrounded by a bunch of hypocrites—all except for Grandma—and I detest hypocrites."

He gazed out across the water, squinting his eyes. "You're in good company then."

"Meaning?"

"Jesus didn't take to them very kindly, either."

She looked up at him. She thought he was making fun of her, but his face was quiet and sober. The hazel eyes were not teasing. She looked down at her watch. "We'd better be getting back. I've still got a big day ahead of me." As she turned to go, she caught her foot on one of the rocks and started to fall. In a flash, Vic reached out to grab her arm and steady her. She fully expected him to take her in his arms—and for a split second she wanted him to. She stood there for a moment looking up at him. Soft hazel eyes looked steadily back at her. "Thanks," she whispered, then pulled free.

Later, she scolded herself for being so vulnerable. She would have to be on her guard constantly. No Benny here to keep watch out for her. When she arrived back at the hotel, she marveled that this Christian had not once preached to her or dictated his demands on her life. That in itself was a miracle.

Roshelle opened the door of her room to see Mitzi sitting on the bed, meticulously painting her toenails. She lifted the brush in one hand and the bottle in the other, as if in a salute. "Ah, she's back from her first date. And now tell Mama Mitzi all about it."

Roshelle pushed the door shut with her hip. "There's nothing to tell. We drove to the lake and had a picnic and came home."

Mitzi finished her little toe with a flourish and replaced the brush in the bottle. "The guy is so good-looking, how did you keep from just melting away?"

"I kept an ice pack on my head," she commented dryly. She opened the closet to pull out slacks to wear to rehearsal.

Hobbling over, walking on her heels, Mitzi said, "Truly, Roshelle. His eyes remind me of old Paul Newman movies. They're so. . .so bottomless. How can he be a kook and be so dreamy?"

Roshelle hated it when Mitzi spoke her very thoughts. "Would you help me find a blouse to match these slacks? I have to be at rehearsal."

"You have almost an hour and you have three blouses that match those slacks." She leaned against the wall beside the closet. "Do you kind of like him? Just a little bit?"

"He's okay." She pulled out the silk paisley with the huge puffy sleeves. "Does this one go?"

"Yeah, but you look better in the mauve."

"Which mauve?"

Mitzi reached around and rummaged through the blouses. "This one." She extended the blouse, then put it behind her. "And I'll give it to you when you tell me what he's really like."

Roshelle reached for the blouse, but Mitzi stepped away. "If I knew, I'd tell you," she protested. "The guy's a closed book."

As soon as she said it, she realized what a dumb statement it was. She had asked him little or nothing about himself because she was scared to ask. But Mitzi was right about the eyes. Roshelle knew leering eyes. She knew condemning eyes. She knew troubled eyes. But never had she seen such peaceful eyes. And they were bottomless. Like you could get lost in them.

Mitzi was now across the room waving the blouse. "Does Mama Mitzi have to teach little Roshie how to *open* the book?"

"Mama Mitzi better give over the blouse if she doesn't want to eat it *and* have her fine little pedicure stepped on." She stomped in Mitzi's direction.

In a flurry of giggles, Mitzi sprinted for the bathroom. "Since you don't know how to even read a book, tell me one thing. If he asked you out again, would you go?"

Yes, yes, her mind cried out. But she stifled the words. Aloud she said, "I might."

The blouse came flying through the air—hanger and all. "That's all I wanted to know."

"Mitzi Wilson, you're impossible. Help me find my shoes."

ﻬ

With a brief good-bye, Vic left for Tulsa later that week. Roshelle breathed a sigh of relief. Now she could let down her defenses. Since opening night she had carefully avoided singing "In the Garden." Usually she stayed with something more rigid, like "A Mighty Fortress Is Our God." But even then, Vic's presence in the room always gave her spooky sensations. She wondered why he continued to show up. Until the day he left town, he attended every show.

Night by night the size of her audiences grew. As Mitzi so aptly said, it was absolutely "titillating" to see the warm response. From L.A., Newt called with updates on the upcoming recording sessions. He, too, was delighted with the Vegas success.

"Hey, sweets," he said, "you know Ann-Margret was discovered in Las Vegas. Don't happen very often, but methinks it's happening now."

They were down to talking about song selections for the CD when Newt suggested she rent a place in L.A. "You'll be here for a while, till we get this CD cut. No sense in you women hanging around in a dead hotel," he said.

It was a novel idea and one she'd not thought of before. After all, there was money now. More money than she'd ever seen while singing with Benny and the band. Why not rent a place and sort of set up housekeeping? The idea was strange and nice all at the same time. Later, she went to Mitzi's room to run the idea by her.

"You bet," she agreed. "A Malibu beach house would be to my liking."

Mitzi had been at the pool most of the afternoon and was fluffing her short black hair with a large gold hotel towel. She'd managed to gain a luxurious tan in the few weeks they'd been there. "With a pool, naturally."

Roshelle laughed. "I don't think we're quite to that point yet. But we could get a place and have a home base. That makes sense, doesn't it? I mean, even if we go on tour, which Newt says we probably will if the CD takes off, we'll still need a place."

Mitzi turned to her, peeking out from under the towel. "Are you trying to convince me or you? I'm fine wherever you put me."

That was so true. Mitzi was like a little flower blooming through the cracks in a boulder. Roshelle never saw her get ruffled. She envied her friend's even disposition. . .her quietness. Roshelle's nerves seemed to be in a constant jangle and the only time she was truly calm and happy was during a performance.

"Newt says he can talk to a realtor friend for us and maybe find a condo or something. And there *could* be a pool, maybe even a yard."

"Cool." Mitzi was now in the bathroom and turned on the hair dryer, thereby ending the conversation for a few moments.

Roshelle continued to see a little place that would be her own. She sighed and lay back on the bed. Maybe that was what she needed. A place to put down roots, instead of bouncing all over the country like a Ping-Pong ball. Maybe then she'd have more of a sense of peace.

Rolling over, she grabbed the phone to give Newt the go-ahead to begin the search.

❧

Roshelle's last performance at the Supreme Royale was both exhilarating and frightening. Frightening because she had no idea where her career would take her from this point. The questions tugged at her mind as she readied herself for the show.

As sort of a gift to celebrate the success of the run, Newt had secured a wardrobe stylist for her. Louis Sarviano was his name, and he had created a stunning black, sequined gown as one of her outfits for the closing night. It was strapless with trails of black organza draping from the back to the floor.

When Mitzi first learned about Louis, she giggled. "Want me to hang around in case he tries to tuck a dart in the wrong place?"

Roshelle laughed, too, but she did indeed want Mitzi to be there for every fitting. Louis had laughing blue eyes and dark hair that hung in curls down the back of his tan neck. His open smile revealed a set of wonderful dimples. Roshelle was ecstatic that Newt had sent him up to Vegas just for her. Louis was a professional, and he knew how to make her look good. But then, that was his business—making people look good on stage.

She turned around in front of the three-way mirror in awe of the image before her. She looked like a million and felt the same.

As soon as her feet hit that stage, it was as though they were sprinkled with magic dust. She danced almost as much as she sang. The dress was more like her skin, and it moved with her every move. Her husky voice was never more strong, never more powerful. Her confidence soared.

Traditionally, she opened with the jazzier numbers to set the tone. From there, she slid into the blues, where her voice melded with the trumpet in an aching ballad. The long, wailing notes wove a web around her audience and fastened them to her. They forgot their cocktails and the clamorous casinos, as she spun out the sad words of the love ballads. She hung on to every note, not wanting them to end. . .not wanting this magical night to end.

Much too soon, the piano was being rolled to center stage for her finale. She tossed the hand mike to the closest engineer and sat down on the padded bench. Without a thought, her fingers traveled up and down the keyboard. And, unbidden, "In the Garden" came rolling forth. She wanted to stop it, but it was too late. As before, she once again felt herself sitting as Rachel in the little church in Sandott. But rather than feeling a godly presence, there was Uncle Jess's eternal scowl denouncing her, condemning her. "You're nothing but a Jezebel," the words flew at her. "Your soul's bound for hell, girl. You'll never amount to anything!"

The emotional blow was so crushing, she could barely finish the song. The response, though, was not diminished, but she could barely hear the warm applause. Mitzi had to support Roshelle's weight as they headed to the dressing room after the third bow.

"Three curtain calls, Rosh. Just like I said." Her voice was edged with fear. "Let's get you in here and let you rest. A magnificent performance. Absolutely magnificent."

After Mitzi had settled her in the room, Roshelle looked up at her. "Can you get me something to use to gargle? My throat feels funny. Kind of scratchy."

Chapter Six

She and Mitzi were both deliriously happy with the cozy little condo Newt found for them in Anaheim. With a pool! "Nothing highbrow," Newt had told them, "but comfy."

First on Roshelle's agenda was to purchase her own piano. The room they designated as her studio was painted in the palest banana yellow and furnished with inviting pastel seating pieces and white lacquered coffee tables. Splashes of California sunshine poured in through tall windows that were flanked by bookshelves—shelves that she planned to fill with wonderful books, in addition to all her music.

There in her "studio" with her new piano, she poured herself into her work until she knew every nuance of every song scheduled for the upcoming CD. She'd been practicing her numbers nonstop since she arrived in L.A. In spurts of new inspiration, she was even penning lyrics and melodies of her own.

When Newt presented her with the recording contract, she used it as an excuse to call Benny to ask his advice. She closed the door to the studio so Mitzi couldn't hear. Mitzi would want to talk to all five of the guys; Roshelle needed to talk to Benny alone.

He gave a whoop when he heard her voice. "I hear you knocked 'em dead in Vegas, Rosh! I knew you would." It was as though her last angry tirade with him had never happened. What a teddy bear he was. "Now you got a contract with the Laurel label. I mean, you're on your way."

When she asked him about the fine print and secret clauses, he simply told her to trust Newt. "He's the best in the business I ever saw, angel. He'll do you good. You don't have to sweat that."

She wanted him to tell her to send him a copy to look at or even to say he'd fly out and take a look. But he didn't.

"You'll have to fly out soon and see our little place, Benny. I have a home just like normal people. Mitzi and I are buying furniture and houseplants and fixing it up spiffy."

"Hey now, ain't that right uptown. A place of your own? Careful or you'll get domesticated on us."

"Not hardly. So when can you come out?"

She could hear him mumbling something as he thumbed through the dogeared calendar he always carried. "Newt's got us sewed up for another six weeks or more. Not even breathing room. Sorry, angel. Not soon, but then that don't mean never. We'll be heading out that way sooner or later. We always do."

He was right. But he sounded so vague.

"You still there, angel? You're so quiet. Do you think I don't want to see you? If so, you're wrong. I miss you like crazy. But I just don't see how I can. . . ."

She took a deep breath and straightened herself. "It's okay, Benny. Really. Just come when you can. Okay?" She knew Benny. He kept everything buried.

"That's my girl. We sure will. We'll all be on your doorstep when you least expect it. Then you'll have to scramble eggs for the whole bunch."

For his sake, she managed a light laugh as they said their good-byes. She knew the separation was killing him, but he was holding it in. And she kept making it worse. And why? Why did she even think it would be better if he came? She pushed her fingers to her throbbing temples. Perhaps it was like being weaned from a security blanket. She'd leaned on him totally for almost five years.

She moved from the phone to the piano and began another strenuous session of work. That night she took several sleeping pills to get to sleep.

The Laurel recording studios were in the Valley, only a few miles from Newt's office. Roshelle could remember when a recording studio was the most exciting place on earth to her. But that was before she tasted Las Vegas. Now it seemed a cold, mechanical, and impersonal place. She'd never thought herself to be claustrophobic, but the day of the first recording session, she wondered. Once the mike was adjusted, the headset in place, and the door of the cut room closed, her throat seemed to close also. If it hadn't been for the friendly engineer smiling at her from the sound room, she might well have given up and quit. He reminded her of Gary McIntyre, the guy who taught her the ropes back in Tulsa, all those many years ago. Everyone called him Mac. She and Mac had become good friends. His favorite saying to her was, "Remember me when you're rich and famous!" And he always said it like he meant it.

After the first session, which she felt to be a total flop, she bucked up with new resolve. It would require even harder work and concentration than she'd imagined. No spotlights, no black sequined dress, no dancing feet, no cheers, no applause. She was totally alone in that room.

But if this was the way to gain the success needed, then she would rise above it! If it meant she must work twice as hard, then she would work twice as hard. Whatever it took, she was ready. By the final session, she was gaily bantering with the soundmen, asking them myriads of questions in order to learn how to best work with them and the equipment.

Vic was right about the computers. Extraordinary sounds came from the keyboards and the results were exciting. As they worked with her—playing back numbers after the mixing was completed—she, too, could marvel at the end result. And hearing the end result made the recording sessions easier and easier to master.

Mitzi seemed to know even before Newt or the recording company when, weeks later, the album reached the top ten on the charts. It took off faster than any of them expected or predicted. Roshelle was still in bed the morning Mitzi came dancing in, waving the trade magazines. She always read two or three and meticulously compared notes.

"We made it. We made it!" she shouted. "Rosh, wake up. You're on the top ten. Look at this."

Roshelle willed her eyes to open as Mitzi yanked open the draperies. The sprightly girl whirled around a few more times, then plopped down on Roshelle's bed. "Look here. Here it is!"

Roshelle rolled over and grabbed at the magazine. She squinted to see through blurry eyes. "Well, I'll be." There it was—number seven on the chart. She reached for the tumbler of water on the bedside table and sipped. The water soothed it temporarily, but the nagging little scratchiness refused to go away. She would ask Mitzi to get her more lozenges later. Mitzi was bouncing so much that Roshelle could hardly drink or read. "Will you sit still so I can read this?"

"Sit still? How can I sit still?" She jumped to her feet and twirled around, humming the winning cut on the CD. "How can you just sit there? You're famous, Roshelle. This is what you've been waiting for. Aren't you thrilled?"

"I am thrilled, Mitzi. But I'm still not quite awake. Is there coffee?" She padded into the bathroom to splash cold water on her face. Why wasn't she more excited? Her song on the top ten. . .top in the entire nation. She had always thought that would send her into spasms of ecstasy.

"Of course there's coffee. I'll get you a cup."

"No need to bring it, Mitzi. Give me a few minutes and I'll be down."

She could hear Mitzi singing and hopping all the way down the stairs.

All of them—the people at Laurel, Newt, she, and Mitzi—had all watched the song climb on the charts, like an owner watching his horse at the Kentucky Derby. The reviews had been great since the beginning. "Brightest up-and-coming young singer," some had said. One described her voice as a "gentle, sultry mix of New York and Oklahoma." "Warm and personable," another said. Newt had already begun lining up publicity people to work on the "angles," as he called them.

Now, talks with the recording company president included discussions of the next CD *and* a music video. It was a heady thought.

Recording company president, Mr. Laurel, called that morning before she had finished her second cup of coffee and conveyed his heartiest congratulations to her. Then he invited her to a party given by another Laurel label recording artist. Roshelle wasn't sure she wanted to go, but later, when she talked to Newt, he said she had no choice in the matter.

"Now, sweets, do I care if you want to go or not? The press will be there and it's high time to get your pretty mug out in the public's eye. In fact, I think we'll have Louis concoct a ravishing little outfit for the evening." He rattled off the address of Louis's Beverly Hills studio as Roshelle motioned for Mitzi to hand her a pen and some paper.

What had made her think it would always be her and the boys when she reached this point? She had never had a clear vision of herself without Benny by her side. Stupid thinking. As with the recording sessions, she had to rethink everything. But, she would do it.

Late that afternoon, when she and Mitzi returned from the fitting at Louis's, they staggered into the front door, weighted down with packages. Every time they went out, they purchased another item or two for the house.

Mitzi was busy extolling the good looks of Louis and Victor Moran. "Victor has the clear hazel, bottomless eyes that seem to look right through you. But Louis. . .whew! Louis has eyes that sparkle, dance, and shine all at once. And that gorgeous hair. Mmm, all those curls." Mitzi pulled groceries out of a sack and put them up in the cupboard as Roshelle unwrapped the soapstone carvings they had picked up at a darling little shop near Louis's studio.

"Vic seems so serious and Louis is always cutting up," Mitzi went on. "Which one do you think is the better hunk, Rosh? Give me your honest opinion."

Roshelle was studying the carvings and deciding where in her studio she would put them. She'd also purchased several new books, and now she picked one up and leafed through it.

"Rosh, are you ignoring me?"

"Hmm? Why, heavens no. I'd never ignore you, Mitzi."

"That's a flat-out lie. You're ignoring me now. Why don't you want to tell me who you think is the better-looking guy?"

"Because it doesn't make a bit of difference what I think, that's why." The blinking light on the answering machine caught her eye and she punched the button.

It was Newt. "Hey, sweets, know of a lady by the name of Rayford? Cora Rayford, from some place called Sandott, Oklahoma? I don't know how she got my number, but she wants to talk to you. Naturally, I didn't give out your number. She says it's very important. But then, that's what they all say," he quipped, and then left the number and hung up.

Roshelle slowly sat down at the bar beside the kitchen phone. "I wonder how she tracked me down?"

Mitzi pulled her head out of the refrigerator. "Rayford? Wasn't that your name before you changed it?" She straightened up with a cantaloupe balanced in her hand. "Hey, Rosh. Is Cora Rayford your mother?"

Roshelle felt her stomach churning. She could only nod.

Mitzi came over and put her arm around Roshelle's shoulders. "Is it that bad? You look sick."

"I feel sick. Wonder what she wants?"

"Hey, I left home, too, remember. But I've gone back a few times. It didn't kill me."

"Wonder what she wants?" Roshelle repeated as though she'd not heard.

"Maybe she's ill or something. Want me to dial it?"

"I wish I never had to talk to her again ever."

"Your own mother?"

Roshelle nodded.

"She beat you or something?"

"No. It's not that simple. I'll call her from my room. Thanks, Mitzi." She felt her friend give her a squeeze and, as always, it made her want to curl up like a baby and cry, just cry until all her tears were spent. That is, if they ever could be spent. She sometimes felt she had a big enough reserve to last a lifetime.

By the time her mother's voice came on the line a few minutes later, Roshelle was in a cold sweat.

"Rachel? Well, finally. It's taken several days and a host of phone calls to find you. You'd think you could at least give us a number where we can reach you. This has caused me a great deal of trouble. Always so much trouble."

"My name's Roshelle now, Mother. Roshelle Ramone. Legally."

"I've never heard of the name Roshelle. But Rachel is a good solid Bible name. And it's the one I chose for you the day you were born."

No sense in trying to argue, she chided herself. "Newt said you needed to talk to me."

"Newt. Is that the name of the man I talked to? Your agent? What a rude man he is. Well, whether or not you care at all, I thought it was only fitting that you know. Your uncle Jess is in the hospital. They don't expect him to live. If you want to see him again—and it's only proper that you would—you need to come home right away."

Home. What a funny word for her to use. Home. It sounded almost like a joke. She wanted to laugh right out loud. Or did she want to laugh because Uncle Jess was finally down and almost out? She could see a little humor in that.

What should she do? It was expected of her to be there. How could she not go? As much as they all already despised her, if she didn't go and he died, they'd have that much more to hold against her.

"I have an important party to attend Saturday night. I'll fly out early Sunday morning."

"Party? What kind of party?"

Roshelle ignored the question. The words and tone sounded no different now than when she was fifteen. "Is Uncle Jess in Tulsa?"

"That's right. In Tulsa."

"I'll be there on Sunday."

"You can't come tomorrow? The doctors aren't holding out much hope."

"Impossible. Sunday's the earliest."

"Want to give me your number so I can let you know if anything happens?"

Not a chance, she breathed inwardly. "I'll stay in touch." She quickly hung up before another word could be said.

Chapter Seven

The recording company's party was a new adventure in her new life. People she'd read about, people she'd seen on TV, those whose albums she'd listened to—there they were, mingling and talking and having a great time. And she was part of it. The entire evening was like a dream.

Roshelle had finally talked Newt into serving as her escort so she wouldn't be alone. For all his tough business dealing, Newt had turned out to be a good friend. Old enough to be her father, he provided a measure of safety for her.

In his classic '58 Thunderbird, which he said he loved more than his third wife who was honestly his favorite, he drove clear across town to fetch her and take her to the home of Blaine and Gloria Bonaros in fashionable Bel Air.

Blaine was one of Laurel's long-standing recording artists. Many gold records hung on his walls. As Newt nosed the white Thunderbird up into the driveway, the guard at the gatehouse checked their identification before opening the iron gates. The driveway led them over arched stone bridges where swans and ducks glided in the quiet pools below. Small waterfalls were strategically placed here and there. Lush gardens, set about with formal hedges, banana palms, bamboo, and flowering trees of all kinds, flanked the drive.

Roshelle felt herself gasp as the house came into view. A stately mansion of English tudor style, it look as though it had been plucked up from the English countryside and set here—except for the palms, that is.

"Don't let it swoon you," Newt said with a little sniff. "They put their pants on one leg at a time just like you do."

She looked over at him and smiled.

The valet parked the car while Newt took her arm and led her to the front flagstone entryway. He handed a card to the butler at the door and they were welcomed in.

In her mind, Roshelle had tried to imagine such a house as this, but failed miserably. Now, as she walked through it, it was still beyond belief. However, rather than garish as she had expected, it was decorated with subdued colors, solid dark wood, and tasteful furniture pieces.

Sounds of laughter, conversation, and music echoed through the house, as they were led down a long hallway into a wing of the home. The room they entered was a good deal more informal than the main part of the house. Wallpaper in a soft celery green was set off with flowered borders. The light oak floors and tall, uncurtained windows gave the room an airiness, even though it was filled with a crowd of mingling party-goers.

Roshelle was sure that in the daylight not only would sunlight flood this room, but the view of all the outdoors as well. At the far end of the room, the floor raised into a platform where a combo was playing soft dance music. Through the French doors she could see several couples dancing on the lighted veranda. Past the veranda's balcony, she could see the round cupola of a garden gazebo. Perhaps one day she and Mitzi would have a place like this.

They were quickly greeted by the host and hostess, as well as by Mr. Ted Laurel himself, all of whom gave warm welcomes and the kisses on the cheek and hugs that Roshelle had come to expect. She was nervous as a cat. Obviously sensing her uneasiness, Newt stayed at her elbow and introduced her to those she didn't know.

In all her years of traveling on the road, she'd never touched hard liquor. But, as the frosty little glasses were being passed around, Newt handed her one and she drank it. Sweet and cold, yet warm, it created a bubbly feeling inside.

There was one familiar face in the crowd. Louis Sarviano came up to say hello. His hug had a bit more feeling than the others. "You look absolutely wonderful tonight, Roshelle," he said, kissing her warmly on the cheek. "But then I've never seen you when you didn't."

"You can say that because I wear your designs," she said, wishing she didn't blush so easily.

"I was not looking at the dress, m'love," he said softly into her ear.

He and Newt fell into talking business talk and, as they moseyed through the crowd, Louis seemed to stay with them.

The most glorious part of the evening came when Mr. Laurel, who, as he told her was now to be called "Ted," went to the platform and stopped the party for an announcement. He motioned for Roshelle to come to where he was standing. She wasn't sure she heard correctly in the midst of all the clamor but, as everyone quieted, Newt gave her a little shove.

Then, Ted Laurel, president of Laurel Recording Company, proposed a toast to their newest star. The adrenalin rush was equal to the one she had at her closing night in Vegas. The applause. . .the attention. Off to the side of the room, near the tall windows, was a stunning white grand piano. Waving toward it, Ted asked her to play a few cuts from the CD. Later, she couldn't remember why she didn't want to go to the party in the first place.

After that, she was asked to dance by several of the men present who, previously, hadn't noticed her. Photographers were everywhere. "Learn to keep smiling," Newt had instructed her. And she did. She would. She would learn it all. Whatever it took, she'd do it.

Louis was also one who asked her to dance on the veranda. But, unlike the others, he had an excellent sense of rhythm. They glided together as though they had practiced for years and she found she quite enjoyed being in his arms.

✿

"Hey, sweets, you was great tonight," Newt told her as he steered the Thunderbird up into her driveway. "Really great. They loved you. You didn't need to be scared."

"I wasn't really scared."

"Petrified?"

She giggled, feeling the effect of the drinks. "That's closer to it."

"Well, the next party that comes around, one of those handsome, hairy-legged young male creatures will be escorting you instead of a crusty old codger like me. They all had their eyes on you."

She giggled again. "Some real hunks, for sure."

"What time are you flying out tomorrow?" He pointed to his watch. "Correction—today."

The happy bubble burst as she suddenly recalled what lay ahead—a trip back to the past—and she was frightened. At first she had wanted Mitzi to go, too. But there were still so many details to be taken care of before the tour and before the video shoot. Newt asked that Mitzi stay here to catch up all the loose ends. It seemed the worst possible time for Roshelle to be going.

"My plane leaves at nine."

"Wish you didn't have to go now. But, family is family. This is your uncle, right?"

She nodded mutely. Her stomach was churning again. Was it too much food and too many drinks? "My father's brother."

"You gotta be true to family if you can," he said.

Right, she thought. *True to family, even though family was never true to me.*

Newt came around to open her door and led her up the front steps and helped her inside. Mitzi was asleep; the house was quiet.

"Hurry and go see your old uncle and get back here so we can continue the business of making you famous. . .and me rich." He gave her a little hug and planted a kiss on her forehead.

After he left, she promptly went to the bathroom off her bedroom and threw up. A gruesome way to end her gallant evening. The remainder of the night was miserable as well, but she dared not take sleeping pills for fear she'd oversleep the next morning. Sleep was fitful. There were dreams of Uncle Jess. . .and of her mother—together.

In the morning she realized she hadn't even begun to pack for the trip. Mitzi said it was because, psychologically, she was trying to avoid the thought of going.

"Right," Roshelle retorted softly so as not to disturb her aching head. "And who hired you to be my analyst?"

Mitzi was helping arrange a few things in the suitcase. "I'm everything else around here, so you might as well add analyst to the list."

"Thanks a whole bunch." Roshelle was in the bathroom grabbing cosmetics and putting them in the overnight case. "Where are those lozenges we bought?"

"Down in the kitchen."

"Would you get them? I don't want to forget them."

"Your throat still sore?"

"A little."

"Hadn't you better have a doctor look at it?"

Roshelle peeked out the bathroom door. "So now we add nurse to analyst?"

"Not a chance. I'm too squeamish. When I heard you in here throwing up your shoes last night, I wouldn't have come in for anything."

"Just get the lozenges, please!"

Mitzi dropped the nightgown she was folding. "All right. All right."

The overnight bag was ready. What else would she need? How could she know what to wear when her mother disapproved of everything? She pulled open a bureau drawer and rummaged through it. Her hand hit something hard. She pulled out a book from beneath the undergarments. The Bible from the Miami hotel! She had almost forgotten about it. As she put in on the bureau, it fell open to where the first violets from Vic were pressed. The pages were stained where the little blossoms had been crushed. She ran her finger over the stain. The words she touched almost jumped out at her. Psalm 69:30. "I will praise the name of God with a song, and will magnify him with thanksgiving."

A shiver ran through her entire body. She slammed the book shut and dropped it back in the drawer.

Mitzi came bounding back into the room and tossed the package of lozenges into the suitcase. "Say, I was just thinking. Isn't Tulsa where that Victor what's-his-name is from?"

Roshelle closed the filled suitcase and picked it up. "Mitzi, my dear. Sometimes you just talk too much!"

Chapter Eight

Roshelle collapsed into the seat of the Tulsa-bound plane. She was near exhaustion, having worked so hard for so many weeks. After asking the flight attendant for a pillow, she tucked it under her head, leaned against the window, and gazed out at the quiet clouds.

She should never have let herself be talked into going back. She hadn't been back since the day she packed her things and crawled out the window. Cora Rayford didn't know her daughter could climb out on the back porch roof and shin down the railings. Actually, Roshelle had done it many times. But this time it was for good. No more would she be grounded for days at a time.

She tried to picture Uncle Jess. What would she say to him? The hate for him still burned inside her. If it weren't for Uncle Jess, her father might still be alive today.

The plane droned on above the fleecy clouds. Her heavy eyelids closed and she was in the basement of the small white church in Sandott. The summer days there were so hot. She'd gone down in the basement to get cool and play . . .to get away from the summer heat. Then footsteps on the stairs. She had to move back into the shadows; she wasn't supposed to be there. Mother would be mad, maybe even use the lilac switch on her legs. She pushed her back against the cool wall behind the stacks of folding chairs.

Uncle Jess. . .it was only Uncle Jess. She started to move, then stopped. Another voice was there in the dimness of the basement. Another voice whispering the name "Jess" over and over. And he said her name back. . . "Cora." The two forms stood close, very close. She put her hands over her ears to shut out the sounds of their embraces and their kisses. She didn't want to hear.

What would Daddy say? The question screamed inside her young mind. She sat very still, not moving, even though her stomach felt like she was going to be very sick. Suddenly, Roshelle jerked her head up. The plane. . .she was still on the plane. She excused herself to the rest room, where she could catch her breath and freshen her makeup. She let cool water run over her clammy hands. That horrid dream! She'd thought she was rid of it for good. If only she didn't have to go back.

❧

Tulsa had grown and changed and yet was still much the same. She drove around for a time in the rental car, just looking. A new exchange on the inter-state caused her to totally lose her sense of direction. But, as she drove the streets, she could still find her way around. The city was perfectly laid out in neat mile squares.

The bar where she had landed her first singing job was gone. It was now an Italian restaurant. Strange. Across town, the recording studio where she had cut so many ad jingles was still there. In fact, it appeared to have enjoyed a face lift. She smiled as she drove slowly by, remembering. Maybe some of the guys were still there who would remember her. . .like Mac. She toyed with the idea of stopping by the next day.

She chose a hotel near the hospital. If she were checked in before visiting the hospital, perhaps she wouldn't have to go out to Sandott at all.

The hotel was nice. Not the Supreme Royale, but nice. Benny would have liked it. Here she was—back in a hotel room again. But now she was really alone. From her window she could actually see the hospital. A scary feeling crept over her. She should have asked for a room on the other side of the hall.

Her mother was expecting her and she couldn't put it off. She had to go over there and face this—alone.

The tailored navy dress she'd chosen was as conservative as she could get and still be herself. A last glance in the mirror didn't give her much courage. She was ready, but she couldn't walk out that door. Why was she so filled with dread?

What if. . .? She went to the bedside table and opened the drawer. As she expected, there was a Bible. She picked it up and flipped through the pages. She remembered having a favorite verse when she was only nine years old. But where was it? And what made her think it would make any difference at this point?

But she kept flipping pages. It was in the New Testament—that much she remembered. Matthew, Mark? At the end of one of the gospels, and she remembered it was in red. Ah, there. Matthew 28:20. "And, lo, I am with you alway, even unto the end of the world."

"With you always. With you always." She was in the swing in the back yard, swinging higher and higher, singing her own little song about Jesus always being with her, always. "Always" was an important word to a nine-year-old girl.

She closed the book. She couldn't explain it, but now she could walk out that door.

Hospital smells were high on Roshelle's list of least likely favorites. She was thankful that she at least had taken the time earlier for a sandwich. She slipped a lozenge in her mouth. Perhaps if she stayed over a couple of days, she could drop by one of the nearby clinics and have her throat looked at. They'd probably give her an antibiotic to get rid of this lingering infection. *And* probably tell her to rest more and stop working so hard.

"Jess Rayford," she said to the lady dressed in pink, sitting at the information desk.

"Reverend Jess Rayford?" the lady asked.

"Yes. Reverend." Roshelle stifled a comment.

"Eighth floor. Check with the nurse at the desk. There's limited visiting."

Her mother had warned her that he was pretty bad off. But it hadn't truly registered in her mind until that moment. She stepped off the elevator at the eighth floor and the nurse at the desk wanted to know if she was a relative. She only nodded.

"To your left. Room 844."

The room was overflowing with flowers. Just as it should be for the respected pastor of the community, she thought grimly. The fragrance was like a funeral. Roshelle's palms were damp.

Her mother was there beside the bed. She looked the same—prim, proper, and in control. There was a moment before her mother detected her presence. A moment in which Roshelle let her eyes move to the bed. . .to the person lying in the bed who bore little resemblance to the harsh man who took over her life following her father's death. It was not the man who condemned her every action and word. It was not the man who seemed to take delight in making her life miserable. This was just a tired old man lying there, very close to death.

Her mother turned then and saw her. "Rachel. So you did come." She rose and came across the room to give her daughter a light hug. One would have thought they parted a few days ago, rather than several years ago.

"I said I would come."

"Yes, but. . .well, never mind. You're here. That's all that matters now." She turned back to the bed. "He's much better today. Much better. I know he might not look very well to you. You've been away for so long you don't even know what he's gone through. It's been so hard on him these past few years. But he's hanging on. Yes, sir, he's hanging on. The doctor said he'd not seen such a strong will in a long time."

She still had her hand on Roshelle's arm, but it was as though she were talking to someone across the room. "It was touch and go when we first brought him in. Had to call an ambulance to bring him here. Heart trouble. It's his heart. It was so awful. I thought sure. . .we thought he was a goner for sure."

Her mother let go of her then and moved back toward the bed. This was as much of a welcome as she was going to receive. Well, what did she expect? Ticker tape parades? After all, she was the one who left.

Her mother motioned for Roshelle to pull up another chair beside her. Dutifully, Roshelle did as she was bidden. "He won't know you," her mother said, still looking at the old man in the bed. "He's not roused since the surgery. But the doctors say he will. He will. It's just a matter of time." She smoothed the skirt of her dress. Cora Rayford always wore a dress. . .nice dresses.

"Just look at all these flowers, Rachel," she went on, waving her hand. "Everyone loves him. Everyone. The entire town is concerned. Mr. Farnum at the bank keeps asking if he can do anything. He's given me as much time off as I need."

Her mother had always hated the thought of working outside the home but, after her husband died, she had no choice. However, the bank seemed to be a proper place for a person like Cora, who cared about looking proper.

"Why, I can hardly keep up with all the get well cards that have come," Cora continued.

"Why should you?" Roshelle asked.

Cora stopped short and turned to look at her daughter. "Why should I what?"

"Why should you have to keep up with the cards? Doesn't he have a secretary at the church?"

"I should have known you'd say something like that." She stood to straighten the sheets, then poured water into a tumbler, even though the man in the coma would not be taking a drink any time soon. "You really aren't our dear little Rachel anymore, are you?"

"My name is Roshelle."

"Well, Roshelle, or whoever you are, we are all the family your uncle Jess has. Why would we want to let a secretary handle things? Is that how you think of family? You just turn your back and let other people take over?"

"Might be less painful." In the room together for five minutes and already they were at one another's throats. Nothing had changed.

"Painful?" Cora pulled a tissue from the box on the bedside table and touched her eye. "You want to talk about painful? You have no idea the pain you've caused us. Your uncle Jess was worried sick after you ran away. I lay awake nights wondering where you were. Wondering if you were dead or alive."

"For the first year and a half, I was right here in Tulsa." She remembered the little upstairs apartment she shared with her best friend's older sister.

Most nights she cried as she slept on the floor of the living room. Some nights she was afraid they would find her and take her back, other nights, afraid they wouldn't. And they didn't. Later, she learned through her friend that Uncle Jess convinced Cora not to search. "She'll come home when she gets cold and hungry," he had said.

When Roshelle heard that, it put steel into her backbone as nothing else could have. She knew she'd never go back.

"Did you expect us to go looking through every sleazy bar in Tulsa?" her mother asked sharply. "Is that what you wanted of your family?"

"It was a pretty nice bar actually. The guy who owned it was kind and big-hearted. He loved the way I sang. He gave me a chance."

"There is no such thing as a nice bar. You know that. And *how* you sing has never been the problem, Rachel." She reached up and patted her graying hair. "It's *what* you sing that was always the problem. Those crude, lewd lyrics. Your grandma Riley would be shocked if she ever heard you—"

"Let's leave Grandma out of this since she's not here to speak for herself." Roshelle vacillated between wanting to scream and wanting to cry. She stood up and stepped to the window. How could she get out of here? "So where's Janey? I thought she'd be here." Her little sister was the only one of the family she really wanted to see.

"She couldn't get a sitter. And she goes by Jane now. Even her husband calls her Jane."

"Sitter?"

Cora enjoyed playing the game to the hilt. "Of course, you wouldn't know. She's married and has a baby. Since you weren't here, she had to ask a friend to be her maid of honor at the wedding. It broke her heart. Truly broke her heart."

The door opened and a nurse pleasantly informed them that the visiting time was over. The interruption gave Roshelle a moment to savor the thought that she was now an aunt. Little Janey was actually a mother. Cute, perfect little Janey. One of the few bright spots in Roshelle's dark childhood world. In spite of the fact that all of Janey's golden qualities were constantly brought to Roshelle's attention, she still adored her younger sister.

"We'll be in the coffee shop," Cora told the nurse. "Please call us there if there's any change."

"Of course, Mrs. Rayford," the nurse answered as she drew the curtain around the bed.

❧

The coffee shop was crowded. Roshelle was craning her neck to look in the room to see if there were any empty tables when she heard a voice from behind her down the hall, calling her. Like a call from out of her past. "Rachel. It's really you. I can't believe it. Welcome home." Her younger sister nearly knocked her over in a bear hug. Now this was a welcome. Roshelle didn't even mind the stares.

"I know it's Roshelle, but it'll take me awhile to get onto that." Janey stepped back to look. "You're beautiful! Just like I knew you'd be."

"Hi, Janey. Thanks." But it was Janey who was beautiful. Tall and slender like their father. Dark shiny hair like his. And the doelike eyes. "You grew up while I had my back turned," Roshelle told her.

"I want you to know I've missed you," Janey said, her eyes misting.

"I've missed you, too." She grabbed Janey's hand. "But Mother said you couldn't come this afternoon."

"When I found out you were coming, I took Darla to Al's mother's and came as soon as I could. I wouldn't have missed seeing you for the world."

"We're blocking the doorway, girls," Cora said in her usual curt manner. "Let's get through the line and find a place to sit down."

"Darla?"

"My baby girl. You've got to see her, Rachel. Roshelle," she corrected herself.

"Some of my friends call me Rosh."

"Rosh? I like that. Can you come out and see our place? Meet Alex and see our baby? Your little niece?"

"Out where?"

"Girls, please. We can talk at the table."

Janey pulled Roshelle over to the deli counter. They ordered premade sandwiches and coffee. "We have a house in Sandott."

When Roshelle heard the town's name, her heart sunk. She shook her head. "I don't know, Janey. There's so much going on. I've got to get back as soon as possible."

They sat down at a small table by the windows. It was as if Cora were not there.

"I'd bring her to you, but when I go to see Uncle Jess—"

"What does she look like?" Roshelle wanted to know.

"Beautiful, of course." She opened her purse and pulled out a little album full of snapshots. Janey and Alex and the baby. In a little house in Sandott, Oklahoma. So cozy. And she seemed content. Unaffected Janey. Like Mitzi, she was always so unaffected.

Roshelle wondered why she couldn't be the same way. But she wasn't. There was no use pretending. This place affected her. In the worst way.

"You cut a CD, didn't you?" Janey said when the photos were put away.

Roshelle nodded. She heard Cora clear her throat in disgust.

"I've been watching for it. I knew it would come. Sooner or later, I knew it would. Just like you always said you would." Was that admiration in her sister's eyes? "Now one song is climbing, right?"

Roshelle pulled the wrapping from the sandwich that looked a trifle squashed. "We just learned that it's in the top ten."

"Jane Rayford," Cora butted in. "Are you listening to—"

"Ingram, Mother. The name's Ingram. You were at the wedding, remember?" She smiled kindly at Cora and turned back to Roshelle. "Top ten? In the nation?" She threw her head back. "Can you believe this? My own sister. So where are the photographers and news reporters?" She fluffed her curly hair and glanced over her shoulder. "Are we being watched? Will I be interviewed in one of those tabloids?"

Cora let her spoon clatter into the saucer by her coffee cup. "Well, I should hope not. Haven't we had humiliation enough with this skeleton in our closet?"

Roshelle recoiled, but Janey remained cool. With a pat on Roshelle's arm, she said, "And this is only the beginning. I'm so proud of you. Al and I pray for you every day."

Praying for her? To succeed? She covered her sister's hand with her own. "Thanks, Janey. I appreciate that." And she meant it. Janey seemed to make the other unbearable things fade into the background.

Chapter Nine

The clinic was down the street from the hospital, a few blocks from the hotel. Bright lavender, purple, and yellow pansies in the clinic flower beds bobbed their heads in the morning breeze. This was a perfect opportunity to take the time to get this sore throat taken care of. There was never enough time in California when she had so many deadlines to face.

She called first thing that morning and the appointment was set for ten. Her wait was brief. Dr. Beasley was a gray-haired, friendly man with full cheeks and wire-rimmed glasses. An ears, nose, throat specialist, she was told. He did all the normal, noncommittal "hmming" that doctors always do when they look at you.

"I know I've been overworking," she confessed to his unspoken questions. "I know I probably should rest more. But there's never enough time."

He nodded and looked a little more. "We'll do a couple of tests. How long will you be in town?"

"I'm not sure. I have to get back as soon as possible." Honestly, she didn't know how she could stay another minute. Janey kept begging her to drive out to visit their "place" and Roshelle was running out of excuses why she couldn't.

"If I get the reports back this afternoon, where can I contact you?" he asked.

He scribbled as she gave him the hotel name and her room number. "Since you're here temporarily, I'll ask them to hurry on this."

"Is it strep?" She'd heard awful things about strep throat. It must be more than just an infection or he would have said something.

"I'll call you as soon as we know."

Why can't they just tell a person what's wrong? she wondered as she drove out into the busy traffic. It was unnerving to be left hanging. She turned in the direction of the recording studio. It would be fun to go back and look around. To remember those early days. RIGHT ON TRACK RECORDING STUDIO the sign read. It was the same sign. She used to ride the bus out here when she had scheduled sessions and Mac would sometimes drive her home. All the guys were kind to her. Just like the guys in the band. She shook her head. No sense in thinking about the band again. It only made her depressed and sad.

The business office was done in tones of mauve and violet—restful and inviting. "I'm looking for an engineer by the name of Gary McIntyre," she said to the young receptionist.

The girl reached for the phone. "Can I give him your name?"

"You mean Mac's really here?" She felt like laughing.

The girl gave a questioning look as she picked up the phone. "He's back there. Your name, please?"

"Just say 'an old friend.' " This was too good to be true. She'd never dared hope he'd still be around. Maybe some of the other guys were, too.

"Gary," the girl was saying. "Someone to see you. An 'old friend.' " There was a touch of sarcasm in the tone, but Roshelle didn't mind.

The side door to the office opened. "Naw. Tell me I'm dreaming. I don't believe this." The barrel-chested Mac gave a throaty laugh and grabbed her in an unrestrained hug as the receptionist watched. "Our little Rachel. Only not so little." He stepped back and took a look. "Whew, not so little. Big star now, eh?"

"Well, I'm getting there."

"We knew you would. We all knew you would. Come on back. I don't have another client for a while." He guided her through the door back to one of the studio control rooms. His domain. "Hold the calls," he said over his shoulder to the receptionist. "When I first saw your photo on the album, I knew Roshelle was you. I'm so happy for you."

"Thanks." He was rooting for her and he'd noticed the new album. It made her feel great.

"What in the world would ever bring you back to Tulsa?"

"An emergency. My uncle is ill."

"You're in touch with your family?" Mac was well aware of her home situation.

"I am now."

"You don't sound too happy about it."

She tucked a strand of hair behind her ear and perched herself on the stool he pulled up. She gave a little sigh, not knowing how to answer. "It was a bad time to leave L.A., and. . .well, nothing has changed here." She brightened. "Except I find out I'm an aunt. My kid sister got married and has a little girl."

Mac gave a wide grin. "I'm married, too." He pulled out his wallet and showed the typical family photo—lovely wife and two darling toddlers. "She's the greatest," he declared, pointing at the photo for emphasis. "Best thing that ever happened to me."

She made the necessary polite remarks. All these happily married people were making her nervous. She looked around at the control room. "The place looks great. You're staying right on top of all the latest technology, I see." She patted a nearby computer console.

"Can't afford not to. We're doing big things in here now. Some pretty important people pass through these doors. And the videos. You should see our videos, Rachel. You'd be impressed."

"Roshelle."

"Oh yeah, Roshelle. Pretty name."

"I'm already impressed. I'm impressed that you're still hanging around here."

He straightened. "I've outlasted all the guys you knew, plus three owners. Can you believe that? Three owners. I sort of come with the furniture." He chuckled at his own joke.

Roshelle gazed through the soundproof window to the cut room where she had recorded ad jingles, all the while dreaming she was cutting her own album. Now that dream had come true.

"The newest owner has some bucks," he went on. "This is actually his second studio in town. Has an office in the Clancy Towers building."

"Mmm. Sounds like he does have a few bucks. You better be nice to this one."

"Hey, this is the easiest guy to be nice to you ever saw. Great to work with and knows this business inside out and upside down."

"Really," she answered absently. Time was getting by and her mother expected her back at the hospital within the hour.

"At one time he owned big casinos in Miami. Worked with all the big name stars."

"Miami. Right. And then he worked his way up to this recording studio in Tulsa. That makes a lot of sense." She couldn't keep the sarcasm out of her voice. "Why would anyone leave Miami for this?"

Mac ducked his head. "He got saved."

"He got what?"

"Gave his life to the Lord. Changed him completely."

"Is this guy. . .?" But the question was never finished. From the control room window she saw the door from the reception area open. There stood Vic. She felt the color drain from her face.

Mac jumped up. "There's Vic now. You'll have to meet him."

There was no back door, no escape route, no way out. Vic's expression was a combination of surprise and sheer delight as he saw her standing there.

Mac stepped to the door and motioned to Vic. "Hey, bossman. There's someone here I'd like you to meet."

Vic strode down the hall toward them. "Roshelle. What a pleasant surprise."

"Hello, Vic."

Mac's hands dropped at his side. "You two know each other?" He slapped his forehead. "I should have known. Victor Moran, you know everybody! But I bet you didn't know little Rachel here, I mean Roshelle, recorded her first songs in this cut room."

"I had no idea. But I'm pleased."

"I've got to be going." Roshelle felt cornered. She never dreamed she'd see him here. "I'm expected at the hospital."

Vic's face registered his disappointment. "You just got here and now you have to leave."

"I just dropped by to take a look. Curiosity. The place looks great." She moved toward the door. Past Vic. He reached out his hand. She didn't take it.

"How long will you be here? A few days?"

"I have to get back to L.A. soon. Newt's scheduling a tour and we hope to squeeze in the video filming before that. There's so much to do." She successfully moved past him into the hall.

"Let me give you my home phone number and my pager number. If you have a minute before you leave, let's get together." He pulled a card from his pocket and wrote on the back and handed it to her.

She slipped it into her purse. "Bye, Mac." She gave a little wave. "It was great to see you again. Thanks."

"You're welcome here anytime, Roshelle. Congratulations on your success—and all the successes to come. I know there'll be many."

Mac stayed in the control room, but Vic walked her through the reception area and out into the parking lot to her car. "So this is the studio where you got your start."

"If you can call car dealership ad jingles a beginning."

"To paraphrase Zechariah, four and ten, don't despise the day of small things." He opened the car door for her. "Everyone has to begin somewhere. I came to Tulsa almost like you did—with very little. But the Lord has blessed me."

She slipped into the hot car, turned the key, and cranked up the air conditioner. "I guess I'll see you around. We seem to have a way of running into one another."

He gave his slow smile. "We do, don't we? Don't forget. Call me if you have a minute. Call me if you need anything."

She nodded and pulled the door closed.

*

Uncle Jess's condition was unchanged. The room was the same as the day before. Her mother looked the same, but in a different dress. Cora held a devotion booklet in her hand. It appeared she had been reading to Uncle Jess before Roshelle's arrival. The room was close and depressing. Some of the flowers were wilting.

She looked at her uncle's pale quiet face and tried to remember how animated the face had been as he slammed his fist on the pulpit and preached hellfire and damnation to his attentive congregation. Or how angry he had looked when he reprimanded her. She remembered his coarse, loud voice. Never gentle. Never quiet. But that must have been another person. Not this old man lying here sick. It was difficult to sort out all the tangled threads of memories. There were knots and snarls all through it.

"How is he?" she asked politely as she came in and sat down.

"Stable, the doctor says. He seems to be out of danger now. He roused a bit in the night."

"Will Janey be coming later?" she wanted to know.

"Her name is Jane. She said she thought you were driving out to see her this evening."

"I never said that," she defended herself. Odd that it was acceptable for Janey to change her name, but not for Roshelle to change hers. But, that's the way it always had been. Janey, the sweet one, the good one, the right one. And yet the two sisters had loved one another in spite of it all. Now that's what Roshelle called a miracle.

"Alex said they were going to have a barbecue in the backyard in your honor and have a few friends over. Grilling steaks, I believe he said."

Roshelle felt her face flush with anger. Her mother was probably at the bottom of this. She'd call Janey when she got back to her hotel room. Between the two of them maybe they could get it straightened out. "There's no way I can—"

Her mother looked at her sternly. "I would think it's the least you could do for your sister, since you weren't even with her for her wedding or the birth of her first child."

"I'm sure there are sisters the world over who have been unable to be together for every occasion, but it doesn't cause a major disaster in the family."

"Unpreventable separations are quite different from this situation. It's quite clear you could have been here had you really wanted to be. But you preferred your wild life to family."

Cora had such an uncanny way of heaping on the guilt. Nothing Roshelle said in her own defense made any difference. Rather, her defenses seemed to open the door for her mother to further condemn. It was hopeless.

She thought about that a moment as she listened to her uncle's steady, but labored breathing. It really *was* hopeless. She was stupid to stay here. For the first time, she admitted the truth—that she had come here with a measure of hope that there could be a reconciliation. How foolish she'd been.

She stood to her feet. "I'll be going now," she said evenly.

Her mother barely glanced at her. "Sit down. You just got here."

"I have some things to take care of."

"Things that are more important than family, obviously. But then that's how it's always been with you, Rachel. Thinking of yourself first. Family never meant a thing to you."

Roshelle felt the twinge of pain as she bit into her bottom lip. She turned and walked out of the room.

Chapter Ten

There were two messages at the hotel desk: one from Janey and one from Dr. Beasley. She'd call the doctor first. That was the more important thing. Now she could get the needed prescription and some relief from the pain. No reason to go up to her room since she would have to go out to pick up the prescription anyway. She made the call from the lobby phone.

"Oh yes, Miss Ramone. I'm glad we caught you before you left town. Are you nearby?"

"At the hotel."

"Good. Could you come back by the clinic? I'd like to talk to you. How about half past two?"

She felt her nerves go taut. This was strange. Doctors are busy people. They don't have time for chitchat. What was the matter? She wanted to ask him why, but she was afraid to ask. "I can be there."

"Super." Was his voice overly friendly? Just her wild imagination. "I'll see you then."

There was nowhere to go to kill the next thirty minutes, so she went to her room and paced. She turned on the television and quickly vetoed that idea as she snapped it back off again. If she were home, she could be pounding out her emotions on the piano. As she paced, she hummed, then sang the lyrics of her newest song. It was a great love ballad. Perhaps with Newt on her side, she could talk Mr. Laurel into using it on her next album.

She would also talk to Newt about calling Benny and the boys off their tour so they could join her as she began her nationwide tour. She made herself dwell on every happy, exciting thing she could possibly think of. She changed out of her slacks back into the navy dress she'd worn Sunday afternoon. Then it was time to go to the clinic—alone again.

※

"You're a singer, right?" Dr. Beasley asked as he ushered her to a chair in his office.

"I'm a singer. A professional singer. Recording artist. Stage star. You name it. And I'll be a better singer as soon as I get this sore throat cleared up. Can you help me or not?"

"Are you singing on a regular basis at this time?"

"Is singing almost every night considered regular?"

Dr. Beasley nodded. "I think so. In a smoke-filled atmosphere?"

"You hardly ask patrons in a Las Vegas casino not to smoke."

"No, I suppose not."

She waited impatiently, wishing he would get to the point.

"Miss Ramone, I'm afraid this problem is not going to just 'clear up.' I've detected nodules on your vocal chords."

A dark silence hung between them momentarily. She tried to clear her throat and the pain there suddenly intensified. "Nodules? Like growths?"

"Yes, like little growths." His voice was calm, steady. "We see this many times in singers who abuse their voices."

"But I don't abuse my voice!" she protested. "I'm just singing. Is there anything wrong with that? I love to sing. Singing is my whole life." First her mother, and now this. She felt the anger smoldering. It wasn't fair.

"Miss Ramone, please. I'm not accusing you. I'm trying to explain—"

"Explain what? What are you telling me? What does this mean?"

"First of all, you'll need to give your voice a rest. Stop singing for a time."

"That's impossible," she snapped.

"Next," he said, ignoring her answer, "I recommend surgery to have the nodules removed."

No. This couldn't be happening to her. Surgery. Someone cutting on her throat. She couldn't bear the thought. No. She fished a tissue from her purse.

"Even with surgery we cannot guarantee that your vocal chords will be normal. But, without surgery, the problem could grow much worse."

Why was she sitting here hundreds of miles from people who cared about her? Alone. Always alone. Benny on one coast, Mitzi on the other. No one here to help. No one. She pulled herself together. She'd survived before. She'd survive again. Somewhere deep within her was that resolve. That stage smile.

"Do you have a physician you want me to contact in Los Angeles? Miss Ramone? I said, do you have—"

"No. I've not been to a doctor in years. I'm so healthy. I've always been healthy. Never sick."

"Perhaps you'd like to schedule the surgery here." He nodded in the general direction of the hospital. The hospital where her uncle now lay near death. "We have excellent facilities here. You'd be well taken care of."

Roshelle straightened her shoulders, squeezing the soft tissue in her hand. "Thank you, Dr. Beasley. I'll be in touch with you if I decide to have the surgery done here in Tulsa." She stood on unsteady legs.

"Please do that. But don't wait too long. Meanwhile I'll give you a prescription that will ease the discomfort to some degree." He scratched out the note and handed it to her. "This should help. And, with proper rest, you should be fine."

"If the surgery is not done?"

"Worst case scenario?"

She drew in a breath. "Yes."

"If the nodules are malignant, the cancer could spread." He shook his head. "You don't want to take that chance."

૪૦

Later, she wasn't sure how long she'd been driving around the city. Her mind was encased in a gray fog and nothing was clear. She stopped at a small park where children were playing on the swings and jungle gym. The heat assaulted her as she stepped out of the air-conditioned car, but she was oblivious to it.

The park was resplendent with dark green cedars, sprawling magnolias, and shady maples and oaks. She strolled among the trees that shaded her from the hot afternoon sun. Squirrels looked at her quizzically, then chittered and scampered away. The blue jays scolded and dive-bombed the squirrels.

In the midst of a cluster of trees was a green, wrought-iron bench. She made her way to the bench and sat down slowly. A lemony fragrance wafted down off the waxy white blossoms of the magnolia. Their beauty and serenity seemed to mock the utter confusion and turmoil in her brain.

It wasn't fair. Why should life play this cruel trick on her? "God, if You're punishing me, You've sure picked a stinky way to do it," she muttered.

From high above her, she could hear a mockingbird singing. She craned her neck to find him. There he was, atop a cedar tree, on the topmost, tiniest branch of the tree. Towering above all other surrounding trees. The branch looked much too fragile to hold the bird. But he didn't care. Nor did he care if there was, or was not, an audience to hear his lovely music. He simply sang.

"That's me," she whispered as she watched the small bird. "That's me. I'll sit on that topmost tiny frail branch. I don't care if it breaks. I don't even care if I fall. I don't care about anything except my singing. You and me, Mr. Mocker. We'll just sing our hearts out as long as we can. I'll sing till I drop."

૪૦

It was growing dark when she found herself back in the hotel parking lot. She dreaded going back to an empty hotel room. As she opened her purse to pull out the room key, Vic's card tumbled out on the floor. She stooped to pick it up. "Call if you need anything," he had said.

"We'll see if Mr. Christian really meant what he said," she said to herself as she headed to the lobby phone. "Or was he blowing hot air?"

The moment he heard her voice, Vic said, "Great. You've changed your mind. Can I meet you at the hotel? I'll be right over. Wait in the lobby."

His eagerness was a bit overwhelming, but she waited. She could see him as he parked out front, then walked into the building. He walked with purpose and determination. One might label him as a young executive who knows where he's going. He was wearing a cool-looking print shirt with casual slacks. There was always an impeccable look about him, whether he was in a suit or not.

For a moment he stood glancing about the vast lobby area. When he saw her, his face lit up and he quickly stepped toward her. She ignored the flutter of excitement she felt at seeing him again. She didn't dare *feel* anything right now.

He reached out his hand to where she was sitting on one of the plush lobby couches. This time she took his hand and let him help her to her feet. "Thanks for calling," he said.

"I had sort of a change in plans. I found I did have a little free time after all."

"I'm glad. Have you eaten?"

She shook her head, wondering if she could eat now that she knew why her throat bothered her so. Part of her wished she'd never learned the truth. Ignorance could be bliss, after all.

He took her to a quiet restaurant, a place like she expected he would patronize. Nothing raucous.

"How's your uncle?" he asked as they were seated.

"Stable is what the doctors say."

"Was he ill long?"

"I haven't any idea. I'm not in contact with my family."

"I'm sorry to hear that."

"Don't be. It's much better this way." She thought of her mother again. "Much better."

The waitress interrupted as she took their order. Vic ordered prime sirloin with tomato sauce, but Roshelle wanted only soup and salad.

Changing the subject, he said, "Mac tells me you left home before you ever graduated from high school."

She felt her face flush. "Did he tell all my secrets? I hope he told you I took the GED and received my diploma before I was seventeen."

"Actually, I couldn't get much out of him at all. He seems rather protective of you."

She smiled thinking of Vic prying to find out more about her. Then she wondered why he would even care to know. "As my mother would say, I ran away—straight into a world of sin."

"Mac said you only wanted to sing."

Unexpected tears burned in her eyes as she nodded. "Singing was all I ever wanted. Even now."

He reached out to take her hand, but she pulled it back. "Are you all right?"

"It's been a rather emotional trip for me. I'll be all right." She struggled to regain her composure. She didn't need him feeling sorry for her. "I wanted to sing, but my family never understood. My uncle constantly preached about the sin of singing demonic lyrics."

"That must have been hard on you as a kid. Preached? You mean, he's a preacher?"

"That's what he calls himself. I have other names."

"You attended his church, I take it?"

"Most of my life."

The food was brought to the table and, as he had done the day of their picnic, Vic insisted on blessing the food—out loud. Roshelle's first reaction was embarrassment. But the sound of his voice in simple prayer had a quieting effect on her.

"What about your father? How does he fit into the picture?" he asked after he was finished with the prayer.

"Daddy," she said. "Well, Daddy's hard to describe." She was hedging. She'd not talked about her father to anyone for so many years. "He died suddenly when I was only nine."

"I'm sorry. Was it hard on you?"

"Devastating. He was my ally."

"Against whom?"

"Mother mostly." She studied his reaction to this and waited for a retort. But he quietly soaked in the information with no comment.

"What was he like?"

"Quiet. Kind." Sort of like you, she wanted to say. The thought startled her. She pretended to be concentrating on cutting a cherry tomato. Then she added, "Never condemning. Never argumentative."

He started to ask another question, but she interrupted him. That was enough. "But what about your family?" she asked quickly, to steer him away from more questions.

"No preachers, that's for sure."

"Lucky you."

"There's probably room for discussion there, but I'll let it pass," he said with a smile. "My father was into money and business and all the trappings. And my very materialistic-minded mother prodded him on. There's plenty of money in Miami real estate. And I followed right in his footsteps."

"And Mac informed on you, too. He said you owned a couple of Miami night spots. You actually *owned* them?"

He nodded and smiled. "That I did. Or they owned me."

"Either way would be fine with me."

"I thought so, too, for a while."

She wanted to know what happened. How he came to throw it all away and move to Tulsa. But, on the other hand, she didn't want to hear some preachy story about how he saw the error of his ways. Boring, boring. "So you grew up around Miami?" That would keep the conversation safe, she thought smugly.

"West Palm Beach for several years, then Miami."

"Don't you miss the wonderful beaches and the water? How can you stand being a landlocked Okie?"

This brought a chuckle. "You've hit a soft spot. I do miss the ocean a great deal. But I travel, so I try to fit in a day at the beach whenever I'm close to one, such as the one at the lake," he added, referring to the day of their picnic.

She didn't want to talk about that day, either. "So why would you choose Tulsa for a base for your recording company? You could live on either coast."

"That's the point. I travel from coast to coast so often that being situated in the center is ideal. The recording industry is doing well here. No big union problems."

She nodded. Everyone in the industry understood the strong unions in Los Angeles.

"Plus the fact that I like it here. It's a nice city."

Ugh, she thought silently. She couldn't wait to get out of here and back to L.A.

&a.

After dinner, he drove to the river and they walked out on the pedestrian bridge. Luckily, the water was up, otherwise the smell of fish would have been overwhelming.

"The nearest thing Tulsa has to the beach," she remarked as they looked out across the water. She remembered the night she strolled out on the beach alone. How clean and beautiful it was. How good it smelled.

She had let Vic take her by the hand as they walked up the stairs and across the street bridge, then down again to the river bridge. Now that they were stopped midway on the bridge, she didn't try to pull away. It was as though she needed to hold onto someone. . .something. . .to try to forget what Dr. Beasley had told her that afternoon.

The bridge was almost deserted. "Monday night is definitely not the most popular night at River Parks," he commented, not looking for an answer.

Monday. It was still only Monday. She gazed out at the shimmering lights reflected on the water. Saturday night at the party seemed ages ago. A soft breeze had come up and there were flashes of lightning off to the south.

"Maybe it'll rain tonight," he said, pointing at the pink lightning.

"Could be heat lightning. With not a drop of rain."

"Heat lightning? What's that?"

She looked at him. His face was softened in the moonlight. "I forget you're not from here. Sometimes in the summer, when it's the hottest, flashes of lightning will flare up, but there's no rain. Daddy used to say those clouds were the 'empties.' It can drive a farmer batty if he's needing a good summer rain."

He looked back out across the water at the clouds. "Hmm. Fascinating. God's handiwork. I marvel at all His creations. The water, the trees, the flowers, the birds, the animals."

Now her hand was enclosed in both of his. He turned to look at her again. "And you. You are one of God's lovely creations. He created such beauty in you, Roshelle, and in your marvelous silken voice."

He brought her hand to his lips and softly kissed it. Then his arms were around her, pulling her gently to him. She could sense his warmth, his tenderness. Softly he kissed her cheeks, caressed her hair, and held her close. A passion welled up in her like nothing she'd ever known before, confusing her.

He lifted her chin and kissed her firmly on the lips. She was enraptured as she eagerly returned his kiss, inhaling his clean, sweet aroma. The opposition she'd so carefully built up against this man was melting away in a matter of moments.

She caught her breath and pulled away, fighting to regain her composure. Her heart was thundering. She wanted to push him away, but she was fearful her legs would not hold her.

"Your hair glows in the moonlight," he whispered as he ran his fingers through it. "Silky. Like the silken sounds of your beautiful singing."

Now she was able to step back from him. "I think I'd better get back. Doesn't the park close soon?"

He glanced at his watch. "You're right. We're about to break curfew." Quietly, he put his arm around her, gently cradling her shoulders as he walked her back to his car.

❧

Both spoke little as he drove from River Parks to her hotel. But when he stopped the car out front, he paused before getting out. "Roshelle, there's something troubling you. Something deep inside. Is there anything I can do?"

She stiffened. How could he possibly know? No one could know. She'd already decided it would be her secret to keep. There was no need to tell anyone. "I've already said I have a few family problems," she said quickly. Send out a decoy to keep him off track. "This trip—coming here—has been difficult."

He wasn't buying it. "No one has a perfect family. I sense it's something deeper."

"There's nothing." She had to find her stage personality. The stage smile. But it was almost impossible—after his kisses and his embrace.

He reached across the car to take her hand. "Please promise me—" he started.

"I'm not real good on keeping promises," she quipped lightly. "I think I've broken almost every one I've ever made."

He ignored her. "Please promise me, if I can ever be of help, that you'll call me." He squeezed her hand. "And meanwhile, whatever it is, I'll be praying for you."

She pulled her hand away. "I'll try to keep that in mind."

Why did he have to be so persistent?

He stayed close by her side as he walked her into the hotel. Stepping inside the heavy front door, Roshelle was shocked to see her mother sitting there in the lobby.

Cora rose to her feet and walked toward them, disapproval and disdain written clearly on her face. "It's about time you showed up."

Chapter Eleven

"Mother. What are you doing here?"

Cora didn't bother to give Vic a glance, but glared at Roshelle. "Your uncle almost dies, and you're out gadding about town. I've been looking for you since late this afternoon." She pointed to her watch for emphasis. It was nearly midnight.

"You have no right—"

"Plus Jane was devastated when you didn't show up for supper at her house. She'd invited friends in and was so disappointed. She spent the evening crying her eyes out because you hurt her so. Have you no feelings at all?"

Janey's phone message from this afternoon. Roshelle had forgotten all about it after she talked to Dr. Beasley. Poor Janey. "How's Uncle Jess now?"

"For all that you care, he pulled through. He took a turn for the worse just after you left. It was probably the bad spirits you bring in with you. I tried to call you to let you know, but you were nowhere to be found. Obviously, you had better things to do than to be concerned about your uncle. After all he's done for you."

"All he's done for me?" Suddenly, anger was smoldering inside her like a rumbling volcano. "All he has done for *me*? Please, please tell me what that could be." She felt her body trembling. Vic moved to take her arm, but she shook him off. "What did that wretched, hateful man ever do for me? Please tell me. I'm consumed with suspense. If he dies in the next five minutes, I will not have lost a thing!"

"Rachel, your attitude is despicable," Cora said in a controlled icy tone. That was always her ploy when Roshelle lived at home—to rouse her to a state of fury, then to act calm and shocked. "You never could hold your temper, Rachel. Always flying off the handle."

Roshelle's voice was loud. People were looking, but she no longer cared. The volcano was spilling over. It was hot and it was terrible. "I tell you what. I'll take my bad spirits, my despicable attitude, and my rotten temper to where you never have to worry about them again. Now, please get out of my sight."

For the first time, Cora looked up at Vic, but said nothing. She looked back at Roshelle. "Your uncle was right about you all along."

Roshelle clenched her fists to keep from clawing and slapping. "Get away from me."

She watched as her mother walked out with her head held high. When she was out of sight, Roshelle stumbled to a nearby couch. Vic took her arm and assisted her.

She sat there stunned, willing her eyes not to shed the tears that were stinging there. She would not let that woman make her cry one more time.

"Not a pretty sight, huh, Mr. Moran?" she mumbled. "And you ask me if something's wrong?" She gave a dry laugh.

"Roshelle," Vic said softly, "you can't let this awful hatred and bitterness continue to build. It'll eat you alive."

"Right. So show me the switch and I'll sure be glad to shut it off."

"The Lord can help you to forgive. To release it. To unload that weight of guilt."

She scooted over away from him. She should have known that, sooner or later, he would start preaching. Guilt, he says, as though she were the guilty one.

"Proverbs says we are not to despise our mothers when they are old. I had to use that verse myself so I know—"

"You don't know anything. Nothing at all. You think you can slap a little Scripture on me like a bandage and it will make everything all right?" She jumped up. "You're no different than she is." She waved in the direction where Cora walked out. "I don't need your phony, plastic religion. For once, Mr. Self-righteous, the perfect Christian doesn't have all the answers. And this time God Himself doesn't have any answers for what's troubling me."

She didn't bother to wait for the elevator, but ran up the service stairs. She was breathless when she reached her room. Quickly she packed her bags and called for the airport shuttle. There were regular flights to Dallas. She'd worry about connections to L.A. after landing in Dallas. By then, she'd be far away from this horrid place—forever!

❦

The DFW airport was fairly empty in the wee hours of the morning. As soon as her flight to L.A. was confirmed, she called Mitzi, awakening her. The sound of her friend's voice was like a refreshing breeze blowing into her cluttered mind. Mitzi could get awake quicker than any other person she'd ever known.

After Roshelle told her the flight number and time of her arrival, Mitzi said, "Newt will be so glad you're coming back this soon. Mr. Laurel, too. They're already talking about shooting sites for the video."

"I'm ready."

"Sure was a short stay. Did everything go all right?"

"As good as could be expected."

"That bad, huh?" Mitzi could see right through her.

"Pretty bad."

"How's old Uncle Jess?"

"I don't know. And I'm not sure I even care."

"It really *was* bad."

"What about the tour? Are the details being hammered out?"

"Hammered is a good word. What a ton of work. I'm not sure who's on the phone the most, Newt or me."

Roshelle was amazed at how well Mitzi had taken the reins of the business matters. "Has Newt contacted Benny yet?"

"We're not that far into negotiations."

"Have him hold off. I need time to sort things out."

There was momentary silence on the other end. "I thought this was the moment you'd been waiting for, Rosh. The moment when the band could be—"

"I know, I know. I can't go into it now, Mitzi. We'll talk when I get there. Okay?"

"Okay. Whatever you say. I'll be at the airport to pick you up."

"Mitzi? Thanks for everything you've done. Everything you do!"

"Hey! You know it's only because there's no one else dumb enough to get mixed up in this zoo." She gave her silly laugh and was gone.

Roshelle bought an entertainment magazine and a cup of coffee and sat down to wait. She preferred the empty airport to the lonely hotel room back in Tulsa.

She flipped through the pages, looking for people she knew. People she'd met on the road, in Las Vegas, and now in L.A. She sucked in a little gasp as she saw her own picture on one of the back pages. It was only a blurb, but there it was. In a few paragraphs, it explained in detail that she was from a small town in Oklahoma and that she had run away from home at an early age. She'd never tried to hide anything, but it was uncanny how they could dig into a person's past and publish it across the country. Someone at the party last Saturday night had told her, "Don't worry when they write what's true about you, worry when they start writing things that aren't true."

Maybe Janey was right. Maybe they would track down her family in Sandott. Wouldn't Cora have a fit? Roshelle couldn't help but smile just thinking about it.

But now Janey and Alex—that was another matter. She never wanted to hurt Janey. But she guessed she already had without even trying. She had failed to call her sister back and clear up the plans for last evening.

She could hear her mother telling Janey, "Rachel would rather go out on the town with a man than spend an evening with her own sister." Or to be more correct her mother would say, ". . .than to spend an evening with her own family."

But that wasn't true. If she'd had a few minutes alone with Janey, she could have explained. Well, not explained totally, but partially. That she couldn't bear to go back to the town of Sandott—ever.

When she got back to L.A., maybe she could call Janey's house. Or even write a little note of apology. But then, with Cora always telling her side of the story, what good would it do? It was useless for Roshelle to try to justify herself or to make lame excuses. And she was weary of doing so.

❧

When the pilot announced they were descending for entry into Los Angeles, Roshelle experienced a new rush of joy. She had everything planned out and she'd rehearsed it along the way. There was no way she could now travel with the band. That was a given.

Benny knew her too well. After one performance, he'd know something was wrong. Correction. After one short rehearsal, he'd know. As soon as Benny found out she'd been told to rest her voice, there would be no more singing. She knew that much for sure. Benny could be very persuasive. But quitting was exactly what she refused to do. She would never quit.

For her, to sing was to live. If she had no more voice, she'd just as soon leave this old world. "I'll sing till I drop," she muttered to herself as she pulled her carry-on out of the overhead compartment.

Sure, Benny would be upset at first that she didn't bring them on board, but he'd get over it. Just like she got over his not coming to be with her in Vegas. That's the way things were in this business, tough for everybody. A person just had to make do.

Mitzi was there at the terminal gate, waiting. Reliable Mitzi. Roshelle gave her a hug. "It's great to be home."

"You were gone only a couple of days."

"Are you sure? It feels like a couple of years," she said. And it had. "Plus the fact that it's great to have a home to come home to."

Mitzi laughed. "You might not be so glad when you see how much has to be done in so short a time."

But she was glad. She wanted to fill every minute of every day so full that she would be exhausted every night. And then sleep like a baby. "What's first on the agenda?"

Mitzi, who now had her driver's license, was weaving through the dense L.A. traffic like a pro. "Newt wants to see you as soon as you get unpacked."

"That I can do."

"He has several fitting sessions set up with Louis for your outfits for the video. He has that agenda at his office. I can't remember when they're all scheduled."

"Filming isn't like stepping into a cut room, is it? Where I can wear my old grungies." A surge of excitement shot through her, as she thought of the upcoming video.

"No. Not like that at all." Mitzi glanced over at her and smiled. "So how was Oklahoma?"

"The same."

"I'm sorry. Sorry it was hard on you. Was your uncle better?"

"This is crazy, but I was never sure. I guess I should have talked to the doctors myself. But I kept taking my mother's word for everything. And I can't always believe her. Anyway, he never roused. Never even knew I was there. It was useless to go. I wish I'd never let her bully me into going in the first place."

"Did you see Mr. What's-his-name with the violets?"

"Actually, I did."

"You're kidding." Mitzi almost drove off the road. "Are you kidding me?"

"I am not kidding."

"Boy, I guess what they say about a small world is really true. Where was he?"

"I stopped by the old recording studio where I first started singing umpteen years ago and, lo and behold, he is now the owner of the place. And he walked right in while I was there."

"Blow me down."

"I agree." Blown down and blown away, Roshelle thought to herself. She had already planned how much she was going to tell Mitzi. So much and no more. Enough to be safe. No need to tell her about the dinner. About the kiss on the river bridge that still burned fresh in her memory. About the argument with her mother. Or the anger she now felt toward Vic. To find that he was nothing but a two-faced hypocrite just like all the rest of them.

Mitzi asked a few more questions about the trip. Roshelle gave a few more vague answers and then turned the conversation back to upcoming business. Dear, polite Mitzi, let it stay there.

❧

Home looked better than ever. Even though she had a meeting scheduled with Newt, she went into her studio and sat down at her piano for a few minutes. She had to get her fingers back on the keys. To play a few powerful numbers. Ones she could really bang out. Songs with rhythm, with a beat, with heart. She made the place reverberate with melodies and reveled in the sense of power it gave her. She sang a few choruses and her throat felt fine, just fine. She was in great shape.

"Are you going to change before going to see Newt?" Mitzi was leaning against the door frame of the studio door. "He won't recognize you in that."

Roshelle stopped playing and looked down. She was still wearing the navy dress. It was a bit rumpled and she was tempted to throw it in the trash. "Don't worry. I'll change."

She dug in her closet for the brightest outfit she could find—the black stretch pants, cobalt blue blouse with the billowy sleeves, and her highest heels. She tied her blond hair back with a designer silk scarf and placed a bright blue, broad-brimmed hat on her head. Now she felt more like herself, she thought as she donned her sunglasses and headed out the door.

❧

In spite of the smog, Southern California had never looked more beautiful. Carefully, she wove through the traffic on the Santa Ana Freeway toward the Valley.

The pictures of myriad stars in Newt's outer office welcomed her back. She stood there a minute, looking around. He'd not put her picture up—yet. But he would. She'd see to that.

The front desk was empty. Sometimes Newt had a girl in as a receptionist/secretary, sometimes he didn't. Usually he ran them off with his gruffness and his penchant for working all hours of the night and day. "This business don't take no holidays," he'd say. "We don't keep no hours."

But he did keep hours—all twenty-four of them. Newt had also never been able to keep a wife. Someone told her he'd had four. He was too attached to his business to have any personal life.

His office door was ajar so she knocked, then peeked in. He barely lifted his head from the papers in front of him. "Ah, there you are. Get yourself in here. We've got business to attend to." He waved her in and motioned her to a chair. A fat chewed cigar was stuck between two fingers.

"Just what I wanted to hear." She seated herself in a leather chair across from his cluttered desk. Newt's office was a mess, but he stayed on top of each minute detail.

He looked up from the work. "What about your sick relative back home? Everything okay?"

He was just being polite, in the brusque way that Newt had about him. He didn't require a full answer, so she simply nodded. "Everything's fine. Mitzi said you had fittings scheduled." She pulled a calendar from her purse. "You want to give those to me first."

"Man, oh man." He shuffled through the papers. "We got so much going on with you, sweets, I hardly know where to start." He pulled up a paper from under the stack. "Here, I'll just give this to you. You keep track of when you and old Louie can get together. That will be one more thing off this desk."

He sailed the fitting schedule across to her. She grabbed it and looked it over. The first session was tomorrow. She'd fill in her calendar when she got home.

"Mitzi tells me you're having second thoughts about the Camp Band. What's up? Why the switcheroo? I thought I heard in your voice you wanted to be back with those boys—wanted it in a big way."

This was the speech she'd rehearsed on the plane. She'd have to be convincing. "The sound I had with Benny," she said slowly, carefully, "and the sound I've developed since I've been singing on my own, aren't quite the same."

"Got your own style now. Is that what you're saying?"

Maybe this was going to be easier than she thought. After all, what did Newt care who she used. "That's right." She gave a little nod.

"Sorta like you outgrew his little bebop band?" He raised one eyebrow.

She sat up. "Oh, no. I didn't mean that at all. Benny doesn't have a bebop band. He's a great musician and a sensitive leader." She stopped short. Had he purposely trapped her?

"A great musician, huh? Sensitive, huh? But you don't want him?"

"No. I mean, it's not like that. I'd like to begin with a new group. . .put together a new band to back me. One that I could have fit in more with my sound. And they wouldn't already be known as a band, like Benny's is." The whole speech was falling apart. She wasn't sure if she was making any sense at all. But no way could she travel this tour with Benny Lee Camp. That's all there was to it.

Newt was still studying her face. "I see. You're the rising star now. I think if you want a new band, we can put together a little band for you. We'll need backup vocalists anyway. So we'll start scouting for the whole herd at one time."

"Will I have any say in choosing them?"

"Opinion, yes. Final say? Probably not."

She gave a little sigh. At least her opinion would count. That would do for starters. And did she want to travel by bus again? he wanted to know.

She shook her head. "Not if I can help it. I think I've paid my dues in the bus torture scene. I'd like to graduate up to flying."

"More expensive, but more expedient." He made notes as they talked.

She gave him her full attention as he began explaining the locations for the video shoots. She made notes in her calendar as he named the days they would devote to the project.

"Hopefully, if the weather cooperates, we'll have this wrapped up before the October tour begins. If not, you'll be flying back and forth to get it finished."

"No problem. I can manage that." She'd been waiting for the right time to mention her new song. Finally, he brought up the subject of the second album.

"I've written a new song, Newt. What are the chances of Mr. Laurel's letting me use it on the newest CD?"

He stopped shuffling papers and leaned back in his chair. "Good girl. You been doing some writing on your own? Old man Laurel will be glad to hear it. Is it a religious song?"

She felt herself stiffen. "Religious? Are you kidding? Of course it's not religious. What a goofy thing to ask me."

"It ain't goofy. Ted Laurel wants you to have one religious number on your next CD. Says you got a bit of a reputation for singing one at the clubs and it's sorta become a trademark of your show. Know what I mean? After all, even Elvis sang religious songs."

A trademark? She couldn't believe this. "I can't. I won't. He can't make me, can he? It's not in the contract or anything." Now she really wished Benny would have looked over that contract before she signed it.

"Of course it's not in the contract. But we didn't figure you'd have a conniption. You sung 'em all over the country for every joint between here and Tuscaloosa." He waved the chewed cigar at her. "How was we to know you'd get bent all out of shape about putting one little religious song on a CD?"

"This is different."

"Women," he muttered. "Never can figure 'em out."

"This is one time I put my foot down. Absolutely no religious songs on my CDs." Her promise to Grandma Riley was for ending performances only. That was all she had promised. She never promised to put one on every record she cut. Her trademark indeed! She'd have to put a stop to that notion immediately. She'd rather be an out and out rank sinner than to be a hypocrite, having people think she was something she wasn't.

"So what about my song?" she asked again. "What are my chances?"

"I'll feel him out and let you know what he says." He ran his fingers through his graying hair. "Only now I'll have to figure out whether to tell him about the new song before or after I tell him you refuse to sing one itsy bitsy little religious number."

But she knew Newt was a manipulator and a negotiator. He sounded miffed, but he was in her corner. If anyone could pave the way with Ted Laurel, Newt could do it.

Chapter Twelve

Rodeo Drive smelled of money. The Beverly Hills Hotel rose to a majestic height and commanded acres of space at Rodeo Drive and Sunset Boulevard. The unmistakable green and pink stucco surrounded by giant palms and lush colorful foliage spoke of elegance and exclusivity.

As Roshelle drove by, she tried to imagine the hundreds of famous faces that had entered there through the years. She had often told herself she cared nothing about all the trappings of fame, that her only passion was to sing. But now she realized the money was nice, very nice. It felt great to be able to buy the things she'd always wanted.

The name SARVIANO ORIGINALS was scrolled in bright red letters across the front of Louis's studio. Roshelle found a parking place nearby and hurried up the front steps for her early morning appointment. As she understood it, Louis had already met with the producers of the music video and costumes had been discussed. Her input was needed.

Now that Roshelle and Louis had been working together for a while, Mitzi was no longer asked to come along as a chaperon. She breezed through the shop and into the back as though she'd been doing this forever. It seemed so right, so natural.

"Hello, gorgeous," Louis called to her as he emerged from a group of bustling workers and racks of dresses. "How's my favorite up-and-coming singer?" He reached for her hand and pecked a kiss on it. "You're looking wonderful as usual."

Roshelle was trying to learn to keep all the gushing industry remarks in perspective, but it sounded so soothing to her ears. "Thanks, Louis. Am I late?"

He released her hand gently. "Perfect timing." His laughing eyes danced and the dimples appeared. "But I wouldn't mind waiting for one as lovely as you."

He had a way of making her blush and when he noticed, his eyes were all the merrier. "What's first on the agenda?" she asked.

"This way." He placed his hand on her waist to guide her back to his office. There they looked over sketches and fabric swatches. He explained what the producers had suggested for each cut on the CD, then he asked her pointed questions. On a yellow legal pad, he took down her comments as she voiced her thoughts and opinions.

Several dresses for the concert tour were ready and each needed a fitting. Little work was needed, however, because he now knew her size and her tastes. Each dress was spectacular, but when he brought out the jade green with the flared mermaid skirt filled with ruffles, she gasped with delight.

"This is wonderful. Too, too wonderful." She ran her hand over the glossy material, which was almost iridescent as it shimmered in the light.

He smiled. "I thought you might like this." He put it up to her. "Perfect with your light skin. When I saw this fabric I knew immediately that I wanted to do something a little special for you."

"A little special? This is more than a little special."

She hurried to the dressing room to slip into it. It fit perfectly. This dress would be a show-stopper for sure. Outside, Louis helped her up onto the small platform before the mirrors, where he could check out every seam. She felt as though her heart were absolutely going to burst. She danced across the platform and laughed as she went. She was floating on a euphoric cloud.

Louis sat back and watched, laughing with her. "It moves well, right?"

She twirled a couple of times and let the ruffled, flared skirt fly. "Perfectly." She looked down at him. "You are truly a genius."

"Even a genius needs something to work with, love. And you are a beautiful creation for me to clothe in my beautiful creations."

❦

The fittings took all morning. As they were finishing up, Louis casually asked if she would have lunch with him.

His invitation was a surprise. She was brushing her hair in front of one of the many mirrors and she brushed back the soft bangs and watched as they fell back on her forehead. "I didn't know busy people like you stopped for lunch," she said.

"You can bet it takes something—or someone—quite exceptional to cause me to stop."

His eyes were always laughing, so it was difficult to tell if he meant it or if he were just going on. But then, what if he were just going on? So what? She had no one to go to lunch with, and it might be fun. Work couldn't always consume her.

The restaurant he chose was just down the street and they walked the distance together. He tucked her arm in his as they strolled together. "I've been listening to all your songs on the CD and I think they're superb," he said, waving his free hand to emphasize the point. "I can see why Ted Laurel is so elated these days. I've not seen him this bubbly in months. You have a natural talent. . .," he paused as he searched for the word, "refreshing, I guess one could say. We hear so much of the other, you know, mediocre singers who are pushed into the spotlight. You seem to be soaring."

Was this true? Was she different? Did she possess a natural talent that could take her to the top? She loved to hear him say it, but was it true? And how could she know?

They chose to sit in the garden amidst the orange and lemon trees beneath the pink-and-white-striped umbrellas. She scanned the menu and marveled. Most of the things listed she'd never tasted, so she deferred the ordering duties to Louis. His favorite, he explained, was escargots baked in baby russet potatoes with hot garlic butter. She flinched, but found it was indeed delicious. She would even learn how to eat like a star.

Louis was a jovial companion and he kept her laughing throughout lunch. His lighthearted and nonsensical bantering was in stark contrast to the heaviness she'd encountered in Tulsa.

He was careful to watch the time, though, and didn't let lunch take her afternoon or his. As he walked her back to where her car was parked, he thanked her with a light kiss on the cheek. "Do you like the beach?" he wanted to know, as he opened the car door for her.

She nodded. "I love the beach."

"How about a Sunday afternoon at the beach? Will you go with me?"

The invitation was tempting—just what she needed—but she remembered the hectic schedule facing her. "I have no idea what's coming up—what all Newt has planned. When the shooting begins, he says we work straight through until it's done."

"And your tour begins soon after, right?" He wet the tip of his finger with his tongue and pretended to be writing on his palm. "Let's see, make a note to fit in time to have one short fling with Louis Sarviano."

She laughed. "I'm sure I'll have a few free moments somewhere, I'm just not sure where. I'll know more next week. Perhaps by the next fitting session." She slipped into her car and looked up at him. A lock of the curly dark hair had carelessly fallen on his forehead. She found herself comparing his face to Vic's, then quickly shut out the thought.

He reached in the car window to take her hand. "Let's shake on that. One of those free moments belongs to me." He squeezed her hand, then let her go. His laughing smile was etched in her brain as she drove home.

Louis was a highly successful man in the industry, in fact, top of the line in his business. He'd probably met hundreds of stars and yet he wanted to be with her. She was amazed.

❧

With joy and exuberance, Roshelle threw herself into the filming sessions. Up early, into bed late, she loved every waking second of the work. The drama of acting out the parts fascinated her. Other singers had advanced from singing into acting, perhaps it would happen with her as well.

These were the thoughts that ran through her mind while she was on location, lip-synching her own songs as the tapes were rolling. One location was on the craggy rocks above the pounding surf near Santa Barbara. The rugged beauty of the area was magnificent. The wind wildly blew her hair, but it was just the effect the producers wanted.

Roshelle made up her mind she would ask around about acting school. She wanted to know more and more about this business of acting, as well as music. She already knew how to put herself into the mood and message of a song and probably it wouldn't be much different to put herself into a character and act out a part. She savored the delicious thought. There was so much to this magical kingdom—and she wanted more!

Phone calls and cards had come from Victor Moran. She sent the cards back and failed to return the calls. Hopefully, their paths would never cross again. Seldom did she think about Dr. Beasley's words spoken to her that day in Tulsa and his warning went unheeded. She worked hard to forget everything that had happened in Tulsa. Only late at night, when she had trouble sleeping, did she feel the fear creep back in. The pain pills helped some, but the discomfort in her throat never went away completely. Staying busy was the answer; sometimes using sleeping pills was part of the answer as well.

One sunny Sunday, she called Louis to let him know she had the day free. She hesitated at first to call, wondering if he'd been serious, but his infectious laughter and quick acceptance extinguished her doubts.

They took the Pacific Coast Freeway to Laguna Beach, where their lunch was served on a brick-tiled patio overlooking the azure Pacific. The restaurant patio was furnished with white tables and chairs, each chair padded with a bright blue cushion. White grilled ironwork fences enclosed the eating area, with pots of red geraniums perched on each support post. Down from the restaurant, Roshelle could see hundreds of sun worshippers enjoying the sandy beach and the magnificent waves. The lazy atmosphere relaxed her right down to her bones.

"You look even more lovely with that half-smile on your lips," Louis said as he sipped his wine. "Tell me what you're thinking."

"To be truthful, I wasn't thinking. I feel so rested here, it seems like work just to think."

He laughed. "You have been working hard, Roshelle. You need to take time for yourself. Like me. I give myself several play days each month."

"Play days?" She stirred a glass of iced mocha, having chosen to forego the liquor.

"Days in which I do nothing but play all day. Deep-sea fishing, snorkeling, scuba diving, swimming, tennis, you name it."

"Your play sounds as hard as your work," she retorted. Louis exuded a sense of vitality and kinetic energy. He made her feel excited just being around him.

He cocked his head as if to think about her remark. "I suppose you're right. I don't do anything halfway. I work hard and play hard."

After they had finished their cold plates consisting of cheeses, melons, boiled eggs, and slaw, Louis took her hand to walk down to the beach. He told her funny stories of the stars with whom he had worked and stories of how he started his business as a boy in high school.

"Think about it," he said, as they spread their bright towels on the warm sand, "a boy who thinks about, talks about, and sketches women's dresses isn't going to be all that popular, right? Right. And my little Italian mama wanted me to open a restaurant like my uncle Primo. My big old papa, he just says, 'Please boy, do *anything* but draw pictures of ladies nighties.'" He laughed at his own pantomime to describe his father and she laughed with him. She doffed her white eyelet coverup, and he gave a whistle. "Love that swimsuit, Rosh. Looks great on you."

She flopped down on her stomach on her towel. He pulled the bottle of tanning lotion from her bag, poured an ample handful, and proceeded to apply it to her back in gentle circular motions. "I didn't have too much support for my singing when I was a kid, either," she told him.

"You don't say," he said as he continued to apply the lotion down her shoulders and arms. "As beautiful as you sing, I would think your family would have been very proud."

"As long as I sang what they wanted me to sing, I was okay."

"And what was that?"

"Church music."

He gave a little grunt of understanding. "Ah, and that's all? Nothing else? No other kinds of music."

"You got it."

"What a pity." He gave her a little shake. "Come on, Miss Ramone, you need to learn how to float the waves."

"But I was just getting comfortable," she protested, not wanting to move. She had sunk comfortably into the depression of the soft sand and felt she could sleep the afternoon away.

"But the waves are calling." He then flopped her over and before she knew what was happening, she was bundled up in his muscular arms and he was headed to the water.

At first she fought and protested, then she laughed and giggled. He carried her right into the warm foamy waves. "Hold your breath," he warned as he plunged them both into the ocean water. She screamed with delight.

They spent the afternoon playing in the waves. He taught her how to ride the waves in and commended her for her quick learning. She told him about learning to swim in Grandma Riley's pond and how adept she became at diving off the old wooden dock. "I should have been born by the ocean," she said as they ran dripping to the towels. "I feel cheated." She sat down and pushed her hair back out of her eyes.

"But now you have the happy California sun and surf at your doorstep to make up for it," he said. He wrapped an extra towel around her shoulders and as he did, he easily pushed her back on the sand and leaned across her and began to kiss her. "And you have Louis to make up for another lack in your life, too," he whispered to her between the kisses.

At first the fiery kisses were exciting to her, but as they became more demanding and intimate, she tried to push him off. "Please, Louis," she protested. "This is too soon. Too fast."

He stopped kissing her, but his face was close to hers, his blue eyes still dancing. "Fast is how things are done here," he said softly. "And I'm not used to any woman saying 'stop' to me."

"This one is saying 'stop.' Please."

Reluctantly, he loosened his hold, but kept his arm around her. "Sort of an old-fashioned girl, aren't you?" he said with a touch of amazement.

It was odd to hear him say that. She wanted to think she was as contemporary as all the others in this business, but maybe she wasn't. If Benny were here, he'd take this guy to the laundry and hang him out to dry.

He lightly kissed her nose. "All right then, I'll take things a little slower from now on," he said.

The incident put only a small damper on the rest of the day. In spite of the scare, Roshelle was still glad she went with him. Learning to float the waves had been worth it.

❧

Yet another appearance in Vegas was squeezed in, for which she was thankful. She needed to be sure, before the tour, that she still had the punch it took to deliver the goods to a live audience. The response left no doubt in her mind. Due to the album, the crowds were bigger than ever. Newt also wanted a chance for her to work with the new band and the backup singers. He even flew to Vegas to catch one of the shows so he could see for himself. He gave them all a "thumbs up."

"Guess you were right about needing a new sound," he told her after the show. "This band is terrific."

She chafed at his comments, feeling guilty for having cut Benny out. She'd not talked to him for weeks and she avoided asking Newt about the Camp Band at all. It was less painful that way.

The first week in October, she flew to Cleveland for the first leg of the tour; Mitzi was by her side. The tour was vastly different than traveling by bus to noisy clubs where few people listened. These were concerts where the people purchased tickets just to come and hear her sing. She often thought of that mockingbird on the tiny tip-top limb. She was shaky at times, but she would sing her heart out.

Each night she was in a different city. Toledo, Detroit, Columbus, Pittsburgh—the cities all began to bleed together after awhile. The spotlights, the applause, the heady music, the well-wishers, the autograph seekers—it was infectious and intoxicating.

By the end of the second week, Roshelle was beginning to feel the effects of the strain. She was backstage after the show in Minneapolis when she realized she was out of pain medication. She'd been in touch with Dr. Beasley only to refill the prescription; eventually, she'd have to see a physician in L.A. in order to get the prescription there.

She had gone to great lengths to hide the pills and the phone calls from Mitzi. Dear Mitzi, who knew more about her business than she did. Why hadn't she kept closer watch on the pills? She was angry at herself and her nerves felt jumpy. She was starting to slip out of her finale dress when suddenly there was a knock at the dressing room door. Mitzi ran to get it.

"It's security," she called back over her shoulder to Roshelle. "You know anyone by the name of Ingram?"

"You know all the people I know," she snapped back. "You tell me."

"Ingram, Ingram," Mitzi said, then shook her head. "Sorry, Miss Ramone doesn't know anyone by that name." She closed the door.

In a moment there was another knock. Roshelle could hear the voice of the security man again. "This Ingram dame says she's a sister to Miss Ramone."

Roshelle jumped up from where she was sitting. "It's Janey!"

Chapter Thirteen

There was a tumble of laughter and introductions as Janey was let in with the sleeping Darla slung over her shoulder like a sack of flour. The other shoulder was weighted down with a diaper bag.

"Did you jostle through that crowd with the baby? Your arms must be killing you. Here, lay her down on the settee. What are you doing in Minneapolis? Are you alone?" The questions spilled out of Roshelle as she felt new bubbly joy rising up inside her. Her own little sister, right here in Minneapolis.

Carefully, Janey unloaded the precious bundle. Almost before the baby was down, Mitzi was kneeling down by the settee. "She's beautiful," she said as she touched the cheek, red from where it had lain against Janey's shoulder. "Isn't she beautiful, Rosh? Your own little niece." She looked up from where she sat on the floor. "I want to have at least four."

Rosh was surprised. "Four babies?"

"Sure. Why not?"

Mitzi had never spoken of her own future plans in life. She was so intertwined into Roshelle's business, the subject never came up.

"We're here visiting Alex's parents when we saw in the paper about your concert," Janey explained. "I had to come and see. You're wonderful! Just wonderful. And all those people love you."

"You *paid* for tickets?"

"Of course. How else do you get in?"

"Silly girl, if you'd called, I would have given you tickets."

"It was hard enough just getting back here," Janey said with a little laugh. "Besides, Mom explained that it was almost impossible to get hold of you, so I didn't even bother."

Roshelle felt a twinge of uneasiness. In keeping distanced from her mother and Uncle Jess, she'd inadvertently cut Janey off as well. But she never meant to. "I'm so sorry I didn't call you back when I was in Tulsa in August," Roshelle began to explain.

Janey waved away the apology. "Hey, I knew you were busy. It was Mother who insisted I have the little dinner."

"Mother? But she said—"

The rousing Darla interrupted her. The tiny face screwed up into the beginnings of a cry. "She'll be ready for a bottle," Janey said, digging in the bag.

"Oh, can I?" Mitzi asked. "How about if I take Darla into one of the other dressing rooms so the two of you can talk awhile."

"Better than that, can you come over to the hotel and stay for the night?" Roshelle asked.

Janey shook her head. "Alex is waiting. We have to get back to his folks' place. We agreed that I'd come back and let you see Darla for a few minutes. I wasn't even sure I could get in."

"I'm sorry," Roshelle apologized again, thinking of her little sister struggling to get in to see her. If she were in her shoes, Roshelle wasn't sure she'd have bothered.

Roshelle watched as Mitzi eagerly took baby and bottle off by herself. "I can do this. I had scads of younger siblings. I was raised as a baby-sitter," she said proudly as she marched out the door.

"Janey, I did plan to call you that night. Something came up."

"For such a versatile singer, you sure are hung up on one note. Is that the only song you can sing?" Janey gave her sister a hug. "Forget all that. Let's talk about this dress. I can't believe how beautiful you look." She put her hands on Roshelle's shoulders and turned her around slowly. "Is this made just for you? I mean, you don't pick these things off a rack somewhere, right?"

"It's made exclusively for me. I have a wardrobe stylist who works with me."

Janey mouthed the words "wardrobe stylist" without speaking, then rolled her eyes. "And all the band and the singers. Do you travel with all of them?"

"All over the country."

"I'm so proud of you. I have your CD and play it constantly. I love to think back and remember how you used to sit at the piano and sing for hours. I knew you would be great. I've told Alex all about you. He's proud of me for having a sister like you."

Janey's open adoration was making her uncomfortable. She steered Janey toward the settee and motioned for her to sit down. "How's Uncle Jess?" she asked to change the subject. She stepped behind the screen to slip out of the dress and into her satin robe. Sitting at the dressing table, she began dipping into the makeup remover and smearing it on her face.

"He's better. He rallied soon after your visit and went home the next week. He still uses a walker, but he's stronger every day."

"But Mother made it seem. . ." She didn't finish.

"He was dangerously ill. She was right about that. The first reports weren't good at all. We were all pretty frightened."

"Okay, that was genuine. What about her telling me that you cried all evening because I didn't come out to Sandott to see you?"

Janey smiled. "That was one of her exaggerations. If I'd known, I'd have told you there was no pressure on you to come. I didn't realize what she was doing."

Roshelle marveled at her sister's serenity. "What you call an exaggeration, I call a lie. How can you stand to live near her?" She knew the answer to that question before she spoke it. After all, Janey always got along with everyone.

"It's not always easy," Janey admitted. "But you know how hurt and wounded she is. You probably know much better than I do."

Hurt and wounded? Cora Rayford? Hurting and wounding *others* was closer to the truth.

"She's harder on herself than anyone," Janey went on. "She blames herself for so many things gone wrong. The guilt's beginning to take its toll."

"You'll excuse me if I don't get out my crying towel," Roshelle remarked, grabbing for a tissue and waving it.

"Everyone makes mistakes," Janey countered. "She did what she thought was right."

"Please, spare me." Roshelle swiped at the remover, whisking off the heavy stage makeup. "She's as hard as nails. What she 'thought was right' nearly drove me to suicide. She and Uncle Jess are both the type who know how everyone *else* should live. They're miserable, so they set out to make life miserable for everyone else."

Janey rose and stepped over to the makeup mirror. "It's not an unsolvable problem." She gave a little laugh. "Mother detested Alex when I first met him and she tried every way in the world to scare him off. But we hung in there. Now she brags about her intelligent son-in-law. Alex and I are praying for the Lord to heal her wounds and change her life. To bring her joy back again."

Roshelle gave a snort. "Again? What makes you think she ever had any?" She glanced up in the mirror at Janey standing behind her. She regretted the words as soon as she saw the look on Janey's face. She whirled around. "Hey Janey, I'm sorry. I love you, Sis, but please don't come in her harping about Mother. Frankly I don't *care* if she changes from the mean witch into the kind witch. I work hard each day to not even think about her *or* Uncle Jess. Their ideas of religion make me ill."

Janey gave a little sigh. "I know sometimes they don't do a very good job of it." Then she smiled. "But that's what I love about Jesus so much. He doesn't let us into heaven on the basis of how other people live out their faith."

Roshelle was relieved that Mitzi and the baby came back in at that moment. Mitzi held up the empty bottle like a banner. "She took every drop."

"Thanks so much," Janey said. "I never expected a ready-made baby-sitter backstage."

"This was a pleasure. What a little doll," Mitzi said, planting mushy kisses all over the baby's face. "She's so good. All the noise in this crazy place, and it doesn't faze her."

"You don't have to tell me," Janey said, chuckling. "I'm already convinced."

"Rosh, you have a darling niece," she said to Roshelle, who was now changed and in her street makeup. "Here, hold her a minute. I didn't mean to hog her."

Darla was cooing and chewing on her fist. Roshelle breathed in the good aromas of baby as she took her into her arms. "She looks like you," Roshelle told Janey.

"That's what everyone says." The pride was evident in her voice.

Roshelle caressed the baby's hair with her lips. She had almost forgotten the exquisite downy softness of a baby's hair and skin. "Mmm, you smell so good and feel so soft." And Darla replied with a little gurgle that sounded almost like a laugh.

"I must get out to where Alex is waiting," Janey told them. "He's a sweet, patient guy, but I'm not sure he's *this* patient."

Reluctantly, Roshelle handed the baby back. There's something about a baby, she thought, that speaks of peace and quiet trust.

There were hugs, a few tears, and sweet good-byes. Roshelle gave Newt's office number to Janey and said, "He always knows where I am. If you need me, call him."

"I will, Rosh," Janey said with a catch in her voice.

￼

The momentum of the tour continued to build and reviews were strong and positive. There 'were big cities and midsize cities; there were large civic centers and smaller theaters; there were lavish dressing rooms and more decrepit dressing rooms; there were receptive audiences and then there were wild audiences. For the most part, she was received with open arms. She gave phone interviews, backstage interviews, and even a couple of hotel lobby interviews. Almost overnight, it seemed that the whole world wanted to see and talk to Roshelle Ramone.

As the mild fall weather turned sharply cooler, the tour advanced southward. For this, Roshelle was thankful to Newt. He now knew how much she detested cold weather.

Suddenly one night they were in Miami, and she remembered back to the time they played the nightclub in the beachfront hotel. That was the night Benny got so bent out of shape because of Vic. Poor Benny. And Keel met her out on the beach and, in his left-handed sort of way, tried to talk her into marrying Benny.

She thought of Benny and the band and wondered where they were and how they were doing. She supposed a girl could do a lot worse than marry someone like Benny. He was steady, reliable, and fiercely loyal. Her conscience pricked her now whenever she thought of how she avoided calling him before the tour and she had to continually remind herself why she hadn't. But the guilt never lessened.

And it was in Miami where she first met Victor. It occurred to her that he might try to see her again here in Miami; it seemed like something Victor Moran might do. She had an idea he probably tracked the route of her tour. He had finally stopped trying to call her and the lavender cards had stopped coming as well. That was a relief. At least she thought it was a relief. Sometimes, as she directed Mitzi to return one, she found herself wondering what he might have written inside.

But, thankfully, Vic wasn't in Miami and after the Miami stint, Newt had scheduled a few days' break. Heaving big sighs of relief, she and Mitzi caught a plane for L.A.

"I think I'll sleep for days," Roshelle said as the plane touched down in beautiful Southern California.

"I think I'll grill a chicken and eat the whole thing." Mitzi seemed to hate restaurant food worse than any other part of the tour. Not that she was a big eater, just the opposite. She was a picky eater and enjoyed her own cooking more than any other. In the few short months since they'd had their own place, she was constantly throwing together superb dishes.

Roshelle was always surprised at how "homey" Mitzi was. And yet she braved the traumas of travel like a trouper. She needed to do something special for her friend to say thank you. Now that there were a few free days, perhaps there would be time to shop for a nice gift for Mitzi. But, before she could purchase one, she, herself, became the recipient of a gift.

The evening they arrived home, Louis Sarviano came to visit. She and Mitzi were in the living room with their feet up, going on and on about how good it was to be home. In spite of her protests, he insisted she change and go with him to supper. Roshelle knew what that meant—dress *up*.

Mitzi seemed amused at the whole thing. "Want me to help you pick out your outfit? Or stay here and entertain your guest?" she asked with a smile.

"Help me pick out an outfit, *then* come back and entertain my guest."

Mitzi giggled as she loped up the stairs, two at a time.

They decided on the silk, double-breasted, pale pink coat that went best with her pearls. Dressy, but still comfortable.

Louis took her to one of the "seen and be seen" spots in Beverly Hills and she was not sorry she had accepted his invitation. In fact, as soon as she was seated in his Porsche coupe, he began his light, funny bantering and she realized she had actually missed him.

The evening was beautiful and the maitre d' quickly knew that Mr. Sarviano wanted a table for two on the restaurant terrace. Ever since the day at the beach, he'd been every inch a gentleman, as though he wanted to respect her wishes.

Following dinner, he took her on a drive to the beach. There, on a spot overlooking the moonlit water, he presented her with a diamond bracelet.

"It's just a little thing," he said, almost apologetically, "but somehow I wanted to give you a token of how much I care about you."

Roshelle was stunned. This was so sudden. She looked at this wildly handsome man with the dimples, flashing smile, and dark curls. Any woman in her right mind would be thrilled to be seen with him, let alone receive his attention in this way.

Before she could speak, he had the bracelet out of the box and was fastening it on her wrist. It fit perfectly.

"Your wrist is so tiny," he said, kissing her hand softly. "I knew to get a small size."

"Thank you, Louis. It's so beautiful. I don't know what to say."

He put his fingers to her lips. "You don't have to say anything right now. Just give me a chance."

"A chance?"

"A chance to get to know you, for you to know me. A chance to build a relationship."

"That's going to be difficult with the schedules we keep." She wasn't even sure she wanted to give him a chance. Her mind was spinning.

"Difficult, maybe. Impossible? Never."

She looked at the bracelet on her arm, sparkling even in the dim light of the moon. "I can't keep this, Louis—"

"Nonsense. This is a gift to show you I care. It has no strings attached." He lifted his hands up in surrender. "What do I have to say?" His eyes danced as he laughed. "You've done a number on me, Roshelle. And I didn't even realize it until you were gone all those weeks." He reached out to take her hand again, touching the bracelet. "I'm falling in love with you, Roshelle. If I hadn't thought I'd scare you completely away, it would have been a ring rather than a bracelet." Then he kissed her. Not with the violence she had experienced on the beach, but gently and sweetly.

❧

The next day, when Mitzi saw the bracelet and heard the news, she was ecstatic. "Rosh, you've blown this guy away. All these dames he's been working with for years, but you walk in and knock him cold in one swoop. Way to go!"

"But, Mitzi, I'm not in love with this guy. He wants to build a serious relationship and I want to build a career."

Mitzi gave a flip of her hand. "Get to know him, marry his money, and sing for a hobby."

"You're no help." She perched on a kitchen bar stool and watched as Mitzi whipped up a soufflé for their breakfast.

"I'm kidding, silly." She whipped the eggs with a vengeance. "Just because a guy likes you, or even falls in love with you, is no reason you have to *do* anything. Just let it ride and see what happens. In fact, the next time he asks you out you could say, 'No, read my lips, spelled N-O!' "

Roshelle took a swallow of hot coffee. "Of course, you're right." She laughed. "I hadn't thought of that."

A phone call from Newt interrupted their conversation. "Hey, sweets! Got a meeting lined up for you this afternoon. A recording company interested in you cutting a CD for them."

"But Newt, I'm signed with Laurel."

"Only for two. Life will go on after the second album, you know. I've worked with this guy some before. He knows his business. This afternoon at three. Okay?"

"I'll be there."

She hung up as Mitzi pushed the steamy soufflé in front of her. She stabbed at it with her fork. "And I said I was going to rest for these few days."

"No rest for the wicked," quipped Mitzi as she touched the gleaming bracelet dangling on Roshelle's arm.

❧

Roshelle rolled up the sleeves on the long, loose-fitting jacket she had pulled on over her gabardine slacks and her checkered shirt.

As she headed for the front door, Mitzi called out to her. "Wait a minute. Where are you going in that getup?"

"To Newt's office."

"I thought you said he had a guy interested in working with you."

"He does."

Mitzi stood leaning against the door frame with her arms folded, shaking her head.

Roshelle looked down at her outfit. "Not right, huh?"

"Not unless you're applying for housekeeper."

Roshelle sighed. "Must be a backlash. Never thought I'd tire of pretty dresses and spike heels."

Mitzi walked over and put her arm around Roshelle's shoulder. "Come on. Maybe Mama Mitzi can help little Roshie find a compromise."

Later, when Roshelle stepped out of her car in the parking lot at Newt's office she felt much more sure of herself dressed in the navy-and-rose, floral-print dress with a sweeping skirt. Mitzi helped her fix a lacy rose ribbon that caught her hair at the nape of her neck. With a bit of new excitement, she strolled into the familiar cluttered office.

There was now a young girl at the desk, which meant Newt was trying out another one. Before the girl could even announce Roshelle's arrival, he was hollering at her to come on in.

She walked through the door to see Vic sitting there, smiling at her.

Chapter Fourteen

"Hey, sweets, you're looking great." Newt came from around his desk to give her a hug. "Come on in here. I want you to meet an old business friend of mine, Victor Moran." He led her to the leather chair beside Vic and seated her there.

Her body was tense. She'd been put on the defensive and she didn't like it. What right did he have to come here like this? "Your 'old business friend' and I have met," she said, not bothering to keep the ice from her voice.

"That right?" Newt was back around the opposite side of the cluttered desk. He sunk into his squeaky chair. "Mr. Moran never told me that."

"Mr. Hardcastle never asked," Vic said in that quiet, even way of his.

Roshelle had never seen Newt ruffled, but now he seemed to be stifling a grin. It made her even more irritated. "What's going on here?" she demanded.

Newt, obviously sensing her irritation, shrugged to show his innocence in the matter. "This is a business meeting, sweets, pure and simple. Mr. Moran here called and asked if we could talk about your cutting a CD for his company."

"But his company puts out religious music."

"I told him you wouldn't be too keen on the notion," Newt said. "If you won't do it for Ted Laurel, I was sure you wouldn't do it for no stranger. That's what I told him." He punctuated the remarks with the chewed cigar and leaned back in the chair. "Course that was when I didn't know he wasn't no stranger."

"You told him exactly right," she said, not looking at Vic.

"Hey now, slow down," Newt said. "The guy's come all this way. Why not let's give him a chance to speak his piece."

"Let's do," Vic agreed.

Roshelle allowed her silence to indicate her reluctant agreement.

"I've come to offer you a contract to cut a CD for the Moran label of all inspirational songs." Vic drew a paper from his pocket. "I have all the paperwork right here."

"I looked at it," Newt put in. "It ain't bad."

She took a breath to speak, but Vic jumped back in. "There are so many hurting people out there, Roshelle," his quiet voice went on. "I saw how your voice and your style can touch listeners. That night in Vegas, you were able to touch them in the midst of all the clamor and hoopla. They were deeply moved." He paused a moment. "But I not only heard it, I felt it, too. An album like this could help so many people."

"Aw, come on, sweets. What's a few religious songs? Even Elvis—"

"I know, I know. Even Elvis Presley sang religious songs. The answer is no."

"But you been singing one a night for years," Newt protested. "It don't make no sense."

"I won't be a hypocrite." Now she looked at Vic. "I told you the very first time I met you why I sing a hymn after every performance. I promised my grandma Riley before she died that I would. But I didn't make her any promises about records. The more I do this, the more people will think I'm some kind of religious spokesperson, and I'm not. I don't want to be known like that. And you're tempting me to even give up singing hymns in live concerts. It's already causing misunderstandings!"

She stood as she turned to Newt. "And you should have known better than to have even considered it. The next time please check with me first, or I'll. . . I'll be looking for a new agent." She shut the door hard as she walked out.

"The nerve of some people," she muttered as the receptionist stared at her.

❧

She fussed and fumed all the way back to the house. She was sorry she ever called Vic when she was in Tulsa. Sorry she ever went out with him. And sorry she ever let him kiss her. She wished she'd never told him anything about herself. "Me? Helping hurting people? What a laugh."

As soon as she stepped in the front door, Mitzi was calling to her. "Newt wants you to call right away. What happened when you were there? The old toughie seems almost beside himself."

She threw down her tote bag on the couch and dialed the number. She was even angrier at Vic for making her upset at her own agent.

"Look," he said as his voice came on the line, "I'm really sorry, sweets. He never told me you two knew each other. And I never knew none of this stuff about your old dying granny. You oughta tell me these things. I can't read your mind, you know."

She was sorry she'd blown up at Newt. It certainly wasn't his fault. "I'm sorry, too, Newt. Sorry I let that guy get me rankled at you. But you have to watch his kind. They can be really sneaky."

"Right. I ain't used to working with no religious folk. In fact, I worked with Moran before he got religion."

"Really?"

"Yeah, when his old man was still bankrolling him."

"Why did he stop? The father, I mean."

"The way I heard it, when Moran got religion—it was in all the papers—

his whole family disowned him. Pushed him right out of the nest and took away the gravy train. One day he was a millionaire playboy with a few Miami nightspots as his toys, the next day, a penniless nobody."

Roshelle tried to assimilate this information into the midst of the anger she was feeling. After all, what did she care what kind of family he came from or what kind of treatment he'd received?

Newt didn't stop to catch his breath before he jumped into the next subject. "But I called to tell you terrific good news. This'll make you forget this afternoon ever happened." He let a meaningful moment of silence lapse to emphasize the buildup. "You ready for this? I got you on the Freddie Fremont talk show."

She let out a squeal. "Oh, Newt, you're great. When?" Fremont's late night show was a prime-time spot.

Mitzi was standing nearby with a questioning look. Roshelle mouthed, "Freddie Fremont show," and Mitzi gave a whoop.

"The week after the tour is finished. Perfect timing, if you ask me," Newt was saying.

"Perfect," she agreed.

Before hanging up, Newt asked, "Say, just for the record, what did the religious dude mean about that night in Vegas? I mean, he must have felt or seen something."

"Newt, my friend, I have no earthly idea. Must have been his overactive imagination."

But, as she hung up the phone, she knew that was a lie. Vic was talking about the moving of the Holy Spirit. She'd felt it many times as a girl, before Daddy died. And she'd felt it that night in Vegas.

❧

Roshelle made sure before they went on the road again that she was well stocked with her pain medication—along with the blessed sleeping pills.

The last part of the tour was a swing through the south, and it was almost better than the first. Now she felt more like a veteran; now she knew the ropes. Both she and Mitzi were learning how to cope with the demands of the grueling pace.

Two weeks before Thanksgiving, the tour came to a close. Their last night was a whiz-bang show in New Orleans and Roshelle was ecstatic. As Newt had said, it was the perfect time to be on Freddie's show.

She was more nervous backstage at the television studio than she'd been at her own concerts. She studied her dress in the full-length mirrors. The black velvet, fitted bodice had a sweetheart neckline, puffed sleeves, and a touch of golden lace at the dropped waist. The full skirt of gold-dotted black taffeta shimmered and swished as she gently turned about.

Suddenly, she was terrified—she was a singer not a speaker. Even though she'd gone over things with Newt and the public relations people, she still felt uneasy.

Her biggest fear was that he'd ask her about singing the hymns and so she came up with several rational answers to give him. But she needn't have bothered, because the subject was never touched. Only later did she realize that people like Freddie cared little about such matters.

Her entry song was received with enthusiastic applause by the live studio audience. That was the best part of the show.

When she was seated, Freddie asked various general questions about her exploding career. They talked about the tour and its success and the album and its success. The name of the album was mentioned several times, as was the title of her hit song. These are the things Newt said were important.

"Your fans gotta know what to go buy," he had told her during the briefing.

Just when the interview seemed wrapped up and she was happy about every part of it, Freddie said, "And now I understand there are wedding bells ringing in your life."

Nothing he could have said would have shocked her more. Her mind went blank. This had not been rehearsed. It hadn't even been discussed. "You must have the wrong woman," she said when her composure was regained. "Marriage is low on my 'things to do' list."

"Aw now, come on. You don't need to be shy with us. Everyone knows you and Beverly Hills's most eminent dress designer, Louis Sarviano, are a hot number these days."

Louis? How could anyone know of us, she thought to herself.

"How handy to have your own designer as your mate. Seems to go together rather nicely, I think," Freddie went on. "Did he design this little number you have on?" He waved his hand toward her black dress.

"No," she answered quickly. "He didn't." How could she clear this up before it went any further?

"But he has designed many of your stage costumes, right?"

She nodded. "Louis is a genius when it comes to dress designs, but—"

"And he had something to do with this little number, too, right?" He reached out to where her arm was leaning on his desk and touched the diamond bracelet.

Roshelle thrashed about in her mind for something to say, while striving to maintain her stage smile. "The bracelet was a gift from Louis, but it's not what you think."

"What *I* think?" Freddie turned to the audience. "Just look at this hunk of ice," he said as the nearest camera zoomed in on her wrist. "And she wants us to think this isn't serious." He got the ripple of laughter he sought and appeared pleased.

And Newt had told her that Freddie was a friendly interviewer, she thought.

He obviously sensed her discomfort and was going for more. "We'll try to get the famous Mr. Sarviano on here in a few weeks to tell his side of this story. What do you think?" The audience cheered and applauded. He turned back to Roshelle with a sardonic smile. "Personally, I think the two of you would make a striking twosome." Again he fished for audience response, and again they applauded their full agreement.

"Much as I'd like to play along with this little game," she said with more force than before, "I'll have to tell you that I have no intention of marrying Mr. Sarviano. We're friends and friends only."

"But he has asked, we understand." Freddie was relentless.

"No," she could say quite honestly. "He has never asked. There's no place in my life for marriage at this time."

It seemed like an eternity before he finally said, "We'll be right back after this announcement."

Due to the live audience, Roshelle had no opportunity to say to Freddie what she was thinking and she was quickly escorted off.

❧

Mitzi had made the decision to stay at the house and watch the airing from there. Roshelle had agreed. "No need for you to follow me across town," she'd said. "Take a break."

As she drove out of the Valley and back across L.A. in the late night hours, she continued to wonder how Freddie could have known about the bracelet. Not even Newt was aware of the gift.

Mitzi was at the door to meet her when she came in. "Are you all right?" Her friend was nearly as upset as she was.

"I think so." Roshelle threw her wrap across the chair and collapsed onto the soft couch. "Can you believe that guy? Creating a story and then using it to bait those people in the audience."

"Well, fasten your seat belt, Rosh. That was mild compared to this."

Roshelle straightened. "What are you talking about?"

Mitzi reached into the nearby magazine rack and pulled out the latest tabloid and held it up for her to see.

Roshelle's hand flew to her mouth. "Oh, no! Mitzi, no."

The headlines screamed, LAUREL'S NEWEST RECORDING STAR FINDS THE LOVE OF HER LIFE. Beneath the headlines were photos—several photos. One was of her and Louis eating on the terrace at the Beverly Hills restaurant the night he gave her the bracelet. Several were of the two of them running and laughing on the beach. But the worst photo of all was the one of the two of them lying entwined on the towels at the moment he kissed her. The caption beneath read: "Lovely new recording artist, Roshelle Ramone, romping at Laguna with internationally known Louis Sarviano."

Chapter Fifteen

The cold truth slowly seeped into her brain. In a matter of days, this tabloid would be on the shelves of every grocery store in every city in the nation. And where there was one, there would be ten more with the same story. Like wildfire in an Oklahoma hayfield in August, there was no way to stop it.

She felt sick and saddened. This wasn't how she planned to be known throughout the country. Suddenly, she realized how inexperienced and vulnerable she really was. She'd been told this was a crazy business, but she hadn't counted on its being this crazy.

Slowly, she stood to her feet. "I think I know who's at the bottom of this," she said. "I have a phone call to make."

She closed herself in her studio and dialed Louis's number. "Do they pay you for divulging the information or do you just stage these little acts purely for pleasure?" she demanded as soon as she heard his voice on the line.

"Roshelle? You sound unhappy. Tell Louis what's the matter."

"How could you do this to me? You staged this whole act and then called the photographers to stand by to get every shot they needed. Now it's not only aired on prime-time, live TV, but in every trashy tabloid from here to Long Island."

"Now, now," he cooed. "It wasn't quite that cut and dried. Nothing I ever said to you was a lie. I care for you a great deal."

"You expect me to believe that after all this?"

"Sweetheart, calm down. Don't you realize this is the best thing that could have happened to you? I know at least a dozen other greenhorns in this business who would give a right arm for this kind of publicity. I thought you'd be thrilled."

"You thought wrong," she snapped back.

"Roshelle, having your name out there just isn't enough these days. You have to create a gimmick, something to rouse interest. Even if you and I never saw one another again, this gives your public something to think about. . .something concrete to connect with your name.

"Excuse my modesty," he went on, "but being connected to the name of Sarviano will take you to the heights quicker than twenty successful albums combined. And I *do* care about you, that's why when the public relations people suggested to me—"

"You have the audacity to tell me they asked you to do this?"

"They merely asked my opinion about the best way to market you."

"Market me?" She felt like screaming. "Market me? I'm not a pound of sausage."

"In this business, you are closer to that than you might want to think, my dear." He paused a moment. "When they asked me, I felt you would be safer with me than anyone. And I truly did it because I care about you. I wanted to help you get off the ground quickly."

"But the album and the tour. . .it was all doing great. My music is all I need."

"Of course it is." His tone was patronizing. "Your music will take you a long way *after* the public knows who you are. Now they do."

Roshelle was at a loss. He had shot the release valve right off her head of steam. Nothing made any sense. Did it matter what people thought about whom she was with? He was right about everyone knowing her name through this. But what about the picture of them kissing? It was all terribly confusing.

"Let me take you to dinner tomorrow, darling. We'll talk and I'll try to explain to you how this business really works. Obviously, no one else has cared enough to do that."

"I'm not sure, Louis. I'll call you tomorrow and let you know."

❧

A call in the wee hours of the morning roused her from a drugged sleeping pill-induced sleep. She could hardly get her bearings. She struggled to remember what city she was in and wondered why Mitzi wasn't taking the calls. But, as she pulled the receiver down to where she lay on the pillow, she realized she was home. Then she realized if she'd let it go, the answering machine would have caught it.

Suddenly, the sound of Benny Lee Camp's voice on the other end snapped her into reality. "Benny, where are you? I'm so glad to hear from you." His deep voice was like music to her ears and she was close to tears. Then she listened a little closer.

"You got ice water in your veins or what?" His voice slurred from the effects of too many drinks. "I tole the boys over and over that you'd call as soon as you could. But you never did. You never did. You think I care about being on your stage and riding on your name? Is that why you left me in the lurch? That why you didn't call me?"

"Oh, Benny. It isn't that at all." She grabbed pillows and stuffed them behind her back so she could sit up. She willed her mind to clear.

"What d'ja think? That I'm some kinda mooch? I'm no mooch, Rosh. I just wanted to help you. Tha's all."

"Benny, you're drunk. Stop talking like a drunk. Talk sense."

"I tole the boys that other dolls might go to Hollywood and go off the deep end, but not our Roshelle. Not our angel." She heard his voice catch. He was crying. "No, siree. Not our little angel. But I was wrong. Dead wrong."

"Benny, stop it! This is crazy." She was sobbing. "I never meant to hurt you."

"I never minded so much when the tour started and you didn't want us. But, when I saw Fremont's show tonight. . . . You gonna marry that slimy weasel, Sarviano, Rosh? Huh? I thought you wasn't gonna marry anyone. You said you wasn't."

"I'm not, Benny. I'm not. I'm not going to marry anyone. Don't believe all that garbage. It's all for the press. . .for the publicity. You should know that. Benny, please listen to me."

She could hear him crying like a little baby, then the line went dead.

She didn't know from where he was calling. She could call Newt and find out. But then, she'd still be talking to a drunk man. She had to wait until he sobered up and then try to talk to him. Now, more than ever, she wished she'd called him first. . .just to talk. No matter what she told him about getting a new band, he would have accepted it, but this. . . .

"Roshelle." Mitzi was tapping at the door. "You talking in your sleep again?"

"I guess I was."

She pushed her head into the bedroom. "Pretty articulate for a dream. Sounded more like you were talking to someone on the phone after it rang."

"Oh, Mitzi," she groaned. "That was Benny."

"Don't tell me he saw the show?"

Roshelle was crying again, and she hated herself for it. All she could do was nod as she blew her nose on the tissue Mitzi handed her.

"The guy loves you, Roshelle. He's always loved you."

"He was drunk," she said as she gave a little gasp.

"That's understandable. After what he saw. Plus the tabloid stories. He's probably seen them, too."

"What am I going to do?" She punched at the pillow in her lap. "I've made a mess of everything."

"No you haven't, Rosh. You haven't made a mess of everything. First of all, you can't talk sense to a drunken man who's trying to drown his sorrow because his love's been spurned."

"I didn't spurn his love," she said through the sniffles.

"Okay. Let's just say you never encouraged it. That's hard on a man's ego. But his ego is not your concern now. Nor can you help what Louis did—or

Freddie, either, for that matter. Right now, you can go back to sleep and rest. Next week you begin cutting the second album and that's where your heart really is. . .in your music. Just try to keep focused and stop letting all these people drive you to distraction."

"You're right, Mitzi. You're absolutely right. I can't let every little thing knock me down." She gave Mitzi a little hug. "I don't know what I'd do without you."

"Come on now, Rosh. You'd do just fine. You have more spit and vinegar than you give yourself credit for."

Roshelle wanted to believe that, but she couldn't. She didn't have much resolve left at all.

The rest of the night was virtually sleepless. She paced the length of her bedroom. When she and Mitzi first designed the room in soft tones of mint green and peach, she thought it was lovely. But tonight it wasn't lovely at all. The sheer beauty of it was mocking her.

She seemed to be doing everything wrong. How could she be making so many crazy mistakes? It didn't matter that she wasn't in love with Benny Lee. She loved the person that he was and she hated herself for having hurt him.

And the truth was, she didn't really know how much longer she would be singing anyway. With each passing day, the pain in her throat increased and someday there'd be no more running from the truth.

※

The next morning she called Newt to ask the hotel where Benny was staying. "Sorry, sweets, they done checked out. They're on the road today." But he gave her the name and number of the hotel at their next stop.

She thanked him and then said, "Newt, is it too late to change my mind on doing a hymn on the next album? Like Ted wanted," she added in case he needed to be reminded.

"It ain't too late. Just like a woman. But it ain't too late. I'll call him and tell him right now. You know the title yet?"

"I'm. . .I'm not sure."

"He'll probably want to know. They're already doing layouts for the cover. I hate to press you, but. . ."

And she hated being pressed. "Oh, all right. Tell him the name is 'In the Garden.' "

Newt gave a little chuckle. " 'In the Garden'? Funny name. You sure that's a religious song?"

"Trust me, Newt."

That's that, she thought as she hung up the phone. Vic had said hymns would help hurting people. Maybe in some way she could make up for having hurt Benny. . .maybe.

&

The first day of the recording session was agony. A singer could do a lot of glossing on stage to cover up for a few faults, but the recording studio was like a refining fire. Late in the afternoon, her voice cracked and began to give out. She saw the pained look on the face of her soundman.

"Want to take a little break, Miss Ramone?" she heard him ask through her headset.

She shook her head. She'd push until she got it right. During breaks she downed pain pills and went right back in to work.

She requested that the hymn be left until last. The recording was already several days past schedule because so many songs had to be redone and Mr. Laurel was none too pleased.

"But he's a patient man," Newt told her on the side. "Don't let his gruffness fool you. He wants you to shine." But even Newt looked a little worried.

Finally, it was time to tackle the hymn. It had to be done and she dreaded it. She had no idea of what she was afraid.

For hours they worked. "Sorry, Miss Ramone," said the technician, "but it has no life. I know it's supposed to be a hymn, and hymns are more reserved, but you still need to put your whole self into it."

Why had she ever agreed to this fiasco? They were dead words to her. A sultry love song she could belt out, but this. . .?

Mr. Laurel was called in and Newt as well. They sat down together to talk it over.

"I wanted you to do a religious song," Ted Laurel told her, "but I don't want you to bomb the album."

"Remember what that religious guy said?" Newt put in. "The one who has the studio in Tulsa? He said you made people cry. How'd you do that?"

Roshelle thought back. "For one thing I played my own accompaniment."

"You did what?" Ted asked.

"I played the piano myself as I sang."

"Well, why didn't you say so? We'll get a piano and move you into a bigger studio. That's simple. And what's this about some dude in religious recording? What's his name?"

"Victor Moran," Newt supplied the information.

"Call him. He knows more about this stuff than we do. Maybe he'll help us on this."

Roshelle panicked. "No, please—"

Newt touched her arm and gave her a look that said, "Don't ruffle any more feathers!"

She clenched her teeth and sat back quietly as Newt called his secretary to get Vic's number. In a matter of minutes, Mr. Laurel was talking to him on a conference call.

"I know this is a rather odd request, Moran. But I need a little favor," Mr. Laurel said in his usual blustery manner. "I'm willing to pay whatever it takes. Can you fly out here and help us with this religious number that Ms. Ramone wants to do?"

Roshelle didn't even need to listen. She knew what Vic's answer would be. He was on the next plane out.

Chapter Sixteen

Victor Moran had a perfect opportunity to say "What changed your mind?" or "Glad you finally came around." But he said nothing and just set to work.

He checked out everything. First, he had private conferences with the soundmen and technicians, then he went over every note of the arrangement. They moved production to the larger studio with a grand piano. Finally, everything was ready.

"Only one more thing," he said to her. "Let me pray for you before we begin."

She froze. If there were snickerings among the crew, she never heard it. He unobtrusively sat down beside her on the piano bench and took her hands. It was probably the simplest prayer she'd ever heard. He asked for the power of the anointing of the Holy Spirit to be on her. And he asked it in Jesus' name. Then he smiled at her and walked out.

The soundman held up his hand and she watched as he brought it down. Suddenly, her fingers were moving easily over the keys and there was no pain in her throat. Her clear, strong, contralto voice never broke.

> He speaks, and the sound of His voice
> Is so sweet the birds hush their singing;
> And the melody that He gave to me
> Within my heart is ringing.
> And He walks with me, and He talks with me,
> And He tells me I am His own,
> And the joy we share as we tarry there,
> None other has ever known.

Easily she breezed through all the verses and twice again on the chorus. She barely remembered the recording and she didn't ask if it was a take. She knew it was. And she knew the prayer had everything to do with it. There were wet eyes in the sound room.

Blustery Mr. Laurel was saying, "Nice little song, Roshelle. Real nice song," as he gave her a condescending pat on the shoulder.

Newt, who was never without something to say, said nothing.

She thanked Vic.

"My pleasure," he answered simply as his hazel eyes studied her. "You were great."

She heaved a sigh. It was over. Maybe now she could have some peace.

&

Roshelle tried repeatedly to contact Benny, but he refused her calls. Feeling that there was nothing else she could do, she finally gave up. What was the use?

Now all the tabloids announced that she had been jilted by her lover, the famous Sarviano. She had refused to see him again—other than for fitting sessions, that is. And, even then, he tried to tell her how much better her career would be if she linked up with him. He was probably right but, to Roshelle, it just wasn't worth it. One day she carefully wrapped the diamond bracelet and dropped it off at his studio.

The holidays came and went unceremoniously. In fact, Mitzi decided, of all things, to spend Christmas with her parents, so Roshelle was alone.

Album number two, turned out to be even more successful than the first and, several times, Newt tried to talk her into doing an album with the Moran Recording Studio.

"You're really good at that stuff," he said. "You even put a few goose bumps on this tough old hide of mine. Why, I always did think," he added, jabbing the air with his cigar, "that everybody oughta have a little bit of religion."

She ignored him. A little bit of religion. . .was that what she was doing? Funny. That was what she'd always accused Uncle Jess of having—a little bit of religion.

&

"I'm going out," Mitzi announced to her one rainy evening in late February.

"Out?"

Mitzi was dressed in a flowered jumpsuit with a perky ribbon in her hair. She looked like a teenager flushed with excitement. "Uh-huh. Out." She was grinning.

"Like on a date?"

"Like on a date!"

Roshelle was shocked. Mitzi never went anywhere unless it was running errands for Roshelle. Where could she have met anyone? "Do I know him?"

"As a matter of fact, you do."

Now her curiosity was thoroughly piqued. "Who?"

"Wait a few minutes and you'll see."

When the doorbell rang, Mitzi laughed and said, "You can answer it if you want."

Roshelle opened her front door to see a gangling, grinning six-foot Keel Stratton standing there, shaking off the rain. She couldn't believe it. "Why you goofy kid." She reached up as he leaned down so she could give him a hug. "What in heaven's name are you doing here?"

"I came to see Mitzi."

"No, I mean in California. Are you. . .is the band booked out here?" she asked hopefully, as she closed the door. Maybe now she could finally talk to Benny.

Keel shook his head. "I quit the band, Rosh. It sort of fell apart."

"Oh, no." She started to ask about it, but then she watched as his face lit up when Mitzi walked into the entryway.

"You two going to stand out there and talk all night?" Mitzi asked.

"Mitzi!" Keel stepped past Roshelle and grabbed Mitzi and swept her up in his arms. Then he kissed her soundly.

Slowly, Roshelle was beginning to understand that this had obviously been going on for quite some time.

As they sat down to talk, Mitzi served coffee and nut bread. They explained to Roshelle that they'd kept in touch by phone and letter ever since Roshelle's first stand in Reno.

"I was always crazy about her," Keel said, with his arm around Mitzi's shoulder, "but it just wasn't the right time. Now, with Benny drinking more and more, it's just not worth it to hang around the band. Plus, I'm tired of traveling." He looked deep into Mitzi's smiling black eyes. "I just want to settle down."

"How long have you been out here?" Roshelle asked, wondering if Mitzi had been sneaking around about this.

"Just a few days this time. But I've been out here a couple of other times before to see Mitzi."

"We didn't want to upset you," Mitzi put in. "He also came to my folks' place for Christmas." She grinned. "And they love him almost as much as I do."

"So, what are your plans?" Roshelle asked, as though it weren't obvious.

"We're going to get married right away," Keel said. "I've waited for her long enough."

They were waiting because of me, Roshelle realized.

"First thing for you to know, Rosh, is that I'll continue to work for you. I'll come here to work in the office every day just like always. Nothing is changed in that respect."

Nothing is changed? More like nothing will ever be the same. She had leaned on Benny and then he was gone. Next, she leaned on Mitzi and now she was gone. How crazy could she be? Nothing was certain except that she had only herself.

"Think about it, Rosh, old girl," she chided herself after the happy couple had left for the evening, "even if old Newt dropped dead tomorrow, you would still have to go on." Go on. That was it. That was her life. Corny as it might sound, the show must go on.

❦

The wedding was a small affair. When Roshelle met Mitzi's parents, she wondered why the girl ever ran away. Mr. and Mrs. Wilson were a light-hearted pair, full of good humor. Looking back, Roshelle wondered if it had been more a case of "leaving home" rather than what Mitzi had called "running away."

Mr. and Mrs. Keel Stratton found an apartment in nearby Garden Grove. Keel snagged a job in a music store and did an occasional weekend gig. He even signed up for a few college classes. Roshelle had never seen Mitzi happier and she knew they would get along fine.

"She'll make a great wife," Roshelle told Keel following the wedding. "She cooks like a dream."

To which Keel replied, "I wouldn't care if she couldn't boil water."

❦

The house was an empty shell without Mitzi there. Mitzi insisted, in agreement with Newt, that they run ads to find her a new "secretary," as they called it. But what they meant was a live-in companion. That made Roshelle feel like a candidate for the nursing home. In all honesty, she wanted someone there with her, but she didn't want anyone to know. At times the cavern of loneliness was so vast and so deep that she felt she'd been falling forever.

Newt, in the meantime, was planning another tour. There was no way she could ask Mitzi to go. By tour time, Newt insisted they find someone to at least be with Roshelle backstage on tour. She acquiesced. It turned out to be Blanche, an older sister of one of the backup singers. She was single, in her forties, and free to travel. When Roshelle interviewed her, she found her to be kind and compassionate.

The weekend before the tour began, Keel and Mitzi invited Roshelle to their house for Sunday dinner. Roshelle brightened at the thought of enjoying Mitzi's cooking once again.

"But on one condition," Mitzi said in a teasing tone.

"Conditions for a dinner invitation. Now I've heard everything," she shot back. "You've been in this business too long. Okay. What is it?"

"We've found a neat little church and we want you to go to Sunday service with us."

"Oh, Mitzi, give me a break." That was all she needed. Now these two.

"Every church isn't your uncle Jess's church, you know," Mitzi said. "Why not come and visit, just for me?"

Roshelle thought of all the selfless giving Mitzi had poured out in those weeks and months that they were together and there was no way she could refuse.

❧

The church was a sprawling building of the traditional Southern California Spanish style. Greeters at the door were congenial as they handed out bulletins and shook hands, making everyone feel welcome. People in the foyer were chatting and children were running everywhere.

"It seemed to us like a family church," Mitzi was saying, noting all of the couples with small children. She gave Roshelle a little jab in the side. "Did I tell you Keel wants four kids, just like I do?"

"Good thing you agree on the small stuff," she quipped as she glanced inside the sanctuary. She was dreading this. As they were seated in the soft padded pews, Roshelle glanced through all the announcements to have something to do. She stopped as she saw the title of the sermon: "The Myth of Hypocrisy."

She knew every selected hymn by heart—and all their verses. She supposed it was like riding a bike in that it just comes back to you. How she had always loved those old hymns.

Never once during the sermon did the pastor yell or beat on the pulpit. Rather, he spoke gently and kindly. The sanctuary itself was filled with the sound of the soft rustling of Bible pages turning as everyone had a Bible and was following the Scriptures he selected.

"Through the years," he said, "we've come to think of the word hypocrisy in only one vein. We've thought of it as people who act one way in church and another way out of church. We've almost taken delight as we gleefully point fingers at other people.

"The word *hypocrite* is a Greek word," he explained. "In the Greek theater it was their name for the actors. In order for the audience to see them, the actors wore large exaggerated masks. Therefore, a hypocrite was the person who played a part and wore a mask."

Like a stage face, Roshelle thought to herself.

"Basically the word simply means a person who pretends to be something he or she is not. Whether it has to do with church or not." As he spoke, the young pastor strode about the podium, directing his remarks to all parts of the church and at times turning around to speak to choir members who were seated behind him.

"We all wear masks," he went on. "Some of us wear heavier masks than others, depending on the measure of hurt we've experienced. Masks seemingly hide our pain. But living behind a mask can be lonely, frightfully lonely. Most of us are less than honest with our spouses, our loved ones, and our closest friends."

Mitzi reached over and squeezed Roshelle's hand.

"The good news is that the saving power of Jesus can cut through the heavy, exaggerated masks that we wear and that through an honest relationship with the Father-God, we can drop all the pretense and stop the hypocrisy."

Roshelle crossed and uncrossed her legs as she tried to get comfortable. For her, the service couldn't be over soon enough. She'd never before thought that perhaps she herself was a hypocrite. Hadn't she always said how she hated hypocrites? And yet she now realized that she wore the biggest mask of all—hiding her real feelings, hiding her fears, hiding her illness. She wanted out of that church fast.

Politely, she ate with Keel and Mitzi, but soon after dinner was over, she excused herself. "I still have a million things to do before the tour," she said.

"I'll be over tomorrow to help you pack," Mitzi said as she waved good-bye at the door.

❧

Blanche was a fairly good companion backstage and was ready to take care of all the details. But she didn't know the ropes like Mitzi and she wasn't fun and silly and painfully honest like Mitzi. The farther along the tour went, the more Roshelle missed her dear friend. The loneliness was almost unbearable. Most nights she cried herself to sleep; the pain in her throat intensified as well.

It was halfway through the tour when it happened, in a theater in Philadelphia. She had made it through only the third number when she collapsed in a heap in front of hundreds of her fans.

True to her word, she sang until she dropped. The only trouble was, as she realized later, she'd never planned what to do after she dropped.

Chapter Seventeen

Total rest, she was told—a frightening thought. Suffering from exhaustion, the papers reported. The rest of the tour was canceled and Roshelle was sent home. Newt was concerned; Mr. Ted Laurel was furious.

"Why didn't you take better care of yourself?" he bellowed. "You young stars are all alike. Think you don't need to eat or sleep."

Mitzi wanted to come and be with her, but she was now pregnant and suffering with the worst case of "all day" morning sickness. Roshelle could hear the torment in her friend's voice. "You need me, but I can't be there, Rosh. I'm so sorry. Every time I walk more than two steps at a time, I throw up."

Roshelle kept insisting that it was all right. In fact she felt worse for Mitzi than she did for herself.

The hours were unending. Blanche came in and out like a mother hen, fussing over her and bringing her all kinds of great things to eat.

But the nights were the longest. She listened to music; she played the piano; she read books; she paced the house—nothing helped. The agony was too much; the loneliness was too much.

"Uncle Jess always told me I'd be punished by God," she said to the silence. "Well, God, if You take away my voice, I guess that's about the worst kind of punishment I could ever imagine. Without my voice, I'm nothing. Nothing."

From the bathroom cabinet she took down the bottle of sleeping pills—her friends, the sleeping pills. Why wait? Why continue suffering? It was too late for anything now.

She took the bottle downstairs to her studio. Probably she should write a note to Mitzi first, thanking her. . .and something to Janey. But then there was Benny. If only she could apologize to him. . .tell him how very sorry she was. Tears were streaming down her face as she thought of him.

And Vic. She sat down at the piano and let her fingers trail lightly over the keys, picking out runs and chords. Vic had always been such a gentleman. . .so kind. . .so peaceful. Somehow she needed to apologize to him. . . and to thank him.

Strains of "In the Garden" spilled forth into the room. Total rest, the doctor had ordered her, but she couldn't stop the singing.

"And He walks with me and He talks with me. . . ." She desperately needed someone with whom she could talk and walk. Someone who would be there always. Everything in her life was plastic and phony. . .and empty.

"Do You do that God?" she asked as her fingers continued the soft melody. "Are these words true? Do You walk and talk with people? Can that be real? That would be so wonderful. So wonderful to never be alone."

Suddenly, she was sobbing—sobs that were wrenching her insides. "Help me, God, please, help me. Please tell me I'm Your own, like the song says. I'm so lonely and so scared. I can't go another minute without knowing if You're there."

The sobs continued to shake her body until she was entirely spent. . . exhausted. The arrangement of the song was still on the piano and these words leaped at her from the page: "The melody that He gave to me. . . ."

She stared at the sheet. "Oh, God. That's it. You gave me the melody. *You* gave me the melody. You don't give and then take away." In a rush she ran up the stairs—just like Mitzi—two at a time. "You are with me. You are. I know. I can feel it!" She wanted to dance and jump and sing all at once.

There, in the bureau drawer beneath all the clothes, there it was—the Bible. What did that verse say? The one Vic was always giving to her? She knew right where to turn. . .where the violets were. . .where they had stained the page.

" 'I will praise the name of God with a song,' " she read aloud. "I will. It says 'I *will*.' " Suddenly, she was scouring Psalms for other verses that talked about singing. There were scores of them. Psalm 59:16 said, "Yea, I will sing aloud of thy mercy in the morning. . . ."

She sprawled across the bed with the Bible in front of her, reading verse after verse, weeping as she read. "I will, Lord. You give me a chance, and I promise I will sing of Your mercy in the morning—every morning. Very loud!"

The next morning, after sleeping with no pills, she called Mitzi. "I'm going to Tulsa," she said. "There are a few things I need to take care of."

Quietly, Mitzi answered, "I thought there might be."

Next, she called Vic to let him know she was coming. "I'll need your help to get through this," she said meekly.

"I'm here for you. I'll meet you at the airport."

≈

The moment Vic caught sight of her, he ran to her and wrapped her in his arms. "I've been so concerned ever since I heard—"

She put her fingers over his lips and then stood on tiptoe to kiss him. Surprise registered in the hazel eyes but only briefly. In a flash, he was kissing her fully with all the passion of a man who had patiently waited for his love and now the waiting was over.

Once in the car, she explained the real cause for her collapse. "Not just exhaustion as the paper said."

"I knew there was more," he said.

"I must talk to Dr. Beasley, to let him know I'm back and to schedule the surgery. But first I have things to do in Sandott."

"Alone?"

She reached for his hand. "Would you go with me?"

He kissed her hand. "I never want to leave your side."

She smiled at him. "One thing at a time."

❧

The Oklahoma countryside was lush and green. The lacy pink-and-white blossoms on the dogwood trees seemed to float in space. Redwood trees spread their branches everywhere. The beauty of God's creation was overwhelming, as though she'd never seen it before.

The little white church was much the same. When Vic drove into the small graveled parking lot, she sat there staring at it. "I grew to hate it so," she said softly, "and them."

"Them, who?"

"Mother and Uncle Jess."

She stepped out of the car as he opened the door for her. "Down in the basement," she said. He took her arm to steady her.

The side door was unlocked and, being a weekday afternoon, the place was deserted. He walked with her down the stairs. Everything was smaller than she remembered.

"I came inside that day because it was so hot outside. Down the steps here. There were old toys down here even though the place wasn't used much. I liked to play here, but Mother always told me not to. We lived a few doors down the street."

Vic switched on a light. The basement was much different now. . .light and airy. Concrete walls were painted in soft pastels; colorful partitions divided the room into classrooms.

"Tell me what happened," he said as they descended the last step.

"I was over here. . .behind stacks of folding chairs, hiding. I heard someone coming. I was scared. But it was only Uncle Jess. So I started to jump out and say "Boo." But then another person came down. It was Mother. They whispered and hugged and kissed in the dark. It was so awful. I felt like I was going to be sick, but I couldn't move." The tears began to flow.

Vic helped her to a small chair and made her sit down. "Then what happened?"

"It seemed so long. . .a long, long time." She gave a sigh. "Finally, they left."
"Is that all?"

She shook her head. "No." There was no way to stop the flood of tears or the deep sobs. "That night, I told Daddy. I told. I was so sorry I told. I didn't mean to tell. But I did."

"What did he do?"

"Nothing, then. He was so sweet and so good. He didn't say anything. He just held me close. But the next day he died. He died, Vic. . .and I killed him. They said it was a heart attack, but I never believed that. I told him the awful truth and it killed him!"

Vic put his arms around her and let her cry. "You were just a little girl, Roshelle. A little girl. You didn't do anything wrong. Do you hear me? You didn't do anything wrong."

"I hated Mother and I hated Uncle Jess. But it was me. I blamed them, but I did it. I killed him. Oh, I've wished a million times that I'd never told him. Why couldn't I have kept the awful secret?"

"Darling, listen to me." He took her shoulders and pulled her back to look at her, wiping the tears from her cheeks. "Your loving heavenly Father would never hold you accountable for that action. You were only a child. You've been focused on the wrong thing all these years and it's destroying you. That guilt is too much for you to bear."

"Help me, Vic. I want to be free. I want to forgive."

"The only thing you're accountable for is accepting Jesus."

"But I've done that. . .when I was only eight." She pointed upward. "Upstairs, there, at the altar."

"Well then, it's time to clear this up, once and for all. Come here." He took her hand and led her to a little altar. A bright red cloth covered it, an open Bible and a vase of wilted flowers adorned it.

Together, they knelt down; together, they prayed. Later, when Vic helped her to her feet, the awful weight was gone—completely gone. The relief was ecstasy. *Dear God, maybe singing wasn't the only thing there was to life. . .to living. Maybe there was more, so much more—such as people, wonderful people.*

He held her close. "Roshelle, I knew you were so tormented. I wanted to help, but I didn't know how."

"You've helped more than you'll ever know. Someday, I'll tell you all about it. Now, let's go pay a visit."

As they walked from the church, Vic stopped and pointed. "Look, Roshelle." The sidewalk from the church to the parking lot was lined with tiny clumps of lavender violets. He released her hand to reach down and pick a single flower. He pressed it into her hand and then kissed her. She smiled up at him through her tears.

"When I was unable to speak of my love to you," he said, "I prayed the flowers would speak for me."

&

"I've been an old fool," Uncle Jess told them as they sat with him in his small living room. The walker that he still used on occasions was nearby. "Your mother always loved me, Rachel, ever since she was in grade school. But I was older and thought of her as only a little kid. She was broken-hearted when I married. I thought she'd never get over it." He gave a shrug. "And I guess she never did."

Roshelle watched this old man in amazement. How could this be the man she'd been afraid of for all those years? "So she married Daddy instead?" she asked.

He nodded. "That she did. Out of anger and spite, she married your daddy. But then, when my Sally died, Cora wanted to divorce your daddy so we could get married. Me and Sally never had no kids, so I was all alone. But Cora was pregnant with you." He rubbed the gray stubble on his chin. "I couldn't never let her do that. Think how it would look. Well, she was more broken-hearted than ever."

Roshelle felt Vic squeezing on her hand. "Poor Mother," she heard herself saying. So this is what Janey meant about Cora's being wounded. But Roshelle never knew. No one ever told her.

"Roshelle thought she was responsible for her father's death because she told him she saw the two of you together," Vic explained to Uncle Jess. "Did your brother know about Cora's love for you?"

Uncle Jess gave a raspy little laugh. "Yep, I'm afraid he did. Everybody in four counties knew Cora loved me."

Vic gave Roshelle a knowing look. She sighed. All these years. The torture, the nightmares, the hate, the pain—now it was over.

"Then, when your daddy died, I was so guilt-ridden," Uncle Jess went on, "I felt I had to keep a tight rein on you." Grief lined the old man's face. "As I rode in that wailing ambulance to the hospital, I kept thinking, 'Lord, don't let me die. I can't face Jesus till I tell little Rachel how sorry I am.' Can you ever forgive me?"

"Last week, I might not have been able to, Uncle Jess, but today I can say 'Yes' and mean it. I do forgive you."

Tears coursed slowly down the leathery cheeks. She went over to him, sat down by him, and hugged him.

He reached around and patted her. "Your mother, bless her soul, in spite of all that's happened, she still loves me. I was so blind. Guilt and pride kept me from marrying her before. But, after coming so near to death's door, I've made up my mind, if she still wants this old coot, I'm going to marry her."

Roshelle looked back across the room at Vic and smiled. His eyes were wet as well. "Looks like we might be having two family weddings," he said softly.

Chapter Eighteen

Her first awareness was that Vic was by her side. The fuzzy haze of anesthesia hung thickly in her mind.

Vic kept repeating, "Not malignant. The growths were not malignant, Roshelle." From a deep hollow well, she could faintly hear the words and the joy in his voice. "They got it all. You'll be fine. Just fine. You'll be singing your silken melodies in no time."

From the first intense pain that she experienced as she began to regain consciousness, it seemed impossible. But his words encouraged her daily. One of the first things she saw were the charming bouquets—at least a dozen—of violets all about the room. She gazed at them and marveled. Such love, such sweet love.

At first, she wasn't able to talk at all. After a few days she was able to manage a coarse whisper. That was the day Vic handed her the phone saying there was a special call for her. It was Benny Lee! She cried for sheer joy—and it hurt to cry.

"Don't cry, angel," she heard his booming voice say. "Vic explained everything to me. You done it so I wouldn't know, you silly kid." She could hear the catch in his voice.

"I'm so sorry, Benny," she said in her loudest whisper. "I'm so sorry I hurt you. I never meant to—"

"If only you'd told me, I would have tried to help. You silly, sweet, beautiful kid. I'll always love you, Rosh. But the Good Lord's provided just the right man for you."

She looked up at Vic and whispered, "Yes. The perfect one for me."

"That makes me happier than anything, Rosh. Just to know you're really happy." He took a breath. "Now listen, the boys and me are gonna get together and come out and see you soon. Real soon. Okay?"

"Okay, Benny. Thanks. . .for everything."

Vic took the phone and hung it up. Then he sat close to her on the edge of the bed.

"How long," she whispered, "before I can sing again? What does Dr. Beasley say?"

"I guess I didn't think to ask that question," he said. "I was more concerned with questions like, 'Is she all right?' " He kissed her forehead as he spoke the words. "Are you in a hurry?"

"God told me *He* gave me the melody. Now all I want to do is give them back to Him—singing songs to His glory."

He wrapped his arms around her and held her close. "I know the perfect recording studio who wants to offer you a lifetime contract."

Looking up into Vic's eyes and feeling the peace, strength, and love flowing from him into her own heart and being, she happily exclaimed, "I gladly accept that offer!"